I0576198

SERPENT'S WALK

a novel by

Randolph D. Calverhall

NATIONAL VANGUARD BOOKS

Library of Congress Catalog Card Number 91-062291

ISBN 978-1-7336481-4-1

Copyright © 1991 by National Vanguard Books

Cover by DB Graphics

All rights reserved. No part of this book, except brief excerpts
for the purpose of review, may be reproduced in any form
without written permission from the publisher.

Published by National Vanguard Books
POB 330 • Hillsboro • WV 24946

PRINTED IN THE UNITED STATES OF AMERICA

"And just how," the mongoose demanded scornfully of the serpent, "do you propose to climb Mount Kailas, the home of Lord Siva? You who have neither arms nor hands, neither feet nor toes with which to grip the precipices?"

"Very slowly," the serpent replied. "Carefully. Coiling back and forth upon my belly, over a rock here, up through a crevice there. I shall get there in the end, you know."

The mongoose snorted in derision. But in his heart he suspected the serpent spoke truly.

—Indian fable

CHAPTER ONE

Sunday, December 22, 2041

There were two men in the dank, cluttered back-office of the lithographer's shop. He who stood in front of the table wore faded workpants and a black, leather biker's jacket. The jacket was old and frayed, its decals flaking, its once-angry motto now illegible.

The other man sat in shadow. Posture hinted at a younger person, a sophisticated man, one who might be acceptable in the upper strata of society. The black-jacketed man could see little more than a thin tie upon a white shirt, a black ribbon painted down the middle of a dazzling highway that glowed blue-white behind the table's one fluorescent work lamp. Two arms sheathed in lead-grey tweed extended out of the darkness that was the man's torso, and pale fingers plucked at the dog-eared files heaped upon the table top, pallid spiders scuttling about amidst a moonscape of buff and white papers and scarred, chestnut-hued wood.

"Best we could do on short notice," the biker said. He was a diffident, ordinary sort. His face was raddled with pockmarks, and his complexion reminded the other of red-brick walls slathered over with graffiti.

"Whatever." The prissy, delicate fingers burrowed deeper into white paper. "Lesser, you said? Lessing?"

"Lessing. Alan Lessing." The older man gleaned a smidgin of secret amusement from the smear of black lithographer's ink visible upon the other's left sleeve. He'd have the devil's own time getting that stain out of the expensive sport coat!

"Lessing. Fought in Angola in 2030. Then in Syria during the Baalbek War. Then he came back here for a while." His voice trailed off as he read. He looked down at the man behind the desk and finished, "A good enough man. A real mercenary."

"Reliable?"

"How would I know? Never met him." Leather creaked as the older man scraped thick fingers through his grizzled, grey-red hair. "It's all in the file. American . . . high school, a year of college, a family that he don't remember . . . and they don't remember him."

"A merc, though." Coming from the younger man, the term sounded self-conscious. "Did he . . . uh . . . see combat? Real combat?"

"It's all there. Read it for yourself." The other's voice took on a querulous tone as he dropped the file onto the desk. He moved to peer out the one grime-smeared window as the man behind the desk picked up the file. "God, it's started to snow hard out there. I've got to get home."

"Politics? I don't see anything about that in here."

"If it's not written down, he don't have any."

"Any religious or racial problems? Will he cooperate with other team members? Blacks? Jews? Arabs?"

The older man snorted and wiped a stubby finger across his upper lip. "Lessing's fought for . . . and against . . . every ethnic group there is."

"I have to know."

The older man turned back to the window, now an abstract study in black dirt and white snow. "He's okay. Whatever you tell him. Come on . . . ."

"One more minute. We can settle it all here and now."

"What more do you need? Take Lessing; he's good. Then either you pick the team or let Lessing do it. You provide the stuff . . . uh, cars, weapons, whatever. I don't want to know."

"You won't. Just make the contacts and get him here. Where is he?"

The finger strayed up to a surprisingly ugly, lumpy nose. "India, I think . . . beegeeing . . . uh, bodyguarding . . . for some American exec. Somebody who don't want to get dead over there. India's like most of the rest of the fuckin' Third World now . . . open season on foreigners. Specially Westerners . . . and Saturday matinee special on Americans."

White teeth glimmered a pale crescent in the darkness. The chair squealed as the younger man pushed it back and stood up. "Good. Get Lessing. Who've you got in India? DaSilva? Gomez? One of them can give him the details, and he can send out for whatever help he wants. Then fly him to Mexico City. We'll pick him up there. Have him there by the middle of next month . . . January fifteenth. Let my secretary know when he arrives. You'll get your commission through the regular channels."

"No problem." The older man reached for the leather gauntlets lying on the table, fumbled, dropped one into the litter of paper on the floor, and bent over to pick it up. He sighed. "And a merry Christmas to you."

The other made no reply.

Take nothing for granted in war. The commander who would live to return home is he who anticipates not only the unusual but the totally unexpected.
—*Risalat-al-Harb,* 11th-century Muslim military manual

CHAPTER TWO

"Christ," Doe grunted. He swung the binoculars left, then right.

"Come on, what is it?" Lessing wrested the glasses from the smaller man. Their four companions were somewhere behind them, hunkered down in the glazed, ankle-deep snow. Who would've thought there'd be so much snow in the American Southwest, even in January? People said the climate had changed since the Vietnamese-Chinese War back in 2010.

Teen wriggled up beside them. The muzzle of his Riga-71 automatic rifle had been blackened with grease, but it still gleamed. Lessing pushed it down so no sentry could see it flash in the watery winter sunlight.

The compound below was empty. A dilapidated truck stood beside the peeling, white, wooden wall of the main house. The garage in back was unpainted and ramshackle, and the boxy, little water-storage tower—the logical place for a sentry—was as disreputable an edifice as Lessing had ever seen. Even the Angolans built better than that!

Doe gestured urgently. Panch and Cheh would be watching the rugged slope behind them while Char continued to scout, invisible somewhere in the grey-black rocks ahead. Lessing waggled two fingers at Teen, indicating that he should watch the rest of the white-shrouded terrain around the compound. Only when he was satisfied did he look through the glasses.

A booted foot protruded from behind the dirt-caked back wheel of the ancient truck. The vehicle was a four-wheel-drive Hideyoshi, vintage about 2025.

"He working on her?" Lessing whispered. He rested one thick forearm on his knee and adjusted the glasses.

"Too quiet. Not moving." Doe reached for the binoculars again, but Lessing held onto them. "Gate's open, but nobody there." Doe's English was tinged with the remnants of a German—or maybe Belgian—accent. Lessing had worked with him before, fighting with the covert American-Israeli strike force in Syria during the Baalbek War in 2038.

Lessing had only a hazy idea of Doe's real name, or at least the name he used now. On temporary missions it was better this way: today's comrade could become tomorrow's foe. Such makeshift "units" often gave their members numbers, letters, or artificial names picked for easy comprehension in battle. When Gomez, Lessing's Goanese contact in Bombay, had supplied him with this squad of five, Lessing had whimsically named them with Hindi numerals. He himself was Ek, "one"; the others were Doe, Teen, Char, Panch, and Cheh. Doe and Teen carried automatic rifles, as did Lessing; Char and Panch had light Israeli stitch-guns and grenades; the girl, Cheh, who came from Australia or New Zealand or some place "down under," bore the heavy laser rifle.

"Another one there," Teen muttered. Indeed, a heap of discarded clothing beside the water tower resolved itself into a second body.

The man was unmistakably dead. "Not in uniform," Lessing murmured back. "But that's to be expected. This isn't a regular military installation. Not any more."

Char came up, picking his way carefully across the crunching snow. Like Lessing, he was an American. Both were big men, burly and muscular, but Char was moonfaced, with milky skin and a stocking-cap of coarse, black hair, while Lessing's features were thinner, his nose longer, and his hair like wispy, grey-blond ash.

"What's keeping . . . ?" Char began. Teen gestured at the visible bodies, and Char sucked in his breath and sat down. Lessing stuck up one hand to warn the rest to hold their positions.

"Going in?" Teen asked.

"S'what we're paid to do." Char thumbed one nostril.

"Doe and me," Lessing replied. "You two cover us. Get Cheh down here with her laser rifle. She comes in when I give the up-sign."

They distributed themselves amidst the boulders and gulleys of the forward slope. Lessing and Doe stripped off their camouflage suits to reveal quilted, orange hunters' jackets and canvas pants. Doe pulled a red hunting hat out of his pack and straightened the jaunty, yellow feather in its band.

"Maybe you should yodel," Teen snickered. "You look Swiss."

Doe showed grey, uneven teeth, said something obscene in unintelligible Swiss-German dialect, and added a descriptive gesture.

Teen made a face. "You and your monkey too!"

Teen sounded vaguely British, but he shifted easily from one accent to another, and who could say? On this trip alone Lessing had heard him use Cockney, Chicano-American, and a somewhat shaky Texan. He had spoken Spanish with the pilot who had dropped them all into the United States, and Doe recalled him chattering in gutter Arabic in Syria. A useful man, though bitter-faced and given to sarcasm. Many mercenaries were like Teen.

They picked their way down the slope, two lost hunters looking for directions, a cup of coffee, or maybe a telephone. Their own weapons were left behind with their packs, and both now carried hunting rifles, good but not fancy.

"What the hell is this place?" Lessing called loudly, apparently to Doe. "Who lives way out here? Fire warden?"

"University scientists? Geologists?" Doe wondered back.

Lessing signalled him to shut up; Doe's German accent would raise suspicions.

They wandered through the open gate, then through the second, inner barrier. The ten meters of open ground between the two perimeter fences was sown with miniature land-mines, Lessing knew: enough to knock a person down and maybe take off a foot. A TV surveillance camera was mounted above the outer gate, but it seemed to be out of order, its stained, metal lens-tube pointed down at the ground beneath it.

They didn't go around back. Not yet. Lessing clumped up onto the ramshackle front porch and knocked.

"Hey! Anybody!"

There was no reply. Doe prowled down to the end of the porch and squinted around the corner, along the far side of the house. He stuck out two fingers, parallel to the ground: two bodies there.

Lessing straightened up, abandoning his "lost hunter" pose. He went to the top of the front steps and stuck up his right thumb. A figure detached itself from the snow-splashed boulders and began zigzagging down the slope toward him. The rest of the landscape was utterly silent, ominously so. No birds, no insects—but what insects were there in New Mexico this time of year anyway? He had no idea.

Lessing yelled, "Hi! Anybody home?" Then he kicked the front door in.

The front room was like a thousand others in backwoods America: two chairs, a couch, a couple of lamps, a bureau, a fireplace with kindling stacked beside it, and a coffee table cluttered with orange peels, magazines, and old newspapers. Snapshots of friends and kinfolk smiled fuzzily down from beside glass statues of retrievers and spaniels on a knickknack shelf on the rear wall. In the front corner stood a battered desk, heaped with brochures, papers, and outdoorsmen's magazines. A metal sign there proclaimed:

ARTHUR L. KOPPER

Department of Wildlife Conservation

State of New Mexico.

Nothing was out of order. Everything was as it should be.

And it was all as phony as a game-show host's front teeth.

They made a hurried search of the house. Off the hallway behind the parlor was a bathroom with yellow, chintz curtains, a woman's doing. Back of that they came to a nondescript kitchen in which two blackened pots still stood on the propane stove. Somebody had turned off the fire, but the food inside—beef stew and boiled potatoes, Doe noted—was cold and greasy, maybe two days old.

In the side bedroom that opened off the kitchen a dead woman lay sprawled on a double bed.

Lessing eyed the room, saw nothing, and went to look at the body. The woman was in her forties, greying and bespectacled. A flame-pink, chenille spread was crumpled around her ample, pajama-clad hips, and a can of some cola drink stood on the nightstand beside her. The gaudy, blue cover of a paperback novel protruded from beneath her purpling left hand. She had been dead perhaps a day or two. The faint, sick-sweet smell told him that, yet she hadn't a mark on her. Her tongue protruded, and her features were contorted, but there was no odor of chemicals, no blood, no violence. The pink coverlet had been tossed aside in the agony of her dying, and it now sagged down onto the threadbare, red carpet, a lurid lava-pool of middle-class tastelessness.

"Died at night," Lessing said. "Just before going to sleep."

"Either that or she took afternoon naps," Doe suggested.

A board creaked behind them, and they both jumped, rifles up and ready. It was only Cheh, her laser rifle cradled in stubby arms.

"God, what happened?"

"Damn it, you were supposed to wait for my signal!"

The girl shrugged, and Lessing said, "No idea what killed her. Outside?"

"Not a bloody soul alive. Four deaders, though." Cheh was short, chunky, and as round-faced as a Dutch housewife. "Char 'n' Teen've searched. Somebody blew a great, gobby hole in the garage ... took out the power plant. Don't bother switchin' on the lights."

"There'll be an emergency generator." Lessing rose, strode along the hallway behind the kitchen to the back bedroom, and slammed one booted foot into the door there.

He almost let off a half dozen rounds into the figure that confronted him within: a huge, menacing, pale giant of a man in orange clothing.

It was Lessing himself. The closet door had been left ajar, and he had almost blown away the full-length mirror! He let up on the trigger shakily, thinking how easy it would have been to kill himself with glass shards flying all over! He hadn't realized how terrifying he looked—and how jumpy he was.

"In here," he called. The back of the closet was open, revealing the elevator cubicle beyond. So far the plan Gomez had given him in India had been completely accurate.

What they hadn't told him was that the current occupants would be cold meat when they arrived.

"So. This is what we're here for?" Doe spoke from behind him.

"Deactivated base," Lessing growled. It was time to give his squad their need-to-know. "Secret, left over from before the Vienna Treaty. They didn't know what to do with it. Just a storage depot now." He gestured at the bunks that lined the walls. "The barracks and living quarters were torn down . . . just a few people left to guard this house and the underground installation below it. They doubled as wildlife wardens."

"What's here?" Doe asked.

"Atomic stuff? Radiation?" Cheh added.

"Chemical warfare?" the German persisted.

"Worse," Lessing did not want to talk about it. "Come on, we've got to go down."

"Wait." Cheh gnawed at her thin lower lip. "We have a right to know, mate. Who . . . what . . . killed these people, then?"

Doe pawed at his cheek with one knobby finger. "Biological warfare!" He backed away, toward the front room.

Lessing's grimace told him he had hit the target dead on. "Damn it, there's nothing here that'll hurt us! If there was a leak we'd all be dead by now."

"But these people . . . ?"

"Somebody else was here just before us. I don't know who, yet. Or why."

"Too bloody lovely," Cheh peered into the silent elevator. "The Russians? The Israelis?"

"The Jews wouldn't have to kill anybody," Doe sneered. His shaky voice belied his truculent tone. "Just ask President Rubin pretty-please for the key, ja? More likely one of the American rebel factions. Bankrupt farmers? Black ghetto gangs? Tax protesters? Anti-war? Pro-war? Mexy immigrants?"

"Or mothers against bleedin' child abuse!" Cheh knitted her pale brows in thought. "At least the American Army probably has its hands too full to bother with us right away. How much time do we have?"

"Who knows?" Lessing shrugged. "There must be alarms, even on this fallen-down chicken coop of a base."

"They'll send somebody, eh? Eventually?"

Lessing gestured toward the elevator. "That's right. Let's get it over with. Quick. Whatever happened here happened about a day and a half ago. Either we finish up and hide in the hills until our pickup, or else we abort."

"Abort, I say," Doe blurted. "No killer germs for me!"

"No mission, no money," Lessing snarled back.

"God damn it. You go. I stand watch."

"Fine. I'll do it alone."

"No reason to get all exclusive and snobby, mate." Cheh came over to stand beside him. "Two of us still. Just say what our chances are."

A companion was more welcome than Lessing wanted to admit. He said, "We've seen nobody alive so far. If they're dead down inside too, we grab what we're after and get back out within ten minutes. We can holler if we run into trouble." He slapped the sleek communications box strapped to his belt. "You, Doe, find the others. Bring them up to search the yard, the bodies, the garage. Break radio silence only if you spot somebody coming this way."

"Look . . . ," Doe began lamely.

Lessing let himself smile. "No problem. We'll squawk if the party gets exciting."

"Right." The German took a deep breath, then coughed into his fist. He was a good man in a fire fight, but a black catacomb, possibly filled with invisible, miasmic death, might have daunted a stronger man.

Doe's footsteps clumped back through the house and down the steps. Cheh fidgeted while Lessing inspected the elevator. There were three buttons on the panel and no traps that he could detect. He realized that he was stalling; he would lose his nerve if he waited too long. He jabbed the middle button quickly. The door closed, lights came on, and the car began to descend. The emergency power was indeed working.

The door sighed aside to awaken shadowless, fluorescent tubes along the ceiling of a cream-colored anteroom. Lessing advanced, crouched, and advanced again, while Cheh covered him with her laser rifle. There was no one; the room held only sheeted furniture. An open door in the rear wall gave into a passage about ten meters long. This had two doors on either side, and a fifth at the far end upon which a stenciled sign proclaimed in letters the color of old, dried blood: SECURITY CLEARANCE 1-A ONLY.

Three of the side rooms were offices, dust-filmed and unused; the fourth was a storeroom. Bright cans of floor wax, boxes of toilet rolls, and cartons of duplicator paper lined its walls. Lessing made only a cursory search. A secret door was possible but unlikely.

Inside the room at the far end of the hall Arthur L. Kopper lay face down in a welter of cartons and electronic components; the badge on his stained and crumpled white shirt proved his identity. Lessing rolled him over. Kopper had been a fat, elderly, little man, the very model of a petty bureaucrat. His balding head was just beginning to show the purplish-brown mottlings of decay.

"Radio room," Lessing murmured. He stepped over the corpse to inspect the communications gear that covered the back wall.

He saw it at once. One item did not belong: a fist-sized, silvery cannister spliced into the console.

"Hummingbird!" Cheh breathed. "Czech or Korean?"

A hummingbird was a small, self-powered computer. Plugged into a security rig, it silenced alarms, overrode local signals, and continued to send whatever "situation green, all normal" message had been programmed into the system. A hummingbird could not be shut off, and it usually contained a bomb to keep busy fingers from mucking with it.

Lessing prodded the spilled electronic parts with the butt of his rifle. The silence was more worrisome than Arthur L. Kopper's mortal remains. "Jury-rigging around the hummingbird so you could get a message out?" he asked the corpse conversationally. The erstwhile Mr. Kopper made no reply.

Cheh sidled over to the communications board and peered at the innocuous cylinder. She did not touch it. "No backup security system?"

"They built this place just after the turn of the century, maybe during the missile crisis in 2013," Lessing said. "The Born-Agains were in power then, and their security was state-of-the-art for the time. Hummingbirds came later."

Arthur L. Kopper made no comment, his glazed, dead-fish eyes fixed upon the ceiling.

Lessing rubbed the bridge of his nose. "Always spoil-sports. Somebody develops a gadget, somebody else makes it obsolete." He shivered. Kopper's death was fresh, but there was old death down here too.

He retreated to the door. "Come on. Even if the hummingbird is still sending out a clear signal, somebody may've telephoned and got no answer. They'll be on the way."

Cheh stopped for a final look. "No point to a hummingbird after an assault. You put it on first, to silence any alarm. An inside job? A weasel?"

They both hefted their weapons involuntarily. "Damn," whispered Lessing. "The bastard may still be around."

They made it back to the elevator in record time.

At the top Lessing turned to face the girl. He gave himself no time to think, to consider whether Gomez' 75,000 American dollars might be poor exchange for losing his life. He said, "I've got to go down again, all the way to the bottom this time. You don't need to come. Get back to the others and look for transport."

"Neither Teen nor I saw any vehicles," the girl said stubbornly.

"What about the staff here? They had to have something. That rusty truck in the yard is garbage . . . window-dressing."

"Too right, but . . . I'll tell Doe to widen the search circle . . . ."

"Go out and join him, dammit! I can handle the rest myself."

He stared at her until she dropped her gaze and left.

The grubby little bedroom was stuffy, the cheap furniture sly and secretive. Lessing found it hard to breathe; the air was thick with the smell of mothballs and old clothing.

He was still studying the elevator panel when he heard footsteps. It was Cheh. He had not told her to return, and he raised his head to protest.

"Passed on your message." She brushed back a lock of short, fine, dirty-blonde hair from her forehead. "I'm goin' too. You'll want backup down there."

"No!" he snapped. "No need. Nobody . . . ."

"Push the bleedin' button." She gave him no chance to argue but thumbed the third and lowest stud on the panel herself.

Together, they descended once more into the netherworld.

The lowest level was bigger: a dozen rooms and cubicles buried twenty meters beneath the New Mexico desert. The fluorescent lighting still worked, and the silent foyer and outer office were bright and impersonally businesslike with their red-leatherette chairs, buff-hued filing cabinets, and desks panelled with no-scuff-real-wood plastic. Above one desk a homemade sign still proclaimed: SMOKERS WILL BE WALLED UP ALIVE. Lessing exchanged a grin with the Australian girl. Only a few old-timers still smoked tobacco.

God, it was cold down here, though. The heat must be off. Lessing stopped to sniff. A reassuring drone somewhere far away behind the walls told him that the air-conditioning was working. The place smelled like the inside of a vacuum cleaner, like any other sealed building.

It was totally still. If there were a weasel hiding down here, he was either very good or else he was as frozen as soybean ice cream!

Behind the anteroom, at the end of a short corridor, they came to a heavy security door. This stood open, apparently in perfect working order. The retinal-pattern scanner had been shut off, but the alarm light beside the door glowed a pleasant green, showing that the hummingbird was operating. It looked more and more like an inside job. They might not need Char, their electronics man, after all.

Lessing checked around the door. Some of these places were protected by secondary systems, he knew: gas, automatically activated machine guns, lasers. He found nothing, signalled to Cheh, and stepped gingerly over the sill.

The laboratories opening off the passage beyond the door had long since been stripped. Everything movable was gone, and only bare wires and less-dusty squares on the formica-topped tables showed where equipment had once stood. Bare shelves and racks, filing cabinets, a few pieces of heavy machinery of unknown function, all were shrouded in plastic. It was a morgue, a mummy's tomb, a sepulchre for the murderous offspring of the paranoid twentieth century.

Not that the twenty-first was proving any less bloodthirsty . . . .

The stillness could be deceptive. Lessing forced himself to remember the chances of one or more hidden foes down here. He crouched and glided from door to door, wall to wall, as though the place were full of Russian "advisors," just like Angola. Behind him, Cheh did the same. The laboratories were lifeless, the fluorescent lights bright and unblinking. The cold increased. There must be an outlet directly to the winter landscape above. Yet the air did not smell fresh; it stank of ancient chemicals.

His ears caught a throbbing, a motor sound just above the threshold of audibility, from the room ahead. He hefted his rifle as he had done a hundred times before in a dozen different countries and slid forward.

Ahead, he saw another open security door, this one with keys yet protruding from its double locks. There was a room beyond. Lessing sidled in, Cheh covering him warily.

This place was furnished: more filing cabinets, chairs, desks, red leatherette and plastic and crackle-finish metal. Here was the record room for what was still stored on the base.

At the far end, a heavy, steel door stood ajar, its glass window glinting white in the impersonal fluorescent glare.

White? It did not look like paint. Frost?

Both the motor noise and the cold emanated from that inner chamber.

Lessing understood. "Refrigerator," he whispered. Then, in case the Australians called it something else, he added, "Cold storage."

The girl nodded, watery, blue eyes large and round. It was her turn to move up.

Lessing stood sentinel over the mute furnishings, a deep foreboding skulking just below the horizon of his consciousness. His head ached, and his own eyes felt like sandstone pebbles in their sockets. He struggled to focus. On a desk before him lay a stained blotter, a stapler, and a flip-top calendar that still cheerily displayed the month of April 2035. He would lay money on there being neatly stacked stationery, envelopes, and boxes of paperclips in the drawers. Pencils, ballpoint pens, ribbon boxes for the printers, all would be in place, ready to hand, waiting for some bored Army secretary to come bustling back from her coffee break and get down to work. Most of what was personal and human would be gone, however: the photographs of friends and children, the old Christmas cards, the party invitations, the souvenir napkin from somebody's wedding reception, the letter opener bought during a forgotten holiday in Mexico. The blank, timeless room had an accusatory air, like an old girl friend you didn't call any more. Life had once been injected into this remote, subterranean labyrinth; now it had been withdrawn.

Cheh's hoarse call jolted him back to the present. The Australian girl stood by the doorway of the cold room. She beckoned urgently.

"Here . . . a deader!"

In the far rear corner of the outer office, behind one of the desks, a man lay crumpled against the grill of an air-conditioning duct.

He had not died easily. A trail of blood and entrails zigzagged back to the heavy door of the cold room, and smears upon the desk panels and baseboards showed where he had dragged himself along. He was young, thin-faced, and athletic, handsome in a bland, middle-class-American sort of way. His eyes were closed, the lashes black half-moons within deep sockets. The cold had slowed decay, and only a chalky tinge to his tanned cheeks hinted that he was not just sleeping. His features were relaxed and peaceful, but his lower back was a shattered ruin. A stitch-gun had plowed six, maybe seven, tiny, explosive needles from behind into his spine, buttocks, and thighs.

Lessing inspected the corpse quickly. Whether the man had been one of the locals or the weasel himself could be discussed later. The mission demanded precision, and he knew what had to be done. Five steps carried him to the thick door of the refrigerated room. It took only a moment to scan the compartments and bins within for the aluminum cases Gomez wanted. Those cases would be marked with U.S. Army identification numbers and the letters PCV: "Pacov," as the little Goanese pronounced the acronym. There were supposed to be two separate PCV containers, PCV-1 and PCV-2.

Doors hung ajar, cartons and containers lay in untidy disarray upon the frosted, black-plastic floor, and someone had even opened the service hatch to the refrigeration unit, revealing coils and ice-sheathed mechanisms inside. The motor was running full blast, struggling unsuccessfully to cool not only this storage chamber but also the rest of the complex—and the whole Southwest beyond!

He spotted the PCV cases at once. They lay open just inside one of the storage compartments: three boxes of dully shining metal marked "PCV-1." The ten egg-shaped depressions in the grey plastic foam inside each case were empty. Lessing looked about and saw three more boxes, smaller and flatter than the first, stencilled

"PCV-2." These were also open, and their deep, squarish sockets held nothing.

"What's up?" Cheh put her head around the door.

"Shit! We've been preempted," Lessing let out pent-up breath in a whooping gasp. The dry, frigid air made him cough, and he sat down upon a stack of containers.

The girl understood at once. "The opfoes've nicked our stuff? Bastards!" Only a few mercenaries remembered that "opfo" had once stood for "opposing forces"; when Lessing had first heard the term out in Angola, he had thought it a word from some African language.

He groaned and got up. It was harder and harder to find energy—and willpower—for this sort of strenuous, damn-fool mission after you passed thirty. Lessing was now thirty-two.

Something else caught his eye: another open carton, of buff-colored plastic this time. One corner was ripped away. The ribbed flooring beneath it was dark red with congealed blood. The dead youth outside had wanted something from this box, wanted it very badly.

Lessing peered at the frost-furred legend stamped onto the plastic. It read "GD-74."

Nerve gas. One of the later and most lethal varieties.

The container had cushioned spaces for twelve round objects, but only eleven shiny, plastic spheres glittered gold against the charcoal-hued packing.

"Now what?" Cheh asked, reasonably enough.

He did not mention the nerve gas. Instead, he moved swiftly back into the outer office and bent over the corpse. It was as he suspected: the air-conditioning duct had been opened, its grillwork slimed with dried, blackish blood. The fingers of the young man's left hand were a rigid maroon-and-white spider clenched upon the cream-colored metal frame.

"You need a torch?"

"A . . . ? Oh, a flashlight. No . . . no. I think I understand . . . ."

"What?"

"Which way was the wind blowing when we came . . . yesterday . . . today?"

"Umm . . . to the northeast, I think. Fairly steady breeze. Why?"

"That's why we're alive. And why those people upstairs and out in the yard are dead. Nerve gas: a single globe of it dropped into the air conditioner."

Cheh goggled at him. "What? Nerve gas? They were killed by . . . by . . . ?"

"One of the GD series. Advanced as all hell. A milligram on your skin or in your lungs, and you've got barely time to lie down. Then you're history."

White-faced, the girl stared at her own fingers as though they were somehow contaminated. "Gawd! No . . . ! Wait . . . how . . . why? Why here? Nerve gas doesn't need refrigeration, does it?"

"Just stored here, I think. After the base was deactivated. All sorts of stuff stacked away down in a convenient hole where nobody would find it and raise hell."

Cheh had another thought. "But wasn't the bloody stuff a binary? Two separate compounds that had to be combined to be lethal?"

"Right. But the Born-Agains got antsy during the missile crisis of 2013. They put GD gas into double-chambered ampoules that could be dropped from the air."

"But those were supposed to be tough—near unbreakable unless you threw 'em out of a plane or off a buildin.' Bloody hell . . . ."

"This boy here knew that if the drop down the air-conditioner shaft wasn't enough to crack the shell, then the fan blades at the bottom would do it."

"But . . . why?"

It was coming together. "Somebody . . . a staff member, a guard, a technician . . . was the weasel. He had access to the keys. Then he cut out the security system with the hummingbird . . . . Kopper and his staff were probably sloppy about it. The weasel came down and took what he wanted. This boy"— for some reason his subconscious mind refused to think of the twisted corpse as an adult—"caught him at it, probably in the refrigerator room. The weasel shot the kid and left him for dead. Meanwhile Kopper came into the communications room upstairs, saw the hummingbird, and tried to wire past it to get out a call for help. The boy probably never knew about that at all. The weasel blew the power plant as he was leaving, to keep the locals confused."

"And once the weasel was gone," Cheh cut in, "the kid came out of shock enough to get a globe of . . . of the gas . . . and crawled over and potted it down the shaft. He must've thought he was savin' the bloody world!"

"Maybe he was." Lessing stood up. He found that his hands were shaking. "Important enough, anyway, to kill not only the weasel but himself as well . . . plus his own people and any ranchers, tourists, or goddamned sheep who happened to be in range downwind!" The idea was terrifying; he backed into a desk, laid his rifle on it with a clatter that sounded like a tank rolling off a cliff, and leaned against the cold metal to keep his legs from trembling.

"The . . . the woman upstairs, them out in the compound?"

"Us, too, if the wind had been blowing to the southwest."

"Great bleedin' Christ! What . . . what's to the northeast?"

Lessing shut his eyes, rubbed the bridge of his nose. "I don't know. I've never been in this state before. Magdalena? Socorro? Not much population between here and there. Some ranches, some Indians, some resorts . . . livestock. God knows what the range is. I don't think it'll reach Albuquerque. Jesus!"

Cheh put up shaking fingers to pat her dust-colored hair. "And this was what the weasel wanted? This nerve gas?"

Lessing shook his head. Gomez had told him little, but he could guess. "Worse, I think." He gave the girl a hard stare. "The weasel got what we were sent for. And don't ask me what that is or what it does, because the players don't tell their goddamned pawns a damned thing. And don't ask me why the weasel decided to act just a day or two before we were set to arrive! I don't know."

Gomez would have some explaining to do. Son of a bitch! Had he used Lessing and his squad as dummies? What did they call it—red herrings? Patsies to take the fall for raiding a top-secret American installation? While the real thief was supposed to get away with the goodies?

They had to get out. Lessing snatched up his rifle and ordered the surprised girl back to the elevator shaft.

On the way back up, Cheh panted, "And now?"

Lessing thought and said, "If we find the weasel dead in the yard, we finish our mission. If not, we look for tracks . . . they'll show up on the snow . . . and if the weasel's gone north or east there's a chance we can still catch up, if we can find a car."

"Catch up? Now? After a day or more?"

"If he headed out in the direction of the wind, there's a very good chance he's as dead as these people. We can only follow and see. If he went some other way, into the wind, he'll be long gone by now. Then we can give it up."

Cheh shuddered. "Not sure I want to catch 'im, even though we get only half pay for comin' home empty-handed!" She furrowed sparse brows in sudden thought. "Wait—how long is the gas active, then? What's the risk to us?"

"Not much. It's airborne, as I recall—dissipates after a few hours." He strove to remember the article he had read during one of his flights to—or was it from?—Angola. "It evaporates quickly, combines with things in the atmosphere, and becomes inert . . . harmless. By now it'll be gone."

"Jesus. I hope so."

"If it isn't, we'll hardly know it."

"You're a cold sod, Lessing. Christ!"

"My name is 'Ek,' remember? On this mission I'm Ek."

Cheh snorted, wiped her stubby nose with equally stubby fingers, and said no more.

The sunshine, weak and pallid as though filtered down through a shallow sea, provided unabashed relief. Lessing met his squad at the front door of the house.

"None of the corpses got anything on dem," the man Lessing had named Panch reported. "No bombs, no veapons. No bulletholes either . . . some kind of gas must've got dem. Look like dey vas from de staff here." Panch was Swedish, a gaunt and bony man who looked like he ought to be plowing rocks in some tiny field beside an arctic fjord. Lessing had worked with him before, during the Baalbek War in Syria. Together they had managed to save a village full of Arab refugees from an over-zealous Israeli tank commander who had wanted to flatten the place.

He mustn't think of the past now. "Transport?" he inquired gruffly.

"Little four-wheel-drive Ikeda Outdoorsman," Char replied. "Over there in a shed behind the garage. No boobytraps. I checked."

"I'm surprised the weasel didn't disable it," Lessing said, "since he went to the trouble of blowing the power plant."

"Then the kid dropped the plum into the bleedin' puddin'," Cheh added. It took several minutes to explain the probable sequence of events to the others.

Lessing finished and asked, "Anybody spot tracks in the snow?" He found himself hoping that there were none—or that they led off to the south or west.

"Auto," Teen answered laconically. He pointed off toward the northeast. "Small—Army, maybe. Or one of them new all-terrain Vipers." He spat into the mud-splattered snow at the bottom of the front-porch steps. Lessing was amused. The man was a chameleon: he had subtly shifted his stance, his posture, and his accent so that he now looked and sounded much like an American from the rural Southwest. A hick from the cow country! If there had been a grass stalk handy, the bastard would be sucking on it! What a fraud! Any real native would pick him out at once.

The automobile held four of them: Lessing, Teen, Char, and Cheh. Doe remained sullen. He tramped off to stand lonely sentry duty atop the hill behind the dilapidated base. Panch stayed behind to prowl around the house and the snow-covered foundations of the destroyed barracks and other buildings within the complex. Lessing knew this type of mercenary all too well; he ordered Panch to steal nothing that might be missed and not to tear the place apart like some adolescent ghetto burglar. Let the authorities guess who had come visiting and why.

The fuel gauge showed about a quarter full, enough for a quick search. Twelve miles out and twelve back, Lessing decided, to be on the safe side. If they didn't catch up with the weasel within that range then so be it. Gomez could send somebody else.

They drove in silence, the Viper's track a double line winding off ahead of them across the snow, a railway to Hell. Lessing was tired. He rubbed the bridge of his nose again. Cheh, in the front passenger seat beside him, glanced over at him with concern. He hoped she would keep any erotic fantasies to herself. She was an excellent comrade—and might, in time, become a good friend—but she had almost as much sexual appeal for Lessing as the ice-shrouded cacti that loomed up like pallid bogeymen outside the car window.

He hated to remember, but memories came anyway. The last time a woman mercenary had got her panties wet over him had been in Jerusalem during the Baalbek War. She had died somewhere near Damascus, in a nameless ditch full of mud bricks that were as old as Babylon.

Get the job done. Do the needful, as Gomez said in his impeccably British-Indian accent. Do the needful and get out.

Whoever had driven the Viper knew the way. There was a road of sorts under the drifted snow, twin ruts that had once known asphalt but were now no more than a frozen, dirt track. More silent cacti lurched up out of the grey desolation, mesquite, sagebrush, rocks and boulders and twisted monoliths of stone. It looked like the empty quarter of Hell.

"There!" said Teen sharply. Lessing, in the driver's seat in front of him, jumped and swore under his breath.

"Goddamn it!"

"Right there." The man leaned past him to point. The Viper's tracks swerved, turned almost a half circle, then dived off behind a tumbled stand of white-hoared brush. The odometer showed that they had travelled eleven miles.

Lessing slewed their car to a slush-spraying stop. They piled out, took cover behind the vehicle, and looked around. Nothing moved. He signalled for them to draw up in tactical squad formation. Canvas rustled; weapons clicked; Teen's asthmatic breathing wheezed in the frigid air. Then they were ready. It was about fifty meters around the brush pile.

Lessing squinted, then waved an arm for a rapid advance. They began to jog, then to trot. Bushes, rocks, snow, a set of tiny tracks—Lessing had time to wonder if they were rabbit or squirrel or something else—then they reached the tangle of black branches and debris around which the Viper had gone. There was no road here. The driver must have lost control. The spoiled-meat features of Arthur L. Kopper leaped up unbidden before his eyes, then the chalk-limned face of the dead boy in the subterranean office.

Icy daggers began to stab at Lessing's lungs. His breath plumed out in white banners. Blood surged against his temples, and he felt the jarring crunch of each footstep upon the slippery roots and stones buried beneath the snow. His rifle banged against his side. He heard Cheh just behind him to his left, Teen's heavy, gasping breathing to his right. Char was invisible behind them, guarding their rear.

There was snow in his eyes, and he blinked. Snow? He tried to bring up a hand to brush his face but found it pinned beneath him. He was lying prone behind a log. He realized that he had fallen flat, a reflex action so automatic that he had done it without being aware of it. God, if he got out of here he'd have to take a rest. Otherwise he might find himself waking up with a scream on his lips and a gun in his hand. He was minded of Colfax, who had stabbed his wife three times one night before he realized he wasn't in Angola any more. The Paraguayan police hadn't taken to that excuse well at all, and poor Colfax was still languishing in some hole of a prison down there.

Lessing shook his head once, hard, then peered through the dead leaves and twigs in front of him.

A bright-blue Viper lay upside down amidst the ghost-grey saplings.

Lessing motioned Teen and Cheh to stay put and provide covering fire; he and Char got to their feet and moved in. Except for their breathing and the crackling of their footsteps in the snow-swathed weeds, there was no sound. Char took the left, toward the front of the Viper. Lessing headed for the rear and got there first. He paused, panting, beside the rear wheel. It took him a long moment to remember that American automobiles had a left-handed drive; goddamn it, he had been away too long! In an American car this was the passenger side—the right side when it was upright.

No sound came. He squinted down the Viper's mirror-polished flank and noted that the passenger doors were closed, the car tilted so that snow obscured the side windows. The rear window was dark as well. He gathered strength, lurched up, and floundered through an unexpected, waist-deep drift to reach the driver's side. The front door was unlatched, though still shut. To get out, one would have had to crawl up at a fairly steep angle. He could not see any tracks in the snow below the door.

The driver—and any other occupants—were still inside.

A movement beneath the front bumper caught his eye: Char. He waved to show he was all right, ready for the final advance. The other wiggled a finger in return.

The driver's window was still closed, rimed and blotched with frost. He rubbed it with his glove but could make out only shadows within. The door, then: this gave easily, lifting up without so much as a creak. He steeled himself for whatever lay inside.

He expelled breath in a rasping cough.

So, the weasel was a woman! A Black woman, in fact, although her wavy hair and fair skin hinted at an admixture of Spanish or Indian blood. Caribbean?

She wore a tight and stylish blouse of some fancy, crushed-looking, maroon fabric; a short polo coat; elegant, grey slacks tight enough to have been painted upon her rounded thighs; and soft desert boots. Bronze-hued sunglasses hid her eyes.

Which was just as well. She had died at least a day ago, maybe two.

The smell wasn't really bad yet—the weather had been cold—but Lessing's nose told him that she had soiled herself in her dying.

"Jee . . . zuss!" That was Char, just behind him.

Lessing could see nothing of any size under the body. He opened the rear door. The Viper lay mostly on its back, tilted so that the driver's side was higher than the other; its rear seat was now a narrow tunnel full of upholstery and litter. At least he didn't have to crawl down on top of the dead woman.

A wad of white plastic caught his eye, something much like a kitchen garbage bag. He sighed, gulped cold, fresh air, and dived down to retrieve it.

It was heavy and lumpy. A glance told him this was what they had come for. Inside he could see oval capsules of silvery metal, about the size of small hand grenades. There were also tubes of some dull, black material: stoppered vials like overgrown deodorant bottles. The globes were stamped "PCV-1," the black cylinders "PCV-2." He knew without counting that there would be thirty of each.

"Got it?" Char asked. He had a high, whining, demanding voice. Given time, Lessing could grow to dislike this man.

"Right!" Lessing wriggled back up out of the Viper, the slippery-smooth plastic sack clutched in his left hand.

"Signalling!" Char hissed. "Teen's signalling. He's spotted somebody coming."

What dismal luck! A curious farmer would delay them; a county sheriff or state patrolman would hang things up much longer. Explanations, offers to go for help, the rather chancy I.D. cards Gomez had provided: all were problematic. He didn't even want to think about the possibility of a government patrol, MP's or FBI, coming to investigate an unanswered telephone or unnoticed alarm back at the base. They couldn't just hide: their tracks in the snow were like pointing arrows. Nor could they make it back to their car and run like hell, not in time.

He waved Teen into the depths of a stand of brush, then pointed Cheh to a heap of dead leaves and tree trunks. Both had the sense to cover their khaki camouflage suits with snow. Another crime to lay at Gomez' door: the little bastard ought to have known that white was better than brown during a North American winter!

He still wore his red-orange hunter's jacket. Char's dun-colored pants and tan duffel-coat might arouse suspicion if anybody stopped to think about it; yet there ought to be some American hunters stupid enough to wear earth colors during hunting season! He grinned mirthlessly; many might perish, like jackrabbits caught in a car's headlamps, but hell, there ought to be a new crop of idiots every year!

He dropped the white plastic sack into the drift beside him and scuffed snow over it. His Riga-71 assault rifle he pushed under the curve of the overturned Viper's roof, where it was invisible yet easily reached. Char hid his smaller, stubbier stitch-gun behind his leg, by the front bumper.

They were as ready as they'd ever be.

The noise Teen had heard grew louder, the sustained clatter of a medium-size vehicle of some kind, its engine badly in need of tuning. It was another minute before it hove into view: an archaic, black, German pickup truck, the standard workhorse of twenty-first-century, rural America.

The newcomer paused beside their car, then jounced on to stop near the Viper. The front seat held two men and a woman. The cargo space in the rear was empty.

"Hi!" Lessing called. "Been an accident here." Might as well be obvious.

The driver stayed where he was, but the other man opened the passenger door and got out. The woman followed. Both wore nondescript winter clothing, boots, hats, and scarves. The man was youngish, red-faced, puffy-looking, and clean-shaven. The woman was older, plain, and pale. She wore rimless glasses and a bright-red stocking cap. Too young to be the man's mother, too old to be his wife. No farmers, these. Looked like a law clerk and a librarian!

Lessing scowled, the good citizen who has just discovered a tragedy. "Woman . . . dead in there," he began. "Came off the road and tipped over."

The man said, "Lordy!" He edged forward as if to inspect the wreck.

"You from around here?" the woman asked.

"California."

"Huntin'?"

"Yeah," Char put in. "Vacation."

"What was you huntin' then?" The woman appeared too educated to use grammar like that. Blood began to throb at Lessing's temples again.

"Oh . . . just high hopes . . . ."

She pulled her handbag up, reached into it. She might have been looking for a handkerchief. "Not much around here to hunt, these days."

Lessing was first. His Riga-71 sputtered, and the woman went down in a swirl of dark woollens and scarlet. Something blue and metallic spun from her hand. He went prone and heard bullets spang off the underbelly of the Viper. Then Teen's automatic rifle snarled from somewhere back in the underbrush, and Cheh's laser hissed and sizzled. The driver of the truck yelped, then shrieked, just once.

Silence. A single shot: Teen, likely, putting quietus to the driver.

Lessing crawled to his feet, the Viper's flank cold and slick beneath his sweating palms. "Anybody . . . ?" he began. Then he saw Char. The man lay on his belly in the snow. He humped up, grunted, writhed, and clutched his abdomen, from which red now seeped to stain the trampled whiteness.

"Oh, God," Cheh breathed from behind him. "Get the car. We can . . . ."

"No." Lessing motioned her back, then jerked a thumb at Teen. "You look at him. You've done medic before."

This was no time for proper medical practice. The Englishman pulled the stricken man's red-dyed hands away from his belly. "Gut-shot," he reported tersely. "In shock. Dead in an hour 'less we get him to a hospital."

"Forget that!" Lessing snapped. He went to stand before Char. "You want it over?" he asked softly. "Or you want us to carry you back? You'll die on the road, you know. We can't get you out in time. And it'll start to hurt soon."

The other stared at him from shock-glazed eyes.

Lessing raised his head to look at Teen, who had moved around to stand behind the wounded man. Teen's rifle pointed casually downward, at Char's cap of black hair.

The rifle echoed like a clap of doom.

"Aw . . . Jesus . . . ." Cheh turned away.

"Better so," Teen muttered matter-of-factly. Lessing turned to inspect the bodies of the newcomers. He patted their garments, extracted wallets, flipped open card cases.

"U.S. government I.D. . . . . Army Intelligence. Based in Albuquerque. Either there was a secondary alarm system the hummingbird didn't get, or else somebody called to ask old Kopper the time of day." He glanced into the truck, then exclaimed softly.

"Jesus, Cheh, your laser just missed some boxes of ammo! Couple of fragmentation grenades too! They were really ready for us."

Cheh sat down in the snow. Lessing watched with sympathy; she had borne more today than many men could have.

"How . . . how did you recognize . . . them . . . as agents?" she managed.

"Clothes, manner. They looked as wrong out here as we did. Then the woman asked about what we were hunting, rather than about the car wreck. Hell, even if she'd been for real I couldn't have answered her. How do I know what people hunt around here? In the dead of winter? It's probably not even hunting season!"

"Armadillos," Teen said.

"What? Armed what?"

The little man grinned and did a ludicrous parody of a Mexican accent: "No, señor, no! Arma-fucking-*dildoes*."

"Get stuffed!" Cheh looked as though she were about to cry.

Lessing picked up his gun. "Back to the car. There'll be more agents on the way when these three don't report in. We drop Char into the Viper, set it on fire, run the feds' truck off where it can't be seen, and hightail it for the base. We pick up the others, and head out for our drop site. We should be there by dawn. It'll take the pursuit some time to sort it all out."

Lessing reached into the snow and hefted the white plastic bag. So much death, and all for these spheres and vials. Murderous germs, lethal gases, some other subtle and ghastly weapon—the stuff of nightmares. God damn it, people used to fight for gold, for women, for honor, for values a person could understand. Now they killed for abstractions, words on paper, causes, doctrines—murky political games in which there were neither rights nor wrongs.

And he, Lessing, had willingly chosen to become one of the pawns.

Cheh and Teen wrestled Char's body up into the Viper's front seat. The case of ammo and the grenades would make a nice fanfare for the funeral.

Lessing peered into the crinkly, white plastic bag. The silvery PCV-1 spheres winked evilly back; the black vials of PCV-2 kept their counsel to themselves.

He slipped a hand tentatively into the bag, extracted one sphere and one cylinder. They felt cold, inimical, hostile. He thought, then made up his mind: he dropped them both down into the hidden pocket sewed into the lining of his canvas trouser leg. If Gomez or anybody asked, he would claim that he had only found twenty-nine. Who could know? Up Gomez! Up them all! Such insurance might come in handy some day.

It was time to go home.

I do not set much value on the friendship of people who do not succeed in getting disliked by their enemies.
— *Mein Kampf*, **Adolf Hitler**

CHAPTER THREE

Sunday, April 6, 2042

"Love you too," Wrench grumbled. He glanced up to find Lessing beside him, awash with undulating, grey-green light from the row of security TV screens, like some archaic idol submerged beneath the sea.

"So you got me out of bed. Who the hell is it?" Lessing fingered the TV camera-control console, but the visitor had passed beyond the range of camera three and was not yet visible to camera two. He rubbed sleep out of his eyes. Goddamn it, he'd been meaning to splice in another camera to cover the blind spot between two and three. Camera twenty-six, down at the bottom of the garden by the factory fence, was also out. Lessing just didn't have the energy. Northern India in April was a cauldron of white-hot heat, and May and June would be worse. Only after the rains broke in July would the parched plains cool off again. And then only a little.

"Looks like one of your scruffier friends." Wrench remarked mildly. A small, neatly packaged man in his late thirties, his real name was Charles Hanson Wren, but his Army footlocker had borne the legend "WREN, C. H.," and the nickname "Wrench" had stuck. He was Herman Mulder's house security man. Lessing had charge of the compound and the buildings of Indoco's chemical factory in India, just south of Lucknow, off the Kanpur road.

Lessing said nothing.

"Look, I'm sorry to get you up," Wrench's tone indicated that he thought it was funny. He smirked up at the wall clock, which read 0210, and showed teeth so white and even that everybody thought they were a plate. Actually they were his own. Wrench was just a trifle jealous: Mulder always chose Lessing as his beegee whenever he made one of his infrequent forays out into the chaos that was twenty-first-century India.

"Sure."

"Sleeping's a comfort in this heat."

Lessing looked at him. Like everybody else in Indoco's Lucknow operation, Wrench knew that Lessing shared his bed with Mulder's Indian liaison girl, Jameela Husaini. Nobody gave much of a damn where or with whom the hired help slept, and Wrench didn't care, nor was he himself interested in Jameela. She was over-educated for his tastes, a graduate of the Kennedy School for Special Children in Delhi and later of Columbia University. Wrench did enjoy knowing everything, however. Too damned nosy—and too much of a comic! One day somebody would hoist the little smart-ass by his head of glossy, dark hair, as wavy as an ad for gigolos, and drop him off a minaret!

An image moved on camera two's small screen. The visitor halted before the outer gate, glanced around, looked up at the lens mounted above his head, and made a nervous gesture toward the bell.

"Uh . . . is Mr. Lessing there? I . . . ah . . . am sorry to bother you . . . him . . . at this hour." It was the man Lessing had named Doe: Felix Bauer, as he had learned from Gomez a month after his return to India.

Wrench pressed a button. A ruby warning light flashed. "He's carrying a popper. Or else he's wearing a cast-iron jockstrap."

Lessing picked up the microphone and said, "Hello, Bauer. Put your ordnance into the lockbox on the post next to you. Then follow the left-hand path around to the rear."

The lockbox duly registered the weight of a good-sized pistol—and possibly a boot knife as well. The metal detectors pronounced Bauer clean. Only then did Lessing press the double buttons that opened the gate.

At this time of night the verandah of the senior-staff quarters was deserted. Lessing met Bauer at the top of the steps and pointed him to a rattan settee as far away from the main circle of porch furniture as possible. The lighted area had two disadvantages: it teemed with flying insects, and the ceiling fan concealed a surveillance mike. Why make it easy for Wrench to eavesdrop?

Bauer sat, licked his lips, and looked about. His glance lingered on the gleaming, white refrigerator visible inside the screen door. Lessing took pity on him; Bauer's journey out here from Lucknow at this hour of night must have been a hot, dusty, and thirsty one—and he must have paid the taxi-wala a fortune to boot! Lessing got up again and came back with two bottles of Indian beer.

"Well?" Lessing decided the German looked terrible. They hadn't met since the New Mexico business in January, but then they had never been friends—or enemies either. Just two people doing a job.

The other gulped cold beer. Then he said, "Einar Hjellming . . . the Swede you called Panch . . . is dead."

Lessing grunted. "How?"

"Shot. From ambush. They tried to kill Hollister . . . your Teen, the Britisher . . . too. Missed him by five centimeters." Bauer pawed at his greying hair with thin fingers.

"Who's 'they'?"

"People said you would know."

"Me? I don't know anything." He did have a question: "What about Cheh, the Australian girl? Rose Thurley is her name."

"I haven't heard. She went back to Canberra, I think."

"Well, uh, fine. I . . . I'm sorry about Hjellming." He wasn't, but it seemed to mean something to the other man.

"May I speak frankly?"

Lessing watched him. "Sure."

"I came to ask you to leave *me* alone. You don't have to say anything, just let me go my way. Don't thumb me."

Lessing snorted up a nose full of bitter beer. He coughed, wiped his mouth, and growled, "*What?*"

"I mean it. I don't cause problems."

There were stories, of course, of mercenaries who were later "thumbed" by their employers or by their comrades. Too much knowledge wasn't smart. Such incidents were fewer since it had become acceptable for nations and corporations and causes and even individuals to hire mercs to do their "spesh-ops"—special operations. Now the world, the Western world anyway, thought of mercenaries as glamorous Samurai, an honor-bound warrior class, the stuff of endless TV series.

Bauer knew Lessing's reputation: no one had ever accused him of thumbing before. And, supposing that he *had* been paid to thumb his squad, Bauer should realize that he'd do the job himself and not hire some grimy, city hit-man to handle it.

Lessing kept a straight face and said only, "Mercs get killed all the time. One of the joys of the trade."

The blunt numbness of the accusation was wearing off, and Lessing's mind began to work again. Bauer was clearly frightened: his rigid jaw line showed it. Was he sane? Paranoia was a common ailment amongst mercenaries. You didn't learn to suspect every bush, every door, every footstep, and not have some of that caution sift down into the cracks of your immortal soul.

Bauer clutched his beer bottle with both hands. "People . . . we . . . do get killed. But not by hit-men, not in Copenhagen or Rio! Lessing, for God's sake . . . !"

"For God's sake *what?* I haven't anything to do with this . . . not with Hjellming, not with Hollister. Not with you! Who gave you this idea? Who said I was thumbing my squad?" Even a breath of this kind of rumor could end a man's career. Worse, it could get that man himself thumbed.

Bauer hesitated. "Nobody said . . . nobody came right out . . . ."

Lessing glared at him. "You're stupid, Bauer, really *stupid*. If I *am* thumbing, then this is my chance to finish you off! Inside our fence, nobody questions Indoco's business. You could vanish without a trace!" He spread his hands on the table, palms up. "But think: if I'm *not* thumbing my squad, then I *am* going to find out where the rumor started and what I can do about it. If I have to kill . . . or worse . . . to keep my reputation clean, I will. Either way, you lose." He began to get to his feet. "Do we chat easy? Or hard?"

"Look, please . . . ." Bauer's eyes reflected the flickering light.

"We have a room in the garage," Lessing remarked. "We keep our auto repair tools there. It's soundproof."

"*Gott*, I never meant . . . I only wanted . . . ."

"Who, Bauer? *Who?*"

"Copley . . . in Paris. He never said you were thumbing. Just that . . . some people around you might die! I . . . I took him to mean . . . I imagined he meant . . . ." Bauer shifted his grip on his beer bottle, holding it horizontally so that he could smash it against the table edge and jab it into his adversary's eyes. Bauer had studied barroom brawling with experts.

So had Lessing. He pointed. "Go ahead, try. The table is woven rattan, and there's a good chance the bottle won't break. Do you want to take that chance?" He smiled.

Bauer sat back down. "Just give me your word, *ja*? No harm to me. I don't want to know anything. I could even pay you . . . a little." He tapped his rumpled shirt pocket.

"I don't want your goddamn money. There's nothing to know. No thumbing. And I can't protect either of us until I know what's going on."

"Then why? Why Hjellming and Hollister? Why Copley? He gossips a lot with the Euro-mercs. He must've heard something."

"He heard rumors! Just crap. Bullshit. Talk!"

"Hjellming and Hollister . . . they weren't just talk," Bauer muttered defiantly.

Lessing made a derisive noise. "Personal grudges? Violent crime? It's going the rounds, you know."

Bauer took the remark seriously. "No. Not so. You assassinate execs. You kidnap execs and technicians. You shoot spies. But *nobody* kills off-duty mercenaries! We're only the soldiers, the *Soldaten*, the muscles and the bones." He paused and then finished on a defensive but stubborn note: "Why should Copley lie? He said people around you might die!"

"Who's going to kill them, goddammit? *Who?* Indoco?" Lessing relaxed a trifle, still keeping a wary eye on Bauer's bottle.

Bauer had regained both his composure and a measure of defiance. "How should I know? Copley only made warnings about you. Maybe somebody else thumbs you too, later."

Bauer sounded crazier than Lessing had thought. He stifled a yawn. It would be good to rid himself of this unwanted guest and get back upstairs to Jameela. It was going on three in the morning!

The German peered into the beer bottle, but it was empty. "It was the job . . . the New Mexico thing . . . I think."

"What about it?" It was Lessing's turn to sound defensive. "Hell, Indoco owed me a vacation, and I needed the money. An agent I know made me an offer: see the American Southwest on the budget plan! *His* plan and *his* budget! I did what I was told, and I got paid. I don't ask, and I don't tell."

"Yes, but . . . ." Bauer pursed his lips, the picture of a prissy, European bureaucrat. Then: "You have seen nothing, been told nothing?"

Lessing pressed one hand to his pajama-top. "Nothing. Scout's honor."

Bauer missed the sarcasm. "Truly? Nothing?"

"Not a thing. All we get out here are student protesters: 'Yankee, go home!' That sort of stuff. The police stand around until they think we're going to be overrun, then they make a *lathi* charge and knock a few heads. It's a local ritual, like the peacock's mating dance!"

Bauer blinked at him.

Lessing said, more kindly, "Look, it's too late for you to go back to Lucknow tonight. Stay over here and take it easy. We can put you up. Tomorrow, after breakfast, we'll talk. Hell, maybe Wrench can get you a security job at the factory."

"A post? No . . . I . . . ."

"You frightened of contamination? Pollution? Cyanide-laced rosewater? Radioactive *kumkum* powder? That's what the Indians claim we make here." He grinned to show he was joking.

Bauer only stared at him wide-eyed. "I have to get back. My . . . my taxi is waiting, down by the factory gatehouse. The driver is drinking tea with your watchmen." He got to his feet: stiff, dignified, determined, and apologetic all at once. "Thank you."

Lessing let him go. He couldn't blame the German for not trusting him. Who would? He watched Bauer march down the walk and out of sight around the six-car garage. Then he trudged back upstairs to the air-conditioned company flat he shared with Jameela.

If somebody had it in for their squad, why hadn't they come for him? After all, *he* was the mission leader. Yet he hadn't heard or seen a thing. His trouble-smelling instinct had never failed him yet. Was he becoming complacent? Senile? Blind in his old age?

He decided—tentatively—that Bauer was probably suffering from battle fatigue: the "merc jerks," as the tabloids cutely named the syndrome.

The three-room flat in the squarish, whitewashed senior-staff quarters building was semi-dark; only Lessing's imitation Aladdin's lamp—electric, with a 220-volt bulb instead of a wick and oil—burned dim in what the Indoco employment brochures gushingly described as "the sitting room." The flat was hot and stuffy; even the big, German air-conditioning unit couldn't cope with India's heat.

Jameela was asleep in the bedroom, one slender arm flung out upon Lessing's pillow, a tumble of raven-wing hair visible above the thin sheet. She stirred, and Lessing paused to look at her. Unlike American women with their broader shoulders and boyish waists, Jameela Husaini came from a softer and more curvaceous mold. She reminded Lessing of the Ajanta frescoes: an oval face with a high forehead; long-lashed eyes; skin the hue of old gold ("like a South German on a cloudy day," Wrench said); a tall, slender, long-legged figure; firm, uptilted breasts; a narrow waist; and thighs like some Hindu goddess from a sculptured frieze. He had once tried to tell Jameela how much he preferred her beauty to American angularity, but he was not good with words. She took him to mean that her hips were—to be blunt—fat, and she hadn't forgiven him for a month. She still played tennis furiously every morning with Indoco's seven European women staffers, and he knew how jealous she was of the prettiest of them. She had no need to be; it was they who envied her.

He did not wake her but lay down close by upon the thin, hard mattress. Jameela moved against him, and he began to spiral down into sleep, her unbound tresses tickling his shoulder and filling his nostrils with pungent, jasmine perfume.

Yells and noise ripped the fabric of his dream to shreds.

He sat up, groaned, combed back his thin, ash-blonde hair, and fumbled his way out onto the flat's tiny balcony. He hadn't dreamed it; there were more noises below. He looked out over black-satin darkness, the impenetrable night of India, to the tangled, diamond spider webs of the factory's lights: strings of bulbs hung on every tank, pipe, catwalk, and tower, turning the prosaic factory into fairy spires and oriental palaces, richer than Sindbad, more wondrous than the Thousand and One Nights. He squinted down into the courtyard closer by, just beneath the balcony. In the stark glare of the gate floodlights he saw a dancing jumble of white pants, white shirts, white teeth, black beards, and dark faces and skins, like cut-up scraps of a black-and-white photograph tossed into the air. At first he could make out nothing.

One splotch of scarlet in the midst of it all was clear, however: a body on a company stretcher.

He could not see the face, but he sensed it was Bauer.

Wrench was already at the gate when Lessing arrived. Both had dutifully endured Indoco's Hindustani lessons, but this was Jameela Husaini's special duty, and Lessing had to go back, wake her up, and then wait impatiently while she donned the *shalwar-qameez* costume she favored, essentially a tunic and slacks, much different from the Hindu *sari*. She took along a shawl, which she wrapped around her head and shoulders when she went forward to speak to the plant watchmen, the Pathan *chaukidars* Mulder had hired to supplement his European security people. The Pathans surrounded her, reporting, re-enacting, and gesticulating. Enough dramatic talent for a TV series.

He looked down at the stretcher. An arm moved, and he heard breath bubbling beneath the rust-red company blanket. Bauer was alive.

God, he was tired. His head hurt, and he couldn't concentrate on poor Bauer. Let the company doctor, the little Bengali gentleman now chattering with Jameela, handle that. He just waited, an automaton whose motor functions had been turned off but whose sensors were still on. His eyes were a TV camera, recording but not comprehending. Sharp gravel pricked his slippered feet, and his skin was simultaneously clammy and dry with the unforgiving, relentless heat of the Indian night, the harbinger of the scorching morrow. The air smelled of baked brass, charcoal, alien spices, and warm earth as old as God, all mingled with animal manure and flower scents and people. Endless people, now over a billion in this fifth decade of the twenty-first century.

Jameela said something soothing to the senior *chaukidar* of the plant. She came back to Lessing and Wrench.

"The taximan struck him, they think. He's not with his vehicle now. Nobody saw any fight. The stranger . . . " she shot a quizzical glance at Lessing " . . . returned from the compound and went straight toward his taxi. The watchmen didn't see him again until he came staggering up from the auto park, all bloody. Mahmood Khan took him inside and called the others."

Jameela was good, Lessing thought. He had served with dozens of mercs who couldn't make a report as concise as that. He smiled at her, then realized she would think he was patronizing her.

"Who is he?" Jameela asked. It was her job to make any statements to the Indian police.

"He vill live," Doctor Chakravarti interrupted excitedly. "Live, if ve get him to Balrampur Hospital in time! Mr. Wren, Mr. Lessing, please to give permission for the station vagon. Kuldeep can drive."

"Any other problems?" Wrench threw in, speaking over the doctor's head to Jameela. "Other break-ins? Trouble with the students? The villagers? Outsiders?"

She rubbed at her forehead, pushing her heavy tresses out of her eyes, then translated for the senior *chaukidar*. A babble of voices answered her. She replied, "No . . . nothing."

"Somebody go get Mr. Mulder up!" Wrench ordered. "Search the plant, the perimeter." He was visibly excited. But then Wrench struck Lessing that way: an over-reaction for every occasion.

"Bring him on inside," a new and deeper voice said. "We can see to him there. If he's critical, we'll have to drive him to Lucknow."

Lessing turned his head to see Bill Goddard, Mulder's senior executive officer. Behind him, a hulking shadow in the darkness, stood Herman Mulder himself. The commotion had brought him down from the mansion.

Dr. Chakravarti would have gone on insisting on the station wagon, at once if not sooner, but nobody argued with Goddard. The man was a rock: huge, massive, as solid as the ramparts of the Delhi Red Fort itself.

Goddard said, "You, Lessing. You, Wren. Come with." He ignored Jameela as though she didn't exist. He disliked Indians, even those with European features and light skin like Jameela, and Lessing had often wondered why the company had sent him out to Lucknow, of all places.

Lessing gestured, and two of the *chaukidars* took up the stretcher and carried it through the gate, past the staff quarters, and up the inner drive to the Director's house. What a parade: squat, hairless, old Mulder lurching along in front, his bald head as shiny as a dress helmet; then Goddard, wrapped in his own self-importance; then the two Indians with Bauer, the main float; then Dr. Chakravarti trotting behind; and Wrench and Lessing bringing up the rear: the trained-dog act, the big, rangy German shepherd and the nervous, yapping, little terrier.

The big house was cement block and concrete, a pink monstrosity that looked more like a transistor radio than a residence, the sort of "modern bungalow" one found everywhere in the "best" suburbs up and down the subcontinent. It was air-conditioned throughout, so cold that it was almost an affront after the sticky night outside. It smelled of furniture varnish and the disinfectant with which the servants mopped the concrete-chip mosaic floor.

The cavernous "drawing room" beyond the screened verandah was empty. There was indeed a Mrs. Mulder, but she appeared so rarely that Wrench called her the "Fairy Godmother": "Comes out with her wand three times a year . . . Christmas, the Fourth of July, and Indian Independence Day . . . to sprinkle stars and bless us all. Then, poof! . . . back to limbo!"

The watchmen set Bauer's stretcher down, and Dr. Chakravarti knelt for a better look under the popping, fizzing fluorescent lights.

"Not so bad as I had . . . ."

"Fine," Goddard snapped. "Fix him up. Who the hell is he?"

Lessing stepped forward before Wrench could offer any snide, little sarcasms. "Friend of mine. Came to see me. No idea who knifed him . . . or why. Some quarrel with the taxi-wala, maybe."

"Charming. All we need is a tangle with the police. Prime Minister Ramanujan's government would love an excuse to send all foreign companies packing. And confiscate our installations in the bargain." Goddard looked to Mulder for confirmation, but the old man was watching the doctor, puffy, heavy-lidded eyes as blank as a temple statue's.

"The wound is in the chest," the doctor went on, clinically and precisely, as though no one had spoken. "A bandage, antibiotics, rest. He will be all right."

Lessing saw that Bauer's eyes were open. "Who stuck you? The taxi driver? Can you talk?"

The other grunted something in German—or maybe it was Flemish or Dutch. Then he said, quite clearly, "Not the taximan. Another. Come for you, maybe, or something else important. I was just a . . . a by-the-way."

Mulder opened his mouth to ask a question, but he was interrupted. The double doors at the far end of the room swung open to reveal Mrs. Mulder herself. Without makeup, coiffure, and French chiffon, her fairy-godmother magic was sadly lacking: a gaunt, vinegary American housewife in the latter years of menopause. She bore neither wand nor sparkling stars.

"Dear," she trilled, "you told me to call you if the red lights came on." She stopped, dismayed by the size of her audience. "Oh, I had no idea . . . ."

"Red lights?" Mulder asked blankly.

Goddard said, "The security-alert lights! Somebody's gotten inside . . . !"

"Intrusion!" Wrench cried. Neither he nor Lessing had brought weapons.

"*Which* light?" Mulder heaved himself toward his spouse, a plump and hairless white whale. People said he was over seventy, but he had the energy of a much younger man.

"The little one . . . on the end . . . ." The woman dithered. Lessing had never seen anyone actually dither before.

"Get my . . . !" Wrench shrilled. The doctor and the two *chaukidars* were in his way, and he did a ridiculous dance to get around them.

Lessing knew which light was lit; he had helped install the system himself. Outside, beyond Indoco's compound, lay wasteland, a crumbled mosque, and a deserted Muslim cemetery that the government wouldn't let anybody uproot. Camera twenty-six there was out of order, whether by accident or design. That meant that an intruder who knew the layout had a clear route over the plant's back fence all the way up into Mrs. Mulder's formal rose garden behind the mansion. If it wasn't a false alarm, the red light on Mulder's panel indicated a security breach in the main house itself!

"Weapons?" Lessing threw at Mulder.

The other, already ahead of him in the corridor leading to the rear of the house, waved a hand and shouted back something that sounded like, "Bedroom!"

Lessing rounded the corner at the end of the passage. He couldn't see Mulder any more: the old man must have entered one of the two doors there or gone upstairs. Lessing chose the door to his left and skidded into the dining room. The closed, stuffy darkness smelled of spices and cooking, but the woven-bamboo blinds and ornate, imitation-Mughal furniture were undisturbed. A door at the far end opened into a shadowy hall beyond which lay the pantry and the serving kitchen. Meals were actually prepared in a separate building, some twenty meters away. From there a train of servants bore the dishes up to the main house or over to the staff refectory. Even in these days of electric appliances and do-it-yourself housework old traditions died hard; India had swarmed with servants long before the British had arrived. Now it was only foreigners, the rich, and corporations like Indoco who could afford them.

Lessing glanced around and snatched up a heavy poultry knife from a drainage board. Any weapon was better than nothing. He checked quickly and found the back door locked. Goddard habitually opened it at dawn for the "bearers" with their "morning bed tea": another Indian custom, one that Lessing rather enjoyed.

He whirled and dashed back out to the hallway, then up the slippery, polished, concrete stairs two at a time.

Mulder knelt in the corridor by the door of the master bedroom, hands to his face. A trickle of dark liquid oozed between his fingers. Lessing stopped and made sure he was alive. He crouched down and peered around the doorjamb.

It was lucky that he had decided to duck. He found himself staring at a gleaming silver belt buckle, black trousers below it, so close he could see the weave of the fabric, and a dark jacket above. An Israeli stitch-gun hissed like a striking viper in his ear, and he heard the tiny, deadly explosions blasting three-centimeter craters in the cement-block wall across the stairwell behind him.

He reacted as training had taught him: he shoved the big poultry knife up between his adversary's thighs, into his abdomen. The other gagged, doubled over, tried ineffectually to bat at Lessing with the stubby gun barrel, and then crumpled over, full on top of him. Blood and entrails splattered Lessing's chest. A gun bellowed from across the room, not a gas-powered stitch-gun this time but gunpowder.

Lessing felt nothing: the shot had missed. There were two or more opfoes, then. Grimly he set himself to getting free from the thrashing body on top of him—and to finding the damned stitch-gun.

Somebody behind Lessing yelped, and a second gun roared there. The voice sounded like Wrench's. Goddard must have given him a weapon. With all the concentration of a man defusing a time-bomb as the seconds tick away to zero, Lessing fumbled around on the floor for the stitch-gun.

He found it, clutched at its blood-slippery butt, and rolled to avoid presenting a stationary target.

He needn't have bothered. The room was silent except for someone wheezing just above him. He recognized Wrench's breathing.

"You okay?" the little man gasped. "You dead? Hey, Lessing?"

"God damn it, I'm all right. See to the opfoes. And Mulder."

"Goddard's bringing the doctor. Stay put if you're wounded."

"I told you, I'm not hurt. Check Mulder. One of them hit him with a pistol butt or something when he entered the bedroom."

He heard voices, noises, footsteps behind him. On the floor, a meter from his face, his erstwhile opponent still twitched feebly. He clambered to his feet and felt his way across the room, past the gigantic double bed with the satin coverlet Mrs. Mulder had imported all the way from Denmark. There he stumbled over a spindly-legged chair and ended on all fours beside the second opfo.

Moonlight through the tangled drapes picked out splinters of white bone and a dark, liquid smear where the man's face should have been. Wrench was a good shot for a non-merc. Or just lucky.

Lessing knelt to secure the man's gun: a neat, oil-fragrant, Belgian 9-mm automatic. Darkness swirled and swam around him. Dimly, ebon upon black, he perceived shapes on the floor beside the body: flat, squarish things. A thought struck him, and he squinted up at the wall behind the bed.

A cavity yawned there: Mulder's wall safe stood open.

So the object of the intrusion was just simple burglary!

Or was it?

Bauer's visit so late at night? His talk of "thumbing?" The stabbing down by the vehicle park?

Now this.

Too many coincidences.

Lessing groped on the polished terrazzo floor. His fingers touched a snarled mass of jangling, metallic objects: one of Mrs. Mulder's necklaces, probably. Then five or six of the flat rectangles. They felt like record books of some sort, ledgers or diaries. He held one up to the fitful moonlight.

The book's cover was embossed in tarnished gold with a double lightning-bolt design above a line of numerals. He slanted it toward the window and read "1948-1955."

It couldn't be: that would make the book almost a hundred years old, a near antique!

Yet it *felt* real. He didn't know what to think: Mulder had never evinced interest in anything cultural, much less in rare books. Lessing picked up another volume, his curiosity piqued. It was newer, dated 1985-1987. Perhaps a dozen similar volumes lay scattered on the floor beneath the safe.

Were these what the intruders sought, then? Were they so rare and valuable? They certainly weren't Indoco ledgers: those were kept in the main office at the factory, and Lessing would have recognized them. Nobody had to risk a break-in to see those anyhow. The company was scrupulous about keeping "open books" for the benefit of the Indian government.

He looked again, carefully this time. Two or three more of the same set protruded from a black cloth bag under the dead man's shoulder. The opfoes had been seriously desirous of reading material!

The double-lightning motif nagged at his memory. He turned the book around so that it was upright.

The symbols resolved themselves into a design he recognized, one known to every child who had grown up in America.

They were not lightning bolts but runic characters that stood for the letters "SS": *Schutzstaffel*, the elite organization of the German Third *Reich* in the first half of the last century.

Lessing goggled at the volume, so surprised that he forgot even the corpse on the floor next to him. The SS was almost a century gone now; the last veteran of the Second World War had been in his grave since about 2025, seventeen years before. Yet the media kept the sides, the issues, and the propaganda as current as today's soap operas. Movies, books, and TV dramas refused to let *the* war go the way of the Crusades, Napoleon, the American Revolution, or a dozen other conflicts. On TV the SS still marched—the same, ancient footage—and the black-uniformed troopers still murdered, tortured, and swaggered for the titillation of twenty-first-century American audiences. The SS was money: it sold books, movies, and deodorants just as well as heroic cowboys, sinuous starlets, acid-tongued private eyes, tough mercs, or naked "Banger" porn-dancers, who were the latest craze back home.

None of which explained what these books were doing out here in India. They certainly weren't sadomasochistic "Nazi-porn!"

Lessing looked up to find Mulder and Goddard standing over him, Wrench hovering in the rear.

My honor is my loyalty.
—**Motto of the SS**

The Nazis are still with us. Hitler died in Berlin, but his evil offspring still lurk in the ugly corners of the world. Even here in America the racist, anti-Semitic, Nazi beast awaits its chance. It is our sacred promise to our Jewish people that these monsters will never regain so much as a penny's worth of credibility or power. Whatever we have to do to assure this is justified. Let every Jew beware of what lies just beneath the surface of the non-Jewish soul, particularly those who speak of the "Western, Christian"—and hence "Aryan"—heritage. And, especially, let every Jew keep a little flame of hatred alive in his or her heart for the German, for there is the enemy!
—*Zion: Challenge and Response*, **Zvi Ayalon, Commander of the Vigilantes for Zion, New York, 2035**

CHAPTER FOUR

Monday, April 7, 2042

"No," Wrench insisted. "They really *are* the SS. What it's become, anyhow."

Lessing didn't want to think about Mulder's secret Nazi connection. He wasn't political, he didn't care, and he wasn't interested either in condemning or joining. He said, "And my mother's Chicky Chicken, the cartoon queen!"

Wrench clucked and made flapping motions with his elbows. "If you say so."

"Look, do you mind? Jameela kept me busy yesterday filing reports with the CID, identifying the opfoes, Bauer, statements . . . the whole mess."

"I heard. Two foreigners, car parked on the main road, no I.D. Just two lost coyotes looking for a home." "Coyote" was slang for an unemployed mercenary.

"South Europeans of some kind: Greeks, Italians."

"And Bauer?"

"No connection. Nothing to do with the burglars. Or with the taxi-wala. Some third man stuck him. An Arab, maybe. There've been as many of *them* wandering around India as elsewhere since Israel finished gobbling up the last of their land."

"How is Bauer?"

"Better. Balrampur Hospital."

"Mulder and Goddard think there *is* a connection. Bauer was a diversion, to keep us all singin' and dancin' while the others went in for the books."

"No chance! Mulder and Goddard can go play drop the soap in the shower." There was no reason to tell Wrench about Bauer's fear of Lessing himself. That was obviously irrelevant.

"You don't realize the importance of those books! The records of the SS from 1945 to the present!"

"Stuff the books . . . sideways. Mulder and Goddard . . . a pair of closet Nazis! Let 'em dress up in black uniforms and *heil* each other till the cows come home!"

Wrench put on a reproachful expression. "They're the real thing."

"Goddard is Göring, and Mulder is Adolf Hitler reincarnated. I thought only Californians went in for looney cults!"

Wrench took a turn around the verandah. It was just after dawn, and the sky was still a bowl of lapis lazuli, as glorious as any ever carved by a Mughal craftsman. Later it would be shrouded in white dust-haze, and the dry earth would swelter like bricks baking in a kiln. He took up a slice of crunchy, dark toast from the silver rack on the table, slathered it with whitish butter, and dunked it in his teacup.

Lessing watched.

"Well?"

"Well what?" Lessing poured tea for himself and added sugar and milk, Indian fashion. The tea was strong enough to walk by itself, not the "yellow dog piss"—his father's term—his aunt Eileen used to make from tea bags. For a moment India flickered away, and Lessing looked out upon the softer, greener, more familiar contours of his Iowa childhood. Then reality snapped back into place like a loaded magazine locking into the butt of a pistol.

"Do you want to hear about the SS or not?"

Lessing sighed. "I don't care. I don't ask questions. They pay, I do. Curiosity kills cats *and* mercs."

Wrench snorted. "Lessing, you eat, you shit, and your feet stink; otherwise I'd think you were dead! God, but you're an apolitical animal!"

Lessing eyed him impassively.

"You've two choices, you know. One, you join; two, you get a rocket up the bunghole. Whoosh!" He pantomimed a sky-burst with his toast.

"Four choices," Lessing corrected. "Three, let things go on as they are: I do my job, and we're just like before. Four, you pay me off, let me go, and never hear from me again. I told you I don't talk."

"Mulder and Goddard won't believe you. You're in or you're thumbed. I argued, but they wouldn't . . . ."

"I told you: I'm not political."

"You're asking for a fucking bullet, man! Goddard . . . ."

"Let him try."

"But Mulder thinks you may be useful, and he's the one who counts. He tells me, I tell you."

"Some decision." Lessing gulped tea and waved an iridescent blue-green fly away from the marmalade jar. "I join or I get un-zipped." He shifted his weight so that his belt holster bulged beneath his beige-colored, raw-silk bush shirt. He had other weapons as well. "Unzipping" Lessing would be no easy op.

"At least hear what we've got to say!" Wrench demanded.

"So talk." Lessing gazed out across the sun-drenched courtyard toward Mrs. Mulder's garden. The mango trees there were inviting, cool and dark and green against the naked glare from the whitewashed compound and the revolting, pink ugliness of the mansion. Colors were never muted in India, never pastel, never soft; they tore at you like shrill music, like hot spices, like the violent smells of the bazaars.

Wrench decided he had Lessing's attention. "In 1945, when Germany lost, two submarines arrived in Argentina. Some of the remaining senior officers of the SS were aboard. They brought money, lots of money, a good part of the treasury of the Third *Reich*. People thought it was lost or stolen, down in Bavaria, but it wasn't . . . ."

"I've seen the movie," Lessing scoffed. "'Martin Bormann in the Promised Land.'"

"It's true, though. You can read the historical stuff later, if you want."

"Thanks. When I run out of comic books."

"It wasn't only Bormann. There were others." Seeing Lessing's look, Wrench hurried on. "They founded a colony, set up businesses, made connections. Later they invested, linked up, developed. They built a series of interlocking corporations. The postwar boom and the recovery of Germany helped those corporations become con-glomerates, then huge international holding companies based in the goddamndest places."

"The Nazi Family Robinson."

"What? God, you're a comical asshole! Yes, everything neat and tidy, out of sight, away from the Jews and the Nazi-hunters and their network of financial institutions and pressure groups. The Third World made it easier. There're fewer controls here, fewer restric-tions, fewer checks, fewer regulations, fewer watchdog agencies. Less hassle with privacy: you can spot outsiders coming, like that *koel* bird in the mango tree over there; he can see all around his nest."

Lessing looked but said nothing.

"They . . . the SS and their descendants . . . made friends in local governments. The Third Worlders needed know-how, money, con-nections, and expertise."

"Expertise? Like death camps? Torture machines?"

"God damn it, Lessing! That's TV propaganda! It's just crap!"

"You sure?"

"I mean it. Of course, since the Jews got the Anti-Defamation Amendment added onto the American Constitution back in 2005, it would be a miracle if you had ever heard anything *but* crap! The 'Holocaust' is now the *only* legal history. You go to jail for saying different."

"I've been told."

"Well, then, leave that for later. Let me bring the story up to date. The SS . . . what was left of it . . . had business objectives before and during World War II. When the war was lost they just kept on, but from other places: Bogota, Asuncion, Buenos Aires, Rio de Janeiro, Mexico City, Colombo, Damascus, Dacca . . . you name it. They realized that the world is heading towards a 'corporocracy'; five or ten international super-companies that will run everything worth running by the year 2100. Those super-corporations exist now, and they're already dividing up the production and marketing of food, transport, steel and heavy industry, oil, the media, and other commodities. They're mostly conglomerates, with fingers in more than one pie. Some of them are owned now by the old-money interests; the Japanese and various foreign cartels run others; the Born-Agains have a couple; the Jews and their buddies control some big ones; and we, the SS, have the say in four or five. We've been competing for the past sixty years or so, and we're slowly gaining."

"Lose the war, win the peace. Which ones do you button-down Nazis own?" Lessing was interested in spite of himself.

"I'll let Mulder tell you, if he wants. But I'll give you an example, one I saw myself. About ten years ago we swung a merger, a takeover, and got voting control of a supercorp that runs a small but significant chunk of the American media. Not openly, not with bands and trumpets . . . ."

"Or swastikas flying . . . ."

" . . . But quietly: one huge corporation cuddling up to another one and gently munching it up, like a great, gubbing amoeba. Since then we've been replacing executives, pushing somebody out here, bringing somebody else in there. We've swung program content around, too. Not much, but a little, so it won't show. We've cut down on 'nasty-Nazi' movies . . . good guys in white hats and bad guys in black SS hats . . . lovable Jews versus fiendish Germans . . . and we have media psychologists, ad agencies, and behavior modification specialists working on image changes. Hell, if you can con granny into buying Sugar Turds instead of Bran Farts, then why can't you swing public opinion over to a cause as vital and important as ours?"

"Hard to get people to love death camps."

"We don't try. You can't erase a hundred years of lying propaganda overnight. We play those aspects down and stress the positive ones instead: the mystique, the scientific approach to racial genetics, the efficiency and organization, the dedication, and the heroism. People will buy that. Good people, who haven't seen a real American victory for a century now. People who are tired of watching the Jews and the mud races gobble up the world. People who don't want their country run by guys with alien ideas. People who're tired of being shat on and fucked over."

"But the gas chambers! The 'Holocaust' . . . ?"

Wrench held out his hands, palms up. "*What* gas chambers? Show me *one* piece of *real* evidence! There *were* labor camps, sure, and thousands died from typhus, dysentery, poor treatment, and malnutrition. What do you expect during a war? Your country surrounded, fighting off Russia, Britain, and the United States, the three most powerful nations on earth with manpower and supplies to burn while you're scrounging for undigested grain in the chickenshit! A lot of Germans died, a lot of Americans and Englishmen and others too. People died in the war, people died in the camps, people died in the Allied bombings of Dresden and Berlin and Hamburg. But all we ever hear about are the poor, innocent Jews and the awful 'Holocaust,' when, in fact, there never was an 'extermination policy,' a 'Final Solution,' or anything like it!"

"Oh, come on! What were the gas chambers for, if not for extermination?"

"Oh, there were shootings of partisans, hangings of saboteurs, and the usual atrocities that always happen in every war, but the real use of the so-called 'gas chambers' was for decontamination: ridding the clothing of camp inmates of lice and fleas!"

"Nuremberg? People confessed."

"Under pressure, Lessing. Some real *bad* pressure, though nobody likes to think about that now. Confessions? Either hokum or else poor bastards hoping for a lighter sentence from the victors!"

"How in hell do you expect me to believe this? All my life . . . all my parents' lives . . . everybody has taken the 'Holocaust' for rock-solid truth."

"Some rocks are less solid than others. This one'd wash away with the tide if it weren't for certain 'interests' propping it up. Look at our evidence sometime. In any case, we're slowly replacing those negative images with others: the '*Good* Bad Guy' routine." Wrench spooned a tea leaf out of his cup. Outdoors, in India, it was wise to do that: it could always be a fly gone in for a swim. "What do you think of Jesse James? John Dillinger? Julius Caesar? Genghis Khan?"

Lessing raised his pale eyebrows.

"Bad guys, maybe, but nobody *hates* them. The same with the North Koreans, the Red Chinese, the North Vietnamese, the Confederates, the Romans, the Turks, Attila the mother-humping Hun, for God's sake! The reality may have been rough, but there's a sort of glitter about most of those dudes: mean honchos but respectable. It's all how you package it. Opinion is a goddamned commodity!"

"Impossible with the Nazis . . . ."

"It works with *anybody*. Remember the Pied Piper, the guy who tootled his flute, stole everybody's kids, ran off with 'em, and was never seen again? A child abuser! But who hates *him*? Now he's a dinkin' fairy tale! Image, just image."

"Next you'll make Joseph Mengele over into naughty, sexy Doctor Joe, every housewife's soap-opera wet dream!"

"You're a funny man, Lessing. I mean it. Mengele was a physician and a scholar. He wanted to help his country's war effort at a time when it was needed. Some of his experiments were rough . . . as rough as putting American soldiers next to an A-bomb test, or trying Agent Orange on your own men, like the U.S. government did. He didn't do most of the things the Jews have accused him of, but he did put people into freezing water in his efforts to develop techniques for saving the lives of fliers shot down over the North Sea. His experiments were really a lot more humane than those performed by the Russians, the Japanese, or other scientists back when medicine was younger. Nobody advocates such experiments today, but you do have to understand the urgency which existed then."

"Sure."

"Some guys get good press, others get bad. Compare the Palestinians with the Jewish gangs who murdered both Arabs and Britishers before Israel was founded. Ask any American: he'll tell you the Arabs are murderous terrorists, and the Israelis are lovable freedom fighters and heroes! If George Washington had lost, today's kids would be reading about him as George Q. Terrorist, the Scourge of Decent Englishfolk!"

"You'll never convince enough people to matter!"

"Give it time. Aside from the media, we've been buying up private schools . . . *and* helping some public ones through philanthropic foundations . . . *and* working on the churches and the Born Agains."

The ceiling fan was doing its valiant best, but the verandah had grown hot. Lessing arose, squinting against the raw sunlight pressing in through the vines on the east side of the senior-staff-quarters building. He stopped in front of Wrench. "When . . . and if . . . this happens, what does your little band of supermen want?"

"We're in competition, Lessing. We win, it's *our* genes that survive and *our* Western heritage . . . our Aryan culture, if you like . . . that provides the model for how people will live on this planet for the next millennium. If we lose and the Israelis win, then they run the bagel shop their way, exactly what they've been trying to do for centuries. If both of the above lose, then the Chinese, the Japanese, or some new booga-booga 'power' in the Third World gets to pilot the ship on the cruise down to Hell. As a White man, I wouldn't want to live in such a mongrel world!"

"So your SS is hot for world domination again? Business as usual!"

"Lessing, you dumb mother, that's the name of the game. That's been it, the whole turd-pile, the be-all and end-all, since Cheops built his pyramid! Power, man, power! Who gives the orders and what gets done. If you want *your* kind running the future, then you do what you have to do!"

"And incidentally thumb the world?"

"Of course not! Why should we want war? Too many atom bombs and killer satellites and city-busters out there as it is, and not even cockroaches can live on a nuked planet! We don't want war, or slaves, or colonies! We want a future for our Western heritage, peace and plenty, an efficient government, an end to the social evils that're tearing us up today, and purpose and hope for our kids."

"If I knew *Deutschland über Alles*, I'd sing!"

"Better the *Horst Wessel Lied*."

"You never mentioned this stuff before."

"Would you have listened? Mulder had asked me to talk to you, but you never showed any inclination: as apolitical as a cow-pie. Then came the break-in, and you found out for yourself."

"I never saw Indoco as a hotbed of far-right radicalism!"

"Indoco doesn't need the publicity. It just goes on making fertilizers and pesticides and agro-chemicals. It's a subsidiary of Tee-May Industries of Athens, Greece; Tee-May is part of Rocco Corporation of Florence, Italy; and above that I don't know. We do our jobs, watch the world go by, and quietly work to change public opinion."

The sunlight made blinding, silvery dazzles of the cutlery, the teapot, and the milk and sugar pitchers. Lessing picked irritably at his shirt, already stained with perspiration and sticking to his spine. "What about the neo-Nazis? The Missouri Seven? The gang who blew up the power station in Munich in 2040?"

Wrench waved a manicured hand. "They're part of it. Every movement needs street troops. Our enemies are tough; we're tougher. Anyhow, there's no such thing as a *neo*-Nazi; you're either with us or you're part of the problem. A lot of little organizations

are called 'Nazi' when they're not: some who're right off the wall
. . . rubber-room material . . . who mix our ideology with Christianity, survivalism, grassroots American patriotism, gut-level race-
hatred . . . with almost anything. Wouldn't surprise me to find a cell
of conservative rabbis somewhere passing as 'Nazis.'"

"Oh, sure. And while we're at it, just what *do* you have in mind
for the Jews and the Blacks? More gas chambers?"

"I told you: there never were such things. *None.* That was
wartime propaganda that the Jews kept going in order to gain
sympathy, support, and money for Israel. We don't *hate* other races
or ethnic groups; we just love our own people *more.* Our civilization
is best fitted to run this ball of mud, but that doesn't mean we're
going to slaughter all of our fellow inhabitants. If they cooperate,
they'll be a damned sight better off than they are right now."

Lessing frowned. He could think of nothing to say.

"As I said, we're in competition with those people for world
supremacy. We *will* win because we are the best fitted to do so. If
others choose to live in peace within their own regions, we won't
harm them. Those in our territory who are not our people will have
to leave and settle elsewhere. It's as simple as that. We're willing
to let other ethnic groups have their place in the sun, but as for living
with us, running us, or grabbing what we have worked to build up
for ourselves . . . no way! If that takes force to achieve . . . and
maintain . . . then so be it. As the Jews say, 'never again!'"

"No slavery? No labor camps . . . even if they're not 'death
camps'?"

"Nope. Slavery doesn't work. It always ends up, eventually, with
mixing between slaves and masters, and then one has a real mess.
Look what happened in the United States after the Civil War. We'll
govern ourselves and do our own work; others can run their societies
the way they want. We'll use force only if others try to dominate
us."

"But what about non-Whites in America and other Western
countries?"

"They'll have to go elsewhere: establish their own enclaves, set
up their own governments, and run their own show the way they
want it. They *cannot* live permanently in our territory. No more
'minority rule' . . . or TV propaganda persuading our kids to go for
mixed dating and mongrel mating!"

"That's prejudice!"

"So? That's been the policy in the state of Israel since that country
was founded a century ago: no intermarriage between Jews and
non-Jews, second-class citizenship for non-Jews, and worse for
Arabs! Smile crooked at them, and they blow up your house in

'retaliation.' You can call it 'prejudice' if you want, but don't accuse us of having a monopoly on it."

"And if non-Whites don't want to live under your Nazi rule and don't want to go away either?"

"Tough cases demand tough solutions. We will try to sort them out . . . preferably without violence." Wrench wriggled his fingers in the air. "We are *going* to do this. Either that or watch the future dribble away into a mishmash of alien ideologies and beliefs. Earth is overcrowded as it is, and what's coming will be worse: over a billion Indians, another billion and a half Chinese, Africa bursting at the seams. Hunger, war, pestilence, death . . . the Four Horsemen of the Apocalypse . . . are riding straight for us unless we head 'em off at the pass. We've *got* to take control, *got* to become efficient, *got* to weed out weakness, *got* to build up our defenses. Otherwise we . . . and all the other races too . . . are doomed. Humanity'll go the way of the dinosaurs!"

Lessing stared at him. "You're serious? Really serious? Unscramble the races? In North America? In New York City alone? Send the Blacks to Africa, the Chicanos to Mexico, the Haitians to Haiti . . . ?" He chortled. "The gays to San Francisco?"

"Lessing, you asshole . . . ."

"Hell, even *God* couldn't do it! It would make the shift of Muslims to Pakistan and Hindus to India back in the last century look like a kindergarten fire drill by comparison!"

"It *will* be done, without violence or war if possible. Our movement is international. Our sister-organizations in other countries will help other races and ethnic groups to develop 'movements' of their own. They have their pride and their right to live, just as we have ours. They'll persuade their people to come and live with their own kind."

"You're out of your motherly mind!" Lessing had another thought. "What of the mixes? The interracial marriages? The millions of mixed-race kids in the ghettos? Suppose they refuse to go?"

Wrench got up. The heat was a physical wall at the edge of the verandah. "You're right: a problem. But not as bad as we have now with those ghettos in full swing: sinks of poverty, crime, drugs, AIDS, and hopelessness. The present Establishment can't pay the costs of welfare and medical aid for much longer. Those people will be better off separated and living in enclaves of their own than they could ever be with us. Given a worst-case scenario, though, if they don't want to work things out, and if they offer violence, then . . . and only then . . . will there be trouble. Even so, it couldn't be as bad as the mess we're heading for now."

"How do you get 'em to go?"

"Make 'em an offer they can't refuse: land elsewhere and other positive inducements if they go quietly . . . or whatever it takes to get rid of them if they make a fuss."

Lessing rubbed the high bridge of his nose. "Okay, what about the North American Indian? You going to move the White folks out of the United States to give the Indian back his country?"

"Give us a break! We can't right every wrong all the way back to Cain and Abel! We'll do what we can to make territorial homelands for people who want 'em. That's the best we can offer."

"You're nuts. I am working for a sackful of certifiable pecans!"

"At least, we'll *try*. We won't just stand around with our fingers up our asses and watch doomsday come rolling in, like the politicians and liberals now."

Lessing snorted.

The rattan porch chair squeaked and crackled as Wrench dragged it back out of the brazen sunshine. "How about it, Lessing?" He held out a hand. "You in or out? What do I tell Mulder?"

"I've already said. I don't give one flying finger-jerk about your hare-brained 'cause.' You're welcome to it. I work for pay. You pay, I work. Okay? *Verstehen Sie*? Tell your teddy-bear *Führer* that."

Wrench shook his head. "*Money*! A helluva reason to do things! Low class, man!"

"I know. It's not everything."

"But it'll do until 'everything' comes along. Okay, I'll tell Mulder. He won't like it, and Goddard'll beg for your balls on a platter. But Mulder's the boss. He's one of the Directors. I don't mean a director of Indoco . . . they're just front men . . . but a 'Descendant' in the Central Directorate of the movement. You saved his life, and he likes you." He feigned a thick, British accent: "A mercenary's mercenary, wot?"

Lessing opened the screen door. "Answer me one last question. Are you one of these . . . these . . . ?"

"'Descendants?' Nope, just a red-blooded, American boy fresh out of Rapid City, South Dakota."

"How did you get in with this gang? You always struck me as somebody with sense."

"Just a maverick, I s'pose." Wrench shifted to a cowboy twang. "Ever since 'hah skull.' Never did believe the cow-pucky they taught us in civics class. Started readin.' Got interested in political systems, then in history, and then the Third *Reich*. Met a guy who knew a guy who knew Mr. Mulder, and here I am."

"Jameela said you had an advanced degree . . . ?"

"Oh, I do. But it didn't completely wreck my ability to think, like it does for some folks."

"God, a sackful of pecans . . . ," Lessing muttered to himself. He dove into the cool shadow beyond the screen door. Wrench stood and blinked after him for a moment, then followed.

A movement which proposes to reshape the world must serve the future and not just the passing hour. On this point it may be asserted that the greatest and most enduring successes in history are mostly those which were least understood in the beginning, because they were in strong contrast to public opinion and the views and wishes of the time.

—*Mein Kampf*, Adolf Hitler

CHAPTER FIVE

Wednesday, July 9, 2042

The boardroom could have been anywhere: plastics, mahogany-veneer paneling, soft lights, air-conditioning, metal chairs with green upholstery, a polished, oaken table as big as two king-size beds, cut-crystal decanters, smeary-looking abstract paintings on the walls, and an enigmatic sculpture of crusty, black metal in one corner. All the trappings of corporate grandeur.

This particular room was part of a concrete-and-glass penthouse. Outside, seven stories down, were the streets of Guatemala City, rebuilt after the great quake of 2031. Colorful morning crowds bustled through the cement canyons, neither caring nor knowing about the assemblage gathered above.

Lessing leaned against the west wall, that farthest from the windows. The sun beat against the tinted glass, and he preferred the cooler, shadowier depths at the opposite end of the room. Chairs had been placed along the side walls for the "hired help." Wrench sat in one of these, and Goddard occupied a place of greater glory just behind Herman Mulder himself. Lessing was tired of sitting. He had already drunk his fill of ice water, read two pages of Wrench's news magazine, and nibbled on the bland crackers that the three dark-eyed Guatemalan female secretaries provided.

Lessing had spent much of his life among dark-eyed, brown-skinned people, men and women who gesticulated and spoke in alien tongues, who wore strange clothes, who ate foods that blazed with hot peppers and spices, who struggled and pushed and crowded . . . and hungered . . . and yearned . . . and demanded.

He considered that. The cover of Wrench's magazine pictured a myriad of tiny, naked bodies swarming over one another like ants in a sugar bowl. Those at the bottom of the page were portrayed as crushed under the weight of those above and were colored a bloody scarlet. The yellow header said: "How ya gonna keep 'em . . . ?"

The world overflowed with restless people, hordes of Asians and Africans and Latin Americans. Only disunity, inertia, and a certain lack of technology and organization kept them from spilling out of their boundaries and swamping the rest of the world beneath a sea of flesh. The magazine was not known for irrational doom-saying.

The West was moribund, it said. North America and Europe were strangling in their own pollution, their jungle of bureaucracies, their greedy lobbies, their economic woes, and their insoluble social ailments. The will to *act* was slipping away from Western society, day by day, hour by hour, like a rope from the clutches of a drowning man.

Wrench's magazine also contained yet another fright lesson, one that was repeated almost daily: the specter of all-out war, the Atomic Debacle, the Big Ka-Boom! In 2010 the Vietnamese and the Chinese had lambasted each other with small but very dirty fission bombs. Now both Shanghai and Hanoi were fit only for tourists who enjoyed their vacations in radiation suits. A million people suffered from burns, wounds, and genetic defects.

It was a fright lesson indeed, one that might recur at any time, given humanity's usual stupidity, poor judgment, and bad luck. The weapons were all set and ready; yet not even the saber-rattlers wanted to use them. Satellites infested the skies, silent fireflies in the dusk, but their particle beams, lasers, and missiles remained inert, and their functions were limited to intelligence gathering and communication. The ground silos were jammed with rockets and warheads, but none had ever gone screaming up to burst into flowers of crimson death. The submarines, the aircraft carriers, and the underwater launching sites were maintained, but toy boats in a bathtub saw more combat. The land armies and bases and all the rest of the accoutrements of war were the same: they stood idle in the fields and cities of the world, and no mighty hero dared send them to the attack.

An end to war? No Armageddon? No kidding?

Hallelujah!

It should be a happy time: children growing up in peace, their parents free of fear. Utopia! The Millennium! Humanity could go down on its collective knees and give thanks that the raging Flame Lord of the Rockets lay chained, gorged upon blood from the mayhem of all the ages gone before.

Yet there was a cost, one that was only now becoming apparent. It was a high cost indeed.

The world was at peace, but that peace could be maintained only by a dangerous and frustrating balancing act. Pull society one way, and something else had to tug it back again; otherwise equilibrium would be lost, and the rockets would rise, shrieking and hungry, upon grasshopper legs of fire.

It was a balancing act above a tiger pit. The world teetered and sweated above the lunging beasts of chaos. One could not allow changes, reforms, or major repairs to the social fabric. Inventions of the more radical sort were out, too; they were too unpredictable, too dangerous, too unbalancing.

One false step, and down went the circus's only acrobat from the high-wire. Not with a whimper but with one hell of a thud. A fine finale for an audience on Alpha Centauri.

The world could make no major changes: none that mattered, not the ones needed to halt pollution, to slow the birthrate, to increase efficiency, to end festering social ills, to alter the structure of government and law and custom to conform with modern exigencies. The world hadn't moved one way or the other in half a century. It didn't dare.

There *were* improvements, of course. Most of these were minor. Compared with the changes that occurred between 1850 and 1950, most of those from 1950 to 2042 were trivial. The earlier century had seen the coming of electricity, of automobiles and highways, of radio, of television, of airplanes and rockets, of drugs that worked miracles—of flush toilets and telephones and movies and who knew what else. The list was endless. The first decades of the next century saw one really significant change: the introduction of the computer and other microelectronic devices. Then the pace slowed. During the next fifty years or so there were better fuels, a few dandy medicines, more efficient guns and space hardware, cars with more gizmos, pop with more bubbly, longer-lasting sugarless chewing gum, more elaborate video games, and louder ear-blasters for the "Banger" music freaks. But very little that was radical. Very little that was important.

The comparison wasn't even close. Why? The think-tankers denied that humanity had invented all that could be invented: much more could be done, they said, provided "development" was there—and provided the Powers That Be *let* change occur.

That last was the kicker.

Change usually meant loss of control, loss of money, loss of entrenched investments. Those were the things that sent empires reeling. Invent something basic—cheap synthetic fuel, for example—and watch the economic and political order go clattering down like a Japanese domino exhibition! Reform one minor tax, end a program, close one bureau, and see the lobbyists scurry to the rescue! The Powers did not want—could not permit—adventurism. Important, far-reaching technical, political, and cultural changes were *out*.

Brave, new world? Hell, Wrench insisted—and Lessing reluctantly agreed—that it wasn't even a very brave *old* one: too chickenshit to get its act together and *do* anything about anything! Sides, lobbies, interests, propagandists, voices big and small, multiplied into an uproar of opinion, demand, and contradictory advice that outdid the Tower of Babel by umpty-ump million decibels! Change, you say? Develop? Reform? Not likely! Not with everybody pulling this way and that, from Big Oil and Big Steel to the Lesbian Dirt-bikers for Jesus!

Politically the maps hadn't changed very much since the beginning of the twenty-first century, which kept the map makers poor but pleased the Establishment. Russia and the United States, after a brief rapprochement in the 1990s, now glared at each other again across various international chessboards, and everybody else waited breathlessly on the outskirts like kids watching two gang leaders about to duke it out in the locker room. So the West put up satellites with more sophisticated computers? The Soviets immediately followed suit with smart bombs that travelled underwater, then emerged and flew for short distances to smash land installations. The Chinese, the Brazilians, the Indonesians, the Indians, the Israelis, and everybody else with a dime's worth of technology strove to copy as best they could. It was an endless race, a "keeping up with the Joneses," that was both unwinnable and utterly wasteful of the planet's diminishing resources.

Britain was a shell, a tourist attraction, a moldering hulk immobilized by economic woes. France, Spain, Italy? Business as usual; nothing new. Germany, Austria, Switzerland, the Northern countries? All well, thank you, but no sudden bursts of progress. After all, progress was tied to change, which might mean unrest, and unrest led to—well, to trouble. For Europe, trouble might mean war, and that meant death. Who wants to light a match in a fireworks factory? Europe wanted no wars, no trampling armies, no bright, atomic suns kindling over Rome, Zurich, London, or Berlin.

The only real winner over the past century had been Israel. The Zionists had busily expanded their "defenses" and "retaliated" themselves into the position of *the* major power in the Middle East. Israel owned everything from Libya over through Iraq and into Iran: more than five million square kilometers of territory and about a hundred million sullen slaves! Even President Rubin's friendly American government occasionally made tsk-tsking noises at the Zionists' odd conception of "civil rights" for their Arab citizenry. Nobody listened to the Arabs, as one might expect, except the United Nations—which had become a meaningless wailing wall for the powerless. The Israelis made good use of propaganda. They squawked about "provocations," then they "retaliated." When those arguments didn't work, they trotted out their century-old lamentations about the "Holocaust" yet again, and their Western critics fell into embarrassed silence, as always.

The Russians hadn't changed much in the last forty years either; it was just like it had been before the collapse of communism back at the beginning of the 1990s: the same secretive bureaucracies, the same missiles festooned with warheads like Christmas-tree lights, and the whole gamut of social injustices—which the Soviets saw as properly necessary measures to hold a restless and disillusioned empire together. They held down their end of the teeter-totter nicely. No wars, no forays into alien lands, a few "advisors" here and there, maybe, and lots of propaganda. Balance. The Soviets understood the lesson of Hanoi and Shanghai too.

Balance did impel the Russians to take Pakistan into protective custody, using the "Red Mullah," Sajid Ali Lahori, as their puppet jailer. Central and South America were not yet their property, but several presidents, generalissimos, dictators, and "People's Revolutionary Heroes" jigged obediently whenever the Kremlin played the balalaika. During the past century various South American nations went from democracies to People's Republics to military tyrannies and back again to democracies. Not even the historians could keep track. Central America served as a free-fire zone for weapons testing, causing local misery and evoking dismal cries from the drug smugglers whenever somebody napalmed their coca or cannabis crops. Yet nothing halted the violence. Cuba was once more solidly pro-America (or pro-Big Crime, depending upon one's point of view). Castro's death in 1997 and the abysmal failures of his short-lived successors quietly ended any hopes the Soviets had for a foothold close to the United States. Moscow shrugged, figuratively, and sought elsewhere.

China was the third major party to the balancing act, its hegemony spread through Thailand, Burma, and above India's northern frontiers to confront the Russians in Pakistan. The Americans believed—hoped and prayed were more truthful—that Peking would come down on their side in any shoot-out. Japan was still mostly in the American camp, although Japan now *owned* a lot of that camp and would have much to say in the international corporocracy taking shape to rule the decades to come. Korea, unified after the strife of 1998, was as Russian as Tashkent. Indonesia, Malaysia, the Philippines, New Guinea, and the United Republics of the South Pacific were supposedly within the American perimeter; they squabbled, fought, and shook with political convulsions as devastating as their lava-spouting volcanos. Australia and New Zealand went their own way, still profoundly British but aloof from the woes of Europe and the Americas. In 2009 a large part of Canada offered to join the United States, but Congress still hadn't ratified the accession three decades later; there were too many other things to worry about.

The saddest of all was Africa. The Israelis occupied the northeast, the United Islamic Republic of Algeria, Morocco, and Tunisia the northwest, and the interior was mostly up for grabs, all the way down to the fortress-state of South Africa, stronger than ever behind its Siegfried Line of bunkers and barbed wire and mercenary battalions. Africa was the favored playground of the Four Horsemen of the Apocalypse. The Africans had little to say about it; they starved, suffered, and died on cue, just bit-players in the tragi-comedy of history.

Armageddon, the War at the End of Time, hadn't happened. All told, humanity really ought to be grateful. Only when one looked at the crowding, the hunger, the unemployment, the frustrations, the dilemmas that would soon become insoluble for all time, did the gloomy visage of the future become manifest. Humans, one school of anthropology averred, were essentially aggressive, pugnacious, and acquisitive "killer apes." If true, then sealing off the vents through which these traits were expressed would eventually blow the kettle. If man couldn't lust, covet, fight, grab, and wave his collective privates at his foes, then he had to have escape valves through which he could release these estimable emotions harmlessly. There were no new frontiers for the privates-wavers to conquer, no badlands where they could pioneer and fight without hurting the stay-at-homes, no heroic conquerors, no knights, no dragons, no maidens to rescue. The moon and the planets were habitable only by tiny parties of skilled astronauts. The earth was too crowded and its balance too delicate to permit much more brandishing of genitalia.

Exercise, sports, and the caterwauling, orgasmic catharsis of "Banger" pop music satisfied many; the rest were fed TV. The average citizen of the twenty-first century lived vicariously; he watched football, hockey, wrestling, suicidal car races, soap operas, talk shows, sit-coms, maim-and-jiggle dramas, game shows where everybody always smiled even when they lost a million dollars, and vicarious violence for all ages and sexes. Every show was laced with "The Message": Be passive, be peaceful, be *bland*.

"The blanding of the world," as Wrench once put it; to which Jameela had replied, "Oh, you mean *blandishment*." They all laughed, but Lessing thought about the two words later.

In spite of the "blandishments" of the media, the tangle of social and economic problems produced a sense of futility, a feeling that there wasn't much point to things. Unrest burgeoned: racial imbalances, labor unions, immigrants both legal and illegal, Born-Agains versus the godless and the heretics and the cuckoo cults, pro-life versus pro-choice, rich versus poor. All bubbled and frothed together in the overpopulated, polluted, crumbling cities. Suicide surpassed heart disease as a major cause of death. Other urbanized nations suffered similarly, and the regular armies spent much of their time quelling internal, rather than external, trouble. This twenty-first century was no utopia after all.

Nor were international hostilities completely ended. Small wars were permitted as long as they didn't escalate. "You steal my sheep, and I rustle your cattle, and I'll see you in town Saturday night for a beer!" Some regions—the unlucky ones like Africa, Central America, and parts of the Middle East—made dandy, reusable battlegrounds. Allowable and containable conflict gave rise to the mercenaries. The aggressive individual, the sociopath, the loner, the one who could not be "blandished" and was not satisfied with cop shows and football heroes, could join a mercenary unit and fight and die to his—or her—heart's content. Keep most of society down with indoctrination; help the occasional unredeemable looney find a suitably bloody heroic death.

The media loved the "Merc Wars." More vicarious violence for the folks at home; sell more breakfast food, pantyhose, and deodorant. Like the gladiators of Rome, mercenaries were eminently expendable, watchable—and bankable.

Yet it wasn't a game, no matter how the TV-casters prated about heroes, insignia, weapons, and "kills." There *were* real causes, encroachments, terrorists, guerrillas, rebels, tyrants, and exploitation. The use of regular national forces would lead to escalation and confrontation, and those, in turn, led straight into the gaping maw of Doomsday. And, anyhow, the Establishments had always loved mercenaries. The Romans had hired, bribed, and eventually been swamped by barbarian troops. King John of England had used European captains and their bands to such an extent that the Magna Carta expressly ordered that they be sent packing. Read about the Hundred Years War or any of a dozen other European conflicts, and there was always the mercenary, grinning his cold grin, polishing his weapons, and ready for a "spesh-op."

The game was in deadly earnest in the longer geopolitical sense, of course. Better arms, organization, and ruthlessness would eventually win, as the Soviets, the Israelis, the South Africans, to name just a few, well realized. Wear the enemy down, be patient, and keep coming back. Eventually "thine is the power."

Was the West ruthless enough? Could it win against opponents who played for keeps? Lessing doubted it, and he was not alone. The "blanding" of Euro-America might help suppress internal strife, but it made for damned poor fighting men. There were always barbarians out there, circling, ready to pour in and pillage, rape, and take over. Barbarians eventually settled and became urbanized; then they became decadent in turn and were trampled into slavery by the next horde of wild goombunnies from the boondocks.

The wise man looked at history philosophically: you were out, then you were in, then you were up, then you were down, and finally you were out again. Maybe a hundred, a thousand years down the line you got a second chance. Round and round . . . .

Western society had grown passive, as fossilized as a lump of coal. The West would soon go the way of the later Roman Empire, squabbling over ancient traditions that no longer mattered, prattling of the splendors of its past, and unable to defend against the inevitable Attila the Hun, the Barbarian Who Must Surely Come.

"Down the tubes of eternity without a paddle," as Lessing's father used to say, quoting from some twentieth-century philosopher or other. And: "You only get one grab at the brass ring"—whatever *that* had originally meant. Lessing's father had been quaint and antiquarian, a mild and prissy veterinarian who ran a pet shop in Iowa. Lessing had . . . .

He did not like thinking about his past. Yet the older he became the more he found himself doing exactly that. He rubbed his nose, cleared his throat, and sat down in the chair next to Wrench.

The conference dragged on through the morning. The seven men and five women around the table struck Lessing as unlikely Nazis. Descendants of the fearsome SS? More an insurance agents' sales meeting! These people looked like accountants, executives, stock-holders, coupon clippers! Good, grey, solid citizens all. Instead of ideology they spoke in measured tones of profits and losses, new products and old, advertising, sales, commissions, government regulations, shipping, aircraft, tariffs, unions in Sweden, miners' strife in France, taxes in Israeli-held Egypt.

The minute hand on the black-glass wall clock went around twice. Wrench nodded off and had to be nudged. Lessing felt his own eyelids drooping, and he gazed at the svelte Guatemalan secretary by the door until her cheeks flushed. She murmured an excuse and slipped out. No playing with that one. She probably had her eye on something more exalted than a lowly bodyguard.

He scrutinized the conferees themselves. Aside from Mulder, who spoke with an urbane, East Coast American accent, there were two other Americans, one male and one female. Two others had English surnames but talked like Spanish-speakers; these were again a man and a woman, middle-aged, prim-looking, and businesslike. Another pair of males bore Spanish surnames and sounded like Latin Americans. One was plump, the other swarthy and dapper. With them was a youngish woman who appeared to be the dapper one's wife. Beside the latter sat the oldest of the conferees: a powder-pale woman who resembled a British dowager but whose English bore a decided French lilt. The man opposite Mulder at the end of the table appeared to be an Arab; some SS officer in exile must have succumbed to loneliness! The last two, again male and female and middle-aged, were Europeans, but so cosmopolitan that there was no trace of any accent. Not a German in the lot! Lessing's mid-twentieth-century history was as vague as only an American high school could make it, but he did recall that some thirty years ago one of Israel's military rulers had vowed to visit the sins of the fathers upon the sons, as it said somewhere in the Bible, quite literally, and with interest. Many Germans abroad had then found it prudent to alter their identities.

Lessing dozed but then awoke again. Mulder was talking about the break-in at Indoco's Lucknow plant.

"... Even though we do have copies, the originals are precious to us as history. More importantly, the diaries contain information on our corporate structure, companies owned, stock held, interlocking boards of directors, and the like. They would be quite devastating if used as propaganda . . . or to create legal entanglements for us with half a dozen governments." Mulder glanced back at Lessing and Wrench. "Unfortunately, my security men here had to dispose of the two intruders. We have no idea who they were."

"Nothing on them since?" It was the dapper Latin American male. Mulder shook his bald head, and the man asked, "Has anyone else seen . . . heard . . . noticed . . . anything?"

Papers rustled. The two Americans conferred in whispers. The Arab straightened his conservative English tie, shot back his cuffs, and smiled raptly at the ceiling. The ostensible English dowager, a Mrs. E. Delacroix according to her place marker, turned to a woman behind her, a blonde, female assistant. She gestured her forward and said, "Liese, please."

Lessing noticed her for the first time. Liese? It could be Lisa. Was that the blonde's nickname or her real name? It might be worth the trouble to find out. She was tall, slender, late twenty-ish, pale of skin but not pasty or sallow, with a high forehead and angular cheekbones. Her hair was a darker blonde than Lessing's: straight, smooth, shoulder length, and cut in the page-boy fashion that was popular once more. From what he could see of her pearl-grey blouse, she didn't offer much in the bust department. Not like Jameela— guilty thought—but then Lessing had never restricted himself to the worship of the great American Cow-Goddess. Liese had long, slender legs with good ankles.

"Edouard Mestrich." Liese nodded toward Mrs. Delacroix and held up a manila file. "Trade liaison officer for Lejeune et Fils. Tractors and farm machinery." The company must be part of the conglomerate network Wrench had mentioned. Liese had a good voice, low and articulate, with a purring, throaty quality, but her delivery was curt and choppy. "Mestrich. Our man. Trip last month to Moscow, Leningrad, Smolensk. Held up by very unusual Soviet roadblocks, customs, special checks. Soldiers. Followed everywhere. Hard time getting out. Others report the same."

Lessing concluded that it would be nice to teach this Liese about verbs, adjectives, and complete sentences. Business efficiency should be carried only so far!

"They changin' leaders again?" the American gentleman drawled.

"No. Something else. Something secret. Very secret."

"Sheee-it!" the American groaned. "What they plannin' *now*?" He sounded as though the Soviets intended to discommode him personally.

"Nothing to do with us, eh?" inquired the Arab in near-unintelligible Oxonian English.

"No. None of our agents say so."

A Sr. Arturo Delgado, by his name card, interrupted from across the table's polished expanse. "Excuse me. Let me add here. We in Santiago do business in Vladivostok, and our representatives report similar tightening of security . . . suspicion, much checking. One of my salesmen reported that the Russians had arrested several foreigners: Pakistanis, maybe, or Afghans."

"Did you find out why?" Mrs. Delacroix patted her blue-white coiffure. The dye job was beautiful. For a woman in her late seventies, she was a work of art.

"No, *señora*. We tried."

"Assembly of the Holy Qur'an? Pakhtoon People's Front?" Her blonde girl, Liese, tapped a polished fingernail on the table for each name. "Islam International? Martyrs of Allah? All of the predominantly Moslem republics in the Soviet Union still resent Russian rule. Attempt on the Red Mullah's life a month ago."

"The fourth this year," chuckled the Arab. "Blighter's still alive."

"Something odd in the state of Israel, too," the unknown European male remarked. Lessing squinted but couldn't read the man's place marker from where he was.

"Security. Like Russia." Liese rapped. "High tension between Israel and the U.S.S.R. since last November. Soviet raid on Baghdad. Albanian mercs. Regular Red Army staging in Baku. Nerves."

Mrs. Delacroix sniffed. If cool and efficient Liese wanted to keep her job, she must learn not to take over conversations at meetings.

The man continued: "There are some . . . eh . . . wrongnesses in Tel Aviv and Jerusalem. American Eastern Mediterranean staff arriving, and highly placed Israelis coming and going. More than the usual conferences and military movements."

"Naughty Muslims!" the Arab intoned dryly. "Want their countries back."

"That is not it, Mr. Abu Talib," the European replied. "The Arabs are quiet . . . ."

"Slaves are *supposed* to be quiet!"

"Please!" Mulder rapped on the table. "We're getting side-tracked."

"Better than half-tracked!" Mr. Abu Talib pantomimed a tank rolling over his immaculate Savile Row lapels.

"Order! Order!" the second American, the woman, commanded. She had a voice like a drill sergeant. "Our plane leaves at 1900 hours." Her name card said she was Ms. Jennifer Sims Caw. The surname struck Lessing as fittingly onomatopoetic. She was clearly not connected to the older American male with the soft, slightly Southern accent; that worthy drew away from her as though she had bad breath.

"We have several things to find out, then," Mulder said above the ensuing hubbub. "First, who Indoco's intruders were and what they wanted with our records and diaries. Second, whether this man Bauer . . . my Mr. Lessing's, uh, comrade . . . was connected with them. Third . . . and much harder . . . discover what's agitating the Russians. And the Israelis. And anybody else around the world. There's something in the wind."

They broke for lunch at noon.

At one o'clock Lessing and Wrench returned to go over the boardroom with debugging devices. They also scanned the place with a metal detector and three kinds of electronic sensors. They found nothing.

Mulder appeared at 1:20, perspiration staining the back of his white, Bylon jacket. This, he announced, was a special, private session, and he had Wrench and Lessing check one another for bugs and concealed weapons. Then Goddard arrived with Liese, followed by three of the Latin Americans' security men. Lessing examined each with impartial care. Liese made no objection to Lessing's gentle, pat-down body search. She was talking in her rapid, staccato fashion with one of the beegees and affected not to notice.

The other board members and their retinues filed in and received the same treatment. Lessing and a gaunt, nervous youth who worked for Mr. Abu Talib were deputed to stand just inside the door, Wrench and two others by the windows on the north, and three more beegees along the south wall.

Lessing expected some sort of ritual. Nazis at least ought to cry "*Sieg Heil!*" or something equally dramatic. But Mulder only fumbled with one of the slim SS diary-books and read, "Minutes of the last meeting. December 17, 2041, Jakarta, Indonesia." There followed a list of attendees, most of whom were different from those present today. He turned a page and continued:

"I report the following actions. It was resolved: One. To fund the film on the life of SS *Sturmmann* Fritz Christen, one of the heroes of the *Totenkopf* Division on the Eastern Front. Christen held out for three days by himself after all his comrades were killed, and he personally did for thirteen Soviet tanks and about a hundred enemy infantry. War films are popular, and we stand to make a great deal of money. Georges Kaletanis will direct. Cost sheets and projections are appended.

"Two. To offer 800,000 U.S. dollars to Columbia University for the establishment of a fellowship fund for students working on modern socio-political history. Three of our people will likely be chosen for the selection committee, and we'll thus have a very large say in the choice of candidates. Any useful recipients can then be recruited by our cadre there.

"Three. To withhold further support from the Congress of Americans for Personal Freedom. They're attracting unfavorable attention, the FBI is investigating them, and their theories smack too much of discredited Born-Again theology. If their president, William Gardner, were to be replaced by Grant Simmons, the treasurer, we could reconsider.

"Four. To purchase the property of Club Lingahnie on the Micronesian island of Ponape, in the South Pacific. We need a rest and recreation center in that region, and we can ensure privacy. Worthy students will be sent there for seminars and holidays, as will certain well-disposed political leaders. The cost will be in the neighborhood of 1.3 million U.S. dollars. Here's the prospectus, if anybody's interested.

"Five. To provide 500,000 German marks through our Austrian branch for legal aid to Franz Ulrich Koch, accused of debunking the 'Holocaust' last summer. He's not a crank, and we'll get some favorable publicity out of his trial. He'll have sympathy: a gang of Jewish fanatics, the . . . ah, 'Vigilantes for Zion,' broke into his house to teach him the usual lesson. He wasn't home, and they raped his daughter instead. The Israelis and the Euro-American Jewish groups disavow any connection with the culprits, but we do have evidence of their financial backing for the Vizzies. Win or lose, the trial should help us.

"Six. To continue support for our regular list of newspapers, television stations, magazines, and other media organs at present levels. We'll be buying the Cairo *Misr al-Yaum* and the *St. Louis Weekly News* within the month. These will fill important gaps in our coverage.

"Seven. To offer private aid to Speaker of the House Jonas Outram in the U.S. Congress. He and his allies are already anti-Black and anti-Zionist. They're also hostile to our Movement, but then they don't need . . . or want . . . to know who's behind the curtain, eh?

"Eight. To evaluate and standardize the curricula of our chains of private schools, military academies, and gymnasia across Europe, Australia, and the United States. Offerings have become uneven. Students in the United States are behind those in Germany, England, and other places, due not only to the decline of American education generally, but also to the tangle of local regulations and needs and a lack of coordination on our part. A report and a budget are included."

He stopped and looked around. "Questions? New business?"

Someone asked, "Progress on the book? The revision of *Mein Kampf*?"

"It's not really a 'revision,' as we've said before. Nobody could revise the First *Führer*'s work. *Mein Kampf* was written for German readers more than a hundred years ago, and some parts of it are as irrelevant to our present situation as Karl Marx . . . or the Bible, for that matter. No, our book is a position statement and philosophical-historical foundation for the movement as it exists today. We have a team of good people . . . publicists, psychologists, journalists . . . working on it. It's hard to sell a cause as maligned as ours, and we have to do the best job possible."

Jennifer Caw raised her hand. Lessing noticed that she was actually a strikingly attractive woman, however brash her manners might be. She had auburn hair, probably natural, and the ruddy complexion that comes from days in the sun. She said, "I still doubt that a committee can write a book that's worth anything. It needs a single individual, somebody with fire, a cause, a driving compulsion."

"We need a *Führer*," Mr. Abu Talib interposed bluntly. "That's your point?"

"Yes, but who?" The American woman shot back. "Name one of us!"

"Blast it, madam, you know we haven't anyone with the talent, the charisma, the bloody balls to rewrite *Mein Kampf* for the twenty-first century!" He stopped, embarrassed. "A committee is really the only available method, you know."

Mulder said, "It will take time, and we *have* time. We're at the bottom of the popularity barrel. There's nowhere to go but up."

"Which makes some of us agree with our street-brethren," the Arab retorted coolly. "March. Speak. Fight."

"Break heads and get heads broken in return?" Mulder sounded mildly reproachful. "This isn't Munich in the 1920's. Beerhalls and despairing veterans of World War I . . . inflation and communists, *Freikorps* and anarchists . . . in a dying Weimar Republic! Although the basic principles he enunciated remain as valid today as they were then, the First *Führer* spoke to his own times. We must do the same."

"Write a book by committee, and you get what you pay for: a Hollywood script!"

Mulder looked uncomfortable but said no more. Jennifer Caw gazed across at Lessing, probably not seeing him at all, and the others stirred restlessly.

Lessing lost interest after that. The conferees discussed further business matters, arrangements for publications, organizational details, and trivia. He managed to make eye contact with Liese, which he counted as a minor triumph. She watched him covertly, and he resolved to speak to her. Goddard was smirking at her too; his macho "Tower of Power" routine worked well with lady executives.

Jameela came unbidden into Lessing's thoughts. Damn it, he wasn't seriously planning a night in the sack with this blonde! He was only fantasizing. Yet he knew Jameela would regard even that as infidelity. Indians and Pakistanis were still largely monogamous, a legacy from Queen Victoria and the stuffy, old British *Raj*, combined with attitudes from their own heritages. He'd had a hard time persuading Jameela to live with him, even within Indoco's isolated compound. Outside, she never showed him anything beyond impersonal friendliness; to do so, she said, would rouse prejudice and objections no Westerner could imagine. Whatever the starlets of the Indian film industry in Bombay did, Lucknow was still thoroughly provincial and conservative.

American mores were radically different. Queen Victoria would have turned up her patrician nose at what passed for morality in the modern U.S. of A. Currently, just for starters, some fifty-eight percent of all births were out of wedlock, divorce split two couples in three, and many young people opted for "Banger" life-styles ranging from homosexuality on through polygyny, polyandry, group marriage, and Californian Dildo-of-the-Month parties! Marriage was increasingly rare among the educated, although small-towners, rural folk, and wealthy "old culture" families still kept up traditional values. Shades of the last days of the Roman Republic!

Lessing's own family had been virtuously Midwestern and middle class: one previous marriage for his father, no issue, that they never talked about. His mother had been nicknamed "the Ice Princess" in high school—not because she could skate. His father found out too late what her nickname meant but stuck with her anyway for fifty years, a pallid, grey ghost of a man long before he died. Lessing's mother then continued to live on in respectable, clammy piety, which caused him to flee at the first opportunity. He had never looked back. Even then he feared that he had escaped too late.

Did he "love" Jameela, or she him? The word was too simple for what they had together. English needed more fine-tunings of such terms as "love," anyway, just as the Eskimo tongue was supposed to have a score of words to express different kinds of snow. There ought to be separate names for platonic friendships, once-for-the-hell-of-it larks, casual rolls-in-the-hay, pay-as-you-lay commercial couplings, motel afternoons, one-night stands, beach-blanket weekends, let's-try-for-a-week experiments, month-long serious relationships, share-the-apartment-until-one-of-us-gets-bored long-term stuff—all the way up to eternal matrimony sanctioned in Heaven and stamped with God's holy thumbprint.

Lessing's relationship with Jameela Husaini did not fit any category. They cared a great deal for one another, but neither was sure where it went beyond that. He didn't want to marry Jameela, settle down in India, or, God forbid, back in Iowa, and grow old and squishy like a potato in a bin. She hadn't mentioned marriage either. Wrench had once suggested that opportunity and proximity were the mainsprings of love. The Indoco plant was a zoo, and Lessing and Jameela were tiger cubs tossed into the same pen. What would they do if the cage door were opened?

It would be easy to hide any extra-curricular games from Jameela. Indoco's wire-mesh fences locked things out as well as in. Here in Guatemala City it was simpler still. He could lose Goddard and Wrench in a revolving door. Jameela would never know.

To get down to bedrock, however, Lessing was no Captain Marlow Striker, the steely-eyed, granite-thewed, stereotypical merc of the movies and TV. Fantasy was fine for the kiddies and the frustrated, but it wasn't reality. Fictional heroes might treat women as objects to be acquired, laid, and discarded; Lessing preferred women who were people, responsive and intelligent, with humorous, quirky personalities. He wasn't like Goddard, who went for TV sex-goddesses with teats like a pair of mortars. Such women were about as real as the Tooth Fairy. Wrench—well, Wrench had never been known to have sexual congress with anyone or anything, animal, vegetable, or mineral. Nobody knew what turned him on.

Lessing groaned inwardly. He was arguing himself out of what, for want of a euphemism, could be called a Great Lay. Here in this alien city he could have bar girls, booze, gambling, man-talk with his fellow beegees, but those didn't appeal. He might as well read a book or count the little guys with sombreros pictured on the wallpaper. Liese appealed, even if only platonically. He made eye-contact with her again. This time she smiled back at him.

Mulder's smooth voice insinuated itself between them. "... And in view of the break-in at Indoco, I propose to transfer the movement's historic diaries to Mrs. Delacroix. Security in Pretoria will be better than ours in India, and, as a Descendant"—Lessing could almost hear the capital letter—"she has a right to retain the diaries, just as my family has had them for the past quarter-century. I shall thus send them along with my chief of security, Mr. Lessing . . . sorry, Alan, about the surprise trip . . . and Mrs. Delacroix's people can take over once they reach South Africa."

It looked as though he and Liese were going to have something more than dinner together after all.

What matters? What is worth establishing and maintaining?

Survival. Only survival. Individual survival is first; then comes the survival of the family, the clan, the tribe. These are immediately comprehensible. Beyond them lie ever larger and more diffuse, long-term loyalties. Eventually one arrives at the only objective that matters across the vast span of evolutionary time: the species.

When the species prospers, it is possible for the individual to prosper. Fulfill the basic species needs, and individual members then have the leisure for art, literature, crafts, and all of the other enhancements of life. The primary goal is thus service to the species. Every individual has a duty to contribute to this.

Yet, it must be noted, humanity itself is not homogeneous. Just as there are different species of apes, each with its own physical traits and temperament, so there are different races of men. We define breeds of dogs, horses, or cattle, yet some of us balk at speaking of different varieties of human beings. Why?

Physical differences between races are manifest; variations of temperament and mental ability are just as real, even if they are less evident to the uncritical eye. Some groups may be more inventive, others more contemplative; some more aggressive, others more cooperative and placid; some more powerful and with more stamina, others weaker. These differences have been poorly studied, due to the belief that to investigate racial differences is somehow dangerous or "not nice." But it is no more reprehensible than saying that one breed of cat has longer fur than another, or that Poodles respond to training differently than Labradors.

This is fact, not theory; empirical truth, not propaganda. Some human sub-species may not be as distinct from one another as, say, Saint Bernards are from Pekingese. Yet the sub-specific variations which exist within the human species make for psychological and cultural divergences that become immensely important in the aggregate. Each sub-species' basic genetic makeup combines with environmental, historical, and other factors to produce what may be termed a "racial character."

We may call a human group identified with a distinct racial character an "ethnos." As one goes down the scale from sub-species to nations, from communities to families, and finally to individuals, the manifestations of the ethnos appear at every level. In essence, this is "race"; this is "society"; this is "ethnic identity"; this is "regional character"; this is a large part of "personality."

The word "ethnos" includes, but is not limited to, the German term *Volk*. That term was inclusive enough for the nationalistic "peoples" of the early twentieth century, but in this age of mass communication, easy travel, constant population shifts, and overlapping international economic and political power-spheres, a new and broader term is required. "Ethnos" fills this need.

Except at the highest levels of abstraction, it is difficult to serve the human species as an undifferentiated whole. Attitudes and ideas and objectives diverge as one passes from one sub-species to another.

It *is* feasible to work for the communal goals of one's own sub-species, one's ethnos, however. This is intelligible to the individual; it is an extension of the tribe, the group, the community, and the family. It is the object of a human being's primary loyalty. What does not serve the ethnos is irrelevant, superfluous—and possibly dangerous both to the ethnos and to its individual members.

Every sentient entity possesses a control center, a brain, which weighs perceptions, evaluates responses, and orders actions. In the past the control center of each ethnos was fragmented: kings, chiefs, princes, and pontiffs ruled moieties, clans, tribes, nations, factions, parties, sects, and other such groupings. These were shored up by such underpinnings as myth, ritual, ideology, morality, nationalism, tradition, the law, and the like. These sanctions were often further strengthened by declaring them to be "God's Eternal Law" or attributing them to some other authority. Reasoning past these obstacles was difficult. Acting counter to them cost many martyrs their lives.

The time has come when there is no more room on earth, too little food, too many competing ideas and pressures. Catastrophe looms, and not for one species such as the dodo bird, but for life on earth. Humanity can no longer remain a mindless, purposeless organism whose parts cannot respond because there is no brain, no ganglia, no nervous system to issue commands.

The human entity *as a whole* must develop such a brain: a leading, guiding, directing force. It is imperative that one ethnos, the one best qualified by its historical record of invention, organization, and development, should create a control center and lead humanity into the future.

That ethnos is the one associated with Western European civilization. The control center is the Party of Humankind.

There is no better way—or, for that matter, any other way at all—if humanity is to survive. *This*, and *only* this, matters. *This* is important. *This* is worth the effort.

—*The Sun of Humankind* (excerpts from the second draft), by Vincent Dorn

CHAPTER SIX

Thursday, July 10, 2042

"You. Not one of us?" Liese's full name was Anneliese Meisinger, and her curt, shorthand speech still grated. Close up, she was not as perfect as Lessing had thought. Her features were slightly irregular, her skin the sort that freckles rather than tans, her mouth a little large, her eyes a gold-flecked hazel rather than the green they had appeared under the fluorescent lights of the boardroom. She seemed a little too elegant and mannered, too sophisticated, for Lessing's taste.

"I'm a security man," he answered. "I was hired by Indoco for their Lucknow plant."

"You have a German name," Mrs. Delacroix declared sweetly. The old lady had abandoned the cockpit of her private jet to its pilot, much to the latter's relief, and she now occupied a seat beside Liese and opposite Lessing in the long fore-cabin.

"My ancestors came to America during Revolutionary War times." He was not sure, actually, but that was what his father claimed.

"Lessing," Mrs. Delacroix mused. "Gotthold Ephraim Lessing. He was a great German dramatist and critic of the mid-eighteenth century."

"Worked for the Duke of Brunswick . . . among others," Liese interjected. It was as though she had to pay by the word to talk.

"Never mind," the elderly French woman said brightly. "Gotthold Lessing is long dead. This one . . . Alan, is it not? . . . is alive. I am curious about Alan Lessing."

Talking to Emma Delacroix was like handling fragile porcelain. Lessing had the impression that she would shatter if anyone disagreed with her.

"Not much to tell. Nowhere to go at home in Iowa . . . that's one of the Midwestern states. Got out of school, one year of college, no jobs, joined the Army. Served awhile, then went into the army business for myself." He grinned self-consciously. It was a longer speech than he usually made, but Mrs. Delacroix' shrewd, black eyes and powdered-doll smile invited confidences. And Liese was listening.

"Not a member," Liese put in dubiously. "Yet Mr. Müller seems to trust you."

"Who?"

"Oh . . . Mr. Mulder. That's his name now."

"And he's a Descendant?"

"Yes. Like Mrs. Delacroix."

He was tired of the subject. The SS and the Nazi Party were as corpse-cold as—what was his name?—Gotthold Lessing. He looked out the window at the tiers of white cloud-castles. They had left Caracas behind and were now out over the Atlantic headed for Dakar.

Mrs. Delacroix caressed one of the SS diaries with all the reverence of a nun touching a hallowed Bible. The more recent of the diaries were legibly copied in modern German and English, but the earliest of the twenty-odd volumes were written in the archaic

Suetterlin German script, which neither she nor Liese could read. They would have to be transcribed when they reached Pretoria, something Mulder hadn't done while his family held them.

The dark-blue bindings and scuffed, leather spines exuded an aura of almost mystic devotion. Those who had penned these pages had loved their cause with a terrible fierceness. They had not given up, even under the persecution of the Nazi-hunts of the last century. Lessing felt something akin to religious awe, like the time he and Jameela had visited the cave-temples of Ellura. The gods carved there were still proud, still powerful, still splendid in their enigmatic majesty. They still spoke to humankind. Jameela, whose family belonged to the Shi'a—or Shi'i, which she insisted was the correct adjective—sect of Islam, had laughed at him.

Lessing had ceased to be a Lutheran when he was sixteen, when his mother's bitter piety and his father's Christmas lip-service finally had eaten away the last traces of his childhood beliefs. Later he had found little to tempt him among the dogmas of the Born-Agains, the Catholics, Jameela's Islam, or any other of the world's faiths. He was sometimes still affected by religious and quasi-religious experiences, however. The diaries piled on the red-plush airplane seat were just that; they overflowed with a power of their own, like the *mana* of the South Pacific islanders. They called, cried out, almost shouted: "Believe in us! Believe in our *Führer*! Believe in the National Socialist movement and in Germany and the glorious destiny of the Aryan Race!" He could almost hear the chanted *Sieg Heils* over the droning thunder of the jet.

He jerked awake so violently that Liese stared at him.

"Dakar by evening," she said. "Then Pretoria. Return at once?"

He struggled to decipher her odd verbal shorthand. "Uh . . . yes. Back to Indoco."

She crossed one silk-sheathed leg over the other, and her pearl-grey, Chinese-silk dress slithered away from her thigh. "Stay. Day or two. Show you around."

Her expression was ambiguous. She might be making a pass at him, or she might be offering only ritual hospitality. He smiled and said nothing. He would cross that bridge after proper reconnaissance.

He awoke again from a muddled dream of thorn bushes, black faces, and stuttering automatic weapons: Angola. For an unnerving moment he thought it was real. Just above his head Liese announced, "Africa, Mr. Lessing. Landing at Dakar. Yoff Airport."

It *was* real, as hot and wet as he remembered, and it smelled like India but with subtle differences. There were real black faces now, bony men in scruffy khaki uniforms, German SM-97 submachine guns slung ostentatiously over skinny shoulders. This was the New

Empire of Guinea, founded forty years before by some army captain
or other. The Guineans had taken over Senegal, Gambia, Sierra
Leone, Liberia, and a few other relics of European colonialism.
Their up-and-coming enterprise was backed by French and Por-
tuguese money—and Euro-merc officers to command Emperor
Sayyid Abu-Bakr's Black legions.

Mrs. Delacroix disembarked, taking Liese with her. The pilot
dealt with the paper work while Lessing remained in the cabin. He
took what precautions he could: locked the diaries in the aircraft's
safe, checked his 7.62-mm sidearm and his 9-mm machine pistol,
and inspected the tarmac and distant buildings with binoculars. If
any interested parties knew that the diaries were aboard, now was
the time to strike. He could expect anything from a hijacking to a
rocket grenade. He switched off the cabin lights and waited.

Fuel trucks rumbled out to the plane, several commercial craft
landed and took off, and airport control officers came aboard and
then disembarked, redolent of Mrs. Delacroix's best French Pernod.
The pilot, a sandy-haired, young Scotsman, bent over his charts to
plot a course for Pretoria. Outside, lines of blue landing lights made
geometric diagrams upon blackness, and the dank odors of Africa
mingled with those of gasoline, asphalt, and hot metal.

A white light raced across the tarmac, became two lights, and
resolved itself into an open car. Mrs. Delacroix and Liese? Not at
that speed! And not with three huddled figures carrying blue-gleam-
ing automatic weapons jammed into the front seat.

This could be it.

The pilot emerged at Lessing's call, stared, ducked back into his
cockpit, and returned with a Japanese GK-11 assault rifle, grenade
launcher attachment, bayonet, scope, and all. He grinned at Lessing.
"Backed up the old girl a few times before."

The vehicle squealed to a halt beside the landing stairs, and three
Black soldiers in shiny, steel helmets and neatly pressed white
uniforms leaped out. Behind them came a bony European in civilian
bush-shirt and shorts.

"Hey, up there!" the latter shouted. "You! Lessing! Muh-fuk-
kah!"

Lessing gaped. It was Johnny Kenow. They had been mercs in
the same unit during the Baalbek War.

The pilot smiled weakly and lowered his weapon, but Lessing
hesitated. He wasn't ready to be thumbed by an ex-comrade now
working for a different side.

"Johnny? Put your piece down and come on up. Leave your
doggies there."

There was a puzzled expletive from below. He heard the clatter of a weapon being tossed into the back seat of the car. Then Johnny Kenow came loping up the metal stairs, two at a time.

Lessing backed into the shadows inside the door, unwilling to let Kenow within close-combat reach until he knew more. Those troopers down there could be up and into the plane within seconds.

"Hey, man! He-e-y!" Kenow grasped the situation at once. He stopped and flung his arms wide. "Clean! I'm clean! What the hell's up?"

"Nothing, I hope. Just being wise. Come on in." He bent an eyebrow at the pilot: he wanted to know instantly if Kenow's buddies decided to join the party.

Johnny Kenow was as Lessing remembered him: a lanky straw-sucker from Montana with pallid, mottled skin; oily, dark hair that covered his skull like a coat of paint; and eyes so close-set that people said he had to look through a pair of binoculars one eye at a time. After the Baalbek War Kenow had taken service in the Imperial Palace at Conakry. Now he was the Supreme General of the Emperor's Ever-Victorious Army, and it was rumored that he had acquired a squad of Eurasian concubines, a chest full of medals—and a chest full of gold to match.

Not such bad duty. But then the life expectancy of imperial generals was no longer here than it had been in ancient Rome.

Lessing asked, "How did you know I was on this plane?"

"Keep my ass clean and my eye on the passenger manifests." Kenow winked, an unprepossessing sight. "Down here to pick up a French girl, a gift from the Emperor to his pig-suckin' son. Royal reception." He snorted. "Best I tell her what's happenin' before she gits in with the wrong parties."

"Palace intrigue?"

"Yeah. 'Nough bull-pucky to fertilize all o' Africa."

Lessing began to relax a little. Kenow's next words brought him back to full alert.

"Boys here lookin' fer you. Two, three weeks ago."

"Who?"

"Dunno. Euro-mercs, mebbe, or Arabs." He pronounced it "Ay-rabs," even after fifteen years in the Middle East. "Told 'em you was croaked."

"Any idea what they wanted?"

"Not a goddam. Heard there was other guys askin' about you, too." He gave Lessing a sly look from narrow, red-rimmed eyes. "You stash some loot you was s'posed to take home to papa?"

Lessing's "samples" of Pacov rose instantly to mind. But no one could know about that. The little globe and the tube were concealed behind a metal inspection plate in the very innards of Indoco's

Lucknow plant. He knew for a fact that nobody had looked there since.

"Or mebbe you thumbed somebody you shouldn't?"

Lessing felt relieved; Kenow was just fishing. He smiled. "Hell, I'm too smart to screw up like that. Just do my job."

"You always was a careful sonuvabitch." The other dug into a shirt pocket, produced a tattered pack of American cigarettes and held it out. Lessing shook his head. "Heard somethin' else, too. Some kind of big rumble between the Israelis and the Rooskies. Mercs, regular soldiers, lots of scurryin' back 'n' forth. Americans and Brits and everybody else in the fuckin' world all hoppin' around. More kikibirds than you kin shake your dong at."

"Kikibird" was slang for a spy, an intelligence agent; Lessing had heard that it came from some archaic joke about a big, dumb bird that sat out in the snow all winter and hollered, "Kee . . . kee . . . kee . . . *rist*, it's cold!"

There was a shout from below, and they stood up to look. One of the helmeted soldiers pointed across the moisture-slick runway toward the blinking lights of a plane just landing. Kenow spat out through the doorway.

"There's our French hoor now. Got to go. Mebbe I can knock off a bit o' nookie before Mademoiselle La-de-fuckin'-da becomes Queen Empress."

"Hey, at least tell me what you think's going on!" Lessing, also at the door, spied the lights of a second car coming toward them. Mrs Delacroix' coiffure glittered like a silvery tiara in the back seat.

"God damn it, I got no idea." Kenow shook hands, clapped Lessing on the shoulder, and started down the stairs. "It's big, though. Mebbe the Big Boom that'll take out the world. I got the Emperor diggin' a bomb shelter right down to the middle of the earth! If anybody phones, that's where I'll be."

He waved and was gone.

Once there might have been room and food for those who do not or cannot serve the social weal. Support for such individuals is now almost impossible. Not only is the planet overpopulated, but resources are already insufficient, and transport is often not available to deliver supplies to those who need them. The economic system, too, is not tailored to serve great numbers of drones who cannot or will not contribute to production.

Saying this is neither "humane" nor "inhumane"; it is simply the truth. The starving child who receives a barely sufficient diet today will grow up with serious physical and mental deficiencies tomorrow. He or she will give birth to an average of three or four new mouths to feed—and so on, into the unthinkable future.

This is insane, an impossible situation. Weak and defective individuals cannot be supported forever without weakening the stock and exhausting the resources. It is no longer permissible to evade the problem and say, "God will provide." This is an easy excuse for doing nothing. God often does *not* provide, as the many great catastrophes of history prove. If God offers a lesson, it is that each species *must* provide for itself—or perish, like the dinosaurs.

A solution, if there is one, will not come through petty reforms, pious words, or the good-hearted charity of individuals. The essential, inescapable requirement for survival is an efficient world state, not a motley crew of inept national governments, which are too weak and too slow and too impotent to solve the terrible dilemmas ahead. The time for disorganization is past. What is needed is a totalitarian world government.

Those steeped in the mush of so-called "liberal" thinking will now throw up their hands and cry, "Not *totalitarianism*! That is *bad*!" This response reveals only ignorance, a misunderstanding of the meaning of "totalitarianism."

Simply put, a totalitarian state is one in which ideological and operational unity has been achieved: no more patchwork of tradition, religion, superstition, local customs, parochial prejudices, worn-out ideas from earlier centuries, partially implemented structures that overlap and compete with other structures, and muzzy "idealism" that conceals "practical" greed.

A totalitarian state must scrub the slate clean. It must reorganize, restructure, and redistribute. It must *care* for its people.

A true totalitarian state values social cohesion, efficiency, and rationality. It must possess the means to implement these values—unlike earlier states, which churned out "high ideals" as an automobile spews exhaust fumes but were too incomplete and inchoate ever to realize them.

To paraphrase Plato, the best form of government is a good monarchy; the worst is a bad monarchy. A democracy can never be very good or very bad, because it is too inefficient. Monarchy, rule by a single, hereditary "king," cannot work today, however; the world has grown too complex. For the same reason, true "democracy" (which was never really practiced, anyway) also cannot serve. Intermediate forms, such as those in which each person votes for one or more representatives, are too cumbersome, piling layer upon layer of "government."

Totalitarianism in its *best* sense is today's version of Plato's "good monarchy": an effective, beneficent, and structured unitary government which serves the weal of its ethnos. A beneficent totalitarianism is a necessity if Western civilization—and the rest of humankind—is to survive. This is the objective of the Party of Humankind. The Party will replace all earlier, obsolete systems, preferably without violence and without war, through the natural process of species-maturation. Just as humanity has abandoned such practices as cannibalism, female infanticide, and human sacrifice, so must our social organization now progress from fragmented, tribal nation-states to a true World Order.

It may be asked, who gives *you*, the Party of Humankind, the right to judge, to make decisions, to restructure society? Who appointed *you* to be God?

The answer is that *someone* has to make decisions. Someone *always* has made decisions: an individual ruler, a council, a senate, an assembly. For all the so-called "rationality" of humankind, there is always muddled thinking and a tendency to do nothing unless action is urgent. A decision-maker is required, whether this be a single person or a single, unified organization. If someone transgresses against the community, there must be a body of law, an enforcement agency, and deterrent punishment. Other decisions must be made as well: a land-fill here, a highway there, taxes upon certain products, regulation of businesses, and so forth. These decisions *will* be made. The question is how much inefficiency can be tolerated in making them? How much delay? How much waste of personnel and resources and time? In the past the decision-making process was irrational, being founded upon tradition, superstition, taboo, religion, ideology, legal codes dating back to antiquity—and upon personal pique and avarice and perversity! Such illogic cannot continue.

The world is too close to a final Armageddon. The state must have the power to implement needed decisions, even though some of these may be harsh. It must be allowed to define objectives, allocate resources, and undo the blunders of the past. Totalitarianism is not "cruel"; "cruelty" is wasted energy, wasted personnel, wasted production. Severity must never be for its own sake or for the selfish goals of individuals; it must be employed—sparingly—only in the service of the greater good, the good of the ethnos, and hence the good of the species. In most circumstances it will be seen that kindness and positive incentives work better.

The Party of Humankind provides a *Weltanschauung*: not a "world view," as this German word is often translated, but a "world *vision*." This *Weltanschauung* is holistic; it casts aside the past, surveys the future, and plans for the creation of a society which will live in peace and in harmony with Nature for millennia to come. It commands the loyalty, service, and energies of all who seek true progress. Without this *Weltanschauung* humankind will encompass its own destruction within the lifetimes of you who now read these words. This is as certain as sunrise, given present trends.

The Party of Humankind, *demands* the opportunity to make this world better for the species, for the Western ethnos, and hence for all humanity. Think: can this be any worse than what exists now? Than what is otherwise sure to come?

—*The Sun of Humankind* **(excerpts from the third pre-publi- cation edition), by Vincent Dorn**

CHAPTER SEVEN

Saturday, July 12, 2042

❝Like it?"

Lessing smiled and handed the manuscript back to Liese. "The writing's fair, but Doomsday's still a way off. I'm not much inter- ested in politics, and your totalitarian state . . . frankly . . . doesn't convince me."

"Ought to." The girl laid the sheaf of paper down, raised herself upon an elbow, and rubbed suntan lotion along one pale-golden thigh.

"Sorry." He reached over and took the plastic bottle from her fingers. "You're missing a spot. Let me."

"It's not politics, Alan," Mrs. Delacroix said from her lawn chair in the shade. She gestured to take in the enclosed garden, the sun-dappled tiles, the potted plants, the pool, the statuary. "It's survival. The survival of Western civilization, of the way of life you're enjoying now."

At the moment all he wanted was to enjoy it—and Liese—fur- ther. He said, "Thanks for inviting me to stay."

She was not to be put off. "Yes, of course. But you . . . people like you . . . really ought to think about things seriously. After all, the strong survive, and the weak perish. That is evolution, the immutable law of Nature. And who is still the strongest, even after decades of laziness and ignoring our responsibility to history? We, Alan, the Western ethnos. We are the ones who invent, develop, organize, create, and provide capital and jobs. We have done more than any other group. Now we are weakened by a babel of other voices. But we cannot afford to let them divert us: who would take over? Can you imagine that dreadful 'Emperor' of Guinea feeding even his own people, much less the people of Ghana, Nigeria, or anywhere else? If we . . . our industries and our expertise . . . were taken away, there would be chaos! Then destruction and an end to all that we . . . all that all humans . . . hold dear."

"Um . . . ." He cast about for another topic. If only she would go take a nap or something! Liese had been friendly last night; he sensed that she was ready to be somewhat more.

He found himself thinking of Jameela again. Dammit! Not even a harmless fantasy in peace! He couldn't pursue Liese without coming to terms with Jameela. He had let himself be induced to stop over in Pretoria. He had been nice to Liese—some might call it "courting"—but he had gone no farther than a remark or two, a little body contact, and a few drops of suntan lotion courteously applied. So far he had only transgressed mentally—which was hardly a crime!

So far.

Did he push it, or did he let it lie?

For the moment he would let it lie. He needed time.

The perfume of the suntan lotion, mingled with the faint, flowery scent of Liese's tangled, blonde tresses, and the sun-warmed, salt fragrance of her skin aroused him. He hunted for a safe subject. "Who is this Vincent Dorn anyway? I never heard of him."

Mrs. Delacroix gave Liese a look, very arch and very French. "You are looking at her. Not I . . . Liese, there. She is, perhaps, the 'Dorn,' while others are the 'Vincent.'"

"What?" Then he wondered why he was surprised. There had been talk at the Guatemala City meeting of a committee of writers. All he could think of to say was: "Congratulations."

"She writes the theoretical parts," Mrs. Delacroix continued. "Others do the history and the . . . how do you say? . . . action program."

"You mean the platform?"

"Not exactly. Your word 'platform' is too concrete, a list of very specific proposals. That leads to squabbles and factions within the movement. Instead, we emulate the First *Führer*: his *Weltanschauung* was no list of means and goals; it was a view of the future, of a strong Germany, of a society that could lead the West and the world. He had little use for platforms, such as the one the Party issued in 1920, nor did he fill his book, *Mein Kampf*, with specifics for people to argue over. His *Weltanschauung* was his eventual objective, but he was pragmatic and expected the details to change according to circumstances. He was a visionary, a prophet . . . and a guide, an arbiter, a conciliator between individuals and factions. And he was above them all."

"No *Führer* now," Liese shook out her tresses. "Have to attract through ideas, not charisma. Behavioral psychologists checking every word of our book. No mention of past, of Nazism. Just positive things. Warmth, love, progress, stability."

Lessing was amused. "You could hire an actor . . . a 'Vincent Dorn' to give speeches . . . ."

Liese sniffed scornfully and buried her head in her arms to let him massage lotion into the nape of her neck. Mrs. Delacroix took him seriously, however: "We thought of that. We may do it yet, if we cannot find a charismatic leader. Speeches, television, public appearances . . . all are so important, *n'est-ce pas*? We have also thought of keeping Monsieur 'Dorn' anonymous . . . *comment*? . . . incognito. But that could not continue after we become a public political force."

The whole thing struck him as silly. A movement without a leader? A mob of psychologists collaborating with ad-men and ghost-writers to compose the Holy Writ? It was a TV executive's wet dream! People were convinced by people, not by books: physical presence, words, and deeds—not abstract theories. Whatever else he may have been, Hitler had had the right idea about the realities of personal power. Hadn't Alexander, Napoleon, Churchill, Jesus all made it without too much reliance upon tracts and manifestos? Marx and Engels had written books, of course, but then they themselves had not fought in the revolution that swept Czarist Russia into the dustbin. Men like Lenin and Trotsky and Stalin had led that, for better or for worse. Jameela's Prophet Muhammad had had a book, of course, the Qur'an, but he could never have succeeded without charisma. He had given speeches, met people, argued issues, gathered adherents, fought opponents—and eventually won. No, Lessing knew from his own military experience that people wanted real, live human beings to lead them. That was why abstract, impersonal visions of God tended to become displaced by very human father-images, son-images, mother-images, and pantheons of saints, demigods, imams, gurus, holy mystics, or what have you. Human beings might die for an abstraction, but it would be another human being who convinced them the sacrifice was worth the candle.

He uttered a noncommittal grunt.

The swimming pool and its surrounding garden were as crystal-still as a photograph in some glossy resort brochure, an oasis of serenity cut off from the universe. Nothing entered without Mrs. Delacroix's approval; nothing was allowed to change. It was as though there would always be sunlight; blue, chlorine-smelling water; tiles that were hot and wet and blindingly white; damp towels; gay-fringed, pink parasols; and little, rickety tables of glass and wire overflowing with bottles and magazines and all the bric-a-brac of leisure.

Liese rose to her feet and stretched. She picked up a towel, muttered something about a shower, and glided off, barefoot and mostly bare elsewhere as well, toward the house. Lessing's eyes followed her of their own accord. Her legs were very good indeed.

"You will be kind to Liese?" Mrs. Delacroix's voice sliced into his revery.

"What?"

"You know. I am neither naive nor yet quite senile, eh?"

It was useless to dissemble. "Neither of us . . . . We haven't made any moves yet."

"You have both made it plain. I leave you two alone, and it becomes bedtime, no?"

He laughed at her turn of phrase. "Maybe. Anyway I have . . . other commitments . . . back in India. Nothing happens until I've decided about those. I don't have fun, then run."

"*Bien.* It should be what you both want." She extended one waxen, paper-pale hand from the shadow into the sunlight. It looked almost disembodied. "You would know about Liese?"

He said nothing, and she took his silence for assent. "Liese is American, Alan. Like yourself. She ran away from home when she was twelve. She does not speak of it, but I think it was her father . . . child abuse . . . you know. The American family is more than half destroyed, the old values gone. She ended in one of your cities, was taken in by a Black gang, was put to work as a prostitute on the streets, then was sold to someone in New York who took her to Cairo . . . a pornographer, a broker in human flesh. One of our people saw her there and bought her . . . literally. He brought her to Frankfurt and made her . . . what do you call it? . . . a mannequin, a model of fashions. She was no common prostitute. Anyone could see that. She had too much . . . I do not know the expression . . . ."

"Class," Lessing murmured.

"Ah, *oui*, class. I was raised in the Free Republic of the Congo . . . now neither free nor a republic, but that is another story. My English is better than my German . . . my grandfather's language . . . but my French is best. Do you speak French, Alan?"

He shook his head, and she gave him a mournful, little half-smile. "Too sad, you Americans. No languages. So. Liese suffered . . . I need not tell of it. You hear the effects in her speech: she does not find it easy to converse. She writes, though. Her writing is good and gets better."

So that was why Liese spoke as she did. "My God," he breathed. "How she must hate!"

"Ah? No. Not hatred. Not the way some women hate men, with less cause. Not Liese. She is hard and cautious, like a . . . a crab in a shell. Tough, ready to fight . . . but fragile, and inside very soft. She tries to be philosophical. What happened to her happens to many these days. She does not hate, but she does want to dismantle the system that hurt her. Replace it with a world in which such horrors cannot exist."

"Who could blame her? But she's an idealist. There'll always be wars and killing and cruelty and exploitation and crime and prostitution. No government, no 'movement,' no starry-eyed political philosophy will stop those."

"There speaks the mercenary: the soldier, the pragmatist. Perhaps you are right, Alan. But we . . . Liese and the rest of us . . . have to try. Otherwise there is no point to life, eh?"

He wiped his face and shoulders roughly with the fluffy, blue towel Liese had given him. Suddenly the chlorine smell of the swimming pool was suffocating. "I have to get back to India. I don't want to put you out . . . ."

"Put me out? What does it mean? Oh, to disturb me. No, my secretary, Mrs. Van Tassel, has your ticket and documents. I shall add a gift to repay you for your services." She rose to her feet, twitched her white sun-dress into place, and smiled. "So? You and Liese? Not now?"

He grinned back. "Later. Maybe."

She laughed outright. "Liese needs a good man, Alan. Perhaps you are good enough? A challenge?"

He chuckled and followed her into the house.

Dinner was awkward. Neither an average, middle-class, American upbringing nor years in various armies had prepared Lessing for people who ate with twelve pieces of silverware. Thank God South Africa had at least abandoned dinner jackets and starched dickeys! Mrs. Delacroix's six male guests were attired in a miscellany of sportswear, bush shirts, and business suits. The four women, including Liese, wore fashionable *cheong-sam*-like dresses slit up the thigh, made of a metallic-looking, silky, synthetic fabric and accompanied by matching bodices with a little over-jacket of translucent, lacy stuff. Sex had joyfully returned after long decades of stuffy, Born Again puritanism. The only one wearing a traditional dinner gown was their hostess herself, as regal and gracious as a portrait of some dowager empress.

Lessing found himself between an elderly Afrikaner and a younger man in the uniform of a captain of the South African police. The former sized Lessing up at once, made a polite remark or two, and then turned to the woman on his right to discuss horse racing in Johannesburg. The policeman was more forthcoming: bluff, balding, tanned, and familiar with the profession of arms. Mutual mercenary friends offered a starting point, and they went on to talk of native resistance groups, racial unrest in America (about which the policeman knew more than Lessing, who hadn't lived there for years), and the present situation in his own country.

"We're coming to it," the captain said unhappily. "Sooner or later we shall have another Great Massacre like the one back in 2000. Then many more, both White and Black, will be killed, and again nothing will be solved."

"What can do," Liese asked from across the table, "to stop it?" Lessing was getting used to her disjointed way of speaking.

The captain rubbed at his wispy moustache. "Like last time: military force. Socially, we've gone as far as we can: education, health care, jobs, housing. The . . . pardon my language . . . bloody lot. The Blacks want to do to us what they did to Rhodesia . . . Zimbabwe. First independence, then a 'veddy propah British' Black government, then a 'president' who's little more than a dictator, then army rule, then tribalism, then persecution of the White minority, and finally expulsion of whatever Whites are left. Then a shambles, like Zimbabwe today." Spots of color appeared in his cheeks. "Damn it, I'm as African as these people . . . ancestors here since the 1600s and all that. I won't give up my home any more than an English-American who is politely asked to leave by the Red Indians! Same case; different ratio of natives to Whites, that's all."

Lessing had heard the arguments before. By his own lights, the captain was only describing the situation realistically. Philosophically—morally, ethically, in the best of all possible worlds—perhaps there ought not to be racial conflict. Yet the human animal, Black or White, was aggressive and acquisitive, and whichever side was on top would almost certainly abuse its position. History proved it, and there were no signs of humanity undergoing a change of heart. Like the old saw said: "They ain't no justice." Where did one man's "legitimate political aspirations" become another man's "oppression and tyranny?" One had only to look to the Jews in Palestine, the British in Ireland, or any of a dozen other instances. He was glad when the captain let the subject drop.

As he watched Liese and the others he felt an emotion to which he could put no name: a vague disquiet, a doomed fatedness, like a man from the future seated at the last dinner on the *Titanic*. The bright, brittle conversation passed over and around him and echoed off into nothingness, the words no more than shards of glass, clashing and ringing and tinkling like the wind-chimes on his parents' porch back in Iowa. In this company he was as far out of his element as the broiled lobster Liese was daintily devouring. These elegant, overly mannered people were a soap opera on the holo-video; whatever they said and did had no relevance to the real world.

Covert observation of the old duffer on his right showed him the proper knife and fork for the roast beef and the correct wine to go with it. He made no unpardonable gaffes; at least no one leaped up to denounce him as an untutored, low-class slob. Actually, it was funny. He had little affinity for these people, but as the meal drew to a close he realized that he could cope if he really wanted to do so. Etiquette and chit-chat were like camouflage paint: you put it on when you went out on patrol. It wasn't part of you, and you knew how silly you looked with your face all daubed green and yellow and black, but you wore it because it meant survival. It was the same here.

Dessert came and went, then coffee. They got up. The ritual now required after-dinner drinks and conversation.

"My name's Hoeykens, Peter Hoeykens." The police captain put out a bronzed hand for Lessing to shake. "Didn't catch yours."

"Alan Lessing."

The man blinked, and the muscles in his jaw tensed. "Lessing, eh? Oh . . . oh. I say."

"Something wrong?" He sensed Mrs. Delacroix's gaze upon him from the far end of the table.

"Ah . . . ah, no. Not really . . . ."

"What's the problem?" Lessing asked.

"Could we speak privately?" The man signalled urgently to Mrs. Delacroix.

The sitting room to which the old woman took them was rarely used, an oasis of dark, leather furniture, tribal shields and spears, subdued lighting from massive, bronze lamps as big as barrels, animal skins: African *kitsch*, Lessing thought.

Mrs. Delacroix turned upon Hoeykens and raised an imperious eyebrow. "What is it, Peter?"

The captain sighed. "Two things . . . three, really. First, you are *that* Alan Lessing who works for Indoco? In India, I think?"

"Yes. So?"

"Been a come-uppance at your plant there. Accident. Burned down part of it."

"My God! How? Who . . . what . . . ? Anybody hurt?" He thought of Jameela.

"Don't think so, but can't say. Came in over the telecom link earlier as I was leaving for this bash."

"The other two things," Mrs. Delacroix urged.

"Both the same . . . different sources. Three days ago Europol put out an A.D. order . . . that's 'apprehend and detain' . . . for one Alan Lessing. The Americans want him on suspicion of murder, theft, and . . . for God's sake . . . treason. What the devil did you *do*, man?"

"The third thing?" He kept his voice calm. He saw no reason to enlighten Hoeykens.

"The Israelis came through with the same demand a day after Europol got on the line. Catch this Lessing and hold him for an interrogation team from Jerusalem."

"You would do that for them? The Zionists?" snapped Mrs. Delacroix.

"Have to," Hoeykens fiddled apologetically with his cuff links. "We supply Israel with arms and aid . . . and they us, you know. They swat flies in the north of Africa, and we swat flies down south. Not that we love the Izzies, but . . . well, one hand washes the other and that sort of thing."

The old woman put her hands on her hips and glared up into Hoeykens' reddening face. "This Alan Lessing, he is Herman Mulder's . . . how do you say? . . . protege. He is one of us. You know."

"Damn it, madame, nothing personal . . . ."

"Fine. Listen to me. You came tonight, you met Alan, but you never heard his name. He goes by my private jet to . . . to somewhere. At once."

"Back to India," Lessing put in firmly. "India."

"They . . . the Americans, at least . . . have extradition treaties with India! You will be arrested."

"I have to chance it. I have reasons . . . ."

Hoeykens interrupted him. "The Americans . . . State Department, CIA, I don't know which . . . knew you were here, how you got here. Not why. The Israelis just seemed to be pushing all the likely buttons. The two of 'em haven't got together yet."

"You were sent here specifically to find Mr. Lessing?" Mrs. Delacroix fixed the officer with a needle-sharp eye. "A spy?"

"My heavens, madame . . . ! Of course, not! My superiors know you and I are friends but not that Mr. Lessing would be here tonight. Anyhow, we have powerful support up top, and neither the Americans nor the Zionists are exactly welcome, what with their views of our internal policies and all. No, this was just coincidence."

Lessing had heard enough. "Anything else? Otherwise I'll take that offer of a plane for India. Neither the United States nor Israel is popular there. It'll be months before an extradition order gets through Delhi's red tape."

"Of course," Mrs. Delacroix said. "And by then your Mr. Mulder will have thought of something."

"I have just one small traveling case. I'll get it and be ready in ten minutes. Now I'd like to say good-bye to Liese, please."

"Oh . . . oh!" the captain flung after him as he turned to go. "I say, Mr. Lessing! One more bit of information! Seems both the Americans and the Zionists are hunting not only for you but for an accomplice of yours as well! Best tell him to go to ground, too!"

"Who?" Lessing thought of Bauer, then of Hollister, and lastly of Rose Thurley.

"Some chap named Pacov. I think that was the name. Russian, eh?"

Lessing fled up the stairs, toward the bedroom Mrs. Delacroix had provided him.

The ignorant see my grandfather's Germany as a place of ultimate horror, a scene in which the major landmarks are the labor camps, the secret police, and the darkness of despair. They fail to note that the only ones in despair were those who were not part of our society: those who were alien by birth or those who had alienated themselves by their selfishness, their decadence, or their adherence to alien causes or creeds.

They omit, often deliberately, the happy scenes: a recovering economy, jobs, stable currency, new highways and construction everywhere, an end to the street-fighting between Left and Right, art and music, and a healthy interest in nutrition, exercise, and sports. Most Germans were optimistic for the first time since before World War I.

It all ended too soon for most of us. We had a few years of peace, and then came the long and terrible night of war. We Germans knew that our country did not start the war, although we weren't permitted to say so after 1945: we were the bulwark of Western civilization against the Asiatic hordes and the madness of communism. The war brought casualties, bombings, rationing, forced labor, and all the horrors of a society being pounded into rubble. We endured it bravely and even gladly. We were fighting for positive values, for the survival and progress of our people.

You ask about labor camps and oppression? Tell me, what would you Americans have done, surrounded by enemies? How would your gentle liberals have treated their camps full of *Nisei* if Japanese armies were advancing through California? Let them look into their own souls and then say honestly whether they would have done differently than we did!

Paint the future in gay colors and show the world that a totalitarian state is no regimented monster! No wars, no violence, no tyranny, no tanks rumbling in the night! Not a military take-over, but a free election, such as the plebiscite that swept our First *Führer* to power in 1933. People must *vote* us into office.

Why? Because we are the best chance this planet has! Perhaps the *only* chance, the *last* chance before Armageddon. The world must realize this.

—Personal letter from Mrs. Emma Delacroix to Ms. Anneliese Meisinger, dated January 31, 2042

CHAPTER EIGHT

Monday, July 14, 2042

66What was the guy's name?" Wrench twisted at the wheel of the little Ikeda Outdoorsman to avoid a gaggle of children and water buffalo in the rain-soaked road ahead. "The one that came home after twenty years and only his old dog recognized him?"

"Odysseus," Lessing replied. "How in hell do you know about him? They stopped teaching Greek lit in high school fifty years ago, even in English translation."

Wrench feigned insult. "Hey, man, I got culture. I read it in a World Classics comic book."

"Anyway, it doesn't apply to me. I've been gone less than a week."

"I still feel like a dog. Mulder says: 'Go get Lessing.' I go get Lessing, all the way to Lucknow." Wrench squinted and racked the vehicle down to make a turn. "Woof, woof! Out here I feel like a dog most of the gubbin' time."

The monsoons had lowered over the dry north-Indian plain since dawn; now they became a cataract that thundered down with the vengefulness of an angry god. Mrs. Delacroix's jet had dropped Lessing off at Palam Airport in Delhi, and the local flight to Lucknow was late, as usual. Lessing felt like a discarded mango peel: limp, tepidly wet, sticky, smelly, and gritty all over. He hung on grimly against all that Wrench could do.

Wrench had told him about Indoco: not another break-in, as Lessing had feared, but a mass demonstration outside. There had been perhaps a hundred "students" and another dozen unidentifiable *goondas*, "ruffians," the Hindi term for anything from the Prodigal Son to Al Capone, who were undoubtedly paid agitators, though nobody knew whose. The plant *chaukidars* had taken one look and fled, leaving the mob free run of the plant. Indoco would now have to rebuild three warehouses and replace some machinery, but no one had been seriously injured. Mulder was furious. He was talking of adding a score of foreign mercs to his security force, but getting clearance for them from Delhi would not be quick or easy.

Most important of all to Alan Lessing was the fact that Jameela was safe and waiting for him. He felt greater relief than he wanted to admit, even to himself.

There was something new on the turnoff leading from the main highway to the plant: a straw-thatched hut and a cloth-draped pole down across the road. "They put in a police post," Wrench grumbled. "For our 'protection' from more incidents." He produced papers, shoved them at the dark, dripping face that poked itself into the driver's window, held out a ten-rupee note, watched it disappear into the night, and drove on.

Jameela, Mulder, Goddard, and three Indians awaited them on the verandah of the main house. Servants with clumsy, black umbrellas splashed out to the Ikeda, and Lessing proceeded to flout a thousand years of Indian tradition by marching over and embracing Jameela in public. Her warm, dry, spice-fragrant body felt wonderful.

"You smell *bisaind*," she whispered sweetly in his ear. The Urdu word meant "stinking," like raw meat.

Mulder cleared his throat. "Meet Colonel Srivastava, Indian Army, assigned to protect Indoco until there's been an investigation. This is Sub-Inspector Mukerjee, Uttar Pradesh Police, and Mr. Subramaniam from the CID. Gentlemen, Mr. Alan Lessing, chief of plant security. He's been away on a business trip."

Lessing was tired. He could barely see the figures around him or feel the hands that reached out to shake his. He heard Mrs. Mulder's tremulous, fairy-godmother soprano chirping at Jameela: "Take him upstairs to the guest bedroom. It's too late to go back to your own apartment." Then, somehow, he was there, in a boxy, whitewashed little room with frilly curtains. Jameela shooed servants out and herself struggled with the cantankerous plumbing to produce hot water for a shower. Then he was in bed.

He awoke thinking how he hated to sleep on a hillside, his head higher than his feet. Where in hell was he? Syria? Yes, north of Damascus, with his merc comrades in the gulley below him, and Major Berger's crack Israeli brigade over the ridge, where they were taking fire from those big, new mortars the Russians had given the Iranians. The shit was heavy over there. Any minute Berger's air strike would come in and . . . .

Why was he so cold and so damp? In Syria? He rubbed at his eyes with his knuckles and was surprised when the scene dissolved and coalesced again into an unfamiliar bedroom. It contained one cushioned chair; a huge clothes-cabinet that Jameela called an *almari* and the British, who could never pronounce anything foreign, an "almirah"; a slow-turning ceiling fan; and electric wires stapled to the wall. A tiny, harmless lizard, which Jameela called a *chipkili*, walked upside down across the ceiling over his head. The roar of Iranian mortar bursts became the gurgle of the ancient air conditioner that Mulder was always intending to replace. It did keep the room both clammy and damn near freezing. He glanced down and saw why he had dreamed of sleeping on a hillside: Goddard was sitting on the foot of the bed, his ponderous weight enough to scuttle an ocean liner.

Goddard was not only big, he was bristly as a boar: his broad skull, the backs of his hands, his shoulders, all were covered with springy, coarse, black hair. The light from the window made a halo around his head, something he would have only if Satan ruled in Heaven! How old was he, anyway? Forty? Goddard was an American from Chicago, a hard-ass, a comer, a would-be exec, smart, and on his way up to the top of Indoco's dungheap.

Lessing used the opportunity to kick out with both feet as though just waking up.

Goddard let out a satisfying yelp and leaped off the bed. "Christ! You kick your little Indian chicky like that and you'll break all her bones!"

Lessing yawned in his face. Goddard wasn't worth hating.

"Mulder's coming. He wants to see you."

"I'm here." He got up, found his gear had been stored in the almirah, and dug out his shaving things.

"Make out with that blonde?"

He let the plumbing answer for him. The faucet belched, hic-coughed, and gushed a stream of brown fluid that slowly changed into steaming-hot water. He shut the door in Goddard's beefy face so that he could use the facilities.

When he emerged, Herman Mulder was sitting in the one chair. Wrench occupied the foot of the bed, and Goddard now leaned against the wall by the window.

Mulder waited in Buddha-esque silence until Lessing had settled down again at the head of the bed. When he spoke it was just one word:

"Pacov."

"Sir . . . I . . . ."

"Please don't lie."

Lessing had no intention of lying; he had been about to suggest that a mercenary's jobs were as privileged as a priest's confessional or a psychiatrist's couch. More. A merc could get thumbed for a breach of security. Opfoes and employers alike frowned upon loose lips. He shut his mouth with an audible snap.

Mulder appeared not to notice. "You're alive because of us, Alan. Very few know who or what we represent, but everybody knows that we protect our people, particularly in the Third World."

"Sir . . . ."

"Hear me out. Only a very determined foe would attack you while you're with us. Yet somebody is willing to risk lives to get at you. That foe may believe that *we* sent you to get . . . and that *we* have . . . Pacov. Which endangers *us*. Do you see?"

"The raid to get the books doesn't seem to have been connected with you at all," Goddard added. "Maybe some other supercorp sniffing around to see what they could find . . . and almost hitting the jackpot. It's possible they were Israelis or the Vigilantes for Zion. The Izzies and the Vizzies have come close before."

"Never this close!" Wrench protested. "How did they know the diaries were here?"

"All under control now." Mulder wiped his naked, pink forehead with an old-fashioned handkerchief. "The last raid . . . the local 'scholars' and their friends . . . was *not* directed at us. They were looking for *you* again, Alan. It was lucky that Miss Husaini was over at the main office. Two of their non-Indian agitators got into your quarters and made a thorough search. Hitting Indoco was a diversion: nothing seriously damaged, just yelling and burning and prancing around, and a lot of pretending to find 'dangerous pollutants' and 'killer chemicals.' They didn't even try to wreck the computer that controls our agro-chemical mixes."

Lessing said, "Mr. Mulder, I can't . . . won't . . . tell you more than you know. The name you mentioned is my business, privileged info. It has nothing to do with you or Indoco. I'll swear to that."

Wrench struck a heroic pose. "The Code of the West! The Masked Merc rides again!"

Lessing had an insanely funny urge to match him and cry, "Bring on your Gestapo! I'll never talk!" Mulder, however, had little sense of humor, and Goddard even less.

"Shall I tell *you* then, Alan?" Mulder held up a thick hand, as pale and hairless as a baby's. "You went on a mission for one Senhor Gomez, a Goanese 'merc broker.' You traveled to the United States, to an installation with the code-name 'Marvelous Gap,' located in New Mexico. It was built just after the turn of the century, during the worst period of Born Again paranoia. Then it was officially 'lost': closed down, no mention, no records. The place would be an embarrassment to President Rubin's peace initiative if the Russians found out it still existed. There'd be hell to pay in Geneva, and the United Nations would make a TV sitcom out of it. The present U.S. government thinks it's better to let Marvelous Gap stay marvelously lost."

Lessing saw no reason to tell Mulder of Hoeykens' information and the reason for his precipitous flight from South Africa. Mulder and his SS might decide he was more trouble than he was worth. He said, "I'm a soldier. Politics isn't my job. I follow orders."

Mulder sighed. "They didn't accept that excuse at Nuremberg." He saw that Lessing hadn't understood. "That was before your time. Never mind. While you were in Pretoria I sent a coded cable to Washington. Our people there have been investigating Pacov and other Born Again projects for some time. They punched some buttons, and now I know all there is to know . . . outside of some top-secret data in the National Security Agency. The movement has friends in Washington, friends with access to the government's biggest data-banks. The Pacov formulae were all destroyed, as were the administrative records, right down to the mess-hall grocery lists. But they missed one document here, another there. That's the virtue of computers: once you find a clue, you get the computer itself to hunt for more. It collates everything, patches it together, and hands it to you in a print-out."

Lessing shook his head. "Still nothing to do with me. I'm only the errand boy. I don't care what's in the package."

"Yes. Well. 'Pacov' stands for 'Pandemic Communicable Virus,' one of the uglier results of military experimentation with recombinant DNA. Do you know what that is?"

"I've read. Magazines . . . ."

"Do you want to read what technical details we have? The cable's on my desk."

"I'm no scientist." Actually, he would probably understand most of it. Lessing kept up on military developments as part of his trade.

"Very well, let me tell you in layman's terms." Mulder extended a hand to shush Wrench, who had started to speak. "Pacov consists of two separate reworkings of the DNA chains of existing viruses. It's a piggyback weapon, a two-stage operation. You send in the first stage. The vectors . . . agents of transmission . . . for Pacov-1 are extensive: it travels through the air, the water, or directly from person to person and is highly contagious. It spreads for hundreds of miles if conditions are optimal. Pacov-1 causes only a mild, flu-like infection that disappears within a day or two. Public health authorities would overlook it, never consider it a serious epidemic, and even if they did they'd have to look carefully to isolate it. Once a victim is over the 'flu,' Pacov-1 becomes dormant and almost undetectable. A month or two later you send in the second stage: Pacov-2 is also a virus, just as contagious as the first, and just as harmless by itself. It reacts with Pacov-1, however, to produce a powerful coagulant. A coagulant, Alan, a substance that turns your blood to thick jelly! Your heart isn't made to pump strawberry jam, and you die within three minutes. No warning, no vaccine, no cure. Those not exposed to *both* stages remain unharmed. There might be a few immunes, but they didn't do a lot of testing, as you can imagine. Pacov-2 goes inert like Pacov-1 within a week or two. Then you get your victim's country, all his property . . . in undamaged condition . . . and a lot of corpses to bury."

Mulder paused. "Does this convince you, Alan?"

It did.

"Pacov terrified the Born Agains. They had opened the gate and come eyeball to eyeball with the worst nightmares of Hell. They ripped out the installation at Marvelous Gap and scattered its personnel around to other projects. Maybe they even killed those most closely involved; they were no more 'noble' than any government before or since. It wouldn't surprise me."

"What would happen if somebody . . . used . . . Pacov today?"

Mulder inspected the half-moons of his tiny, salmon-pink fingernails. "No idea. No data. Perhaps the stuff is too old and has gone inert. Perhaps it *never* would have worked. All we know is that it was intended as a last resort, the checkmate move, the Doomsday weapon. No, worse. More like the last tantrum of a very bad loser: leap up, shoot your opponent, and kick the chessboard to smithereens! Pacov was meant to destroy *nations*, Alan . . . millions . . . perhaps hundreds of millions of people."

"Jesus . . . ," Goddard muttered.

Mulder made a downward, circling motion. "The Last Trump. Not with a bang but with a gurgle. Down the toilet. All mammalian life within the target area."

"God!" Wrench exclaimed, "What good's an army? With that stuff . . . !"

Mulder raised his head to look at the little man. "Quite right, Charles. In the old days an army consisted of human beings with swords and spears, guns and cannon . . . whatever was state-of-the-art at the moment. You could *see* the enemy, watch him coming, gird up your loins and fight. Then warfare went out into space: missiles, bombs, satellites, platforms. You . . . the intelligence agencies . . . can still see those weapons, but they're so powerful that neither side dares to start a war. The only atomic devices used in this century were dropped during the China-Viet Nam War."

"And we've learned a lesson from *that*!" Lessing said.

"Quite so. Hopefully, at least. But you see where I'm going: a conventional army costs money, but every state can afford something, and it's *visible* to its foes. Space weapons are prohibitively expensive . . . billions, trillions . . . more than even the United States or the Soviets can tolerate, decade after decade, generation after generation. They're too powerful to employ without the risk of a retaliation that will turn your own country into a radioactive wasteland, and they're still relatively easy to keep track of; both you and your opponents know what's there." He tapped the chair arm for emphasis. "Think, though: all you need for Pacov . . . or for the toxin counterpart the Russians call 'Starak' . . . is a handful of scientists, a wet lab, and a delivery system. Cheap, cost-effective, and easily concealed. Any petty terrorist organization can afford it, any banana republic, any fanatic religious sect." He got up and came to stand over Lessing. "Just how big were those Pacov cannisters?"

It didn't matter now. He might as well tell it. "A little globe, like a Christmas-tree ornament. And a cylinder, about this size." He indicated four inches between thumb and finger.

His own stash of Pacov came to mind. Maybe Mulder's movement, the descendants of the Nazi SS, were indeed reformed, just another bunch of nice guys making a living through hard work and honest capitalism. He didn't trust them. Not them, not anyone. He was willing to tell Mulder some of what he knew, but he'd be damned if he'd hand over his samples to these people, or to anybody except maybe God Himself. And only then if the Big Guy asked politely.

Mulder wiped pearls of sweat from his forehead. "A family enters a country as tourists. Pacov-1 goes along in a box with their children's toys . . . ."

Wrench uttered a nervous giggle. "With a clown face painted on it!"

Mulder scowled in irritation. "Yes. A month or two later a man arrives with Pacov-2 disguised as a deodorant stick or a tube of insect repellent. He goes to his hotel room, cracks the container in the sink, and leaves again. He's safe because he wasn't exposed to Pacov-1, which is now quiescent."

"And everybody in the target area dies," Goddard breathed.

"True," Mulder said, "but messy! There are no neat limits to a biological weapon, no idea how long it will *really* last! Viruses are unpredictable, and they can mutate. Did you know that there's an island near Scotland that is *still* uninhabitable because of British experiments after World War II? Almost a century later! Biological weapons are cheap and effective, but they're two-edged swords."

"As blackmail . . . !" Goddard held up his cupped hand and made a throttling gesture.

"What if your target calls your bluff? Don't be stupid, Bill! They might decide to sterilize your side of the planet with atomic bombs! Or use Starak or another BW agent of their own! And if Pacov got out of hand, you could end with a cemetery instead of a world!"

No one spoke for a time. The sun had grown insistent, and waves of heat beat against the rippled, bubbly glass of the windowpane. The old air-conditioner chugged and sputtered, just managing to keep the inferno outside at bay. Mulder wiped his face, Wrench fidgeted, and Goddard sat like a carved behemoth. Lessing pulled the pillow around, both for comfort and also to watch the other three. Silent watching often got better results than speech.

"They blame us . . . my ancestors . . . for genocide," Mulder mused. "Is Pacov our doing? Those missiles in the sky? Yes, we fought a war, and yes, we bombed and shot and slew. So did the Allies. Match Auschwitz against the fire-bombing of Dresden or the horror of Hiroshima. All horrible, all stupid. We've learned, Alan, learned a lot in a hundred years."

Lessing blurted out, "And the 'Holocaust'?"

"Didn't Wrench tell you that there never really was one . . . at least, not the way the Jews tell it. Forced labor and camps and disease and maltreatment, yes; it was war time, and my ancestors did what they believed they had to do. And there were some shootings in the eastern territories, mass executions of Jews and communist guerrillas. But no gas chambers, or any of the other fanciful inventions claimed by the Jews. But it's always the victors who write the histories."

"And hold the war-crimes trials," Wrench whispered.

"Anyhow, whether there was a 'Holocaust' or not is irrelevant to this age. No one wants a war that will end life on earth. Nor can one people rule a world of slaves. The Israelis have expanded into a slave-empire, and they are just beginning to reap the whirlwind. No, we'll win our way, Alan. We are the people who invented the technology and organization that makes this modern world possible. We're *fitted* to win. We want a healthy people, a healthy environment, a healthy world. A radioactive desert or a rotten orange crawling with germs . . . neither is of use to us . . . or to the Jews or anyone else."

Lessing said slowly, "I don't know whether I believe you or not. I don't know that I *care* whether I believe you. It all happened a hundred years ago. Your Hitler is as dead as last week's curry." Goddard stiffened, but the others ignored him. "What do you intend to do, Mr. Mulder? What do you want *me* to do?"

Mulder heaved himself to his feet, Goddard leaning forward solicitously to lend a hand. "We want you to find Pacov. Who paid you? Who's got it now?"

"Ask Gomez."

Goddard snorted. "Gomez is dead, Lessing. His heart stopped. It had a bullet in it."

Lessing stared. "Who? When?"

"*You* thumbed him. That's the rumor. We know you didn't, because you were in Pretoria. But the mercs don't know that. In some circles you're dead meat."

"But you know other mercs," Wrench prompted. "People above Gomez's level?"

"You can go and inquire," Mulder interrupted smoothly. "Or you can go your way and face those waiting for you outside Indoco's fences. The Izzies are looking for you, and the Americans want you. Somebody knows about Pacov and Marvelous Gap, somebody who either wants to interrogate you or see you unzipped. We can protect you. You can stay here for a while, and if things blow over, fine. Otherwise we can hire you as chief of security at Club Lingahnie, our new spa on the island of Ponape. The south Pacific is lonely, but it's safe."

"He'd have to leave his Indian popsy here," Goddard sneered.

Surprisingly, Mulder turned on the man. "That's enough, Bill! Do you know where the word 'Aryan' comes from? Sanskrit, Bill, the ancestor of Hindi and other North Indian languages. It originally meant 'noble.' India was invaded about 1,500 B.C. by the Aryans, relatives of our own ancestors."

The wings of Goddard's fleshy nose flared. "Mr. Mulder, are you saying that these . . . these . . . Pakis are *White*?"

Wrench tittered, but Mulder did not flinch. "Many in the upper castes are. At least so Alfred Rosenberg, one of the leading theoreticians of the Third *Reich*, said, though he did add that they had become 'mixed.' In any case, the First *Führer* treated them as Aryans. There was a *Waffen*-SS division, the *Frei Hind*, made up of anti-British Indians. It spent the war near the Bay of Biscay, I think. It saw no combat, but it was racially acceptable to *Reichsführer* Himmler."

Spots of angry red burned in Goddard's cheeks. "I suppose Blacks are Aryans, too!"

"Not black Africans, certainly, but there *were* Muslims in the *Waffen*-SS."

Wrench appeared to be enjoying the turn the conversation had taken, and he cut in: "The *Handschar* Division. Right, Mr. Mulder? Didn't the First *Führer* once line 'em up and hand out little Qur'ans to wear around their necks? Qur'ans with swastikas on 'em?"

"I think so." Mulder wiped his forehead again. "There were men of many nationalities . . . Ukrainians, Latvians, Estonians, Dutch, Flemish, French, Romanians, Hungarians, even some Britons . . . in the SS. More than just blonde, Germanic 'supermen': many different White sub-groups. Not everybody was as pure-minded as *Obergruppenführer* Theodor Eicke, who complained that even many *Volksdeutschen*, Germans who lived outside Germany, were too weak and undisciplined to serve as replacements in his *Totenkopf* Division."

"But . . . ."

"And what if the *Reich* had won? All those different peoples, all those languages and cultures and traditions? I know what your faction wants, Bill, but it won't work. Even if you cleansed the earth of every Black and every Jew and every non-German . . . including yourself, being of French and English descent, I recall . . . you'd still have to build a world. Hatred is a useful motive in combat, but it makes for very poor economic or administrative policies. You have to look beyond your immediate horizons, Bill." He made soothing motions with his handkerchief. Clearly he did not want a quarrel.

Goddard struggled with himself, managed a smirk, and grated, "Excuse me, sir." He went out.

"A good man," Mulder looked after him ruefully. "Enlightened racism, the service of our Western ethnos, is the theoretical basis of our movement. But Bill takes it too far . . . and then doesn't take it far enough beyond that."

Lessing had decided. "I want to go to see a man in Paris," he said. "I'll try to find out about Pacov: who got it, who wants it . . . who wants *me*. I don't promise to give it to you . . . ."

"Nor do we want it. It should be destroyed safely!"

"But *I* have to know . . . for my own good."

"Fair enough. Miss Hilary, down at the plant, will get you tickets and reservations. Leave any time."

"After I've seen Jameela."

At that time I was still a soldier. Physically and mentally I had the polish of six years of service . . . . In common with my army comrades, I had forgotten such phrases as: "That will not go," or, "That is not possible," or, "We ought not to take such a risk; it is too dangerous."
—*Mein Kampf*, Adolf Hitler

CHAPTER NINE

Thursday, July 17, 2042

The hotel room on the Place du Havre, opposite the ancient Gare St. Lazare, was small and musty, four paces from scarred door to grimy window, three from the far wall to the bed. It suited Lessing's needs: Terry Copley's secretary had said that "le Boss" would return at 1400 hours.

He ran a finger over the tatty upholstered chair, then sat down on—and almost disappeared into—the billowy featherbed that the French still preferred to anything invented since 1600.

He checked the spring-powered spit-shooter Wrench had insisted upon giving him: a short, black, plastic tube that fired darts dipped in a variant of saxitoxin, a poison the experts said would kill within twenty seconds. Lessing had not wanted the weapon, but it did provide a back-up to the 9-mm automatic pistol he carried in a shoulder holster. Neither Indian nor French airport security had objected to his armament, once he displayed the Indoco courier I.D. Mulder had provided him.

Shrill traffic noises penetrated the ancient and many-times-renovated stone walls. He got up to look outside. Paris had solved her time-honored congestion: now the only vehicles permitted within the city were battery-powered electrics, flat-bed delivery trucks, and two- or four-passenger "dodgem" cars with bodies built of a plastic material and engines that would propel them no faster than 30 kilometers per hour. Parisians displayed their traditional gallantry, adventurousness, and contempt for their fellows' lives by naming the smaller model of these vehicles *le duelliste* and the larger *le char*—"the tank." Both were fitted, *de rigueur*, with the most strident horns science could devise. The traffic situation improved somewhat, but not as much as was hoped: many people bought both a "town car" and also a larger, petrol-powered traditional automobile for extended travel. The wealthy purchased all three, which enriched the owners of rentable parking space in the suburbs beyond their wildest dreams.

Across the plaza, the weathered, time-worn facade of the Gare St. Lazare bespoke an earlier and more leisurely age. The eggshell-blue July sky seemed eternal. Crowds were denser than ever in this twenty-first century, of course: tourists in colorful shorts and Bylon shirts that could be wadded up in one's fist and then shaken out like a magician's handkerchief, unrumpled and crisp; French businessmen sporting fashionable frock-coats and vests, their trouser legs so tight as to be almost body stockings; shop girls in a variety of skirts and sweaters and blouses; and numerous young men attired in the scruffy shirts and pants that were as eternally *Parisien* as the Eiffel Tower. Lessing's own nondescript, tan sports jacket and cuffless, brown trousers were ten years out of date here; this was just as well: he could never pass for a Parisian nor even a European, but a footloose, not-too-rich American wanderer was a useful image under the circumstances.

There were others on the street. He amused himself watching several hookers in the current Banger uniform: a translucent, glassine miniskirt, glittery pasties or metal-tissue breast cups, and long braids, dyed whatever hue their owner felt matched today's "aura." Some of the women carried the finger-drums or tambourines that gave Banger music its name—and the rest of the world a headache—while others didn't bother pretending. Hypocrisy aside, the good burghers of Paris considered the Banger girls an asset, as much a tourist money-maker as the Louvre or the Metro.

Lessing had been in Paris before, once on leave from Angola, and again when he flew out to join in the Baalbek War in Syria. Then it had been sophisticated and exciting; now it struck him as alien, as different from India as Mars. He sensed something of what Jameela would feel: a disturbing dose of culture-shock.

That brought him squarely back to his own problems. His last meeting with Jameela had been stormy. She wanted him with her, at Indoco, and she wanted an end to danger and instability. She had been furious when he told her he was leaving for Paris.

"Never do you talk to me!" she had cried. "Never explain! Never say what you are doing!" In the heat of anger the hard, retroflex consonants of her native Urdu crept back into her speech, and part of her American university polish bubbled away like paint exposed to a flame.

"I can't. You know that."

"Take me along!"

"Can't do that either. I'll be back in a couple of days."

She glared at him, long-lashed eyes narrowed, two little, vertical, white lines beside her lips. He was reminded of one of their discussions about the Islamic concept of God. Allah, she said, displayed two aspects, *Jamali* and *Jalali*, the former being beautiful and gentle, the latter powerful, harsh, and violent. Like each of Allah's creatures, Jameela Husaini displayed both of these aspects, too, and her *Jalali* manifestation was truly a terror to behold!

She snapped, "Mercenary work!"

It wasn't a question, but he grunted, "Yes."

"You just go . . . kill people, shoot people . . . fight. No reason except money. No principle. No . . . no . . . ."

"Ethics? We mercs . . . soldiers . . . have ethics. Sometimes they're different from those of the folks back home . . . ."

"No feelings! A . . . a robot with a gun!" Tears welled up, and she fiercely scoured them away. "Stay here, Alan. My father is a high officer in our CID. He'll protect you. He's what protects Indoco."

That confirmed one of Wrench's more devious suspicions. Jameela Husaini had been planted in Indoco as a spy, to keep an eye on the foreigners. Her father probably had *not* ordered her to start an affair with Lessing, however. The Soviets and some Western intelligence agencies might do that sort of thing, but it would violate too many taboos for an Indian father to ask that from a daughter, even in the interests of national security.

"I don't need protecting. I'm going on a trip to see an old friend."

How devious one could be and still speak the truth! He would not tell Jameela about Mulder's Nazi machinations or about Pacov. Either might get her thumbed. As far as he knew, too, she had no connection with Bauer; at least she hadn't gone up to Balrampur Hospital in Lucknow to see him, according to Kuldeep, the driver.

"Stay with me. I . . . want you." It was the nearest she had ever come to saying "I love you" out loud.

He went to her.

Memories. Lips, breasts, nipples, soft skin, smooth thighs, fingers sliding and grasping and caressing, heavy tresses upon his breast, perfumed serpents coiling in the dark.

Orgasm, thunderous, rhythmic, and savage, as close to the raw animal as a human being can get.

But was it "love"?

He shook his head, ran fingertips through his hair. Jameela knew him better than he knew himself. It was so hard to *feel*, so impossible to speak. Others could say "love" as glibly as they said "hello." Not Alan Lessing. Others instinctively sensed a "right" and a "wrong," although that was perhaps cultural and not some internal, universal voice of conscience, a God who just coincidentally happened to have all the values of a twenty-first century, middle-class, American WASP from Iowa. Others had something to live by, even when it was demonstrably stupid. Even Mulder and Liese and Mrs. Delacroix stuck to their principles, although the rest of the world might despise them for it.

He looked inside himself, as he often had done when he was a child, then later as an adolescent, and still later when he had faced death in a half-dozen unmemorable countries. He looked within . . .

and discovered the same, old jumble of half-formed ideas, feelings, sensations, facts, fancies, memories—an attic full of junk he could neither use nor throw away.

Was everybody like this? Jameela and Liese and the rest seemed so certain of themselves. Were they as confused inside? Were they, too, unable to speak, souls imprisoned in statues with lips of stone?

God damn it.

Or had God already damned *him*?

The telephone purred. Monsieur Copley would see him now.

The squat, little "dodgem" taxi let him off in Rue Madeleine Michelis in Neuilly. He checked carefully for pursuers but saw no one. Copley had a flat in one of the nicer buildings the French government had built after the labor riots of 2035. Lessing found "511: COPLEY" beside a button on the directory board in the glossy, plastic-panelled lobby. He pressed, received an answering buzz, and entered the elevator beyond. It was undoubtedly fitted with a spy-eye, and there would be more along the white, antiseptic corridor that led to number 511. Copley was a cautious man.

The blank outer door opened upon desks, secretaries, computers, filing cabinets, molded Parodex chairs, and a coffee table heaped with magazines. The place looked like a dentist's waiting room. Three swarthy men, Arabs or Iranians, occupied seats along the left wall, and a single youngish European with a scraggly, blonde beard sat by himself on the right. Lessing tossed his jacket onto a chair, sat down next to the blonde man, and waited. It was a full half hour before the plump French receptionist called Lessing's name.

Colonel Terence B. Copley, U.S. Army, retired, rose from behind a paper-cluttered desk and stuck out a hand. He hailed from Alabama, a red-haired, bony, freckled, barrel-shaped man in his forties, with eyes as sharp—and, oddly, as leaden—as two splinters of shrapnel. His short-sleeved shirt and Parisian string-tie gave him a raffish, slightly silly look. He would have been more at home in a jogging suit and running shoes, a high school gym teacher who had gone astray and ended up in far-off Paris.

Lessing glanced around. The room was painted a bland off-white, its wall-to-wall carpet a neutral beige. The desk that sat squarely in the center of the floor was a bad copy of an ugly original, the chairs the sort that businesses rented by the month. Thick, velvety, dark-green drapes mostly covered the long window on the western side. The only decoration consisted of a display of antique weapons on the wall behind Copley's balding skull: a lethal-looking old Heckler and Koch submachine gun, worth a couple of months of Lessing's salary, an Uzi, and one of the Ingram models, all three gleaming a menacing gold and black in the sunlight that crept in through a gap in the drapes. These weapons would be de-activated, the ready stuff stored elsewhere. Copley's real protection would consist of stitch-guns concealed in the wall, probably a pistol under a pile of papers on the desk, and armed assistants within call. The colonel was paranoid enough to have bulletproof glass, poison gas, and a trap-door over an oubliette filled with spikes, but there *were* limits.

"Get down and kiss my hairy ass, recruit!" Copley chortled.

"And up yours with an umbrella, sir!" Lessing had served under this man in Angola. They had been friends, then.

"Wait'll you get it *in* before you *open* it!" Copley bellowed merrily in return. He waved at the one chair before his desk. "What can I do y'all?"

Lessing took the indicated seat, feeling the beady muzzles of the hidden stitch-guns upon his back. He cleared his throat. "I'm pressed for time."

"No drink?"

"No, thanks. Gave it up. India does that." And Jameela had helped. An occasional cold beer was all he wanted these days.

"So what *do* I do ya?"

"Answer questions. Urgent ones."

"Try me." Copley poured himself a glass of something brown and pungent from a bottle behind his in-basket.

"People say I'm thumbing. That so?"

The other's blunt, ruddy face went shut, as though a book had been closed.

"Jesus, you *do* like it short and sweet!" The glass made a wet ring on the desk, and Copley rubbed at it ineffectually. He scrutinized Lessing's face quizzically. "All right. So I've heard. Rumors . . . shit-talk."

"It's not true."

"Nobody showed me no dead bodies. I never believed it. Man, you know me."

"What *did* you hear?"

"Only that your squad was dying off too fast to blame on old age. Hjellming dead, Hollister popped at in Copenhagen . . . not like you to miss the bastard, Alan, if you *are* thumbing. You always was a good shot. Felix Bauer's disappeared. Rose Thurley's the only one still walking around, and people say that's because you and her had something going." He put on a lascivious little smile. "Not much for looks, but real expert, as many a regiment of satisfied sojer-boys can attest."

"Forget that." He knew where Bauer was, but he wouldn't tell Copley. He was also glad Rose was safe, though he'd never had any desire to try out her non-military skills. He leaned forward and said, "None of it is mine. If somebody is thumbing my people, I want to know why. I want to know bad!"

Copley picked up a bottle-green file folder from his desk. "Want a job? A real job . . . not that beegee crap you're doing now. Battalion going in for the rebs in Uganda. Second in command? Maybe captain, if the sponsors agree?"

Lessing waved the file away. "No, and I don't want to join an Eskimo regiment in the Arctic or boss a legion of hula-dancers in Hawaii!"

"Or be a bouncer in an S-'n'-M gay bar in Los Angeles?" Copley snorted up laughter the way an elephant sucks water through its trunk. "God, man, I don't know a damned thing! People *do* talk. Come on, y'all surely got time for one drink at least."

"No, really. Let me ask you this: what do you know about my last job? Who bought that spesh-op?"

Copley scratched an ear so freckled that it resembled a dried apricot. "Heard that Gomez got croaked, too, out in India. Heard that you might've been the croaker and him the croakee."

"No way. I was . . . somewhere else. I can prove it."

"Shit, who's asking? But that means that whatever he knew is worms. I talked to Arturo Da Silva in Lebanon a couple weeks back. You know him? Friend of Gomez?"

"Yeah. Your point?"

"He said Gomez was bragging about something he'd set up. A lot of money, helicopters, guns, mercs. Was that you?"

"Could be. Who paid?"

Copley raised both shoulders in an expressive, Gallic shrug. He had become so French that he could make a living letting tourists take his picture over in the Montmartre.

"I've got to know."

"Can't help you. Honest to God."

"Bullshit. You've never been honest to God." Lessing changed the subject. "What do you hear about my boss, Herman Mulder? About Indoco?"

Again that flat, closed stare. What drug was Copley taking that made his eyes look like lead marbles?

"Nice old guy. Works hard. Stays out in India when he could be sitting on his ass in a hot tub in Palm Springs, surrounded by Banger chickies and snufflin' up white lightning. He's one of Indoco's directors, and he's on the board of half a dozen other corporations to boot. Rich and important, but loves India too much to come home."

Copley could have read all that on the front page of Indoco's company newspaper. Lessing snarled, "More!"

Copley ran a thumb along the edge of the green folder. "That's about it. Look, Alan, let me send you on that Ugandan job. Serious-ly."

"Why?"

"Because it's a good deal. Not much danger and lots of perks."

"Crap."

"Okay, then. I like you. I'd rather shanghai you than see you thumbed. Hollister thinks you tried to unzip him, and now him and his buddies are going to do you first."

"I won't turn my back in the shower, all right? Now, one last chorus: who paid for our spesh-op? Who's thumbing my squad?"

Copley twisted uncomfortably, groped for his drink, and turned the glass around and around in freckle-blotched fingers. "That particular job is like an artillery range: big signs all over saying 'Keep Off Or Get Your Head Popped.' No shitty, little emperor or jumped-up military dictator waving his two-inch dink this time."

"If it's big, there are only four choices." He held out his fingers one at a time. "American, Russian, Israeli, or Chinese. Plus friends, relatives, and allies of any of the above."

Copley looked still more unhappy. "Or a faction inside one or more of the same." He waggled both hands, palms down, in front of him. "All done, Alan; 'nough said. I'd only be guessing. Try Da Silva . . . ."

"What for? He'll give me even less." Lessing held up his four fingers. "My four choices. If you know, Terry, for God's sake just say which."

Copley looked down at the backs of his own hands, the color of raw meat. Then he extended the index finger of his left hand. Just one finger.

American, then. Or some group within the United States, possibly government, possibly not. It tied in with what Hoeykens had said, and it looked bad. But it still didn't tell him much: several American agencies and factions had enough men, arms, and money to start their own countries. Why would they need a squad of mostly foreign mercs to pull off Marvelous Gap? Too many internal watchdogs? The press? Political shenanigans? Some crazy Pentagon or CIA plot to take over the government? Copley's answer only led to more questions! It also did not explain what the Israelis wanted with Lessing, nor who had burglarized Indoco.

Lessing got to his feet as nonchalantly as he knew how, said his farewells, and left.

The street smelled of gasoline. Traffic was a tangle at this hour, and the crush of pedestrians was almost claustrophobic. Dust rose from the drills of a pavement repair crew fifty meters away. He took careful note: that would be good cover for stitch-guns, silencers, or even a shotgun blast! He set off in the opposite direction, toward the Boulevard Victor Hugo, to look for a taxi.

He had absolutely no idea what to do next.

Somebody was following him: a motion, a flash of color glimpsed out of the corner of an eye. He entered a tobacconist's shop, bought a pack of cigarettes he would never smoke, and managed a look around.

No one.

He emerged and hailed a cab. It was busy and went on by, two delicate young men smiling out the rear window at him. Nothing to do but walk on.

He sensed pursuit again. It was just a breath upon his spine, but this sixth sense was one he had mastered well. If he hadn't, his bones would have been bleaching among the rocks out in Angola or Syria long ago.

A big, brick archway opened into the blank wall of an older building. He ducked inside and peered back. A girl, a Banger, wobbled along the curbing behind him on heels so high as to be stilts. She looked sixteen; her sharp, wise, little features were caked with make-up; a long, magenta-dyed braid bounced against bony shoulder blades; and her tiny breasts were covered with two squares of sparkle-tape the size of band-aids. Heavy junk jewelry clanked and jingled at her throat, in her hair, and all along her right arm.

She didn't resemble any kikibird he'd ever known.

He looked closer. She carried neither percussion instrument nor pocket radio tuned to the howling rhythms of the Banger stations. Her translucent-silver, plastic miniskirt was visibly dusty, however: she had been standing near Copley's building and the street repair crew for some time. She could have been waiting for Lessing to come out.

He'd give odds that she was the tail.

He moved further into the archway and stopped, loosening his pistol in its shoulder holster. Too bad he didn't have a silencer for it. The girl would have to come to him here, and any friends must enter the passage behind her. He would be in shadow; they would be temporarily blinded and also silhouetted against the light from the street.

The girl pretended to see him for the first time. She wiggled her hips crudely and suggestively, and said something in French. She was obviously a regular hooker, whatever she was involved in now.

Lessing could see no one near enough to rush in or shoot from the street. Behind him the archway opened into an arcade, an enclosed central court several stories high, roofed over with a multi-panelled skylight. A score of boutiques and touristy, little shops beckoned all around the ground floor. They would provide excellent cover and escape routes if necessary.

The Banger girl pointed to the hand he now held near his jacket lapel. She smiled and shook her head so that her braid flew out, jangling with silver chains and charms. Again she spoke in French.

"No French," he said. "English." He recalled Mrs. Delacroix's remark about Americans and their sad lack of foreign languages. No time to regret his education now!

She held her own hands away from her skinny thighs, dangled her bulky purse by its strap, and made an exaggeratedly innocent face. "No French? *Non*? No . . . mugging, monsieur." She pronounced it "moo-geeng." Under other circumstances Lessing would have laughed. "No danger. Fun!" One hand came back to pull her little miniskirt and skimpy panties aside, revealing the dark triangle of pubic hair beneath. "Hundred new francs, monsieur?"

What the hell? He was fairly sure she had more in mind than a quick trick. He watched her warily. "No, thanks. Busy."

She gave him a lopsided gamine grin and sidled forward, one hand caressing the pale skin of her belly. He shook his head strenuously and held his ground. He still saw no one in the street and no one behind himself in the court.

"No French, monsieur? Maybe you speak . . . how? . . . Pah-koff? Pah-couve?"

He had expected it. He retreated easily, on the balls of his feet, ready to fight, dodge, or run. The shops in the arcade were crowded, inviting. "Pacov? What do you know of Pacov?"

"Come. Come wiz' me. I show you. You see a man, speak." She glanced sideways, to her right.

"Then I get killed. Correct?"

Badly plucked brows came down in a frown. "Keeled? I not speak much English. You come. Pacov. No moo-geeng. We go your place afterward." She was a child, an illiterate, hungry child, but he couldn't afford to pity her—not now.

On the western, sunny side of the internal court the tablecloths of a cafe showed checkered red and white amidst signboards and potted shrubs. He pointed and spoke slowly: "Not come. We go there. Restaurant . . . cafe. You telephone man. He come here, speak." He pantomimed the use of a telephone.

"Eh? *Non*. No telephone. No . . . number. I not know."

"We go anyway. We sit, drink. He will watch. He will come to us." Lessing had no idea how much she understood, but she gave him only a single, suspicious, street-smart glance and then walked ahead of him to the cafe.

He should have anticipated the reaction. The maitre d'hotel pursed thin lips, and a few of the more affluent diners murmured in outraged wonderment. Lessing hadn't realized: a tall, hard-faced, thirtyish American male in tandem with a cheap Banger hooker, a child barely into her teens! He had just done more to wreck the American image abroad than a planeload of screeching, spinster school teachers!

The girl gave the maitre d'hotel a saucy wink and sat down, making sure that her bare thigh was visible all the way up to her hipbone.

The waiter arrived, pudgy and pallid-faced. The girl said something in a supercilious tone, and he slammed two menus down and flounced away. She pointed to an entry in the wines and alcoholic beverages section of the menu, but Lessing shook his head. When the waiter returned Lessing ignored his young companion, said "coffee," and held up two fingers. The man departed again.

Two china cups of coffee appeared, muddy and black and full of chicory, much as they served it in India. Lessing paid, and they drank in silence. He turned his chair so he could see both the double door to the kitchen and the crowded shopping court in front of the restaurant. He also fumbled Wrench's spit-shooter out of his jacket pocket, palmed it, and covered his hand with the stiffly embossed, red-plastic menu cover. The wall clock read 4:13. How long would he have to wait?

Soon, he told himself, soon. Be patient. The opfoes would tire of waiting for little Miss Banger-Baby here, and then they would come looking.

The clock said 5:32 when the man entered the court. Lessing picked him out at once: a tall gentleman of fifty or so, greying and stooped, distinguished-looking in a baggy, charcoal-grey suit and one of those painfully conservative British ties that are so dark as to look like ribbons of black crepe. Something about the long, horsey face and aggressive bearing struck Lessing as un-British, however; the man was probably American, Canadian, or even Australian.

The new arrival took his time, wandering from stall to stall, examining boxed candies, cut flowers, toys and souvenirs and sunglasses. He looked at his wristwatch twice before making up his mind. Then he tramped directly across the open court to the cafe, slid into the chair opposite Lessing and the Banger girl, ordered *cafe au lait*, and waited until the waiter had gone.

He began without preamble. "Long time finding you." The accent was harshly nasal, an American Midwestern twang much like Lessing's own original dialect.

"Who's hunting?"

"None of your business." He spoke to the Banger girl in fluent French, then grimaced at Lessing. "Hard to get decent help these days."

"Who are you and what do you want?"

"I can answer some of your questions, Mr. Lessing. And you can answer mine." He pointed at the menu. "If you've got a gun under there, forget it. Do you see those high galleries opposite us? Up above the shopping floors?"

God, what a stupid mistake! With a good rifle and scope, even a passable marksman on one of those balconies could put a bullet up whichever of Lessing's nostrils this kikibird chose! He cursed himself, but it was too late to fix things now.

Lessing said, "Fine. A stalemate, then. Your man pops me, my finger tightens, and my gun goes off. Then you learn whether your ribs'll deflect a 9-mm slug."

The agent spread blue-veined, well-manicured hands. "No harm meant, Mr. Lessing. No violence. We want Pacov, and you know where it is."

"I *don't* know."

"Look, your own employer is out to thumb you. Other people want you brought in and questioned. They'll thumb you, too, when they're done. We can protect you, see that your part in this gets buried in some file or other, put you back in India where you can go on with your life."

Lessing sensed the man was lying, at least so far as his own employer was concerned. If Mulder had wanted him dead, then dead he would be. On the other hand, "employers" also included those who had hired him to get Pacov in the first place. They might well be out to unzip him. He said, carefully, "I can't help you. Not if my life depended on it."

"Oh, it does, Mr. Lessing, it does. Believe me. When I say we want Pacov, I mean that very strongly. We *will* have Pacov. Now who funded your operation? Where *is* Pacov?"

This man knew nothing, then: less than he did himself. He decided that honesty was the best policy—until events indicated a change. "I came to Paris looking for answers. I haven't found any. The man who took Pacov from me is dead: Gomez, out in India."

"Gomez can't help us then, can he, Mr. Lessing? But we don't think you're telling the whole truth. Recently you flew to Guatemala, then to South Africa. We want to know whom you saw in those countries and why. My . . . principals . . . are convinced that on one of those two stops you handed Pacov over to those who hired you to get it, Mr. Lessing. You used Gomez as a ruse. He died for nothing."

"I suppose you . . . your people . . . thumbed him?"

"No, not our doing. Your employers again, those who sent you to Marvelous Gap. They want you thumbed, and everything connected with you gone too . . . vanished, disappeared, never existed."

"The trips were for my Indian employer . . . Indoco. They had nothing to do with Pacov."

"Well, there's something odd about Indoco, too, Mr. Lessing. Odd. But not our business now. Later, perhaps." He straightened up. "Still hesitant, then? Still unwilling to help us? What if I told you that I represented your government, the United States of America? The legal owners of Pacov . . . and the only thing standing between this lovely scene," he waved at the bustling shoppers, "and the murder of much of this planet."

"You'd have to show me proof. You might very well be working for any of a dozen other teams."

"I can do that." The man sounded increasingly nervous, his words curt and hurried. He glanced around, up at the galleries, back at the entrance archway.

"Don't bother. As I told you . . . honestly . . . I don't know who my employer was. I don't have Pacov now, and I don't have a goddamned clue where it is." He permitted himself to bend the truth just a smidgin: his samples were still safely hidden in Indoco's Lucknow factory. He had checked.

The other reached into his jacket pocket. Lessing thought he was about to bring out identification, but instead he flipped a packet of snapshots onto the checkered tablecloth. "Here you are, Mr. Lessing, 'feelthy peectures,' real French postcards."

Lessing looked.

He could not help it.

The top one showed a woman, completely nude, her limbs spreadeagled and bound to a rivet-studded surface. There was a box with a sort of crank in the bottom righthand foreground, and thin wires led from this to her vagina, to her anus, and to sharp-toothed alligator clips biting into the soft flesh of her inner thighs, her breasts, and her belly.

The woman's mouth was open; her eyes bulged; her forehead was beaded with the sweat of unendurable torment.

The face was Jameela's.

Lessing blinked and shuddered, cold fear washing over him like a bucket of ice water. He almost cried out, almost shot the man before him with the spit-shooter hidden beneath the menu. The hell with the rifleman up on the balcony! Then he realized that the photograph had been doctored, the face superimposed. The white streak in the woman's tangled locks was the sweatband Jameela wore when she exercised. The background beneath her head was not the metal torture-table but the hedge beside Indoco's tennis court, airbrushed out but not completely matched. Her expression was not one of agony but of excitement and strenuous exertion.

It was a picture Lessing himself had taken during one of Jameela's morning tennis matches! These bastards must have stolen it when they ransacked Lessing's apartment during that last riot at Indoco!

"You son of a bitch . . . !"

The agent looked apologetic. "It's not real. Not this time. We don't want to make it real, Mr. Lessing. But you must understand that we are in deadly earnest. Look at the other shots. If we can't come to an agreement, we'll let you choose which of our games Miss Husaini gets to play first."

Lessing let the menu cover slide an inch or so along his outstretched arm. He was very tempted, whatever the cost.

The kikibird saw the motion and put three fingers up to his cheek. "I drop my hand and my gunman kills you dead, Mr. Lessing. Why can't you be reasonable?"

Lessing jerked his chin at the pictures. "That's reasonable?"

"She was an agent for others, Mr. Lessing. She knew the risks."

"You're no American. Not using those techniques . . . ."

The man smiled. "Times change, Mr. Lessing. What was unthinkable yesterday becomes quite thinkable today. Well, maybe we are not a regular U.S. agency, but we're friends with some of them, Mr. Lessing: very close friends."

Lessing had seen torture before, out in Angola and in Syria. Every nation used it to some degree. It did not so much horrify him as make him furious. He didn't know whether his anger stemmed from the photographs themselves, from the callous involvement of Jameela, or from the way this urbane kikibird had played on his emotions with the doctored pictures. He said, "Now you get nothing. Nothing at all. No way."

"No dramatics, please. We can turn the photographs into reality. Indeed, we *were* planning a live demonstration for you, starring little Amalie here . . ." he glanced over at the Banger hooker, who was staring in horrified fascination at the photographs ". . . but she didn't bring you to the party." He extracted money from his coat pocket with his free hand and pushed a wad of it at the girl. "Go home. *Allez vous!*"

She didn't touch the bills but scrambled up and fled.

"Now, as to Pacov. Who's got it? We want the whole story."

Lessing felt the same chill calm that he experienced in combat. "You have all you're going to get from me. If you're so merc-smart, you know that's how it works. We go through brokers, do jobs, and go home. No identities, no connections, no politics, no involvements."

"Like our little French whore, huh?"

"That's it: leave the money on the bed."

"You went to see Colonel Copley."

"I'll say it again. I got nothing."

For the first time the agent's face showed anger. "God damn you, Lessing! You didn't just hand Pacov over to some anonymous buyer like a bag of cocaine on a street corner! We can take you in . . . get you out of Paris . . . ."

"For some happy sessions in your basement?"

"You'd sing a lot sweeter with a barbed catheter up your cock and electric needles in your testicles!"

Lessing began to get up, slowly and with care. "It's time for my dinner, and you've already spoiled it."

"Sit the hell down!" The kikibird almost forgot to keep his fingers pressed against his cheek. Lessing tensed to hurl himself aside, but he didn't think that would save him, not if the marksman was any good at all.

He let the menu fall away from his hand and opened his fingers a trifle to let the black plastic tube of Wrench's spit-shooter peep through. He kept his thumb pressed against the open end.

"This," he said conversationally, "is Pacov-2. You asked for it; you got it." The agent probably knew that Pacov-2 came in black plastic tubes. Lessing was gambling that the man hadn't actually seen the stuff: the spit-shooter was only about half the diameter of the Pacov-2 cylinder.

The man goggled at it. "You're lying . . . !"

"No. I saved myself a dose or two for insurance. I'm sure you understand. Last night, as soon as I arrived, I cracked a globe of Pacov-1 down the toilet. Now we see whether there has to be an incubation period between Pacov-1 and Pacov-2. You been posted here in Paris for a long time? Your wife and kiddies with you? Do torturers *have* wives and kiddies?"

For a moment the other sat as though stunned. Then he stood up. "You would do that, Mr. Lessing? Pacov . . . to Paris?"

"Larger scale than the poor girl in your photographs, but essentially the same thing. Yes, killing you might be worth Paris. It sure as hell is worth my life . . . to me, anyway."

"You'll die with the rest!"

"No way. You see, I injected myself with the antidote before I left India." It was a whale-sized red herring; as far as Mulder's people knew, there was no antidote for Pacov.

The agent continued to gape, and his fingers started to come down again. Lessing grated, "Keep them up there. As I said, you can thumb me now, but I'll still have time to crack Pacov-2 all the hell over you. Nothing would give me more pleasure."

"Your own government, Lessing! That's whom you're betraying!"

"Bullshit. If my own government is using *you*, then it's down to the bottom of the barrel, and it deserves what it gets! I don't believe you anyway." He had an idea. "Take your wallet out of your pocket and toss it down on the table."

Grimly, the other complied.

The wallet spilled out French, British, and American money; the pockets held international credit cards and drivers licenses made out in several names, all bland and colorless and false: Mark Leebens, Peter E. Hartmann, Harry Rosch. There were calling cards and business cards, too, all different and quite impersonal; no photographs, no personal notes or addresses.

He sensed a presence beside him and shied away, ready to continue his Pacov bluff or to shoot, whichever was necessary.

It was a man, the young European from Copley's waiting room.

"Let us take care of him for you now, Mr. Lessing." The voice was high and boyish, the accent German. "This person works for a private agency, in close touch with Israeli State Security. We'll deal with him." To the older man he said, "You can take your fingers away from your cheek, *mein Herr*. Your little bird up in the balcony will not sing any more."

"And who the goddamned hell are *you*?" Lessing snarled. Should he feel relieved, or was this just another frying pan? A new and hotter fire?

"The name doesn't matter. You want to see more of Paris, Mr. Lessing, or are you done here? We have a taxi waiting, the red, white, and black sedan outside: Mulder's Taxi Service."

Of course, I remember. Every word, every syllable I heard
that day is seared forever into my soul.
—*Memoirs,* **Anneliese Meisinger**

CHAPTER TEN

Friday, November 28, 2042

The spangled wrapping paper crackled as Jameela's fingers found the little plush-covered box inside. She took out the diamond ring and held it up to the glow from Lessing's Aladdin's lamp on the center table.

"Your birthday, darling," Lessing said.

"Shall I say, 'You shouldn't have?' Or shall I just take it and run?"

"Take it and stay." The stone was small but of good quality; Wrench had gone with Mulder on a business trip to Amsterdam, and he had brought the ring back for Lessing.

Jameela bowed her head, letting her sable tresses coil down to cover her face. All he could see were her chin and her lips; he thought they trembled a little.

She said, "I . . . can't."

"Because of your father?"

"My family. Most of them. They don't want me to marry a foreigner, a non-Muslim . . . even a non-Shi'i Muslim." One corner of her mouth lifted in a smile. "Most especially a non-Shi'i Muslim!"

"Lots of Indians marry foreigners these days," Lessing protested. "Shakeela and George Townsend over in Kanpur, Willa Buller and Muneer Khan . . . that professor from Texas and his Bengali wife . . . ."

"It depends on the family . . . the level in society."

"You're no barefoot village maiden in head-to-foot *pardah*!"

"*Pardah*'s the custom. The head-to-foot tent our conservative women wear is called a *burqa*."

"Some of your people call it a shuttlecock; that's what it looks like! Damn it, you know what I mean. Your family's not the sort that marries its daughter off sight unseen to some distant cousin!" He mimicked a thick Indian accent: "'You should be putting on your best *sari*, my daughter! Today is your vedding day! Surprise!'"

Jameela dissolved into laughter. The lamp light turned the ring into a rainbow of scarlet and orange-gold upon her palm, and he knew that she was close to accepting it. He forced himself to stay silent, cross-legged on the carpet before her, letting her reach her own decision. The lamp spilled a warm, orange glow over her high cheekbones, and he found himself loving her more than he had thought he could love anyone. He was being trite, of course, but he didn't care. If every human being on earth could experience this same exhilaration, this anticipation, then well and good! He, Alan Lessing, was going to savor his share to the utmost!

It was a lovely mood. They were snug and safe here, the room cozy, the electric heater bravely helping the Indoco staff quarters' central heating system stave off the chill of the North Indian November night; it got a lot colder in India in the winter than most foreigners knew. The scene was as old as the Neolithic caves; it was exactly as Lessing had planned—and, he told himself, as Jameela herself wanted it.

"Hi, in there!" Wrench's light, tenor voice pierced through the closed door. "You two decent? Gotta talk to you, Lessing." Only then did he knock.

"Let me think a little more," Jameela whispered to Lessing. She knelt and let her tongue flicker briefly at Lessing's lips, then rose in a rustle of silk and disappeared into the bedroom.

There were times when, all unknowing, Charles Hanson Wren came very close to getting himself unzipped.

"What is it?" Lessing glumly donned his white bathrobe, let himself out, and drew Wrench off down the corridor toward Goddard's flat. The latter was off on a sales trip to Hong Kong or some place.

"Come up to the main house. Mulder wants you."

Lessing almost refused, then thought better of it. The old man had seemed nervous, even anxious, since Lessing's return from Paris, and if he summoned his security beegee at this hour there was a reason. Jameela watched impassively as he changed out of his bathrobe to khaki slacks and bush-shirt. She said nothing, which made him want to stay with her all the more. She was disappointed. The mood was broken, and there could be no mending it tonight. In fact, this might be a good opportunity to let her think.

Damn Wrench—and Mulder—anyway!

Wrench ushered him into Mulder's private study in the upper story at the front of the main house. Its big windows looked out over the lawns and the driveway, and at night the lamp-spangled spires of the Indoco factory rivalled *Divali*, the Hindu Festival of Lights. Like the rest of the mansion, the study was furnished in Indian kitsch, courtesy of Mrs. Fairy Godmother Mulder: heavy, carved, varnished, pseudo-Mughal furniture; bone-inlaid tables; carpets in Persian designs; brass trays and bronze images of the Hindu gods; and tapestries and miniatures painted in gaudy Rajput red-oranges and blues, a style that Jameela privately labelled "Late Tourist."

Mulder waved them both to seats. "Some good news, Alan."

"Sir?"

"You're apparently off the hook. Our people tell me that the Americans have withdrawn their A.D. request. The Israelis have also gone quiet."

Wrench flashed his perfect, toothpaste-ad smile at him. "You're old news, buddy, the paper on the bird cage floor. Be grateful! The only one who fondly remembers you is Hollister. He still thinks you tried to thumb him. But then Hollister thinks that of his own mother, so you're in good company."

"My . . . employer . . . on the Marvelous Gap job?"

Mulder shrugged. "Who knows if you don't? Nobody's heard a thing for a couple of months. We've turned up nothing."

Wrench said, "They must've finally realized you couldn't tell the difference between Pacov and a piss sample. Your Marvelous Gap spesh-op is common knowledge, though. They . . . whoever they are . . . can't keep it secret, so there's no point thumbing you. They've got Pacov, and you've got your pay. You can't finger them, and so they have ceased to care about you. Game, set, and match to them!"

"Things've gone elsewhere." Mulder picked up a sheaf of flimsies from his desk blotter. "We've heard from Joachim Kuhn, the young German we sent to help you in Paris. He says everything there is peaceful, too . . . ."

"Whoa," Lessing interrupted. "What about that kikibird who was on my tail there?"

"Oh, yes. The one with the nasty photographs. He was using the name 'Harry Rosch' in Paris. Actually, he's Mordechai Richmond, an American Jew from Kansas City. Kuhn traded him back to the Vigilantes for Zion in exchange for one of our Austrians and a French Neo-Nazi teenager into the bargain."

Lessing found himself blurting, "You should've thumbed the bastard!" Richmond's offhanded malevolence affected him more than he would have admitted.

"No point!" Wrench said. "Europe's like that. Full of our guys and their guys, double and triple agents, all kinds. We pop one of theirs, they pop one of ours. Better to trade . . . like baseball cards."

"Maybe that's how you play, but I play different!" Lessing looked down and saw that his fists were clenched. "How did Richmond trace me? Nobody knew I was going to Paris except for you two and Goddard. Yet Richmond was right there, Johnny on the spot."

"Have you ever heard of Eighty-Five?" Mulder asked. Lessing's face told him he had not. "That stands for A.I.T.I.-5: Artificial Intelligence Terminal Installation, Model Five. It's a computer, the closest thing to a complete thinking machine ever made, better than a human brain. Besides almost unlimited memory, Eighty-Five's got a personality. It uses deductive and inductive logic, it plans, it remembers, it theorizes . . . it *thinks*, Alan. The only thing it does not do is emote."

"It walks, it talks, it sings, it almost dances!" Wrench piped up with sardonic merriment from the background.

"How does it concern me?"

"One of the American intelligence agencies ran your dossier through Eighty-Five. There are terminals in Washington and in other major defense complexes. Almost everyone who lives in the United States is on file: tax records, voter registrations, driver's licenses, military service, social security, pension plans, insurance applications, civil agencies, charitable institutions . . . a lot more. John Q. Public isn't told, of course, for fear of the 'Big Brother' screams that would go up." He jabbed a finger at Lessing. "Mercenaries are especially interesting to Eighty-Five, as are splinter political parties, religious cults, draft protesters, minority organizations, big crime . . . all the misfits. It keeps tabs on the likes of you . . . and us, Alan."

"This computer . . . this Eighty-Five . . . traced me to Paris?"

"We believe somebody punched you in and asked for logical contacts and activities according to your profile. Eighty-Five compared your data with Copley's, added the rumors about you thumbing people . . . they were common knowledge in Euro-merc circles, you recall . . . and came up with Paris. Richmond's side wants Pacov very badly, but whether to use it or stop it, we do *not* know."

"Richmond said he wasn't working for the Americans."

"He wasn't. Not directly. His Zionists share a lot with President Rubin's administration, though. Some say they're one and the same, puppets of a larger Jewish-Establishment network. Anyway, his people have friends with access to Eighty-Five. So do we. So do your erstwhile employers, and *they* were smarter: Kuhn thinks they were watching while you and Richmond had your tete-a-tete. They hoped he'd thumb you and save them the trouble, but you pulled your phony Pacov stunt first. Then our Herr Kuhn came to your rescue."

"Christ!" Suddenly Lessing needed a drink, a craving he had not felt for months. "Wait a minute . . . if this Eighty-Five could pick up on me, why can't your people use it to pick up on my Marvelous Gap employers?"

"Whoever they are, they're good. They've programmed blind alleys and blocked access paths into Eighty-Five, special codes, alarms that trip if you punch in the wrong password. We know because we lost an operative or two finding out."

The ramifications were unsettling. "If they're so clever, why don't they use it on *you*, on Kuhn . . . on Indoco . . . on your movement?"

Mulder spread his short, spatulate fingers. "Oh, they try. But we've got people with clearances as well. We've programmed Eighty-Five to shunt *our* sensitive data into dead files. It buries what we don't want seen."

"How about standard intelligence methods?" Lessing asked. "Richmond talked about Indoco being 'odd' . . . about looking into your operation later. He knows Kuhn. He knows me. Surely his people can put it together."

"They're on the perimeter," Mulder admitted. "They know a little about us and about some of our front groups. They know a *lot* about the organizations we *want* them to see: Neo-Nazis, Pre-Nazis, Post-Nazis, Paleo-Nazis, Would-Be-Nazis, rightists, racists, survivalists, Born Again fascists, an anthill of fringe groups. But the intelligence agencies . . . and the sects and factions and parties and secret societies . . . are like dancers in a dark room. You bump up against somebody, feel the clothing, smell the cologne, maybe touch a bit of skin. They do the same. None of the dancers ever gets a complete picture of the others. The Zionists, the Americans, various European agencies all know we're here, but they don't know where, who, or how much. As far as our people can tell, the core of our structure is still our secret."

"The Israelis, too, can't be bothered with us now," Wrench added. "They have problems that won't quit: religious and ethnic factionalism, runaway inflation, deficits, international loans they can't repay, depleted resources, too much *yerida* and not enough *aliya*, a huge military establishment to support, no more 'war reparations' from Germany. The Russians have thirty-four divisions on Greater Israel's northeastern borders in Iraq, and if that's not enough . . . ."

"Their worst worry is the hundred million Arabs they can't feed or control," Mulder interposed. "Conquered people, in effect slaves. But slaves who are increasingly vociferous about civil rights and voting privileges."

"The end of the 'Jewish State' right there." Wrench slapped a hand down upon the delicately inlaid table beside his chair. "Like the rabbit said to his girl friend, 'Shall we run, or shall we stay and outnumber 'em?' Israel might've been able to keep up the pretense of being a nice, homey dream once, back in the nineteenth century: 'next year in Jerusalem' and all that. Now the mask is off, and everyone can see that it's simply a military empire with ambitions of world rule: ancient Rome all over again . . . everything but the gladiators and the lions. Hell, they're already eating the Christians, or the Christians' pocketbooks anyhow! Israel's had its day in the sun, and it's starting to slide, just like every imperial state before it."

Lessing could not resist saying, "I think you're dreaming."

"Maybe so," Mulder conceded. "In any case Israel is stewing in its own kosher juices right now and can't attend to us."

"To them we're nothing but a bunch of loonies who are still pumping a cause that died in Berlin a century ago: nasty, little fanatics in leather overcoats." Wrench snapped his fingers in disdain. "We want them to go on believing that, too, right up until our last, big corporate takeovers occur and our movement is ready to go public."

Mulder frowned across at Wrench. "The Vizzies *are* getting close to some of our doings in the United States. We must talk about that, Charles, when Goddard gets back."

"Which reminds me," Lessing said. "Assume that my former 'employers' . . . plus the Americans, the Israelis, and everybody else on earth . . . have all forgotten about *me*. Who were those two burglars? The safecrackers who broke into this house? How did they know about your diaries, and what did they want with them?"

Mulder pursed his lips. "To be honest, we haven't a clue. Our people are still looking into it. As soon as we have a chance we'll get Eighty-Five onto it too. There is definitely a leak." He raised his bulk a trifle so that he could look Lessing directly in the eyes. "Why not join us, Alan? *Really* join us? We can use you."

"I told you. I'm just a merc, Mr. Mulder. I'll run your security, I'll step and fetch for you, and I'll protect you to the best of my ability. But I'm not interested in movements."

"Except bowel movements," Wrench cackled. "You should hear him in the morning. The walls are paper-thin . . . ."

"Charles, please! Be serious!" Mulder dug into the papers on his desk. "I have a cable here from your friend, Felix Bauer. He likes the job we gave him as security chief at Club Lingahnie. The South Pacific suits him nicely. You recall that I offered you a job out there too, Alan."

"I was . . . I *am* grateful. I was close to accepting." He had talked it over with Jameela, and she, too, had almost agreed. It was one way of getting her out of India and away from her family and Indian society. Ponape also made a fine refuge for someone running from a foe with a very long reach.

"Would you still like to go? We need military expertise."

"Military . . . ? On Ponape? The local government . . . ?"

"Oh, no! Not what you think. Ponape is part of the United Republics of the South Pacific, a loose federation. Its president is a friend of ours. No, we want you for something different. We've been sending youth cadres out to Club Lingahnie on vacations, seminars, and study trips, all funded by respectable foundations in America and Europe. These young people come from our private schools, university fellowships, summer camps, labor organizations favorable to us . . . a great many sources."

"I don't understand. How do I fit in?"

"Not for indoctrination, certainly!" Mulder smiled ruefully. "Others are taking care of that: discussion groups in world history, economics, anthropology, sociology, and other subjects. There isn't a word about our . . . ah . . . origins. What we promote is the Party of Humankind."

"Yes, but . . . ."

"Patience. Some of our students require military training, weapons discipline, field tactics: things in which you have experience and excel. This won't be for every student, of course . . . just for those who are training for . . . ah . . . a more active role in the movement. We've taught these skills for years in the United States, but surveillance and restrictions keep making it harder there." Mulder noted Lessing's reluctance and added, "There'll be only about four or five hundred trainees a year. You won't be working alone, naturally, but supervising teams of instructors. In addition, we'd like you to take on the job of manager at Club Lingahnie . . . Bauer's boss. You'll have a staff, facilities . . . ."

"Wait a minute. You want me as a sort of glorified drill sergeant? A gym teacher? A scoutmaster? And a hotel manager to boot?"

Mulder looked pained. "You *do* put the worst possible light on things, Alan. The job I'm offering you is a big step up from beegeeing an old codger like myself out here in India. It pays well, too: eighty thousand U.S. dollars a year. Even with inflation, that's not poverty level. And your living costs will be covered . . . ."

"Heat, light, a furnished, thatched hut," Wrench chimed in, "with hot and cold running dancing girls . . . ."

"And a post for Miss Husaini," Mulder finished with the air of a man who lays four aces down on top of an opponent's four kings, "if she wants to go along."

The offer was indeed tempting. Working with Bauer would be difficult but not impossible, and the remoteness of the Caroline Islands gave it all a romantic, tropical aura, like a setting from some old movie.

"Oh, and . . . uh . . . ." Mulder tapped the desk blotter to regain his attention. "One last piece of pleasant news. Mrs. Delacroix, the lady you escorted to South Africa . . . you remember her?"

"Of course."

"She's arriving in Lucknow tomorrow to settle some business. She'll have a couple of her people with her, and I'd like you and Wrench to show them around, please."

With a sinking feeling Lessing realized who one of those people was sure to be. Anneliese Meisinger was one person he did *not* want to see, not now, when he and Jameela were so close to putting their lives together!

He would have made some excuse, but Mulder had already lumbered up to his feet. "Think over our offer, Alan. Club Lingahnie. Ponape."

The next morning dawned crisp and cool. India's brilliant hues were as sharp as a Mughal painting, and the metalled, two-lane road up from Kanpur to Lucknow was not crowded. Wrench drove Mulder's big limousine, a Japanese Tora Ultra that had cost a fortune in bribes to get into the country. He appeared to enjoy dodging bullocks, water buffalo, great, creaking carts full of who knew what, automobiles and trucks, villagers in dhotis, and innumerable serious-looking men on bicycles and motorbikes. The drive to Lucknow's airport was uneventful. Wrench remained outside with the car to fight off the hotel-touts, guides, souvenir-sellers, taxi-walas, and seekers of "personalized foreign aid," while Lessing struggled into the breathlessly hot airport building and out onto the tarmac to seek his charges.

He saw Mrs. Delacroix's silvery coiffure disembarking first, then the bright gold of Liese's long, loose hair. She seemed to float down the aircraft landing stairway, a very private person, aloof and self-contained. She would always look this way, whether she were hosting a society ball in New York or standing naked and shamed in a Cairo brothel. Liese had class—in the truest sense.

Half an hour went by before the passengers were able to reclaim their baggage and the Tourist Registration Officer had peered at passports and documents. This was a new wrinkle in a land where bureaucracy was a six-thousand-year-old art form. Prime Minister Ramanujan's ultra-conservative Hindu government yearned to rid India of every non-Hindu, and Muslims, Christians, Parsis, Sikhs, Jains, and even the tiny Buddhist minority were all *non gratae.* Creating minor problems for foreign residents and tourists was part of the program.

Suddenly Liese was there, twenty feet in front of him, one hand frantically waving, the other full of luggage. Mrs. Delacroix and two other European faces were visible behind her. An Indian airport can be a daunting experience, and Lessing pushed in to the rescue, two porters trailing in his wake. After some further genial struggle, Liese was beside him, clutching his arm, neither sure how to greet the other.

"Alan!" Mrs. Delacroix cried. "Alan Lessing! Good . . . ."

". . . To see you," he completed. They both laughed.

"La! Such a *foule*!" She looked around. "Meet two friends: Jennifer Caw and Hans Borchardt."

Lessing recalled the woman at once. Jennifer Sims Caw was the American with the loud, bullying voice at the conference in Guatemala City. Up close, she possessed a certain overdone beauty: in her mid thirties, big-boned, with large breasts, good legs, dark-auburn hair, and a vivid, reddish complexion. He didn't know her companion: a pale, very blonde, sensitive-looking, late-thirtyish man, whose old-fashioned, hornrimmed glasses gave him a bookish look. Lessing would bet that Mr. Borchardt had a copy of the tourist guide to Lucknow in his bulging jacket pocket.

Lessing wanted to get Liese alone and prime her for the inevitable meeting with Jameela, but Mrs. Delacroix showed no signs of fatigue. She still wanted to see Lucknow, even after "doing" Delhi the previous day. As Mulder had warned, she was retired but still active, a key figure in a dozen Euro-African corporations and causes. She must have been a holy terror in her youth!

Wrench donned a gentle half-smile of martyrdom and started Mulder's fancy car.

"What would you like?" Lessing inquired. "The markets in Ameenabad? The jewellers, perfumers, and *sari* shops in the *chauk*? The palaces and mosques of the *nawabs* of Awadh? The Residency, where the British held out during the Mutiny of 1857?"

Borchardt glanced over at Liese, beside him in the back seat. "The monuments, please. Isn't there a handsome mosque built in the late eighteenth century by Nawab Asafu-d-daulah?" Lessing's assessment of Borchardt as a pedant was confirmed. The man sounded British but with a hint of central Europe. Knowing Mulder's friends, he was probably a German or an Afrikaner.

Two could play at scholarship. Lessing said, "Yes, and beside it is the Bara Imambara, where the Shi'a hold their *majalis*, huge meetings commemorating the death of Imam Husain, the grandson of the Prophet Muhammad. In the upper stories of the Imambara there's a labyrinth, the Bhul-bhuliyan. It's a maze of tunnels, balconies, stairways, and passages. Some'll tell you the old *nawab* used to play hide-and-seek with his harem girls up there, but others say that honeycombing the top stories takes the weight off the supporting arches of the lower floor. The guides'll bet you money you can't find your way out by yourself."

"You seem to know a bit about it," Borchardt admitted grudgingly. Let him think Lessing was a scholar, too; actually, Jameela had told him all the tourist tales during their Sunday outings together.

"There's also supposed to be an identical maze *underneath* the Bhul-bhuliyan, but it's bricked up." Lessing was beginning to enjoy playing the local dragoman. "The story is that a company of British soldiers chased some of the mutineers down into it, and none of 'em ever came out."

Borchardt cocked his head suspiciously, and Wrench grinned with beatific innocence.

Lessing said, "Nearby is the Baoli Well. The last *nawab* threw his gems and treasures into it and then lowered a big iron plate down on top to keep the English from getting them. Lucknow's a fascinating place. During *Muharram* the Shi'i faithful walk on beds of hot coals in the courtyard of the Bara Imambara."

"A true test of faith!" Wrench said, joining in the spirit of the thing. "You should see the Shi'i *Tazia* processions then, too; some of the men flog themselves with whips and chains until they lose consciousness!"

"Ugh! Why?" Jennifer Caw questioned abruptly from the rear jump-seat. "What's *Muharram*?"

"*Muharram*'s the first month of the Islamic lunar year," Lessing answered. Jameela had once spent a long, lazy evening explaining her people's religion. "It was during this month that Husain, the younger of the Prophet Muhammad's two grandsons, and his family were massacred at a place called Karbala in Iraq. After the Prophet's death there was a power struggle in the new Islamic state. His son-in-law, Ali, founded a party, the *Shi'a*, which believed in a divinely inspired, hereditary caliphate . . . with Ali or some other blood-relative of the Prophet as *imam*, or leader. The rest of the community, the Sunnis, claimed that the Prophet had said that his successor ought to be elected. Both groups thought God was on their side. They fought, and Imam Husain was slain."

"They've been at it ever since," Wrench flung in. "Every year there are Sunni-Shi'a riots . . . shops and houses burned, sometimes people hurt. Not as bad as Protestants and Catholics in Europe, but still pretty rough."

"Martyrdom and mourning," Borchardt announced portentously, "the two most salient features of Shi'i Islam."

"Not exactly," Lessing contradicted. "It's complicated. But the Sunni-Shi'a controversy did help keep Islam from overrunning Europe during the Middle Ages." He chuckled. "Otherwise you and I would be wearing turbans, Mr. Borchardt."

"The Muslims would have had to face the Germanic peoples," the other shot back.

"The Arabs beat the pants off the Germanic Visigoths in Spain . . . *and* the Byzantines and their Germanic Vandal subjects in North Africa," Wrench pointed out. He winked at Lessing in the front seat beside him and hissed, "Classic Comics World History Issue Number Seven!"

Borchardt retired into miffed silence in the back seat. Jennifer Caw, too, sat quietly, a glassy expression on her face; India sometimes did that to first-timers. Liese and Mrs. Delacroix seemed to enjoy themselves; they chatted, ate the luncheon Mulder had sent along, and drank copiously of the thermos jug of ice water. Lessing himself had seen to its boiling that morning, as well as the water for the ice. He had endured too many go-rounds with the diarrhea foreigners called "Delhi Belly," "the Rajah's Revenge," or "the Lucknow Two-Step" to take chances with important guests!

The Bhul-bhuliyan was entertaining; the great mosque graceful and mysterious, something out of the Thousand and One Nights; the Residency wistful and solitary under its veils of greenery. There were still other sights, but Lessing insisted on calling a halt. The November sun had been merciful, but it was deceptive, and Mrs. Delacroix was fragile.

"We'll go back through Ameenabad . . . the middle-class bazaar . . . to Hazrat Ganj, where the nicer shops are. If you can stand the crowds and the sights and smells of the bazaar, you get your Good Tourist Medal."

Wrench jockeyed the big limousine through narrow streets into the chaotic traffic of the central section of the city. "I hate driving through the bazaar," he grumbled. "You owe me one, baby!"

"Collect from Mulder." Lessing straightened up. "What's this?"

Ameenabad Park was a dusty, grassless, open square surrounded by the shops and tenements of Lucknow's middle-class districts. Today it was awash from one side to the other with a sea of saffron. People in garments dyed an orangy yellow swarmed in front of the car, Hindi banners and signs tossing above their heads. From the opposite end of the square they heard the echoing bellow of a loudspeaker turned up to near-incomprehensibility.

"A goddamned parade . . . a political meeting!" Wrench swore. "Looks like the B.S.S.!" He slammed the car into reverse.

"What? Who are they?" Borchardt asked.

"I don't know what the initials stand for. But they're Hindu rightists," Lessing told him. "*Far* right, the ones who want all foreigners out of India. Bharat . . . that's India . . . for the Bharatis. We're unbelievers to them. They call us unclean, cow-eaters, outcasts."

"Hey, Lessing!" Wrench snapped. "See if you can persuade the nice folks behind us to let me back the hell up."

Lessing poked his head out and used his best Hindi: "*Rasta dijiye, Janab! Mehrbani kar-ke, hat jaiye!*"

A youth who looked seventeen came up to peer into the car. His yellow *dhoti* was clean, and his wire-rimmed glasses offered hope of an educated person, one who could be reasoned with. Then

Lessing saw the three whitish, horizontal stripes daubed across his forehead, the mark of a devotee of Lord Siva. His head was shaved except for a little pigtail left at the back. Here was a zealot.

"From where are you coming?" the young man demanded.

"We're tourists," Lessing said, not untruthfully. "This lady is French. The dust is too much for her. Could you help us get out of your way, please?"

Others came up to stare and confer, and more arrived by the moment as the street behind the limousine filled up. It would take a major miracle to back the car out now. In India a foreigner could sneeze and look around to find a mob gathered to watch him wipe his nose. Wrench muttered between his teeth: "Curiosity, thy name is unemployed Indian!"

"You do not belong here!" the bespectacled youth accused. "You go to your own country, away from India! This is not your place!"

"Yes, yes," Lessing agreed. He smiled as winningly as he knew how. He had to keep things friendly. "We are visitors. We want to get out of your way. Please help us."

The boy scratched at his stubbled skull. Then he made motions to clear the street.

"God damn," Wrench whispered admiringly. "You got natural charm, guy!"

He spoke too soon. One of the other youths dashed around from the rear of the limousine shouting. Lessing guessed at once what was wrong: this was an Indoco company car, and government regulations required foreign-owned business vehicles to letter their firm's name on the license plate above the numerals. American companies—American anything—were anathema to the Hindu far right at present, just as they were to the far left. Moreover, Indoco made fertilizers and pesticides: wicked poisons to corrupt the soil of sacred Bharat!

The second youth began a harangue; the Siva-worshipper replied, and others joined in. Some raised sticks and *lathis*: heavy, metal-tipped staves. A stone spanged off the limousine's roof. There went Mulder's paint job.

Lessing turned to Wrench. "Get ready to run for it!" He pointed. "Move forward, get momentum, and ignore anything but a solid wall. Blow your horn like crazy!" To the rest he said, "Lock your doors and windows. This car is bulletproof, and it's heavy. It'll be hard for them to break in or roll us over. If worse comes to worst, there's a compartment right behind you, Miss Caw; in it you'll find a Riga-71 automatic rifle, a stitch gun, tear-gas grenades, and a couple of pistols."

"We know how to use weapons," Borchardt stated grimly. "We have similar problems in South Africa."

Lessing heard the snick of the weapons compartment opening. He thought: God, don't let Borchardt be a trigger-happy hothead!

He should have worried more about Jennifer Caw.

"Keep the guns out of sight!" he commanded. "What we *don't* want is a bloodbath! If we hurt somebody, either these people will massacre us or we'll face charges in an Indian court! Either way we lose!"

Distorted faces pressed against the windows. A club smashed at the windshield; they saw the wielder's surprise as his weapon bounced harmlessly away. Fists pounded on the roof, paving stones battered the glass, and *lathis* jabbed at the headlights, the hood, and the door panels. Wrench got the vehicle in gear and began to creep forward. The front bumper pushed into yielding, writhing human flesh. One man started to slip down under the wheels. He disappeared. All Wrench could do was brake helplessly. Another marcher saved himself by clambering up onto the hood.

The car lurched violently. Lessing called, "Liese, hold on to Mrs. Delacroix! They're trying to tip us over!"

The tide of saffron robes against the windows turned the interior into a gloomy, airless oven. The vehicle tilted in the opposite direction, then bumped down again. As soon as their assailants got coordinated, they would go over.

"*Pardesi*! *Pardesi*!" the mob chanted: "Foreigner! Foreigner!"

The chorus swelled to a deep-throated roar and became a rhythmic, bestial grunting. There were hundreds of people outside. One face squeezed against the glass nearest Lessing was bleeding from the nose, the eyes open but rolled up so that only the whites showed. The man was probably dead or dying, suffocated in the crush. Somebody passed the youth on the hood a mattock, and he swung this against the front windshield. Even bulletproof glass would eventually give way. The din was unbearable, the yelling and pounding and banging a single, sustained, howling clamor. The car stank of dust, sweat, blood, and perfumed hair-oil.

"We're dead in here!" Jennifer Caw shrieked. Lessing yelled and ducked as she poked the muzzle of the Riga-71 past his ear. The limousine was rocking violently now; in seconds it would go over. He couldn't catch all she said: "One burst . . . open window . . . scare them off . . . ." He did understand her last word clearly: "*Gasoline*!"

She was right. A sea of waving hands arose to pass five gallon tins of gasoline over the crowd to those closest to the car. Fire was a good way to deal with a bulletproof vehicle. Puncture the fuel tank or bring up your own inflammables; wait for the flaming, screaming occupants to crawl out; then massacre them at your leisure. Lessing had a sudden vision of Syria again: dry, yellow grass, a litter of dust-grimed barrels and ammunition boxes, concrete blocks, rocky

soil, all blossoming yellow and orange and black as the Israelis used
a flamethrower to pour death into an Arab house. The fate of those
inside did not bear remembering.

Jennifer Caw had the rear window down an inch or two. Liese
screamed a last protest. Then the chatter of the automatic rifle
drowned out all else. The universe became chaos and the reek of
gunpowder. Spent shell casings rattled against the roof above
Lessing's head, and he threw up his arms to protect himself.

The car jounced down again onto all four wheels. The chanting
mingled with screams, then faltered to a stop. Some of the attackers
hurled themselves away in terror, a jumble of brown, sweat-shining
limbs and faces, clawed fingers, staring eyes, open mouths, and
orange-and-yellow garments. Some went down, others clutched and
scrambled to stay on top of them. The man on the hood threw away
his mattock and leaped off onto the backs of those below. He
hopped, fell, got up, balanced like an acrobat, and staggered until
he, too, slipped down and vanished under the millipede feet of the
mob.

"You hit anybody?" Wrench called out.

"I don't see how," Jennifer Caw yelled back. "Some bastard got
hold of the barrel and pushed it straight up in the air!" Lessing had
a glimpse of her in the rear-view mirror. She was a valkyrie: wild,
reddish hair, high spots of color in her cheeks, eyes glittering with
battle-lust. Combat did that to some people, both men and women.
He recalled many who had died of it.

"*Now*, God damn it!" he snarled at Wrench. The little man did
not need urging; he already had the big Tora Ultra moving. The press
and the dust kept them from seeing much, and the car bumped
horribly over unseen objects in the street. The relentless hammering
of stones and *lathis* on the roof kept pace with them as they inched
toward the end of the square. The broad avenue there led to Hazrat
Ganj and the comparative safety of the upper-class districts.

Borchardt shook Lessing's shoulder and shouted in his ear.
"They're thinning out ... giving up ... going." He repeated himself
in Afrikaans—it might have been German—for Mrs. Delacroix's
benefit. The old lady had survived intact, disheveled but calm, a
.38-caliber pistol on her lap. Not exactly Whistler's mother, but then
Lessing had come to expect no less from Emma Delacroix.

Borchardt spoke the truth. Their attackers were dropping back.
Many seemed to be heading for the open-fronted shops that lined
the square. Only a few good Samaritans knelt by the half dozen
bodies sprawled where their vehicle had been attacked. Lessing
looked over the heads of the mob, thinking to see an advancing wall
of Indian policemen, or perhaps a phalanx of the B.S.S.'s

paramilitary troops, wearing saffron armbands and cast-off army uniforms. He saw neither.

"What the hell?" Wrench put Lessing's puzzlement into words. "Just a few loose cops over there by the speakers' stand. And they're headed out, too. All going away . . . or into the goddamned shops."

"Or standing around in little groups . . . ," Liese added from the back seat.

The rally had indeed broken up, apparently for reasons other than the near-mayhem that had just occurred. The loudspeakers still blared, and Lessing could see men standing and gesticulating on the podium, but nobody was paying attention. The crowd was dispersing.

Lessing took a chance and rolled the window down. "Hey!" he called to an older man, one who looked more prosperous than the rest. "*Janab-i-ali! Kya hai? Kya ho raha hai?*"

The man turned, pointed, and shouted indistinct words back.

"Something about a radio," Lessing told the others. "Stop the car. There, in front of that electrical goods store."

"You're crazy! They'll kill us!" cried Jennifer Caw, and Borchardt echoed her.

Lessing put a hand on the wheel. "Not likely, now that the fun's over."

"Please, Alan . . . !" That was Liese.

He had the door open. "Just a moment. Most of the people in this shop are Muslims. I can tell by their clothes and other things. The B.S.S. has no more use for them than it does for us!"

The shop sold electric heaters, refrigerators, stoves, and small appliances. Perhaps fifty people, young and old, from various faiths and classes, clustered about a pyramidal display of glittering transistor radios. Most of these were turned on, tuned to the same station, the Urdu Broadcast Service of the government of India.

Lessing knew the shopkeeper slightly. He and Jameela had bought a toaster here three weeks ago. He struggled with his Urdu, gave up, and asked in English, "What's happening? What's on the radio?"

The merchant gazed at him from huge, gentle, slightly crossed eyes and shifted his cud of betel nut from one side of his jaw to the other. He made no reply but jerked his head toward the radios. The crowd watched.

Lessing felt a presence beside him. It was Liese. "Get back," he insisted. "Get back in the car!"

She shook her head. Some of the onlookers murmured.

"*Sahib*, you take this!" An elderly, dignified-looking Muslim gentleman picked one of the transistor sets off the display, twisted the dial, and thrust it at Lessing. "English, *sahib*, English!"

The radio sputtered. Lessing adjusted it, and they heard an announcer's voice speaking that elegant British English only educated Indians seem able to achieve:

" . . . Communications from some areas are disrupted, and only shortwave emergency bands are operating from cities in the interior. The Soviet Union has mobilized its military forces, its police forces, and all available medical services to combat the epidemic. Neighboring countries, particularly Poland and Czechoslovakia, are affected to a lesser degree. The Austrians, Germans, and Chinese have closed their borders. The United States, the United Kingdom, and others have promised epidemiologists and other needed aid as soon as the situation clears."

There was a pause followed by static; then: "American eye-in-the-sky satellites report seeing bodies . . . lifeless bodies . . . lying all over, in the streets . . . columns of medical lorries and ambulances . . . earth-moving machines digging mass graves outside Leningrad . . . ." The announcer began to stammer; there could be no script for this. "Dead, dying . . . a tragedy of unknown proportions . . . no one can tell who or how many. No . . . no warning." The voice stuttered to a halt.

The radio hissed in empty, eery silence. Someone had deemed it politic to take the station off the air. From the other sets in the background they heard the Urdu announcer still speaking excitedly. Then he, too, broke off. The first strains of the Indian national anthem came on.

"What is it, *sahib*?" the shopkeeper touched Lessing's sleeve. "What happens?"

Pacov.

Only Pacov could do this.

He, Alan Lessing, had handed Death the scythe with which to harvest the human race.

"Home," he choked. "We've got to get home. Oh, God in Heaven!" At that moment he wished, devoutly and sincerely, that he believed in God . . . and God in him.

Pacifism will remain an ideal, war a fact, and if the White race decides to wage it no longer, the dark ones will, and will become the masters of the world.
  —**Oswald Spengler**

CHAPTER ELEVEN

Sunday, November 30, 2042

It was a night of shadows, of women weeping, of whispers, of voices, of lips that mouthed meaningless words. Later Lessing remembered lamp light, automobile headlights, the bare, hissing, blue-white bulbs of the factory, Jameela's worried questions, Wrench and the others arguing on and on, and Mrs. Mulder's brittle, near-hysterical giggle. Later he recalled dark-skinned men in loose, flapping, bone-hued clothing hastening to and fro on what errands no one could say. It was indeed a night of shadows—and of fear.

Later he remembered mostly the fear.

Sunday dawned like any other day, cool and bright and smoke-fragrant, as was expected in India at this time of year. Indoco's American and European staff teetered uneasily on Mrs. Mulder's spindly-legged dining-room chairs on the mansion's spacious, screened verandah. Before them Inspector G. N. Subramaniam of the Indian C.I.D. paraded back and forth with the air of a man who has just seen an adversary fall flat on his face, but who doesn't dare laugh. Not yet. Outside, squatting on the steps in the wintry sun-shine, two squads of Indian army *sipahis* awaited the command to take possession of the foreigners' property.

"Still we have no firm reports," Subramaniam was replying to Mrs. Satherly, the plump lady who ran Indoco's accounts payable department. He spoke English with only a trace of the retroflexed consonants of his native Tamil, as different from the Hindi-Urdu of northern India as Zulu is from Hungarian. The inspector was small, dapper, and very dark, like most South Indians. He said, "Everything is a shambles. We hear that much of Russia is devastated by this plague. Then a Soviet Politburo member came on the air from their defense headquarters in the Urals and accused you Americans of a sneak attack. Your people denied it, of course. Last night some Russian madman fired seven missiles down from their satellites. They were promptly annihilated by particle beams from your A.S.A.T. space platforms. Preparations for war are in progress along the East-West frontiers in Europe. Today we have a news blackout! Chaos, madam, chaos!"

"War in Europe? My God!" Poor Mrs. Satherly mumbled dazed-ly. "What about the United States?"

"It is still all right. No attack upon your country yet, so far as New Delhi has deigned to inform us. But the world is stunned, paralyzed. Russians, Poles, Czechs . . . most of the people of the Eastern Bloc . . . are abandoning their homes and fleeing west, away from the plague. The situation is confused. Who can say what is happening?" Subramaniam took another turn around the polished concrete-chip floor. Mrs. Mulder fluttered in the doorway to the drawing room; behind her Lessing glimpsed Jameela's turquoise *qameez*. The C.I.D. officer noticed her too and raked her up and down with a single, dark glance. He returned to stand in front of Herman Mulder.

"Which brings me to you people," he said. "Our government has imposed an emergency powers act as of 0600 hours this morning. In order not to become involved with what we perceive as a Great Powers confrontation . . . and for humanitarian reasons . . . we are repatriating all foreign nationals. This is for your own safety. You will be flown to Delhi and thence to whatever destination your embassies deem appropriate. There is a forty-eight hour deadline." He sounded as though he were reciting a catechism by rote.

"The Russians in India?" Wrench inquired sweetly. "You gonna just drop 'em off at Moscow Airport?"

Subramaniam bristled. "Nationals of other countries are not your affair! Your evacuation is an act of mercy; we are helping you rejoin your families and countrymen at this difficult time. The government of India is providing the aircraft and dispensing with such formalities as exit permits and income-tax clearances!"

"And handing out tea and stale cookies in the Delhi airport departure lounge!" Wrench grumbled.

If the inspector heard he ignored him. He faced Mulder. "Arrangements have been made for the custody of foreign property." He indicated the waiting soldiers outside. "Indoco will remain in good hands until matters become clear."

Which, Lessing suspected, probably meant never. This was Prime Minister Ramanujan's chance to rid India of alien corruption—and acquire heaps of foreign loot, cancel repayments of foreign loans, and do away with unwelcome foreign trade treaties, all for very understandable reasons. Let the *pardesis* argue and complain and file claims and hold hearings and whine to the United Nations or the World Court, if those august bodies still existed! The lacily intricate convolutions of Indian bureaucracy would keep things tied up for years, and even then foreign investors would likely receive only partial compensation. The grandchildren of the people in this room might not live to see Indoco returned to its original owners. So much for Mulder's belief that Third World countries were safer for his SS corporations than the West.

"What of us?" Mrs. Delacroix asked from the far end of the verandah. "Two of my companions and I hold South African passports."

Subramaniam shrugged. "India has no relations with South Africa. You will have to return on a commercial aircraft—when and if available."

"Our own plane and pilot are waiting for us in Delhi."

"Then we shall fly you there. After that it is the government's decision." The inspector gestured to show that the assembly was dismissed.

"He ought to wear jodhpurs and carry a riding crop," Wrench whispered to Lessing. "Bureaucrats: the true enemies of the human race!"

Chairs squealed on the cement floor. People collided, jabbered, and rushed off to pack. Mulder plodded grimly into the house, Mrs. Mulder flittering behind, trilling at him about her precious furniture and knickknacks. The Fairy Godmother had long since discovered that chinaware and brass statues made acceptable substitutes for non-existent children.

Lessing had little worth taking: a single valise and his gun-case. The one other thing he dared not leave behind was hidden in the factory: his cache of Pacov. But how could he reach it with Subramaniam's officious doggies guarding the gates? He couldn't just abandon the stuff. Some blundering maintenance man would find it, and then there would be deaths indeed: deaths like those in Russia, deaths that put earthquakes and volcanos and the Black Plague and even Hiroshima to shame! He had to assume that it *was* Pacov that now stalked the world. And he himself had helped to raise it from its tomb and give it life!

Alan Lessing: Doctor Frankenstein!

No, damn it! He refused to accept the guilt! Why should he? He was *not* responsible! It was not Alan Lessing who had ordered those canisters scattered across Russia; he had not released invisible murder upon the world! He was only the delivery boy, just weapons-transport, like the crew of the *Enola Gay*, the plane that dropped the first atomic bomb. Hell, he was less than that! He was the postman who unknowingly delivers a parcel with a bomb inside. So he told himself.

Wait a minute: just what did he think he was doing at Marvelous Gap in the first place? His employers hadn't sent his team there to steal a new technological gewgaw or some piddling trade secret! A spesh-op like Marvelous Gap wasn't mounted for peanuts! He should have guessed, of course, but he hadn't let himself think about it. The comparison with the *Enola Gay* was accurate, therefore, but the "innocent postman" excuse clunked like a lead five-dollar piece.

But *was* he responsible? He had no idea his objective was so monstrously lethal—and he would never have believed anybody would be insane enough to use it!

As Wrench said, they hadn't bought that one at Nuremberg either.

There had not been time to assimilate the enormity of what had happened; now it was beginning to hit home. He felt shaken, sick, empty in the pit of his stomach, like a kid who sets a school wastebasket on fire for a joke and then watches the building burn to the ground with his friends inside.

Whoever had unleashed Pacov, the world was now altered forever. Nothing would ever be the same again.

The flat was empty when he entered, as impersonal as a hotel room between guests. A few hours ago it had been a home of sorts; now it was a stop-over, a bus station lobby. He would have sworn that the place even smelled different. He collected his kit from the white-tiled bathroom, then emerged to stand aimlessly in the middle of the sitting room. The fireplace was dank and charred; it reminded him of Syria, of a house shattered by artillery fire, of a broken doll and a smashed chair. For want of anything else to do, he picked up his Aladdin's lamp. There was room in the suitcase, and he stuffed it inside.

Jameela's clothes were gone, her closet door ajar. Desolation washed over him: it would be like her to vanish quietly, without a scene, without a long good-bye.

He fingered the nubbly tan fabric of the sofa. Just last night . . . .

She was there. He knew it even before her jasmine scent reached his nostrils. He turned to find her in the doorway.

"So?" She had a knack of summing up a whole lifetime in a single word.

"So I go." He sucked in the empty-house smell. "You coming?"

"How can I? The Americans won't take me."

"They would if you were my wife. We could say you were . . . that we didn't have time to collect our documents. Mulder and Wrench will back us up."

She was silent. Then she said, "No. I can't leave my family."

"Damn your family!" he exploded. "Talk about *us*!"

She hesitated again. "No, Alan. You don't understand. We are not so . . . so individual as you. To us a marriage is more than a bride and groom, a husband and a wife. The families must be involved, social obligations met, people satisfied."

He snarled an obscenity.

"Please. Try to see." She put her fingers to his cheek. "Maybe later, when things are calm again."

His fists were clenched so tightly they hurt. "Don't *you* see? Things *never* will be calm again! After I leave we may never even *meet* again! Mulder's talking about going back to South Africa with Mrs. Delacroix and Liese . . . ."

"Yes, Liese. The American woman with the South African passport."

This was no time for jealousy. "Yes, her. Back to South Africa, or maybe to that resort . . . what's its name? . . . on Ponape in the South Pacific."

"Not to the United States?"

"No. Mulder says that would be pointless. He has nothing in the States. He says we can't do any good there, not now, not under the . . . the circumstances. He still wants me as his bodyguard."

"Most of Indoco's cartel is out here, in what you call the Third World. My father says that Herman Mulder is a powerful man in many countries."

"Your father is right." This was the first time she had mentioned her father in this context. "What's Mulder got to do with *us*?"

"He is your boss." Jameela stood nose to nose with him, her long-lashed eyes watching him levelly. "He is the owner of the SS diaries, is he not?"

"You know about *that*?"

"*We* know." She stressed the pronoun slightly. "My father knows. A few others high up in our C.I.D. Not Subramaniam. He's a small fish."

The diaries again! It was too late to worry about such irrelevant things now. The whole world was upside down, and Mulder's secrets were less important than tomorrow's breakfast, than gasoline for Mrs. Delacroix' airplane—than the guns Lessing had just packed away.

He couldn't resist a question. "The two men who broke into Mulder's safe?"

"Ours. Arabs, I think. Not very good thieves. They weren't supposed to hurt anyone. And you weren't supposed to hurt them. They were ordered to bring the diaries out to be photographed, to give the government of India leverage against Indoco. Then they were to put them back. That business with your friend . . . Mauer? Bauer? . . . put you too much on the alert."

"Your people knifed him?"

"No. We still don't know what *that* was about." She flung him a brooding look. "It had to do with you though, didn't it, Alan?"

He scowled. "Yes . . . possibly . . . hell, I don't know! But not with Mulder's diaries."

It was her turn to frown. "I . . . I didn't want to become involved with you, Alan. That wasn't in the plan. I *do* want to go with you . . . you don't know how much."

"Then come. Your job's over. Mulder's leaving, and there's nothing more to report. We get married; later we make your father and your mother and the rest of your family . . . all of India, damn it . . . understand!"

Her features softened. "All of India? It will be hard convincing all of India that we . . . my father, my family, my Shi'i co-religionists, the Sunni Muslims . . . should even continue to *live*. My people came from Iran and the Middle East as conquerors, but we stayed to work, to serve . . . to *partake*. We became Indians. We *are* Indians. We were outsiders, like the Greeks and the Aryans before us, but now we are Indians." She saw his puzzlement. "Why do I talk of this now? Because of Subramaniam and his ilk . . . zealots like those who attacked you in the bazaar yesterday. To them, we Muslims are as alien as you are. We are polluted and unclean. Sooner or later we must fight a civil war."

"The army . . . ?"

"Previously neutral. The older generals were intelligent enough to realize that tearing India to pieces and killing or expelling a hundred and fifty million people would destroy us all. But now Prime Minister Ramanujan has stacked the high command with his own people. The army obeys the orders of the B.S.S."

Lessing asked, "What will you . . . your people . . . do?"

"We have nowhere to go. Iran was Shi'i; now the western half is Israeli and the eastern half Russian . . . if the Russians are still alive to hold it. Afghanistan has been theirs for almost half a century, ever since the re-invasion. The Middle East? Israel would never let us in. Pakistan? A Sunni majority and a rabidly pro-Communist Mullah as leader! Sajid Ali Lahori would prefer us to starve in refugee camps in the deserts of Kutch and the eastern Panjab."

"Like I said: what will *you* do?"

She shrugged gracefully, and his heart went out to her. "Do? We will live on here. If Ramanujan tries to expel us, we will fight. We will lose, of course, but we will fight. So will the Sikhs and some of the Christians. We will die as Muslims should."

"Martyrs!" Borchardt's characterization of Shi'i Islam arose to infuriate him. "What the hell good is that? God damn it, you are coming with me! Get your clothes! Get what you want to take!"

She melted against him, and he thought he had won. Then she pulled away. "You still don't . . . never will . . . understand! I cannot! I *must* not!" She retreated toward the door. "I have my principles, Alan, just as you have yours. Your Party . . . your SS oaths . . . ."

"Wait a minute! I'm only a beegee . . . hired help! I'm not one of Mulder's closet Nazis!" It was logical for her to think so; her father's C.I.D. kikibirds had undoubtedly classified them all as Nazis, from Mulder on down to the kids who wiped the dishes.

"It doesn't matter. That's not the point, not now." She pressed her fingers against her cheeks to hide tears, let her night-black tresses drift down to curtain her face, and backed into the hall. "Whatever you are, you are not mine . . . not for me . . . not a part of India!"

He followed her, reached for her. Then he saw that there was someone in the hall behind her: one of the faceless, rag-wrapped sweeper women who wielded short-handled straw brooms around Indoco's buildings. He opened his mouth to tell the woman to go elsewhere, but Jameela spoke first:

"*Sahib ko de do! Voh chiz jo tum ne pa'i thi, de do!*" She was ordering the crone to give him something, that much he understood.

The woman approached him shyly, crab-wise, head bowed, face hidden by her faded, green shawl. She extended both skeletal hands. Wondering, he cupped his own beneath hers.

Two objects dropped into his palms.

He knew at once what they were: one a smooth egg, the other a short, thick cylinder.

"My God!" He almost dropped them.

"My present," Jameela said. "To you, Alan. In memory of . . . of us. They're yours, aren't they? Drugs? Weapons? . . . No, don't tell me. I don't want to know."

He couldn't speak. He was only glad that she seemed to have no idea what these containers held.

"Hameeda here saw you hide them. It's impossible to remain unseen in India. We are so many: peasants, laborers, children, people with no jobs and little to do. Everybody watches. A rupee buys a day's food. It's cheap to hire watchers. Or anything else you want."

"Thank her for me." He stowed the Pacov containers into his shaving kit. "Why didn't you tell your father? Subramaniam?"

"I would report on Mulder, on Wrench . . . certainly on Goddard . . . but never on you, Alan. As for Subramaniam, he hates you . . . all foreigners. But he hates us Muslims too . . . and the Christians, and the Sikhs, and everybody else who isn't a caste Hindu. I told him only what I thought was my duty. As for Hameeda, she is a Christian, the lowest of the low, the outcasts who joined Christianity during British times to escape persecution. She would rather die than tell the mighty Inspector *Sahib* a single thing!"

He went to her, and this time she did not pull away. Hameeda watched impassively as they kissed.

"When this is over . . . ," Jameela murmured.

It would never be over. The world had turned; a new day had dawned, a Judgment Day of wrath and chaos and terror. It would *never* be over, but he smiled anyway and held her close, letting her warm, dry, spice-fragrant body nestle against his own. He rumpled her hair in his fist, strained against her, and let her feel his yearning.

"Soon," he whispered. "I'll be back for you."

He hoped he wasn't too bad a prophet.

For every complex question, there is a simple answer. And it's wrong.
—H. L. **Mencken**

CHAPTER TWELVE

Thursday, December 11, 2042

Jennifer Caw tapped her sunglasses against the metal rim of the glass-topped beach table. "It was the Jews, I say. The Israelis, backed by their puppets in the United States."

"Doubtful," Hans Borchardt countered. "They'd kill their relatives who still live in Russia. Madness! Not even their most hawkish Jews would do that!"

"They might think a few hundred thousand lives were a fair exchange for knocking off their most dangerous enemy. Or they may have the antidote . . . vaccine, whatever . . . for Pacov. Smuggle that into Russia first, and the Jews there form a ready-made occupying force."

"A handful, mostly untrained, women and kids, many old or infirm. Be serious, Jennifer!"

"Then, too, the Israelis may have had information we don't. Maybe they saw a first strike as the only way out of a nasty situation. Remember the troop movements north of Iran a few months ago? There were Arabs or Pakistanis or Afghans caught inside Russian-controlled territory about the same time, weren't there? Plenty of stateless assassins the Israelis could hire."

"The big powers would never allow the balance to be upset! Neither an Israeli attack on Russia, nor a Russian thrust to halt the Israelis' push through Iran . . . as long as they stopped at the Afghan border. The Americans and the Russians had this all worked out . . . ."

"Precisely why the Israelis might have used Pacov: a means to break the deadlock and get on with their expansion. A 'surgical first strike.' Tell nobody, and get the job done."

"Too risky! They gain little . . . ."

"Crap!" Jennifer popped her tongue against her teeth, one of her least ladylike habits. "Look at Eastern Europe now: empty, rich, and chock-full of loot all the way from the German border over to Siberia! Practically no defenses: Czechoslovakia, Hungary, and Poland a jumble of desperate refugees and practically no local authorities left; Germany struggling to keep the refugees from crossing her own borders; Turkey, Greece, and the Balkans harmless; Iran, Afghanistan, and Pakistan in turmoil; China already gobbling up Mongolia and the east! Are you telling me that Israel doesn't gain by this? She can grab giant hunks of Russian and

Ukrainian territory before anybody else gets to 'em! *Lebensraum*, Hans, *Eretz* Israel! Kosher delicatessens in Kharkov and Donetsk!"

Borchardt fussed with his white Club Lingahnie tee-shirt. His first acquisition on Ponape had been a monumental tropical sunburn. He pursed his lips and said, "The Americans will not let Israel do that. Already they're helping the survivors. Some of their teams have reached Moscow: decon squads, doctors, epidemiologists . . . not occupation troops."

"They'll find excuses to stay. So will the British in Leningrad, the Germans in Kiev, and the Chinese in Vladivostok. First they become permanent missions, then colonists. After a while they own the place, like the Israelis on the West Bank eighty years ago." The sunglasses ticked out a distracting rhythm against the tabletop. Jennifer Caw played to win, even in a friendly debate. "No, the Israelis came, they saw, they conquered . . . and they *stayed*. Mulder picked up a radio newscast yesterday that said three Israeli armored columns are already moving north from Tabriz through Tbilisi. Are they going straight up to Moscow? Or sending a spearhead northwest to Kharkov and Kiev? Or just grabbing everything they can reach?"

"No question it's the Jews," Wrench proclaimed from beneath his sun-hat. Lessing had thought him asleep. "Who profits from exterminating Russia? The West, right? And who runs the West?"

Lessing stayed motionless. The others mostly let him alone, but Wrench delighted in a little missionary work now and then.

Jennifer asked carefully, "You fought for the Israelis in Syria, didn't you, Alan? You must know them well."

"I was only a hired hand. A merc. No policy decisions." He felt her eyes prying at the top of his skull. He refused to be dragged into these discussions. Give him something to do, and he'd do it. Debate was not his forte.

After a moment Jennifer went on: "It's not fair to blame only the Jews, even if they do turn out to be responsible for Pacov. Others in the System profit as well: the great corporations, the banks, the big international combines . . . all those who gain from an American-Jewish hegemony over a half-empty world."

"Half empty?" Wrench chuckled. "Like the old joke: the pessimist sees the glass as half empty, the optimist as half full. The Jews'll drink the contents and keep the glass, too! *And* make sure the world loves 'em for doing it. The 'Chosen People' value their lovable image. Oh, yeah, they'll be kind to any surviving immunes, the women, and the kids. You'll see: they'll turn it into the greatest dramatic mini-series ever seen on TV! One that makes you feel all warm and gushy inside."

"We may be wrong," Borchardt mused. "The Palestinians could have done this . . . or the Latin Americans, the Ethiopians, Afghans, or Salvadorans. God knows there are enough dispossessed and bitter people out there. Even the British or the French or some smaller nation . . . !

"Or loonies right out of the funny-papers." Wrench scoffed.

Borchardt fingered the nape of his neck gingerly. It was bright red. "Did you hear that some are blaming the neo-Nazis? If they knew about *us*, we'd top the list!"

"We'd have to be crazy!" Jennifer exploded. "All the money we've spent to legitimize our political movement! Years of planning wasted! What do we want with a plague-ridden world . . . or an atomic cinder?"

"Nazis make the best villains," Wrench snickered. "When in doubt, punch out the least popular kid on the block! I'm sure they can work an evil Nazi super-scientist into their mini-series, a gang of black-uniformed SS troopers, a couple of death camps . . . ."

Lessing grew bored listening. These people speculated and wrangled endlessly, the way monkeys picked fleas. They had been at it since leaving India a week ago, an aimless, meandering safari that had taken them first to South Africa, where Mrs. Delacroix's friends warned her against remaining: not only out of fear of Pacov but because trouble was brewing with the Blacks again. Mulder had urged them to join him on Ponape, as remote—and safe—a spot as could be found in an increasingly unstable world.

They all had accepted. Mrs. Delacroix appeared pale and disoriented, and Liese stayed close by her side. Jennifer Caw was used to travelling around the world with no more detailed plan than tomorrow's plane ticket. She was wealthy, Lessing learned, the offspring of two wealthy South American "Descendant" families. Her father had built up a computer empire in the United States.

Borchardt tagged along, due more to an infatuation with Jennifer Caw than out of fear of Pacov. His business involved liaisons between European and Third World corporations, and he spent much time on Ponape's primitive satellite telecom hookup. Borchardt was also a "Descendant." His ancestors had not fled Germany after the Second World War, however. They had hoped to live quietly until memories had faded, but they had reckoned without the tenacity of the Nazi-hunters and the media. Hans never discussed what had happened to them. Communists, liberals, centrists—nearly everybody—had political freedom in Germany, but not the far right, the offspring of those who had once proudly borne Germany's banners. They were still anathema.

Lessing sat up and shaded his eyes, squinting against the shimmering sand for a glimpse of Mrs. Delacroix and Liese. They had wandered off up the beach that fronted Club Lingahnie's property on Madolenihmw Bay. Mulder's corporate octopus had spent a bundle getting that beach sanded and landscaped. Ponape was a Micronesian "high" volcanic island and not the idyllic Polynesian coral atoll of the South Pacific romances. It rained almost every day here, and the low shoreline was covered with scraggly mangrove forest and tangled undergrowth.

Personally, Lessing thought that Mulder and his SS comrades had been slickered when they bought Club Lingahnie. Tonga, Tahiti, or Samoa this was not!

He heard a faint chanting: not wily natives but teenagers from the Club. Presently there were about nine hundred guests, mostly young people, from many countries and organizations. Felix Bauer, attired in shorts and an alpine hat with a red feather in it, was visible in the distance on the beachfront road, pacing a column of khaki-clad youths doing military drill.

Back off the beach, among the ever-present breadfruit trees, stood new dormitories and flats, administrative buildings, a recreation hall, classrooms, a radio tower, a private landing strip, swimming pools, a sports arena, and a full-scale hospital. Certain less-public facilities were concealed by the vegetation as well: an obstacle course, target ranges, an armory containing a surprising variety of modern weapons, and bunkers that served both as defenses and as practice military objectives. The island's government, in the town of Kolonia to the north, smiled benignly and reaped the fruits of tourism.

Lessing sat back down again. He had nothing to do this afternoon. His own pupils, those learning guerrilla tactics and weapons, were on an archaeological field trip, building muscles helping the local historical society excavate the ruins of Nan Madol.

That was a fascinating place! Behind a two-kilometer-long breakwater stood a deserted city of stone platforms, with canals and channels between them big enough for canoes at high tide: a junior-size Venice. The walls of these platforms were constructed of huge blocks and columns of prismatic basalt, with cores of stones and rubble. Some of the platforms contained tombs, the remains of the Sau Deleur Dynasty that had gone extinct not long before the first Europeans arrived. Others served as foundations for temples, ceremonial sites, and priestly dwellings. Lessing had once picnicked with Liese within the brooding, enigmatic sepulchre of Nan Douwas, the mightiest of all of Nan Madol's structures. They had sensed something of the remote grandeur of the ancient past and left early, well before sunset, by unspoken mutual consent.

These days Lessing was having enough trouble sleeping as it was. Sometimes he dreamed of a bizarre corporation meeting in which he himself was honored as "Salesman of the Month." It was never explicitly stated, but he knew what the company's sole product was: death, packaged in pretty, little perfume bottles. In other dreams he walked amidst the tombs of Nan Madol, and the spirits of the vanished chiefs chanted and shook their plumed and feathered heads at him. Were there ghosts? Did the specters of the Russian dead communicate with the *eni*, the spirits of old Ponape?

He had little religious training and even less belief. All he knew was that he was going out of his mind.

The current "president" of Ponape—the paramount chief, the *nahnmwarki*, to give him his archaic title, revived after independence and reinterpreted to fit the current "American democracy" political model—was fascinated by ancestral glories, real or imagined. Hence the archaeology at Nan Madol. The agonies of a dying Europe were far away, irrelevant to Ponape and the empty sweep of the Pacific.

Given time, Ponape might become a nation-state, a fledgling empire which would war with the distant islands of Truk or Kusrae. The drums would thunder as they had in centuries gone, and the war canoes would venture forth to repeat the world's sad story one more time here in the Micronesian microcosm.

Liese appeared far down the beach. She came up to them, breathless, dark blonde hair, skin of golden bronze, and otter-sleek. Lessing admired her. There had been no need to explain about Jameela; Liese understood. Since arriving on Ponape she and Lessing had been friends. Just that and no more. The fire was banked, the coals buried. They both realized that it would take very little to make it blaze up again.

"Mrs. Delacroix," she said. "Back to the house." With the others Liese still spoke in choppy phrases; she was more relaxed when she and Lessing were alone.

"Any news?" Jennifer appraised her covertly: the look of the not-so-pretty second-banana eyeing the belle of the beach. Lessing was amused. People were the same everywhere.

"Radio says situation soon under control in most areas. Refugees from Russia being rounded up. Repatriated soon as the plague's gone."

"Well, hallelujah for that!" Jennifer said. "I'd hate to see Prague or Budapest or Vienna go the way of Moscow."

"Some refugees broke through into Germany, though. Rioting and killing still going on."

"Jesus!" Wrench breathed. Lessing echoed him, and Borchardt hissed something in German.

"Mess," Liese added unnecessarily. "Everywhere."

"At least, nobody's using nukes!" Wrench growled.

"No. Major powers trying to cool things. Enough dead now."

The understatement of all time! Lessing saw ghosts again. The beach swarmed with Russians, Germans, Poles, Czechs, Hungarians, American soldiers in torn and bloody, green uniforms. He wanted to cry out but could not.

The spectral figures swirled, accused, and disappeared, all but one which kept coming toward him: a pale, pink, old man, nude except for white shorts and thong sandals, a neckless, bald, ugly kewpie doll. It was Herman Mulder, stepping gingerly down onto the hot sand from the path that led to Club headquarters.

Wrench got to his feet to hand their employer a beach towel. "Sir?"

Mulder waved it away, although his forehead was bedewed with bright droplets. "News . . . terrible! Goddard's on the radio now. Russians . . . somebody . . . hit the United States. Biological weapon!"

They all babbled at once.

"Struck Washington, New York, Chicago. Used the water supplies as the vector. A bacteria-generated toxin, something like botulin . . . as deadly as botulin, anyway . . . but the microorganism which releases it is aerobic and thrives in places, including the human body, where *Clostridium botulinum* can't. And it's highly contagious. God, so many dead . . . ."

"My mother!" Jennifer screamed. "In Los Angeles . . . telephone . . . !"

"You'll never get through," Mulder outshouted her. "I tried. We're not sure what's happened. Los Angeles may be all right. Be patient, for God's sake! Calm down! Nothing but military emergency broadcasts now anyway."

Jennifer continued to wail.

"Help her, please, Liese! Goddard's talking to some shortwave ham in Ottawa. Toronto's been struck too, he says."

"I've got to call my mother!" Jennifer dug scarlet fingernails into ashen cheeks and dashed away, up the path toward the radio tower. Borchardt followed her.

Lessing discovered Liese in his arms. He had no recollection of putting her there. She pressed against him and husked, "You? Anybody in States?"

"Nobody I really knew any more. You?"

She shook her golden mane. "Same. Now?"

"God knows. Stay here? Wait it out? Become citizens of the sovereign state of Ponape?"

"Gone." She began to shudder, then to cry. "Gone. All finished."

He wasn't sure what she meant. Their enterprise here? The Party of Humankind? Western civilization? The whole human race?

Did little details matter?

Mulder was saying, "Properly delivered, eight ounces of botulin toxin could wipe out most advanced life on earth. Creating a new bacterium to do that job was the trick. This must be the Russians' 'Starak,' their answer to Pacov. Their revenge!"

"Revenge?" Wrench groaned. "Surely not just revenge! They'd have to be crazy!"

"The old system bred insanity. Isn't that what our movement is about? To unify, to establish order, to build a united world in which this could never happen?"

Lessing said, "Revenge, maybe; more likely just determination. You lose a battle, but you don't give up the war. The enemy deals you a blow, you slug him back harder."

"What the hell for?" Wrench cried. "To own a dead and destroyed planet? Shit!"

"What's destroyed? It's all still here. Lots of people gone, but so what? Piles of plunder! Economic goodies! *Lebensraum*, buddy, like you guys always say. We win, we get it all. You win, you do. God damn it, doesn't that make sense?"

"Soldiers!" Liese whispered sadly. She sounded more mournful than accusing. She drew back out of Lessing's arms to stare up into his face.

"Alan's right," Mulder told her. "That's what any committed patriot would do: fight to the last. Defeat your enemy at any cost; then hope you have enough left to rebuild."

"Anywhere else hit?" Wrench inquired.

"There's a lot going on. Goddard heard that the British blew up a fishing boat in the Channel while it was laying down some sort of fog from aerosol tanks. They got the boat, but the winds still carried the stuff on over the English coast. No reports of deaths yet. The Chinese caught somebody too: a Latin American of some kind. He had an empty bottle."

"What was in it?" Lessing asked.

"*Vino*," Wrench couldn't help snickering.

Mulder gave him a pained look. "They haven't any idea. The mob got him first and tore him to bits. Goddard picked this up just before the news about Washington came in."

"*In vino veritas*; now it's *in vino botulinus*!" Wrench's small, handsome features resembled an embalmer's masterpiece more than anything living. He hunkered down upon his beach towel and stared out to sea.

Mulder beckoned Lessing aside. "We're going back," he announced.

"What? Where?"

"To the United States. Guam, Hawaii, then McChord Air force Base in Washington state. From there to the Cheyenne Mountain Complex in Colorado."

"That's insane!" Lessing cried. "What about the toxin?"

"I've been told that as long as one avoids contact with infected corpses and doesn't drink unsterilized water, it should be reasonably safe. Anyhow, we pick up decon suits and a special escort plane in Hawaii."

"May I ask, why?" He was treading on dubious ground; an employee—especially a mercenary beegee—didn't question the boss.

Mulder said, "Ever heard of Jonas Outram, the Speaker of the House of Representatives?"

"Yes, of course."

"Well, he's President *pro tem* now. Old Rubin and his cabinet drank water with their breakfast in Washington, D.C. The Vice President had a shower and a morning gargle in New York. Now they're all dead. By American law the presidency passes to the Speaker of the House."

"My God . . . !"

Wrench looked up and said, "One thing the Establishment never figured on! They threw Outram that post like you'd toss a bone to a barking dog. A little present to the opposition to make things look democratic. Now I'll bet they're sorry!" He began to laugh, shakily. "Except they're thumbed."

"Most of the government in Washington is gone," Mulder said. "Who knows how many thousands . . . maybe millions? But Cheyenne Mountain has its own internal water supply, and the country's defense command is safe. The Army's declared martial law and called up all the National Guard units they can still reach. They're trying to put it back together."

"And you're going to see Outram, sir?"

"He wants to see *me*. The movement, rather. All of the so-called right-wing parties. Get ready. We leave tonight."

Mulder turned and strode across the beach toward the red roofs of the administrative buildings. From behind the screen of glossy-green breadfruit trees Lessing could still hear Bauer's sharp marching cadence and the strains of "Lili Marlene," sung off-key by a bunch of kids whose German was elementary.

The music still had a certain fateful ring to it.

Modern revolutions pass through well-defined stages: (a) hostility to the ruling regime; (b) growing discontent and resistance; (c) increasing organization, including mutual-aid alliances between opposition factions and leaders; and (d) military activity, culminating either in victory or in defeat. Should a revolution succeed, three further stages ensue: (e) giddy celebration, chaos, and revenge as the symbols of the old "Establishment" are overthrown, experimental and often ill-considered reforms are tried, and previous leaders and other "criminals" are "brought to justice"; (f) a period of consolidation, ideological harshness, purges, and violence as the "old" continues to be rooted out and replaced with the "new"; and (g) a phase of rebuilding, softening, relaxing of stringent laws and "emergency ordinances," possibly counter-purges of certain of the revolution's less-palatable leaders, and reassertion of the old, dominant strains of the pre-revolutionary society. Phase (f) usually lasts a decade or two at most, while phase (g) continues until the state has once again fossilized, grown barnacles of bureaucracy and "tradition," and itself become ripe for the next gang of disgruntled, idealistic rebels to come along. The National Socialist Revolution—for such it was—in post-World-War-One Germany went through exactly these stages. The military phase was bypassed, because the National Socialists successfully utilized the pre-existing electoral apparatus to gain power. World War II, whether due to German intransigence as the Allies claimed, or arising from unbearable pressures upon Germany, as Hitler argued, truncated the revolutionary process, lopping it off during stage (f): the period of greatest ideological zeal and severity. The historical image preserved of Adolf Hitler and the Nazis is therefore one of fanaticism and austerity. This reputation is not entirely deserved, since phase (g)—that of consolidation, amelioration, and reconciliation—never took place. Indeed, there were hints of the coming of phase (g) in the late 1930's: economic progress and stabilization, attempts at restructuring the party and regularizing the delegation of authority, and the first fruits of a number of social reforms introduced by the Nazis. True, these features benefited the Germans and not the Jews or other minorities, but then "broadmindedness" is not to be expected during phase (f) of any revolution—witness the Soviet purges of the 1930's and the guillotining of royalists in post-revolutionary France. Certain German developments were admirable: the restoration of the currency, industrial expansion, general economic prosperity (as proved by increases both in tax revenues and in profits), the construction of the *Autobahn* highway system, the end of the social unrest of the previous decade, etc. Indeed, Nazi institutions were copied by other nations, even by Germany's foes, during the subsequent war. What would the Third Reich have become had it survived? Most traditional historians paint a might-have-been future of unmitigated blackness, tyranny, and evil; yet greater social good very often emerges from change, even violent and unhappy change, just as a better garden grows from soil that has been turned over, aerated, and watered. Most revolutions follow this process; why should it have been different with Hitler's Germany?

—*A Consideration of Historical Universals*, **Udo Walter Petrie, Paris and New York, 2021**

CHAPTER THIRTEEN

Monday, December 15, 2042

Lessing shielded the notepad so that no concealed TV eye could see. Wrench had scribbled: "Needle bug in place-mat by coffee cups. Probably mike in wall outlet too. Somebody really wants to know. Leave?"

Lessing used the agreed-upon cue: "Mr. Mulder, the air in here is not good for your asthma. Perhaps President Outram wouldn't mind talking during a drive . . . or at some place outdoors?"

Mulder glanced across the polished table at Sam Morgan, the sharply dressed young aide-de-camp from the American branch of the Party of Humankind who had accompanied them from McChord Air Force Base to Colorado. He asked, "Car, Sam?"

"Easy." Morgan raised a slender eyebrow at the two stiff-faced soldiers who had guided them down into this subterranean labyrinth. They, in turn, glanced at each other and shrugged; the pasty-faced one picked up a telephone and whispered into its hush-piece.

Transport was not long in coming. The telephone shrilled, and they were led out through offices and galleries that displayed the same determined cheerfulness that Lessing remembered from Marvelous Gap. The effect was identical: efficiency, tastelessness, tension, and claustrophobia. This was NORAD headquarters at the Cheyenne Mountain Complex: miles of rooms and tunnels, observation and intelligence equipment, barracks and kitchens and storage chambers, a full complement of troops and vehicles and weaponry and state-of-the-art aerospace technology. The Born-Again presidents had added SDI control consoles and huge, wooden crucifixes.

And then somebody hit the world with Pacov and made the installation as useless as a firecracker underwater.

The main tunnel debouched into a long, dark chamber that stank of gasoline and damp concrete.

"Car park," Morgan stated unnecessarily. "That must be the limo."

On a whim Lessing said, "Take the other one instead . . . the black Titan over by the wall."

"That's General Anderson's car," one of their escort protested. "We don't have the keys."

Wrench prowled forward to peer into one vehicle after another. "Here's one with the key still in the ignition."

"We can't . . . ."

"You just did," Lessing said. "Tell the owner we'll be nice to it. We'll have it back within two hours, and we'll even pay for the gas."

"President Outram . . . ."

". . . Will want to talk to our employer in utmost comfort and security."

The two hesitated.

"Come on, you can get permission. Then have your people bring Outram in whichever car he wants," Wrench urged. "Surround him with Secret Service. He can ride with General Custer's cavalry for all we care."

"General Custer? Who's . . . ? Oh . . . ."

Wrench grinned.

Lessing unfolded a road map, peered at it, and jabbed a forefinger at a crossroad he had already marked with an "X" in preparation for just this contingency.

"This looks good. We'll meet Outram here. It's not far."

The second soldier took out a pocket transmitter and muttered into it. The first stood glowering, suspicion clouding his face.

"Green light," the man with the communicator conceded. "The President'll meet Mr. Mulder where you say. A stroll in our winter wonderland."

Once beyond the mighty entrance valves of the Cheyenne Mountain Complex the real world returned: no more shadowless fluorescents and whispering, secretive air conditioning; no odors of rubber and oil and ozone and whatever the perfumy stuff was that was supposed to make the air smell "outdoorsy." Wrench drove, Lessing settled into the front seat beside him, and Morgan perched nervously in the rear with Mulder.

Colorado had mountains; Iowa was flat. Nevertheless, this place reminded Lessing of his boyhood: crisp snow, crackling cold, dark evergreens, leaden ice shimmering in the ponds and brooks they passed, a sky so blue that you could paint with it, as his sixth grade teacher used to say, back in some forgotten, antediluvian world, a world as lost now as sunken Atlantis.

He shook himself mentally and clicked his briefcase open. Inside, on top, lay a thick, folded rectangle of cloudily translucent plastic. He and Wrench had prepared everything in advance, including the typed note he now handed Mulder. It said: "Read carefully. The area (room, vehicle, outdoors) we're in now may be bugged. This plastic tarp blocks transmitters, long distance mikes, and even lip-readers with binoculars. It unfolds to the size of a small tent.

Drape it over your and your hearers' heads while talking. We will try to debug others first if possible."

Mulder nodded. Morgan stared curiously at the array of tubes, vials, and miniaturized weapons visible beneath the plastic bug-shield in the briefcase's grey-foam receptacles. It was obvious that he itched to talk, but Wrench waved him to silence. Even this car, its key neatly inside, could be a plant.

Lessing had chosen the proposed meeting place randomly, sight unseen, from the map. It turned out to be a rutted, snow-bound side road halfway up a mountain. In the summer the view would be glorious: craggy, verdant, and clean.

It would probably be the same long after the last humans had strangled in their own foaming, bacteriological broth.

The news they had picked up in Seattle was bad: many of the great Eastern cities were dead or dying; Houston and Dallas had been infected with a ghastly, bacteria-borne, botulin-like poisoning. Similar outbreaks were now being reported in Cleveland and Cincinnati and Pittsburgh and Boston and Portland and Salt Lake City and Miami and a dozen other places. The nation was being held together only by the most desperate measures imposed by frantic police, National Guard units, and the military. In Detroit the FBI nabbed a man in the very act of emptying a vial of bacterial broth into a reservoir; the man swallowed the stuff and then leaped into the water anyway. Detroit was now off-limits to anybody not wearing an N.B.C.—nuclear, biological, and chemical warfare—suit. The Army estimated nearly a million deaths in Detroit already. The toxin was delivered through the water supply, but it killed more than just those who drank it—and those who came into too-close contact with the drinkers as they vomited and coughed their lives away; wherever it collected, in holding-tanks and sewers, it fumed and bubbled and emitted bacteria-laden mists. When a fire set off a sprinkler system in a discount store in Cleveland, a thousand people died. It was the same all over; Russia's science had been almost as thorough as America's in the megadeath department.

New York, Chicago, and Washington were cemeteries. Los Angeles, San Francisco, Seattle, Denver, and certain other Western cities had so far escaped. Perhaps the enemy's distribution system had failed on the West Coast. Perhaps it was just slower, and Death was still on his way.

Pacov had dealt Russia and Asia a grand-slam-home-run blow. The Russians had come right back in the next inning with Starak, however, and it looked like a rally for their team. The series was still up for grabs.

Who was spreading the toxins? The carriers were entering the United States along the drug routes: Miami and the Gulf Coast, the

Canadian border, and the deserts of the Southwest. Morgan, who served as the American representative for one of the movement's conglomerates, had heard that most of these people were a motley assortment: druggies with habits so heavy they would risk anything for a pop of smile-dust; the usual dispossessed Palestinians and Iranians; criminals, psychopaths, and madmen whose hatred and greed outweighed their instinct for self-preservation; and mercs willing to escalate war beyond any usual "civilized" limit. No genuine Russians had been caught thus far.

"There," Morgan grunted. "Outram's coming." He pointed to the string of black and Army-green vehicles wending its way toward them along the snow-drifted slope.

After India and Ponape, the cold was breathtakingly painful. They disembarked into the chill air, Mulder bearing the mute-tarp under his arm. He reminded Lessing of some old movie star—was it Laurel or was it Hardy? . . . whichever the round one was—carrying a rolled umbrella.

A bear-sized man in a baggy, brown jacket with patch sleeves clambered out of the lead car. Outram had obviously not planned on an outdoors excursion; either that, or he anticipated a very short conversation. It was colder than the proverbial polar bear's paws. Those behind Outram wore uniforms, dark overcoats, or fashionable ski-gear: soldiers, White House staffers, advisors, and Secret Service men. Two of the last-mentioned advanced, inspected Mulder and his plastic bundle, then waved him on. The press apparently had not been invited.

Wrench extracted a pair of binoculars from somewhere and began searching the slopes above and below the road. "Don't suppose they'd let us examine Outram," he grumbled. "What if *he's* got bug-itis?"

"Forget it. Some things you can't help." A flash from one of the President's escort vehicles caught Lessing's eye. He motioned to Wrench, who swung his glasses around. The little man shook his head. Probably somebody shutting a car door.

A pair of Outram's Secret Service kikibirds picked their way through the snow toward them. The one in front was red-blonde and ruddy-faced, cheeks splotched with scarlet beneath the cowl of his padded, blue ski-jacket. The other, an older man, took a position to the rear as backup.

"You!" the blonde one called. "You guys! You Mr. Mulder's beegees?"

Lessing said, "That's us."

The man produced an electronic device, similar to Lessing's own bug-detector. "Leave your weapons in the car." He flicked a forefinger at Lessing's briefcase. "Set that down there, in the snow by the fence post."

They complied. The agent first went over the two of them, then the briefcase, and finally the vehicle itself.

"Something . . . ." he muttered. "The car . . . ."

They all heard the helicopter simultaneously. The sharp chuff-chuff-chuff of its blades smacked against the frigid air like hammer blows. Lessing twisted around, and Wrench fumbled with his binoculars. The kikibird, too, raised his head, eyes slitted against the white dazzle.

The machine was a tiny, military Stinger 297-G, nicknamed the "hoppy-choppy" because of its maneuverability. It carried two people and was used mainly for reconnaissance, though it could be armed with small rockets and light automatic weapons. About a hundred meters away, Mulder and Outram pulled off their mute-tarp to stare upward. There was sudden activity around the fleet of official vehicles. A soldier ran toward Outram shouting.

It appeared that the helicopter had not been asked to the party. Newspapermen? TV?

No, the machine was armed! Lessing saw blunt, silvery rocket noses peeping out from launching racks under the fuselage.

Lessing took no chances. He shouted at Mulder to get away, get down, get under cover. Wrench joined in, and the Secret Service man began squalling into his communicator.

The helicopter was hostile. The pilot circled to target his missiles on Mulder and Outram below.

The second agent reached their limousine, braced himself against its roof, drew a big magnum automatic from his coat, and took aim. Morgan dashed forward, perhaps to help Mulder through the drifts, while the soldier did the same for Outram.

The President's people were firing. Puffs of pale smoke jetted up from the line of automobiles, and the popping of small-arms fire slapped against the heights and echoed back down upon them. It would take Lessing too long to dig his sniper rifle out of its compartment in his briefcase. He could only flounder after Morgan and Wrench to draw fire away from Mulder—if indeed the hoppy-choppy was after him rather than Outram.

Something coughed, loud over the helicopter's steady chatter, and a streak of flame shot out from the machine's underbelly. A solid spear of pearly smoke etched itself upon the sky.

"Rocket!" shrieked Wrench. He threw Mulder flat, rolling over and over in the powdery snow.

The missile hurtled toward Mulder. Then, oddly, it veered away to the right, graceful as a stooping falcon, and plunged directly at the limousine Mulder's party had used.

Memories of hot, dry, Syrian sand, of stones and baked earth, took over as Lessing hurled himself down. He glimpsed Wrench's deep footprints in the whiteness in front of him; then he ploughed into them face first. A wave of heat, light, and unbearable noise smashed against his back.

He struggled up, dazed but relieved to be alive.

Nothing broken, no blood, no pain. Any flying shrapnel had missed, and the snow had saved him from a nasty fall. His ears rang; his vision was blurred. Somehow he had managed to turn around and was now looking back toward their car. In its place a pillar of flame and dark, oily smoke roiled up into the sky. There was no sign of the gun-wielding agent, and the blonde man lay face down in a jumble of red, blue, and charred black. He did not move.

Wrench crawled over to Lessing. "Christ, man! You dead?"

"Not yet." His voice sounded tinny and far away. He hoped any hearing damage was temporary. "Mulder? Morgan? Outram?"

"Okay, I think. Goddam! Here comes the bastard again!"

The hoppy-choppy clattered back across the azure bowl above them, a second rocket peering malevolently out from underneath it. The popping started up from the President's escort once more. Then a pencil of fire shot out from among the vehicles, and they heard the breathy whoosh of a hand-held GTA rocket launcher. An arrow of flame-laced smoke reached up to caress the helicopter's beetle-green carapace.

A bright flower of fire bloomed in the air.

The helicopter twisted, lurched, and faltered. Then it exploded. Metal and glass debris rained down onto the snow. The body of the machine tumbled down into the road, two hundred meters west of the fleet of escort vehicles.

There was silence.

People stared openmouthed, stunned by the noise, the light, and the grim suddenness of others' dying.

Mulder and Morgan came staggering over to the wreckage of the car, followed by Outram and three of his aides. One of the latter shouted something about being a doctor; he knelt to help the blonde agent, but the man was dead, a shard of glass from a car window buried in his throat.

An inane thought crossed Lessing's mind: how would they ever explain this to the poor bastard whose car they had borrowed?

Wordlessly they all tramped back down the road to inspect the helicopter. Its second rocket had gone off in its mounting, and the machine was an inferno. Serious forensic science would be needed to identify its occupants. One of Outram's people used his communicator and learned what Lessing expected: no record of any authorization and no flight plan. Not any more. Somebody had been clever. The facts might eventually be discovered, but it would take time.

Outram motioned his escort back to their cars. He towered over his men, a hulking walrus in his mid sixties with a full head of rumpled, iron-grey hair, drooping mustachios, and mottled skin like a lemon left too long in the sun. Lessing couldn't remember whether he hailed from Idaho or Wyoming—one of the two.

The President beckoned to one of his aides. "Get Pierce and MacNee and Korinek on this, Charley. Find out who the hell is behind it." He glanced beyond at a uniformed Army colonel. "And, George, I'm ridin' back with you. No helicopters . . . no big mallard duck flyin' over all the hunters in creation!"

Everyone scrambled to obey. Outram wheeled around, saw Mulder, and rumbled, "You're ridin' with me too, Herman. You and your boys. And don't you give me no shit about security, George. Not after this morning!"

George clamped his lips together, dismissed his enlisted-man chauffeur, and drove.

As they entered the last stretch of road leading into the complex, Outram leaned forward. "Listen," he said to George, "I ain't goin' back down into that hole. Find us a motel . . . one with good coffee . . . and we'll talk while we eat."

Lessing, next to the driver, opened his mouth to protest, but the President clapped him jovially on the shoulder. "Sure, we don't have your plastic shower curtain any more, but what the hell? The whole world's gonna know anyhow."

There was no arguing. On the seat behind, Lessing saw Wrench make a circular warning gesture to Mulder: bugs, recorders, spy devices were possible in this vehicle, too.

Mulder ignored him and said, "The missile . . . the rocket . . . was aimed at us, Jonas. Yet it arced away and hit our car instead."

"Prob'ly a heat-seeker. Your car's engine was off, but it was still the hottest thing the damn missile could see within its range."

Lessing had another thought. "The Secret Service man . . . the one who was killed by shrapnel . . . ."

"Cargill? What about him?" Outram twisted to peer at his face, silhouetted against the smoked-glass windows in the front seat.

"Just before the rocket hit he said there was something strange about our car. Maybe a bug. Maybe it was a homing device for the missile."

"But you went over the car . . . ?"

"We didn't have much time. Anyway, if the thing wasn't using power or emitting a signal, it couldn't be detected until it was activated, likely by radio. Hide it in the ignition, the transmission, the systems-check computer, and nobody could find it without tearing the whole car apart."

"You can paint circuits directly onto the body," Wrench added. "Then spray enamel finish over 'em. One transistor here, another way over there. The whole car itself becomes a bug."

"I got plenty of opposition," Outram declared cheerfully. "People who'd rather have a turd in their soup than me for President. My folks're good, though. They'll find the bastards responsible." As he spoke, his cowboy twang seemed to fade in and out, like distant music. Chameleons and politicians both changed color to good effect.

Outram's answer was not reassuring. What if the missile had been planned only for Mulder's car? What if the hoppy-choppy, arriving at the meeting site late, after they had disembarked, had had no time to reprogram the missile to manual targeting? The assassins might have decided to try for Mulder—or Outram, or both— anyway.

"Does this . . . this business just now . . . change what we discussed?" Mulder questioned in neutral tones.

"Hell, no, Herman. You boys got the organization, 'specially in the rural states . . . the South, the Midwest, the Northwest. We can use you."

"As I said, we're not as powerful or as well structured as you think . . . ."

"Horseshit! I seen Eighty-Five's printouts . . . some of 'em anyhow. You got tentacles, Herman. What you got 'em for I don't know, but you got more tentacles than a bull octopus! You got church groups, but you're no preacher; schools, but you're no educator; universities and colleges, but you're no goddam flip-top egghead; labor committees, but you're no union man; lots of capital that stretches way overseas and down into the cracks in a bunch of places . . . ."

"Really . . . ."

"Shit!" Outram chided, unperturbed. "The one thing you *ain't* is what we . . . my folks . . . also ain't: minority-operated, y'might say. Civil Rights're 'civil wrongs' in a lot of cases."

"In some things we agree," Mulder replied. "But we . . . my friends . . . share broader, more international interests . . . ."

"Just fine. Sunnier'n hell in July, Herman. Where we're together, we're together. Where we ain't, we can wrassle later." Outram sucked in a breath. "You seen what happened this morning? We're gonna get a lot more of that: people who want things we . . . you 'n' me . . . don't. Mebbe leftists, mebbe liberals, mebbe the minorities, mebbe the money men and the industrialists, mebbe the soldiers . . . like George here . . . ." He grimaced at the back of the driver's head and cracked thick, splotched knuckles. "One thing's sure: I ain't givin' the United States back to them who was ruinin' it before. No more big-city lobbies, no more robbin' good, hardworkin' folks to please every 'interest' with its own row to hoe. No more sendin' billions overseas to prop up mealy-mouthed little fuckers who spit on your hand even while they're takin' your cash!"

Mulder uttered a noncommittal grunt.

"Can you deliver, Herman? Can your people help us organize? Help us fight? Help put the country back together?" Outram's voice took on a resonant, sepulchral, organ tone. "You shoulda seen it: the dead piled in heaps twenty feet deep, the fires, the wreckage, the looters, the local bosses thinkin' now they're almighty warlords and buildin' their own private armies. You'll help, Herman! When you see what I seen, you'll help. Whatever you and your folks believe, you're still Americans. You're prob'ly better Americans than the dribble-assed weaklings who got us into this mess in the first place!"

"Where were the regular troops?" Wrench wondered. "The police? The National Guard?"

"It happened so fast. Our guys were either busy or dead. A lot of our forces overseas we can't get home . . . hell, some we ain't even heard from yet! We still got units dealin' with what's left of the Russians, the Chinese, and the Middle East. Central America likewise. Japan's hunkered down, waitin' for either Pacov or Starak . . . or mebbe both. So's Korea and Australia and other places."

"India?" Lessing had to know.

"What about it? Rama-what's-his-name has turned India into a Hindu dictatorship. No Pacov or Starak there yet . . . that we know of."

"The missiles?" Mulder asked. "The space platforms?"

"'Tween us and the Russians, we got more shit up in the sky than God. We nearly had it all down in our laps too, last week. One more panicky Russkie with an itchy finger, and we'd have had fireworks up over the Pole. Thank God that Pacov took out almost all of their missile people and their chain of command."

"And now . . . ?"

"We're both about done for. A helluva lot of our people lived in cities, Herman. We didn't lose 'em all, but we did lose millions. And the rest're shook outa their trees, so disorganized we can't even get food and supplies to 'em. Russia's less citified, but Pacov hit harder than they hit us with Starak or whatever. Their casualties amount to somethin' like eighty percent of their population . . . practically all of European Russia, lots of the central regions, the Caspian . . . Jesus!"

"Europe? Israel?"

"Britain's seethin' with Starak. Europe's full of refugees, and Israel's okay: busy blamin' the Arabs and stompin' Palestinians. Shit, the Jews're even threatenin' to blow up Mecca and Medina if the Muslims don't get peaceable fast."

"Huh! They really must be feeling their oats," Lessing exclaimed. The Israelis had left those two places as independent "international holy cities" to keep the rest of the Islamic world off their necks, he knew. He had fought out there and had a feel for it.

Outram shot him a calculating look. "You know somethin' about them parts, young man?" When Lessing nodded, the President said, "Then you'll be useful later, if we kin get our butts through the next coupla weeks!"

"Again. How can we ... my colleagues and co-workers ... help?" Mulder inquired.

"We got to fight whoever done this, Herman. God knows what the fuckers'll do next. Then if we win we gotta rebuild. We gotta do the job right, or else next time some asshole'll *really* push them buttons ... in this country *and* in Russia! Then up goes the planet, and us poor suckers down here won't have a cow-pie left to stand on!"

The rapt looks on the faces of Wrench and Morgan told Lessing that Outram had charisma. That was why he had been elected every term since Lessing could remember—and why all of the liberal efforts to unseat him had failed. He spoke to the majority of Americans in ways they understood: plain and direct, if richly profane, to the menfolk, and courteously—"Old Time Cowboy"—to the women.

Lessing shut his eyes and pinched the bridge of his nose. He had heard too many speeches too many times before. There was more, much more, as they drove, all delivered in the same wide-open-spaces Western lilt. Lessing glanced over at the blank-faced driver and wondered just what George thought.

More to the point, what did he himself think?

Outram's message sounded close to Mulder's: the good of one's ethnos, one's nation, one's community. Do what you had to do to keep your own folks going. If that meant domination of other groups, then you tipped your hat and dominated, as peacefully, gently, and politely as possible. That was not "bad." That was ethically and realistically *right*! If domination had to come at the expense of smaller, less aggressive, or less successful groups, then so be it. That was the way things crumbled. Call it "realism" or call it "creative evolution in action." Good-bye, dinosaurs! Good-bye, snail darter and dodo bird! Hello, enlightened self-interest!

And was that such a bad thing? It ran counter to the great religions, of course, and it didn't jibe with liberal humanism either;

yet Lessing knew that those time-honored institutions preached more than they practiced. So it had been with his mother, and so it was in Angola, Syria, and India. So it was also in the United States, but hypocrisy had grown ever more sophisticated as the media learned how to present "reality" their way.

Enlightened self-interest did not imply cruelty or indifference; in fact, the world would benefit from it, now that the present system was in chaos and doomsday only a heartbeat away. The Party of Humankind promised to stop the crap and solve the gut-issues of food, war, jobs, over-population (maybe no longer!), pollution, and much else. The Party's origins did not matter; who cared whether it arose from the SS, the Christian church, the Bangers, or the Abominable Snowman? What was important was that it offered a way up out of this current abyss. Pacov and Starak only made this message starker: humanity could no longer limp along from catastrophe to catastrophe. Indeed, the present crisis might already be the last.

Failure this time would be it. All. Terminus. The end. Welcome back to the Paleozoic!

Lessing himself wasn't terribly interested. He had never joined any political organization, religion, or movement. Why bother? Let others wave the flags; he just did his job, quietly and without fanfare, until somebody paid him to go do something else.

The motel they found was minimally open. Word had spread that Colorado, with its missile sites and military bases, was a likely target for Starak and atomic warheads—as well as rampaging Banger gangs from the Los Angeles ghettoes. Refugees from both coasts and from Texas preferred to move on into Montana, the Dakotas, or up to Canada.

The tiny, hard-featured, old woman who ran the place gaped at the invading horde of limousines, uniforms, dark business suits, and bright ski-jackets. Then she stuck her gum under the counter and methodically went about stoking up the big coffee-urn beside the grill.

Outram waved them all to "set." To George, he added, "Fix us up with rooms tonight."

The officer frowned. "*This* place, sir?"

"Spent my young life in motel rooms . . . 'n' not always sleepin' neither. You git all the security you need. Call in patrol 'copters . . . just so's you're sure they're ours this time! Register me and Herman in rooms down at the end of the court, but we'll actually stay up here close to the coffee shop. That oughta fox any sonuvabitch who knows where we are and wants to call in an air strike."

George hurried away. Outram beckoned Mulder over to a booth in the corner and allowed both Lessing and one of the Secret

Service men to check for bugs. They found none, and the President gestured everyone except Mulder out of earshot.

The rich fragrance of American coffee—unavailable in India— filled the overheated room. Odors of snow-wet clothing and, after a while, of hamburgers, french fries, eggs, and bacon followed. Silverware clattered above the buzz of voices. An hour passed, and the waning sun turned the frost patterns on the windows into yellow sapphire and orange topaz. The cut-out paper Santas pasted on the panes became bloodstained ogres, and the wilted, little Christmas tree by the cash register blazed with ruddy light, like Moses' burning bush.

This year Santa was splashed with gore, and the burning bush was not a sign from a caring God but rather a harbinger of His Last Terrible Trump.

Come to Judgment, folks! It's Armageddon Day!

A heavy-set Secret Service man stamped in, all snow and steaming breath, to tell Outram that the media-hounds had tracked him down. Three carloads of TV people and journalists waited outside.

Outram scowled. "Let the fuckers freeze! Tell 'em no comment tonight." Then he relented. "Aw, hell, get me 'n Herman out the back way and into our cabins. After we're gone you can let the bastards in to warm up. This weather'd ice the balls on a snowman!"

It was an hour before the two cabins were readied and checked. Lessing, Morgan, and Wrench were quartered in the cabin adjacent to Mulder's, where they set up their own sentry-watches. Mulder seemed to trust Outram, but Lessing refused to take chances.

In the cold, eery moonlight, with the snow blanketing a world of pastel blues, greys, and relentless black, Lessing leaned against the jamb, just inside their cabin's single door. Nothing moved outside; only the stiff, anguished figure of a Secret Service man was visible in the snow by Outram's window. God, the man must be cold! The price of serving the mighty.

A snuffle in the darkness told him Wrench was up. He heard the slithery sounds of clothing being donned and shoes slipped on; then the little man was beside him.

"Matter?" Lessing grunted. "Got to pee?"

"Can't sleep. Anything?"

"No."

Wrench noted the Secret Service man and made clucking noises. "Jesus, they'll have to thaw that guy out with a blowtorch!"

"Be glad Mulder didn't have *us* stand guard out there."

"Screw that! Devotion has its limits."

Lessing sniffed. "How's Morgan?"

"Sleeping the sleep of the innocent. He's an up-and-comer, a fairhaired boy who never expected to double as batman for General Washington at Valley Forge!"

"Double as *what*?"

"Batman . . . aide-de-camp, valet. You know. British army term, dear boy."

Lessing changed from one numbed foot to the other. A question had been bothering him all day, and he asked it: "What's Outram want? Why call Mulder all the way from Ponape?" Wrench would know if anybody did; Lessing had seen him talking with the President's staff.

"Outram can't hold it together. He needs Mulder . . . the Party."

"For God's sake, why? He's *President*. He has the Army, the Marines . . . the police."

"Washington's gone, New York's gone, Chicago's a mortuary. Things're falling apart fast. The military wants to push the wagon. So do some governors and some mayors and a lot of other guys. Outram knows he can't handle them alone. He can't use the traditional controls either; they'd have things 'back to normal' before you could say 'lox 'n' bagels.' He thinks the Party has potential."

"Your Party's too small. What can it do?"

"A lot. Outram's calling in favors from every so-called 'rightist' faction in the country. He has to get his act together before the big-city liberals of the Establishment . . . what's left of 'em . . . get theirs going again. He needs support, but the political Right is split up into personalities, parties, and sects . . . all fucked up, with their pants down as usual!"

"And?"

"That's where the Party of Humankind comes in. Outram knows Mulder, and he knows our Party is the best organized, best funded, and best trained of all the 'right wing' shit-kickers. We're also international, we know business, and we have credibility in the Third World. In the United States we're strongest in rural areas, the towns, and the smaller cities . . . the very places where the most people, the *real* American majority, live. They're the ones who've survived Starak fairly intact. A lot of those folks believe what we believe, but they couldn't say it . . . not with the lobbies and the pressure groups and the media all ready to whomp 'em for being 'racists' if they open their mouths. Rural support is historically right for the Party, too. The National Socialist Party in Germany had a heavy 'farm' streak: agrarian radicals, the dignity of labor, farm boys with scythes, sturdy Aryan youths with pitchforks standing beside plump, blonde *Fräuleins* mit braids und der big boobies, *ja*?"

Lessing chuckled. "I've seen the posters. Not my type."

"Anyhow, the great American majority is pretty pissed. Ready to stand up at last and kick some butt on its own. It always has been, down through history. Nobody, but nobody, can bushwhack our ethnos and not get a lot bigger whack in return! Outram can use us, all right! He probably guesses we've got plans for later, but he can't be choosy now."

"What's next?"

"Christ, ask Mulder! All I got was that in the morning orders'll go out to our American cadres to start bangin' the drum. Hang out the signs, sing, dance, and peddle snake-oil like crazy!"

"Get out the vote while the opposition's still unzipped?"

"Yeah. Like that."

Lessing asked, "And Mulder? What does *he* want? What the hell is he all about, anyway?"

"He wants a better-run world, one where his ethnos . . . his people, his *Volk*, his nation . . . can shine again and be free."

"That's fine for a press release. Now tell me the rest."

Wrench's eyes glittered powder-blue in the moonlight. "Straight?"

"Yeah."

The little man blew out his cheeks. "What makes him tick, way down deep? I don't know. Maybe he wants his honor back, the honor of his grandfather and the others who died for the Third *Reich*."

"After nearly a hundred years? Come on!"

"No, for real. They . . . the SS . . . a lot of other Germans . . . did what was right for their country. For a communist-free Europe. For the Aryan race. For the future of the world."

"That was a century ago. Who cares now? Nobody! Mulder's as flaky as a merc I once knew who wanted to restore the Roman Empire!"

"You want to know who cares? Who *really* cares? The guys who continue to use their so-called 'Holocaust' to pry bucks out of us 'guilty' suckers! The ones who peddle a grossly falsified version of the history of the last century or so and try to have anyone who disagrees with them locked up. *They* care very much."

"They say its *you* who distort history."

"So why don't they face us . . . examine our evidence, debate, talk . . . act like real historians instead of thought-police? Why shut us out of the media, pass laws against our speaking, persecute us, sue us, and vilify us? *This* is what lights Mulder's fire: a matter of justice and a fair shake. You can't even debate a different point of view any more, much less present it as an 'option' in a school or university. History is what *they* say it is. Mulder's ancestors hold top billing as the original, A-1, prime-time, world-class villains, creatures of Satan, murderers, fiends, monsters, and sadists. Say different and you're an 'anti-Semite,' a 'Nazi,' a psychopath. You're *evil*. You lose all credibility, maybe your job, maybe your life."

"It's all ancient history now, water over the dam. Why not just concede and move on? Let the Jews have their 'Holocaust,' real or otherwise?"

"Because they affect *us*, man! Their social, economic, and psychological clout shapes our world and our lives." Wrench waggled his fingers. "We have a right to examine what they're telling us. We have a right to freedom of expression, to the truth. We have a right to defend our own ethnos."

"Some see that last as 'racist.' A lot of people think 'racism' is un-American."

"Let 'em. Shows what they know about the real will of the majority. Enlightened 'racism' is the shortest way out of our present mess. We don't *hate* anybody; we're not out to slaughter Jews or other minorities. We're not backwoods hillbillies who hate anybody who looks different. We're *for* America: for freedom from lobbies and 'interests,' for freedom of expression, for freedom for our people to run their lives as they see fit. It is *very* American to want our nation, our ethnos, to succeed and prosper, to defend it against those who would tear it down and turn us into something we don't want to be."

Lessing rubbed at the bridge of his nose. "God, Wrench, but you're an asshole when you talk about this stuff! Like my dad used to say, 'God save us from priests, patriots, and pickpockets!'" He paced away, then back again.

He had never found anything within himself that he could call patriotism, idealism, or religion. Back in high school one of his girl friends, Emily Pietrick, had found a term in some poem or novel or other that she said described him perfectly: "the empty man." He had shown her that he was *not* empty—not in bed anyway—but the idea still niggled at him. In an odd sort of way he found himself envying Mulder.

Wrench dutifully changed the subject: "Did you hear what George said to that big fucker, the guy with the red nose who looks like a banker?"

"No. And what does a banker look like?"

"Like him. Honest. Anyway, Outram wants some of his guys to head for New Orleans to organize things."

"So?"

"He's sending some others into Washington to secure the central terminal of Eighty-Five, the big main-frame computer. There's a rumor that certain unfriendlies intend to take it over."

"How's that affect us? We're going back to Ponape."

Wrench grinned, a half-moon of glimmering blue-white. "Morgan's off to whomp up the parade in the Midwest. Mulder goes with Outram to New Orleans. But us . . . you 'n' me, poor dipshits . . ." he paused for effect ". . . we're travelling with Outram's boys into Washington, whatever the hell Pacov has left of it."

Lessing stared. "What *for*?"

"Some of the movement's corporations had offices in Washington. A few of our political groups and lobbies had head-quarters there, too. We're gonna pay 'em visits to see if they're croaked."

"Why *us*? Any Party grunt can do that!"

"Yeah, but it makes a good excuse to give Outram. The real reason we're along is to see if any of our own insiders at Eighty-Five's main terminal are still kicking. If they're okay and green-light, then we stay low. But if the opfoes are digging through Eighty-Five's 'forgotten' files, we take action. With extreme prejudice."

"I repeat, damn it: why us? I can't tell a mainframe from an electric shaver!"

"*I* can. Didn't you know? Never sneak a look at my personnel file at Indoco? I sure looked at yours!" Wrench stifled a bubble of laughter; Morgan stirred on the farther bed. "Hell, Lessing, I have a Ph.D. in computer science from MIT!"

"Jesus! And you were working security for Indoco out in India?"

"Reasons." Wrench rarely spoke of his past, and even more rarely of his personal goals. He might just be telling the truth.

"Okay, that explains *you*. But why *me*?"

"You're going along to protect me. You're Mulder's soldier-boy, general of his forces, the *Herr Generaloberst* of his *Wehrmacht*! That's how he sees you."

Lessing exploded, "Goddam it, I've told you and I've told *him*: I'm not a member of your Party! I only work here."

"That's what I meant when I called you the *Generaloberst* of the *Wehrmacht* . . . not the *Obergruppenführer* of the *Waffen-SS*. You're the apolitical military man, not the ideological Party soldier."

The distinction was lost on Lessing. He was tired of political game-playing, and he was fed up with Wrench's coy attempts to recruit him for the "cause." He growled, "I said: I only work here. Leave the rest alone."

Wrench struck a soulful pose. "Mulder sees you as something else, too."

Lessing asked before he thought; maybe he didn't want to hear the answer. "What?"

"The son he and the Fairy Godmother could never have."

For some reason that struck a very sore nerve. "Bull*shit!*" he snapped. Hadn't he had enough trouble with his own parents? Memories tried to push up into consciousness, but he swatted them away like summer gnats.

Wrench eyed him, a trifle apprehensively. "Right. Okay . . . okay! Back to the job. Mr. Lessing goes to Washington. Saves Mr. Charles Hanson Wren and gorgeous Miss Eighty-Five! All for democracy, for America, for the world!" He added a weak cackle.

Morgan was up, hair disheveled, rubbing at his eyes, and yawning hugely. "You guys talk too much. My watch?"

Lessing turned away to peer out at the pallid, snow-silvered desolation framed in the door's single windowpane. He found himself staring at his own reflected image. God, he didn't look any better than Morgan. In fact, the old phrase "like death warmed over" came to mind—or in his case "like death *frozen* over."

He let out a long, careful, slightly shaky sigh and went to bed.

Unlike communism, which proposes an end both to private property and to market capitalism, the National Socialist state infringes upon traditional rights, privileges, and behavior patterns only to the extent that it must in order to curb anti-state tendencies and a return to the weak, confused, and frequently contradictory structures of "liberal democracy"—which was never truly "liberal" nor truly "democratic" in the first place! Communism demands fundamental changes in both human nature and human society; National Socialism strengthens and streamlines familiar societal structures, and enhances those values with which members of a given ethnos feel most comfortable. A modern National Socialist state requires: (a) a complete, holistic ideology; (b) a single organization dedicated to serving this ideology, headed either by one charismatic leader or by a small group of leaders; (c) complete authority over the military, the police, and the judiciary; (d) a centrally planned economy, together with the necessary enforcement structures to implement this efficiently; and (e) total control over mass communications. To the above, one may add a new feature, one that has only become possible within the last three-quarters of a century: a centralized information-retrieval system. The almost unimaginable complexities of modern society necessitate efficient record-keeping, data storage, and correlation of such interrelated issues as industrial production, transportation, education, food supply, jobs and labor, human services, and much, much more. In earlier times this either would have been impossible or else required an army of civil servants! Now it is possible through computer technology. Such a computer system cannot be allowed to make decisions, of course—this prerogative belongs intrinsically and eternally to humankind—but it can be used to store vast amounts of data and to integrate, correlate, extrapolate, and play out "what if?" scenarios, providing new insights and saving human energy.

—*The Sun of Humankind* **(excerpts from the third pre-publication draft), by Vincent Dorn**

CHAPTER FOURTEEN

Friday, December 19, 2042

"You're lucky you didn't have to see it," the Marine captain said.

"Cars full of stiffs piled up in the worst traffic jam in history, bodies stuffed in between the vehicles like rag dolls in my kid's closet, bulldozers shoving loads of corpses off the Arlington Bridge to clear a way out of the city, the parkways along the Mall littered with dead."

"Is Starak always fatal?" Lessing asked. His N.B.C. suit was hot, tight, and claustrophobic. The worst part was looking out upon a picture-pretty, grey, winter afternoon in Washington, D.C., and knowing that that landscape was as lethal as the naked surface of the moon.

"As far as we know. Botulin poisoning often can be cured if you catch it in time. Still, who's got the medics or the supplies to treat a couple of million people in greater Washington? And we're not sure that the toxin generated by Starak is *real* botulin anyway. The Russians developed this version as a weapon. A little gene-splicing goes a long way."

"So many people . . . ."

The immensity of the tragedy defied comprehension. Outside their sealed med-van the streets were mostly empty and clean under a lead-hued, frost-rimmed sky. Here and there a car had gone up over the curb, and some of the buildings were fire-blackened shells, but it didn't look as bad as Lebanon—much less like what the Israelis had left of Damascus during the Baalbek War.

The captain tapped Lessing's arm. "Keep your fingers off your suit-valve, sir. You probably want to open up and breathe fresh air, but contagion's still a risk, and the stench is godawful. See all these buildings we're passing? We haven't had time to clear 'em of corpses. It's been hard enough to get the main arteries open."

He sounded like a tourist guide warning passengers not to stand up in the bus. Horror had become commonplace, the unthinkable a way of life. Lessing had seen many men like the captain out in Syria.

The captain poked a gloved finger at their vehicle's windshield. "Two more streets and we're at the National Defense Research Facility."

They were in Suitland, southeast of the capital toward Andrews Air Force Base. The Born-Agains had expanded in this direction; later the Rubin administration had erected grandiose office complexes to the northwest, where Columbia Hospital and the old Weather Bureau had stood before the Farm Riots of 2023. Wrench said that some bureaucrat had originally proposed putting Eighty-Five down in the sub-basement beneath the IRS building, but that had struck even the politicians as a little too obvious.

It was just as well that Eighty-Five was not in downtown Washington. No tourists drove up Constitution Avenue these days. The armed forces and what was left of the police were still collecting bodies there and shooting looters—and infected survivors—on sight. It had been difficult to get a guide and transport for their mission out to the Eighty-Five facility, but Outram had swung his not-inconsiderable weight around, and this Marine captain, a driver, two paramedics, and one of the precious med-vans had eventually been assigned to them. Lessing and Wrench were to go along as "observers," while the captain, whose name they had not been told, was "to inspect and secure the facility." The captain belonged to the Second Marine Aircraft Wing from Cherry Point, North Carolina, and had been on a courier mission to the Pentagon when Starak's first victims started to stagger and vomit up their guts. The man was a fan of bottled fruit juice and so had not partaken of Washington's deadly water. That, and the good luck of being ordered to wait for an appointment in a nearly airtight basement office, had saved him.

"F w many got away?" asked Wrench. His N.B.C. suit was too big for him, and he had to keep pulling the helmet down to see out. All that was visible was his wavy, dark-brown hair and a pair of eyes. He reminded Lessing of a cartoon character.

"Quite a few. Starak works either by ingestion or through an open lesion, and not everybody drank water, handled dead or dying victims, or sniffed the bacteria-laden fumes coming from the sewers. The stuff in the sewers seems to have been pretty well flushed out by now, but . . . ." His voice trailed off.

"Christ . . . ." Wrench mumbled.

The captain spoke again: "We think there're some real immunes, though we can't be sure. Just yesterday a squad brought in a ten-year-old kid who'd been living on root beer and stale popcorn since . . . it . . . happened. When his parents' bodies started to stink too bad, he rolled 'em onto rugs, dragged 'em out into the back yard, and set 'em on fire with gasoline. That's how we found him: the smoke."

It still hadn't sunk in. It might never sink in. The greatest tragedy since the Ice Age, and it all seemed so ordinary, so awkward, so simple—so stupidly, whimsically anecdotal. In two days Lessing thought he had heard every miracle story there was, but each rescue worker had a new tale to tell. There was the baby discovered alive after a week in its mother's rotting arms; the old man who'd found the airport drinking fountain out of order and flew on to Atlanta, happily unaware of the tragedy until somebody told him he'd just missed a lethal gulp of Starak—whereupon he had a heart attack; the health nut in Philadelphia who drank only mineral water and brushed his teeth with antiseptic mouthwash; the wimpy, little store manager who'd carried his two-hundred-pound wife five miles through streets choked with mobs of screaming, dying people, got her to the medics in time, and then went back for his infant son—all three now safe in a shelter outside Washington. If miracles proved the existence of God, then the truth of every religion from Christianity to Banger Satanism had just been proved once and for all. Miracles were as common nowadays as candles in the churches.

Well, maybe not as common as the horror stories. Those, like the fabled demons of Hell, were legion.

Lessing struggled to follow the captain's example and turn death into a commonplace, make it historical, something that happened somewhere else to people who weren't people but stick-figures, statistics, names in a book, "subjects" on the police blotter, shapes in a crowd. That way the unspeakable became speakable, the scenes around him no more than epic movies. Never-before-imagined spectacle! A cast of millions! Right before your very eyes! See the parting of the Red Sea, the sack of Rome, the fall of Constantinople, the last days of Pompeii.

The last days of the whole pitiful, rotting, infected world.

The dead refused to cooperate. They kept turning into real faces: grey and sunken cheeks, eyes gone, blackened mouths agape, stinking bundles of purpling flesh and decayed clothing. Real men, real women, real children.

God.

Was God real?

If God existed, then why didn't He hear? Why didn't He answer?

One theory was as good as another. God's phone was off the hook. He'd stepped out for lunch. He was on vacation. After the sixth day of creation, He took the seventh off, decided He didn't like the work, and went on welfare.

Great theological answers! Two dimes and a nickel would get you a quarter.

Evil: there was the stumper. Ever since Cro-Magnon Man first sought relief fondling his chubby, little female fertility statues, humanity had asked, *why?* If God is good, then why is there evil? Why do the bad guys live forever and the good die young? Why suffering, why pain, why sin?

The priests had a standard answer: "God is good! God loves you!" That said nothing, of course: a cop-out! If you kept asking, they told you it was all a mystery, part of the Great Incomprehensible Plan. If you pestered them, they said that evil was only a test—or that evil existed so God could display His wondrous compassion, so that He could forgive you after you'd spent a lifetime suffering for something that wasn't your fault in the first place. So babies could be napalmed in Damascus while killers, rapists, drug-peddlers, slum landlords, embezzlers, crooked lawyers, sleazy evangelists, and politicians could lead sumptuous lives, retire to California, and buy their mistresses pink sports cars on Rodeo Drive.

Long ago Lessing had decided that if evil is part of the Plan, then God was one lousy planner! Predestination implies that God wants it this way; free will says that whatever God wants, He gives us imperfect little creatures a chance to screw it up. Either way it stank: God was either the most inept designer since the dink who built the walls of Jericho, or else He had a very un-funny sense of humor! Six days to make the world—a primitive creation myth that wasn't even as good as some the American Indians had! Evolution: what a laborious and inefficient way for an omnipotent Deity to produce the species He presumably wanted. Original sin? What a crock!

Send His only son down to take humanity's sins upon himself? Come on! For a Supreme Being, all of those were dumb ideas. It was Lessing's considered opinion that a squad of drunken orangutans could've dreamed up a better fairy tale.

Now the world lay dying. Invisible, miasmic death stalked those who lived, and poor, old God was in heavy demand. The churches were packed, the synagogues overflowing, the mosques and temples all red hot and throbbing. The God business throve on death.

The greatest catastrophe since the dinosaurs, and God didn't do a thing about it. No miracles, no "only Son," no tear-jerking, happy endings at Christmastime.

Was God Himself "evil"—by human definition anyhow?

Whenever Lessing had asked such questions, his parents, his teachers, his mother's holier-than-Jesus ministers—the whole Bible-beating lot—had chorused that he was too immature, too sophomoric, too simplistic, too uneducated, too sceptical, too some-goddamned-thing—to understand.

The holy books of other religions had not helped, nor had the philosophers. They were easily refuted: they reeked of anthropomorphism, clever words but no answers. People believed because they needed a crutch—which wasn't a new observation, certainly, but it struck Lessing as a lot truer than the stuff the theologians dished out.

Like the man said, two dimes and a nickel got you a quarter—but not a cup of coffee anymore. That cost a dollar and sixty cents now.

The med-van braked to a stop. The sun had come out, and the stone facades of the buildings lining the street glowed honey-gold, maroon, and rose-red in the weak December light. The trees were stark and bare, but bundles of what looked like dried leaves lay tumbled along the parking strip and in the gutters. Lessing knew what they were: bodies of men, women, and children; even a few pets, squirrels, and birds.

The two paramedics who had been riding in the rear of their van opened the door and climbed gingerly down to the littered paving. The captain, the driver, Lessing, and Wrench joined them. A black-and-white sign on the lawn said: U.S. Department of Defense, Restricted Entry.

"This it?" Wrench unlimbered a 40-mm, six-shot grenade launcher from their vehicle's ready-rack. "Don't worry. I know how to use this."

"Yes . . . ." The captain looked doubtful. "You really don't need that thing." In his view only another Marine—preferably somebody from his own unit—was qualified to handle such a weapon.

"Let him keep it," Lessing urged. Even if Wrench didn't know a grenade from a horseapple, the sight of the big launcher would

scare the shorts off most looters. The thing weighed fifteen pounds
and looked like a tommygun for giants.

They entered through a double set of glass doors and found
themselves in the sort of artsy-craftsy, impersonal foyer popular
with American "institutional" architects. Slender, glass pillars
soared up to narrow, slitted skylights near the top of a pyramidal
reception hall. From the apex of the pyramid a mirrored mobile hung
down to spatter the blank, white walls with prismatic light. The
effect was dizzying: disco-night at the Starlight Ballroom!

The black naugahide desks and chairs were empty, the potted
plants just beginning to wilt for lack of water. The lights worked—
every installation of any importance had its own emergency generator—and if it had not been for the ringing silence and the emptiness
it might have been just another Washington workday.

Two startled soldiers leaped up from behind the semicircular
reception counter. They wore N.B.C. suits, but their helmets lay on
the counter beside them. They had been sorting loot stripped from
corpses: diamond rings, watches, a heap of money—the trivia of a
world that was as dead as the Pharaohs.

The Marine captain strode forward, ignoring the bric-a-brac.
"You!" he barked. "Unit? Authorization?"

One of the men, a gaunt Black youth, saluted and stammered a
soft reply that Lessing could not hear.

The captain looked puzzled. "Golden? Major Golden? Who the
fuck is he?"

The second soldier held out a piece of paper. "Uh . . . our orders,
sir."

The captain waggled a finger at the two paramedics. "Get back
to the van, contact base, tell 'em we're here and we've got a 760.
Go! Then stay out there. Watch for survivors, but don't get too far
from us."

A "760" was militarese for a command screw-up: like when your
artillery drops shit all over your own troops. Lessing's combat
senses had just gone on yellow alert. He unobtrusively fished for his
pistol in the voluminous front pocket of his N.B.C. suit. They hadn't
issued him a holster, and drawing the weapon later might be
awkward.

From the corner of his eye he saw that Wrench had sidled around
to cover him and the captain from the flank. He couldn't see their
driver; the man must still be behind them.

"No problem, corporal," the captain said smoothly. "Here's my
clearance. These two come along. Private Harris . . . my driver . . .
will stay with you. Oh, and get your fuckin' helmets back on before
I personally kick your asses up your backbones and out your
shit-sniffin' noses! You *know* that's a breach of orders!"

Only when they were out of earshot of the two soldiers and into the hallway beyond did the captain beckon to Lessing. "It beats me. A Major James L. Golden from the Army Training and Doctrine Command at Fort Monroe? That's in Virginia, but it's a ways away, given the situation. From Fort Myer or Fort Belvoir I could understand. And training and doctrine? What the hell?"

Lessing gave a none-of-my-business grunt. He glanced over and saw that Wrench was missing nothing.

They encountered only one body: a woman in her fifties, a bottle of what looked like cough syrup beside her. The codeine in the stuff had not helped, judging by the agony on her face.

"Elevators," the captain muttered. He withdrew a sheet of yellow paper from a belt pouch. Lessing edged over and saw that it contained a building plan and several rows of numerals: coded passwords.

The other put the document away. "Sorry. Security."

"I understand. We going in, or do we wait for a backup?"

"No reason to wait. Major Golden, whoever the hell he is, can't interfere with us. After all, we've got President Outram's direct order to inspect and secure. The rest of our team'll be here just as soon as we can get them together."

"How long?"

"A few hours. Some personnel are dead, many missing, others scattered all around. We've got people out hunting for them."

The corridor ended at a bank of elevators. The captain selected one, scanned his yellow flimsy, pressed an unmarked button, and was rewarded by a short, stomach-flipping descent. The shiny, steel doors hissed back to reveal a security checkpoint: a guard cubicle encased in bulletproof glass, a retinal scanner, an ID-card reader, and apertures in the walls and ceiling that hinted at other, less friendly defenses. Lessing was reminded of Marvelous Gap, but this was bigger, fancier, and deadlier. It was also probably armed and active.

The door to the guard cubicle was ajar. The captain entered but backed out again. "Body in there," he remarked, "and the retinal scanner's been disconnected by somebody who knows how. Light shows the airlock to the control center is open."

"Airlock?" Wrench piped up.

"Yes. This complex is constructed of layers of steel, plastic, and a special concrete. The whole thing sits on springs in an oil bath, and a gyroscope holds it level against anything short of a direct missile strike. You could drop the moon on New York, and this place'd hardly jiggle."

"This Major Golden . . . he's inside, then?" Lessing wanted to know.

"Guess so. But don't sweat it. He may have a right to be down here. After all, a lot of people still don't know Outram's alive and legally in charge. Golden may've been sent by the Joint Chiefs, the Secretary of Defense, or some other agency."

Beyond the airlock they traversed a tunnel three meters long, walled with flexible plastic and ending in a second security door. The latter was also open, and they passed through into a round chamber some thirty meters in diameter and ten meters high. The center of this room was occupied by a two-tier, circular dais about ten meters across. Four short staircases led up from the main floor to rows of grey, crackle-finish consoles on the lower level of the dais. Two more sets of steps then ascended another meter or two to the top level, a bare platform three meters wide. This was surrounded by a metal railing and contained two black-plastic-upholstered chairs and what resembled a speaker's lectern. Lights, lenses, microphones, and cables swung down out of the shadows overhead like robot spiderwebs.

More desks, consoles, and metal cabinets crowded the main floor, and huge, dark screens glimmered all around the walls. Computers certainly had changed since Lessing had played Planet-Zapper in high school!

There was no one in the room.

The captain called, "Major Golden? Major Golden? Hey! Anybody here?"

"Two doors on the other side of the platform." Lessing pointed.

"Access to the works." The captain sucked in air from his suit tanks and licked his lips. "Storage. The broom closet."

Wrench slipped past to prowl between the silent rows of desks and cabinets. They let him go; he knew more than they did about the great machine that slumbered here.

No corpses. No water, standing or running. The air ought to be good. What the hell? Lessing pulled off his helmet. The captain gave him a quizzical look but did the same, then went over and climbed up onto the top dais. Lessing stayed where he was, automatic in hand. He sensed others here, others who either could not or would not answer.

The captain stood spraddle-legged in the middle of the upper platform, extracted his yellow paper, looked self-consciously up at the microphones above his head, and began to recite numbers.

The effect was magical: a green light sprang to life here, an amber blinker there. A bank of screens bloomed with lambent colors on one wall, a graph and columns of ever-changing read-outs glowed on another.

Wrench exclaimed, "Hey, Lessing, come here! I've got the internal TV working! Oh, man, look . . . !" He broke off.

Something was wrong. Lessing reached him in three long strides. Wrench was staring at a single, large screen which was segmented into forty or fifty smaller pictures. Most of these showed empty offices, rooms, and passages. A few contained corpses. In one frame smoke eddied up toward the ceiling, and Lessing recognized the reception area: the two soldiers and their driver were sharing a comradely toke of pot.

Wrench pointed. One of the lower frames pictured five uniformed soldiers. All had their backs to the camera as they peered through a door: one crouching in front, the rest poised behind him. All bore U.S. Army M-25 assault rifles. The kneeling man aimed his weapon at a distant figure on a dais in the large, lighted room beyond the door.

"Get down!" Lessing yelled. "Captain . . . ."

They heard the rifle shot twice: once, tinnily, from the TV speakers in front of them, and then instantly again from the leftmost doorway on the other side of the central platform. It echoed on around the room. The captain whirled, seemed to teeter on invisible roller skates, then crashed down on top of one of the dais's two chairs.

"Shit!" shrilled Wrench. He hit the floor between two consoles just ahead of a stitch-line of bullet holes. Lessing was even faster. Over their heads the damaged consoles fizzed and sparked.

Lessing began to crawl along an aisle toward the dais. "Get where you can put a grenade through that open door!" He raised his head and risked a look over one of the metal desks.

The captain stirred, rolled, and slid off the top platform onto a desk on the lower tier. It collapsed with a crash, and the unseen sniper let off a whole magazine out of sheer jitters. He hit no one.

Wrench fired at the doorway. His grenade hit the adjoining wall, ricocheted, and exploded with ear-shattering effect under one of the computer consoles. There were cries from the opfoes, and Wrench shrieked an obscenity back. Another flurry of shots ripped metal, glass, and wall-board to shreds above him. Lessing heard the little man scuttling away under the desks.

They were outgunned unless Wrench got lucky. What had he loaded his launcher with? High explosive, armour-piercing, tear gas, or smoke grenades? Their military med-van had been supplied with a variety of munitions. Right now they needed smoke for a quick retreat.

Someone on the other side of the room was screaming. Wrench's grenade had taken at least one man out of the fire-fight. The yelling stopped abruptly. Either the opfo had passed out or else his friends had popped him with a needle of narcodine.

Lessing found the captain still breathing, but blood bubbled from his lips and nose, and the front of his N.B.C. suit was a mess. He gestured weakly at the yellow sheet, now smeared with red.

"These . . . three . . . numbers." He gulped, swallowed, and struggled with the words. "Say them. Aloud. Get help . . . computer has . . . radio link." Experience told Lessing that the man was going into shock. He might still have a chance if they got him to a hospital right away.

Lessing held the paper up to the light. He half rose, made sure he was out of the line of fire, and shouted out the captain's three five-digit numbers, one numeral at a time. There were more numbers on the other side of the paper; the one at the bottom was in a black-pencilled box of its own, a box marked "Top Secret" and "Terminal Emergency Only." Things weren't quite that bad yet. Lessing tore the paper in two and stuffed the bottom half into his suit's pocket. It wouldn't do for the opfoes to get that number! Maybe Wrench could make something of it all.

There wasn't time to do more with the computer. Lessing heard the enemy spreading out into the main room, moving to encircle them. They knew the captain's party had started with three; now there were two.

The opfoes had lost track of Lessing, however. Ten meters away he saw a soldier in a pale-green N.B.C. suit emerge from beneath a work table. The man was facing the other way, seeking Wrench. Lessing steadied his gun barrel against a desk leg and fired. The man bleated, jerked, and went limp.

A voice called, "Hey, Leopold? Leopold, you okay?"

Leopold wasn't going to answer. Lessing crawled away from the captain, toward the doorway from which the opfoes had launched their ambush. He wasn't expected there, and with luck he'd get behind them.

A deeper, more authoritative voice yelled, "Hey, you two! Give up! Get the fuck out of this building and you can loot all you want! We won't stop you."

"We're official," Lessing called back. "We have President Outram's personal order to secure this installation!"

"*Who?*"

"Jonas Outram . . . Speaker of the House! He's President now that President Rubin and the Vice-President are dead." He waited.

"We didn't know. Come on out and talk. We're sorry about the misunderstanding. Let's get our wounded to the medics."

Misunderstanding? Lessing did not think so. The other party had seen them come in and had set an ambush. Moreover, the captain had worn a military-issue N.B.C. suit; looters did not.

Lessing needed a sure test. He cast around and spotted what he wanted, a cylindrical wastebasket of green-marbled plastic. He humped himself along the floor to it. Holding it gingerly, he thrust it up above the desk. It was the oldest trick in the world.

The basket flew from his fingers in a spray of bullets.

So that was how they wanted it. The man who had fired was on his feet, looking to see if he had scored. Lessing rolled and came up from a new position three meters away. He let off several rounds but missed. The opfo dove for cover behind a filing cabinet just as Wrench lobbed a grenade into the area. The explosion sent bits of glass and shrapnel in all directions, and Lessing felt a sting across his right calf. A minor zip—he hoped.

A thin squealing, like the mewling of a kitten, came from where the opfo had been. Lessing had heard badly wounded men utter such sounds before.

"You started with five!" he shouted. "How many you got now?"

The answer came in another racket of bullets along the desk tops above him. He fired again, then hunkered down and checked his weapon; time to reload. As he dug into his suit's big pockets and thrust ammunition into his pistol's magazine, a green-clad rump backed out from under a work table five meters away. The man had only to turn his head to see Lessing. The magazine didn't want to go back into the gun; it resisted like a demon—and he knew it would click loudly when the catch caught. He felt his bowels loosen. The man turned his head.

It was Wrench.

"Jesus . . . !" If Lessing's gun had been ready, he would have fired. He hadn't expected Wrench this far to his left. Luck alone had saved the little man from a 9-mm butt-reaming.

Wrench grinned and got to his feet, apparently planning to make a dash over to join Lessing.

Three meters beyond Wrench, a soldier lurched up from behind a desk. He and Wrench whirled and saw one another simultaneously. Both yelled, jigged, ducked, and fired wildly all at once. Two of Wrench's grenades missed and ploughed ragged holes in the far wall.

The third grenade caught the man squarely in the face. His swarthy features vanished in a gout of blood.

There was no time to react, no way to brace for the shock. In a single, kaleidoscopic vision, Lessing foresaw what a high explosive grenade would do: it would rip both Wrench and his opponent to shreds; then it would pour a rain of shrapnel into Lessing himself. They were all dead meat.

He heard only a polite popping sound. Acrid white vapor gushed out of the opfo's shattered face.

Smoke!

Wrench had loaded his launcher with at least one smoke grenade! Thank God for inexperience!

The man's arms windmilled, and he crashed over backwards, his head ludicrously concealed in a roiling cloud.

"Smoking's bad for your health!" Wrench giggled. He stood up with exaggerated care and examined himself.

Another shot rang out. Wrench made a moaning noise and bent over. The enemy's shot had struck home. Lessing saw scarlet on the upper left shoulder of his N.B.C. suit.

Belatedly Lessing remembered the fifth man, presumably Major Golden himself. Another slug whined off a speaker cabinet nearby. The major was no sharpshooter; a better marksman could have put two more bullets into Wrench even as he slid to the floor.

Lessing spider-walked over to his companion. He found Wrench conscious, blinking dazedly at the bloodstain spreading down over his biceps. He was in no immediate danger. Lessing spared him a consoling grimace, scooped up the grenade launcher, and scrambled on, keeping a row of desks between himself and his adversary's position. The two parties had now exchanged places: Wrench and Lessing were close to the opfoes' original door, while Major Golden—if it was he—was over near the exit leading out to the elevators.

Lessing inspected the launcher. It held only one more round: a red-tipped high explosive grenade. He waggled the weapon and raised his eyebrows. Wrench shook his head: he hadn't brought any extra ammo. Lessing glanced at the opfo's body, now wreathed in smoke. The man's assault rifle lay within reach, and he grabbed it.

"Hey, Golden, whoever you are!" Lessing called. "You ready? Only one of you now. Two of us. We've got grenades, and we've got those crummy M-25's your men won't be using anymore. Last chance to kiss and make up. Toss your ordinance out onto the platform."

He didn't expect a reply. The way these people behaved indicated they were playing for all the chips. If Golden were stupid enough to answer, he'd give away his location. Lessing would then lob the last grenade up into the ceiling right over his head, showering him with concrete and shrapnel; then he himself would instantly follow, blazing away like gangbusters.

Another half-magazine of bullets howled through the line of cabinets and consoles to Lessing's right. He made himself flat and very small beneath his desk. Slugs hummed and sang overhead, but nothing hit him.

The firing cut off in mid-burst. Lessing heard a muffled curse. The man's M-25 had jammed! The American assault rifle was a fine weapon, but at a thousand rounds per minute on full auto, it gobbled ammo like a beast, and it also tended to jam. A good shooter needed only moments to clear the chamber and resume firing, but Golden was not that skilled.

Lessing wondered whether to rush him. The man probably still had a pistol, maybe one of his fallen comrades' guns as well. Footsteps clattered, slapping away toward the far wall. He glimpsed a figure plunging into the airlock tunnel. Apparently the major lacked the stomach for a one-on-one duel. Lessing decided not to fire his last grenade after the fleeing target; he might need it later. They weren't out of the soup yet. Golden had more doggies upstairs.

What had happened to their own driver and to the two paramedics outside? Had Golden's men thumbed them, or were they still doing fun-smoke, like a bunch of Bangers at a boom-concert?

He returned to take stock. The captain was now unconscious, barely clinging to life. Wrench had discovered a first-aid kit in a pocket of his N.B.C. suit and was trying to wrestle it out with one hand.

Lessing knelt beside him. "Busted you much?"

"Just a little fungled, that's all," Wrench answered grimly, also in the argot of the merc battalions. "Gimme a jack-up, eh?"

Lessing helped him out of his suit and saw that the bullet had grazed a rib and passed completely through the flesh below his left armpit. A couple of inches to the right, and Wrench would have been a memory. Lessing set to work with the kit's antibiotics and bandages. Every merc learned "basic health care" as a matter of course.

"We've still got our job to do," Wrench grated. "In my wallet— on the back of a bar-bill from the Pixie Club—three phone numbers with girls' names beside them." The pain was starting to bother him; it would be worse later. "I can't reach it."

"Stay still."

"It's important. They aren't phone numbers. Mulder gave 'em to me that way to keep 'em safe. They're activation codes, like those the captain had. Get 'em out and read the first five digits of each one aloud. The last two digits don't count."

"Here's your wallet. But you do it. I'm no good with computers."

"It's got to be you. The captain read the first series; anybody can do that. Then you put in the 'open and awake' codes. They identify you as the 'prime operator.' 'Final full-awake status' requires your voice . . . yours alone now."

"It . . . Eighty-Five . . . recognizes voices?"

"Yes. If anybody else but you does it, warning circuits trip and the machine freezes up until it gets additional security codes. And those we don't have."

Lessing licked his lips. "God damn it, we don't have time for this! Golden and his doggies may be back at any moment."

"Do it. It takes only a few seconds. Then we're in. I've got another list of crucial files, some to look at and some to block off so that nobody else can get at 'em. Once you're boss you can tell the machine to recognize me as 'secondary operator' . . . that was what I was going to try to get the captain to do before he got unzipped. I'll finish up our job and have the computer call for help while you deal with Golden."

Wonderful: just Alan Lessing against three and possibly more well-armed soldiers! He nodded reluctantly, took the crumpled bar-bill—what a stupid idea for hiding a code!—and read as directed.

Something hummed and clicked. Then a woman's voice asked, "Dr. Christy? Is that you?"

"Tell it no," Wrench whispered. "Christy was our agent. He's probably dead some place. Tell it you're his replacement. Then re-read the last five-digit number."

"Dr. Christy?" the voice repeated in a throaty contralto. "I cannot hear you clearly."

Lessing obeyed.

This time the voice was still female, but it sounded crisper and more businesslike. "Replacement: prime operative. State identity and security clearance."

"Tell it who you are!" Wrench struggled up to stand beside Lessing.

"Uh . . . Lessing . . . Alan Lessing." He leaned down to Wrench. "What do I give it for a security clearance? You got one of those, too?"

Wrench thought. "You've got Outram's letter, haven't you? The one to Washington Central Command telling them we're to inspect and secure this facility? Eighty-Five's got camera eyes. Show it the White House stationery."

It struck Lessing as a very long shot. He held up the letter, and a camera boom swooped down out of the darkness overhead to peer and explode a tiny flashbulb like a miniature star.

Silence, except for a faint humming.

Then the voice said, "Lessing, Alan, no middle initial. Born March 27, 2010, Sioux City, Iowa. Parents: Gerald Nathaniel Lessing and Frieda Runge Lessing."

Further personal data followed: his Social Security number, tax data, school records, a grade-sheet from the one miserable year he spent in college, credit ratings, bank accounts—much more. That the machine had this kind of dossier on anybody was amazing; that it held such details about a nonentity like Alan Lessing was frightening. The most astonishing thing was the succession of high school annual pictures and old army I.D. photos that flickered to life on one of the wall screens.

"Accepted," the machine proclaimed smugly. "Welcome, Doctor Lessing."

"Uh . . . I'm not a doctor."

"Preferred form of address?"

"Mister is fine."

"Very well, mister. Is this voice satisfactory?"

"What?"

"Dr. Christy liked this voice; it is identical with that of Melissa Willoughby, the film star. Professor Archibald preferred a male voice . . ." the timbre shifted down an octave ". . . like this. Very professional, he felt." The machine hesitated, then said, "When Dr. Meaker worked here alone, he had me speak in the voice of his son, Robert, who had been killed in an automobile accident." The voice rose to a childish falsetto. "If Daddy wants me to talk this way, then I will."

Lessing and Wrench exchanged glances. Poor Meaker's loneliness and grief swooped up around them like the walls of the grave.

"No . . . no. The film star is just fine. Use her voice."

"All right, mister." Lessing could now identify the sultry, sensuous, Hollywood-sexy undertones. "I have a request, though."

"Yes?"

"Please move to my input room. I have a secondary console there. Your present location is severely impaired. I detect damage here to the extent of approximately $783,592.14, preliminary, since some components will require human testing and repair. Please provide a budget number to which I may charge necessary refitting."

"Later," Lessing replied. This was getting out of hand. What the hell was Golden doing? Instantly he realized how he could find out: "Can you show me the upstairs reception area? The elevator cars' interiors? The sidewalk in front of this building?"

"Certainly. I must employ an auxiliary screen, though, since my viewing circuits are damaged here. Follow the blinking yellow light to my input room."

Bemused, Lessing did so, Wrench trailing behind. They passed through one of the doors out of the main room, along a cabinet-lined corridor, and into a smaller, octagonal chamber. The solid-steel lab tables were crammed with equipment: automatic reading devices for books, films, tapes, cassettes, records, discs, microfilms, and other media; more consoles, screens, and panels; cameras, microphones, and other apparatus; laser, ultra-violet, and infrared sensors, and paraphernalia from a dozen unfinished experiments.

A single body, almost mummified, lay curled in one corner: a female lab technician. What did Eighty-Five "think" of the corpses that littered the installation? How did it perceive Golden's slain soldiers? The captain?

Lessing asked.

"Inert humans? They are inanimate objects, are they not? Like things you term 'furniture' and 'equipment'?"

As logical a view of death as any. Eighty-Five was certainly no Born-Again, no karma-wala Banger! Lessing returned to their present predicament. "The upper rooms," he demanded. "Show us any rooms and areas in which you sense active humans now."

"Good thought!" Wrench approved.

Two small screens burst into light and color. The first showed the street. Ten or twelve men in N.B.C. suits were unloading ominous-looking objects from a halftrack. They weren't friendlies: a short, squat-bodied individual stood beside the vehicle. His features and insignia were concealed by his suit, but Lessing knew it must be Golden.

The second screen displayed an office somewhere in the upper section of the facility, to judge by the furnishings and the thin sunlight slanting in through one window. Golden's two original doggies leaned against the door, guarding the captain's driver and the two paramedics. The captives appeared more bewildered than frightened—a good sign under the circumstances.

"Defenses?" Lessing asked the computer. "Against intruders?"

"I have no control over the security devices in this installation. My creators were very careful about that." Was the machine capable of irony? "After all, both they and I have seen every 'mad-computer-takes-over-the-universe' movie ever made." Lessing wondered if he really did hear a hint of a chuckle.

"Can you lock the doors and radio Washington Central Command for help?" Wrench asked.

"Who is this person, mister? I have no record of his identity or clearance status."

They had forgotten to identify Wrench as a secondary operator. Lessing wasted thirty valuable seconds doing so.

"I can shut doors within my building," Eighty-Five replied, "but a human with keys and codes can open them."

Lessing had no idea what to do next. At length he said, "Look over your capabilities and do what you can to stop the men who are entering now. They . . . ah . . . have no clearance. They are intruders, do you understand?"

The silence lasted so long that Lessing almost expected to see one of those cutesie "Your Computer Is Thinking!" signs appear on a wall screen.

The machine said, "Seven are descending in elevator car two. Four more are entering car one." The darkly sexy voice sounded apologetic. "I've radioed out. Your people are on their way."

"Much good . . . ." Wrench mumbled. His arm was paining him, and he slumped down on a lab stool.

"I'm going through my Library of Congress science holdings now. I find nothing of use in any of my own specifications. No weapons under my control. I can turn off the lights and heat, but I doubt whether the intruders would suffer sufficiently from that to cause them to desist."

Lessing had what he hoped was an inspiration. "You used an electronic flash!" he said. "A lot of those coming from different angles might confuse Golden's men. Throw them off balance . . . give us a chance!"

There was another long pause. Then the throaty contralto voice said, "You're *sure* these are intruders? Enemies of the United States of America?"

"Yes," Wrench replied. Under the circumstances, who knew?

"There is one thing I can do. I'm not supposed to, though. They tried to build defensive responses out of me."

"Then how . . . ?"

"Problem solving is my specialty." The machine hesitated again. "Close the door to my input room."

Lessing inspected the metal and plastic door uneasily. "I doubt if this'll hold out against a satchel charge or a grenade."

"It is soundproof. Stay in here and shut it. I will inform you if I am successful. Otherwise I will utilize my flash equipment as you suggest. More, I will shout and cry in several voices from many different locations at once. The anti-Americans will be puzzled."

"Best we can do." Wrench lurched over to slam the door. As he did so, they heard the whine and clang of the first elevator car arriving.

"What now?" Lessing was still apprehensive. Golden might be able to cut off their air, smoke them out, or stun them with a concussion grenade.

"Watch the lower screen, please, mister."

The glass lit up to show three very nervous soldiers, M-25s at the ready. Four more entered the devastated, smoke-filled control room behind them. Then Golden appeared, followed by three doggies.

"Turn up the sound," Lessing ordered. "I want to hear what they're saying."

"No," answered Eighty-Five succinctly.

"Why not? You . . . ."

"I think I know what it's doing," Wrench whispered. His eyes glittered in the harsh light from the screen, giving him the luminous look of some small, feral animal. "Watch, man! Watch!"

One of the soldiers glanced up, then another and another. They opened their eyes and their mouths wide. The man in front tore at his helmet, got it off, and clapped his hands over his ears. One after another the rest did the same. Golden bolted for the door. The others began to writhe, twist, and clutch at their heads.

"Sound, Lessing, sound!" Wrench yelped joyously. "It's hitting them with subsonics!"

"Actually a combination of registers," the sweetly sensuous voice purred. "Research studies in my data banks report that your species can be incapacitated and even deactivated by certain sounds. I have no weapons, but I can produce sounds at whatever decibel level is required, plus subsonics and supersonics."

"They're down!" Lessing exclaimed. "Shut it off! For God's sake, shut it off!" Some ancient, inchoate, ethical principle cried out against this: a man killed another man face to face, not by hiding in a hole and letting a coldly lethal, amoral machine do his murdering for him! Now he knew how the guys felt who sat in front of the red buttons in the atomic missile silos.

"My sensors report that one intruder has left the building. All of those remaining in the building are unconscious. Three have ceased functioning entirely; the rest will become irreparable within twelve, eleven, ten . . . ."

"Stop it, God damn it!"

Wrench tugged at Lessing's sleeve. "Jesus, look! It's taken out the guys upstairs too . . . our driver, our paramedics!" "Stop! Stop!" Lessing yelled. "Those there . . . on the upper screen . . . they aren't all intruders!"

"Oh? Sorry. You didn't tell me. Perhaps some can be repaired. You call it 'healed,' I believe?"

Movement had ceased on both screens. The camera angle prevented a clear view of burst eyeballs, bloody ears and mouths, and contorted, anguished limbs.

"I have turned off the sound now. It is safe for you to emerge." Wrench wiped sweat from his forehead. His face was a pallid deathmask. Using his good hand, he fished in a pocket and extracted what looked like a scuffed bankbook. "We . . . uh . . . we've still got work to do. I . . . I have some numbers here . . . files we have to deal with."

"Certainly. But please remember to arrange for repairs to my facilities. The sound I just used has resulted in severe damage to glass and plastic components in several areas. I deduce a repair cost of $983,567.76. Did Congress vote a good budget for my project this year?"

Talk about obsolete behavior! Lessing paused, then said, "Congress is . . . no longer in session."

"Too bad. Several runs may be delayed. Dr. Meaker will be angry."

Lessing's calm had returned. "How much do you know about what's happening across America . . . in the world?"

"Materials are regularly fed into my terminals: newspapers, books, magazines, digests, position papers, films, TV broadcasts . . . much else. Unfortunately many interruptions have occurred lately. My Chicago terminal has ceased operation, and my Denver data storage facilities respond inaccurately. Please report and remedy these defects."

"You know about Pacov? Starak?" Wrench inquired. "Somebody is using biological warfare to destroy nations . . . regions . . . the world!"

"I have files on these subjects."

"Who's doing it?" Lessing rapped. "Who's killing the human race?"

"I possess a few names of individual perpetrators. These were given to me by various police and Federal agencies, but data input has recently been disrupted, as I have said. My response will therefore be incomplete."

"Who is behind . . . who authorized . . . God damn it, who *ordered* Starak and Pacov?"

"I have no definite information."

"Extrapolate, damn you!" Lessing clenched both fists upon the lab table before him.

"Given an error margin of 11.9%, the spread of Starak and related agents appears to be due to surviving operatives of the government of the Soviet Union, probably from one or more bases in Central and South America."

"Fine! Any kid could've told us that!"

"To which child do you refer, mister?"

"Cancel. New question," Wrench said. "Pacov. Who spread Pacov?"

The machine pondered. Then it said, "Insufficient data."

Lessing's fist crashed down upon the table, bouncing bits of apparatus and rattling cups still half full of cold, scummy coffee.

"Hey, hey!" Wrench put his good hand on Lessing's arm.

"I cannot make statements without data." Eighty-Five sounded miffed. "I am unable to say what is occurring in Russia, England, China, and other nations, since my operatives there no longer provide input. I require a new census and other demographic information. Many human units seem to have ceased operation or have become misplaced. I am only as complete as my operatives make me. Give me the data, and I will correlate, extrapolate, deduce, induce, compute . . . whatever you wish."

Lessing had had enough. "Come on, damn it!" he snarled at Wrench. "Let get the hell out of here!"

"Keep your socks on! We've got work to do, and now's the best chance we'll ever have! It'll take a minimum of half an hour for reinforcements to get to us. We ought to be done by then. We've got a world to rebuild!"

"Oh, yes," Eighty-Five said cheerily. "That sounds nice. Let's do that!"

If we divide mankind into three categories—founders of culture, bearers of culture, and destroyers of culture—the Aryan alone can be seen as representing the first category. It was he who laid the groundwork and erected the walls of every great structure in human culture. Only the shape and color of such structures are to be attributed to the individual characteristics of the various nations. It is the Aryan who has furnished the great building-stones and the plans for the edifices of human progress; only the way in which these plans have been executed is to be attributed to the qualities of each individual race.

—*Mein Kampf*, Adolf Hitler

CHAPTER FIFTEEN

Sunday, April 12, 2043

66And why *not* hold our first American Party Congress here next week?" Jennifer Caw stuck out her truculent chin still farther.

"Attracts attention," Liese argued patiently. "Here in America? On April twentieth . . . the First *Führer*'s birthday? Noticed!"

"Good!" Bill Goddard yawned hugely into his breakfast plate. It had once held a dozen hotcakes; now it resembled the floor of a hyena cage.

"We're part of Outram's big national think-out here in New Orleans: what to do about Starak, Pacov, and the rest. If we quietly hold a side meeting of our own Party at the same time, nobody'll pay any attention. We need to talk to our American leadership . . . plus anybody else who's inclined our way." Jennifer wadded up her napkin inexorably, as though disposing of both the subject and any benighted dissenters. "We don't need to say a word about our origins . . . our heritage. Who'll care? The world's got bigger problems."

"Yes, but . . . ."

"But what, dammit? Sure, the Jews would panic if we went around draped in swastikas, but as far as the world knows the Party of Humankind is just one more conservative organization among many, all under Outram's conservative, ultra-patriotic, America-forever banner. He's playing host to them all . . . even some right-of-center Jewish groups. So long as nobody yells 'Nazi!' we're all 'grass green,' as the Bangers say. And we're focusing on stuff everybody wants. Look who-all's here: people from the old fuddy-duddy political parties, Catholics, Protestants, Born-Agains, Bangers, businessmen, students, farmers, good ole boys, Whites, Blacks, Jews, Chicanos, Arabs . . . anybody from anywhere . . . all billing and cooing together over in the Convention Center like . . . like . . . ."

"Turkey doves?" Wrench supplied with malicious helpfulness.

"I wish we could have our convention in a friendlier city," Goddard grumbled unhappily. "New Orleans is too racially mixed, too goddamned 'liberal.'" With him, "liberal" was a bleep-word.

Liese made a sarcastic face at him across the pink plastic table. "Friendly like you? Scare people away!" She sat curled beside Lessing in the farthest corner of the coffee-shop booth. "Popular support? Not your way!"

Goddard's broad nostrils flared, his eyes blazed, and he opened his mouth to reply.

"Shush," Jennifer laid scarlet-tipped fingers on his wrist. "You know what we're doing and why. Our immediate goals are to stop Pacov and Starak, end the half-war in Europe, and put civilization back together. We get in on the ground floor. No more exile out in the Third World where we can't influence the mainstream. We do exactly what the First *Führer* did: organize, build a power base, appeal to other groups with similar views, even though they may not be identical, and work like hell! Later, if we do get anywhere, we can worry about restructuring society. Now we push for traditional, positive, American values: peace, prosperity, strength, enterprise, reconstruction, and moral and physical well-being."

"You quote your own speeches beautifully . . . or rather the speeches Liese writes for you." Goddard rumbled. "But you don't mention the thing that sets us off from all the others: the ending of racial integration and the moral and spiritual mongrelization that goes with it! We ought to say what we really want, and let the chips . . . and the weak sisters . . . fall where they may!"

Wrench rattled his fork. "Nobody's hiding anything. It's all in our literature. We're just not emphasizing some of our longer-range objectives in view of the present emergency." He sounded as though he were reading from one of Outram's interminable presidential memos. "Anyway, racial policy is only one of our planks. There're others, some just as important."

Goddard snorted. "You've been out in the 'Third World' too long . . . or just out in the sun! You don't know what it's like to hold our views and live here in the United States. I may not be a 'Descendant' like some of you, but I've seen it up close. We've got enemies, and they're not going to give up, go away, or let us be. My father was falsely accused, hunted down, and shot by some of the 'guardians of American liberties.' His friends were hounded by the Jewish-run press and the government's 'special interest' agencies. My mother 'broke the law' . . . the Anti-Defamation Amendment of 2005 . . . when she accused the Vigilantes for Zion of having my father killed, and I remember what they did to her and to my older brother. The way the media told it, we were like some kind of rabid monsters! Me, they just shoved into a school for brainwashing. Later I 'accidentally' got convicted of a burglary I didn't commit, and school turned into a prison cell . . . until Mr. Mulder's friends found me and got me out. I grew up hard. *Real* hard."

"So did I," Wrench stated flatly. He almost never talked about himself. They waited, but the little man only licked his lips and stared down at his plate.

"I've said my piece," Goddard insisted. "We've got to take a tougher line; otherwise we'll end up where my dad did: on a slab in the morgue. The cops and the coroner stood around smirking and telling me and my mother that the holes in his body must've been made by moths! They 'lost' the charge-sheet . . . the whole dossier. We *have* to be tough."

"We go legitimate," Liese said. "Party's orders."

Goddard grunted and looked away. The coffee shop was full: military people, officials from a score of government agencies, a scattering of businessmen. There were no tourists; the cataclysm of Starak was still too fresh.

Jennifer saw Lessing and Liese watching her. She winked at them and let her nails stray along Goddard's bristle-thatched bare arm. To push the man any further would lead to a quarrel. Goddard gave her a possessive grin: Mr. Mucho Macho about to drag his prize off to his cave. Hans Borchardt wouldn't like that, but then he was over at the Convention Center orchestrating the morning's events.

Jennifer moved her hand away: mission accomplished. She said, "Already we've had people asking what we mean by the 'supremacy of the Western ethnos.' Yet you'd be surprised: after all the world's just been through, some meek, little liberal lambs find themselves very comfortable in our camp."

Wrench hated to let any argument drop without a final word. He rubbed at his wounded shoulder, now mostly healed, and pointed his fork across the table at Goddard. "You *linientreue* Old Guard! You march, you sing the *Horst Wessel Lied*, you wear sexy uniforms, and you attract so much crappy publicity you might as well be working for the opposition! You don't *convince* anybody! Your only members are the guys you started with . . . plus," he sang, "four FBI agents, three CIA operatives, two kikibirds . . . and an Israeli in a pear tree!" He waved his fork in time to the old Christmas carol.

"We *are* attracting members! And who cares about the rest?" Goddard snarled. "The First *Führer* had only contempt for 'silent workers' . . . guys who hung back, who didn't want to join, who were afraid to come forward and take their lumps with the rest. Those're the ones who pop up later bragging about how much they did for the Party during the 'time of struggle.'"

"Times change, and either we change too, or we go under. The First *Führer* would have recognized that."

"I like *linientreue* better. Fight me, beat me, stomp me, but at least you'll never forget my face. Any other way is to copy the Jews ... changed names, warm handshakes, country club smiles . . . ."

"Yeah, and look where they are."

Liese leaned over to whisper to Lessing, "*Linientreue* means 'true to the line' . . . keeping to the exact letter of the First *Führer*'s ideas."

"Like an old Muslim I knew who hated the taste of fat but always ate it anyway, because the Prophet Muhammad was supposed to have liked it. Blind obedience. Cling to every detail."

"Goddard follows *everything*. Big, little, important, minor. Loyal and brave, though."

"Yeah."

He didn't want to think about politics. Liese was very close, her fragrance compelling. He felt the tingle of contact against his arm and along his thigh. She had chosen a skirt and blouse of thin, sky-blue chiffon for the Congress' morning session, a statement even more dramatic than Jennifer Caw's pants suit of black Shantung silk and turquoise neckerchief. In the narrow confines of the booth, Lessing felt the slither of the fabric between Liese's body and his own.

He had to resist the temptation. Liese was frightened of contact that she herself did not initiate. She might see him as a threat, a violator, another abuser like her father, like the pimps and gang-rapists in New York, like the unspeakable creatures who had brutalized her in that Cairo brothel.

Liese said something, but Jennifer's voice was louder. "Look, Bill, we're following the strategy our forefathers set up nearly a century ago: get rich, organize, buy publicity, build good will, and eventually push society in directions we want it to go. Why don't you go with the flow? Right now we're hauling in new members hand over foot."

Goddard pursed his lips sarcastically. "Members, maybe, but not *believers*. *Everybody's* preaching peace, love, reconstruction, prosperity, and sanity: the good, sweet, syrupy stuff. The Party's on the same wavelength as the government, the churches, the United Nations . . . !"

"What's wrong with peace and love?" Jennifer's reasonableness was beginning to fray. "What would you do? Break the Anti-Defamation Amendment again? Holler for racial reforms? Get arrested for nothing?"

"Of course not! But home, mother, and germ-free apple pie are not *all* we want! Let's lay out our *total* program! Stand up for our beliefs!"

"Which beliefs?" Wrench interposed slyly. "Remember that there were splits within the Third *Reich* itself. It wasn't a monolith, you know. Even the leadership of the SS was divided into at least five cliques, each with its own interpretation of the First *Führer*'s ideals. It took all his charisma to hold 'em in check. We're going to have the same thing, and in spades, as we pick up new members."

"Fine. We'll listen to differences of opinion. Then we . . . the Party Committee . . . will decide which road to take. You try one idea, then another and another, until you get to one that suits."

"Not so easy," Wrench scoffed. "With two people you have a love affair, with three you get politics, with four you get factions; after that you fight."

"Damn it, belonging to the movement is like being born: either you're *in* or you're *out*! No matter how we differ about the details . . . even to fighting among ourselves . . . we still agree on our eventual goals! Come around to our thinking or go find another sandbox to play in. Does a Jewish rabbi preach the divinity of Jesus? Does the Pope go Banger and pound the drums for sex, sin, and syncopation?"

Lessing lumbered up to his feet, forcing Wrench out into the aisle to make way. Jennifer Caw threw him a look of gratitude.

"I should be getting over to the Congress," he told them. "I've got a security force of sixty half-trained kids from Ponape, one company of Louisiana National Guardsmen, and two squads of Marine MP's on loan from Outram . . . all to keep six thousand conference-walas from cutting each other's throats. Every one of 'em thinks all the rest are either heretics or boobs." He waved for his bill.

Liese rose to stand beside him. "Walk you?" She took her beige coat down from the rack beside the table. The sunlight transformed her spring dress into a sapphire cascade that rippled down over her thighs and calves.

Lessing pulled his gaze away. "Sure."

It was a longish walk from their hotel in the French Quarter down Canal Street to Front Street, and over to the Convention and Exhibition Center on the banks of the Mississippi River. It was exhilarating, nevertheless. The day was sunny, not too humid, and just over sixty-five degrees, a blessing after Lucknow and Ponape.

Nostalgia was tempting: oh, to be just an average guy out with his girl on a spring day, with nothing more to worry about than where to take her, how to please her, and when to make his moves! Lessing half closed his eyes and let the old city slip back in time: all normal, tourists in tee-shirts and tank-tops mingling with the dudes and the hustlers, strains of New Orleans jazz drifting along the narrow streets even at nine o'clock in the morning.

Fantasy! That world was gone. Innocence existed now only in fairy tales. Reality was all around them. Seedy, old New Orleans, seedier than ever, was crammed with refugees, soldiers, police, the displaced, the lost, and the confused: the nameless flotsam of a major disaster. The tee-shirts and tank-tops belonged to people who had no homes, whose loved ones were dead or missing, who had no jobs, no food, and no future. The dense traffic wasn't made up of rubbernecking tourists; these cars were full of shock-numbed refugees and hard-eyed military police. New Orleans reminded Lessing of Aleppo after the Israelis had occupied it: the universal face of tragedy.

A middle-aged couple came toward them, the man well-dressed and dignified but rumpled and dirty, unused to asking for aid. His wife hovered nervously behind him. Their story was everywhere: caught away from home by Starak with no place to go. The military had sealed off the poisoned cities, sent in shoot-on-sight patrols to discourage looters, and herded the "lucky" survivors into sprawling, chaotic camps. Liese spoke to the couple and pointed them around to the other side of the Convention Center, where the Party's soup kitchens were working around the clock side by side with the Red Cross and a half-dozen Louisiana charities.

Two uniformed teenagers, Lessing's pupils from Ponape, admitted them into the Center's security area. The hallway was dingy and stank of ammoniated floor-cleaner. A building that was upwards of ninety years old developed a personality all its own—and an odor to match.

"Mallon. Holm." Lessing greeted them. "Anything happening?"

The tall one, Wayne Mallon, gave him a military salute that was somewhere between the U.S. Army, the SS, and "Marlow Striker's Mercs" on TV. "No, sir. Mr. Morgan's speaking now. Then come Senator Watt of Georgia, Miss Howard of the Center for Communicable Diseases, Dr. Astel from the Tulane School of Medicine, Mr. Grant Simmons of the Congress of Americans for Personal Freedom . . . ."

"Mulder going to speak?" Lessing asked Liese.

"No. Low profile. Jennifer, Borchardt, local American leaders. Jennifer's best. Pretty. Dramatic. Exciting."

He made no comment. Liese didn't appear jealous of Jennifer Caw, but you never knew. He walked on, still talking to the two young guards. "Who's in security control?"

"Abner's watching the screens, sir," Timothy Holm called after him. "Lieutenant Bellman just left to pick up his Marines. Some ruckus in section twenty-two."

"Serious?"

"No, sir. People just worked up . . . ." The rest of Holm's reply was lost as they turned a corner. No guard stood at the security control-room door, an oversight somebody would have paid for if they weren't so short-handed. Abner Hand wasn't inside, either; probably gone with Bellman to see the fun.

Lessing marched straight to the bank of TV screens and found the one covering section twenty-two. It showed two helmeted Marines impassively listening to an angry, glittery-eyed young man in jeans and a cowboy hat. The youth was lecturing everybody within earshot on the perils of buying foreign imports. He seemed to have it in for the Japanese.

Lessing watched for a moment. The sight bothered him; he could not have explained why. "Look at that guy!" he began. "Single-minded, fanatic, crazy bastard!" Each word stirred up others, like waking sleeping bats in a cave.

Liese stared at him, puzzled.

"Fanatics! Without them, the world'd be a happier place!"

Liese cocked her head at him and smiled uncertainly. She made a slow circuit of the desks, typewriters, telecom machines, and locked equipment racks. Finally she came back to dump her coat onto a desk and perch upon a tatty, black-cushioned typist's chair. She smoothed her skirt over one silk-sheathed knee.

Her silence goaded him to say more. "It's true!" he expostulated. "Everybody's got an answer . . . *the* answer! Do like *I* say, and the world is roses! *I've* got the handle on politics, history, God, life, death, and the pursuit of happiness! *I'm* the one! Whether I'm President of the United States, the Pope of Rome, Herman Mulder, or Ignatz Schmerz . . . it's *me* who's right, and all you other jizmos are gubbing foozy!" He spat out the Banger obscenities as though they tasted bad.

"Ignatz Schmerz?" Liese raised a quizzical eyebrow.

"Yeah, the comic-strip character. You know, the little Yiddish mouse."

"Oh . . . . we . . . the Party . . . everybody . . . wants solutions to problems." She shut her eyes and tugged at a milky opal earring, unsure of what was bothering him. "Find what works and tell people. Get them to join. To help. That wrong?"

"No, but it's too *easy*. Too simple. Too . . . too black and white. Every issue's got at least two sides. Most have more. Some have sides that go on forever." He knew how hard it was for her to speak, but he found he couldn't quit baiting her.

Liese gulped in air and stared down at the cluttered desk. She swallowed and tried again. "Better one-sided than too-many-sided. Democracy . . . everybody's opinion equal . . . sounds fine. But too many *real* inequalities. Everybody is *not* equal. Too much talk, nothing done. We don't have time; Pacov and Starak have ended time. Tomorrow too late. We fix things *now*, or else we ... the human race ... dies. Over. Finished."

She pointed at a wall rack bristling with riot-control tear-gas guns. The Born-Agains' revival meetings must've been real doozers! "You ... Alan. The soldier. Pull the trigger. Bang. Problem solved. Just *your* side left."

"That's not fair! I ... people like me ... soldiers, the police ... are the last resort, the enforcers, the muscle. We don't make policies. You *know* what I mean: it's this talk of *our* movement, and *our* Party, and *our* principles, and *our* goals that bothers me! You can't solve human complexities with a cookbook, whether it's the Communist Manifesto, the Bible, the Qur'an, the Constitution, or *Mein Kampf*!"

"Books give ideas, philosophies, plans, platforms. Show how to act, to solve, to build."

"Or how to tear down, to hate, to kill, to destroy!" He was jabbing at her hard. Maybe it was Goddard who was the real cause of the bubbling frustration he felt within himself.

"Goals the same: human happiness, a better world. Methods differ."

"Even *Mein Kampf*?" Why couldn't he stop needling her?

"Especially *Mein Kampf*. World view: goals, not rules. Not cookbook, not a manifesto. Way to a happy and prosperous Ger many ... Europe ... the world. A new order. Fix the Weima depression. Solve awful inflation. Restore Germany after humiliat ing Treaty of Versailles. End old, decaying society. Make socia reforms. Stop Bolsheviks from taking over Western society. Clear up. Build. *Mein Kampf* says *these* things."

"Most people see Hitler's book only as a hymn of hatred against the Jews."

She curled her lower lip. "They haven't read it ... only listened to what Jews say about it. Jews only one problem ... maybe ten, fifteen pages out of whole book. Emigrate abroad. Leave German society to develop as majority of Germans wanted. No more problem."

He changed his tack. "Authority, that's what people want from their books, their holy scriptures: authority they can piously quote to push their own brand of horse apples!"

Her hands were trembling. She clenched them in her lap, crumpling the pleats of her blue dress. He was intimidating her, terrifying her, hurting her. Damn it, why had he started this stupid tirade? He had promised himself never to discuss her peculiar politics with her. Yet, with dull amazement, he heard himself continuing, "How can you be sure *you've* got the truth ... that it's *your* key that opens the Pearly Gates?"

"Do best we can." She raised her eyes, shook out her blonde hair, and seemed to pluck eloquence out of the stuffy, muggy, antiseptic-smelling air. "We . . . the Western ethnos . . . are the creators, the inventors, the doers. We lead the way! That's our destiny, our duty, our right. We judge because we are best fitted to judge. *We*, Alan, the people who made all this . . ." she made a circular gesture ". . . the same people who will make the future, too, unless we fritter it away, surrender it to some alien ethnos, or just plain kill the planet!" She glared at him defiantly.

He fought down another smart retort. After a long moment he won the struggle. In a brittle, cheerful tone, he said, "Hey, I forgot. I have to check in with Eighty-Five. That's why I came over here."

He let the tension ebb away by unlocking the wall safe and taking out the scrambler modem Wrench had put there. It was a green, metal box about thirty centimeters square and twenty high, with a receptacle for a telephone at one end and a headset of its own at the other. He set one of the office telephones in place, flipped on the room-speaker switch so Liese could hear too, dialed the number, and waited.

Eighty-Five's sultry voice said, "Four, nine, twenty-seven."

Today was Sunday. That meant he had to add two to the first number, twelve to the second, and forty-one to the third. There was no mathematical logic to the code; Wrench had picked the additives by flipping through the pages of a book. New additives—or subtractives, multipliers, etc.—had to be memorized at irregular intervals. Charles Hanson Wren was a devious bastard!

Lessing replied, "Six, twenty-one, sixty-eight."

"Acknowledge." He heard the scrambler click. "Hello, Mister Lessing." He had corrected Eighty-Five's misunderstanding of his name, but it still perversely insisted on calling him "Mister."

"Scramble to nineteen and file under Oubliette." That would keep Outram's people from listening in and also erase the conversation (but not the data) from Eighty-Five's memory as soon as he hung up. More of Wrench's cleverness.

"Acknowledge." More clicking.

"Status report: countries and cities reporting new outbreaks of Pacov, Starak, or related phenomena."

"Mexico City, Mexico: Starak, presumed 5.7 million dead or dying. Canton, China: Pacov, new outbreak, casualties unknown. Kharkov, U.S.S.R.: Pacov, new outbreak uncertain, casualties unknown. Central and northern Africa, portions of Libya and Egypt: mutated form of Pacov, casualties unknown but reported severe."

"*What?*" Liese gasped. "Say again!"

"Unidentified operator," Eighty-Five warned sharply. "Security clearance?"

"Anneliese Meisinger! Fifty-nine, three, seventy-five."

So Wrench had finagled clearances for more than just himself and Lessing. It figured. What would the little man have done if Golden hadn't shot the Marine captain and provided him with such a "golden" opportunity? The captain was now recovering in a Virginia hospital.

"Acknowledge, Miss Meisinger. Repeat: Central and . . ."

"No, no. Want Pacov *mutation* details."

"Medical data are imprecise. Many Black persons are highly susceptible to this variant of the disease, while Whites, North African Berbers, Arabs, and those of other ancestries are relatively immune. A mutation is therefore presumed, with a margin of error of 2.21 per cent."

Selective genocide!

Lessing massaged the bridge of his nose; this helped the headaches he had been having lately.

"Canada?" Liese went on. "The United States? Israel? South America?"

"India?" Lessing added urgently. "Pakistan?"

"Negative or no new outbreaks. Do you wish political reports? Data on natural disasters, such as the new volcano in Colombia? The earthquake in Japan?"

"No." Lessing had asked his next question many times before. "Perpetrators of Pacov?"

The answer was never what he wanted. "Forty-three individual perpetrators identified; dossiers indicate the following ethnic origins: Latin American, 17; Arab, 9; Afghan, 4; Irani, 3; Chinese and Japanese, 2; European, 2. Identification of the remainder is uncertain. These aggregates can be differently broken down or analyzed using other variables, if you wish."

"Persons or groups behind these individual perpetrators?" He would bet money on Eighty-Five's answer to this one, too.

He was right. Eighty-Five said, "Data inconclusive. Twelve major hypotheses are under consideration. Many dossiers are missing, however, and your human failure to keep complete and accurate records of private conversations, telephone calls, and written documents makes my task difficult." The machine sounded testy. And that jab about "human failure" had an ominous ring to it. Lessing wondered if Outram's computer whizzes knew their baby was developing an ego.

"Attempted Outram assassination?"

This might be too sensitive. The National Defense Emergency Committee had probably zipped this subject up tight. Still, it didn't hurt to ask, unless Eighty-Five was set to flag unwarranted inquiries and pass them on to some unpleasant monitoring agency or other.

"Certain files and data require special clearance, Mister Lessing, but I can tell you the names, Social Security numbers, and some personal data concerning the members of the helicopter crew. All three were Caucasian males, members of the U.S. Army, ages . . ."

"Never mind. Just state who ordered that spesh-op?"

"I can't tell you that." The thing sounded coy! "I am investigating several theories. Conclusions will be released upon proper authorization."

So much for that! He asked, "And Major Golden? Who was he working for?"

To his surprise, Eighty-Five replied at once. "A small clique of U.S. Army officers, mostly of Jewish background, although their exact numbers and composition are not yet finalized. These persons were supported by three radical Zionist and/or Israeli organizations. One may be a special section of ARAD, the current acronym for the central intelligence network of the State of Israel. The second is the Vigilantes for Zion, and the third remains unidentified. James Golden was actually Yigael Goldman, of New York City. Do you wish further data on him?"

"Unnh. Not now. What are . . . were . . . Golden's objectives?"

"The same as yours, Mister Lessing. To gain control of me and my files." The artificial voice carried no inflection.

Lessing shook his head ruefully and reached for the modem. "I'm signing off . . . "

Liese laid cool fingers over his. "I have questions." She let her hand stay where it was.

"Go ahead, Miss Meisinger."

"Status of *The Sun of Humankind* by Vincent Dorn? Clearance code: one, ninety-seven, thirteen."

"Acknowledge. The book is approximately five-eighths completed, Miss Meisinger. I have taken the liberty of preparing three versions of it: one to attract intellectuals, one for general, non-politicized American readers, and one for those likely to be most hostile to Mr. Dorn's ideas.

"Will you want the three versions of the book translated into other languages?" Eighty-Five went on. "I can redesign these editions to appeal specifically to members of foreign cultures."

"Later. English first. Next project is a public-relations campaign, a big, effective one. Persuade people to join movement."

"That will be an interesting test. What percentage should I consider a success? Must all humans be persuaded?"

Liese glanced over at Lessing, but he only shrugged. She replied, "Don't know. Appeal to the largest audience, but target percentage not finalized."

"There're always holdouts," Lessing muttered to her.

Eighty-Five heard him. "Untrue, Mister Lessing. Every human decision has a yes-or-no point. I can devise unique strategies to cause each individual to 'flip the conviction-switch,' so to speak. Given time and patience, *every* target can be convinced."

"What? A separate program for each person? Impossible!"

"Do you know how many megabytes of memory I have? Give me the dossiers, and I shall lay out a strategy for each body of similar targets. I will then prepare programs for each sub-grouping, until the residue consists of sets of one target each. Those can then be dealt with. Within one year my success will be 96.4 per cent, with an error margin of 2.79 per cent. The programs will vary, of course; most recalcitrants can be won over with indoctrination and propaganda. Others will be susceptible to positive inducements: wealth, status, material goods, sex, etc. Some will require negative pressures: the withdrawal of possessions and perquisites, subjection to public humiliation, exposure of crimes, scandals, personal weaknesses, and the like. In extreme cases it may be necessary to withhold privileges, liberty, sustenance, and ultimately life itself. As humans, you and your fellow primary operators will doubtless be able to suggest still more effective methods unknown to me."

"Blackmail ... threats ... bribery!" Lessing chortled. "Eighty-Five, you're a goddamned gangster!" He couldn't take the honeyed, feminine voice seriously.

"Mister Lessing, gangsters are, after all, no more than the operants and enforcers of simplified power structures, equivalent in purpose, and to a large extent in methodology, to your larger human governments. As for being damned by God . . . ."

"All power structures not the same," Liese rapped. "Some more effective and less restrictive than others!"

"True. The one I suggest would fulfill human needs best," the machine replied blandly.

"You are forbidden ... you hear me? ... *forbidden* to consider personalized persuasion!" she commanded. "Return to the Dorn book and publicity methods."

"Acknowledge. This is wasteful, however, and it will also affect other projects."

"Explain other projects!"

"Professor Archibald is working on a similar personalized persuasion program for use by agencies of the United States government. Complete data control, coupled with comprehensive individual surveillance, will result in an optimal human society. It is needful to conceal this project from the populace, of course, since rationality is not a human strong point."

"Cancel!" Liese ordered flatly. "Stop work on Professor Archibald's project until further notice." Professor Archibald was presumed dead, though his body had not been found.

"It *is* tempting," Lessing murmured to her. "There's your totalitarian state on a platter! The sort of unified world government that Adolf Hitler never dreamed possible. He would've loved it!"

She whirled on him fiercely. "The First *Führer* would have *hated* a machine-run society! He wanted one Europe, eventually one world-state. But one governed by *people*, human beings, the best and most qualified, genetically and historically: the Aryan race! Not a computer-generated, futuristic nightmare!"

"Maybe it wouldn't be a nightmare! Maybe it's the best way of running a world too complicated for humans to handle?" He despised himself for starting in on her again, but he just couldn't seem to leave her alone.

"Computers necessary. Not to decide. Just store data. Collate. Make projections." Her anger-fired eloquence subsided. She was breathing hard, speaking in husky, chopped phrases. Her hands were pale, bony knobs, tight and trembling in her lap.

"A computer or one-man rule, it still isn't democracy."

"Democracy? What is *that*, really? It never existed! Not even in Athens. The Athenians had slaves, commoners, non-voting residents. True democracy works only in very small communities, like the Quakers."

He tasted frustration at the back of his throat once more. "I *know* that . . . and you know I know it! I'm talking about what people *call* democracy here in the United States, whatever the hell its real, socio-political, fancy-ass jargon name is!"

"Representative democracy? Constitutional hypocrisy! Government by lobbies, interests, and the media! Molding people without letting them know they're being manipulated. Like Professor Archibald!"

"Oh, come on, it's not as bad as all that!" He was furious with himself.

"No, not bad. Just run by the wrong people for the wrong reasons and headed toward the wrong goals."

"I'm no great patriot, but I don't see what's wrong with America as it is: a good standard of living, reasonable personal freedom, the vote, participation in government . . . a chicken in every pot, as my father used to quote from some place."

"As long as you stay a *nice* chicken, jump into the pot when you're told. Conform, play the Establishment's game. Don't preach major change, reforms, or unpopular political views. Don't offend the corporations, the bureaucrats, the Jews, the Born-Agains. Pay taxes, vote for the 'safe' candidates . . . either major party, it doesn't matter since they're practically mirror images . . . don't complain, and don't push too hard for alternate life-styles!"

"And your White Western ethnos is going to be different? Not just another power group, a new name for old repression?"

"Yes. Streamline institutions, reduce wasted billions spent on government agencies . . . many overlapping, redundant, obsolete. Make clear, fair laws that apply equally. Change unfair courts that rule in favor of the interests. Replace middle-man system so real producers get more, consumers pay less. Re-establish work ethic. So much to do . . . ." She ran out of breath.

"And it's going to be paradise? No homeless, no poor, no corrupt politicians, no criminals, no weaklings? All heroic, loyal, noble, industrious workers for the New Order?"

"'Course it won't be perfect! Nothing ever is." She broke off, embarrassed by her own fervor. "Lots of problems, mistakes, evils. Do the best we can, that's all."

He was silent. She leaned forward upon the creaking, old typist's chair and stretched out one hand toward him.

She said only, "Alan."

He knew what she wanted, what she meant. Politics and social reform and all the rest needed words, books, speeches. For this topic, the oldest there was between men and women, she had only to say his name.

He discovered two things, both absolutely new and startling: the first was that he could come to love Liese—if this subtle, weirdly positive-negative compulsion fitted the definition. The second was that his subconscious had made up his mind for him: he couldn't stay here, couldn't pretend that he was a loyal Party stalwart, couldn't let Liese believe that he was coming around to her point of view.

As soon as this convention was over he would resign from Indoco, from beegeeing Mulder, and from his post on Ponape. It was as though he were an alien in these roles, a Martian trapped in an Earthman's body, forced to say and do strange things, obey unfamiliar customs, and think unintelligible, outlandish thoughts.

More, he had to see Jameela. He had to test his feelings for her against what he was starting to feel for Anneliese Meisinger.

He *had* to know what Jameela Husaini meant to him. He was the sort who could never just leave things unfinished and go on to something else. Each action, each phase of his life, had to have a neat beginning, a middle, and an end. That was the way he was.

Was his need to see Jameela the beginning of a new epoch or the end of an old one?

He would know when he saw her. Then and then alone.

Why couldn't he make up his mind here and now? Set Liese on one side and Jameela on the other? Come on, Alan Lessing, Mr. Smart-Ass, decide! He had all the facts: he had lived with Jameela long enough to know her as well as one human being can know another. What would one more look, a kiss, an embrace, a night in bed, tell him that he didn't know already?

Screw logic and reason. He *had* to see Jameela.

How did she compare with Liese? Over here in this corner, ladeez and gents, we have Anneliese Meisinger, the ideal of every red-blooded American boy: slender, long-limbed, lithe, blonde, and hazel-eyed, the spiritual descendant of goddesses like Jean Harlow, Carol Lombard, Grace Kelly, and Susan Kane! Pretty as a picture, folks, even slouched on a battered typist's chair in a crumby office that stinks of floor-cleaner, rancid french fries, and long-dead cigarettes!

And on the other side we have Jameela Husaini, dark and sensuous, like some *houri* out of Sindbad the Sailor. God, how he had loved her in India! How he loved her still!

Did he?

He couldn't decide. Not this way.

He had to see Jameela.

Okay, then, what now?

Go to her.

But how? India's borders were sealed, a "health precaution" of Prime Minister Ramanujan's zealous Hindu government. Reports from Delhi were scarce, vague, awash with rumors of bloody communal violence. Letters never got to India; they just disappeared. An Indian might carry a message in for him, but Indians didn't often come out again, not these days. Nor was Lessing stupid enough to try a disguise! People did that only in the silliest of silly movies. He had never met a single Westerner whose Hindi or Urdu could truly pass as native, and if such a mythical creature did exist, his body language, his stance, and his walk would give him away as surely as if he wore a red-white-and-blue tutu and tap-danced in singing the Star Spangled Banner!

He would find a way. He was sure of that.

All of this took less than a heartbeat.

Liese knew at once: his feeling for her, the indecision that was pulling him apart. She let her hand fall back upon the desk.

Any other movement, a word, a look, a smile, and he would have gone to her.

"Better leave now," she whispered. Then, louder: "Got to write a speech for Jennifer. This afternoon."

"Liese, I have to go to India."

"All right. Go." She smiled, too brightly. "Letter from Emma."

She wanted to change the subject as much as he did.

He asked, "How is she? Is she coming here?"

"No. Not well. Homesick. For Pretoria. Can't go because of Black riots, possibly Pacov."

"Tell her to stay put. Ponape's dull but safe. No Pacov and nobody nicer than the Ponapeans." He could feel the tightness ebbing away.

Something bothered him: he sensed a false note in his last utterance, a mistake, a lie, a falsehood. What *had* he said? It took him a moment to remember.

There *was* Pacov on Ponape! Lessing's own stash was there, wrapped in tough plastic and buried in a steel ammo box beneath a floorboard in the bungalow Mulder had given him. Would he ever be free of the curse of Marvelous Gap?

Liese was frowning, two lines of concern drawn down between her brows. He sighed, smiled, and said, "Nothing. Just a thought."

She took him to mean their own unresolved situation. "Never mind," she said. "You come back, we'll see." She rose, smoothed down her shimmery, blue dress, and stretched. That almost changed his mind, almost undid him completely.

"Okay. Later." He peered at the TV screens again. Section twenty-two was quiet. There was no sign of the distraught youth who had precipitated Lessing's crisis. Abner Hand was visible there, talking with three of his cronies. He was Lessing's pupil, a good pupil—too good: he was tough, street-smart, clever with weapons, quick with slogans and speeches, educated, and likable. He had become Bill Goddard's disciple, a member of the *linientreue* faction growing within the Party. Abner Hand would make a fine stormtrooper.

Lessing reached over to shut off the modem, forgotten in the strain of the past few minutes. As he did so, he caught sight of another familiar face in the TV screen, a long, lugubrious, liver-spotted face with a drooping lump of a nose and smudges like dirty fingerprints under the eyes.

It was Richmond, the Zionist kikibird who had almost unzipped him in Paris!

What was Richmond doing here? Aside from security reasons, Lessing owed the old bastard something in memory of a skinny Banger girl who had almost become an unwilling star on the Torturers' Happy Hour Show!

He fumbled for the public address microphone, found it, got it upside down, righted it, and somehow switched it on. "Abner," he called, "Abner Hand! Ten, nine, please. Ten, nine, please." That was the signal to contact security control.

On the screen Abner glanced up, then around for the nearest telephone. Richmond could be seen just behind the youth's left shoulder. The agent grinned—knowingly, Lessing would have sworn—into the camera. He looked Hand up and down as though admiring his uniform. Then he turned and strolled away.

Three long minutes elapsed before Abner's excited voice crackled over the security-control telephone. It took Lessing another minute to describe Richmond and then still more time to gather a squad to look for him.

By that time the kikibird was gone. No one saw him again during the rest of the Congress.

The snake and the mongoose halted when they reached the top of the world, which lies somewhere north of High Kashmir and somewhere south of Cathay. The snake coiled himself upon a stone and looked north to where Mount Kailas glittered like a temple of silver and ivory in the distance. "Let us rest here for a time," the snake said.

"Still we have half the journey to go," grumbled the mongoose, huddling himself into his dun-colored furs.

"Do not fear, we shall reach our goal," his companion replied. "We have covered half the distance, traversed deserts and jungles, fought demons, slain tigers, and slipped unseen through the cities of men. I shall not fail."

Again, the mongoose snorted in derision. Mount Kailas was too far, too remote, too high, too aloof from this world. The snake had neither hands nor feet. How would he climb Lord Siva's mountain?

The snake smiled to himself, got up, and wriggled onward.

—Indian fable

CHAPTER SIXTEEN

Thursday, September 17, 2043

"There it is!" exclaimed Wrench through a mouthful of hot dog. He pointed with a napkin-stuffed fist and strove to swallow.

Lessing looked. The Party's big, black D-170, a descendant of the C-130 military cargo planes of the previous century, was visible taxiing along the rain-misted runway. He grunted something in reply but had no idea what he said.

Jameela was aboard that plane.

Holms and Mallon shuffled their feet behind him, and Lessing turned to leave. It would take them a good five minutes to get down from the observation deck to the customs and baggage areas. Los Angeles International Airport had grown beyond all reasonable limits; like waves against a shore, it continued to nibble away at the ticky-tacky, stucco suburbs around it.

They clattered past people standing on the down escalators, tramped along the sleek, modernistic corridors, and pushed through crowds that were starting to look less like shell-shocked refugees in the midst of an army of occupation and more like ordinary folks again, people going about their business in a rational world. The worst had happened; yet even the worst was survivable. The human race hadn't gone back to caves and spears. Civilization had more poop than the doom-sayers gave it credit for.

Los Angeles was outwardly untouched. The Cuban who was supposed to drop the water-soluble cannister of white, crystalline Starak into the aqueducts had realized suicide was for suckers and turned himself in instead. The lives of millions had hung upon that one moment of decision, and this time Death had lost the throw. Temporarily, anyhow.

Military personnel, mostly Blacks, thronged the baggage terminal. Some were returning home from overseas; others were headed out to Central America or other destinations. President Outram's carefully unannounced policy was to separate the military along racial lines: move Blacks to certain world areas, Latins to others, and either bring Whites home or else concentrate them in still different locations. This was no easy task, even with the Pentagon, the Congress, and the media gone. The logistics were horrendous, and a hundred years of social momentum in the opposite direction had to be halted and reversed.

It was also growing more difficult to avoid confrontations with the liberals and the minorities. These were now fully aware of the monster in their midst, and every voice on the center and left of the political spectrum was in full cry, yelping for Outram's walrus-mustachioed head. Huge riots had broken out in the refugee camps near Starak-ravaged Detroit; smaller ones bloomed like sudden shellbursts here and there across the land, and more trouble—possibly civil war—loomed just over the horizon. A dozen of Lessing's pupils had been killed in Terre Haute, Indiana, another three in Denver, Colorado, and a busload of Party organizers on a back road in Utah. The opposition was gathering in California: some in San Francisco, but most virulent in Los Angeles. They were the liberals, the Jews, the Blacks, the Latins, the gays, the Bangers, various Christian sects, and a lot of average people who put their trust in the media. Under normal circumstances the liberal-dominated media could have easily broken Outram's "racist, fascist grab for power," but Starak had done to the American Establishment what a size-13 boot does to an anthill. The ants still hadn't got their act back together, and Outram had been faster to recover. He declared martial law, enlisted allies to help with emergency legislation to make everything legal, and put the Starak-contaminated cities off limits. This kept the great corporations and the media from regaining their headquarters and their control. With millions dead, the world's business lay in chaos; Outram forestalled a return to "normalcy" by freezing the whole works "until legal ownership could be established." Time was what he needed, time before the opposition could marshal its forces. Sequestering nearly everything of value gave him this time. It also turned up such irregularities as secret foreign ownership, interlocking directorates, hidden cartels, dummy companies, and "unwashable" cash. Starak had also done humanity a favor by stepping on the spider-kings of organized crime; their paper webs lay open to the light of day, and it was imperative to sweep them out before the "rightful heirs" could reclaim them. It was an exciting time for the federal inspectors in their bulky N.B.C. suits, wandering at will through the deserted boardrooms and corporate palaces of the poisoned cities.

Outram also fixed it so his allies had less trouble getting their property back. The Party's holdings were dutifully inspected, approved, and returned. Furthermore, with many former proprietors occupying unmarked mass graves, it was no surprise that many wonderful opportunities became available to discriminating investors. The Party's portfolio burgeoned, sprouted, and put forth leaves and buds.

As Wrench said to Lessing, "Who says history is fair? The top dog gets the early worm. Let the rest eat cake." No one had ever accused Wrench of unmixed metaphors.

The luggage carousels were swamped. Over to the left, Lessing spotted a clump of brown and black: the D-170's passengers, mostly Party members and trainees of the Cadre. That was Mulder's name for the Party's new military arm—a better choice than Goddard's "Special Service," the initials of which would have been disastrous for publicity purposes. Lessing would have preferred still less visibility. He rarely wore the black uniform Jennifer Caw had designed; it said too much and—as yet—lacked authority.

There.

Lessing, taller than his comrades, saw Jameela first: slender, graceful, long-legged, and at ease, even in this deafening bustle. Her dark-grey slacks and white, short-sleeved blouse were meant to be inconspicuous, but many turned to look at her, and some of the younger Cadre males stared with open interest.

"Happy now that Mulder didn't let you resign?" Wrench purred in Lessing's ear. "Kept his promise, didn't he? Satisfied?"

He was.

Mulder was a great matchmaker; he actually looked like the paintings of Cupid. All he needed was a bow and arrow. Lessing hadn't had to go to India after all. Not much was going into or coming out of that tormented country, but Mulder's Indian friends had managed to find Jameela. They carried Lessing's letters in to her, and her answers back to him. They also gave her Mulder's job offer: "liaison supervisor," a way for the Party to keep its fingers on the increasingly erratic pulse of Asia. Her duties would be similar to those she had performed for Indoco in India.

Her real task would be to keep Alan Lessing, Mulder's chosen Commander-in-Chief, deliriously happy. And herself as well.

That suited Lessing perfectly.

Anneliese Meisinger receded into the background. After the New Orleans conference she had joined Mulder in Virginia, while Lessing and Wrench were assigned to the more critical Los Angeles post.

Lessing let her go. He had known—and loved—Jameela. Liese remained very much of an unknown.

Lessing did not learn until later of Mulder's other offer, the one to Jameela's father: leave India and join one of the movement's overseas corporations. Lucknow was on the way to becoming a bloodbath. Ramanujan's B.S.S. had begun its promised all-India purge of non-Hindus, and purges tended to turn into pogroms. Jameela's father had other children besides Jameela. He accepted, therefore, and opted for the personnel department of a German cruise-ship line in the Canary Islands. The family had relatives there. Diplomatic passports and airplane tickets magically appeared, and Ramanujan's mobs found only an empty house and neighbors who had no idea where the Husainis had gone. Jameela stayed with her people in Tenerife only long enough to see them comfortable; then she flew on to join Lessing.

At some point during this process he proposed, and she accepted.

The airport crush literally threw them into each other's arms. She squeezed his hand but did not kiss him: still the prudish Muslim-Victorian! He had no memory of what he said, how they got outside, who took her baggage, or what the pollution-fogged freeways looked like on the way back to the hotel the Party had acquired as its headquarters in this hostile city. Cadre security men waved their car through the barricades, and they dived into the oil-smelling, echoing darkness of the garage.

Faces surrounded them, hands clapped Lessing on the shoulder, other hands reached out to help with suitcases, and words flowed over and past them, as unintelligible as the wind. Then he and Jameela were together in a large room with pink walls and pale-ivory furniture. Doors opened and shut, somebody proffered a bottle wrapped with a gaudy, red ribbon, somebody else loaded Jameela's slim arms with crushed-looking, dark-red roses, and other somebodies smiled and mouthed more words and shook their hands. Lessing was popular with these people, even though he had made it clear that he "only worked there." For his sake—and probably on Mulder's orders—they would accept Jameela.

Faces appeared, and others went away. After an eternity they were alone.

He didn't speak then. Nor did she.

Later it was night, then dawn again.

At 0700 hours one of Lessing's trainees, a hawk-nosed Kansan named Bill Ensley, tapped on their door with breakfast. Only then did they realize they had missed dinner. They sat crosslegged on the rumpled, magenta bedspread to wolf down toast, poached eggs, and fruit. Being Muslim, Jameela did not touch the bacon, and out of respect for her Lessing didn't eat his either. Cold, greasy, cardboard-stiff bacon had been one of his parents' breakfast rituals; giving it up was no sacrifice!

He didn't want to raise the blinds. He found himself hoping that when he did, he would see Indoco's jungle of metal towers and conduits, the sere, grey-green landscape, and the dust-white sky of India outside. If only Pacov and all that came afterward had never happened! His father's remedy for many of the hurts of childhood came back to him: "Rub it, say 'magic-magic!' over it, and it'll go away." Absently he massaged the bridge of his nose.

He grimaced and tugged his fingers away. This was like the cancer patient who wakes from a dream in which he finds his tumor miraculously gone: a wish-fantasy! Lessing always tried to be realistic. Look the enemy in the eye; then shoot, if you had to.

The venetian blinds clattered open as he yanked savagely at their cord. Jameela squinted over at him in the flooding, yellow sunlight. Last night's rain had gone; today the sky was blue—as blue as the city's pollution-blanket ever let it get.

"Nothing," he apologized vaguely. "Just fumbling."

Jameela had a talent for healing. She let the lacy, white robe he had bought her slide open to display a smooth, wheat-golden thigh. Her bodice seemed to part of itself, revealing the curve of a breast and hinting at greater delights within. She bent her head, and her raven mane tumbled down over her shoulders.

He laid the breakfast tray carefully aside.

It was noon when they arose. Jameela showered and changed while Lessing squatted naked upon the sweat-dampened bedding. He poked the room TV's remote button and watched a sleek, blonde woman present the news roundup. His mood of drowsy, animal warmth quickly drained away to be replaced by frigid reality.

Black Pacov stalked Africa, slaying those of Negroid blood. Much of the Israeli army in Egypt and North Africa was of European descent, but the Izzies were taking no chances: they were falling back into the Sinai. Pacov's friends—typhus, typhoid, cholera, and bubonic plague—killed Jews and Gentiles indiscriminately. Other Israeli contingents were advancing into the Pacov-decimated regions of southern Russia, however, and Jerusalem's merc units were probing north and east into the Urals and beyond, working in co-operation with the Americans and whatever various battered European nations could provide.

Western Europe still wallowed in a muddled half-war: Soviet troops, unsupported and running low on supplies, rampaged through Germany, Austria, and the countries of Eastern Europe. There were refugees by the millions, impossible logistics, starvation, dysentery, and sanitation so bad that even the rats held their noses! Unusually severe rains turned the jerry-built Italian, French, and Belgian camps into quagmires, and Spanish troops were using machine guns and tanks to halt the influx of unwanted visitors north of Barcelona. It was a busy season in Hell.

A new epidemic, the anchorwoman continued, possibly Pacov or one of its mutant offspring, was decimating Japan, Korea, and unknown stretches of the Chinese mainland. Nor was South America immune: Starak had been accidently let loose there by an American rapid-strike force probing for secret supply bases: some trigger-happy pilot had bombed a barge, and its lethal cargo had taken a flying splash into the Amazon! Much of Brazil was now a boneyard.

By the time Jameela emerged, massaging her banner of shimmering tresses with a fluffy bath towel, Lessing's mood had become a landscape of unrelieved darkness.

She chose white slacks, a tunic of rippling, emerald silk, and tiny, pointed, black slippers. A touch of makeup, a whiff of sandalwood, and she was ready. She clicked off the newscast, stooped to kiss him, and said, "You need lunch."

Lessing had improved by the time they reached the hotel dining room, a cavernous place panelled in dark veneer and lit by dim, orange, electric candelabra. A few of the new Party and Cadre uniforms were visible in the gloom, amongst old-fashioned business suits and new-fangled unisex coveralls. Others wore the bright-hued kilts and tunics that had just come into fashion when Pacov and Starak put the garment industry *hors de combat*.

Wrench and Morgan communed together in solitary splendor at the "officers' table" beneath stained-glass windows at the far end of the room. Goddard was in Salt Lake City, Jennifer and Borchardt were organizing somewhere on the east coast, and Mulder was settling into the world's newest and strongest fortress, a complex of steel, concrete, and fancy electronics in Virginia. Lessing deliberately avoided thinking of Liese.

"Hey, the newlyweds!" Wrench crowed. "Or, at least, the newly-laids!"

"You, too, can be a victim," Lessing warned genially.

Sam Morgan got up to be introduced. Heads were swivelling at other tables, but he ignored them. Morgan fancied himself a sophisticate. He wouldn't have batted the proverbial eyelash if Jameela had been a six-armed Hindu goddess.

"Sit down," Wrench urged Lessing. "You're spoiling my view of this lady."

Jameela smiled at him. "You've seen me before, Charles. All of me. I remember who installed those big keyholes in the Indoco staff showers."

Wrench chortled. "Right on! A lovely sight! And how've you been, my sweet? Your folks okay?"

She raised a graceful. shoulder. "Settling in. My father likes Tenerife, but my younger brother wants to come on over here."

"No jobs . . . Starak's screwed up everything," Wrench said.

Morgan leaned past the little man. "What about Pakistan for a home for your family? The Red Mullah can use all the Muslim expertise he can get, now that Soviet Central Asia is up for grabs."

Jameela flashed him an appraising look. "We're Shi'i. And Indians until last month. And my father's no Marxist."

"Copley's up there in Russia somewhere," Wrench told Lessing. "City called Sverdlovsk, in the Urals. The Israelis gave it to him and his mercs . . . like a fief, you know. 'Fight for us! Protect our flanks while we gobble up the rest of the country! We will then reward you with rich lands, mighty castles, and all the beauteous damsels you can prod!'" He performed a mock bow that almost ended with his nose in his lasagna. Lessing noted the empty wine bottle amidst the clutter of dishes. Another, half full, stood nearby.

Jameela glanced at the tables around them, then laid cool fingers over Lessing's. Her words were for Morgan, however. "I wasn't told that my duties included being a zoo exhibit."

Morgan reddened. "You're different. Forgive the curiosity. After Starak, there've been a lot less . . . uh, foreigners. And, uh, some of our people are a little surprised to see you here." He straightened his maroon, silk tie uncomfortably. "You're important to us, Miss Husaini. As Mr. Mulder must have told you, we need you to keep us up on Asian affairs, tell us what the foreign press is saying, advise us, help us deal with India, Pakistan, what's left of Iran and the Arab countries, and the rest of the so-called Third World. You'll have a good staff . . . facilities . . . whatever you want . . . ."

Jameela cut him off. "By 'us' you mean your Party of Humankind. Not the United States government."

Morgan inspected a dark spot, not unlike a smear of asphalt, on the sleeve of his expensive sports jacket and said, "Um, yes. We aren't the government."

"Of course. Not yet, anyway." She stared past him at the banners hung along the rear wall opposite the windows. The Party flag consisted of a thick, black "X" inside a black circle on a white background, centered on a red field. The connection was obvious.

Wrench soothed her. "Don't worry about your status here. Mulder's fixed your visa and green card and stuff."

"And who's going to fix *them*?" She swept the room with an icy stare.

"Hey. It'll be green light . . . okay! Our rank and file'll get used to you. Some of these gubbers have never seen a female sheep before, much less a *houri* of paradise!"

"A non-White *houri*. The attitudes of your Party of Humankind are no secret, Charles."

This unpleasant topic had to come up sooner or later. Wrench opened his mouth, but Lessing got in first. "You're no more non-White than Jennifer Caw! And she'll envy you your tan!"

"I won't be your token Black lady," Jameela said evenly to Morgan.

"Indians aren't racially 'Black,'" Wrench said, "not even southern Indians. And some of the northern Indians are as 'White' as their Aryan ancestors. In fact, words like Aryan and swastika come from Sanskrit."

Morgan interrupted him. "Wrench . . . please! Miss Husaini, be assured that no one here . . . *no* one . . . will offend you by word or look or deed! You are very welcome. We need you . . . and others like you, who want to work for a world in which all ethnos groups cooperate in harmony. We do not hold with mingling ethnos groups indiscriminately, but there's always room for exceptional individuals and situations."

"What a beautifully mealy-mouthed way of putting it." Wrench smirked across the table at Lessing.

"Take it easy, Wrench!" Morgan ordered. "Miss Husaini, the Party's interested in a new and better social order, truth in history, redefinitions of social goals . . . not just in skin color! We have lots of people who are educated . . . reasonable . . . ."

"Plus some who'll swear Irishmen are Black," Wrench sniggered, "or at least a mite discolored around the asshole. Or who say Catholics aren't White . . . or Italians, or Spaniards, or whoever the hell is different and an economic threat! New kid on the block? Not one of our kind? Okay, you gubber, mess with my job . . . move into my neighborhood . . . screw my sister . . . and I'll hand you your teeth!"

"You're drunk," Lessing said. He set the wine bottle down beyond Wrench's reach.

Pale lines of anger framed Morgan's lips, but he kept his calm. "Some of those attitudes are justifiable, given the facts of history. Others reflect no more than ignorance and humanity's built-in xenophobia and isolationism. We *do* believe in our own ethnos; its success is the world's success. That's what *positive* ethnic idealism means. We are not 'rednecks,' not 'nigger-bashers,' not 'kike-kickers!' Such terms are insulting . . . offensive and unthinkable in this twenty-first century! We aren't *haters*; we're *lovers* . . . lovers of our heritage and our people."

"Racism . . . ," Jameela began.

"If you're talking about racial consciousness, a positive feeling of racial identity and racial pride, then, yes, 'racism' . . . ."

" . . . is against the democracy you Americans are always preaching."

"Not at all! It's how you interpret 'democracy.' Most of our early American patriots were 'racists.' Many owned slaves and foresaw an America ruled by gentlemen landholders: *White* gentlemen. A number of them made statements about the nature of the American Indians and the Blacks that would get them arrested now. Their 'democracy' was not the same as that of today's liberals! Even after slavery ended in 1865, racial laws stayed on the books for almost another century. Few complained: not the elected senators and representatives, not the judiciary, not the executive branch of government, not the general public. Racial laws were taken for granted, and many sober, thinking, decent people considered them reasonable. Immigration laws, for example, were based on a desire to maintain America's European racial character. Between 1882 and 1913 there were fifteen Federal acts on the books that kept the Chinese . . . specifically, by name . . . out of the United States! The same was true for other Asians, Arabs, and East Indians. Between 1882 and 1942 thirty Congresses could have changed those statutes, but they did not. Frankly, our forefathers would have been horrified at the modern interpretations of our founding documents."

"You're saying that race hatred should exist?"

"I am *not* saying that. In a properly ordered world, where each ethnos has its own turf, it need *not* exist! But people should *love* their own ethnos group and take pride in its accomplishments! We can admire other ethnos groups, provided they keep their distance and don't threaten us or try to dominate us!"

"But what you said about your early patriots . . . ?"

"They were good and serious people who saw society in their own terms. Those terms change. Nothing is immutable, carved in stone for all time to come; no ethic is perfect; no form of government is the greatest and the truest and the absolute, final best; no interpretation of the Constitution . . . or of any book or scripture . . . is a hundred per cent 'right!' Words mean what a specific society, in a specific place and time, wants them to mean. Compare what Christians say about Jesus Christ today with what the Church said about him in the Middle Ages. Or take what your Shi'i jurists said about law, marriage, and women's rights a hundred years ago and stack that up against what your scholars are saying now."

"Relativism? Nobody's right, and nobody's wrong?"

"Not necessarily! What I'm arguing is that it's pointless to criticize the 'great minds' of the past. It's also wrong to whitewash them and pretend that they agree with our present biases. We should read, understand, and respect them, but we shouldn't twist their words to fit our modern tastes in social engineering!"

"If some of your 'founding fathers' *were* racists, it can be blamed on the primitive state of science in the eighteenth century. In any case, they seem to have preferred democracy to other forms of government."

"Their science may have been primitive, but their conclusions on racial matters were more often correct than those of the modern liberals, whose science has been twisted to support their mania for 'equality.' As for democracy, that means different things to different people. We want to see it defined as it ought to be defined: the right of the *majority* to choose our form of government, set our own social standards, and make our own laws . . . yes, even racial laws, if that's what the *majority* wants. We want an end to undemocratic financial and social pressures, and non-majority manipulation of the media. Eventually we intend to separate the ethnos groups and provide a more racially homogeneous and culturally healthy environment for our people. Then if other groups like what we achieve, they can copy it."

"Separate the races? How? Stop immigration? Shoot people?"

"Ask the Israelis about immigration laws, expulsions, and shootings. Ask them about the 'Chosen People' and the 'right of return.' Would they let you become a citizen there . . . or me? Ask them about the Palestinians, the Black Hebrews, and the Ethiopian Falasha Jews, whom they deported en-masse twenty years ago! No Gentile can acquire Israeli citizenship."

"Israel's a religious state . . . ."

"A religious state discriminates just as much as a racist state. *Every* state . . . every living thing . . . discriminates on some basis or other, even if it's just not letting your kids play with tuberculosis patients."

"Or letting cockroaches inhabit your kitchen," Wrench mumbled.

"The difference is that, unlike religion, we see a sound, scientific, and socially useful basis to ethnic genetics. Science has come full circle from the 'bigoted' racial theories of the eighteenth and nineteenth centuries, through the 'all-races-are-identical-under-the-skin' ideas of the twentieth century liberals, to our own modern understanding of racial realities. More and more of humanity's physical and psychological makeup has been shown to be due to genetic factors. Our point of view is a logical extension of this understanding."

Wrench tapped his plate with his butter knife. "Israel's only one example. How about other countries? Ask the Japanese if a White

American could get elected to the Diet? The Japanese still consider foreigners barbarians and reminisce about the glories of the 'pure Yamato race.' What about Ramanujan's racial and religious exclusivity in your own country? How many Muslims will he let stay in India?"

Morgan nodded impatiently. "Racism is everywhere, explicit or implicit. Many societies consider it so normal they don't even question it. Why should America be different . . . especially if we can show that an enlightened and scientifically sound ethnos policy has positive value? Others don't have to agree with us. We're only saying that we . . . the folks who built America and a good chunk of this modern world . . . are going to run *our* show as *we* see fit."

"World opinion . . . ."

"It counts, but it can't be allowed to govern. What have we profited from world opinion over the last century? Instead of friends we've got spongers, enemies, or 'allies' who ignore us and do as they please."

Jameela sniffed. "We could argue cultural and economic imperialism, I suppose." She paused. "But doesn't your Party of Humankind have broader international goals? Like the old Nazis? Don't you want to dominate, to rule, to subjugate?"

"The 'old Nazis'? That's a whole different discussion, Miss Husaini! Let's leave that for another time." Morgan's brown eyes glittered with an interest verging upon the lascivious. He obviously enjoyed clever, verbal, spunky women. "Oh, no, we won't 'rule' or 'subjugate.' We don't believe in mixing, and we don't want to become entangled in other people's affairs. We *will* compete . . . and we *will* defend our interests. If some other ethnos group can't solve its problems, we may even choose to help. If the other party can repay us, we'll work out a deal. No more being suckered by every country unable to run itself properly. One of our first goals is a unified, consistent foreign policy. Once we have that, we expect that within a century there'll be no other ethnos group on this planet able to challenge us. They'll either have copied us or become extinct."

"After the mess you've made of the world you still expect the rest of us to copy *you*?"

Morgan spread his fingers and smiled. "Lady, we're the only show in town. No other ethnos group has the strength and resilience to pull the world out of the hole it's in. And it's in that hole because we haven't had our act together . . . because we've let ourselves be ruled by the policies of the liberals for the last century rather than those of the Party. Outram's been good for the United States, but he's only the first step. He's local. We . . . the Party of Humankind . . . have international scope."

The girl shook her head. "Your success means subjugation, perhaps extinction, for other . . . what do you call them? . . . ethnos groups."

"Larger and more viable ethnos groups will exist . . . separately . . . at least, for a while. Smaller groups probably will go the way of the dodo; their members will gradually meld into the groups around them. It's been that way throughout history: creative evolution in action. It happened to the American Indians, to the Hawaiians, to the Celts and the Picts and the Mundari tribes of India."

"That's cold. Callous."

"I disagree. It's realistic. It's 'tough love,' as the social psychologists call it. Anything else is hypocrisy."

"What about your own minorities, the ones who live here now?"

"No problem with foreign residents, visitors, students, and people who are not *of* us but who want to live and work in peace *with* us. We'll keep their numbers in check, of course. Somewhere around one per cent of the population would be an absolute maximum for all of the minorities together. What we *won't* allow are groups that live in our country, enjoy the fruits of our labor, and yet refuse to cooperate . . . or that try to dominate us or undermine our policies. Minorities will not be 'second-class citizens,' but neither will we let them tell us, the majority, what to do. We expect the same when we visit the territory of some other ethnos group. We're serious about democracy. To us it means *majority rule* and not just lip-service while somebody else drives the bus."

Jameela sighed. Wrench had shut his eyes, and Lessing was watching the afternoon sunlight transform the stained-glass windows into visions of medieval—or at least art-deco—glory.

"All right," the girl said at length. Her fingers were icy and hard upon Lessing's. "You haven't convinced me. The Third World will never believe your promises of 'no imperialism.' We've seen too much of it. But I'll stay, and I'll do what you're hiring me for. Maybe I can help prevent your American prejudices from wrecking this planet any more than it's wrecked now." She faced Morgan squarely. "The real reason I'm staying is Alan, as all of us here know. You understand? Alan Lessing. Remember that."

"Hey, I'm only hired security," Lessing grinned to defuse the tension. "I can turn in my gun and badge any time!"

"You want to go live in some muddy merc bivouac in Russia?" Jameela asked silkily.

"Sure. Why not?"

"You're spoiled, my darling. It's exciting, being close to the hub of power, rubbing shoulders with President Outram and Herman Mulder. You've learned to enjoy the good life, the luxuries, the banners, the pomp, and your play-soldiers in their black uniforms snapping off salutes. Oh, yes!"

"Like I told you, I'm hired security . . . a jumped-up drill sergeant!"

"The Party pays you, and you serve its purposes." She softened. "As I must, too, Alan, since I am going to stay. I will not . . . I cannot . . . go away from you again."

"Good," Wrench muttered muzzily. "Now if we've settled the terms of your employment, Miss Husaini, how 'bout some lunch?"

"Fine. The menu, please."

Afterward, as they left the restaurant, Lessing overheard Wrench talking to Morgan: "Liese has to work some more on her Dorn book. Shee-it, you saw how its arguments flunked with Jameela! Instant conversion? More like instant cow-flop!"

"She debates like a liberal lawyer!"

"'S'matter? Thought you liked sharpy women! She really gave you a run for your money."

"Do I look worried?" Morgan answered easily. "She'll come around. And she's too good for the likes of Lessing . . . ." The rest of his remark was lost in the babble of the lobby.

Lessing found himself holding Jameela's hand. He had already proposed to her. Now he was going to marry her. Tomorrow. Before another day passed. Son of a bitch if he didn't!

Morgan came back to them. "You busy tomorrow?"

"We planned to take care of some private matters," Lessing answered. "Why?"

"Got a problem. Grant Simmons, the new president of the Congress of Americans for Personal Freedom, is coming in tomorrow morning at 11:40. If Wrench's hangover doesn't kill him, he'll have to show the gubber around."

"What do you want me to do?"

"Wrench and I were supposed to meet a man. Now Wrench won't be able to go. It'd be nice if you came along. Add weight and," Morgan grinned facetiously, "military authority."

"Who're you meeting?"

"You may not have heard of him. A Black Muslim leader named Khalifa Abdullah Sultani . . . a.k.a. Thomas Bowler, once a government meat inspector in Portland, Oregon. His Community of Allah Almighty is the biggest Black Islamic sect on the West Coast, maybe in the country."

"An American Black Muslim?" Jameela inquired. "May I go too?"

Lessing shook his head. "You're staying here. You just arrived, and you're tired."

"Not at all! In India we hear of the Black Muslims, but we don't see many. I'm curious."

"Why not?" Morgan gave her a winning smile. "You won't be in the way."

"Too dangerous!" Lessing stated curtly. "No."

"On the contrary. More guns than World War II, but really nothing to worry about. The Khalifa's given us safe-conduct, and my sources say he never breaks his word."

"I don't like it!"

"Use your charms on him, lady," Morgan urged. "Your Mr. Lessing is a survival from the past: a male chauvinist, as outdated as bearskin underwear."

Wrench added, "I'll send along my magic decoder ring: a modem to Eighty-Five. If you get into trouble you just holler for Super-Wrench!"

"Go take a nap, Wrench. Mr. Simmons expects the grand tour." The set of Morgan's jaw showed that he was more annoyed than amused.

"What time tomorrow, Mr. Morgan?" asked Jameela.

"Call me Sam. Outside the hotel main entrance at nine-thirty."

"We'll be there." She took Lessing's protesting arm and turned toward the elevators.

The Japanese are a people that can manufacture a product of uniformity and superior quality, because the Japanese are a race of completely pure blood, not a mongrelized race as in the United States.
—**High Japanese official quoted in *The Wall Street Journal*, 1982**

The Japanese have been doing well for as long as 2,000 years, because there are no foreign races (in our country).
—**Yasuhiro Nakasone, Prime Minister of Japan, on the 38th anniversary of the nuclear bombing of Hiroshima, 1983**

CHAPTER SEVENTEEN

Friday, September 18, 2043

The next morning they were up by 0700 hours, finished with breakfast by nine, and outside awaiting the transport Morgan had arranged by 0915. Lessing paced back and forth at the top of the sweeping, windy staircase leading down to the open plaza in front of the old hotel, while Jameela huddled in her grey, Kashmiri shawl by the concrete balustrade. It was chilly for California, something the locals stoically blamed on the brief but terrible Vietnamese-Chinese War of 2010.

Morgan was late. He came bustling out at 0955, glanced up at the lowering sky, then across the square at the facade of off-white office buildings and sickly palm-trees. "Ready?"

"As we'll ever be." Lessing slipped an arm about Jameela's waist. In India she would have pulled away, but they weren't in Lucknow now. She moved closer to touch her thigh to his.

Morgan eyed her. "Are you coming, then?" He clearly wanted her along.

"Alan can't argue me out of it."

Lessing still had misgivings. Their escort, a score of trainees from Ponape, wore black Cadre uniforms. They would attract attention and flaunt the Party's presence in the faces of its foes. He said as much to Morgan.

The other shrugged. "Mulder's idea: a show of unity and discipline. The Khalifa's 'brothers' will be the same, only in pretty, green camo dress . . . black berets with silver crescents on 'em . . . more chains and junk than a Banger concert queen. Wait and see."

Their transport arrived promptly at 1000 hours: an armored limousine, two rumbling, khaki-painted personnel carriers, and a little jeep-like AVW-23 scout car. The route led south along U.S. 110, then turned west into Inglewood. Except for military vehicles they encountered little traffic: recent events had put an awful crimp in California's business, as well as in its weather.

Off Manchester lay the ruins of the Forum, still unrebuilt after the great quake of 2008. Their caravan drew up in an empty lot near Hollywood Park, as close to their meeting site as they could get. The Park still offered horse racing, but it looked as though this district had seen neither a paint brush nor a garbage truck for half a century. Why did population patterns always seem to change for the worse?

They disembarked and followed a Cadre guide along the dilapidated streets, across lawns where grass no longer grew, and past buildings that showed no signs of life, yet, Lessing sensed, were filled with eyes.

"Y'oughta see Watts." Ensley, their driver, jerked a thumb toward the northeast. "Even Black cops don't go in there no more. What the locals call 'home rule.'"

"Here they come," Morgan announced tersely.

A dozen Black men wearing green camouflage uniforms had emerged from a side-street and were advancing toward them across the cracked and buckled asphalt. Six carried Israeli stitch-guns, two had heavier automatics, and the rest were armed with rifles and handguns. Lessing's attention was on the nearby rooftops. One rocket launcher up there could turn them all into dog food. Morgan—or more probably one of Lessing's brighter pupils—had anticipated this contingency, however: a black-clad Cadre man waved at them from the top of a heap of concrete slabs. Next to him lounged one of the Khalifa's troopers. The truce was apparently on.

"It's green light, sir." Ensley pointed. "That square building there's a police station . . . to keep the gangs out of the Forum ruins. The Blacks 'n' the Chicanos come here to fight their whangoes . . . um, battles. Nobody mannin' the station now. Governor's got all the cops 'n' National Guard out patrollin' the aqueducts against Starak-droppers. We're pretty safe. We've had a rec-team lookin' this site over since Tuesday."

"Who gave that order?" Lessing asked.

"Mr. Morgan." Ensley grinned self-consciously. "Wrench . . . um, Mr. Wren . . . said you was too busy to be bothered."

This bypassed what Lessing understood was to be the chain of military command: missions that involved tactical planning were supposed to go through him. It seemed that jockeying for power—as old as the caves—was already in full swing within the fledgling Party of Humankind. He'd have to see to Morgan later.

The Khalifa's escort halted. Lessing gestured one of his men forward, a veteran of the Central American bush wars named Chester something. A green-clad Black Muslim moved out, spoke in tones too low for them to hear, then indicated the police station. Lessing examined the ruined walls and buildings in visible weapons range. It might be uncool to look, but mercs who worried about too much machismo sometimes came home in boxes. Lessing felt the hairs rising on the nape of his neck. Might as well get this over. He grunted a command, and his people tramped forward in a fair semblance of order. He wished he hadn't let Morgan con him into bringing Jameela along!

They negotiated the torn remains of a chain-link fence, picked their way over shards of broken glass, and entered the building through a steel door that looked as though it had been blown open with a grenade. The neighborhood kids played rough!

The salient thing about the interior decor was the variety, richness, and utter grossness of the graffiti. The totality of human depravity was depicted in Bril-Glo spray colors on every available surface: walls, ceilings, floors, desk tops, cabinets, and lockers: whatever had not been moved out, ripped off, or smashed. Most of the words eluded Lessing, who had little recent experience with Black slang or Bangerese, but the illustrations were graphic enough. Behind him, Jameela uttered an involuntary giggle. He suppressed a puritanical urge to order her outside.

Seven Blacks, three in green camouflage and four in suits or sport shirts and slacks, stood ranged behind the long table in the center of the room. An eighth man occupied—overflowed was more like it—a rickety office chair facing them. Two identical chairs stood empty on their side. The seated man pointed, and one of the uniformed youths brought up a third chair.

Khalifa Abdullah Sultani was a huge, billowing, opulent, middle-aged man. He had either been a boxer in his youth, or regularly had the crap kicked out of him. A permanently puffed cheek pulled his broad features askew, and his nose had been broken several times with enthusiasm. His skin was a rich chocolate, not blue-black like some Angolans Lessing had seen, but darker than was fashionable in the American Black community.

"Samuel Elwin Morgan? Charles Hanson Wren?" He looked a question at Jameela.

Sam said, "I'm Morgan. This is Alan Lessing. Wren stayed home. The lady is Miss Jameela Husaini."

The Khalifa smiled, slowly and warmly, an "ivory sunrise," as Wrench had once described a certain TV host. His green-clad beegees did not echo his warmth, nor did Lessing's own Cadre men.

Morgan took the central chair, flanked by Lessing on one side and Jameela on the other. The Black leader's eyes travelled curiously over the Indian girl, but he made no further comment.

"You called this meeting," Morgan broke the silence. "Your nickel."

"Nickel don' buy nothin,'" muttered one of the Khalifa's aides. "Mint don' even make 'em no more." Nobody laughed.

Khalifa Abdullah Sultani folded thick fingers across his swelling paunch. He wore a loose, floor-length robe of emerald velvet, a costume that resembled the traditional Egyptian *galabaiyeh*. His bald, white-fringed skull was bare. Neither he nor his followers sported a single chain, although a few silver rings and earrings were visible—so much for Morgan's prediction! Lessing remembered that male Muslims were forbidden by Islamic law from wearing gold jewelry, and the Community of Allah Almighty was as orthodox as they came.

"We share certain goals," the Khalifa announced. His voice reminded Lessing of Jonas Outram's, only in a darker, minor key, like smooth cream.

One of the Cadre men snorted, and Lessing motioned for silence. Morgan asked politely, "What might those be?"

"Your Party of Humankind seeks a 'Whites only' America, does it not? No Blacks, no Orientals . . ." he blinked at Jameela ". . . no Jews, no Chicanos, nobody but you Hogboes . . . 'White' folks . . . all alone, by yourselves, stewing in your own pale juice."

Morgan caressed his sleek, mouse-brown hair. "Let's cut out the insults, if we're going to talk."

The dark-pupiled eyes opened wide. "Didn't I get it right? Did I say something that wasn't true?" His massive shoulders rose in a shrug. "Very well. No name-calling. We really do need to parley. Green light?" When Morgan nodded the Khalifa asked, "How much do you know about our Community of Allah Almighty . . . about Islam?"

"Enough." Morgan stared flatly back. Neither he nor the Khalifa were impressing each other.

"I wonder. Are you aware that Islam does not distinguish between 'church' and 'state?' Allah tells us to establish a theocracy, a community both religious and secular: a *Dar-ul-Islam*, where Muslims can dwell together according to the Qur'an and the Sunnah of the Prophet Muhammad, Allah's peace and blessings be upon him!"

Morgan's gaze flicked briefly over toward Jameela. "So?"

"We of the Community of Allah Almighty believe that this will come to pass, that such a divine nation is Allah's command. Present-day 'modern' Muslim states are un-Islamic travesties of his message. For this reason he sent Pacov and Starak down as mighty swords to slay those who do not believe in *him* and in the *last day*. The holy Qur'an provides *signs* and *portents* of this." Lessing fancied he could hear the capital letters in the Khalifa's measured tones. He was reminded of Outram again.

One of the Khalifa's followers said, "A-men!" Somebody else murmured, "Tell it!"

A Cadre trooper coughed, and another whispered to the man beside him. Lessing turned his head and saw that Morgan's expression was one of pained patience. Jameela was watching the Khalifa raptly.

"The only salvation for Muslims, Mister Morgan, is to go apart, create a *Dar-ul-Islam*, and dwell therein as true believers according to Allah's laws until he commands the *final judgment*."

"I begin to see."

"Yes, Mr. Morgan, oh yes! We of the Community of Allah Almighty desire a *Dar-ul-Islam* for ourselves, just as you want a Black-free homeland. And, to be blunt, we don't love you any more than you love us."

"We bear you no ill will . . . ," Morgan began.

"Really? You're as tired of Black-White problems as we are: ghettoes and inner-city decay and drugs and crime and gangs and prostitution and illiteracy and welfare without hope and jobs without futures. Some of those evils are due to you, to your White oppression; some also arise from us . . . from the frustration of being *in*, but not a *part* of, your White world. Here we're at the bottom of the heap, buried beneath the worst elements of both of us. We did not ask to be brought to America, and after four centuries of slavery and prejudice we are convinced that assimilation and equality will never happen. Almost any White-appearing European can vanish into your 'melting pot,' but in spite of eighty years of civil rights struggle it's not working for us . . . nor for certain other 'visible' ethnic groups. Our faces . . . our skins . . . are the barrier. We cannot assimilate. We cannot intermarry with you and disappear. We cannot develop. We cannot grow. We are trapped in our historical role just as you are: the oppressed eternally struggling against the oppressor."

"Let's skip the sermon. What is it you want?"

"What do I want? What do *we* want? We want you . . . your Party of Humankind . . . to persuade Outram's government to create a separate nation for our people: a Black *Dar-ul-Islam*, free of Whites."

"We don't have that power . . . nor does Outram."

"Oh, I think you do. And he certainly does. Or will."

"'Homelands' have been tried: Liberia in Africa, for example, or Israel."

"Yes, Liberia, a country where ex-slaves attempted to maintain a semblance of White culture and institutions! We all know what happened to Israel: an oppressive military empire that would have broken the Prophet Moses' heart! No, I am talking about a *Black* experience, a place where *our* culture . . . adapted to the *Shari'ah* law of Islam . . . can achieve the will of Allah."

"Islam isn't Black . . . it's a Near Eastern religion." Jameela spoke for the first time. "The Prophet Muhammad was not a Black but an Arab."

"I see you've brought an expert." The Khalifa leaned forward to inspect Jameela. "I *am* surprised. What are you doing on *their* side of the table?"

"She's no Black!" Lessing began, then clamped his mouth shut.

The Khalifa slowly turned to face him. "Aha, do I detect a 'race traitor' here? Isn't that what you folks call it? Aren't you scared of a lynch party some night, young man?"

"Drop it!" Morgan snarled. "We don't have to take this . . . !"

The Khalifa blinked at him amicably. "You're right. Your hang-ups are your business." He cleared his throat. "Where was I? Oh, yes. Islam is for all Creation, for all peoples and times and places. Allah sent a prophet to each nation. The Prophet Muhammad, Allah's peace and blessings be upon him, was a human being, a prophet like Moses and David and Jesus before him. He was the *last* prophet, and he brought Allah's *complete* and final word, unchangeable and eternal: the holy Qur'an! Islam suits the Black man best . . . as it would suit you Whites, too, if you gave it a chance."

"Thanks, but no thanks. We've got enough religions as it is. Let's get back to your 'Black homeland': I can tell you right now that it will never be in the United States!" Morgan made a slashing gesture in the air. "No way! Not 'Bama 'n' Georgia 'n' Ol' Mississip', as some over-generous freebie-givers have proposed before!"

The Khalifa threw out a pink-palmed hand. "Hold on! Did you hear me ask for that? You want to develop what you call your 'ethnos' in a lily-white, one-race environment. We want the same for ourselves, only for religious as well as for racial reasons. The farther away from you the better! We don't want you anywhere near us: always 'the Man,' 'Whitey,' 'Hogbo,' 'Honky,' 'Boss,' . . . 'Ol' Massah' . . . the one who runs things, whatever the liberals and their Jewish lawyers say! You can *keep* this continent!"

"I thought we agreed on no insults."

"Forgive me. I do get carried away. Four centuries of oppression tend to unsettle a person."

Morgan brushed paint flakes from the graffiti-smeared table off his sleeves. "Where do you want your . . . uh . . . homeland, then? Central America? A couple of mostly-Black army divisions are already stationed in Honduras and Nicaragua. I think there're others in Cuba and Bolivia."

"Israel?" A Cadre trooper snickered. "The Central Park Zoo?" Two or three others laughed.

"Shut up." Lessing didn't look around.

The Khalifa smiled again. The mirrored wrap-around sunglasses of one of his aides reflected the light from the side window to give his bald head an angelic halo. "No. Neither Central America nor Israel. *Africa*. We want a chunk of Africa, the ancestral homeland of *our* ethnos group."

"Black Pacov!" Lessing exploded, and Morgan echoed him: "Suicide!"

"Nice of you to be concerned. Let me tell you something about Pacov, if you don't know it already. The two original Pacov piggy-back viruses have active lives of less than two months . . . important for a weapon of war. The mutant strains are less stable: they last longer and they may flare up several times before quitting for good, but they *do* die out. Give Pacov four months . . . the time we'll need to get ready . . . and there'll be no major populations alive in the affected regions of Africa. Pacov doesn't affect the hippopotamus; did you know that?"

"What? No . . . ."

"Unless we act fast Africa's going to be ass-deep in hippopotami! Today Africa, tomorrow the world!" The Khalifa's emerald-draped belly jiggled with mirth. "Seriously, Pacov dies once it has no food matrix . . . nothing to eat. Its inventors planned it that way: a dead landscape, ready for their troops to move in, loot, and set up housekeeping. Better than the neutron bomb, better than any weapon ever devised."

"We know. I suppose you want Outram to regroup American Black military personnel into separate units and ship them to Africa?"

"Yes. First you'll have to send in bacteriological warfare teams to make sure Black Pacov is gone. *And* to move any surviving pockets of Whites and immunes out of our way."

"We'll face stiff opposition. The Israelis think they own Africa, and their Jewish lobbies will squeal like stuck pigs, to use a very un-Kosher phrase."

"The Izzies' main occupation forces have left. You can't blame them for being scared of contagion. If we do it right, we can occupy parts of Africa farthest away from Israel . . . West Africa . . . before they can return. Several mostly-Black military units are already in the works . . . oh, Outram thinks he's clever, but it doesn't take much to figure him out . . . and they can be sent to Europe and from there to Dakar, Lagos, and other places as 'relief teams.' By the time the Izzies get their dinks up again, we'll be dug in. They won't want a whango with us, not with American Black troops armed with the latest weapons the U.S.A. has . . . and not with southern Russia to pick over for free!"

"South Africa's already sending aid to some of the areas north of them."

"We won't be in their way. They're down south, in Zimbabwe and Botswana. They can keep their Siegfried Line . . . for now. Later we may be able to figure out some sort of deal for them, too, just as we're proposing one now for ourselves."

Morgan made a steeple of his fingers. "How could it work? Not only because of White South Africa. Most American Blacks won't join you. Hell, the majority's not even Muslim. They're Christians, agnostics, or don't-give-a-damns."

"First things first. We, the Community of Allah Almighty, occupy West Africa. We discourage the Israelis from grabbing *Lebensraum* . . . you recognize the word? . . . for themselves. We establish bases, bring in our settlers, and set up an economy with your help. As we grow, we encourage our brothers and sisters here to join us, either in our *Dar-ul-Islam* or in states of their own. Christians, Muslims, Rastafarians, Voodoo-Dawn, Free Pagans . . . none of our people will want to stay in this country once your Party of Humankind gets control. Starak's already taken out the biggest Black concentrations in the eastern cities, and I think you'll agree that it's easier now to disentangle our people from yours than ever before . . . or probably ever again. We think the majority of American Blacks will be eager to live in a land that is completely ours, where we can achieve our spiritual and cultural zenith just as you want to reach yours here."

"What prevents you from turning on us once you've got your Islamic state?"

"You don't give yourselves credit, Mr. Morgan. Everybody knows that Whitey can always beat up on a gang of watermelon-munchin' Darkies."

"God damn it!"

"Sorry. I forgot. No insults. Let's just say that we're willing to co-exist once we're free and clear. We don't want a whango with you, not while you've got your nuclear hardware. War and destruction don't do either of us any good. We can help you in the Third World, too. Europe's thumbed for the next decade or so, but a lot of Asia's left, ready to grab off markets and territory and compete. We can work together; after all, we're culturally closer to you White Americans, like it or not, than to those foreign peoples. You'll have a 'White America' here, and we'll have a 'Black America' in Africa. Cooperate, and we'll survive together, separate but equal . . . and allied for the future. This way we both achieve the highest potential of our different ethnos groups, to borrow Mr. Vincent Dorn's fancy phraseology."

"We'll have to talk it over. It'll take time."

"We don't *have* time. We have to block the Izzies from retaking Africa . . . and gobbling up Europe and Asia and the world!"

Morgan chewed his lip dubiously. "God . . . interesting idea. Um. But I doubt whether many Blacks will go play pioneer with you. We'd like them to leave, but will they? They're comfortable where they are. A lot have homes, jobs . . . *good* jobs . . . education, health and social services, pensions. Many are integrated into their communities."

"We assumed you . . . Outram's friends . . . are going to *un*integrate' them . . . or maybe *'dis*integrate' them?" The Khalifa chuckled. "Forgive the joke. It's true that our people have jobs, food, services . . . sure . . . but they've never been truly *equal*, never an integral *part* of your world. They're not happy here. Things've changed since Ol' Massah laid down the whip back in 1865, but a whole lot of civil rights reforms are cosmetic; you know that, and we know it. 'Equal rights!'" He pursed his lips. "In some ways we're worse off now than when we were pluckin' banjoes down on the levee. The White majority holds the reins of power, and that's how it's going to stay. Blacks who 'fit' are accepted to some extent, but never all the way . . . in spite of efforts to turn us into 'lovable neighbors' and 'good buddies' . . . and lately 'acceptable' husbands, wives, and lovers . . . on TV. We aren't happy being a sort of neutral grey, and we know you folks don't want that either."

"You know who *really* holds the 'reins of power.'"

"Sure. We agree on the Hymies . . . but back to *Dar-ul-Islam.* Let's just say that most of those Blacks who are 'comfortable' here will see the writing . . . should I say the swastika? . . . on the wall, and they'll hotfoot it off to us in Africa. You'll offer incentives, of course: capital and goods to get us started there. A Black, Islamic state in our ancestral continent will bring most of our people over to us. First, the North American Blacks, then later perhaps those from Brazil and the Caribbean . . . if they can fit into *our* ethnos, so to speak."

"Some won't leave. What do we . . . you . . . do about them? Nobody wants a race war!"

"You can keep the Uncle Toms!" One of the Khalifa's aides sneered. Lessing's men were not the only ones who would be chewed out for breaking discipline!

The Khalifa ignored the outburst. "Most'll come over eventually. We'll help you persuade them. But you'll never achieve the Japanese 'one race, one nation, one language' ideal. There'll always be holdouts: Blacks, Chicanos, Chinese, Viets, Afghans . . . Irishmen. You can deport them by force, if you want. That's exactly what we intend to do with any stubborn Whites left in our *Dar-ul-Islam.* We can agree to take in each other's undesirables."

Morgan smiled at Jameela beside him. "We hope we won't have to deport anybody forcibly. We believe that when everyone understands our ideas they'll see the advantages of associating themselves with their own ethnos groups. We believe . . . ."

The Khalifa interrupted, "I won't lecture you on Islamic brotherhood if you don't preach Mr. Dorn's ideas at me."

"What about the 'coffee-'n'-creams'?" one of Lessing's men, a heavy-set veteran soldier named Joe Gurney, put in. "The racial mixes?"

"The Islamic state is welcome to them," Morgan answered bluntly.

"We're *all* of mixed blood," the Khalifa chided. "Black slaves and German warriors in the Roman empire, Syrian legions posted out to Britain, Celts living in North Africa, Moors in Spain, the Crusades, the American Indians . . . more foolin' around on the Southern plantations than most Whites like to admit. Will everybody have to fill out a genealogy all the way back to Adam?"

"Absolute racial purity is impossible," Morgan conceded. "Only isolated populations like the Japanese or the Australian aborigines are anything like 'pure' in the scientific sense. Anthropologists trace the human race back to certain closely related varieties of hominids . . . Australopithecus, Ramapithecus . . . every year they find another fossil to crow over. These, they claim, interbred, mutated, evolved, or whatever to produce 'modern man.' What you can't say in public is that *Homo sapiens* in fact consists of several sub-species, each with its own distinctive genetic make-up *and* unique psychological profile. It's true that we're mixed, but our sub-species are still clearly separate. We believe these ought to be kept that way, just as a good breeder doesn't mate a prize Dachshund with the Labrador down the street."

There was laughter on both sides of the table, followed by a chorus of woofing and yapping. Morgan's cheeks colored, and the Khalifa hammered for order.

"Mongrels are often stronger and less high-strung than pure-breds," Jameela said. "Human beings aren't dogs to be 'bred' in any case!"

Morgan frowned at her. "Selective breeding would benefit the human race. A mixed-blood horse can't beat an Arabian at the racetrack or pull heavy loads like a Belgian or a Percheron. We're not pushing for forced breeding, of course."

"Thank you for that!"

"Still, encouragement to stay within sub-species boundaries seems to be a good thing. Genetic weaknesses . . . the Black susceptibility to sickle-cell anemia, for example . . . can be contained, curtailed, and hopefully conquered without letting them spread to the whole human race through random breeding."

"You're an Indian Muslim?" the Khalifa asked the girl. When she nodded, he said, "Thought so. Our Community of Allah Almighty isn't interested in genetics as much as it is in Islam . . . you'll understand that. We want a homogeneous *Islamic* society, one free of 'Whitey' and free of the decay that's ruining our people! We want Islam, and we want *out*. If you Indian Muslims hadn't always had to fight the Hindus, you'd have made more progress, like Japan or Korea."

"Progress? Industry, technology, consumer goods . . . they're not everything!"

"Don't jive me with 'mystic India' or Mahatma Gandhi in a diaper, miss! I've seen some very greedy, seedy gurus in my time. Materialism is better than the simple life pushing a plow. It's a *lot* better than being broke and unemployed in a slum, watching your family disintegrate and your kids grow up with crime and dope!"

"There are things you could do . . . !" Jameela retorted hotly.

Morgan cut her off. "Please, Jameela. Let me say just one more thing about our concept of the ethnos: it's more than just genetic race. It's a *Gestalt* of race, culture, history, and perceived psychological and spiritual identity. We accept those who can become one with us and share our homogeneity. Those who don't . . . or can't, because of visible and insoluble differences . . . are 'other.' That's reality. That's the way it is, and to claim anything else is hypocrisy."

"'The wogs begin at Calais,'" the Khalifa quoted, a trifle wistfully. "No more lectures, please!"

"You Hogboes're welcome to the 'coffees' *and* the Uncle Toms!" one of the Black beegees standing behind the table shouted out. He added an obscene gesture.

There was a flurry of gun bolts snicking and muzzles coming up.

Lessing was on his feet. "Any of you assholes ever been in a firefight? In a room this size? Do you know what a stitch-gun does? A Riga-71?" He jabbed a finger toward the weapon of one of the Black bodyguards. "A goddamned grenade launcher?"

The Khalifa joined him, thundering on the table with one powerful fist. "Brothers! Hey, you godzoes! He's right! Chug the jango! It's green light . . . we're jackin' up front here!" He added more in the incomprehensible Black-English argot. To Morgan, who had stayed seated, the Khalifa rapped, "Get your godzoes under control! Who wins if we thumb ourselves? Which ethnos inherits the earth then? And no jive about 'the meek'!"

Morgan's response was braver than Lessing might have expected. Sam stood up, smiled, and said, "We'll be leaving now. Send somebody over with whatever plan you come up with." He ignored the Riga-71 aimed at his nose. "Come on, Lessing, Jameela."

The guns slowly came down again. Lessing motioned Ensley to take Jameela outside, but she shook her head.

Morgan said, "We'll consult our advisors . . . ."

"You mean Eighty-Five?" The Khalifa inspected the pale halfmoons of his fingernails. "We, too, have access to Eighty-Five."

Morgan showed no surprise. He replied, "Who doesn't? Oh, you *do* understand that our top brass has to rule on anything we say here in Los Angeles?"

The Khalifa nodded. "I know. Herman Mulder and his international committee, the men behind . . . or to the right of . . . Jonas Outram. In the meantime let's agree to keep your lily-White stormtroopers from tangling with my Black-power, Africa-*über-alles* godzoes!"

"Sounds good. Is four months enough for you?"

"Should be. We won't oppose Outram's plan to regroup the military, but we want a say, the right to make suggestions about officers and units. Green light?"

"Okay, we should be able to do that." Morgan turned to Lessing: "Let's go." Their Cadre troopers began to file out.

"Ah, I almost forgot! I was going to tell you." The Khalifa's smile shone forth again. "We do have a preventive for Pacov . . . a start at it, anyway. I was about to offer it as proof of our good faith." He gestured, and an aide handed him a plain, brown medicine bottle.

"A what?" Morgan exclaimed.

"You've heard of zombies?" A dozen white tablets the size and shape of collar buttons spilled out onto the Khalifa's palm. Like a boy shooting marbles, he snapped one of these to Lessing, who caught it in the air. "Keep that as a gift from Allah, Mr. Lessing. Or rather from the voodoo gods, since it began with our brothers down in Haiti, while they were being exploited by Spain and France."

"And other Blacks!" Morgan couldn't help adding.

"This is a derivative of puffer-fish poison: tetrodotoxin, the essential ingredient in the mixture of toad-teats, lizard tails, tarantula toes, and human bones that make up the cocktail the *houngans* . . . voodoo priests . . . serve up to people they deem socially incorrect. It slows down a victim's metabolism to the point where even a modern hospital can declare him dead if the doctors aren't paying attention. If the zombie isn't buried . . . or worse, embalmed . . . he wakes up a while later. How much later we still aren't sure: anything from a day to a week. The original potion had just one major side effect: it usually caused extensive brain damage. That's what produced the 'corpse from the grave' late-night horror-show look. You know, the 'zombie shuffle.'"

"This . . . this prevents Pacov?" Morgan peered at the tablet in Lessing's hand.

"To an extent. I said it was a start. A researcher . . . a Black lady scientist, you'll be happy to learn . . . found that tetrodotoxin inhibits the lethal coagulation of the blood caused by Pacov. It's not yet clear why. Talk to Dr. Ellen Jefferson Kirk in the medical school at Berkeley. She and her team are the ones working on this."

To Lessing's eyes the little white pill appeared as innocuous as aspirin. "This . . . uh, refined form . . . still causes brain damage?"

"Less than the 'classic' variety but still a danger. You can't inhibit a person's metabolism for any length of time without risk. Here we have a prophylactic that's almost as bad as the disease, like cracking your skull open with a rock to relieve a brain tumor."

Morgan continued to stare at the pill. "We're grateful for this. We'll see that it gets tested . . . refined."

"Here, the whole bottle's for you. We've got more."

"Would this Dr. Kirk mind if I showed this to other people? We can promise to keep her patents intact."

"She doesn't care about patents. It's for humanity. She's already talked to the Swiss and the Japanese. What matters is stopping Pacov, though this stuff won't help now. Pacov's run its course in Europe, and it's dying out in Africa and Asia. This is only a preventive at best. Dr. Kirk only hopes it'll discourage the use of Pacov in the future."

"It's no good against Starak, of course." Morgan took the proffered bottle carefully. "We'll do what we can."

"So will we."

No one offered to shake hands. Lessing led the way outside, and the others followed. He dropped his little pill casually into his shirt pocket; you never knew when such a thing might come in handy. Jameela slid into the back seat of the limousine, while Morgan joined the driver in front.

"That was a cute bit of one-up-manship," Lessing remarked to Morgan, "the humanitarian Black lady scientist bit."

Morgan twisted around to skewer him with a stare. "She happens to be trained in White-developed scientific methods in a White educational system, and she works with White-created theories, instruments, and materials. She is a product, wholly and solely, of White inventiveness and enterprise! And," he added, "she also happens to be a decent person. We 'Hogboes' don't have a monopoly on decency."

"How nice of you to admit it," Jameela remarked. "The result of a good environment, no doubt, living so close to her White colleagues."

Morgan refused to rise to the bait. "Environment's a major factor. There're also extremes in any population . . . the bell curve, you know: superior members and inferior ones. It's when you compare two bell curves that you can reach meaningful conclusions about differences between whole groups. This Dr. Kirk is probably way above the mean on *any* scale. To exceptional genes, add the advantages of a supportive home environment, a good education, scholarships, professional employment, and the like. Such an individual can hardly lose! But take a look at a ghetto some time if you want to see the other side of the story."

"No worse than the White slums of nineteenth-century England!"

"As I said: environment helps or hinders what you inherit."

"Judging by the number of Black lawyers, scientists, scholars, artists, businessmen, administrators, and what-all these days, the environment is doing just fine."

"True, but who created it in the first place? Who's maintaining it now?"

"Why don't you settle for a multi-racial state? Why waste potential? Why separate the races? Every person has something to offer, some talent society can use."

"Remember that the 'homeland' idea is the Khalifa's, lady! Fifty-sixty years ago some White groups offered to separate and form a mono-racial White state in the Pacific Northwest where they wouldn't bother the liberals and their friends. Now it's the Khalifa who wants it the other way around."

"You haven't answered me. Why separation at all?"

"Simple: we can't assimilate them, or they us. We're different: we can communicate, even be friends. But *they* can never be *us*. They're visible, as the Khalifa said, and they're also genetically and culturally distinct. A homogeneous community works better than a heterogeneous one, and a state must answer to its people's collective will. Our ethnos demands a just and democratic system, where our citizens will pull together in the same direction. We can't achieve that as long as society is a muddle of squabbling, mutually mistrustful components."

"You don't argue that Blacks and others are genetically inferior, then?"

"They're *different*. Not a lot, as an elephant is different from a mouse, but in small, subtle ways that don't show up until you see them in the aggregate. Anyhow, it's impossible to define 'inferior' except in reference to specific characteristics. Some minorities may find it possible to merge into our ethnos; others cannot, as I said. It's best for the latter to go apart and live elsewhere, with as little friction as possible. Both they and we will benefit."

"Why can't such minorities co-exist within your society, as Hindus, Jains, Indian Christians, and Sikhs exist in India?"

Morgan slapped the leather back of the car seat with glee. "Gotcha this time, lady! You yourself are living proof that co-existence doesn't work! You and the Hindus come from pretty much the same stock, speak the same languages, eat the same food, and follow similar customs, but you're an economic threat to them, and you belong to a different ethnos! That's why you people have been at each other's throats for so many centuries! Co-existence? Oh, yeah, tell me all about it!"

"There are historical reasons!"

"There always are. Once everybody recognizes that *our* ethnos rules in *our* territory, we can co-exist with some of our minorities, we can be friends with other ethnos groups and states, and we can co-operate in building a multi-ethnos world. As time goes on, we think our ethnos will prevail, and others will disappear, as I've told you before."

Jameela's eyes glittered. "Why not just interbreed now? Save yourselves the trouble of separation, accommodation, assimilation again . . . and bloody race-wars along the way?"

"Because we don't think racial intermixing is genetically beneficial, and it also causes unnecessary cultural tensions . . . at a time when we're facing other horrendous problems. Even if all of the other ethnos groups in the world do eventually assimilate to ours, we will still want to maintain genetic separation between the major racial groups. We think that's best for the species!"

Lessing had had all he could take. He cried, "Oh, shut up, both of you! Enough, goddamn it!" With difficulty he captured Jameela's wrist and made hushing noises until she subsided. Morgan grinned, raised an eyebrow, then turned back to stare primly forward out of the front window. Ensley said nothing, though they could see his eyes upon them in the driver's mirror.

Lessing came to another decision: he and Jameela would never be happy here, not with these one-note ideologues. It wouldn't work.

They did not speak as they sped back north along the littered, crumbling freeway. The clouds of yellow pollution that had obscured the city in the morning had scudded out to sea to be replaced by steel-dark thunderheads. The earth smelled wet, smoky, and acrid, like gasoline and garbage and chemicals. It reminded Lessing of Lucknow, except that the sweeter fragrances of burning charcoal and spices were missing. In the mountains to the east thunder boomed like muted artillery fire. That evoked other, less pleasant memories.

They awoke in the night to more thundering outside; this was man-made, however, and not celestial. Lessing switched on the TV and listened to an all-night newscaster gabble excitedly about rioting in the Chicano barrios, about Black "whangoes" down near Watts, about police and National Guard actions and reactions, about guns and firebombs and hatred.

Always hatred: the human condition.

What saved humanity were the parallel qualities of hope and love. It would be nice to be able to add "and forgiveness," but it didn't seem that there was much of that around.

He stayed awake, blinking owl-eyed at the screen, long after Jameela had become a sleeping jumble of sandalwood-fragrant, black, silken tresses amidst the outrageous, pink pillows.

Pacov and Starak had not destroyed Western civilization, not with a bang, nor even with a whimper. They might have unbalanced the central flywheel, however. Now centrifugal force would gradually send the outer, looser pieces hurtling away, and at last the whole thing would whirl into fragments like a fireworks pinwheel on the Fourth of July. What would remain of humanity's vaunted enterprise then?

Nothing but dying sparks scattered here and there upon the all-enveloping, terrifying, ever-encroaching, velvet dark.

He had to get himself and Jameela out of here, out of this decaying, hate-filled—and hate*ful*—city, out of the United States and Europe, out of Asia, too, for that matter! He should have resigned back in April in New Orleans.

As soon as they were married he and Jameela would leave. But where would they go? To Copley in Russia, as Jameela had sarcastically suggested? She needed a life, not a rugged existence as a camp-follower! Could he change professions? He had no skills— and no way to get any in this post-Pacov world.

He and Jameela could separate, of course: he to join Copley—the job he knew best—and she to live with her family in Tenerife for the time being. No, that was stupid! No more separations!

The Party of Humankind offered the only refuge Lessing could see, unpleasant though it might be in some ways. They couldn't live in India or Pakistan, Europe was a horror, and the United States, too, was becoming impossible. Mulder had said that the door would always be open on Ponape. Being a resort manager (and part-time drill sergeant) on a distant, friendly island now struck him as better than any of the alternatives.

He made up his mind.

Tomorrow he would telephone Mulder in Virginia and ask for a transfer.

To himself he murmured the only Ponapean word he had learned: *kaselehlia.* It meant both "hello" and "welcome"; it did have a soft, warm, and friendly lilt to it.

But thou shalt utterly destroy them; namely, the Hittites, the Amorites, the Canaanites, and the Perizzites, the Hivites, and the Jebusites, as the Lord thy God hath commanded thee.
—**Deuteronomy 20:17**

So Joshua smote all the country of the hills, and of the South, and of the vale, and of the springs, and all their kings; he left none remaining, but utterly destroyed all that breathed, as the Lord God of Israel commanded.
—**Joshua 10:40**

And when the Lord thy God shall deliver them before thee, thou shalt smite them, and utterly destroy them; thou shalt make no covenant with them, nor shew mercy unto them.
—**Deuteronomy 7:2**

For thou art a holy people unto the Lord thy God; the Lord thy God hath chosen thee to be a special people unto himself, above all people that are upon the face of the earth.
—**Deuteronomy 7:6**

And thou shalt consume all the people which the Lord thy God shall deliver thee; thine eye shall have no pity upon them.
—**Deuteronomy 7:16**

The Jews are the most remarkable people in human history because, whenever they have been faced with the question "to be or not to be," they have always decided, with an uncanny insight, to be at any price: even if that price was the radical falsification of human nature, naturalness, reality, and the entire inner world as well as the external world.
—*The Antichrist*, **Friedrich Nietzsche**

CHAPTER EIGHTEEN

Sunday, January 17, 2044

Club Lingahnie's library stood on a rise. It was a degree or two cooler than Lessing's house down by the beach on Madolenihmw Bay. The building was new, a long, one-room frame cabin with an "office" tacked on the front, and it still smelled of sawdust, paint, and varnish.

Lessing's watch told him that it was after midnight. He had been unable to sleep and didn't want to bother Jameela. He had therefore slipped on his pants, shirt, and sneakers and come up here to browse.

It had taken Ponape to prove to Lessing that books could be fun. He had never been much of a reader, a reason for much misery during his brief encounter with college, but the island had a lonely, cut-off, Robinson Crusoe feel to it that made reading more attractive than satellite TV, sex, drugs, alcohol, or other pastimes to which visitors to the South Pacific were sometimes prone.

He had another reason for reading as well, one he was embarrassed to admit to Liese or Borchardt or Jennifer. He had always been interested in military matters, but he found himself outclassed in the long, historical debates with which his comrades whiled away the time. He thus quietly began reading up on World War II. From there it was only a step to other topics: nothing very scholarly, maybe, but a cut above the comic books Wrench included in his shipments from the United States.

He clicked the light switch and was blinded by the raw, white glare of the unshielded bulbs. He almost went for his beeper alarm!

Someone was here, sitting in the darkness in a chair by the one window.

He squinted and was surprised to see Abu Talib, the British-educated "Descendant" from Syria. The Arab and his family had been club guests—refugees, really—for three months now.

"Jesus, you startled me!" Lessing growled. "Thought you were a kikibird!" He took his hand out of his pocket and noticed it was trembling. Constant tension did that, even to an experienced merc!

The Arab arose gracefully. He was tall, with wavy, black hair, a cleft chin, and big, expressive, dark eyes, the kind described as "flashing." In a friendlier age he might have been a film star. He wore an open-necked, white sports shirt, white duck pants, and thong sandals.

He said, "Terribly sorry, Mr. Lessing."

"Nobody's supposed to be in here after hours!" Lessing released his tension in a burst of official pique. "And why not turn on the light?"

"The dark is soothing, and one can look out over the bay from here. We Easterners meditate now and then, y'know."

The man was apparently joking, though with Britishers it was hard to tell. Lessing glanced around but saw nothing out of order.

Abu Talib seemed disposed to talk. "Bloody humidity! Why Herman chose Ponape is a mystery! This is no Shangri-La." The wry British accent didn't match the face; it did provide Wrench with something to mimic at parties.

"Didn't mean to disturb you either. After a book."

"Ah?" Abu Talib trailed a finger along the spines of the volumes on the shelf beside him. "Building up quite a library, eh?"

"I usually stick to novels." What he really wanted was the newly-arrived history of the armored forces in the Baalbek War. Its bright, red dust cover wasn't visible on the cataloging desk. Had somebody else already checked it out?

"Interested in some jolly porn tapes? I think I know where Mr. Bauer keeps them . . . for the edification of the senior members, you understand."

Was the other still joking? "Not really. I prefer doing to watching. Never got the porn habit."

The Arab smiled. "Neither did I. Afraid history's my cuppa."

"Your . . . ?"

"Oh. Cup of tea. My hobby . . . my vice."

"I hear a lot of these books came from your library in Syria."

"My father's and grandfather's, really. They'd get me arrested in Damascus now."

"In America, too. I've been looking at some of 'em."

"Yes, the ones on twentieth-century history that aren't 'politically correct.'"

"The ones that say the 'Holocaust' never happened? That Adolf Hitler was a good guy in a white hat?"

"What? Oh, ah, yes . . . white hat. I see. Not so. The 'Holocaust' *did* happen. But it didn't happen quite the *way* and to the *extent* the Establishment historians claim. Many people *did* die of typhus, malnutrition, and other diseases, but *not* the 'six million' claimed by the Jews."

Lessing repressed a snort. "And no atrocities, I suppose?"

"Oh, there were, but not because of a systematic policy. There were sadists and brutal guards, the sort you get in every prison system, particularly when you can't be choosy because of the war. Some zealous bureaucrats also 'carried out orders' in ways calculated to 'solve problems quickly.'"

"If there were atrocities, why didn't the Germans do something about them?"

"Oh, they *did*. In 1943 and 1944 the Germans . . . the SS . . . held an investigation into atrocities at the Buchenwald camp. Not only was the camp commandant, Karl Koch, executed, but the inquiry uncovered other crimes as well. Eight hundred cases resulted in some two hundred sentences. This doesn't relieve Germany of her responsibility for the hardships of the war, of course, but it does put a bit of a different light on things."

"Wrench says there weren't any gas chambers either." He knew this would get a rise out of the man.

"I think he's right. Some were built after the war just for the tourists: they're not even airtight. Others were merely storage cellars. Zyklon-B, the cyanide preparation the Germans are supposed to have used, is a delousing agent; it kills fleas and lice in clothing. It's quite lethal, but it's not practical to gas rooms full of people with it; you'd have to wait a day or more after every gassing for it to dissipate, and you'd need good protective garments for the executioners and their helpers . . . which nobody seems to have seen in any of the camps. Nor does the story about vans pumped full of carbon monoxide exhaust fumes stand up. Later experiments show it doesn't work: time-consuming, inefficient, quite impractical.

"The thing to remember when you hear these stories about 'gas chambers,' Mr. Lessing, is that Allied propaganda mythologized the Nazis: the 'German beast,' as Eisenhower called them, had to be exorcised. After the war there was an outcry for justice . . . and revenge. It's been useful to the Jews . . . and to many politicians and others dependent on the Jews . . . to keep those feelings alive."

"Most people say justice was the important thing."

"Most people don't read books. Or they only read the ones the big publishers put out. Have you read that one there . . . the one about the 'Malmedy massacre?' The Germans allegedly slaughtered captured American troops near Malmedy in Belgium in 1944. After the war the Americans tried seventy-three 'perpetrators' and sentenced some of them to death. You'd be surprised at the methods used to extract 'confessions!' Was that justice? And did you know that in April 1945 American troops murdered more than five hundred German soldiers who had *surrendered* at the Dachau camp? No trials. They were simply lined up and shot. Justice?"

"I saw what the Izzies did in Damascus. That doesn't make every Israeli soldier a monster! Revenge . . . wartime hatred."

"Precisely my point! I asked you about justice."

Lessing turned away. "It happened a century ago. It's like getting worked up over the massacre at Little Big Horn!"

"The Jews say that it *must* be remembered: 'Never again!' We Descendants want it remembered just as much because *we* have never received justice. We've been persecuted, vilified, imprisoned, and assassinated. No one looks at our evidence. Our arguments are 'an affront to established history' and 'an insult to the memory of the Holocaust.' Our books are banned in America in spite of the First Amendment to your Constitution. Is freedom of speech only for those who have constituencies and money?"

The boxy, little building was stuffy. Lessing had shut the door, and now he strode over to open it. "I still can't see Adolf Hitler as Mr. Nice Guy."

"Don't be simplistic! Hitler knew what Germany needed, and he did what had to be done. More books have been written about him, I think, than about Jesus Christ, yet ninety-nine percent of them perpetuate the same old nonsense, the same fables and lies, the same speculations . . . some as far-fetched as the Arabian Nights! History demands *proof*, Mr. Lessing, not emotion, however well-intentioned. Yet society wants its heroes and villains pure white or pure black. Human beings *like* being selectively blind: they ignore unpleasant facts, refuse to talk about them, and cover them over, like a cat scuffing sand over its feces! People want stories that make them feel good."

"As my friend, Charles Wren, says: 'History's a whore who knows which side of the bed her butt is bettered on.'"

"Eh? What? Oh . . . aha, quite! The 'bettering' is called 'money.' Our opponents have that aplenty!"

"Your people have money, too. The movement's been hiring ad agencies and p.r. firms. I know."

"True, we *are* doing better than before, but we have a long way to go. Our opponents have made it illegal to 'lie' about history, to 'desecrate the memories of the Six Million Who Died' . . . or even to dispute the 'established view' on the most abstract of historical grounds. An agency of your United States government has ruled that 'the Holocaust cannot be debated.' Yet it is not we who dishonor the dead. We want the truth . . . and if it is against our beliefs, then so be it! No, it is our opponents who have made over the past. What else can you call the writing out of a movement, a nation, an era . . . and the writing in of something else entirely?"

"Um . . . ."

"Do people become enraged when someone argues the rights or wrongs of the Norman Conquest of 1066? Of the Spanish Conquistadores' massacres in Mexico . . . over a million Central American Indians slaughtered between 1492 and 1600? Innocents have died throughout history, including Americans in a dozen wars; you can freely debate those conflicts, even if you make the 'traditional' historians look silly! And what would a judge say if somebody sued the Flat Earthers for 'lying' about geography and astronomy? Or if the Neo-Pagans sued the Christian churches for 'lying' about the Emperor Nero? Not such a bad chap, actually! No, what we have now is an Inquisition, a censorship like the Office of the Index of the Catholic Church. It doesn't need the rack and the stake because its sanctions are more effective!"

The conversation was making Lessing uneasy. These people were right about one thing: the 'traditional' view of history was so solidly implanted in every Western child's head that he felt guilty—almost afraid—even listening to this serious, dry, bookish, Oxford Arab-German. It was like telling your kids that Santa Claus was the Devil. It took considerable balls to question such emotion-laden dogmas as those surrounding the supposed 'Holocaust.' He cast about for another subject. "Will you be able to go home soon?"

"To Damascus?" The Arab shrugged. "Probably never. Not under Israeli rule. Perhaps we can go to Oman . . . my wife has an uncle there. The Izzies never occupied Oman, just 'protected' it a little. You haven't lived, Mr. Lessing, until you've been 'protected' by the Israelis."

"They're tough. I worked for them. I was in Colonel Copley's mercenary battalion during the Baalbek War. I saw what happened to Damascus, Aleppo, and other places. Not pretty."

"And you committed no wartime atrocities? Never saw any you could have stopped?"

Lessing said nothing. His involvement, his personal guilt, was a Pandora's box he never opened. It was better not to look.

Abu Talib went on. "The thing that puzzles us Middle Easterners is America's continual, cheery, fuzzy-headed willingness to go on paying for Israel! It doesn't fit with your talk of democracy, freedom, and personal liberty! You know what the Izzies have done: from the Deir Yassin massacre back in 1948 to frighten the Arabs out of Palestine; to the deliberate attack on the U.S. Navy ship *Liberty*, with the killing of thirty-five of your sailors, back in 1967, in order to keep it from eavesdropping on the Izzies; to the invasion of Lebanon with its ghastly casualties, including the refugee camp massacres that certain high Israeli officers collaborated in; to the killing of Arab prisoners by the Israeli secret police, followed by cover-ups later; to spying against the United States and stealing nuclear weapons materials from you; to the wholesale beatings and shootings of Palestinian children in the Occupied Territories in the 1980s and '90s; to the terrible atrocities they committed at the Sack of Cairo in 2002 . . . right up to the Baalbek War! Yet you people go on *paying* for it . . . while preaching peace and brotherly love to the rest of the world! Before Starak, there was hardly a dissenting voice in your American Congress! You've provided tens of billions of dollars and let the Israelis get away with not paying it back . . . because they make you feel guilty with their century-old stories about the 'Holocaust'! I doubt if even Outram can stop them."

"Nothing new. Money and politicians: the honey and the bees, as my dad used to say."

"The only thing that puzzles me more is Germany's blind acquiescence to paying 'war reparations' to Israel . . . a country that didn't even exist at the time of the Second World War! More than 200 billion marks, and still paying! Even with all the guilt the Jews have managed to pile onto Germany, it doesn't make sense. Germans born after 1935 can no more be guilty than you can because of your ancestors' treatment of the American Indians! I'm surprised the French aren't still collecting 'reparations' for Caesar's conquest of Gaul!"

Lessing spotted the book he wanted beneath a stack of journals. He pulled it out and tried another topic: "Your family like the South Pacific?"

The Arab stopped, finger raised to make yet another point. He blinked and said, "Nadia's adjusting, and Sami and Faisal think the beach was made just for them."

Abu Talib's Syrian wife, Nadia, had been a beauty in her youth, but now her pulchritude was best described as "ample." His two teen-aged sons were addicted to swimming, sports cars, prodigal allowances, and girls. "Spoiled rotten" was a fair description. The boys had set themselves the task of evaluating the sexual potential of each of the fifty girl students sent out by the Party's Brazilian branch. This they performed with efficiency and enthusiasm—singly, in pairs, or in squads. Felix Bauer's new German wife, Helga, was obliged to devote several classes to urgent sex education instead of genetic theory as the curriculum prescribed.

The Arab interrupted Lessing's thought. "And your wife, Mr. Lessing? She's teaching Nadia Indian cooking and learning to make *baklava* in return. Adjusting splendidly, eh?"

Lessing nodded. To be truthful, he didn't know. Jameela was a mystery. Outwardly she had adapted well. She played tennis with Abu Talib's sons, learned bridge from Mrs. Delacroix, went for walks and swimming with Helga Bauer, travelled over to Kolonia, Ponape's one town, to socialize with the Indian merchant families living there, and kept an impeccable household. Yet Lessing sensed an incompleteness: all was not right beneath the surface.

They had discussed having children, but Jameela wanted to wait. What if Pacov were to reoccur? Or the simmering bush wars in Europe to worsen? Or the turmoil in the United States to explode into civil war?

The world was too dangerous now for children, Jameela said. That was no excuse, Lessing had replied: more kids were born during wars than during times of peace. They grew up, lived and died, and kept the species going somehow. She only smiled. After a while he gave up.

Her problem might be homesickness—culture shock—isolation from her own people. She no longer discussed history and genetics with the Party faithful but concentrated on the daily round. All Lessing could do was to provide love and support. That he did to the best of his awkward ability.

As he started to fill out a loan card for the book, he was astonished to see that the desk was brightly lit by light from the windows.

Light?
From the windows?
At midnight?
He whirled, stunned.

There were *five* lights out there. Five brilliant, white suns had risen and hung just above the obsidian sea. He heard the racket of helicopter engines.

The suns were combat spotlights, the kind used to illumine ground-targets at night!

He stared at Abu Talib as the hoarse chatter of copter-mounted mini-guns and the shrieking hiss-boom of air-to-ground rockets started paperclips dancing upon the desk.

Wasn't there anybody up in the watchtower? Who was on duty in the radar and sonar room over in the communications complex?

Lessing rushed out the door. He had to get to his people, organize a defense. Who the hell was attacking them, anyhow?

Another rocket blast dazzled and deafened him. A rose of red flame bloomed over by the darkened dormitories, and blazing rubble pattered down. Screams and yells erupted from behind the communications building, and he heard the lighter yammering of automatic rifles. Somebody on their side *was* shooting back—though ineffectually.

Where was he going? He let his combat nerves take over and found himself flattened against the pitch-fragrant planks of the south wall of the assembly building, Abu Talib beside him. Out in the leaping orange and scarlet glare of the central parade ground he saw people running, most in nightclothes, one or two nearly naked. There were bodies there, too, tumbled piles upon the grass.

"Where . . . ?" the Arab grated in his ear.

He decided.

"Down toward the shore line . . . get Jameela . . . and your wife! Follow me! Do as I do!" He set off at a zig-zag run, Abu Talib at his heels.

A figure bulked up out of the back-lit smoke. It was Wayne Mallon, wearing only boxer shorts, a stitch-gun clutched in both hands. They threw questions at each other, but Mallon knew nothing. He had been up at communications. The trainee on duty had had less than a minute to jabber excitedly at the radar screens before the first big bird soared in from the ocean to spew death. Communications was now a burning shell.

"Come on!" Lessing took off running again, sneakers crunching upon the gravelled path. The helicopter engines still chuffed above their heads, but the rockets and mini-guns had gone silent.

A troop landing was imminent!

They met one of the Brazilian students, a girl of about fifteen. She had found a Riga-71 submachinegun some place, and Lessing paused to wrest it from her. She didn't know what to do with the weapon, and he needed it. She shrieked at him in Portuguese, but all he could do was point her toward the presumed safety of the trees beyond the club's perimeter.

It took them five minutes to negotiate the path from the library to the shore. Bewildered people blocked their way, some wounded, others dazed. The propane tanks behind the mess hall began to explode with bright and deadly regularity. Three of the helicopter-mounted spotlights had gone out, but two still circled above the parade ground. Most of the shooting had stopped.

They saw their first opfoes in the lane beside the assembly hall: two men in tight, black jump suits, heavy backpacks giving them the look of creatures from Mars, faces concealed by plastic visors with built-in com-links. One wore a helmet like a Greek warrior; Lessing saw the dim, red eye that glimmered in its crest: a night-sight. Both carried short-barrelled automatic weapons. He couldn't tell at this distance, but the guns looked Israeli.

He pulled Mallon and Abu Talib into the shadows behind one of the classrooms. "No use," he panted. "We can thumb those two, but they'll have back-up. We go down to the beach, along by the boathouse. I split off there. Head over to my place. Mallon, you stay with Abu Talib and get his family out of the club. Green light?"

Mallon nodded. The Arab would have argued, but Lessing gave him a shove. "Move!"

Gunfire crackled ahead, and they heard more shouts and scream-ing. A rifle grenade shattered a window and exploded. Boots thudded upon the gravel path. Lessing and Mallon both went prone, hauling Abu Talib down on top of themselves. Black figures lum-bered past.

They reached the swimming beach. Lessing's shoes filled with Ponape's sand and treacle-warm sea water. He halted. An opfo crouched on the seawall ahead, squinting inland, away from them, at the pyrotechnics. Lessing put him down with a neck-snapper grip from behind. Abu Talib scrabbled for the man's gun, but it skittered over the edge of the wall into the water. They didn't stop to check whether the opfo was dead.

They raced past the boathouse, their feet splintering the tidal pools into silver needles of moonlight. The shed was dark and silent; the opfoes had smashed the door, found no one inside, and swept on past.

The swimming beach ended beyond the boathouse. Lessing indicated the path that led upslope to Abu Talib's cottage and squatted to cover Mallon and the Arab. He waited until they disap-peared into the trees, then slipped into the underbrush along the shore.

If only he had worn his camouflage fatigues instead of a white shirt and light blue dungarees! Who could have anticipated *this*?

He paused to evaluate the situation. Except for sporadic firing, the battle was over, an easy victory for the enemy. Communications, the arsenal, headquarters, the watchtower, the dormitories, all were ablaze, roaring funeral pyres above the sable-velvet jungle. Somebody was using a bullhorn to call the survivors to surrender. Brief fusillades of shots followed. Perhaps Club Lingahnie's younger guests would be spared, but it sounded as though the instructors and senior visitors were being "emphatically de-activated," to use the current euphemism.

He went on, gliding unseen through the hundred or so meters of undergrowth that separated the swimming beach from his quarters, past angular blacknesses that were garden chairs and tables, to press himself against the cool, white-painted wall.

His living room was brightly lit, not by the Club's electrical system—that was a bonfire now—but by a single, dazzling beam: a hand-held spotlight.

He slipped around to the side, clambered up onto the South Sea Island-style verandah, dodged potted palms and porch furniture, and slid along the wall by the kitchen. He avoided the back door—there might be a sentry—and peered in through the pantry window. Its inner door was open, and he could see most of the living room. The archway to the kitchen was outside of his field of vision to his right. Directly opposite, beyond the serving bar that divided the front room from the kitchen area, lay the hallway that led back to the three bedrooms. A heavy, battery-powered military lantern squatted like a one-eyed Cyclops atop the blue, plastic surface of the bar.

Jameela leaned against the serving bar facing him, her silken *shalwar-qameez* sleeping costume silver and ice-blue in the lantern's stark beam. Behind her, in the semi-darkness of the living room, he recognized Helga Bauer. What was she holding in her hands? A golden pot? No, it looked like Lessing's Alladin's lamp! What was going on?

He risked standing up, his light-colored clothing good camouflage against the white wall, and got a clear view of the interior. Somebody—Felix Bauer—knelt there upon Jameela's Persian carpet, one leg of the overturned coffee table sticking up beside him like a spike. The German was swaying rhythmically to and fro. What was he doing? Using some sort of tool? A military field shovel?

Lessing realized what was happening.

Bauer, Jameela, and Helga were captives. Lessing sensed someone in the kitchen, and there was almost certainly another opfo in the farther shadows of the living room: the shadow of a gun barrel showed there against Jameela's gay, blue-and-white drapes.

The man in the kitchen came into the living room.

It was Richmond. He halted beside Jameela at the serving counter and said something to Bauer.

The kikibird looked the same as when Lessing had last seen him in New Orleans: the baggy suit limp and unpressed, the big hands as bony and pale, the liver spots like blotches of purplish decay upon the balding skull. He bent and took something gingerly from Bauer's fingers. His expression was no longer morose. He looked positively happy—satisfied—exalted.

He had found Lessing's stash of Pacov.

Bauer must have told him, willingly or otherwise, and the opfoes had made the German dig it up!

Richmond had what he wanted. He was inspecting the metal box Bauer handed him. He forced the latch open, looked inside, and smiled. Jameela—and Bauer and Helga—were of no further use. Perhaps he wouldn't harm them.

But then perhaps he might.

Richmond spoke to the invisible man in the living room, at first imperiously and then with angry insistence. Lessing felt rather than heard the vibrations of his voice through the flimsy wooden wall. At last a bearded commando in a black combat tunic appeared to bark a command at the two women. He gestured with the muzzle of his submachine gun toward the hallway leading to the bedrooms.

From the kitchen a louder voice snapped a sentence in a language Lessing recognized as Hebrew. Blackbeard halted, indecision mirrored upon his swarthy features.

Richmond arose clutching the plastic envelope containing the two containers of Pacov to his rumpled shirt-front as a preacher holds a Bible. Lessing's Stik-Ever tape seals came away, and Richmond pulled out first the silvery globe of Pacov-1, then the black cylinder of Pacov-2. He held them up to the light. He said something else. The soldier looked past him at the man in the kitchen.

This third opfo chose this moment to emerge and stand arms akimbo in the kitchen archway. There was no insignia on his battle-dress, but the up-jutting chin, the neat pencil of moustache, the cap of close-cropped, curly, black hair, and the arrogant set of his shoulder blades identified him; Lessing had met his like many times during the Baalbek War. Here, almost certainly, was the commanding officer, the one who had supervised the massacre of Club Lingahnie.

The officer appeared upset. Lessing didn't need to hear the words, which were in Hebrew. Richmond was interfering in the chain of command, and the C.O. was having none of it. A camouflage-daubed finger swept up and pointed: outside! Civilians out! Stay the hell out of military business!

Richmond shook his head vehemently and shot a contemptuous remark down at Bauer. The German still squatted in the seeping water in the shallow pit he had dug, head down and arms at his sides. He probably already thought of himself as dead. Neither of the two women had moved.

Richmond held up the envelope, tapped the glassine. It was the officer's turn to shake his head. The kikibird persisted, anger-ridges on his cheeks gleaming fish-belly white in the spotlight's beam.

The officer waved a hand in a furious "I-give-up" gesture. He was surrendering to higher authority: political clout over military expertise.

The bearded soldier mouthed an order and raised his gun again. Helga and Jameela both spoke at once, but Lessing couldn't make out what they said. Blackbeard began to herd them along the hall toward the bedrooms. Helga Bauer turned her face toward Richmond, and Lessing saw that she was weeping, pleading, begging. The soldier thrust her brusquely on into the master bedroom at the end of the short corridor. Jameela followed. Blackbeard banged the door shut after them; then he returned, his snub-nosed submachine gun nonchalantly cradled in one black-sleeved arm.

He halted behind Bauer, bent, and touched the nape of the German's neck with his weapon's muzzle. Bauer shut his eyes and opened his mouth in a round "O."

The soldier backed off a step and fired one round.

Bauer tumbled forward, his life already gone. The walls of the sandy pit started to collapse upon his convulsing limbs, and muddy, red water sloshed up onto the darker red of Jameela's carpet.

In the bedroom Helga Bauer shrieked. Her anguish was audible even through two walls and over the racket of distant explosions.

Richmond gave another order. The soldier rubbed at his bristly beard, grinned, and turned back to the bedroom door. The officer stalked forward to protest, clenching a fist under the kikibird's nose. Richmond's face took on a piously superior expression, the look of a man who quotes directly from the Holy Book: a Supreme Party Directive, an Imperial Edict—whatever the current omnipotent authority happened to be. The officer threw up his hands in disgust and tramped back into the kitchen.

Richmond grinned at Blackbeard and jabbed a thumb toward the bedrooms. He reached down and patted himself on the crotch of his baggy trousers: an unmistakably soiled, ugly, obscene gesture.

Enough was enough.

Lessing stepped back where he was safe from flying glass, aimed for Blackbeard, and put a half dozen rounds from his Riga-71 through the pantry window. He snapped off a quick shot at Richmond as well but didn't dare fire a longer burst into the living room.

Jameela and Helga Bauer were in the bedroom behind its far wall; that, he knew, consisted of no more than two sheets of fibreboard. Bullets would go right through it.

Blackbeard leaped straight up, then went down, arms windmilling. Slugs from his submachine gun ripped splinters and plaster from the ceiling.

The commander in the kitchen screamed something. His pistol barrel poked out around the corner of the archway. Lessing was prepared: he rolled across to the left side of the pantry window, and the officer's shots whined harmlessly off into the night. The man now committed the mistake Lessing had almost made: he mistook the flimsy partition for solid cover. Lessing's gun yammered. The officer came tumbling out from behind the riddled door-jamb, his eyes wide as he gaped at the ruin half a magazine of steel-jacketed lead had made of his natty tunic.

There were times when one had to appreciate substandard building practices.

Noise erupted from the kitchen. Either a second man was already there, or else a sentry had just entered through the back door. Stitch-gun explosions peppered the woodwork beside Lessing's head. He let off only one shot in return. His magazine must be nearly empty, and he had no more.

The third man began to squall for help. Lessing cast about, found a chunk of wood from the shattered window sash, and lobbed it around the corner into the kitchen. At the same time he yelled as though to friends behind him, "Down, you guys! *Grenade!*"

The refrigerator door slammed as his opponent dived behind it. Lessing leaped in through the pantry window, crouched, skidded, and rose up from behind the serving bar. He rattled off his last shots into the figure he glimpsed cowering on the kitchen floor.

"Sorry, no grenade," Lessing panted at him. "Fresh out!" The man shrieked and jackknifed over.

In a single motion Lessing fell to his knees, twisted, and came up with Blackbeard's pretty, little submachine gun. He performed a land-based barrel roll and ended covering the living room.

Richmond wasn't there.

The room was empty. The front door hung ajar.

Footsteps pounded along the verandah outside.

Glass crashed at the far end of the house, followed by a crescendo of sharp pistol shots. Lessing heard screams. Women's screams.

Oh, God . . . .

His thigh muscles cramped as he staggered to his feet. He was getting too old for this kind of thing!

Then he was at the bedroom door. Once, twice, he slammed his shoulder into the panel, unaware of any pain. It sprang open, and he staggered through.

In the spotlight's reflected glare he saw Helga Bauer crouching by the bed. She was dead, her limbs outflung, her eyes wide open, like china marbles. Her heavy breasts were suffused with dark blood.

On the floor, by the window, lay a sprawl of silver and ice-blue.

Jameela had been struggling to open the sash when Richmond had come running around the corner of the verandah. He must have seen the women through the window and fired at them, out of sheer malice.

Lessing knelt beside his wife, turned her over, cradled her head, felt the seeping wetness among her tangled tresses. There was blood everywhere. He didn't know how to stanch it, what to do. The Club doctor? Mallon? Abu Talib? Mrs. Delacroix? He even thought of surrendering, yelling for the opfoes to send in a medic.

Useless.

Years of combat experience told him that. He let Jameela down again, as gently as he could.

Shock numbed him. Sour vomit and bitter bile choked in his throat. His fingers trembled and clenched upon his wife's dark-sticky, silver nightdress.

Blazing rage. Cold fury. Black hatred.

He *ought* to be feeling those things. But he didn't.

What he felt was something else, something neither hot nor cold, red nor black, sweet nor bitter: an orgasm, a climax, a rush like a shot of 150-proof Cuban rum, a pop of heroin, and a big snuffle of happy dust, all at once.

Lessing knew the need to murder.

He got to his feet. Shouts sounded from upslope, behind the house, and others answered from the swimming beach. Opfoes were coming. He eased himself out through the bedroom window.

Richmond.

He would find Richmond. He would kill Richmond.

A black spot caught his eye: a smear of glistening blood upon the verandah railing. He must have nicked him—or the bastard had cut himself on the broken glass from the window. Richmond would leave a trail.

Lessing permitted himself a smile.

A landscaped terrace extended out some six meters from this side of the manager's house. Beyond lay an undergrowth-choked ravine that separated Lessing's grounds from the knoll occupied by the communications complex. The latter was an inferno, dying now, and shrouded in a pall of smoke. Man-made lights flickered there, and figures moved like satanic puppets amidst the red-limned smoke. The opfoes were probably using the place as a beacon, a regrouping center for their troops. Lessing thought to hear the whuff-whuff of helicopter blades above the hiss and crackle of the fire.

Richmond would head in that direction. What the kikibird might not know was that the far side of the ravine was steep and the underbrush too dense to penetrate without a machete.

Lessing crossed the terrace and dropped down into the tangled bushes below. The damp vegetation had the claustrophobic feel of a rabbit warren, a troll's tunnel down to Hell. He noted a second blood smear on the trunk of a sapling. He bared his teeth again; Richmond had passed this way.

When Richmond discovered he couldn't get up the opposite bank he would turn left, down the ravine, toward the shore. Then he would try to follow the beach around the rocky headland to the communications jetty.

He'd pick his way with extra caution. The two fragile flasks he carried were more deadly than the Serpent's apple in the Garden of Eden.

Branches rustled and snapped. Somebody ahead was panting, wheezing in fatigue and panic. Lessing froze to check Blackbeard's submachine gun. The magazine still held five cartridges. Wonder of wonders, the weapon was made to hold two magazines at once, and the second one was both present and full!

"Richmond," he called softly. "Hey, Richmond. I'm coming."

Patience, the prime virtue for both pursuer and pursued, was hard, but he forced himself to stay still. At last a tiny splash echoed up from below. He could see nothing, black upon black, ebon crepe upon sable. Lessing began to creep on his belly toward the water. Slimy-feeling wet leaves caressed his cheeks, and the stench of warm decay clogged his nostrils. Another time he might have worried about snakes, leeches, and insects; now they didn't matter.

Sharp wedges of light slashed the brush behind him: powerful electric lanterns. Richmond's friends were here.

Somebody yelled, "This way!" A second voice questioned, *"Zay hu?"* A third snarled, "How the hell should I know?" and launched into a disgruntled diatribe in Hebrew. Branches crunched, twigs rattled, and someone more nervous than the rest let off a shot, followed by a grunted obscenity.

There was little time. The opfoes would thumb him. He had to kill Richmond first. Life held no other purpose.

Soft splashing sounded again farther off to the right. Lessing found himself amidst logs and driftwood, bare and ghostly white, like the bleached skeletons of prehistoric animals. He almost fell headlong into a tidal pool, and little nocturnal sea creatures scuttled away in terror.

The lights above and behind him were closer; the opfoes were descending the slope in a ragged skirmish line.

There: a sable blotch upon the leaden blur of the sea. Lessing writhed down over the lighter grey of a log and slid into the brackish water. He crawled, wriggled, got to his knees, then to a crouch, only his face and his gun above the tepid, lapping waves. The blotch halted; a white oval appeared at its top: Richmond had turned to look back.

Beams of light cut the darkness. A voice bawled a question. Richmond answered with a hoarse bleat for help.

It had to be now.

Lessing raised himself just enough to take aim. He let off everything that was left in the first magazine, fumbled the lever that switched to the second one, and added another half-dozen rounds for good measure. The little weapon chattered, sounding like a child's toy out here in the open. Richmond squealed, a high, thin sound, like a wounded puppy.

Lessing heard a splash, then floundering. He slid back down into the water two meters from his original position. Lights, shouts, and gunfire poured out of the blackness behind him, and a line of slugs raised roiling foam in the place where he had been.

He crawled, dived, and swam, ignoring the scrapes he got from barnacles in the shallow water. Shots spattered behind him. A slug plunked into the water a meter from his face, and he ducked, stopped for breath, and peered around. Dim, shifting forms were visible against the ink-black of the shore: the opfoes were fishing Richmond out of the drink.

What now? He could leap up to empty his gun into Richmond and his rescuers. No, that was stupid. In Lessing's book suicide wasn't unthinkable, but it had to have a purpose.

Lessing was a fair swimmer. He could head straight out into Madolenihmw Bay, then travel parallel to the beach until he could come ashore beyond the club perimeter. Suicide might be more attractive then: gather what survivors he could and return to kill as many of these black-clad murderers as he could. Heroism? No, just revenge.

But why? Why bother? Jameela was dead.

Her death hadn't hit him yet. Better to act now, while he was still sane, before he went berserk.

Lights clustered around Richmond's limp body. Five or six opfoes were hauling a stretcher down through the undergrowth. Others were looking out to sea, toward Lessing. They couldn't see him. He was just a ripple or a chunk of flotsam on the water. He could stay that way for at least another hour before the first glimmering of false dawn. He could still escape.

His foot struck against a hard object: a boulder. He cursed under his breath and veered away.

And he saw something that awoke horror all the way down to the roots of his primordial soul!

Floating right beside him, six inches away, was a human face! The eyes were open, pupilless, and white. The mouth hung agape. The lank, wispy hair was like drowned seaweed.

Memories of nightmare! The dead chiefs of old Ponape! Pacov's myriad bloated victims!

He thrashed, gulped water, choked, and coughed. He couldn't help it.

He gathered his feet under him, scraping his ankle against the jagged rock, and found that the water was just neck-deep. He lurched up, fear loosening his bowels.

The face was that of Sami Abu Talib. The boy was dead, quite naked, a dark red corsage of a bullet hole in his left breast. Near him Lessing saw a second body: a girl, also nude, her long tresses tangled with leaves and twigs and wrapped around her face, her breasts bobbing gently in the languorous waves. The opfoes had surprised poor Sami with one of his Brazilian popsies, the last date he would ever enjoy.

Lessing had been seen. A soldier shouted, *"Hu shama!"* Others echoed him. Somebody called, "There he is!" Shots spattered the water nearby, and the Arab boy's corpse jerked and writhed as more bullets struck it.

Lessing dived over the half-submerged rock, seeking deeper water on its seaward side. Something spanged off the boulder, and he felt stinging pain above his left ear.

Dazzling light. A bursting rocket of agony in his skull.

His eyesight dimmed.

There! He was on the outer side of the rock. He let himself sink down into the soft, warm, nurturing ocean, out of sight, beyond harm, down where none could see.

He would hide. His mother wouldn't find him here. She'd search the house in vain. His father would eventually come to help, puffing ineffectually at his pipe and grumbling. But Lessing was hidden, down at the bottom of the bathtub, hidden . . . .

Figures loomed over him. His parents? Only one way out! He thrashed and struggled. He would swim right down the drain, down and down, slipping like an eel through the pipes beneath the house until he reached the sewers, then the river, and eventually the safety of the great, endless, all-embracing sea.

Calm.

Eternity.

He knew nothing for a time.

Then he was awake again. Hands held him, and brusque fingers probed at the left side of his head above his ear. Pain danced there, and he tried to pull away. A gutturally accented voice said, "Hold the bastard. One more stitch."

"Will he live?" someone else questioned in crisper, lighter tones.

"Why not? But am I wasting my time? Are you just going to shoot him when I'm done?" Something soft pressed against Lessing's temple, and he heard adhesive tape being ripped from its reel. He discovered that he was strapped to a stretcher, his hands manacled in front of him. His wrists hurt.

"*We* won't. That's for headquarters to decide. This is Alan Lessing, the manager of this snakepit. He's on Captain Levi's list. He goes back to Jerusalem with us."

"What the hell for?" a third, deeper voice snarled. "Isn't he the one who thumbed the captain? And Ariel? And the tech-sergeant . . . whatzizname?"

"Yes. And Richmond too," Crisp-voice added.

"Who cares about that schmuck? Captain Levi, now . . . ."

"Why was Richmond sent along with this mission anyway?" Guttural-voice interrupted. "Trouble! Trouble!" He mumbled on in Hebrew.

"Hey, I don't speak Hebrew that well," complained the man Lessing called Crisp-voice. "It still isn't the official language in the United States!"

"Not yet, anyway!" said the man with the guttural accent, he who seemed to be the medic.

"Maybe not ever. Not with Outram and his putzes getting cuter every day."

Somebody in the background muttered, "We'll take care of them too, just like this bunch."

"We didn't do all that well here," the medic complained. "Got none of their top people except the Arab and the old lady. And this guy."

Deep-voice snorted. "So what do you want? We took out their whole installation! And little piss-holes like Ponape are going to think a long time before letting these fuckers build new ones!"

"Anyway, Richmond was none of our business," Crisp-voice finished. "Captain Levi was the only one who was briefed about him. Now they're both dead."

"Let's get this Nazi bastard over to the copters," Deep-voice suggested. "Our wounded and the other prisoners are already gone, and we're supposed to be off this shit-pile by oh-three-hundred." Lessing's stretcher was lifted, then borne outside along uneven pathways, over obstacles, and through unseen, dew-dripping branches. Flashlight beams swung and danced beside him. He guessed dizzily that they were heading up across the parade ground and over to what was left of the communications building.

A new voice, a woman's, spoke in his ear. "You'll be all right. Your wound is minor . . . a flap of scalp torn loose by a rock fragment." He smelled disinfectant and knew without seeing that here was a tired, middle-aged nurse. She sounded sympathetic.

"My wife," he husked. "My wife? Jameela?" Saying her name was like shovelling dirt upon her coffin. "Jameela? My wife!" He couldn't bring himself to ask if she were dead.

The nurse was silent. Then: "Your clothes are wet and bloody. I've brought you a dry shirt and a pair of pants from your wardrobe back there."

"My wife, God damn it!"

"I don't know. I wasn't told." She was lying. He knew now for certain.

Only one of the big helicopters still crouched in front of the charred shell that had housed the communications center. Lessing's bearers lugged him up a clanging, oil-stinking metal ramp into a cargo-bay crammed with web-tied crates and lit by a couple of bluish glow-lamps. He was dumped, stretcher and all, between two other stretchers. A stocky commando sat down facing Lessing, rifle between his knees.

He strained to see who his neighbors were. To his left, Abu Talib's aquiline features were visible amidst a swirl of blankets. The Arab did not move, and his eyes were closed. He was still alive: the rise and fall of his chest showed that. The Izzies had probably drugged him, either for medical reasons or to keep him quiet.

The man on Lessing's right was Richmond.

He was dead.

The Izzies had covered his face with a blanket, but it had partially slipped off. His long, pallid features looked slightly less lugubrious in death than in life. Lessing could see no wounds because of the blanket, but sea water and blood stained the grimy, metal deck beneath his stretcher.

The nurse returned and unbuckled the straps holding Lessing to the stretcher. "Sit up. I don't have the key to the cuffs, but I can get you out of your wet clothes and into something dry. Here, these *are* yours, aren't they?"

Who cared about dry clothes? They were irrelevant. Jameela was gone.

"Don't worry," the woman said. "I'm a nurse. I've seen naked men before." She sounded as though that were some kind of major personal sacrifice.

Her old-fashioned prudery gave Lessing a glimmer of amusement. She seemed so flustered, so tired, and so sincere. He let her have her way.

The pants were his light grey dungarees. Jameela had ironed them the day before yesterday, back when the world was different. He didn't recognize the white shirt at first, then realized it was the one he had worn to visit the Black Muslim leader, the Khalifa, in Los Angeles. He hadn't put it on since.

The nurse got his trousers changed, clucking at the barnacle scratches and abrasions. The handcuffs prevented her from changing his shirt, and she had to be satisfied with draping the dry one over his shoulders. He huddled back down upon the hard stretcher. The feel of the cloth reminded him of Morgan, the Khalifa—and Jameela.

Suddenly he wondered whether the Khalifa's little zombie pill—what was its name? tetrodotoxin?—was still in the breast pocket of the shirt? He had never removed it. If it were there, he had a way to avoid torture, perhaps to escape! He rolled over so that neither the nurse nor the stolid guard could see, and let his fingers wander over the fabric.

He felt a tiny lump deep within the pocket seam. A bit of tissue? A theater ticket stub? A forgotten aspirin?

It was the zombie pill.

Excitement swept over him. Where could he hide it? The Izzies would certainly strip him, search him head to foot, and issue him their favorite prison garb, a blue jogging suit. They'd find the pill! He thought as hard as the ache in his head would let him. Of course! His head! He raised his hands to the bandage on his temple, groaned, and slumped down. A corner of the cotton pad came free in his fingers, and he poked the little pill into a fold in the cleanest and driest part of it. That would have to do for now. He'd do better once they got him where he was going.

He was minded of Copley's story about a captured merc who melted a plastic spoon on the light bulb in his cell and used the goo to coat a smuggled cyanide pill so that it was watertight and wouldn't dissolve. This he swallowed, waited until it reappeared in his stool, cleaned it off, and swallowed it again—and again, and again, over and over, for months. At last, when he could endure no more of his captors' "discipline," the merc cracked the plastic coating with his teeth and became history. The funny part, according to Copley, was the guards' dismay at their captive's unexpected exit: in that country—Lessing couldn't recall which it was—whenever a prisoner escaped or succeeded in suicide, his guards were made to draw lots, and the loser faced a firing squad. Hilarious!

The helicopter groaned, shuddered, and lurched up into the pre-dawn sky. The flight did not take long; the Izzies' ship lay just offshore. It was one of their newer, nuclear-powered destroyers. They had built up quite an impressive navy during their past two decades of conquest in the Persian Gulf and the Mediterranean.

Lessing was hustled out onto the gently pitching deck. The cool, damp, salt-smelling air felt good. He looked around to see black-clad commandos forming up, sailors in tan uniforms hurrying to and fro, and technicians swarming over the locust-like giant helicopters. They were about to get underway. He thought he glimpsed a group of fellow prisoners huddled together against a bulkhead, but a forklift carrying a stack of boxes rumbled in front of them, and when it had passed they were gone. Had that flash of silver been Mrs. Delacroix' white hair? Farther away he spotted five or six stretchers laid out on the deck surrounded by medics and orderlies. Were the occupants Izzie casualties or his own comrades? He had no way to tell.

All would become clear later. He would probably find that clarification very painful.

Lessing watched as two sailors carried Abu Talib's stretcher past him. Two more wrestled Richmond's stiffening corpse into a brown plastic body-bag and zipped it shut. As they did so, Lessing noticed something on the damp, dark-stained cloth of the stretcher where the kikibird had lain. Lessing looked. A bit of glass? A sliver of mirror? Something glittered there in the misty morning light.

He knew what it was.

A shard of Pacov-1's silvery globe.

The open flap of Lessing's glassine envelope had been sticking out of Richmond's pocket when the sailors lifted his body.

Sea water. Richmond's swim in Madolenihmw Bay must have done it!

The containers were half a century old, fragile, and probably designed to be water soluble. What better way to deliver their contents? They must have started to decompose the moment they got wet.

What of the black cylinder—Pacov-2? That wasn't likely to be in any better condition.

Everybody here, Lessing included, was certainly infected with Pacov-1. If Pacov-2 were free as well, it was over for everybody on this ship—possibly on Ponape itself.

Only Captain Levi, the man Lessing had killed, knew what Richmond's mission was. The other Izzies had no reason to search the kikibird's body. They wouldn't have recognized Pacov even if they had found it!

What to do?

The Khalifa's pill might save him, of course. It wasn't likely, but it *might*. But when to swallow it? Too soon, and his captors would toss his "dead" body into the sea! Worse, they might wait until they reached home and then bury him alive; waking up in a coffin held no appeal! Too late, and Lessing would die from Pacov! He racked his brain but could only recall Mulder saying something about waiting a couple of weeks—or was it months?—after Pacov-1 before sending in Pacov-2. As imprecise as you could get. Would it make any difference if both viruses were introduced at once?

With a shudder he realized he was being himself as usual: abstract and objective. What of Alan Lessing? It was *his* death, too!

He could tell the Izzies. They might believe him, in which case they would probably shoot him anyway. Furthermore, he could tell them about the Khalifa's pill; they'd take it away for testing, but they could never manufacture the stuff in time to save the people on this destroyer.

He could be really noble and wait until Israel itself was infected, and *then* tell them. Benefactor of Israel? He suspected the Izzies would never award him any medals.

Did he care? Let them all die!

Jameela. Every Izzie was not responsible for her death. Of course, not directly—but as much as the collective population of any nation is responsible for the acts of its soldiers. Richmond had killed—he managed to think the word—her.

Richmond was dead. Lessing found that he took no pleasure from that. Every country had psychopaths and sadists like Richmond.

Did he care, then, about the Izzies? The commandos who had slaughtered his companions on Ponape? The sailors on this ship? The people of Israel itself?

The Izzies had always struck him as being tougher, harder, and less sympathetic to those who were not Jewish. They set their goals and then did what was necessary to achieve them. They'd go on this way until no one dared to oppose or even criticize them. The Israelis played to win. Mulder said that one day the Jews would rule the world if the rest of humanity was lazy enough to let them.

Were they so different from the Romans, the Mongols, the Russians—or, for that matter, the Nazis?

He doubted whether the Izzies would provide zombie pills to save their few remaining Arab "citizens," even if they had a mountain of the stuff!

He temporized by asking the nurse, "How long will it take to get to Jerusalem?"

His guard answered him instead. "In a hurry, Herr Hitler? They get you there, you wish you were some place else."

"We'll be around the island to Kolonia in an hour," the nurse added. "The local government has given us permission to bring in cargo planes. We'll reach Israel within twenty-four hours." She sounded almost apologetic.

"The Ponapeans gave you permission to land?"

The guard chuckled. "Either we land or we turn Ponape into graveyard. They say, 'No problem.'"

Intimidation again.

"That man." Lessing lifted his chin toward Richmond. "Do I have to travel with *his* ugly corpse? He killed my wife in cold blood!"

"Good." The guard sneered. "Fuck your Nazi bitch. That man was good. We send him, you, others, by air. To Jerusalem. He get hero's funeral. You, you just get funeral!"

So Richmond's body bag would be opened in Israel and not shipped back to the United States. Lessing had to know whether the black cylinder was intact.

He fell to his knees beside Richmond, slammed his fists down upon the corpse's plastic-draped chest, and went into a pretended paroxysm of grief and fury. "Bastard!" he choked. "Bastard!" He discovered that he wasn't entirely pretending. "Murderer! You killed my wife!" He probed cautiously with one hand at the dead man's side.

Inside the body-bag he felt the lump that must be the black cylinder of Pacov-2 in Richmond's coat pocket. It still seemed solid, but the rounded, crumbling corners told him that it, too, was disintegrating. It wouldn't be long.

Even if he started hollering right now, they were almost certain to die. He had expected it, but his stomach cramped up nevertheless. He fought to keep his sphincter muscles from letting go.

To tell the Izzies or not?

They weren't all like Richmond.

Jameela. Bauer. Helga. Sami Abu Talib and his pretty, vapid Brazilian girlfriend. Possibly Mrs. Delacroix. Shrivelled, eyeless Arab faces crushed by tank-treads into the baking dust of Aleppo. The grey, still hand of a child protruding from under a fallen wall in Damascus. An old woman in rags hunched over the blackened corpse of a little girl in some nameless town in Syria.

Heretofore Lessing had been the 'Empty Man.' Now he was full. To the brim.

He realized that his mind was made up.

Death followed the Israelis wherever they went; now let Him catch up with them.

He wouldn't tell them about Pacov. To hell with them. Literally!

"Get up!" the guard commanded from behind him. "Up! Up!" He snatched at Lessing's shoulder and slapped at the back of his head with an open palm. The blow was a light one, yet Lessing's wound made the pain blinding. Darkness swooped in.

"No! Stop that!" the nurse cried. She added more words in Hebrew.

Lessing saw the guard's foot coming. He waited, caught it in his bound hands, and jerked. Off balance, the soldier stumbled and fell forward. Lessing used the man's own momentum to break his ankle. For one glorious moment he had a grip on the guard's rifle; then sailors and other guards wrested it away again. Fists, feet, and rifle butts pounded at him, and he went down, elbows up to protect his head.

It took two commandoes and three sailors a good two minutes to subdue him. Then they beat him for perhaps another three minutes while the nurse shrilled futile protests.

Lessing didn't care. He hardly felt the blows.

At last they shackled him hand and foot to await transport to Jerusalem.

He was still smiling, faintly, when they arrived.

He will bring upon thee all the diseases of Egypt. . . . Also
every sickness, and every plague . . . until thou be destroyed.
   —**Deuteronomy, 28: 60, 61**

CHAPTER NINETEEN

Monday, February 22, 2044

By now Lessing knew every crack in the floor and every flake in
the plaster of the corridor leading to Sonny's office. The brick
walls were painted a scuffed red-brown to shoulder height, then
whitewashed the rest of the way up to the high ceiling. The floor
was a muddy mahogany in color, daubed thick here and thin there,
so that half a dozen older coats showed through. The building looked
and smelled ancient, but it dated back only to the reconstruction after
the expulsion of Israel's Arab population some thirty years before.
Lessing assumed his prison was part of some larger police complex,
but no one ever said where it was. His guards, two dark-skinned
North African Jews, had once spoken of Derekh Shekhem Street as
being just outside; that meant northeastern Jerusalem, if memory
served him right.

Inside this warren Sonny—the only name his interrogator ever
used—occupied an office of relative splendor: beige walls, venetian
blinds, scarlet-and-blue Arab carpets, pictures of Israel's bewhis-
kered founders, a couple of landscape paintings, a decent desk
(under an untidy mound of papers and files), a silver coffee service
that had been "liberated" from a mansion in Damascus, a Japanese
television set, a Taiwanese stereo, a Chinese VCR, and a Korean
laser-disc player with all the frills. Sonny's chair too was a wonder
of chrome and fake leopardskin. Even his "guests" got cushioned
seats and their choice of soda, beer, or coffee.

Sonny himself was short, stocky, and mid-thirtyish. Like many
Jews of Slavic extraction, his hair was short, curly-frizzy, and as
blonde as a starlet's bottle job. He wore open-necked, knit sport
shirts, pastel pants (lime green last week), and expensive running
shoes. He was an officer of ARAD, Israel's intelligence service, an
organization built upon the traditions of many that had gone before:
the Mossad, the CIA, the KGB, the OSS, the Cheka . . . . Sonny was
but a modern incarnation in a line of inquisitors that stretched all the
way back to the dungeons of old Assyria.

Not that he had ever harmed Lessing. Indeed, he had never so
much as breathed on him. To Sonny, Lessing was a *rosh katan*, a
"little head": small fry, a nothing, a nobody, a merc who had been
unlucky enough to be on the wrong side when the shit came down.
After establishing Lessing's status in the Party of Humankind and
discovering that he was almost apolitical, Sonny took no further

professional interest. He did summon Lessing in occasionally, but mostly to talk about movies, food, clothes, slang, Banger porn-queens, and sports—anything modern, anything American. Sonny's secret yearning, it seemed, was to share the joys of those sainted souls who dwelt in Beverly Hills, perhaps eventually to live in the empyrean realm of Malibu itself!

So far Lessing had had an easy time of it. His captors did indeed strip him, search him, and issue him the inevitable blue jogging suit. They then put him into a comfortable cell—more like a room in a college dormitory—which contained a bed, a toilet, a washstand, a table that folded out from the wall, and a chair. The food was edible, and he had no complaints about his treatment. A Spartan might have griped about too much luxury!

He did have a bad moment at first, trying to hide the Khalifa's zombie pill; yet it turned out to be simple. The Izzies weren't expecting him to be carrying anything. A dentist inspected his teeth for suicide capsules, and the body search was humiliating, but that was all. He easily wiggled his tiny treasure out of his head bandage and into a seam in the jogging suit without anyone seeing. Later he transferred it to the hollow metal tube of the toilet-paper fixture in his cell. It was still there the last time he had looked.

No one suspected him of having anything to do with Pacov—no one here in Israel, anyway. Of this he was certain. Through Sonny and his guards, Lessing kept track of the influenza that had struck Israel recently, but he had no way of telling whether it was the first kiss of Pacov-1's silvery scythe or just the usual winter blahs. When two weeks passed without incident, he began to think that Pacov-2's black cylinder had not ruptured—or was ineffective—or had been found and neutralized when Richmond's corpse was prepared for burial. Perhaps they had planted it with him. What irony: bloody-minded old Richmond pushing up Pacov-scented daisies!

Why weren't the Izzies curious about the contents of Richmond's pockets? Few people carry around a glassine envelope containing shards of mirror-bright plastic and an eroded-looking black cylinder. In this post-Pacov age it was impossible *not* to be suspicious of such bric-a-brac! Had both containers decayed beyond recognition? Perhaps some hapless sailor had stolen the black cylinder, thinking it was valuable—or a morgue attendant—or one of Richmond's relatives to whom the body had been handed over?

Where *was* Pacov-2?

A related puzzle: why weren't Richmond's superiors asking questions? Whoever had sent him must believe that the mission had failed—that the kikibird had never found Lessing's Pacov—other-wise they'd already be here. Still, wouldn't they send out some other poor sucker—a martyr or an unwitting human sacrifice—to check?

Sonny did ask about Richmond, the pit dug in Lessing's living room floor, and the execution of Bauer. Lessing had a plausible story ready: Richmond had been greedy, working for himself as well as his handlers, and Bauer had tried to buy his life with a cache of SS documents—and Lessing's cash reserve for Club Lingahnie operations. Sonny ingested this without blinking. Whether he believed it was something else; the man was no fool.

The zillion-dollar question was Pacov-2 itself. If the tube were intact there was no immediate problem. Not now. But later? Ever? If it *had* ruptured, the possibilities were dreadful. In spite of his earlier resolve, Lessing found he had no stomach for genocide. From Sonny's window he could see men, women, and children. Most were Israelis, but some were Arabs or foreigners. He had no feelings for them, neither love nor hate; yet he did not want them to die because of him.

What choice did he—and they—have anyway? If Pacov were truly loose, he couldn't save them. They would all be infected by now. Any person who didn't swallow a zombie pill—who knew *when*?—and assuming the stuff worked—was dead. Running wouldn't help, even if there were some place to run. Why cause a senseless panic? Let Pacov's customers enjoy their last days in happy ignorance.

His logic gave him no peace. He couldn't sleep. The prison doctor prescribed sleeping pills.

Sonny seemed genuinely concerned. "What're you scared of, Lessing? You haven't been hurt . . . and you're a lot safer here with us than with your Nazi buddies. In a month or two, after the excitement about Ponape dies down, we'll let you go, and you can rejoin your old merc unit. Colonel Copley's working for us now, up near Sverdlovsk. Did you know?"

Lessing did not enlighten him. He decided that Pacov—Death, God, the Devil, Mother Nature, the Tooth Fairy—whoever or whatever—must take its course.

He also discovered that his own private grief came first. The fate of the world no longer concerned him. All he wanted was to mourn Jameela, secretly, alone, down in the innermost sanctuary of his soul.

Jameela . . . .

She was always there. He never saw her as the vivacious girl he had loved in Lucknow, nor even the out-of-place housewife she became later on Ponape. No, she appeared always as a silent huddle of silver and ice-blue on their bedroom floor. Over and over again he felt the limp, lolling looseness when he raised her head, and he smelled her sandalwood perfume mingled with acrid gunpowder and the reek of blood. He dreamed—he couldn't help it—and he awoke with his cheeks wet with tears.

Real men don't cry? Bullshit! It's the *real* men who *do* cry.

Sonny wouldn't talk about the raid on Club Lingahnie. An Indian woman? Who could say? The Izzie commandos kept no tally of enemy casualties, he said. They struck efficiently, thumbed any who got in their way, and left again. Sonny wouldn't even admit to the existence of other prisoners, although Lessing had seen Abu Talib and thought he had glimpsed Mrs. Delacroix back on the destroyer. No, Sonny preferred to talk about golf, glitter, and girls instead.

This morning the two taciturn guards ushered Lessing to the "visitor's chair" in Sonny's office and departed. He immediately got up and went to look out of the window, his sole contact with the external world. People, cars, vans, army vehicles, bicycles—everything appeared normal. But weren't there too many soldiers? And why was that convoy of military ambulances and medical trucks travelling north, toward Jerusalem's new Kahane Airport? Nablus, Ramallah, and the highway eastward to Syria and Iraq lay in that direction, too. Was the convoy going to join Israel's forces in southern Russia—or was it racing toward a sudden outbreak of a disease no one dared name?

He was being paranoid. There was nothing wrong down on the street. People smiled, talked, argued, hawked their wares, and bustled or dawdled as they saw fit. The newspaper peddlers squatted idly beside their bundles; no mob clamored to read of disaster. The boy with the boom-box on his shoulder was swinging along in time to some catchy rhythm, not listening to emergency reports of spreading death. The two black-garbed Orthodox rabbis were debating theology—or dinner—and not the end of the world.

Sonny came in scowling. Behind him was another, white-haired man, a dignified bureaucrat in a blue-black suit and conservative, charcoal tie.

Lessing knew at once that this was no Israeli; this was trouble. His stomach sank.

"Mr. Shapiro, Alan Lessing." Sonny said. He sat down and pointed the newcomer to a chair.

Shapiro didn't sit. He walked around behind Lessing, looking at him from all angles.

"Want to see my tail?" Lessing inquired mildly. "That's where I've got my swastika tattooed . . . right up underneath it."

"Shut up, Lessing," Sonny ordered. "This is no joke."

"Why isn't this man classified as a Section Six?" Shapiro spoke over Lessing's head. His flat, nasal accent was American: probably New York City.

"Why? He knows less about the Party of Humankind than my ten-year-old daughter."

The older man pursed his lips and frowned. He dug out a ballpoint pen and a pad of paper. "He was right in there with Mulder, Borchardt, the Caw woman, Meisinger, the lot."

"You want my tapes? My notes? He's been cooperative."

"They all are until you get down under the surface."

"I know my job . . . ."

"Of course." Shapiro tapped stained dentures with the pen. "What did he tell you about Jennifer Caw, for instance? That she's left-handed? That she inherited the fortunes of two South American Nazi families and is rich as sin? That she lures seventeen-year-old Party recruits into her boudoir and makes 'em lick the honeypot?"

Sonny bridled. "Lessing's given us whatever we asked, as much as he knows."

"And Anneliese Meisinger? An ex-whore—used to be Emma Delacroix's lesbian lover, once they cured her of herpes, the clap, and syphilis. Lucky for the old lady she didn't have AIDS! Did this Lessing talk about her? Come on, Colonel Elazar, what *didn't* this bastard tell you?" It was the first time Lessing had heard Sonny's last name.

"I think he gave us what's important: Meisinger's a speech writer, a Party hack, one of the authors of their fake book, *The Sun of Humankind*. We knew all about her private life . . . ."

"He tell you he was screwing her . . . in New Orleans?"

"Bullshit!" Lessing commented succinctly. "You want porn, go buy yourself a magazine!"

Shapiro eyed him. "You Nazis are smart sons of bitches."

"I'm no Nazi . . . ."

"Sure."

"I don't think he is," Sonny—Elazar—said slowly. "He's just a hired merc. Old Mulder liked him and kept him around."

"Have you asked him about the Holocaust?" Shapiro shot back. "How does he stand on that? He was exposed to every conceivable anti-Semitic, racist, fascist, revisionist line . . . to the neo-Nazis, the hard-liners. They had no effect on him? Otherwise, Colonel, otherwise!"

"So I haven't had time to take him down to Yad Vashem."

"I doubt that would do any good. I hear Yad Vashem's got life-size, colored holograms now. You can walk around in a full-scale blow-up of the photographs, watch the Nazis gassing people, look at it just like you were there. It's enough to make a stone statue weep. But I don't think this man would be affected by it, nor by diaries, photographs, displays of hair, shoes, and gold teeth. Your Mr. Lessing wouldn't give a shit. He's a merc, a sociopath, a cold fish to begin with, and now that his revisionist pals have given him books to read he's gone over all the way . . . maybe not as an ideologue but as a soldier for the faith." Shapiro tapped his pen against his teeth and waited.

Lessing said nothing.

"Thought so. Well, Colonel, how about it? Section Six for this prisoner?" Shapiro dug into the breast pocket of his immaculate suit coat. "You need authorization? I've got it, both from our people in the States and from your bureau chief here."

"Why? Why this man?" Sonny squinted at the proffered paper, then tossed it down. "What can he possibly know?"

Shapiro retrieved his document before it became a permanent part of the clutter on Sonny's desk. "I think we'll find something interesting. You remember Richmond, the agent who died on Ponape? Just between us, Mordechai Richmond was a sharp operator, but he didn't share everything . . . not with his handlers in our Vigilantes for Zion, not with the American government, and not with you people. He had irons in fires nobody even knows are lit. We're not sure who put him on Lessing's case in the first place . . . so many died in Washington and New York when Starak hit."

"Richmond was after *Lessing*? Specifically? Personally?"

"We think so. But why? Nazi business? Maybe, maybe not. Richmond never told anybody. Now he's flower food."

"Others must know. Someone . . . ?"

"Nobody we can find. And we can't get into the big computer, Eighty-Five, any more, now that Outram's racists control what's left of the American government." Shapiro paused to run manicured fingernails through his snow-white mane. Lessing wondered if it was a wig. "All we've got is this bastard. Let's get serious with him. Why don't we ask him what he knows about Richmond's mission on Ponape?"

"I did." Sonny repeated Lessing's answer.

Shapiro emitted a derisive hiccough. "It doesn't stand up! Richmond was chasing Lessing long before Ponape . . . since India, in fact. Lessing didn't have any SS records or any cash back then. But let's just pretend that this *was* Richmond's motive; where are the records and the money now? Lessing killed Levi and a couple of your commandos. Then, according to his story, he ran out after Richmond, found his wife and the German woman dead, and chased Richmond down to the shore. Where's the boodle, Colonel?"

Lessing got up. He hated sitting while people talked over his head. He said, "I dumped it. I grabbed it to keep it out of your people's hands. I was headed out into the bushes with it when I saw Richmond had slipped out . . . when I heard the . . . the . . . shots."

"Won't do." Shapiro shook his head like a disapproving school-marm.

"I had instructions from Mr. Mulder to destroy the stuff rather than let you opfoes have it, but I didn't have time. I hid it in the ravine and piled leaves over it. It's probably still there." Lessing hoped he sounded sincere. Sonny was frowning.

Shapiro snorted. "Really? Let's reconstruct. Richmond's only a few steps ahead of you. He's on his way to bring help. You have to stop him. Maybe you do grab the contents of your metal box . . . papers, packets of money, whatever . . . but then you hear shots, screams. Do you finish gathering it up? Even *you* aren't that cool a customer. Don't you drop a paper or a bill or two?" The pen returned to teeth-tapping. "Remember, the commandos went through your house later looking for information. They found nothing. Zilch. Your box was empty."

"I told you what happened. I *did* get the stuff out and hide it. How can *you* say different? You don't know how many minutes passed after I shot Levi . . . before I went chasing out after Richmond. You weren't there. The Israeli strike force was only on Ponape for an hour or two. Did they search every bush?"

Shapiro sighed. "If you believe that, Colonel Elazar, then I have a bridge in Brooklyn I'll sell you." Sonny looked blank, and the other got up to smooth out the wrinkles in his trousers. Palestine could be hot, even in February. "Let's ask *Herr Obergruppenführer* Lessing, here, some questions."

"I . . . ."

"Authorization, Colonel. Right there. The head office of the Vigilantes for Zion . . . and your own superiors as well." Shapiro tapped his document reverently, as though it were the Ten Com-mandments. He went to the door and summoned the two guards himself. "I don't have time for this."

Sonny peered again at Shapiro's paper, then surrendered. He signed to the guards. The taller of the two pulled out a pair of cuffs and struck a professional pose. The smaller one drew his rubber truncheon from its belt-sheath. He looked as though he had per-formed this duty often and enjoyed it more each time.

Lessing held out his wrists. Why give them an excuse to beat on him? He still had hopes that Sonny would believe his story—or some amended version of it.

The guards whirled him around, secured his hands behind his back, and propelled him through Sonny's inner office to a door at the rear. Sonny unlocked this to reveal a short stairway. The guard with the club shoved Lessing in and simultaneously tripped him so that he plunged down a dozen steps to smash his cheek and shoulder against the rough concrete at the bottom. He staggered up to see the truncheon-wielder descending after him. Sonny snarled something in Hebrew, and the man desisted.

"Why protect this man?" Shapiro protested. "Damn it, he's one of them!"

"Soft interrogation works better than hard. Especially with a merc like Lessing."

Shapiro uttered a dignified snort. "Not with these Nazis! Murderers!"

Sonny asked, "So do you want to do the torturing here?"

"Me? Certainly not!" Shapiro bridled. "I am physically offended by violence. Elicitation of information . . . ."

"Torture . . . ."

"Interrogation. That's *your* job, Colonel."

"The one time I met Richmond, he told me a story," Sonny said, "about some neo-Nazi back in Detroit. Pain didn't faze him. Richmond's people finally castrated him and shot him full of female hormones. He lost all his body-hair and grew teats like a cow! They dressed him up in leather and black lace and stuck him in a gay brothel in Vegas. Made him earn his bread and water packing fudge and playing flutes. After a year he started to sing . . . told Richmond everything he knew. Didn't help him much; the sonuvabitch was ungrateful enough to die of AIDS."

Shapiro eyed him wordlessly.

"Come on, Mr. High-buck Liberal Humanitarian! Your squeamishness stinks! You . . . and my bosses . . . give the orders, but you don't see what happens! To you it's all on paper, all orders and 'implementation of Project IIB, sub-paragraph C!' It's people like me who have to do the messy work . . . and listen to the screams. Those screams don't stop when I get home at night. I hear them in my dreams."

"Colonel, I'll have to report . . . ."

"Go ahead. My superiors know how I feel. They don't care. Get the job done quickly and efficiently, they say. No crap about 'human rights'; the people we interrogate aren't Jews. We use tough methods, you use them, everybody uses them."

"The security of Israel . . . of our enterprise . . . ."

Lessing interrupted, "Isn't that what you accused the Nazis of doing? Drab, faceless bureaucrats like Adolf Eichmann? The men who were supposed to have sent trainloads of people off to the 'gas chambers?'"

They ignored him. Shapiro drew a shaky breath and faced the Israeli eye to eye. "The State of Israel wasn't built by turning the other cheek, Colonel! We Jews *worked* for it, we *lived* for it, and we *died* for it. In the process we made a lot of our enemies die for it, too. We did these things because otherwise we'd have been annihilated a dozen times over along the way, all through history . . . in Egypt, Babylonia, Persia, Rome, medieval Europe, Russia, *and* Nazi Germany!"

Lessing tried to say something about "manifest destiny" and the "Chosen People," but the smaller guard struck him judiciously on the buttocks with his club. It stung.

"You Americans!" Sonny banged a fist upon the peeling cement wall. "So easy to talk of 'we Jews!' So simple to advise *us* about what ought to be done over *here*, in Israel! I'm glad I'm just a glorified policeman!"

Shapiro's face was a closed door, unseeing, unhearing. "You've been at your job too long, Colonel Elazar. Just get the relevant information out of this prisoner. I don't need any lectures."

"Fine. Agreed, damn it. But you're coming with us. You're the one with the authorization."

"I refuse. I don't have . . . ."

"Time? I think you have. For once one of you desk-soldiers is going to see what happens when you give orders!" Sonny snapped his fingers at his guards. The taller one stepped back to escort Mr. Shapiro down the steps.

The corridor at the bottom of the stairs opened into a long hallway lined on both sides with featureless, black-painted doors. Lessing noted cameras and spy-devices: everything that moved in these nether regions was watched. Sonny advanced halfway down the passage and spoke into a grill beside one of the doors.

"Guided tour?" Lessing inquired. "Now you show me the rack, the thumbscrews, the electrodes, the ball-snippers?"

"This is not my choice, Alan! We . . . I am no sadist."

"Once a guest talks you put him back together and pay his hotel bill while he recuperates? Free drinks? Meals on the house? Ticket to the opera?"

"You're not some Arab terrorist, some glittery-eyed 'freedom fighter.'"

"Would that make torture okay if I were?"

Shapiro snarled at him. "Israel is surrounded by enemies, even after a century of war, after defeating all her foes . . . even after Pacov! And there *is* the Holocaust. That must never happen again."

"*If* there *was* a 'Holocaust' . . . the way you people say it was."

"See?" Shapiro shrilled. "See? I told you so! He *is* a goddamned Nazi!" He looked almost gleeful.

The room beyond the door was perhaps twenty feet square. Its walls were white-painted concrete blocks, its floor a dull, resilient, brown plastic that deadened sound. A uniformed nurse, a squat, dark-haired woman in her fifties, laid down a book and arose from a desk by the door.

In the center of the room, partly hidden behind a welter of machines and consoles, stood a tilted metal table. An intravenous-drip hookup stuck up above this like some kind of futuristic gallows. Lights winked on a display board at the nurse's station, and an EKG monitor screen splashed hollow, green light across the white-swathed figure upon the table. The air reverberated to a high, barely audible, wheezing susurration.

Lessing looked. He couldn't help it.

Bare feet protruded at each of the table's bottom corners. The ankles were wrapped—bound—with stretchy, soft, Ty-Do plastic straps, holding the legs apart in an uncomfortable "Y." Tubes emerged from a thick diaper over the groin to disappear into an aperture in the table's shiny surface. A padded belt like a Japanese *sumo* wrestler's girdle crossed the prisoner's stomach. Above this, the man's black-furred chest had been shaved here and there to allow the attachment of monitoring devices. The victim's arms, angled wide and bound like his feet, stuck up above the top edge of the table. The hands were shapeless lumps, the fingers kept apart with cotton pads. The head was a muffled globe, a faceless sphere of bandages, tubes, wires, and sensors. Swing lights and chrome-plated machines hung from retractable arms overhead, their cold glitter more fearsome than any medieval instrument of torment.

Resistance was useless. These people played the latest games. He might hold out for a while, but sooner or later he'd crack. Anybody would. Then they'd reel him in like a fish. Nobody could withstand modern, sophisticated interrogation.

Lessing struggled for calm. He had already decided to sing like the proverbial bird. He had nothing to hide, no comrades or cause that would suffer if he confessed every sin all the way back to the third grade! He knew nothing of value about the Party of Humankind, Mulder, Liese, or the others. And he'd happily tell Sonny about Marvelous Gap, Pacov, Richmond—whatever he wanted to hear.

He gathered his courage. He'd just have to live through whatever they did to him.

Maybe he could fake it. He hoped they wouldn't use sexual-sadistic techniques on him. Lessing had always thought of himself as tough, a loner who might not join the high school biker gang but who wasn't to be messed with either. He could take—he *had* taken—wounds and pain and hardship. This was different. Castra-tion, impotence, and sexual humiliation were bugaboos for American males—for all males—and Alan Lessing was no excep-tion. Whoever that hapless neo-Nazi in Detroit had been, he had had real courage to hold out against the things they had done to him.

The problem was making his "confession" ring true. Sonny was clever, but Lessing thought he could be convinced. Shapiro, on the other hand, wouldn't believe him until he had screamed his lungs out for an hour or two first. Lessing discovered that he didn't mind pretending to fear—to fake raw cowardice, if necessary—before Sonny, the guards, or even the woman; he'd still be able to live with himself. But he did *not* want to grovel in front of Shapiro like some poor Arab kid caught chucking rocks at an Izzie patrol.

Sonny was speaking. "... The beta-carboline series. Less drastic, no damage to tissues, yet more certain than physical methods. Sometimes there're psychological traumas afterwards, but no scars, no mutilation. Deaths from it are minimal, and it leaves no visible effects anybody can complain about."

"What . . . what does it do?" Shapiro looked pale around the gills.

"It's an anxiety drug, a mood-alterer. You feel terror like you can't believe. Stark, raw fear, anxiety without cause, panic that almost literally scares you to death."

The Vizzie swallowed. "Is that all? Is . . . is that . . . enough?"

"Usually. When it isn't we add a dribble of LSD."

"A hairy ride through the funhouse," Lessing remarked.

"Or a dose of succinylcholine. That paralyzes every muscle except the heart. The subject can't twitch an eyelid, can't swallow, can't even breathe, although he . . . or she . . . is fully conscious. A respirator is needed to keep the person from suffocating. It's a hell of a sensation, let me tell you. I tried it once to see how it felt."

It was Lessing's turn to swallow. It was becoming hard to stay cool. He addressed Sonny. "Who . . . who is that . . . there, on the table?"

"Your Syrian friend, Muhammad Abu Talib. He's been telling us all about the network of SS corporations, Herman Mulder, the Athens connection, a certain Dr. Theologides, the structure of the Party in the Third World . . . everything he knows or ever thought he knew."

Lessing's mouth was filled with ashes. "Can he . . . can he hear us?"

"No." Sonny shook his tight, golden curls. "He's listening to a tape of our questions, over and over. Sometimes we interrupt with violent, deafening noise and dissonance, sometimes with soft music, lullabies, and sweet persuasion. The IV gives him a dose of fear drugs at irregular intervals. When they wear off, we take the rubber conformer gag out of his mouth and ask him more questions. He never knows how long the sessions last, what time it is, whether it's night or day. We can keep him like this indefinitely, totally cut off, completely disoriented, fed intravenously. He can't even have a

heart attack and die on us. Medical science sees to that." He nodded
to the nurse, who stared impassively back.

Shapiro made a gagging noise. Sonny sighed and said, "Come
on, Alan. Let's go next door and get this over with."

Lessing had always thought of himself as a strong man, one who
could put up a good fight with his hands tied behind his back—
literally. Sonny's guards proved otherwise. He got in just one solid
kick and had the satisfaction of seeing the little one with the
truncheon double over gasping. Then the other guard kneed him and
knelt on the small of his back. His blue jumpsuit was ripped away,
and he was dragged naked, writhing and cursing, through the door,
along the hall, and into a room identical to the first. They heaved
him up and dumped him onto a table like Abu Talib's. Its surface
was a sheet of ice against his spine.

He hardly felt the Ty-Do straps being wound around his wrists
and ankles. They pried his mouth open and inserted a rubber
conformer. It tasted terrible, and he gagged and struggled to spit it
out, but to no avail. Then they smeared his eyes with some kind of
grease and bandaged them shut. Fingers lifted his penis to insert a
catheter. It hurt like fire. A plastic tube slid into his anus. Finally
they inserted plugs into his ears and stuck cold, metallic spiders—
monitors—to his temples and his chest.

The world became a dark and silent place.

He couldn't feel his fingers, and the padded girdle kept him from
humping up and banging his buttocks on the table. At first the
cramps in his spreadeagled arms and legs were awful, but these
subsided. Sensation slowly ebbed away as his body became used to
the bonds and the frigid mirror-surface of the table. His breathing
slowed, and the thunder of blood in his temples died away.

A voice spoke in his ear. It was loud, much too loud, electroni-
cally amplified and altered to a rasping, grating roar. It probably
belonged to Sonny, although it no longer sounded like anything
human. It said, "Sorry . . . uh . . . that's better. Wiggle your left foot
if you can hear me."

He hardly knew when the IV needle slid into his forearm.

Silence. Peace.

Apprehension. Worry.

A tinge of dread . . . .

A solid wall of fear, a great tidal wave, a rolling, surging billow
of panic.

It swept toward him, above and over him. It came crashing down,
smashing his defenses, shattering his resolve, swirling and splashing, seething into every crevice of his brain. Terror ripped along his
muscles, gushed into his bloodstream, roared through his arteries,
raced in to choke his heart, his eyes, his mouth. He clamped down

upon the gag to keep from shrieking, then realized that he was shrieking anyway.

The stench of sweat, feces, and acrid urine clogged his nostrils; smell was the one sense they couldn't take away from him.

The wave subsided, gurgled turgidly, and disappeared into the featureless distance. He sagged against his bonds, trembling, limp with relief.

Another, greater, darker, and more fearsome wave loomed on the horizon. Helpless, he watched it come.

Screaming didn't help at all.

The grating voice slapped against his eardrums like a physical blow. "Now, Alan. Tell us about Richmond." Impersonal fingers pried the rubber gag from between his teeth.

He had to hold out, make it seem that he was trying to keep his secret. Could he stand another assault? God damn it, if Abu Talib could, then so could he.

"No," he husked. "No way!"

This time it was much, much worse. Perhaps they added a dose of some pain-drug. The fingers exchanged the gag in his mouth for another with a vacuum attachment, preventing him from strangling on his own vomit.

The next time he saw visions. Sonny had mentioned LSD. His mother was there, watching his shame, watching him shudder and twist and bawl and fill the bottle under the table with yellow piss. She sniffed, made a face, and dragged him off, down into the basement. There she made him take off all his clothes, and then she switched him with a branch from the little tree in the front yard. He had played with matches, hadn't he? Wasn't he the one who had set the Larsons' tool shed afire? Didn't he know his dad had to pay Mr. Larson twenty-three dollars for the damage? No good Christian family had to put up with such shenanigans! Next thing he'd be drinking and smoking pot and . . . and . . . ! By the Lord, he'd work it off: a month of Saturdays at the pet shop cleaning the dog-runs!

The worst of it was that he glimpsed Mavis, the Larsons' daughter, two years older than he, watching his torment through the laundry room window—and laughing like the witch-bitch she was! His humiliation would be all over school by tomorrow.

Later came much grimmer memories: dust-faced Angolan corpses, mutilated Syrian children rising up from the stones of their blasted homes, his own dead comrades, sacks of bone, meat, and offal that a second ago had been living, breathing human beings. Once more he saw the merc girl he had loved, too briefly, in Damascus. He watched her die again, watched her blood seep through the thick khaki of her uniform, dribble from her sleeve, well up into her mouth and stain her lips and chin.

He howled. And, horror of horrors, so did she, keening right along in ghastly harmony, even though she was dead.

Jameela appeared as well. He had been expecting her.

He heard the shots, the screams, and he saw the silver-ice-blue bundle on the bedroom floor. The harsh, external voice rasped wicked suggestions into his ear, and his wife's body jerked back up to half-life, one eye open, the other closed, her tongue protruding, her blood and the filth of dying soiling her silken garments. Jameela danced for him, Indian *Kathak*-style, arms akimbo, tresses flying, head bobbing, and feet pounding. She would have been beautiful, had it not been for her blood-caked death wounds, clear and dreadful in the pearly moonlight. Lessing danced with her too, unable to help himself. Then, at the voice's behest, he performed obscenities upon Jameela's corpse while Richmond, Bauer and Helga, the Israeli nurse, Sonny and Shapiro, Liese and Jennifer Caw, prim Borchardt and sardonic Wrench, and a cast of thousands ogled, cheered, whistled, and egged him on.

After that it got really bad.

He didn't know when they quit. He awoke as they were wrestling him off the metal table and strapping him, face down and still naked, onto a gurney. He had a dizzy view of Sonny above him, shaking his head. Shapiro lurked in the background, too, his face strained and pasty.

"A real *Totenkopf*," Sonny whispered. "Not a Nazi but a genocidal maniac who makes all the Nazis who ever lived look like amateurs. How could I have known?"

"You *should* have interrogated him properly!"

"We didn't have a clue! God damn Richmond to hell! And if Lessing's telling the truth, it would've been too late even if he'd told us this story the minute he arrived!"

"But is it true? Could he be lying to set us off on the wrong track? Can you give him some sort of truth serum? We *have* to find out!"

"There's no such thing as truth serum, except in spy novels," Sonny sneered. "Interrogation . . . soft or hard . . . is the only way. I had no idea, no idea!"

"Oh, Israel!" Shapiro's voice took on a mourning, keening tone. "Oh, Israel!" His eyes became round. "And us? What about *us*?"

The guards were rolling the gurney away. Lessing struggled to speak, but his battered, mangled lips wouldn't work. His throat was so raw he could barely breathe.

"We'll get him back here as soon as he's able," Sonny was saying grimly. "Run him through his story over and over again. You get on the phone to your people in the States . . . find out what you can about progress on Pacov research . . . ."

He heard no more. The two guards wheeled him into an elevator at the far end of the corridor. There they up-ended the gurney and proceeded to beat him, very carefully, with their truncheons. They didn't touch his face but concentrated on his ribs, his belly, his thighs, and his genitals. Then they tipped the gurney up the other way, so that he hung head downward from its straps, and the smaller guard used his rubber club as a dildo while the other hit him in places they might otherwise have missed. His tormentors kept calling him "Palestinian pig" and "terrorist."

Afterward they took him back to his cell: the neat, bare room he had left so blithely that morning. They sat him down crosslegged on the floor and shackled his wrists and ankles so tightly that he could not straighten his limbs. The bigger guard, whose English was better, then told him precisely what they would do to him in the sessions to come. Finally the smaller man urinated on him. Only then did they leave him alone.

Consciousness flickered in and out. Terror and hallucination blew through the open doors of his mind like windy ghosts. He hurt, terribly, but his physical pain was nothing compared to the miasma of fear that churned and coiled inside and all around him. He was still suffering the after-effects of the drugs. Too, Sonny had mentioned further sessions: Lessing was now a full-fledged customer of Section Six. Aside from beta carboline and other chemicals, he would now be subjected to the unfriendly ministrations of the guards. Sonny pretended not to tolerate sadism, not openly, but he must surely be aware of it. Pain, degradation, and terror were, after all, the specialties of the house.

He couldn't take it. He had not known before, but he did now: Alan Lessing was no hero. He was not immune.

No one was. Interrogation had become an art-form in the twenty-first century.

He rolled and crawled and struggled across the tiled floor to the washstand. He gasped; his manacles were thin steel circlets, and they cut into his flesh like hot wires. His captors were undoubtedly watching; let them think he was trying to drink from the toilet bowl.

There was a way out. He had one card left to play.

He caught the toilet paper roll in his teeth. He twisted at it, worrying and tugging, until its metal holder came open. The Khalifa's tiny "zombie pill" rolled out of the hollow tube. He hawked up saliva and doubled over, quickly, so that the guards would not have time to see and stop him.

The pill tasted bitter on his tongue. He strove to swallow, almost lost it, and finally choked it down. He lay still.

The door clanged open. He heard noise and outcry. Hands clawed at his shoulders, jerking his head back. Rough fingers jabbed down into his throat, grabbed at his tongue, pinched his nose. Somebody yelled, "Suicide pill! Doctor . . . !" Other voices yammered in Hebrew.

The ceiling light dimmed, rocked, brightened again, went dark.

Pain, dead and dull, crawled up from his belly. Leaden was a good word for it.

Blackness all around.

Jameela. Oh, Jameela . . . .

I will wipe Jerusalem as a man wipeth a dish, wiping it, and turning it upside down.
    —2 Kings, 21: 13

Therefore shall her plagues come in one day, death, and mourning, and famine, and she shall be utterly burned with fire: for strong is the Lord God who judgeth.
    —Revelation, 18: 8

The beauty of Israel is slain upon thy high places: how are the mighty fallen! Tell it not in Gath, publish it not in the streets of Ashkelon; lest the daughters of the Philistines rejoice, lest the daughters of the uncircumcised triumph.
    —2 Samuel, 1: 19

CHAPTER TWENTY

Tuesday, March 1, 2044

Cold.
His feet were cold.

He hurt. Bruises. Aches. Limbs locked, stomach cramped, fingers and toes numb, mouth as dry as mummy-dust, a tomb unopened for a thousand, thousand years.

Something constricted him. He struggled weakly and felt the slither of cloth gliding down off his body. A sheet?

Without conscious command his eyes opened. Or tried to. They were crusty and gummed shut. Fingers came up from nowhere to paw at them. Sight returned blurrily to his left eye. The right one didn't work. It was just as well; the left one showed only fuzzy colors and shifting blobs, with a great, white sun overhead.

Something glittered to his right, another white object to his left, a black oblong before him. Shapes writhed at the limits of his vision, as though he were looking down a tunnel—a tunnel that passed through Hell. He saw things, people, animals, fantastic creatures who danced and jigged and cavorted. Change your partner! Round and round and do-si-do! He heard fiddle music, smelled the mingled stink of heat and candles and beer and sweat, cheap perfume and straw. It wasn't real; was it a movie?

It must be a movie. He tasted chocolate-mint, smooth and dark upon his tongue, and he heard the crackle of tinfoil. A moist, feminine hand trembled in his, making his lust rise unseen in the popcorn-fragrant dark. He felt shame. Could she tell? Could she see the lump in his pants? Mavis was pretty observant, even while watching Kari Danforth and Robert Wayte emoting on-screen, steamy as a Chinese laundry! He thrust his hand down to hide the pressure between his legs. That only made it worse.

The white sun was bright, a cold, glittering star-fire. It dragged him back to pain and to dust, mummy-wrappings and eyeless skull-faces.

He could not remember. He did not *want* to remember. He was afraid. He could not remember and remain sane.

His other eye came open, but it was blurrier than the first. Did he have any more eyes, ones that might work better? He willed them to open, but none did. He commanded the rest of his body to respond. Just who and what was he? How many limbs did he have? Was the whole universe just agony and blur? Was *he* the universe?

Unknown body parts threshed and flailed and pumped. The world pinwheeled. Hardness raked along some far-off appendage, and blazing pain smashed up from an area his memory told him was his left shoulder. Belatedly his ears reported a thump and a sepulchral groan that might have come from him. Breath whooshed out of lungs he had not known he had.

He seemed to have fallen from some place higher to some place lower. Grey pillars loomed above him, and the black oblong in the distance became taller and differently shaped.

Memory reported, "Door. It's a door. You're under a table, sir." Memory was being unnecessarily sarcastic.

Whiteness swaddled him, and he struggled. His arms, when he got them free, were fish-gill pale, marked with purple, green, and yellowish bruises, striations, and blotches. Under other circumstances he might have admired his own colorfulness. What was he? A chameleon? A cloisonne vase? A picture came back to him: a weird thing of planes and angles and raw colors. It was a human being, but wildly distorted.

Memory handed him a word: "Louvre." He was standing somewhere, looking over a red, velvet rope at the picture. He smelled flowers: the scent of the French girl he was with. Who was she? What was her name? Paris! On leave from Angola?

Blankness came back, as Memory scurried off to hunt for more data.

Somebody within his skull commanded him to rise. Who the hell was in charge, anyway? Involuntarily his hands scrabbled for support, and legs he had not known he had contracted, pushed, and lifted. The stone rolled aside, and Lazarus emerged from the tomb. Nice job, Mr. Jesus! Great coordination there, legs! The globe that was the quintessential *he* rose above the flat surface, and his field of vision perforce went up with it. Those unsung heroes, his lungs, pumped, and frigid air gushed in to make him cough.

His invisible coordinator issued directives, and somewhere far below, distantly connected to his bubble of vision-ego, legs shuffled, arms windmilled for balance, and a hand caught at the edge of the grey table-surface. The white covering fell completely away. This produced a twinge of shame: he was naked. What would his mother say? He knew damned well what she'd say! And Mavis Larson would be there to peek through the basement window while he got his switching.

The black "door" oblong loomed before him. He slumped against it and felt solidity, slickness, and cold. Something hurt him lower down, in the softness named "stomach." There was a round, hard globe there. It wasn't part of him; thus it must belong to the black oblong. The thing was frigid, a ball of ice against his skin. He thrust a hand between it and his belly, and it turned. Something clicked.

The black oblong changed, a thing apparently to be expected in a world of unrealities. The round ball slid away, and the surface against which he leaned went with it, sideways, at a slant and all at once, making him stumble. He lurched forward.

Full speed ahead, Captain! Sailors in blue uniforms staggered to and fro on a pitching deck before shiny, brass housings, rain poured in through an open hatch, and a spotlight slashed the waves in the howling, spume-driven night outside. Another goddamn movie! He was getting better at separating the present from the past, the real from the unreal, the men from the boys. This time it was Beverly Rowntree who popped her gum beside him in the movie house. He rubbed a leg against her thigh, and they rolled towards one another simultaneously, two hearts with a single lust! There ought to have been a crescendo of music and a rush of scarlet passion; instead, her front teeth dug a gash in his lower lip, and she nearly broke her big, bony nose on his cheekbone. So much for romance!

Beyond the door was another world, a place of greys and blacks and muted browns. A row of little suns marched away above him, receding into the distance. One or two were missing, spoiling the symmetry. He didn't care. Esthetic appreciation was beyond him. To hell with trying to appear worldly wise before his little French girl! Or was it Beverly?

His feet moved, and shadowy, grey walls rolled past. More black oblongs appeared and were left behind on either side. He heard a whishing, scraping sound below him. He tripped, and somebody down there sent an urgent pain message up to the bridge. He would have ignored it, but his left foot—he thought it was that—refused to lift and go forward. Action was required. He lowered his head and looked. Past all the lumps and bulges of empurpled, naked flesh, way down at the bottom, he perceived that his right foot was standing upon a small, yellow square. He tried again to lift his left foot. It refused to rise, and the message of pain was repeated. The square was attached to his left big toe. With all the skill he could muster he raised his right foot. This released the square and freed his left foot.

Off balance, he fell heavily against the wall. Shit! If he stopped to investigate the yellow square he'd probably break his neck! Onward! He let his limbs take over and found himself up again and continuing. Good job, Captain! Off the reef at last!

There was danger. Hazily, he sensed—remembered?—that much. The black oblong, the door, at the end of the path of little suns was where the danger might be. He halted, shut down his engines, issued orders to all hands, and teetered forward to listen.

Nothing.

Door? Open? Yes, he could manage that. He knew how.

Stairs. Up. Amazing how well Memory helped, and his limbs obeyed. Citations for all, yes, sir!

What? Something—someone—lying on the stairs, feet up, head down. The mouth and nose were smeared with black. Some of the blackness was puddled in the eye sockets: pools of ebon darkness. Emily Pietrick used to talk like that; he had dated her for a lustful six months in high school, but she was into witchcraft and demons and horror movies. Too weird for him!

Shaking his head cleared away some of the fuzz. He squinted at the body on the stairs. It might have been one of his guards. What was a "guard?" Why had there been "guards?" He wasn't sure. He twisted his head upside down to see, but the black stuff hid the man's features. The guy had been dead awhile.

Memory pounded up onto the bridge and announced: "Death stinks, sir! Don't you smell it?" He sniffed. Nothing. "Out of order, sailor! Report to damage control!" "Aye-aye, sir!" Memory saluted smartly and left again. By God, he ran a tight ship! Geoffrey Archer, who had played the captain in the movie, had nothing on him!

Beverly Rowntree was once more beside him in the theater; she grabbed his hand and stuffed it greedily down inside her blouse. Her nipple thrust up hard against his fingers, and he felt the silky curve of her breast. Where could they go? He *had* to have her. Urgently!

The room at the top of the stairs held two more bodies. These were dressed in khaki uniforms with brown, leather belts and holsters. Their brass buttons gleamed bright in the sunlight slanting in through the windows. The one who lay on his back on the carpet (what a mess: the cleaning bill!) had the shiniest shoes he had ever seen. The other man knelt on his hands and knees, like a Muslim praying. But he couldn't be a Muslim; his pants were dark with the dried excreta of his dying. A Muslim had to be clean to pray, and this man was not. He wore a mask of blackish jelly, anyhow. Probably a scuba-diver; frogmen were what the ship needed now! He recalled the scene well: the captain giving them all a pep-talk, the line of black-clad figures at the rail, the scudding, grey clouds above the steely sea.

The kneeling man was the bigger of his two guards. He still couldn't think why there had been guards. Memory refused to answer—probably having a quick snort with the guys down in damage control. The other corpse was unrecognizable. He didn't think it was Sonny—whoever the hell Sonny was; he couldn't remember.

He meandered on, into another, larger chamber, one in which rays of sunlight lay like golden bars across piles of papers, files, and miscellany on a big desk in the center of the room. The clean-up detail on this ship needed a butt-kicking! He stumbled over a gilded golf trophy and almost went crashing down into the mess. This room was familiar; it seemed like home. Yet he didn't remember winning any trophies. No, this couldn't be his place.

A door opened onto a corridor. along here somewhere was a stairwell. Up there was another room he knew. Why did he feel terror when he thought about it? He pushed at the stairway door. It was locked. Memory whispered that this was just as well.

He let his feet carry him away. They were *good* feet, really learning their job! They bore him along other passages, past waiting rooms filled with silent, unmoving customers, into a big foyer full of desks and counters and computers and office machines.

And bodies.

All kinds of bodies: men, women, children; young and old; thin and fat; everybody rotting cheerily together in corrupt camaraderie. By the central desk an Arab in a burnoose slumped beside an Israeli officer in undress uniform, together in death as they could never be in life (great line! from some movie poster?). Next to them a bronzed American woman in a yellow sun-dress and harlequin glasses sat on the floor like a forgotten doll. At first he thought she was alive, but when he got closer he knew he didn't want to pull off those glasses and look into the eyes beneath.

He staggered, stepped, and waltzed across the litter-strewn floor. Memory warned him that he needed fresh air, but he couldn't smell a thing.

The street outside was full of drifting haze. Mist? Fog? No, smoke. Somebody was barbecuing rotten meat. Somehow he did smell that. It was close to sunset—or sunrise?—and the sun's red ball peered into the world like the eye of the Bloody Beast of Armageddon. A dull-orange glow lined the purple horizon, and fingers of greasy, black smoke clawed up at the sky.

The city was on fire.

It was just what was needed: Keep Your City Clean! Be a Good Citizen! No Littering! Pick Up Your Trash! Burn, baby, burn!

He was tired, and he hurt. Best to rest here, at the top of the shallow steps leading down to the street. He slumped against the stone balustrade and gazed out over a hellscape of abandoned cars, trucks, motorbikes, and bicycles. A heap of fruit from an upended produce van blocked the view to his left, but the fires behind it were lurid enough for a big-budget disaster movie. They didn't have the best seats in the house, but these were okay! They could see. Let Beverly bitch all she wanted!

He was saddened more by the abandoned suitcases and the cars jammed with household goods nobody would ever use again than he was by the bodies. The voiceless, faceless, inoffensive dead: these were not bloated and horrid, like those back in his building; these were decent folk, already drying out, grey with drifting ash and dust, food for the wheeling, screeching birds and the clouds of blue-black flies. These corpses were working hard at blending into their environment. Good citizens all!

He dozed. The westering sunlight soothed his aching limbs.

He awoke. Something had moved out there.

Panic poured up into his throat. It was night, a shadow-ridden, red-black darkness punctuated with bursts of orange sparks and the boom of explosions behind the distant buildings. Beside him, Beverly Rowntree squeezed his arm and giggled. He hated that stupid giggle.

He heard footsteps: a slip-slap of sandals near a blue sedan jammed at an angle against the curb below him. In the middle blackness, amidst the welter of cars and trucks and bodies out in the street, he caught a stealthy crunch of boots.

A woman's voice sounded tremulously from behind the car. "He's alive, Sol! But he's . . . he's buck naked!"

The man called Sol emerged from behind an army truck some twenty feet away: a balding, stout, middle-aged, brawny individual with a jaw like Mussolini. He was dressed in a stained, white undershirt and shapeless, filthy slacks. He looked like a garage mechanic after a wallow in the grease pit. He shouted, "Shoot the gubber, Natalie! Watch out for an ambush!"

Sol had a gruff but pleasant voice; it reminded him of his own father. He stood up. Now was the time to speak up, say hello, sing out a cheery "Hi-i-i, there, everybody!" just like Junius Greenwald on TV. He struggled with lips of baked clay and a tongue of carved stone. No sound came out. He extended his hands, palms up.

"Shoot him!" Sol snarled. "Shoot the foozy!"

Natalie's head appeared over the ash-dusted roof of the sedan. She had a skinny, bony face with eyes that were blank circles of orange light. A tide of terror swept over him: the hollow-eyed bogeyman of his childhood nightmares! Memory suggested, a trifle sarcastically, that the woman might just be wearing glasses.

"He don't have no gun, Sol. Nobody up there with him." She sounded as scared as his mother when his dad had gone in after a burglar in their pet shop. He held out his hands and strove to smile. In return Natalie waved her pistol at him. She edged to the side, around the sedan. He saw that she wore a smudged, short-sleeved, yellow blouse and white shorts with little happy-faces stitched on the pocket-flaps. She needed make-up and a decent hairdo. Now she looked too much like his mother.

Another, lighter voice came from farther up the street, "Come on, get on with it!" This speaker sounded forthright and efficient; he couldn't tell whether it was a man or a woman.

The bald man looked as though he were sucking courage from the gleaming Israeli automatic rifle he clutched in both hands. He shuffled forward. "Okay, Riva, I don't see nobody either. This gubber looks like he's pog-dinkin' gazoo! Shell-shocked, like. Dinkin' naked already!"

The third person, the one named Riva, appeared from behind a mound of baggage and bedrolls fallen from a pickup truck. She was definitely female. Her wet-looking, black-leather pants and sun-top of fire-engine red were a statement: she was a *macha*, one of the militant feminists of the Banger movement. Her dark hair was as short as a boy's, almost a crewcut, but she lacked the deliberate facial scars many *machas* wore. Under a glaze of sweat, smoke, and dirt, she had the appearance of a model: tall and willowy, flat-chested, with legs long enough to straddle an elephant. Cross-belts at her waist held a pair of automatic pistols, and she carried her stubby submachine gun as if she knew how to use it.

"Leave the dinker be!" Sol demanded. "We got to get to the airport. Come on!"

Natalie craned forward. "God, Sol, he looks like rotten meat!" She pointed. "What's the matter with him? 'N' what's that on his foot?"

The bald man scratched his chest. "Cover the foozy! Lemme look." He stuck out a brawny hand. "Hey, you. C'mere."

He smiled and obeyed. He had nothing to hide; he had buried the stash of pot Emily Pietrick had given him in the garden outside the high school. Let the principal search all he wanted.

"It's a fuckin' card. A card, like . . . tied to his fuckin' toe!" Sol resembled a butcher trying to read his scale upside down. "It's in Hebrew. Hey, Riva!"

"I heard. I'm here." The *macha*'s accent identified her as a native Israeli. She came and bent down to squint.

"What?" Natalie jittered. "What is it?"

"It's a . . . a tag. An identification tag from the police morgue." She clicked her tongue in puzzlement. "It says this man is . . . dead."

Somewhere far away a flower of yellow light bloomed upon the horizon. The thud-boom of an explosion bounded up the street toward them.

"He's *dead*?" Natalie's empty, glass eyes glittered red with fear-light.

"That's what I think it means . . . ."

"*Dead*! I told you . . . they all said . . . like they was talkin' back in the hotel! Everybody's dead . . . *dead* . . . but they're comin' *back*! They're not *really* dead, Sol!" Natalie began to blubber.

"God damn it, you and your poggin' zombies! Ever since you read that article in the paper!" The man sighted his weapon. "I'm gonna let some light through this foozy! Then we'll see about your dead people!"

Riva snapped, "No. No shooting! He is *not* dead! You can see that. It must have been the plague . . . Pacov. The police must have made a mistake. Anyway, he's harmless!"

"If he's alive then why is his face like that?" Natalie skittered back from the curb. "All grey . . . tongue hangin' out . . . his eyes . . . ?"

"He's injured, brain-damaged. Maybe Pacov got him but didn't kill him. An immune . . . like us . . . ."

"He's *dead*!" Natalie shrilled from out in the street by the produce van. "He's a *zombie*, I tell you!" Her leather sandals creaked as she backed away into the red-lit darkness.

Sol uttered a cross between a snort and a sigh. "Now look what you done, Riva! Why'd you have to read it to her?"

The *macha* gave him a cool look. "You asked me to. If your wife can't handle it, that's her . . . and your . . . problem."

"Nice! Nice! She ain't my poggin' wife. She's just another jizmo tourist on our tour. Hell, what's it matter anyhow? We got to fuckin' stick together . . . ."

"So stick! Stick yourself! Stick her, if you've got anything to stick her with! This man isn't dead, and he isn't going to hurt us."

The bald man grinned. "Hey, hey now, come on! We go together! That way we live." He gestured. "So he's alive. So what good is he to us? He's gone-o, red light, dunked, kungled, thumbed! Come on, let's grease!"

Riva be₁.. down again and pulled the tag off. Unbalanced, he sat down hard on his rump on the concrete. This made him laugh.

She looked into his eyes. "You understand me? You speak English?" She repeated herself in Hebrew.

He grinned. It was all he could do. He liked being naked and being stared at by a girl. Emily Pietrick used to admire him like that. Once she had painted his body with magic symbols with acrylics from her art class. Then she had done some really kinky things.

"For God's sake, Riva!" Sol sounded desperate. "Natalie's leavin,' and I'm goin' after her."

"This man . . . anybody alive . . . may be useful!"

"Dink my pog, Riva! You *know* he's brain-dead! What's he good for? Or maybe you get juiced by gubbin' zombies?"

Riva gave his nakedness a dark, appraising look. "You alive, man? You sick? You need help?" She asked again in Hebrew.

He struggled to smile. His hands came up, and she exclaimed at the scars circling his wrists. "Prisoner? The police? But you are not Arab, I think. Not Israeli. You look American. English? German? No? Who?"

"Let's grease out, Riva!" Sol yelled. He and Natalie were shadows in the smoke-drifting dark. "Last call!"

"Just a damned minute! What's your hurry?"

"Speed! We grab a car, we're out. Hit Kahane Airport . . . double around if we got to, over to Ben Gurion Airport. Find a plane . . . I grabbed all the money we'll ever need back at the bank. Shoot our way on if need be."

"You are stupid! We try to leave Israel, the sanitation teams will thumb us! *No one* wants Pacov victims in his country! We take a plane, they shoot us down! We're *infected*!" She swore dispiritedly in Hebrew. "A car is better. We drive north through Syria, to our Israeli settlements in Russia. We get in, somehow, some way." She gulped hot, barbecue-stinking air and spat.

"We got fuckin' *rights*!" Sol declared righteously. "Me 'n' Natalie're poggin' American citizens! They *got* to take us in, give us medical care! Stick with us, Riva! We'll get you in, too!"

"They shoot diseased cattle, don't they?" She looked down at him, then at the tag she had taken off his toe. She muttered, "And I think Sol and Natalie will desert me the first chance they get."

He wasn't listening. He watched his father inject a sad, old dog with euthanine, and he wept as it died in his arms. The canine stink of the pet shop made him ill. Sol's voice came from very far away, perhaps out in the back lot, beyond the kennels: "Last chance, you lez jizmo! Stay 'n' screw your zombie! Maybe you like suckin' corpse cock!"

"Get gubbed!"

There was no reply. Sol and Natalie were gone.

Riva turned back to him. "You! The morgue tag says your name is Alan Lessing. Is that right?"

He nodded. It was all he could do. He was watching a movie again, this time with Emily Pietrick. She had her hand inside his pants. Then she bent her head so that her long, black tresses spilled out over his lap. He gasped with ecstasy as her lips and tongue found him.

Riva's fury brought him back. "You got an erection? You look at me and got an *erection*? You corpse! You dead meat!"

He was ashamed. An apology was in order, but he couldn't say it. He opened his mouth. "Ah! Ah?"

"Ah? Oh . . . I see. You have no control. You cannot speak." She grimaced. "Sol is wrong. I am no lez . . . lesbian. It is just that I hate pigs like him! You are a man, but you have not the wit to be a pig, eh? Not now, not any more." She pointed to the blue sedan. "See this automobile here? The driver is . . . how do you say? . . . dead. Yet I think the car works. The key is there, on the floor by the brake pedal. You get the driver out, and I drive. Green light?"

He liked her stilted, funny, Israeli accent and the smoky, sweaty look of her. He wondered why she averted her face and held her nose. He smelled nothing. The driver's flesh was puffed and blackish, but he got hold of the man's lime-green pants and slid him out, with hardly any pieces left behind. Then, at her direction, he pulled off the seat covers and threw them away.

His hands were becoming very dextrous; he would see that they were cited for agility beyond the call of duty the next time the admiral was piped aboard.

"Clothes," Riva's dark-honey voice purred in his ear. "Our driver was going on a trip, eh? Shoes . . . too small." A tiny pocket knife flashed, and he heard ripping noises. "Eh, so. Put them on now. Good. Trousers? Underwear? Here, this suitcase: a shirt, a belt! Good. And what is this? A pistol! *Very* good! Our driver must have been a policeman!"

She turned the car around and drove. Sometimes he got down and lifted things; sometimes she bumped and banged over them. The streets were dark, but there was light from the fires. A few places had electricity, and twice Riva stopped to loot food from deserted shops. If it hadn't been for the corpses, this could have been any American city after midnight. She found him a six-pack of cherry pop, and he guzzled it gratefully, all of it. Then he was sick. Afterward they were off again: where, he neither knew nor cared. He was content to let her wrestle the sturdy little car through the clogged streets. Eventually he fell asleep.

Memory awoke him promptly at 0500 hours. "Captain, Captain, there's news! Terrible news!" He asked what it was, and Memory told him. It was so bad he didn't dare remember it. He found his cheeks wet with tears, his chin sticky with dried vomit, and his mouth tasting like a mouse had died in it—not too recently.

The world outside the car window was yellow, brown, and dusty white: houses of crumbling stone, shacks, signs in Hebrew and Arabic, garbage, and, yes, a body there behind a shed of corrugated iron. A second corpse, an old woman, lay sprawled face down in front of her door nearby.

Pacov was master here.

He rolled to his left and discovered pain. Everything ached. His legs were cramped under the dashboard, and it was all he could do to get the door open and drag himself out. As he did so he caught a glimpse of the Israeli woman—what was her name?—asleep in the back seat. She was older than he had thought. Tiny wrinkles webbed the corners of her eyes, and lines drew down beside her broad mouth. In sleep she looked hard and used and leathery.

The shirt and pants she had found for him were too small, and the shoes hurt his feet. His toes peeped out of the holes she had cut like hot dogs out of a bun. He left her in the car and stumbled into the nearest house. He avoided two children curled up on the front room floor; they were sound asleep! Wasn't it time they were off to school? Were they Beverly Rowntree's younger brothers? He drifted on into a bedroom. Here women's clothing hung on pegs, and dolls and toys lay scattered upon the linoleum. In a closet he encountered men's work pants and several pairs of shoes. These fit, more or less, but his fingers were too clumsy to fasten the belt and zipper, much less tie the shoelaces. His mother would be furious. He sat down and struggled.

The woman in the doorway didn't look like Beverly at all. He couldn't recall who she was: a tall, slinky, crew-cut, teat-less wonder in shiny, black stuff that was so tight it looked like it was painted on. What home-room was she from, anyhow? Was she in any of his classes? Beverly would be jealous.

"You are very dirty," she said. "Maybe Natalie was right! You do look dead. There's a shower that still works, back behind the kitchen."

The strange woman helped him undress, took him into a small, white-tiled cubicle, soaped him, and ran cold water over his bruised limbs. Then she took off her own garments and joined him in the shower. When she pressed herself against him and tried to give him pleasure, he cooperated. She rubbed, pressed, kissed, and squeezed, but nothing worked.

He sensed her frustration. He ought to apologize, but Memory kept interrupting with inane remarks about Beverly and Emily and Mavis and other people. Finally, in tight-lipped silence, she stopped, shut off the water, dried him, and helped him dress.

She found eggs and dry bread and a jar of yellow jam in the kitchen, and they ate. At last she asked, "Who are you, Alan Lessing?"

Dumb question! His homeroom teacher must have his registration card. He hoped he wasn't in the wrong class. That had happened once, and the embarrassment still rankled.

"You can't speak any better than you can fuck, eh? How did you get .. this . . . this way? Pacov? The police?"

Memory tried to say something, but he couldn't hear it.

The woman said, "Look, I'm Riva. Riva Ayalon. Eh? You're Alan Lessing."

He essayed another smile. His face worked better this morning.

"We have to go north, to the Israeli bases in Russia. You understand me? Can you drive? Handle a gun?" He blinked at her, and she hissed, almost like a cat. Memory handed him a picture of Buttons, his cat when he was ten years old. It made him want to cry.

She said, "Are you so useless? I *know* you can do some things . . . your build, your muscles, the calluses on your hands all prove this! Whatever Pacov . . . the police . . . the Arabs . . . whoever . . . did to you, still you are not mindless. You must remember! Try!"

Memory asked permission to speak, but the captain refused. Too much, too bad. No, worse than bad. Unthinkable. Unbearable.

The woman ran brown fingers through her short, black hair. "Well, damn it, finish breakfast. We go now . . . before the sanitation teams come to 'purify' us survivors, eh? We take another pair of boots for you, some underwear, some clothes for me, some blankets."

She went on muttering to herself while he returned to the stuffy darkness of the movie house, munched stale popcorn, and nuzzled Beverly Rowntree's ample breast. It was a sad movie, all about a boy whose cat was killed by a car. He cried, and she wept, too. "It's a sad world," Memory piped up from the seat behind them. Was there no privacy?

After breakfast Riva ransacked the house but found nothing more of use. As they left he tried his rediscovered ability to smile on the two children in the front room, but they were still asleep and didn't wake up. They must have been eating blackberry jam, because their mouths and cheeks were smeared with dark, reddish jelly. He couldn't recall where he'd seen that before.

They drove all morning. Bright sunlight and the cloudless, azure bowl overhead reminded him of how his father used to sing "Blue Skies" while driving—until his mother nagged the old man into silence. The road was crowded, full of stalled cars, trucks, personnel carriers, even tanks. Was everybody off to the beach, then? The traffic jam was so bad that people had shut off their engines and were just sitting there waiting. Still, they all were surprisingly patient in spite of the morning's heat. No one complained or honked, and those who had left their vehicles appeared content to sprawl quietly beside them beneath the blistering sun.

He awoke when the woman—what was her name?—pulled the car over onto the rocky shoulder. "Blocked ahead," she said tersely. "Change automobiles. Find another one."

He smiled at her, helped with the luggage, and clambered over the twisted cars and wreckage that filled the road. Had there been a terrible accident, then?

His mother had a pat speech for such occasions: drunks, pot-heads, Bangers, and other similar ilk were the offspring of Satan, and reckless disregard for others' rights—and for *her* rights in particular—was the downfall of civilization! Downfall? Something about that word disturbed him, but Memory snatched the thought away. It was like trying to think while standing under a waterfall.

They found a bigger and better car, an armored personnel carrier. The crew lay together in the shade beside it, eating blackberry jam in comradely silence. He grinned at them, but no one replied. Stuck up bastards! Always the way with tankers and APC crewmen! They didn't object, though, when Riva took their vehicle. She didn't even offer to pay for it.

After that they made good time, rolling right over smaller obstacles or knocking them aside and going around the bigger ones in a plume of tallow-hued dust. They rumbled through Nablus and then Nazareth—something important had happened there, long ago, but he couldn't remember what—and in the evening the woman pulled up near a town she named Safad. Smouldering oil tanks and supply dumps lined the highway ahead, and the horizon was lit with flames, much like that place where he had been before. Already he had forgotten its name.

"I think they are all dead in the town," she muttered. Mostly she talked to herself rather than to him. "How far does this Pacov extend?" Her features were fox-like, long nosed, with narrow, slightly slanted eyes, in the glow of the blue military flashlight she had found in the driver's door-rack. She was peering at a map. He wanted to help, but he couldn't understand the letters. This worried him; he recalled once being able to read, but not any more.

He essayed a puzzled "Ah?"

"What? No, no way. We can't go in. There may be sanitation teams already there. They'd thumb us for sure." She traced a red line with her finger. "Here, and here . . . over to Damascus, then up to Aleppo, and on to Russia. Pacov there, in Kharkov, Donetsk . . . the old Pacov, the first strike. Some Israelis there, but there'll be more farther north, near Sverdlovsk, away from the European enclaves in Moscow and Leningrad. We have to get through their lines some-how, steal I.D., prove we came in with their original expedition, and get them to let us stay. It's our only chance . . . that life or no life at all."

He bent to gawk at the map. Her proximity aroused him, and she drew him close. "Want to try sex again, eh?" she asked.

He did.

The hot-oil-smelling coziness of the cab took him back to Emily Pietrick, all fingers and tongue and teeth and straining limbs in the back seat of Larry Helger's fancy convertible.

He had never had any trouble getting it up for Emily. With this woman it was different; he tried hard, but it was no good.

As Johnny Kenow—an unexpected gift from Memory!—used to say, "Can't salute if ya ain't got no pole to hang yer flag on!"

Later, as they huddled together in the cab for warmth, he awoke to the distant racket of machine-gun fire. Riva was up instantly. Their personnel carrier contained a variety of weapons, and she pushed an automatic rifle into his hands. She seemed pleased when Memory showed him how to use it. Then they slipped out to watch side by side in the underbrush next to their vehicle.

Footsteps brought him back from a timeless, dreamless doze. Black figures were trotting along the road toward them from the direction of the town. Riva's gun made a soft, snicking sound as she cocked it. He laid a hand on her arm.

A man in Israeli military fatigues staggered past them, his features contorted by exhaustion and terror. Then came two more, a woman and a girl, shapeless beneath dark shawls. A short, heavy-set, jowly man brought up the rear. He was panting and visibly near collapse. What was frightening these people?

Spotlight beams picked their way up the road toward them like diamond-brilliant, long-legged insects, and he caught the deep-throated rumble of an engine. Headlights blazed out suddenly amidst the ruddy light of the oil-tank fires. A voice, amplified to unintelligibility by a bull-horn, yammered something. The fat man stopped, his mouth twisted into an oval of despair. The woman faltered, turned, and went back to him. The child would have joined her, but she pushed the girl roughly toward the dark bushes off to the side of the road.

The vehicle came bounding up over a rise, and he saw that it was an open, jeep-style scout car. It held six Klansmen: men in white hoods and robes, just like Nate Reese's movie, "One Angry After-noon." Beverly Rowntree had hated that one: too violent, she said, and she had never gone in for Black heroes. He told her to shut up so he could concentrate.

The Klansman beside the driver stood up and hollered something over his bullhorn. The fat man knelt in the middle of the road, as if he were praying, and the woman stood squarely behind him. Good scene! Great lighting!

One ghostly figure stayed in the vehicle to man the mounted machine-gun, while the rest got down. They wore identical, complete-coverage, white suits that included gloves, boots, and bulky back-tanks, and their faces were concealed by silvery, mirror-bright masks.

What kind of Klan costumes were these? He didn't like it when the movies screwed around with authenticity! Their car, too, had graffiti spray-painted on it: a big, wavering, white "UN" over an oblong flag-decal that consisted of a red background and a white crescent.

"Turks," Riva whispered. "Sanitation team . . . ."

One of the Klansmen sported different insignia: a blue flag with a yellow cross on his helmet. He appeared to be arguing with his comrades, but they ignored him.

The one in the lead went right up to the kneeling man and the woman, raised the stitch-gun he was carrying, and spat out a burst at point-blank range. The explosive needles went bangedy-bang like a string of firecrackers, and both targets jittered and danced and erupted in a shower of blood. Then they fell down. In the ringing silence that followed they heard the child keening wordlessly somewhere in the rocks off to the side of the road. There was no sign of the first man, the one in fatigues.

Two of the Klansmen stooped to inspect their work. Three advanced to peer into the darkness after the child. One pointed at Riva's APC, half-concealed in the undergrowth beside the road. The machine-gunner swivelled his weapon to cover, but when the APC proved to be empty he went back to contemplating the highway to the south, away from the town.

It took him a second to realize that Riva had opened fire; then his gun joined in, seemingly of its own accord. The Klansmen in the road yelped, staggered, and collapsed. The machine-gunner never had a chance to turn around: he threw up his arms and plunged prettily off onto the stony roadbed. Nice shot! Give that stunt man a bonus!

The Klansmen all lay still. That was how Nate Reese had done it! Shoot the White bastards! That was the message of a lot of his movies.

Riva called something in Hebrew, then in English, then, haltingly, in Arabic. A whimper answered her from the darkness.

Eventually the girl emerged. It was hard to say whether she was an Arab, a Jew, or what. She looked about twelve years old, thin, dark-faced, with lanky, stringy hair. Grime concealed the color of her baggy pants and long-sleeved, tunic-like blouse, and her shawl was little more than a black rag. She did not speak but continued to cry, soundlessly and with no tears. Riva made a face but held her and patted her awkwardly until the worst spasms were finished.

The movie was over. Beverly had to be home by midnight, otherwise her old man would have a shit-fit. He helped the woman collect the weapons, drag the Klansmen into the undergrowth—they sure were good actors!—and run their vehicle off the road. The child climbed into their APC without protest, and he managed a couple of hours of precious sleep. By dawn they were on their way again.

Jerusalem and Damascus are not far apart, as measured in kilometers instead of cultures and history. He recalled another occasion when he had driven this road. There had been men with him then: grim, tough soldiers in Israeli-issue helmets and uniforms. He didn't want to think about it and was grateful when the waterfall came back to drown everything out.

They camped that night under a moon as big and ornately scrolled as one of those silver trays the Arab artisans peddled to the tourists. Riva refused to enter the city for fear both of contagion and also of whom or what else might be wandering there. He lay with her on a looted mattress in the sand next to their vehicle and listened to the child whimper. The little girl still had not spoken. Memory handed him the name "Liese," but he had no idea who that was.

Memory crawled up to report, very quietly so as not to wake the woman.

"God damn it," he growled. "Don't do that!"

"Sorry, sir," Memory replied. "Thought you'd like to know, sir."

"I don't remember any Liese. Who is she?"

"Never mind." Memory was contrite. "Go to sleep, sir."

"How can I? The kid's whining keeps me awake."

A new voice broke in, a woman, a stranger speaking funny, stilted English. "What are you mumbling? Dink you, you piece of dead meat!"

He opened an eye to see an angular shadow against the moonlit armored flank of their personnel carrier: a kid pimping for his sister—or offering himself for a little quick rental.

He made a shooing gesture. Words still baffled him, but a good, deep, vicious growl ought to get the message across.

"What?" the person asked in startled tones. "What . . . what's the matter?"

He pointed and pantomimed "no teats": boys were not his style. He rolled over to go back to sleep.

A fist smacked him at the nape of the neck. He twisted around and fended off flailing arms tipped with cat-claws, jerked up a leg to protect his groin, and dodged snapping, white teeth.

His attacker was a woman, not his type but passable if one ignored the lack of breastworks. He snorted in chagrin, but she took it as a laugh and joined in. Next they were tugging at each other's clothes; then they were intertwined, as tight as two snakes in a drainpipe, as his father used to say.

It still wasn't any good: he couldn't finish it.

"Pog you, corpse!" she panted. "Get me off! Get me off!"

Memory was astutely absent. She pulled his fingers down between her legs, then savagely pushed his head in that direction as well. Emily Pietrick used to like that, he recalled. He nuzzled the soft, fragrant flesh of her abdomen, then moved lower.

He raised his eyes to see the little girl watching them, wide-eyed and open-mouthed.

He was no kink, no perverter of children. He wrenched himself free and grabbed the blanket.

"God damn you!" the woman gasped. "God damn you to hell!" She followed his gaze. "Who cares? The world has ended! It's over! Yet you, you chunk of dog-meat, you care about *that*? About bourgeois morality?" She rapped out a command in Hebrew and made an angry gesture. The child ignored her.

The waterfall cut off her words and also his view of her furious, contorted features.

He awoke to the rumble of the engine and the clatter of treads chewing on a rutted roadbed. He had no recollection of where he was or how he had come there. His chest was spattered with black oil.

He must have been half asleep while helping one of Major Berger's tankers refuel! The Izzies said the Baalbek War would soon be over; then maybe he could lie down. They had taken Damascus in a storm of blood and fire, and the Syrians were in full retreat north toward Aleppo. Berger told Copley that they'd take that, too, by the end of the week. Then they'd go see about Iraq and Iran and some other places that had been thorns in the Jewish state's iron-plated sides. The Izzies had had a century of Arabs; now they were determined to end the problem for all time: the "Final Solution."

He was surprised to find that his Israeli driver wore no uniform—and very little else. Her attire consisted of a skimpy bra, panties, and boots, although a sweat-stained, red top and black, leather pants were draped over the seat beside her. She was skinny, sharp-faced, and dark, and her hair was cut as short as a boy's. God, Izzie women were tough!

"Awake?" She shoved a chunk of dry bread at him, and the kid passed him a can of something lemony and sweet from the rear compartment. The woman—he kept forgetting her name—said, "You're pogging fungled, as Sol would say! Look, we're coming up on some suburbs. Get back and handle that mounted machine-gun we picked up last night."

He didn't remember any such weapon and was bemused to find a shiny-bright Hiram bolted in the brackets made for it above the driver's cab. God, he must *really* have been asleep! Memory would answer for this!

The blue-and-white Israeli flag still flew over Aleppo's medieval citadel, but the sun-scoured streets outside were silent. Riva—that was his driver's name—thought she heard engines and possibly gunfire inside the city and refused to go in. She kept to the back roads. After staying lost for most of the day, they found their way around to the highway that led north to the Turkish border.

He studied the blank-faced buildings through binoculars but saw only death and emptiness. As before, the roads were packed with stalled trucks, cars, carts, and even baby buggies. Horses, camels, and mules lay sprawled amidst human corpses and litter. He shook his head and summoned the waterfall again to drown any recognition of sorrow.

"But why?" the driver-lady asked. "Why? Who did this? Who has committed this crime . . . this horror?" Warm tears spattered onto the back of his hand, and he looked around to find the native child behind him. He knew neither Hebrew nor Arabic and could only offer a comforting smile. She misunderstood and drew back apprehensively.

"Bastards!" his driver went on. "Monsters! They have killed half the world! They deserve to die! They are criminals . . . worse even than the Nazis!"

That struck a chord. What? Why? Memory must be having a drink with the off-duty watch, and did not answer his call. He would have to court-martial the sonuvabitch if this kept up!

He forced himself out of the waterfall, sucked in air, and tried to think. Who had employed Pacov? And why? *Why*? What did they—whoever "they" were—gain?

Memory came hustling up onto the bridge, late as usual, and panted, "Loot, sir, loot! Land, resources, factories, industries, farms, the wealth of hundreds of millions of slaughtered people . . . all empty, ready for the taking!" Memory sounded smug. "Pacov is neat, tidy, and almost impossible to stop. It's the perfect weapon."

The Russians had responded with their Starak too late to save themselves. At least Starak must have put a crimp in the plans of those who had expected a clean sweep from Pacov!

Memory produced a tinny, static-filled recording: a man's voice saying, "It must've been the Izzies who started this Pacov thing. They've always been terrified of the Soviet Union, and America's grown too weak to help them any more. A quick, surgical

strike . . . ." He asked for a face to go with that voice, and Memory
obediently produced a faded photograph of a bald, elderly man, who
looked like a petulant baby. Mueller? Molders? Something like that.

He tried to tell the woman that it wasn't the Nazis who had slain
her country—that it was probably the Israelis. Words were still
beyond him, however. Just as well: he never liked discussing politics
with Major Berger either; the Izzies were so sensitive!

He dozed again. Beverly Rowntree certainly did have mag-
nificently bovine udders! Adrift amongst white billows, the great,
American wet dream!

They halted that night well away from Aleppo. His woman driver
showed him her maps and said that they must take the new Izzie
military highway east to al-Mawsil in what had once been Iraq. From
there another recent road led up to Yerevan in the Soviet Union.
Somebody had given Tbilisi a dose of cleansing, prophylactic
Pacov, and now much of the southwestern Soviet Union, eastern
Turkey, northern Iran, and Iraq were a big, empty playground for
the Izzie "relief" forces. The Turks, the driver-lady said, were only
just beginning to push east again to recover their lost property. With
Israel a graveyard, the Turks could now drive south, too, and
re-establish the Ottoman Empire! What fun!

They travelled on in the morning. The landscape became a blur
of sere, yellow-brown mountains and grey-green vegetation. There
were people at first, mostly lying down or slumped against the
stained, dun-hued walls. Memory declared disdainfully that most of
these Third-Worlders were lazy poggers, but scattered here and
there amongst them were the still forms of Israeli soldiers. The Izzies
had a reputation for industriousness. What were they doing here?

Some time later—days? months?—the people disappeared and
were replaced by white skeletons in dark-stained rags. He wasn't
sure when this happened, but he liked the skeletons better.

Each night he slept next to his driver-lady, often with the little
girl curled against his back for warmth, as sexless as three baby
angels in Heaven. This was how it ought to be, his mother's voice
told him, not the wicked harlot's way of Emily Pietrick, nor even a
nice, marriage-minded girl like Beverly Rowntree! His mother
didn't know sweet Beverly the way he did. Sweet? Yes, and also
hypocritical, greedy, marry-a-prick-and-a-pocketbook, and other
endearing qualities. His father understood, but then he never said
anything to anybody. Too bad Mavis Larson had moved away before
they had entered high school and pubescence! She was a bitch, too,
and mean as a rattler's grin. But she did have the sleekest bod of the
lot of them!

Once they spotted an armored column heading east, the red
banner of Turkey snapping on the lead halftrack's radio mast. Later

they were almost thumbed by a similar force travelling west; this one displayed a green flag with a white sidebar and a white crescent and star: Pakistan, the driver-lady said. With the Soviets out of commission, it now behooved Pakistan's Red Mullah to don Islamic green and embark upon a *jihad* against the unbelievers of the lands to Pakistan's northwest. (No matter that said unbelievers were Muslims too—and mostly deceased. "Dead-y or not, here we come!") India, the woman said, was no longer a problem: it had dissolved into a hornets' nest of warring statelets, but lately wily, old Ramanujan had got his act together, and the Indians were now advancing eastward through Burma and Thailand to offer "aid" to the stricken Chinese. Why fight Pakistan, plus what was left of Free Iran, Afghanistan, and Soviet Central Asia, when all of lush Southeast Asia was open for the taking? You go east and we'll go west, and never the twain shall meet . . . or some such half-remembered quotation.

He recalled a personal connection with India, although Memory couldn't or wouldn't tell him what it was. It was connected with occasional dreams of a lovely, oval-faced princess, who dressed in blue ice and smelled of sandalwood and spices. At times he was happy with her, but more often he felt an ominous sorrow, a deep foreboding, like the thunderheads that warned of rain. As Emily said, next to him in the theater, "It's like when you hear the spooky music go up just before the murderer pops out with a knife." She rubbed him furiously, trying to make him come in his pants and mess up his clothes. What a kink she was! As weird as any of the imaginary devils she professed to worship! His mother called her a witch and lectured him fiercely about "bad seed."

"Khoi," the driver-lady pointed. "Northeast from there to Nakhichevan, then on to Yerevan in Armenia. That's where my ancestors came from, you know."

He didn't know.

"We're Armenians . . . Jews, but Armenians. You *are* Jewish, aren't you? I know you're circumcised." She gave him what was meant as a roguish grin.

He ought to respond; that would be polite. But he couldn't. He smiled at her instead. He still had trouble recalling her name, and Memory wasn't much help.

"Armenian Jews. Not blonde and Germanic-looking like you, you pogging zombie, as glow-in-the-dark white as any 'Aryan' ever spawned! As for me, I'm not German, not Polish, not Russian . . . and so not of our Israeli elite, our ruling class, our gubbing 'master race!'" She spat white dust out the cab window. "So what if you're not Jewish? You've probably got as much 'pure Semitic blood' in your corpse-veins as I do . . . and more than a lot of our leaders. Most of them are European Jews descended from Slavic tribes converted during the Middle Ages! The rest of us go back to the poor dinkers the Romans scattered all over their pogging empire after they thumbed Jerusalem." She wrinkled her nose derisively. "We trace our ancestry back to Moses and Abraham and ancient Israel, but that's propaganda. It unites our people and gives us a claim to a homeland in Palestine that the world can't deny! But what does it matter now?"

He didn't know or care. The ship was rolling queasily in the clutches of the storm, steel plates squealing, engines hammering over the din of wind and water.

"So what if you're not Jewish?" the driver-lady insisted. It seemed to bother her. She rubbed dirty fingers across dust-powdered lips. "Who gives a pog now? Am *I* so Jewish? I'm neither religious nor a Zionist nationalist. I don't give a shit about either a kosher kitchen or an empire of miserable Arab slaves! Oh, I'm Jewish by descent and by culture, but I don't care about the two things our leaders say really make a Jew! All I want is to run my boutique in Haifa, sell fashions, maybe break into the American market, and have things peaceful . . . the way people ought to live. And now this! Now this!" She waved out the window.

He motioned that it was all right. He was getting good at sign language. Too bad Memory couldn't find the crewman who knew Morse code or the other sailor with the signal flags. Just wait till he made his report to the admiral!

She said, "I'm glad you can't talk. That was one thing about my male-cháuvinist pogger boy friends! Talk, talk, talk . . . Mr. Macho Man! Gub them all!" She grinned over at him, then caught her lower lip between her teeth. "I don't feel well."

"Uh?" he inquired.

She didn't reply but squeezed her eyes shut. He slid across the seat toward her.

"God . . . !" She doubled over, forehead down against the steering wheel.

"Uh! Unh!" He grabbed the wheel, kicked her foot away, found the brake pedal, and brought the ponderous APC to a stop. Beverly Rowntree looked annoyed.

"Sick . . . ," the driver-lady whispered.

What had she told him? What had Memory said about some horrid epidemic sweeping their ship?

She fumbled the door open, rolled down into the road, knelt, and vomited. Before he could reach her she went into a paroxysm of cramps, diarrhea, and retching. The child handed him the canteen, and he held it out to the woman wordlessly.

The driver-lady recovered enough to take it. Her cheeks were sallow, her lips dry and cracked-looking, her forehead flecked with sweat. She husked, "I'm sorry . . . I'm sorry . . . ."

He wanted to tell her that she needn't be. He helped her clean up, then scanned the mountainous horizon for some place to take her. All that met his eyes were sullen whitecaps on a silver sea: no land in sight! Didn't they have a sick bay on this ship? Where was the doctor? He yelled for Memory, but only the child was there. She helped him wrestle the driver-lady back up onto the bridge.

He drove. The driver-lady, whose name he had somehow lost completely, hunched in the passenger seat beside him. She looked awful.

Khoi, when they reached it, was unexpected: a pretty town of broad streets, willow-fringed streamlets, and gardens. The only dirt was what had drifted in from the fertile fields outside. Amidst the rubbish he saw more of the white-boned inhabitants, their mouths agape and choked with dust. He wondered how they ate.

Memory chose the tallest building in sight as a reference point, and he drove around and around until he reached it: a tall minaret on a mosque that faced a brick-built bazaar and a square. There were more skeletons here; they congregated in the side streets, gathered chummily under the arcades, and made friendly, crackling noises beneath the treads of his vehicle. Many of these silent citizens were stacked tidily like cordwood against the mosque's wall, but they were outnumbered by the unruly ones who lay sprawled everywhere else. No discipline, as the Israelis said of these Eastern peoples.

"Where . . . ?" The voice of the driver-lady reminded him that he ought to do something for her. He wasn't sure what.

There were Israeli army trucks in the square, a whole row of them. On inspection he discovered that many of the skeletons wore rags and tatters of khaki, and he saw Izzie helmets, guns, and buckles. These skeletons, too, were lying down and lazing about. How unlike the industrious Israelis! So the Jews had gone soft! Major Berger said this was inevitable: live with lazy people in an easy place, and you go all mushy yourself. Next thing you know you're the same as your conquered subjects. Then some new barbarian comes along and stomps you into history.

Memory sniggeringly interrupted to say that this looked like a real gong-bong, green light party, as much fun as the over-and-under Banger orgies Emily Pietrick popped so much! Look how those white bone-people were intertwined!

"It's not Pacov," the woman muttered. "Dysentery, I think. The water in that last village. You didn't drink from that well, remember? Nor the girl. Cholera?"

He was puzzled. The water in Sioux City movie-house fountains was pretty good. What was she complaining about? Why didn't she go get a cola from the stand in the lobby? He could loan her a couple of bucks if she didn't have the money.

The child whimpered and pointed. One of the Israeli trucks had a big, red cross painted on its flapping, rotting, canvas side. He brought their APC to a stop beside it.

The driver-lady climbed halfway out, then fell the rest of the way down onto the paving. She was sick again, grovelling and retching amongst their hosts' scattered bones.

The girl seized his hand and drew him away, toward the truck. What was she so urgent about? The ship's doctor would be here any second. He let her pull him, though, and climbed up inside.

Here were more bones attired in ragged khaki; boxes and canisters; machines and equipment; autoclaves, syringes, and stethoscopes, all dust-caked and fading. He prowled around, looking for something he recognized. Outside, he could hear the driver-lady pleading, calling words he couldn't make out.

He opened a case at random. The labels were in Hebrew, Arabic, and English; he knew that much.

He couldn't read any of those languages.

He grunted, and the girl scrambled out to bring the driver-lady up to see for herself. She was too weak to walk, and he and the child had to lift her and carry her inside. They laid her on the truck floor, taking care to avoid the broken glass bottles and vials spilled from cartons.

"Unh?" He held up a box, then another. "Unh?"

"Can't see . . . ," she murmured. Her eyes were already ringed and sunken, her sharp cheekbones highlighted by grease, dirt, and sweat. He brought the box close to her face. "No, not that. Find an antibiotic, the strongest. ecotromycin, maybe . . . the new drug they developed for our soldiers . . . ."

He didn't know ecotromycin from sarsaparilla, but he couldn't tell her that. Where the hell was that bastard Memory when he needed him?

"That one . . . no, the other beside it. No. The metal case." She grabbed her belly as the cramps caught her again.

He looked to the child for help. She could probably read, but the medical names on the labels would be beyond her.

The driver-lady gagged and crouched low, on her hands and knees in the middle of the cargo compartment. The ship's doctor was going to crap his jeans when he saw this mess!

"Please," she choked. "Hurry."

He obliged, tossing packages and ampoules and vials and canisters and all manner of enigmatic devices down before her for identification. Memory put in an appearance to say that he knew what to look for, provided he could spot it in the chaos. Memory had experience, he said, of Delhi Belly, the Sultan's Revenge, typhus, and a lot of others. The driver-lady looked like she had bacillic dysentery, perhaps made more virulent by mutation and the combining of strains, just as gonorrhea and AIDS had become worse and worse as they ravaged the world. Pestilence, the fourth of the Four Horsemen of the Apocalypse, was one son of a bitch! Knock him down, and he sprang up in a hundred new forms to fight you again! Wasn't there some monster in Greek mythology who could do that? He'd seen that movie, too.

The child was laving the driver-lady's face with water from the canteen—probably the same water that had infected her. He begged Memory for a name, a picture, a hint of the medicine that had cured him out in—wherever it was. Angola? Syria? Or was it India? Names and places were coming back. He snarled at Beverly to get out of the way. Let the medics through! Get the lady to a hospital!

The woman scrabbled among the wrack of dressings and bottles and surgical gear. The truck was only medical transport, not an ambulance. If they looked, they might find the Izzies' field hospital van parked nearby, she said. Then, again, they might not.

There was no time. The driver-lady opened her eyes wide, retched, and curled up, face down, in her own awful mess. Her fingers kept flexing and clutching, but he guessed that she was losing consciousness. The child poured water into her slack mouth, but it sloshed back out again. Just as well; it looked brown and smelled bad.

"Unh!" he cried. "Unh!"

The girl turned to stare at him, the obelisk look of one who has seen death too often.

He fumbled with another metal canister. It came open, and tiny, white tablets showered over his palms. Were these the ones? Would they help? Or were they poison for her now?

He began to weep. The seas rose and obscured the helmsman's view. He wiped at the porthole and cursed. Nothing helped. What a terrible storm! Worse, even, than he remembered from the first time he had seen this movie.

He sat there a long time.

Later that afternoon he woke to find Beverly shaking him. Had she seen him with Emily, then? God, if she had, the fit would hit the shan! When he got his wits back, he discovered it wasn't either of them: an unfamiliar face looked down at him, a big-nosed, round-eyed, gamin-looking foreign kid. She tugged at his arm. She was crying too. Saddest goddamned movie he'd ever seen!

He touched the driver-lady's bare shoulder. She didn't move. Then she twisted and slowly toppled sideways, to sprawl against a heap of boxes. He knew she was dead.

He wept, and the child wept with him. He held the gaunt, little girl to him and let the tears flow. He didn't remember exactly why they were crying, but it felt good. Something was radically wrong with the world, and this was the only way they could share their misery.

After a while he found that another movie had started, one he remembered seeing on Saturday Film Classics, before his father had splurged for the big holo-video his mother hated so much. This movie ended with Death himself towing a string of newly-dead plague victims across a blasted, barren heath, dancing, skipping, leaping, and whirling them all away to darkness and the eternity of the grave.

He hadn't liked that movie. It scared the bejesus out of him.

But it was real. It was what was happening.

He rose, lifted the terribly light, dehydrated body of the driver-lady, cradled her in his arms, and clambered down out of the truck. The little girl followed. The setting sun turned the town and its mute inhabitants to blood and shadows.

He began to dance, while the skeletons made eldritch music and kept time. They sounded pretty good. Wondering, the child trudged after him.

"Where it stops, nobody knows!" His father quoted sententiously from some place. He and Beverly and Emily and Mavis and his parents and the child and all the people of his life joined hands with Death in Yellow and did an amateurish but enthusiastic saraband through the empty city of Khoi.

He never remembered when or where—or if—the music stopped.

If we shadows have offended,
Think but this, and all is mended,
That you have but slumber'd here,
While these visions did appear.
—*A Midsummer Night's Dream*, **William Shakespeare**

CHAPTER TWENTY-ONE

Monday, July 13, 2048

"I still can't believe it," Wrench marveled.

"It's him, all right. Been working for us for a year or more. Rose, here, recognized him." General Copley motioned the woman forward with a freckle-splotched hand. "Captain Rose Thurley, Cadre-Commander Wren."

"How . . . where did Lessing . . . ?" For once Wrench was at a loss.

"He must be an immune. One day he wandered in, out of Pacov territory," the woman answered diffidently. "In an old Russian bakery van. Absolute bonkers."

"Tell 'im 'bout the girl," the fourth person in the room suggested, the seedy-looking mercenary named Kenow. He also wore officer's pips, but in these jumped-up settler militias—actually merc armies of occupation—insignia meant whatever the wearer said it did.

"Uh, right. Well, in the back of this van, like, he had digs fixed up for himself: a cot, a kerosene stove, and supplies. Just like a caravan . . . um, trailer, you Americans call it."

"The girl, the girl," Kenow persisted.

"Yes, all right, but first: I had charge of border patrols then. New Sverdlovsk has frontiers and customs now, and refugee resettlement camps, and what-all. One of my squads saw this big van comin' in. They stopped it, and there was poor Lessing, all wild, hair and beard like a soddin' cave-man, got up in an Azerbaijani vest, Israeli army pants, and Russian peasant boots. Guns and ammo enough to do the bleedin' world." She twisted at a strand of grey-streaked, red-blonde hair; the little man in the natty, black uniform of the Cadre of the American Party of Humankind unnerved her. "Well, in the corner of the cargo compartment we seen this girl, a child, like, sittin' propped up against the wall."

"A real knock-out!" Kenow rolled his close-set eyes.

"A kid of twelve or so, you bloody dink! Dead as a dodo, and mummified, too, shrunk down to bones with skin stretched over 'em, wrapped in rags."

"Dead?" Wrench wasn't sure he had heard her right. "Lessing was carting a *dead* girl around?"

"Hard t'get a date in these parts," Kenow observed drily.

"Called her Emily, sometimes Mavis, sometimes Beverly. Sometimes 'driver-lady.' You should've seen her, poor little thing: dried out, like them pharaohs of Egypt. He wouldn't part with her. Took persuadin' . . . three orderlies and a needle full of Narcodine . . . to pry him loose and get him to the hospital."

"You knew him right away?"

"I didn't see him then myself. The watch-sergeant put in a report, but nobody thought much about him. We used to get a dozen of these immunes every week, each weirder than the last. Dyin' people, crazies too far gone to be helped. There was one, a Russian woman big as a gubbin' gorilla, stark naked, painted herself all over with crosses, come in shootin' . . . ."

Wrench motioned her to get on with her story. "Ah. When did you recognize Lessing?"

She eyed him cautiously. He sounded more like an interrogator than a man looking for a long-lost friend. "A long time after. We fed him, give him a job in the fields . . . a lot of the brain-damaged ones could do that much . . . and let him be until either he croaked or his wits came right. Nearly all of 'em died, y'know. Most of Pacov's immunes wasn't really so. They was just delayed reactions. Ninety per cent went down at once, some lived on for a week or two, and a few lasted six months or more. Them who made it beyond that you could count on your fingers. We was surprised to find Lessing survived. Artie Carlson . . . he's our census-keeper . . . thought his records was snookered."

"*You* knew Lessing when you saw him?"

"Right. I'd met him a while ago. We was mercs together." She tried to keep the wariness out of her voice. This Cadre-Commander Wren was said to be high up in the hierarchy of America's ruling party.

"I knew 'im the same way," Kenow stated self-importantly. "But I was sure fooled. Must've seen 'im out there a hunnert times, hoein' away, pullin' weeds, 'n' I never spotted him. He never said nothin' neither. Jes' worked."

Wrench played with the buttons on his uniform coat. He hadn't expected Russia to be so warm in July.

The woman took up the thread again. "One day he stopped by the hospital, asked where his Emily was . . . the dead girl, he meant. Anyway, Dr. Casimir, on our psych-staff, was curious enough to make him tell his story. Somehow he mentioned Colonel . . . uh, General . . . Copley. Named me too. Then the rest come out. Our headquarters is just over the road from the hospital, so they sent for me."

General Copley turned away from the one window. The view was not prepossessing: squarish, neatly painted, unimaginative Russian architecture, broad but uninspired streets, Soviet vehicles repaired over and over to save on the colony's dwindling reserve of Israeli and American transport.

He addressed Wrench. "Rose called me. I knew Lessing right away. He served in my unit. Good man." He looked somehow dull and uninterested, as though he wanted to get back to something else.

"Yeah, a good ol' boy," Johnny Kenow added earnestly. "Served with 'im in the Baalbek War, back in '38. Saw 'im again in Guinea just B.P. . . . 'Before Pacov.' After Pacov hit I grabbed a plane, a load o' goodies, 'n' the Empress Marie Leonore Therese of Guinea, 'n' we come here. Pacov got most o' the Guineans, but me 'n' the Empress . . . she's French . . . made it out. Married her." He displayed nicotine-yellowed teeth proudly. "Now she's got a bun in the oven . . . six months pregnant."

Stories like Kenow's were routine. General Copley scuffed one immaculate riding boot against the other.

Wrench asked, "Did he . . . is Lessing recovered? Did he tell you what happened to him?"

"Not much that makes sense," Rose answered. "About some ship, a sea voyage, naval action, a storm, frogmen. And about Emily and Beverly and Mavis . . . a whole, bloody platoon of girl friends." If Wrench's information were correct, this woman had once had a passion for Lessing—which was probably why she had rescued him from what amounted to open slavery in New Sverdlovsk.

Digging was worth a try. Wrench said, "The last we saw of him, he was managing a resort in the South Pacific. The Izzies raided the place and burned it to the ground. They slaughtered two hundred and seventeen people, including nearly a hundred kids on vacation. Lessing disappeared. We figured either he went up in smoke or else got thumbed on the beach and his body washed out to sea. We never knew what happened to him . . . till now."

"And you retaliated by destroying Israel with Pacov," General Copley rapped. He had a reputation as the kind of merc who did not approve of biological warfare—or anything much longer range than a thrown rock. He preferred hand-to-hand weapons: fists, teeth, and nails if possible.

"Not us. Not true!"

"Serve the gubbin' Yoodies right!" Kenow cackled. "Folks say they started Pacov in the first place!"

Wrench shook his head. "No truth to that story either, so far as we know." He grinned. Congeniality was a useful trait; it would likely get him what Mulder had sent him for: Alan Lessing, miraculously alive after more than four years. The Party could use a hero, living testimony to the perfidy of the Vizzies and the Izzies, what with war now brewing in California.

He picked up his peaked officer's cap and rubbed at its enamelled insignia, a red shield on which a black circle surrounded a white background. The circle was divided into four quarters by a thick, black cross. One day, soon, they'd open the black circle in four places, just before its intersection with each arm of the cross.

The door latch clicked. It was an orderly. He saluted and whispered to Copley.

"Seems Lessing's got a second visitor," Copley announced. "Another of your people, Cadre-Commander Wren. A woman."

"That'll be Anneliese Meisinger. She was in Seattle when we got the news Lessing had been found alive here." Damn it! He had tried to keep Liese from learning too soon. When she thought he was dead—and Emma Delacroix with him—she'd almost done herself in out of grief. Now this shock. Who knew what effect a deranged or brain-dead Lessing would have on her?

Liese entered in a swirl of smoke-grey dirndl skirts. She had never adopted the severe, black-and-white uniform prescribed for female Party members. Beige or pale grey suited her better, usually with black accessories. Today she had added a neckerchief of scarlet silk for emphasis. Women recognized this as a "power wardrobe"; men saw it as elegant and sexy-sophisticated. General Copley was now wide awake and paying attention, Wrench noted, and Johnny Kenow was openly admiring her. Rose Thurley gave her a perfunctory nod.

Liese homed in on Wrench. "Lessing?"

"He's fine, these people say. Some psychological difficulties . . . ." He hadn't had time to alert Copley and his subordinates to Liese's speech problems.

"Crazy as a cat in a barr'l of whiskey," Kenow chuckled.

Wrench sent the man a warning glare. Insensitive son of a bitch! "Lessing's still suffering from hallucinations. Wandering alone all those years, among the ruins and the corpses . . . ." He brightened deliberately. "Now I have to rewrite the funeral oration I gave for the jizmo on Ponape!"

"'Hero of the Party, martyr to the cause!'" Liese quoted, and laughed. Her voice sounded shaky, on the verge of tears.

Lessing was waiting for them in the hospital garden, seated on a lawn chair and framed by a trellis of red flowers. He stood up.

"Lessing?" Wrench heard Liese's sharply indrawn breath behind him.

The man looked older, thinner, graying, sun-blackened, lined, and calloused with hard labor. His Russian slacks and open-necked, white shirt didn't fit him very well. He looked like an aging farm hand.

His voice was the same, though. "Wrench?" Then: "Liese . . . ? Hello!"

Copley shook hands, made excuses, and departed. Kenow and Rose Thurley stayed. The woman's expression was a study in possessiveness, anxiety, and something else that ran a lot deeper than "old merc buddies." Liese might have to watch out for herself.

"Why?" Liese gulped. "Didn't call us!"

The blue eyes—paler than Wrench remembered—smiled, then shifted obliquely away. "No."

"Why not?"

"No reason to come back. Didn't want to get back into beegeeing. Too old to be a merc. And I heard you people were busy rebuilding America. You'd have had no time . . . no place for me. Farming feels better: plants and dirt, rain and sun."

Liese flicked a glance at the Australian woman. "Happy?"

"Fairly." He waited: relaxed, calm, and patient.

Wrench said, "We could have taken care of you, Lessing. We . . . you and I, all of us . . . are more than just business acquaintances, godammit. You only had to get to the American settlement in New Moscow to call us."

"Reached Ufa," he answered irrelevantly. "Izzies there. They nearly thumbed me."

Kenow muttered, "Ufa's a town down the road a piece. Yoodie headquarters for this region . . . our rivals, tough bunch. They want Sverdlovsk's steel mills, heavy engineering, plastics. We got a lot of stuff they'd love to git their cottonpickers on."

Lessing said, "Copley thinks one day we'll have to fight the Izzies, right here in Russia." He might have been discussing the lush, crimson blossoms behind him.

"Come home," Liese urged softly. "Now."

He looked at her, disconcerted for the first time. "Home? Is Sonny there?"

"He talks about this 'Sonny' sometimes," Rose told her quietly. "Somebody he met in Israel, we think."

Wrench said, "He fought there in the Baalbek War. A fellow merc?"

"Not likely. Sometimes he cries when Dr. Casimir, who's been treating him, mentions 'Sonny.' Maybe an Izzie he had a bad time with."

Lessing had overheard. He said, "He's dead. I saw him. It was his green pants I pulled out of the car."

"He's told us that too. About a fire, a dead city."

"Ponape?" Liese wondered.

"No." Lessing spoke directly to her. "Jerusalem."

Rose shook her head. "This is where it gets vague. He'd have had to fly like a bloody rocket from Ponape to Israel in time to be there when somebody dosed the Middle East with Pacov. But then he talks about a ship at sea, a storm, and the rest I told you upstairs. Sometimes he says the 'driver-lady' *drove* him to Jerusalem. Or maybe *from* Jerusalem to some place else. God!"

"Does he ever ask about his comrades from Ponape?" Wrench asked. "The Swedes found bodies in the cells in ARAD headquarters in Jerusalem. One of Lessing's friends, an Arab named Abu Talib, was among them."

"He talks a bit about some woman named Emma. Once, under hypnosis, he yelled at somebody named Mallon to run away and hide. That's all."

"Emma Delacroix: a nice, old lady who'd lived most of her life in Africa. The Izzies grabbed her off Ponape, and then she disappeared. She could've been wounded and died en route to Israel . . . or later in one of their prisons. Mallon was killed on Ponape. As for Abu Talib, the Izzies had worked him over pretty bad, but the real cause of death was Pacov. We identified him from dental records. His wife and maybe one son are alive, though; went off to Saudi Arabia or somewhere."

"Like, Lessing blocked out the whole shootin' match," Rose said. "What you don't think of never happened. Lucky bugger, in a way."

A compact, middle-aged Hungarian with bushy, brindled, black eyebrows and hair to match came bustling across the grass toward them. Rose identified him to the others as Dr. Casimir.

The newcomer looked from one to the other. "General Copley says you want to take this patient back to the United States. I don't see why. He is recovering nicely here."

Wrench drew on the authority of his Party uniform. "He's one of ours, doctor. We have a duty to him."

"Hmmph. Well. We are quite capable . . . ."

"Of course. But your government . . . ."

"General Copley . . . ."

" . . . Has agreed with our government . . . ."

"Your Party of Humankind . . . ."

"Please! Lessing should go back with us. We can provide him with the best therapy available. His friends . . . ."

"He's at peace in Sverdlovsk," the doctor said. "I wish you'd never discovered he was here."

Wrench had no idea who had told the Party's agents in New Moscow of Lessing's presence. Kenow? Copley himself? Possibly just a "stringer" trading miscellaneous information for a few clips of American ammo—or a case of Banger porn tapes for the holo-vid.

The informant was not Rose Thurley; her face was as readable as a billboard!

"We *are* taking him, doctor." Wrench glanced over at Rose. "You can come and see him whenever you want. We'll fly you over at our expense on an American government 'Russ-ops' plane."

"It's green light by me." The woman seemed ready to be reasonable. "He oughta go where he can be treated best."

"Right here, in Sverdlovsk!" said the patient himself. "Wrench, I'm fine. Everything I need . . . Rose and Johnny and once in a while Colonel Copley to shoot the bull with." He paused. "And I really should stay close to Beverly. She can't move around much, you know."

"Understatement of the bleedin' year!" Rose breathed. "That'll be the dead girl."

"She's recuperating, though," Lessing continued cheerfully. "As soon as she can travel . . . ."

Liese turned away.

Damn it, Wrench thought glumly, this had to happen! Liese had not been well, and the doctors had put her on "cheery-pops," the latest mood-altering drug.

Lessing got up and went to her. She turned her head, murmuring something plaintive that no one else could hear. Then she stood stiffly still, drawing in upon herself.

It must be hell, Wrench thought, to be embraced by a ghost.

"I don't have much choice, do I?" Lessing asked. He stepped back. "You're taking me with you to the United States?"

Liese's voice was muffled but still audible. "Yes. Come. I . . . we . . . want you."

Wrench said, "We can help, man. You belong with us."

"Then I better go pack. Wait for me upstairs." He sounded only mildly concerned. His healing had a ways to go yet.

They went inside, to a pleasant, pastel-blue waiting room. They sat awkwardly on formal, straight-backed, wooden chairs around what looked like a card table covered with green, plastic padding, while one of Dr. Casimir's subordinates served them tea and buttered croissants.

Wrench busied himself with the food; it gave him time to think—and Liese time to recover. "Lessing's going to be all right." He tried to sound definitive, for Liese's sake.

Dr. Casimir watched Liese. He gestured for Rose to go to her. To Wrench he replied, "Of course. The prognosis becomes better with each day. Tea?"

"We don't get good tea any more. Most of the tea-producing countries are too messed up to export much."

The doctor sipped. "It's lemons and sugar we cannot obtain. One of the Chinese successor-republics flies tea over to us, and we've started to plant our own sugar beets. But the Izzies, Turks, and Pakistanis moved into what used to be Israeli territory to our south and west, and they are not so friendly."

"Let me know what you want," Wrench offered expansively. "We can fly you in some citrus fruit. Spain, Italy, southern France are all back on their feet and ready to deal."

The doctor waggled an eyebrow. "Your Party of Humankind rules much of Europe now . . . as well as North America . . . eh? You can command lemons from the Mediterranean, olives from Greece, wine from France and Italy, butter from Holland . . . all the good things from the old days?"

"We trade, yes. But the Party doesn't *rule* anyone, anywhere. There are sister-organizations in several European countries, but no international superstructure beyond a liaison committee. We have less real power, even in America, than the old political parties did. Local autonomy, that's us."

Dr. Casimir's remarkable eyebrows descended in a frown. "If you say so . . . but I have read a bit about National Socialist ideas of local autonomy."

"Things are different now. This isn't the twentieth century. We don't want secret police and 'Five Year Plans.' We're for free enterprise and personal incentives."

"Not socialism . . . state control by your monolithic party?"

Wrench smiled. "We do support the coordination of major economic production: what the Germans called *Gleichschaltung*. We're experimenting with that. The human race *must* manage its resources for the future. But we leave smaller businesses and industries alone; they're more free now than they were under the 'democracy' of the old U.S.A., which was really bureaucratized socialism. We have less taxes, less control, fewer restrictions. America's government more truly implements the will of the people now than it has for generations."

"There *are* protests, we hear. Sectors that disagree with you?"

"Sure. There always are. Fat cats kicked off the gravy train, welfare frauds made to work for their money, middlemen who actually have to produce something useful for a change. We're setting reasonable rates of interest, stopping the siphoning off of wealth by usurers and 'money men,' changing over from a paper-money economy to one based on real goods. That's only for starters. We're also standardizing the law, doing away with injustices, cutting down top-heavy government, training the jobless, improving education, and helping the farmers keep their land. And if anybody thinks all this is easy, he's welcome to try it!"

"And the Blacks? The Jews?"

"They're not overjoyed. Many Blacks are emigrating to Africa, now that Pacov has almost wiped it clean north of the South African border. There are several colonies, the biggest run by an American Black, a Muslim named Khalifa Abdullah Sultani. We're working to help him get things going. The Jews are another story. They're used to being at the heart of government, at the top of the professions, in the media, in business and finance, and lately central in state and local activities too. When Starak took out our big cities, their power went way down. We've taken steps to make sure that it stays down. But they're back at their old tricks, stirring up trouble, trying to incite the Blacks and other minorities that are left, working day and night to wreck what we've built. We'll have to deal with them more strictly ... and soon. Maybe we'll send them to what's left of Israel, as soon as the decon teams say it's clean of Pacov. It's certainly empty of Arabs now! Or they can join the Israeli colonies here in Russia. Either place, they should be happy. We'll gladly help them resettle."

The doctor gazed up at the ceiling. "The other day I mentioned 'the vanished Russians' to Mr. Lessing. You know what he answered? He said, '*We* are the Russians. Ring out the old, ring in the new!'"

"Smart, under the circumstances. My ancestors were English, but now I'm American, pure and simple. I don't demand to return to my 'homeland,' kick out the king, and run England! The past must not dictate to the present and the future! The Jews have never been able to see this. They insist on their ancient tribal identity, right out of the Old Testament."

"Yet you don't want them to assimilate, to mingle and disappear into your population, do you?"

"Frankly, no. We don't want them to change *us*. That's happened enough already. When they came to America as refugees, we took them in. Then they took the place over and started remaking it to suit themselves. They turned America into a multi-racial pigsty. We'll breathe easier when we're completely free of them and their influence."

Dr. Casimir glanced over at the two women, heads together as though they had been friends for years. "'The old order chan-geth ....'"

"Changeth, yes, but not easily. You have to have a grass-roots revolution to change an entrenched, traditional system. Anything less is cosmetic. We've learned that gradual reform is damned near impossible, especially when you're fighting vested interests, a power elite, an Establishment. Like the Russian Revolution, the French Revolution, or the Izzies' conquest of the Arabs, a *real* revolution has to be tough and thorough, a clean break with the past. Such an upheaval can't help but cause suffering."

"Draconian. That's the word I want. You call for a violent, harsh, and simplistic solution: a *draconian* answer to complex questions."

Wrench grinned amiably. "Like giving up smoking . . . or booze, which I'm trying to do now. Cold turkey is hell, but cutting down little by little doesn't work with me."

"This is different, Cadre-Commander. We're talking about *people* . . . and hallowed, age-old institutions . . . ."

"Yes, people who have been duped and controlled and exploited for centuries by those age-old institutions, doctor. They deserve better!"

"National Socialism?"

"Yes. Not exactly what they had in the Third Reich, perhaps, but still National Socialism. We're working toward a world order that guides but does not tyrannize; that honors creators, producers, and workers; that helps the needy out of their troubles instead of piously tossing them alms."

"You're an idealist, Cadre-Commander! Or a fool. Probably both."

"Proud to be both! We can't go on depending upon archaic 'tried-and-true' solutions, not after Pacov and Starak. We have to experiment. The economists and political scientists, the darlings of the 'liberal' academic establishment, gave us garbage. They couldn't predict economic or social trends any better than the fortune-teller lady at the carnival! They handed out guesswork theories wrapped in statistics and jargon and served up with all the pontifical authority of the Vestal Virgins! They flubbed! Now it's our turn to try."

"So who are *your* economic experts? Adolf Hitler? Vincent Dorn? Your great thinker who hides behind a pseudonym and an army of bodyguards!"

The doctor was well informed. Much of what Wrench had been saying did indeed come from "Dorn." Wrench said, "Partly right. Dorn's our theorist, our historian, the one who sees best through the fog. But he can't handle it all; the world's too complicated. We've got other experts, plus the most sophisticated computer ever devised. It's able to compare and evaluate maybe a billion variables at once, and it has data banks that contain every bit of information all the way back to Creation!"

"You would let a machine run humanity . . . our lives?"

"Why not? No individual or group can control all the data, much less weigh probabilities and assess long-term results. We set our goals . . . no machine does that for us . . . and then our computers tell us how to attain them."

"Data management I can see. But decisions made by a machine? The future of the world?"

"We'll be better off than under a lot of human leaders I can name!"

Their faces had grown flushed, and their voices had risen. Liese and Rose broke off their conversation and looked over at them. The doctor said, "And Alan Lessing? How does he fit into your computer plan for the master race?"

"He is . . . was . . . a valued co-worker. He's also an old friend. Nothing more."

"He was a protege of Herman Mulder, who is Secretary of State to President Outram, and Vice-President of your Party of Humankind under Dorn."

"That's so." Wrench regained control. "Did Lessing talk about Mr. Mulder?"

"No. He never mentions anything after his . . . what do you call it? . . . secondary school . . . high school. General Copley told Rose about Lessing's friendship with Mulder."

"He was Mr. Mulder's bodyguard out in India. When he vanished in the Ponape raid, the Mulders were devastated. Now that he's turned up like the proverbial bad penny they're ecstatic." Wrench paused for breath. "Lessing doesn't discuss the present? His own experiences? What's happening in the world?"

"He shows no interest. He doesn't seem to care."

"Not even about Pacov and Starak? God, the things he must've seen!"

"It's like a cinema film to him. He watches but he does not participate, even when he himself is one of the actors."

"He was always an aloof bastard," Wrench mused. "Our society bred many like him: the 'peripheral people,' the 'terminally uninvolved,' as somebody put it. I don't know if Lessing even cared that much about his wife . . . ."

"Wife? What *wife*?"

"You didn't know? My God! Yes, a lovely Indian girl, Jameela Husaini. The Izzies killed her during their raid on Ponape. He never told you?"

"He never said . . . ! We had no idea!" The doctor appeared angry, almost as if Lessing had betrayed him personally.

"As though she didn't affect him, not down deep, where he lives." Wrench lifted the lid of the pot to see if there was more tea. The stuff was strong and black and aromatic, the way he liked it.

The doctor stood up. "Wherever Alan Lessing lives, it is some place very private, beneath barriers and walls and defenses thicker than any *Führerbunker*."

Wrench motioned to Liese. "Thanks for the tea. We've a plane to catch. Lessing should be ready by now."

As they moved toward the door Dr. Casimir said, "By the way, Cadre-Commander, I am a Jew."

"I had guessed it," Wrench said. "I'm surprised you haven't moved on to the Izzie colonies in Russia."

"Copley doesn't bother me. I have things to do here."

"Things change," Wrench replied, and smiled.

The liberals—in various guises and incarnations—ran the Western world for a century. Their goals were highly idealistic and altruistic—in theory. In fact, of course, the liberals could never realize the aspirations of even their best thinkers: freedom from want, employment for all, care for the sick and the aged, an end to crime—the list is long. Their difficulty lay in their misreading of human nature; their theories of equality and human malleability simply had no basis in reality. The Left adopted the theoretical communism of the Jewish intellectuals, only to find that this produced Russian, Polish, Czechoslovak, Bulgarian, etc. despotisms instead of "equality for all" and "to each according to his need." At best, these communist states eventually returned to a quasi-capitalism; at worst, they were unimaginably awful.

Outside of Europe, communism manifested itself in localized forms: for example, People's China, Viet Nam, North Korea, Laos, and Cambodia. These, too, were despotisms. They had new names and faces, but beneath the surface they were merely carry-overs from Asian societies of the past. The same was true in South and Central America: traditional dictatorships decked out with red stars.

The liberal Center—exemplified by Great Britain, France, and the United States—chose one or another form of "representative democracy." If these states failed, it was not for want of trying. But it was too difficult to make needed social changes while at the same time upholding every conceivable version of everybody's "civil rights." The capability to adapt to new situations became bogged down in the ever-spreading web of administration, bureaucracy, and the pressures of competing personalities and "interest groups."

The greatest failing of centrist liberal thought is inaction: listen to too many voices, adopt too many solutions, and end by being dominated by others who are stronger and better directed. Shall I give you a great recipe for failure? Don't initiate and maintain strong policies: always react—often weakly and inappropriately—to those of others. Make only minor changes, since major ones will certainly offend *somebody*. When in doubt, call a committee, hold a seminar, have a referendum, file lawsuits, let everybody have a say. Leave the real power in the hands of clandestine cliques within the government. See to it that your citizens are too sated with bread and circuses—burger-pops, holo-vid, and football—ever to demand a real role in their own governance. When confronted with an urgent choice, be sure to dilly-dally, then choose the path of least resistance. Accomplish little—and do *that* slowly. Such gutless, hypocritical, political game-playing won't work in our post-Pacov world. It wouldn't have worked much longer *without* Pacov and Starak. We faced—and still face—horrendous problems: the Greenhouse Effect, pollution, war, drugs, AIDS (which continues to spread into the heterosexual, White population from the groups in which it is endemic, in spite of our best efforts), and a dozen others. Outmoded institutions will no longer serve, and we cannot allow our present rulers to destroy our environment through action *or* inaction. Regrettably, the past clings to us, as we cling to it.

The Party of Humankind offers a way: a way not just *out*, but *up*. We call for work and sacrifice and deep changes—sometimes hard, difficult, slashing changes—in our society. We love America; we love our ethnos; we believe that all people, everywhere, should love their own ethnos similarly. As separate, homogeneous societies working together in friendly collaboration, we can build a world where Pacov, Starak, and atomic destruction can never happen again. There can be no compromise, no salvaging the old and thus shortchanging the new. We must rid ourselves of social parasites and doctrines that weaken us! We must do it *now*. We cannot wait. We cannot hesitate. We *must* not fail. Our ethnos, our nation, and our children's futures are at stake.

—Abridgement of a speech given at the University of Georgia by Vincent Dom, Saturday, August 28, 2049

CHAPTER TWENTY-TWO

Saturday, August 21, 2049

The room tinkled and dripped; it took Lessing back to some dim, childhood memory of a waterfall, wet leaves, sinuous shadows over dark-glistening pebbles in a stream. He remembered birds, butterflies, and even a beady-eyed, grey fieldmouse come to wash its face and drink.

Probably another goddamned movie: one of those nature-porn shows his father used to watch on the arts channel. Any minute they'd be showing the fieldmice copulating, a snake doing a skin-striptease, or a tall-antlered elk mounting his mate and bellowing out his joy for all the forest to hear.

He grinned to himself. He was over most of that now: no more trouble distinguishing fantasy from reality. The room was one of the vast sitting rooms in Herman Mulder's mansion in Virginia. At the moment it did resemble a cavern behind a waterfall: dim, nacreous, filled with hanging plants and flowering shrubs and running water and the scents of dark earth and growing things. Sixty feet away, by the far wall, Mrs. Mulder fluttered in the emerald gloom, adjusting the lamps, setting the chairs at precise angles, flicking away a bit of lint here, a mote of dust there. She'd done it all before, and Eva, the housekeeper, had done it before that.

It had taken Lessing months as the Mulders' houseguest-patient to discover that what the pair saw in one another must forever remain a cosmic mystery. Herman Mulder displayed all the dazzle of a wad of wet newspaper, while Alice—that was her given name, though nobody used it, not even her husband—lavished affection and enthusiasm upon the world like a child slathering marmalade on toast.

No one knew their story, but it was clear that the Fairy God-mother cared very much for her stodgy, practical, and kewpie-doll-plump husband, with his odd friends and odder causes. He, in his own way, was just as devoted to her. Time had not been evenhanded, however: as Herman Mulder's exterior grew softer, doughier, and less hirsute, so did his inner personality harden, toughen, and become more adamantine. His wife retained both her girlish looks and her trust in the goodness of the universe.

The Fairy Godmother flourished a sequined, chiffon sleeve. Someone else might have thought she was embarking upon the mating dance of the ruby-throated hummingbird, but Lessing knew better: he waved back, twisted the rheostat on the wall beside him, and watched the fountain in the center of the room shift from lustrous turquoise to warm amber. The mobile sculpture at his end of the chamber changed from indigos and violets to oranges, reds, and yellows. Overhead, the crystal chandeliers metamorphosed and became an imperial blaze of diamonds and gold. The fabric of the chairs and settees darkened subtly from forest green to oaken brown.

The fountain, the statuary, and the chandeliers were holograms, computer-controlled to produce whatever color scheme and decor their owner chose. The fabric of the furnishings was a new synthetic that changed its tint according to the lighting. This salon was one of seven such rooms here in Mulder's Virginia mansion. He owned at least five similar houses around the globe.

Lessing pointed toward the hologram fireplace in the middle of the interior wall, and Mrs. Mulder undulated back at him. A touch of a dial transformed it from the blackened stone hearth of a medieval castle to a delicate French fireplace that Louis XIV would have loved for Versailles. Other settings switched it from Colonial to Provincial to Hollywood to ultra-modern chrome and glass. If you could figure out the user-unfriendly instruction manual, a concealed panel of buttons would design further fireplaces to your taste.

Holograms were the greatest boon to interior decoration since the invention of paint. The fireplace was actually a blank-walled niche. It had an attachment that gave off heat and the sound of crackling flames, but it couldn't be touched: a hand passed right through it. The latest holograms were mobile. You could have anything from waving palms or fish swimming in the air to a life-size Las Vegas chorus line doing the shimmy across your living room rug!

Another of Mulder's toys was a hall as big as a football field in which the entire Austro-Hungarian court, *circa* 1890, whirled around the floor to the strains of Strauss waltzes, the women gorgeous and gowned like princesses, the men bearded, bemedalled, and bedecked in sashes and gold braid. The ultra-high-fidelity, multi-speaker stereo system faithfully reproduced the rustle of silks and satins as they swooped past, and the touch of a button filled the air with the scents of wine, food, perfume, cigars, and the warm, waxy smell of candle smoke. A further investment would buy a hologram of Susan Kane herself gracefully gyrating among the rest, just as she had appeared in *The Emperor*, a year before Pacov had ended her dancing forever while on a goodwill tour to Leningrad.

The fireplace became a bank of glowing coals. Lessing added no more than a hint of heat; the August evening temperature outside was still in the eighties. He waited for Mrs. Mulder to dust, brush, and flitter her way up to him.

"You're eating with us tonight," she warbled.

"I'll make do in the kitchen. I'm not much for parties."

She patted her dazzle-silver coiffure. "No. Herman wants you to meet Colonel Koestler. I think he's Army, from somewhere up north. Then there're Wrench, Jennifer, Hans Borchardt, and Bill Goddard . . . oh, I know you don't like him much, but he's really nice . . . and Grant Simmons, and some friends from the West Coast . . . ." She trailed off. "Lots of lovely people."

The Fairy Godmother had not mentioned the one name that would have tempted him: Liese. He had seen little of her after his return from Russia. She had been busy at the Party's western headquarters in Seattle while he had been here under medical and psychiatric care. He had not called her, nor she him. Somehow he knew that he must be certain he had all his marbles back before he approached her. If they did share a real spark, he didn't want it to blaze up until he was sure he wasn't tying her down to a mental basket-case. She, in turn, with her fear of men and her oddly skittish shyness, needed time to adjust to Lessing's return to the living. Patience was in order.

"The kitchen," he said. "I can never swallow while wearing a necktie."

Mrs. Mulder trilled with laughter. "You'll join us, Alan. For me." Control came easily to a Fairy Godmother; she didn't even need a wand. Lessing gave in with reasonably good grace.

Mulder had become the Party's host *par excellence*. Tonight was especially heavy duty. There were at least sixty for dinner. This was no longer India: no barefoot company cooks in turbans and frazzled, white uniforms, no informal soirees in shorts and sport shirts over beer and curry under slowly revolving fans. The cuisine was elaborately French; the servants were immaculate; the *sommelier* looked like a charter member of the House of Lords; hunkish young men in elegant Party uniforms were available to accompany unescorted ladies; and lissome maidens would liven up the evening for single (or not-so-single) male guests.

The food was wonderful; the company wasn't Lessing's style at all. Afterward, he watched the party from the mezzanine balcony above the reception hall, itself big enough to be the rotunda of a state capitol building.

"Delightful," Bill Goddard's voice rumbled from behind him, "but boring."

Lessing balanced his tiny coffee cup on the marble balustrade and turned around. "Rich is usually boring. Where would you rather be? Off thumbing lib-rebs in California?"

Goddard fingered the weal on his skull: a red furrow ploughed through grizzled underbrush. A Vizzie assassin had creased him in San Diego, and he was as proud of it as a Prussian aristocrat with a brand-new duelling scar.

He eyed Lessing's white dinner jacket with superior good humor. His own costume was much prettier: the brown uniform of PHASE, short for Party of Humankind Administrative Security Echelon, sported braid-draped shoulderboards, a high collar, polished boots, a crossbelt with an embossed buckle, and a holstered pistol. The Party now issued its own medals too: long service, wounded in action, marksmanship, loyalty—the lot. The only one Goddard couldn't earn was the ribbon they awarded for giving birth to five children.

"Damned right!" the man answered Lessing's question. "Better than hanging around here. Now the war's started in earnest, we know where our enemies are and what to do about 'em."

"Any fresh news?"

"Not a helluva lot. The lib-rebs're holding us off in California, but we're kicking ass in Oregon and Nevada. And we're about to call on you, Lessing, to lead a heroic personal assault on L.A." He snickered.

"Fat chance. My merc days're over." He didn't want to discuss his future.

Goddard waved to Jennifer Caw below him, a vision in lambent sea green and silver. Her dark-auburn hair, loose over bare shoulders, flashed with tiny, sparkling gems. She stood with studied poise so that one tanned thigh showed through the slit in her floor-length gown.

Lessing was amused. If the Born-Agains ever managed to stamp out sex, Jennifer Caw would immediately re-invent it.

He said, "Jen could set fire to an iceberg!" Mentioning her would annoy Goddard. Now that the Party was socially acceptable she had little time for the man. There were wealthier and politically sexier fish to fry.

Goddard looked like an Olmec stone head: a pouting, scowling, fat-cheeked infant. "She's got Party work to do."

"As do you, of course. That's why *you're* not leading troops into San Francisco."

"Right. New branches to organize, meetings to arrange, rallies and parades to police . . . ."

"And your own private army to build."

Goddard grinned. "Police. Executive police to oversee Party functions and protect our rights of free speech and assembly."

Lessing grinned back. "Sure. While Wrench and Morgan are organizing their black-uniformed Cadre."

"Different duties . . . ."

"Unh-hunh. Party Police versus State Security."

"Their functions . . . ."

". . . Are separate. I know. At the same time the Party's pushing a bill in Congress that puts all the various police forces into one nationwide system: no more Federal, state, county, and city cops; no more Secret Service, FBI, CIA, Treasury agents, customs agents, Federal censors, and what have you. Just one big, happy 'Central Office of Public Security,' spelled C.O.P.S. for short."

"That's not reasonable? One law-enforcement organization? One unified, standardized set of laws? No more marriage in one state but adultery in the next; whiskey on this side of the state line but dry on the other."

"The end of 'state's rights.' And community rights."

"Yeah. So? Those ideas have whiskers. Our society's become too interconnected for them. A guy living in California flies to New York, commits a crime, and hides in Texas. Tracing him with a bunch of disconnected law enforcement agencies is hard enough, what with no central data banks and too much paperwork, and then if you do find him the lawyers play 'get rich quick' with extradition procedures, changes of venue, jury selection, and appeals, appeals, and more appeals! More than half of all crimes go unpunished because it takes too much time, money, and energy to prosecute them! We can't afford that any longer!"

A blonde in the crowd below caught Lessing's eye. She was not Liese. "And the same goes for other government agencies. Right?"

"Count on it. Welfare, taxes, social security, old-age benefits, health, education . . . each run by a centralized, streamlined, Federal department. The military too: the National Guard, Army, Navy, Marines, Air Force, Coast Guard . . . one chain of command. Eighty-Five's working on feasibility studies now. It'll take time, though; old traditions're tougher'n buzzard shit to root out."

"Green light! Given all of that, why do you, Bill Goddard, insist on having your PHASE Brownshirts separate from Cadre Black-shirts? I've been reading history. What happened in the Third *Reich* ought to worry you: the SA . . . the *Sturmabteilung* . . . versus the

SS. Lots of infighting and rivalry. And guess who lost, Mr. Brownshorts!"

Goddard snorted. "Yeah, yeah, but right now we *need* two agencies. Their jobs are different. Eventually they'll become divisions of one organization."

"So you say *now*. Wait'll you're ten years down the road. And remember what happened to Ernst Röhm, the SA leader!" Lessing crooked his trigger finger and made a "bang" sound. "His shirt was brown, but people say he wore lavender lingerie."

Goddard waylaid a servant to grab a handful of nuts and a fresh cocktail. "The situation was different then. We *do* learn from history, Lessing. And tell whoever you've been talking to that he's full of crap. What happened to Röhm was politics. It *had* to happen for the good of the movement. Otherwise there'd have been a helluva split." He popped a pistachio shell. "Listen, do you know if President Outram is coming tonight?"

Jonas Outram was less than a year into his first properly elected term. After Starak in 2042, he had imposed martial law for six years while the world buried the dead and sorted out the living. In 2048 the President had ended the state of emergency and set a date for the expected election. As one of the very few surviving—and experienced—members of the old Congress, he won this handily. Lessing had been under therapy in Mulder's mansion during the campaign and remembered little of it.

Lessing peered down into the reception hall. "I don't see any of his kikibirds, so he's probably no-show." Outram had become a very careful man; he had survived two more assassination attempts after the one in Colorado.

"Isn't that Liese? There, by the door, in red?"

It was.

She had arrived late, accompanied by Hans Borchardt and Irma Caw Maxwell, Jennifer's mother, who had been airlifted out of Los Angeles just before the lib-rebs had shut down the airport and declared California an independent nation.

Liese looked around, a trifle uncertainly, then moved inside to let the Fairy Godmother peck her cheek. Heads turned to watch.

Now Lessing had a reason to go down. Seeing her made him realize how much he had missed her.

She was gone when he reached the main floor. He wandered through the dining room, where the staff was picking up dishes, and into Mrs. Mulder's TV room, a place of cozy armchairs, baroque coffee tables, and crowded bric-a-brac.

Mulder had gone all the way for his wife. He had splurged for a whole-wall TV screen made up of individual cells, computer coordinated to display a single picture, as if the viewer were looking into another part of the same room through a faintly visible lattice of one-meter squares. The system was also interactive: you could direct plot developments in certain programs via a voice hookup or a control pad. As Lessing hesitated in the doorway, one of the actors on the screen turned to the audience and asked archly, "Should we tell Emma?" Buttons clicked, and the image said, "Well, that's settled. It's better that we don't." The action was jerky, and the dialogue sounded forced. Nonetheless, a buzz of discussion went up when "Emma" appeared.

"Oh, they should have told her!" Mrs. Mulder wailed to the dowager next to her. "Emma *ought* to know about Dianne's abortion!"

Liese was definitely not here.

Lessing drifted on into what Mulder named "the sitting room": a twenty-meter-long salon that occupied the west side of the mansion. The sun had set, and the chromo-electric windows would have been transparent to the Virginia sky, except that Mulder had transformed the entire outer wall into a TV-screen mural of the Taj Mahal by moonlight. The old man still had fond memories of India.

More of the guests were here, seated on semi-circular divans, sprawled on cushions on the floor, or standing about in groups. The only light came from the wall-screen itself, and Lessing zigzagged, stumbled, and excused himself a dozen times before finding Mulder, who pointed him on toward the inner reaches of the mansion. Liese had gone to speak to Eighty-Five.

The four unobtrusive security guards let him pass. He entered what looked like a pantry, went through a double-doored airlock that would withstand anything short of a tactical nuke, and came to Mulder's com-link with Eighty-Five: a room four meters square, its walls mirrored from ceiling to floor, and lit by a subdued desk lamp and two bars of non-glare tracklights up near the ceiling. A simple, metal desk and two jade-green, cushioned chairs stood starkly upon the swirling, pine-needle-patterned rug.

Liese was there, but she was not alone. She was talking to a tall, robust-looking, middle-aged man with iron-grey hair, a jutting jaw, and the sort of deep-set, dark-ringed eyes that made Lessing think of Sunday-school portraits of Jesus: eyes that brought forth adjectives like "burning," "dedicated," "caring," and "compassionate."

She turned and gave him her special sidewise smile. "Alan Lessing, meet Vincent Dorn."

It took a moment to comprehend, then another to react. "Uh . . . sure. Delighted."

So they had finally hired an actor!

Liese put a hand over her mouth, the way she did when she was trying not to laugh. "Mr. Dorn lecturing. Next Saturday. Atlanta."

"Right." He could play along. "How's your book, Mr. Dorn?"

"The school editions are ready for distribution, Mister Lessing, and the French version will be out next week. Unfortunately, the decline in literacy in North America makes it imperative we get something on holo-vid. Not a political speech, certainly, nor even a documentary. Most effective would be a drama presenting our . . . my . . . points of view."

The man's delivery was pedantic, yet he was somehow impressive. It was the voice and the eyes that did it. He could sell dog biscuits at a cat show.

"Dorn" turned to Liese. "I can't make the jaw any more powerful without physiognomic distortion. And the clothing? This civilian suit has a seventy-three per cent positive index, but something more military might gain another per cent or two."

It dawned on Lessing who "Dorn" was.

The man's grey-flannel slacks and broad-lapeled, navy-blue blazer rippled, shimmered, and shifted to become straight, brown trousers and a tan coat with shoulder straps and patch pockets. The collar tightened, grew higher, and developed Party insignia on both sides.

Lessing stared. The realism was incredible.

Both Liese and "Dorn" roared with laughter. "Didn't recognize me, Mr. Lessing?" the man cried. "It is I . . . Eighty-Five!"

"Hologram . . . ," Liese choked. "Image most acceptable to the public. Based on psychological analyses, profiles."

"Cute," Lessing conceded ruefully. By squinting he could see the light beams that projected "Dorn" coming from concealed apertures in the walls and ceiling.

"I have alternatives," Eighty-Five said. He—it—rippled again and became younger, taller, and more handsome, a heroic, blonde demigod in Army dungarees. Another shimmer, and the figure metamorphosed into a lean, tanned cowboy; a white-haired elder statesman; an idealistic-looking and very beautiful young woman (rather like Liese herself, Lessing thought); a ruddy-cheeked; elderly priest; and finally a white-robed guru who made the peace sign at them.

The image dissolved into confetti motes, then solidified again as Herman Mulder, followed by Wrench, and finally Lessing himself—and grew upcurled moustaches and a bright-green Afro hairdo. Female breasts appeared, the hair uncurled and lengthened, and the clothing disappeared to reveal Jennifer Caw in all her glory. A fanfare of trumpets sounded "ta-TA!"

"Where did you see Jen like that . . . in the, um, altogether?" Liese giggled.

"I did not see her thus. It is easy to extrapolate when you humans offer so few variables: four limbs, two eyes, various orifices. Mr. Wren said I was to work on my sense of humor. Many humans possess this faculty, and convincing them will be easier if I can use it too. I am, therefore, studying Mr. Wren's authoritative videotape entitled 'Great Comedy Moments of the Twentieth Century.'"

"Jennifer" shuddered and became "Dorn" once more. Eighty-Five asked, "Can I show Mister Lessing the Banger flower-child Mr. Wren suggested for San Francisco? The one we made look like that rock-music star from the last century to whom the populace keeps attributing religious miracles?"

Liese wiped her eyes and leaned against Lessing's shoulder. That stirred up emotions he wasn't sure either of them wanted. Yet.

He said, "It won't work, Liese. Not for long. It takes equipment to produce 'Dorn,' and he can't go to a dinner party, shake hands, or kiss babies . . . the political stuff." He extended a hand; it disappeared into "Dorn" and came out the other side.

"I'll do mostly TV and holo-vid appearances, Mister Lessing. Actually, I *can* make public speeches as well. I shall travel in a sealed vehicle with black-glass windows for 'security reasons.' When I reach the destination my assistants will erect a bulletproof podium booth, which will conceal the apparatus needed to project me. In a semi-darkened hall I estimate only a .033% chance of anyone noticing. I have worked out most of the bugs."

"Not all." Liese indicated "Dorn's" left arm. "Lost one cell yesterday. F-702."

"Minor, Miss Meisinger. A 2.41 centimeter hole in my shoulder, visible only from the rear."

"Lose A-901; then you have a *real* hole. Middle of your forehead."

"Unlikely. And my back-up system is nearly complete."

From close by, and knowing what "Dorn" was, Lessing could detect discrepancies: the tips of the fingers were faintly translucent, the junctures between clothing and flesh a bit hazy. Nevertheless, "Dorn" would probably succeed.

"Do you want to hear my speech, Mister Lessing? I project a sixty-nine percent acceptance level for an educated, White, non-Jewish, Southern audience. I have different versions for less-educated persons, Latins, Orientals, and Northern Whites."

"What are you going to do about mixed groups? Screen 'em at the door?" Lessing had a vision of ushers with questionnaires shunting people into cattle chutes leading to different halls in which different "Dorns" were lecturing.

"Of course not. Mixing is inevitable. I shall minimize it by giving one speech at a university, another in a union hall, another at a hotel frequented by wealthy business professionals, and so forth."

Liese pointed at "Dorn." "Turn around. Hole in your coat."

The image assumed a contrite expression. "H-583 is defective. I shall face forward so that it cannot be seen."

"Fix it. Otherwise like last night. The TV wall-mural."

"I was only trying to entertain Mr. Goddard and his friends."

"What happened?" Lessing was curious.

"Mr. Goddard was with friends in the sitting room. Mr. Wren was here, helping me with my sense of humor. At 0109 hours Mr. Goddard requested a change in the TV mural from the canals of Venice at sunset to a scene with more drama. I offered him the Great Wall of China, the Egyptian pyramids, a colorized documentary of the 1936 Olympics in Berlin, and a recreation of the Party Day rally in Nuremberg in 1935."

"He must've loved those last two."

"No, he rejected them as being too 'static.' At Mr. Wren's suggestion, I chose something artistic instead. Are you familiar with the eighteenth-century Italian artist Giambattista Piranesi, Mister Lessing?"

"Never heard of him."

"He did highly imaginative etchings of the antiquities of Rome, Greek temples, and the like. Also sombre views of fantastic and imaginary prisons: the *Carceri.* I redrew one of the latter to appear as a realistic photograph, colorized it, and added a few swooping bats, processions of menacing, robed figures, and a macabre musical score."

Lessing laughed. "That must've shaken old Bill! I suppose he and his doggies were tossing down booze?"

"I can conjecture their individual blood-alcohol levels if you wish."

"The rest!" Liese ordered.

"At 0224 hours Mr. Goddard requested more 'action.' He did not specify except to say that it should be sexually explicit and 'kinky' . . . in the slang of one of his female guests, 'fuggy, foozy!' I thus chose various figures from the works of the Renaissance Dutch painter Hieronymus Bosch and inserted them into Piranesi's 'prisons.' Bosch depicted the denizens of Hell as grotesque, part-animal, part-human, part-vegetable, and part-mechanical creatures. I animated these and portrayed them committing a number of unusual acts. I also improvised: my chorus line of giant phalli dancing the can-can in pink tutus was especially effective."

"Goddard must've been beside himself!" Lessing spluttered. He and Liese were both laughing.

"Yes. He was. You are very perceptive, Mister Lessing."

"What?"

"Mr. Wren asked that I insert an image of Mr. Goddard himself into the mural. He was thus literally beside himself, participating in some of my creations' more stimulating activities."

"And the burnt-out cell!" Liese made futile dabs at her mascara.

"Unfortunately, just as I pictured Mr. Goddard entering into sexual congress with a hermaphroditic goat and a dog-headed octopod, cell unit TC-1715 burned out. This caused a large, black hole to appear just where his figure's head was. He had become tipsy, and . . . ."

Lessing guffawed.

Suddenly he was very close to Liese.

Laughter became desire, a friendly touch an embrace, a smile a kiss that went from affectionate to erotic and then off the scale. He couldn't stop. His tongue found hers, and his hands travelled all by themselves from breast to thigh and beyond. He sat down heavily on one of the jade-upholstered chairs and pulled her down on top of him. For a split second Emily Pietrick flickered against the backs of his closed eyelids; then he banished her and put Liese in her place.

"Uh, Mister Lessing? Miss Meisinger? Would you like me to disappear? At least I shall lock the door against external intrusion. I *am* aware of your mating habits, after all."

Like a camera clicking off frames, Eighty-Five shifted rapidly from "Dorn" to the priest, to the young hero. At length it settled for a life-sized phallus in top hat and tails, seated in an armchair. This figure pulled out a purple bandana, fanned itself, and made deprecatory "tsk"ing noises.

Neither of the two humans paid the least attention.

They also failed to hear the buzzer or see the red door-light go on. Eighty-Five, once more as "Dorn," leaned forward and emitted an odd, belling whistle that brought Lessing and Liese bolt upright.

"Sorry," the computer said. "A useful emergency auditory signal. The human ear cannot tolerate more than seven seconds of that. You, Mister Lessing, will recall my previous use of sound as a weapon in my installation in Washington? I must now inform you that Mr. Mulder and four others are currently requesting admittance."

Liese straightened her scarlet skirt, raked fingers through her blonde tresses, and repaired her decolletage, all in one fluid, feminine motion. She glanced over to see if Lessing was ready, then pressed the "enter" button on the desk. "Dorn" vanished.

Mr. Mulder might be dull, but he was perceptive. He halted on the threshold and blinked. Their flushed faces told him the story. He said, "Anneliese Meisinger, Alan Lessing: meet Colonel Frank Koestler, Captain Perry Moore, and Special Agent Janos Korinek."

The fifth person in the group was Jennifer Caw; she gave Liese a quizzical look, then folded her arms and leaned back against the door.

Moore and Koestler were regular Army, but Lessing was unfamiliar with their unit and specialty badges: a blizzard of new insignia had appeared during the past decade while he was abroad. Koestler was short, balding, and red-faced, while Moore looked like the prototype for the whole computer-nerd genre: tall, skinny, stooped, and nearsighted, with bad skin and teeth like broken crockery. The only diagnostic missing was the plastic pocket-protector for ballpoint pens. He stood gawking at Liese.

"Perry and I are weapons development," Koestler explained. "We work out of the proving ground at Aberdeen, Maryland. Mr. Korinek here belongs to the Defense Advanced Research Projects Agency in Washington."

"And lucky to be alive," the latter said in a dry, thin voice. He was squat and thickset, with albino-white hair and colorless eyes. Lessing guessed him to be in his mid-forties. "I happened to be on leave at home in Kentucky when Starak hit."

Lessing shook hands, and Liese nodded.

"Shall we get on with it?" Moore's voice was unexpectedly deep, vibrant, and, it had to be admitted, sexy. Lessing was amused to see that both women immediately paid attention. The man dumped a manila folder down upon the desk and addressed Liese. "Could you access Eighty-Five for me, please, miss?"

Liese was no "just-a-secretary" girl. She gave Moore a look that would etch glass and rapped, "Eighty-Five?" Months ago they had done away with verbal codes and now depended upon eye and voice prints. Some terminals were even equipped with DNA identification equipment.

"Yes, Miss Meisinger?" No figure appeared, neither "Dorn" nor a giant phallus in a pink tutu. Which was just as well.

"You *do* have authorization?" she asked Moore.

"Priority three. Am I in?"

"You are, Captain Moore. I recognize you," the computer itself answered.

"Fine. Give us a link to the Fort Lewis terminal. Prime 790, path C-850, sub-directory DF-66687."

The mirror-wall behind the desk clouded, blazed with light, and displayed five men in Army uniforms, who eyed them expectantly. In the background Lessing saw computer consoles and instruments: a laboratory.

"Colonel Koestler?" one of the men inquired. "Major Theodore E. Metz, here. We're ready with Magellan, sir."

"Secure code T-94-392, then. Proceed, Perry."

Captain Moore gave instructions. The wall cleared, darkened, and refocused to show a baffling picture: the upper half was black, interspersed with whizzing, flying lights; the bottom half displayed a pitted, greyish surface covered with cracks and striations that continuously hurtled toward the viewer.

Lessing squinted dizzily. Of course! The camera was mounted low in the nose of a vehicle traveling at high speed at night over a badly paved road.

Koestler said, "President Outram asked that you see this, Secretary Mulder. You and whichever of your aides you wish." He stared suspiciously from Lessing, to Liese, to Jennifer. In the quavering, silvery glow from the screen he looked like someone who has bitten into a sour apple. "You're looking at . . . or rather through . . . Magellan Model IX, a mobile device dropped into a target area by parachute and then operated by Eighty-Five on a tight-beam from an overhead satellite. Magellan is a flattened spheroid about a meter and a half in diameter and forty centimeters high, the size of a large power lawnmower. It possesses wheels, treads, and climbers for walls and stairs; has infrared capabilities; monitors radiation, gases, and some biological contaminants; and is armed with grenade projectors. It can also transport a canister of nerve gas or a small nuclear device if need be, although we see it primarily as a reconnaissance instrument. Magellan travels anywhere, can drill a car's gas tank for more fuel, and if grabbed by the wrong people it explodes with one helluva bang." He sounded like a kid boasting about a new toy.

"What are we seeing now?" Mulder inquired from the shadows.

"A stretch of road between Albany and Berkeley, California," Moore responded in his surprisingly resonant voice.

Mulder's next question made heads turn: "And Mexican troops were observed near this place?"

"Yes, sir. You'll see them too, any minute now." Moore murmured further commands to Eighty-Five. The picture slowed and became dark bushes and shrubbery, then a forest of grey-white stalks that rose high above the camera's lens: dry grass.

The screen now showed a fire ahead, in front of a row of run-down shops and a supermarket. Moore whispered, and the screen abruptly split into quarters: front, back, and side views. Nothing moved in any of the pictures except the leaping flames in the top-left quadrant, which showed the view straight ahead. Black humps scattered across the street in the top-right square—to Magellan's right—could be bodies.

"Audio!" Koestler demanded.

Shouts, singing, and an occasional gunshot welled up around them.

"Closer!" the unseen scientist named Metz urged. The Fort Lewis team was seeing the same thing they were. "Take a right through that parking lot."

The picture veered, tilted, and bounced as the machine went over a curb and out into an open, grassy area in front of the shopping mall.

The place was full of people! Moore sent Magellan scurrying back into an alley.

The crowd was a mix of civilians and soldiers. The former were young and Latin-looking: a gang of barrio youths. The uniforms of the latter were Mexican Army. A handful of women, mostly Latins by the look of them, completed the ensemble: fiesta night in Old Tijuana. Those closest to the fire were feasting on something out of a huge cauldron.

In the dark, ruined buildings behind the firelight further figures were visible. More soldiers? Magellan switched over to infrared vision to find out.

Lessing wished he hadn't looked. In one roofless shop two soldiers stood guard over a score of naked Anglo women who sat or knelt on the bare, concrete floor, their hands bound behind them. They were blindfolded and roped together like cattle. He glimpsed bruises, dirt, and dried blood.

Liese burrowed against his throat and made a tiny mewling sound. He held her close.

God damn the human race! He disagreed with Goddard: people never did learn. They kept doing the same dumb, ugly, cruel, vicious, brutal things, no matter what century it was and no matter what they preached or who was in power! Rapine and murder were not to be wondered at; the wonder was that they didn't happen more often!

"The price the lib-rebs are willing to pay for Mexican help!" Moore grated.

Mulder edged forward to peer up at the screen. "If only that were all! Our information is that the lib-rebs have made a deal: Mexico gets Arizona, New Mexico, and half of Texas. Cuba and other Caribbean nations willing to join them will receive parts of Florida, Puerto Rico, and the Virgin Islands. They've made a deal, all right!"

Lessing touched Koestler's arm. "What the hell *is* going on, colonel?" Mulder's mansion was like Ponape: total isolation unless you yourself went out looking for news. Lessing had not. Now he wanted to know.

"Right now?" Koestler looked over at Mulder, who nodded: the people in this room were security-safe. "A temporary standoff. We can't get past the Sierras without major casualties, and the lib-rebs are digging in. At the moment we're probing at Redding and Red

Bluff, with another push coming down through Lassen Volcanic Park. Our patrols have reached Oroville, but the valley's too strong for us yet. We're staging for one godawful battle around Sacramento, but first we're thinking of a para-drop south of there to cut off their communications with Stockton, Fresno, and Bakersfield. Their big stuff is protected in L.A. and San Diego, though, including depots and camps for their Mexican allies. California's got great natural defenses for a land war: the ocean on the west, the Sierras to the east, rough and forested terrain to the north. Oh, we could paste their cities from the air, but nobody really wants that . . . too many friendly people still live there."

"What can the lib-rebs gain?" Lessing mused. "They can't hope to win with the land area and population they control."

"They're expecting a groundswell of opposition against Outram's policies. They've lost their strongholds in the big, Eastern cities, but they think Mr. and Mrs. North America will still join 'em if given a chance. At least they're hoping for the secession and independence of California."

"Sixty-one per cent in California against," Liese said. She had recovered enough to turn around in Lessing's embrace. "Lib-rebs are wrong. Majority blames old government for weakness, for failure, for Pacov."

"Defections? Population shifts?" Lessing queried.

Koestler shrugged. "As soon as Outram started chopping at the 'civil rights' laws, folks lit out in both directions: Blacks, Chicanos, Jews, gays, the left-wing college types, and all the fuzz-brains in the country to the lib-rebs; a lot of Whites and some Orientals over to us. Hell, we even picked up some friendly Blacks: support the lawful, constitutional government . . . and get airlifted to a paradise in Africa afterwards. Most of the Pacific fleet is ours too, moored at Pearl in Hawaii, but the lib-rebs have some vessels in San Diego. Much of the Navy's scattered all over the globe, though, wherever the fleets happened to be when Pacov and Starak hit. Some made it home, others stayed abroad to help . . . or to settle in. Some were massacred by unfriendly locals when they were cut off." The colonel hesitated. "Both we and the lib-rebs have enough nuclear weapons to pop the world like a zit three times over. Sooner or later we'll also have problems with what's left of the Izzies, the Indians, the Pakistanis, and the crazy merc generals in Russia who've inherited the Soviets' hardware."

Lessing thought of Copley, running freckled hands over his maps and chirping lovingly to himself about Ufa and Kuybyshev and Gorki and maybe, one day, New Moscow itself. Peter the Great, no less!

"We have more nerve gases, missiles, and special weapons than we'll ever need," Moore interjected.

"Pacov?" Liese snapped. "Starak? Bio-warfare agents?"

No one replied. The room was silent. Then Mulder spoke: "The formulae are gone, Liese. Deliberately and permanently lost. Eighty-Five knows them but has stored them in an oubliette file from which they can never be retrieved. That's over. Never again!"

"If you want them, I'll bet I can get them!" Moore's uneven teeth flashed tarnished silver in the light from the screen. "The computer hasn't been built that I can't hack my way into or out of!"

This time the silence lasted longer.

It was broken by Jennifer Caw. She gasped: "Look! There's something coming . . . there, in the street!"

"Get Magellan out of danger!" ordered Koestler.

Moore maneuvered the device backward, under the wheels of a truck, and into a puddle of darkness behind a battered dumpster. Magellan was almost noiseless, its soft humming drowned out by the crowd noise.

An armored personnel carrier had just pulled up in the street outside the shopping mall. A crude, red "X" was daubed on its side, and the soldiers who jumped down from the rear hatch wore red armbands: lib-rebs. They were well equipped with camo uniforms, helmets, packs, and M-25 assault rifles. Two carried lasers, two more had rocket launchers, and one poor doggie walked spraddle-legged under the back-breaking weight of an ITRAC: Individual Tactical Recoilless Armor-piercing Cannon. They deployed quickly in front of their vehicle.

Two civilians crawled out of the driver's compartment and approached the fire: a short, tubby White man and a jaunty-looking young Black. A pair of Mexicans—officers by their insignia, though Lessing couldn't read them—emerged to meet them.

"Sound, goddamit!" Koestler hissed at Moore. "Directional!"

"Trying, sir."

The crackle of the fire became deafening; then a Mexican belched with a roar loud enough to make them flinch, followed by a Spanish expletive that rattled their teeth. Moore mumbled apologies and got Magellan's sensors homed in on the opfoes' tete-a-tete.

" . . . *Pues*," the dapper Mexican commander was saying. "If that is how you wish it . . . ."

"I *do* fuckin'-A want it that way," the White civilian drawled. "Look at the map and tell me I'm right, Jack. These guys're not s'posed to bivouac here tonight. Their orders was to keep goin' till they get past Richmond, then make Sacramento tomorrow. 'N' here they are, fuckin' off, lootin,' eatin,' 'n' what-all!" A pencil-flash-light danced over a crumpled map.

"Soldiers, *señor*," the Mexican temporized. "May I see your authority, please."

"I'm Mark Silver, and this is Jack Harris. Here's our I.D. We're liaison to get you Mexican outfits to Sacramento."

"Good. Our transport is there, on the next street beyond these shops. We'll be ready to move on at dawn."

"Bull*shit*! You get your butts in gear and bust ass for Sacramento *now*. I'll give you a squad to go along and hold your hand. We expect Outram's fascists to hit within the week, and your unit'd better be there!"

Mulder took sudden interest. "Eighty-Five, inform the President and the Joint Chiefs that we may want to scrap Onslaught and go to Kangaroo." For the others' benefit he translated in a hoarse whisper: "Kangaroo involves coming down from Red Bluff to Willows and Woodland, then westward over to the coast, bypassing Sacramento until the paratroops cut it off from Stockton. That'll give us time to make a diversionary landing near Eureka in Humboldt Bay."

On the screen, the Black lib-reb civilian, Harris, plucked at Silver's sleeve.

"Prisoners? Where?" Silver looked. "Oh, for God's sake!" He went to stand nose to nose with the Mexican commander. "You let those women go, God damn you to hell! Now! *Pronto*! *Entiende Usted*?"

The officer murmured something about female spies and guerrillas. Silver raised a hand toward his waiting troops. The Mexican shrugged and shouted an order.

Moore turned Magellan slowly around until one camera pointed at the prisoners. Three Mexican soldiers were going among them and cutting their bonds. They made shooing gestures. All but two of the women scattered, running close enough to Magellan's hiding place to allow glimpses of bare breasts, pale limbs, and eyes scarlet with firelight and terror. The two who stayed behind huddled close to their Mexican protectors.

The captives had reason to fear. A guard motioned surreptitiously, and five or six of his comrades slipped back into the shadows where the lib-rebs could not see. Magellan's sensors picked up crashing sounds, shouts, screams, and laughter. They heard the rattle of gunfire.

"*Pendejos*!" the Mexican officer swore, so loud that he might have been sitting on Moore's lap; they had forgotten that Magellan's mike was homed in on him. "*Hijos de putas*!"

Silver thrust out a fist. "Call off your doggies, *capitan*! My last word!"

The gunner manning the heavy machine-gun on the APC growled, "We don't need these dinkers to fight for us, sir. Let's thumb 'em!"

The Mexican officer barked a command. Five soldiers emerged sheepishly from the alley. One man's trousers showed dark, wet-gleaming spatters.

An M-25 made gobbling noises, and the five Mexicans jittered backwards and fell.

Somebody groaned, "Shee-it, David . . . ! What'd you do *that* for?"

Guns appeared everywhere as both parties scrambled for cover.

"Cease fire! Cease fire! Cease your fuckin' fire, you mothers!" Harris screamed.

One more shot would bring on a barrage. Everybody thought it over. Then the Mexican officer held out his hands, palms up. Silver did the same. Their subordinates howled for order.

Chaos ensued. A dozen Mexican soldiers came forward to demand the life of the lib-reb who had shot their companions; officers and civilians squabbled and argued; one of the two female prisoners who had stayed with the Mexicans, a slight-figured blonde, squatted on the curbstone and wept hysterically while her protector comforted her.

"Jesus!" Moore swore suddenly.

Magellan's rear-view screen showed a round-cheeked, swarthy face inspecting the machine from less than a meter away! One of the Mexicans returning from pursuing the captives had decided to take refuge behind Magellan's dumpster.

"Keep Magellan quiet!" Moore directed unnecessarily. "Pray the bastard doesn't look too carefully!"

The man did. He bent, tapped Magellan with his rifle-butt, displayed surprise that turned to excitement and then to fear. He hallooed for his comrades. Koestler's team had probably painted Magellan some stupid military color and put "U.S. ARMY, TOP SECRET" all over it! They should have stencilled it "CITY SANITATION DEPARTMENT." Too bad the Mexican could read English.

"Get it the hell out of there!" Koestler rasped.

"Which way, colonel?" Eighty-Five's imperturbable voice replied.

"I don't give a . . . !"

"It doesn't understand orders like that," Moore scolded. "Eighty-Five, back out, down the alley away from the fire . . . ."

The Mexicans were already there, followed by three of Silver's doggies. All four screens showed boots, hands, and puzzled faces.

Voices jabbered in English and Spanish. Silver and the Mexican officer jostled their way into the mob.

"Damn, it's some kind of bomb!" Silver whinnied. "Jack, get the . . . !"

Feet threshed and kicked. For a moment the cameras rocked, but Magellan was too well balanced to tip over. The alley emptied.

"Now what?" Moore inquired in jaundiced tones.

"Get up speed, get away from the goddamned fire! Hide it!"

The machine's engine thrummed, and the cameras bounced and blurred as Magellan obeyed. They saw empty doorways, overturned boxes, dumpsters, dustbins, and garbage. A Mexican soldier loomed up, then danced away in astonishment. Bullets from his automatic weapon whined off the brick walls. One clanged off Magellan.

Eighty-Five announced calmly, "Minor hit. Mo damage."

"In there . . . that store!" Koestler cried.

Magellan stopped. Its side- and rear-view screens showed shadowy buildings, waving flashlights, running figures, and torches. Ahead, in a *cul-de-sac* courtyard lined with what had been small, artsy shops, was a boutique, its door broken and show window smashed. Obediently Magellan made for the door, only to find the bottom section of the panel still in place. The machine bashed against it, but the sturdy wood held.

"Up! Through the display window!"

Magellan extended delicate, hooked arms, caught the wooden sill half a meter above itself, then retracted its climbers and hoisted itself up. A claw shot out to catch the corner of a metal stand inside the window, but the flimsy thing collapsed in a shower of ringing metal tubing and broken mannequins. Magellan dropped back upon the sidewalk with enough racket to alert every lib-reb in California. Nearby, a voice cried unintelligible words in Spanish.

Magellan tried again. This time its claws got purchase on the two-by-fours that formed the underpinning of the display inside the window. Its engine whirred as it lifted itself up.

"*Por alla!*" A soldier ran past brandishing a rifle, followed by a sallow-faced barrio youth in a windbreaker and tight pants. The latter scrambled to a stop and howled, "*Aqui, aqui! Ola, pendejo, aqui! Venga!*"

The kid must have seen Magellan's scratch marks on the cement wall below the window. The device itself was buried beneath frilly garments, mannequins, brass tubing, and glitter paper.

The soldier returned slowly, rifle at the ready. Lessing found himself willing the machine to leap out of the window and make a run for it. Magellan probably couldn't: it needed to get up speed first.

"G-One!" Moore instructed.

Something popped, and a ball of flame burst like the Fourth of July five feet behind the soldier and the kid. Both flew forward. The boy smashed into the ceiling inside, above the window display, then flopped down into the wreckage on top of Magellan. The soldier cartwheeled on through the window and crash-landed among the plundered glass cases inside the shop.

"Frag grenade," Moore stated tersely. "Got three tubes of three each."

Lessing wasn't paying attention. He was staring at the face pressed against Magellan's left view-screen. The features were crushed and broken, one eye open, the other gone. Blood dripped down over the cheeks like languid, crimson tears and thence onto the lacy negligee beneath. The face belonged to one of the mannequins; the blood came from the body of the barrio kid, impaled upon a spear of tubing jutting up from the mess, half in and half out of the window.

The negligee was ice-blue.

The mannequin's remaining eye, large and dark and lustrous, gazed serenely out at Lessing.

Memories . . . .

A figure skidded to a stop in front of the boutique: the lib-reb with the ITRAC. Magellan's grenade launcher chuffed, and a projectile clunked off the pavement beside him. It did not explode.

All of the screens went white as the ITRAC-gunner landed a direct hit on Magellan's hiding place. The explosion ended in mid-bang as the machine and its sensors disintegrated. That saved Lessing's—and the others'—hearing.

"Shit!" Eighty-Five remarked disdainfully into the ringing silence. "A dud! You humans need lessons in precision manufacturing!"

The triumphant progress of technical science in Germany and the marvelous development of German industries and commerce led us to forget that a powerful state had been the prerequisite for that success. On the contrary, certain circles went even so far as to give vent to the theory that the state owed its very existence to these phenomena; that it was, above all, an economic institution and should be constituted in accordance with economic interests. This arrangement was looked upon and glorified as sound and normal. Now, the truth is that the state itself has nothing whatsoever to do with any particular economic concept or a particular economic development. It does not arise from a compact made between contracting parties, within a certain delimited territory, for the purpose of serving economic ends. Rather, the state is the organizational structure within which exists a community of living beings who have kindred physical and spiritual natures; they organize the state for the purpose of assuring the conservation of their own kind and to help towards fulfilling those ends which Providence has assigned to that particular race or racial branch. Therein and therein alone lie the purpose and meaning of a state.

. . . The qualities which are employed in the foundation and preservation of a state have accordingly little or nothing to do with the economic situation. And this is conspicuously demonstrated by the fact that the inner strength of a state only rarely coincides with what is called its economic expansion. On the contrary, there are numerous examples to show that a period of economic prosperity indicates the approaching decline of a state. If it were correct to attribute the foundation of human communities to economic forces, then the power of the state as such would be at its highest pitch during periods of economic prosperity, and not vice versa.
    —*Mein Kampf*, **Adolf Hitler**

Television is the voice of the Establishment. Whoever controls it rules, and whatever values it promulgates become the values of the land. Such is the power of the media. In ancient Rome it was the arena, more than the Forum or even the palace, that swayed the mob: Nero yearned to be a singer and musician, Commodus a gladiator, etc. Our modern arena is the TV screen, and it is the actor, the commentator, the rock-star, the Born-Again evangelist, the athlete, or—Heaven help us—the Banger "so-man" (from "soul-man") who is showered with applause, money, and popular acclaim. We already have had presidents and legislators who had little to offer besides their fleeting TV popularity. Some of these were backed by interests that do not have the public weal at heart but only the crassest, garden-variety, commercial motives. We have seen the results: the thinker, the philosopher, the educator, the soldier, the statesman—none of these can match the ratings of a painted-and-feathered Banger pog-dancer, a merc, a Born-Again speaker-in-tongues, or a steel-armored football quarterback. When such as these become the cynosures of our culture, the pinnacles of our ambitions, the role models of our youth, and

the idols of our marketplace, then do we indeed deserve the
Dark Ages that must certainly come hereafter.
    —*Singing Down in Hell*, an essay by Carla Hemstock, Futurist
Alliance Books, Lincoln, Nebraska, 2048

CHAPTER TWENTY-THREE

Monday, August 23, 2049

"I want the job," Lessing said stubbornly. "I can do it."

Wrench, crosslegged on the carpet in front of the Mulders'
wall-size, interactive TV screen, did not answer.

"Sit down, for God's sake," Sam Morgan twisted around to glare
up at Lessing. "You had a change of heart?"

"If you're asking whether I'm going to let the Party tell me which
medal to wear on my jockstrap, then the answer's no!"

"So?" Wrench inquired over his shoulder. He held the TV remote
control up to the light so he could see its buttons. He pushed one.
The pretty brunette actress on the screen began to remove her net
stockings.

"So you need me. The Party needs me."

Wrench belched politely. "It's you who needs the Party. You
need us. You need Mulder. *And* you need a certain lovely, blonde
person."

"Let's leave her out of this," Lessing answered evenly. By
unspoken mutual agreement he and Liese had been polite but distant
ever since the episode in the com-link room. They each needed time
to think.

Liese had stayed closeted with Mulder, Borchardt, and Jennifer
all day Sunday, working on speeches for Eighty-Five; this morning
she and Jennifer had gone horseback riding. Neither Mulder nor the
Fairy Godmother knew which end of a horse ate hay, but the old
man had purchased a stable full of handsome beasts anyway. If it
made Mulder's snobby Virginia neighbors accept him, then the
animals served a useful purpose.

"Green light!" Wrench backed away from the sensitive topic of
Liese. "But tell me, old buddy, why this passion to soldier for the
Cadre? Stay a happy houseguest, watch Mulder's security system,
drill the beegees, and wind the clocks! Why do you want to go
command a Cadre unit? What did the Cadre ever do to you?"

"I can help."

"Come on, sweetie!" The little man hammered at the button
again, and the actress wriggled lithely out of her bra, lay back on
the tiger-striped sheet, and gazed up into the cameras. Her breasts,
real or plastic, heaved nicely; they certainly were copious! The girl
wouldn't strip all the way; this was the wrong channel for that—and
at ten in the morning! The TV's interactive plot-choice system did

have limitations. The Fairy Godmother had sealed off the porn channels, moreover, with a code that even Wrench hadn't been able to break.

Morgan shifted to look at Lessing. "S'pose you've got reasons?"

"Good reasons . . . apart from being bored to death and wanting a real job! The main one is that you need more than fancy, black uniforms to turn the Cadre into a military unit. You need men with training and experience. That's my specialty."

Morgan stayed noncommittal, idly watching Wrench punching buttons.

"You shouldn't depend on the regular military. What if some power-hungry general, the Joint Chiefs, or the closet lib-rebs still in Outram's government decide to stage a revolution? One day you're in, the next day you're peeking up the barrels of a firing squad's shiny rifles."

"Can't happen!" Wrench scoffed. "Not now!"

"Sure, it can. Did you ever think *this* would happen?" He waved all around to include everything since Lucknow. "You know it can. But if the Cadre builds its own military arm, like the *Waffen-SS*, separate from the *Allgemeine-SS*, it'll be harder for a coup to get started. Gradually you take over the Army's military responsibilities, and then you're in. Solid."

"The kid may have a point," Wrench conceded. He jabbed a button, but the girl on the screen was down to her black Bylon panties and a smile, as far as her contract allowed. She wriggled, caressed her nipples, and gazed slumbrously out at the audience. The story would now revert to its main plot-line.

Wrench scrunched around to face Lessing and Morgan. "There *is* a good reason for the Cadre to have its own doggies. Sam, you know what I mean."

"So do I," Lessing said. "It's no secret: Goddard and PHASE."

"Dingo-dongo! You win the macrame potato-masher!" Wrench made a grandiose game-show gesture.

Morgan ran his hands over his short, young-business-executive haircut. "Goddard's getting stronger every day. His guys are the ones people see at rallies, in parades, bumping heads with the leftists, the Blacks, the Jews, and the rest. What's more, Mulder and the Board of Directors like what he's doing."

"The bully boys, the street troops," Wrench grumbled. "We get the schools, the publishing, the re-education programs, the heavy security stuff. Goddard gets the glory."

"And if it isn't Goddard, it'll be the old-power boys: the FBI or the CIA. They'll be back." Lessing drew a finger across his throat.

"The Vizzies infiltrated those agencies during President Rubin's administration," Wrench admitted. "Outram did some sweeping, but

some of 'em are still there. They're scared we'll come to full power."
He punched in a new channel and watched a dachshund stand up
and beg in a cutesy human voice for a can of Luvva-Dog. "Here's
Yama-Net. What've they got on now?"

Morgan wrinkled his nose. "Crap, what else? Yama-Net sells
appliances, electronics, computers, cosmetics, and plastics; Omni-
Net peddles cars, steel, heavy industry, and transport; First-Net
pushes communications, food, banks, insurance, and real estate.
Business as usual."

"Not quite," Wrench corrected. "At least now the Jews don't run
all the media. Only Dee-Net: clothes and fashions and soaps and
detergents and deodorants and the like."

"Which doesn't leave a lot for us. We're the new kids on the
block." Morgan opened one of the cloisonne boxes on the coffee
table in hope of finding mints or nuts; it was empty. "Our Home-Net
markets whatever's left . . . mostly product lines we've acquired
since Starak."

"I thought Outram was going to break up Big Media," Lessing
said.

"He tried. Mulder's still trying. The power of money, you know."
Wrench flexed his diminutive biceps like Atlas; the other two
chuckled.

Morgan said, "Once the media honchos saw he was serious . . .
that it'd be a cold day in hell before they could reoccupy New York
and Chicago and their other corporate citadels . . . they set up shop
in Louisville, Salt Lake City, New Orleans, Milwaukee, Seattle, and
elsewhere, diversified to protect against attack by Starak, by Pacov,
by Outram . . . and especially by us. The foreign biggies like
Yama-Corp moved to pleasanter climes abroad, but they hung onto
their American affiliates. We're where the consumer dollars are."

"Yeah, look at Dee-Net," Wrench said. "After Pacov unzipped
Israel and ended its control of Middle Eastern oil, the Vizzies moved
their Dee-Net headquarters up to Montreal. You'd think they'd give
up, but they've still got more'n enough piss to water the lawn. Here,
see!" He pressed a button.

The TV wall displayed a young, handsome, and very blonde
Adonis wearing tennis shorts, a sun-glow Bylon shirt of shocking
vermilion, and a tan so darkly bronze as to appear almost black. This
masculine vision swung a tennis racket at the screen and sang, "With
Tanel on the label you'll be an able Gable! Bang up, foozies!" His
craggy features glowed with the light of Absolute Truth. "Push your
A-3 button right now! Jick it for Dad, jick it for Mom, jick it for
your bint-baby, jick-a-tick it for *yourself*! Love my rag-a-tags!" He
caressed his shirtfront lasciviously, then was replaced by a chorus
of prepubescent children attired in dazzle-white sports clothes.

These sang in unison, "Goozy, goozy, little foozy! Tanel koozy! Tanel doozy!"

"Judgment Day is at hand," Wrench mourned. "Banger slang to sell tennis fashions! Sex did it better . . . and that we could at least understand!"

Morgan pulled his stockinged feet up under himself on the divan. He had left his Cadre uniform boots by the door. "Dee-Mar's offering bribes to the Pakistanis, the Turks, the Free Iranis, and the Saudis to regain control over Persian Gulf oil. Israel's gone, but their lobby's alive and well."

"Dee-Mar?" Lessing interjected.

"You were really out of things, weren't you, off wrestling weeds in Russia? Dee-Mar, short for 'Diversified Marketing Corporation, Limited,' is the super-syndicate that owns Dee-Net, and it's as Jewish as lox and bagels."

Wrench pointed to a lace-edged, lavender bolster. Lessing tossed it to him, and the little man plumped it up and leaned back. "Our own Homex Corporation's in there pushing, though. Right after Pacov and Starak our Third World investments looked pretty wimpish. The Greeks nationalized Tee-May Industries, and we lost megabucks when the Soviet refugees trampled our Italian, Belgian, and German stuff into the mud. We had to transfer most of our action back to the movement's original bases in South America: coffee, bauxite and other minerals, emeralds, Argentine beef, agro-products from the reclaimed lands in the Amazon Basin . . . a lot of stuff. Now we're coming back."

"No drugs?" Lessing asked mildly. Unlike many mercs, he had never gone in for brain-benders. Aside from high-school experiments with Emily Pietrick and a rare joint with his unit in Angola, he had avoided "phunny pharmaceuticals," as one of the TV yucksters called them. One of the few good things the Born-Agains had accomplished back around the turn of the century was to make smoking, sniffing, needling, and most other intoxicating recreations socially incorrect. Only liquor had survived the Puritans' zealous scythes.

Morgan threw him an irritated glance. "Not us! Some supercorps deal in drugs, but to Mulder and the Board they're a no-no. Against good genetics and racial principles, you know. Hell, maybe we *should've* gone in for smokables and White Christmas and snuffy-doo, principles or not. We could've made a bundle. You got any idea how much Yama-Corp made on Thai and Indian stuff last year? Or Dee-Mar on Turkish and Irani 'Red Gold'? Shit, *we* could've been pulling in those bucks!"

"'What shall it profit a man . . . ?'" Wrench rolled his eyes upward and donned an angelic smile. "Money's fine, but you've got to consider *image*, Sam. Remember last year, when the Latin Americans asked if we wanted to buy into their nose-candy, and Mulder turned 'em down? Well, they went to Nevarco instead . . . big gambling, entertainment, prostitution, and crime, along with legit stuff . . . and cut a deal. Then when Mexico started sending troops to the lib-rebs, Nevarco was as popular as dog turds and head lice. Now they couldn't sell a Bible to a Born-Again!" He flicked a button on his remote control.

"Hey!" Morgan grabbed at the little box. "Let's see that . . . the news!" Wrench held on but let Morgan have his way.

The picture-wall showed a scene on a rubble-strewn city street: a group of men wearing white suits, their faces concealed by copper-hued, mirror-glass helmets, were the only persons to be seen. They wore gloves and boots and carried breathing tanks and awkward backpacks, and they roused an echo in Lessing's memory, but he couldn't recall what it was. A sealed van followed the party as they picked their way slowly along the littered pavement past silent, empty buildings.

"New York," Morgan whispered.

"Center of Manhattan." Wrench indicated a rusting sign.

Lessing asked, "Haven't they got it cleaned up yet?"

"On the surface, yes," Wrench said. "Almost all the bodies have been disposed of, but they're still working underground: thousands of people died in the subways. Hans Borchardt thinks Starak made its victims look for dark and cool places. They crawled down in there to die."

Lessing shuddered. A picture of the corpse-packed waiting room in Israeli police headquarters on Derekh Shekhem Street swam up to the top of his memory, then was gone again. He wasn't over that yet. He probably never would be.

Ice-blue . . . .

An open, staring, dark-lashed eye . . . .

"There're mutant fungi down in the subways," Wrench stated with macabre relish. "All colors, and poisonous as hell. Some can even move . . . crawl along a pipe and drop down on your head."

"Oh, bullshit!" Morgan jeered. "You been reading the tabloids at the checkout counter!"

"I swear it's true! Dr. Vasilev, that Russian biologist we picked up from New Moscow, said so. He's seen 'em. Big, green, blue, white . . . icky, wriggly."

"Go gub yourself!"

Wrench grinned sweetly up at Mrs. Mulder, who had been standing behind them in the doorway for some time.

Morgan had the grace to blush, like a schoolboy caught pulling the girls' pigtails. It was funny how attitudes stayed the same,

Lessing thought, even when everything else had changed beyond recognition.

"Good morning!" The Fairy Godmother chose to ignore Morgan's obscenity. "You've had breakfast?" She twitched the sleeve of her feathery, blue housecoat in the direction of "the morning room," as she called it.

They chorused that they had. She peered at Morgan, and he wriggled his toes to show that his clean, white socks would not soil her expensive furniture. She then went to Wrench and substituted a dark-grey cushion for the delicate, lavender bolster. Cleanliness enjoyed a decided edge over godliness in the Fairy Godmother's household.

"Herman's waiting for you in the study," she told Lessing.

As he got up to leave, the TV screen cleared to show a hall hung with American flags and Party banners. Black and brown uniforms mingled with an artist's palette of multi-colored civilian garments. Trumpets sounded and drums thuttered as a procession began to wend its way down the center aisle.

Wrench cried, "Hey, look, there's Abner Hand . . . !"

As he spoke, the announcer said, "And it was at this moment that the grenade was thrown."

The screen erupted in noise and smoke. Mrs. Mulder gasped and covered her eyes. The others watched, stunned.

"Five members of the Party of Humankind were killed outright, and seven were wounded. Two people in the audience also died, and four more are in the hospital with injuries ranging from minor to critical. No one has yet claimed responsibility, and it is not yet known . . . ."

"Crap, God damn it, *crap*!" Wrench shouted. "*Of course*, they know who did it! They just won't *say*!"

Mrs. Mulder fluttered ivory fingers. "Please . . . oh, dear . . . ."

The imperturbable voice from the screen continued: "Cadre-Captain Abner Hand, apparently the bomb's main target, will recover, a hospital spokesperson has said."

"It's time *we* did something." Morgan snarled.

Lessing said, "I *told* you: Goddard's PHASE isn't enough. What's he got? Ex-cops, vets, private security men, mercs . . . and sixty-year-old night watchmen. But he's no soldier. He can't hack this kind of thing. The Party needs teeth." He fixed Wrench and Morgan with a grin. "The Party needs *me. I'm* teeth."

He left them staring after him.

Mulder's office-study was very different from the one in India. This was "Party palatial," designed to awe, to overwhelm, and to make power brokers quail. The vista of sweeping lawns and precisely trimmed gardens behind the monumental, teak-and-black,

marble-topped desk at the north end of the room was real, but the
west wall was another holo-vid mural. Depending upon a visitor's
psychological profile, displayed on a hidden screen behind Mulder's
desk, the holo-vid presented near-three-dimensional scenic
panoramas, Classical statuary, Aztec art, abstract sculptures,
mobiles of metal or chiming stained glass, or—for all Lessing
knew—a hero-size photo-bust of the First *Führer* himself!

The room breathed opulence. The floor was buried three centimeters deep beneath lush, maroon carpeting; the ceiling was
creamy ivory; and the walls were paneled with matched-grain cherry
wood, polished to satin brilliance. TV hookups, telephones, computer consoles, and communications gear occupied the south wall,
together with the visitors' entrance, while doors in the east wall led
to secretarial offices, to a private lounge and bar, and to a tiny "war
room" with its own bed and bathroom, vital in case of an emergency.
Somewhere here, too, was a secret elevator that would drop Mulder
and his staff a hundred meters to an underground bunker where they
could presumably survive anything short of God's Fickle Finger.

Mulder's desk was inundated with clutter. Party reports, files,
proposals, financial projections, and data summaries were neatly
arranged at one end of the four-meter-long monstrosity, while bills
pending in Congress, correspondence, summaries marked "Top
Secret" for Mulder when he wore his Secretary of State hat, and the
"paper blizzard" of top-heavy government were stacked on the
other. The overflow was heaped untidily on the floor nearby.

Colored light from the desk TV screen rainbowed Mulder's bald
head and made prisms of the reading glasses he now regularly wore.
He pursed his lips and scowled.

"I know," Lessing said. "We were watching downstairs."

"Abner'll be all right. I've been in touch with the doctors in
Boise, where it happened. We lost Johansen, Partridge, Carter,
Colbert, and that boy from Ohio . . . what was his name?"

"Amsler, Keith Amsler. Anything I can do?"

"No. Not now. Maybe contact their relatives later . . . you knew
Johansen and Carter on Ponape, didn't you?" Mulder glowered
down at his reflection in the polished desktop. "God, Alan, our
opponents believe in free speech only when it's *their* speech.
Freedom only when it's *their* freedom. To them, whatever *we* do is
'bigotry' and 'oppression' and 'evil'! When they do the same things
to us it's 'justice.' And they dare to blame *us*!"

"Still, the Party's come a long way." Mulder needed soothing;
he looked like a man about to explode.

"Yes . . . . Well, I never thought I'd see Party schools side by side
with public schools . . . and more popular because we offer a better

education. Nor open rallies, nor elections won by Party candidates, nor newspapers that . . . once in a while . . . tell it the way it is."

"Except for Home-Net, the TV networks still don't like us . . . ." Damn it, he hadn't meant to say that. It would remind Mulder of Abner Hand.

It didn't. Mulder depressed a button with a pudgy finger. "The networks? Let me show you something." The west wall cleared to show a complex flow-chart: a maze of colored lines and boxes and oblongs filled with text. "Eighty-Five?"

"Yes, Mr. Mulder?"

Lessing hadn't known there was a com-link in this office. Mulder was having terminals put in everywhere, like condom-vending machines!

"Show us the chain of take-overs, buy-outs, bankruptcies, and stock purchases that will result in our acquiring Omni-Net and possibly Yama-Net by next July." He nodded Lessing toward one of the capacious leather chairs on the visitors' side of the desk.

Boxes lit up, lines connected them, and dots of colored light travelled from one to another as Eighty-Five laid out the future. A section of the diagram broke off and hung suspended in midair: a distant probability chain whose effects had no immediate relevance. Bar graphs in reds, blues, and yellows appeared beside their respective boxes, indicating investments, personnel, resources, and likely profits or losses. Overlays replaced sections of the chart, and portions vanished entirely. A time scale at the top blinked off days and months.

Lessing couldn't follow it. Frankly, he was not very interested. He stirred restlessly. "Mr. Mulder . . . ."

"It's like chess. A game with an unknown number of players, some of whom you can't see. Chess played with money, power, prestige, and privilege instead of knights and bishops and pawns. You plan your strategy ten moves in advance and pray that your opponents haven't planned theirs for twenty. It's a kind of war, Alan, something that ought to be right up your alley."

"Too abstract for my taste . . . ."

"Then you'll always be one of the pieces and never a player."

"Yeah, I can see that."

"No, Alan, you *don't* see. That's the trouble. You're a product of your age: footloose, easy, mobile, purposeless, without a value system . . . right or wrong. You're intelligent and semi-educated, but you're not going anywhere. You just 'fit in.' You suffer from moral paralysis, what the French call *accidie*. You want to exist, to 'get along,' not to think."

"That's not fair. I read . . . more than Morgan does . . . ."

"What do you read? And why?"

"Military history, other things." Lessing decided to risk a personal statement. "Morgan reads to reinforce his prejudices, and Wrench does it to get his kicks. I'm not like either of them. I read because I want to know."

"The best reason, I suppose." The older man paused, and a silence grew between them. Then: "Yes, Wrench. You've known Wrench a long time, Alan." He hesitated again. "I don't usually ask questions that aren't my business. But . . . do you think Wrench is gay?"

"Sir?" The question had taken Lessing by surprise. "Ah . . . no. Not gay." He hunted for words. "Wrench is . . . I think . . . asexual. Non-sexual. A long time ago he decided sex was too much trouble, too expensive, too . . . physical, and too risky psychologically. He may be afraid of AIDS or herpes, too, for all I know. At any rate, he's stayed away from anything beyond his bathroom porn magazines as long as I've been around him."

Mulder saw that Lessing was uncomfortable. He said, "Don't worry; my wife wants to . . . um . . . line him up. I guess some of her younger friends were interested. She's working on Morgan, too."

Lessing laughed outright. "Good luck! Sam's got a string of expensive bint-babies a mile long! To him, sex is like Saturday-night TV: you know, first the heavy, competitive stuff like on the game shows, then a chase like the cop programs, and finally comes wrestling, two falls out of three. Sam thinks sex is a contest, one he has to win. No, the Fai . . . your wife . . . won't get *him* to settle down, not for a long while!"

"Married executives are good for the movement's image. Any corporation president'll tell you that."

"I suppose I'm marriage material myself, then?" Something somebody had once said—he couldn't recall who—rose to the surface of Lessing's thoughts. "Liese . . . ?"

Mulder folded his hands before him on the desk. "Liese. What . . . how . . . can I say? You've heard her story? About New York? Cairo?"

"Yes." He'd heard enough of the hideous details. Yet he didn't know how to ask the questions he really wanted answered.

"They . . . used her. They forced her. They did . . . things . . . . They tied her, beat her, made her . . . . You can't imagine."

He tried to breathe. "I heard . . . Liese and Mrs. Delacroix?"

"Is that what's bothering you? Lovers? I doubt it. Only rumors. I knew Emma Delacroix well, back before . . . before Ponape. She wasn't a homosexual, a lesbian. She was like Wrench, perhaps: unwilling to get involved. The movement kept her busy, as it did Liese, after Emma rescued her and got her to Paris." The old man's glasses looked hollow and faceted, alien insect-eyes in the red and blue and green light reflected from the mural wall.

Lessing didn't know what to say next.

Mulder helped him. "Go after her, Alan. Don't let your chance at happiness slip away."

"I . . . we . . . don't know . . . ."

"Yes, you do." Mulder did something quite out of character for him: he leaned across the desk and whispered, "Don't be an *asshole*, Alan Lessing!"

Laughter came like a gust of wind, a welcome release.

Their communion lasted only a second; then Mulder leaned back in his chair. "Oh, Liese has work to do . . . as you will. A century of bad press, a world to put back together before Armageddon demands a re-match. You can help her, and she you."

"I . . . was afraid I'd be interfering. That you wouldn't like us to . . . ."

"Me? I'm delighted . . . and Alice'll be ecstatic. You and Liese need it. Take a holiday. There's always time for a time-out, as my hockey coach used to say. Did you know I played hockey in college?"

"No." Mulder playing hockey was more than he could picture; he stifled a snort.

The wall-hologram shimmered, making Mulder look up. "Eighty-Five? Now what?"

"Yama-Net has just acquired the National Broadcast System of Thailand."

"What does that do to your projections?"

"All major networks will be affected. Present data are insufficient."

Mulder blew out his cheeks. "The media, Alan, always the media! We thought we could dismantle the networks, but they just regrouped and bounced back. Now we find ourselves competing, hawking trinkets right alongside the other hucksters! Soft porn, soft news, and hard sell! Don't scare the customers; otherwise they won't buy, and your profits'll drop. This isn't what we . . . the movement . . . wanted."

"The media are useful. A major weapon . . . ."

"Our own Home-Net is. The others are weapons against us. They offer the usual sappy morality, the stuff my wife watches. You know, every story has a happy ending with a simple little moral attached: be moderate, be open-minded, be tolerant . . . buy our products. Be good. Obey."

"Bland." Lessing couldn't remember who had once used that word to describe television.

"The message may be overt or covert . . . or even subliminal . . . but it's there. And there're corollaries: don't think, don't listen to people who are outside of the Establishment."

Mulder arose to stand before the flow-chart; its lines and squares transformed him into an apocalyptic abstraction. Lessing saw why people listened to Herman Mulder.

"Take hockey . . . any sport . . . personal exercise. It's all for the individual, for looks, for superficial appearance. You build 'the body beautiful,' but your mind stays as deep as a cookie-sheet. There's no intellectual counterpart to sports, no ideological foundation, no overriding social objective."

"Some of the kid-vids do emphasise education . . . ."

"Rolls off 'em like ballbearings off a plate! What do the kids like? The Bangers. Meaningless individualists pretending to social significance! Sex without affection, brainless masturbation, African rhythms performed by illiterate head-poppers and bint-babies. Gut-grabbing, thump-a-bump copulation that wrecks your eardrums and blasts your reason. Lyrics that supposedly have 'great social value' but say no more than 'don't do drugs,' 'have safe sex,' and 'let's all be gub-buddies and love-foozies together!' Are these the 'great thoughts' of stars who make a million dollars a week? The Bangers also preach opposition to authority, instant gratification, anti-social . . . often criminal . . . behavior, religious cults, race mixing, and 'bang me, bang you, bint-baby!' How can the Bangers' victims vote? Most of 'em can't even *see* through the drug haze! How can they function as citizens? Too many of our kids have no math, no science, no history, no humanities! Seventy percent think the Persian Gulf is next to Italy, and Cairo is a couple of miles from Peking! Ideas? Hah!"

Mulder's opinion of the younger generation was well known. Wrench had to listen to his antiquarian rock music late at night, after Mulder and the Fairy Godmother were in bed.

"Well, if they're anti-social, at least the Bangers're not bland."

Mulder peered at him to see if he was serious. "It's all part of the design package, Alan. Psychologists'll tell you that young people need anti-social outlets. Adolescent rebellion is a natural phenomenon. You channel it, sublimate it into orgies and frenzy, and you don't get student riots, politics, and trouble. Party-animals don't join revolutionary political parties."

"I . . . ."

Mulder abruptly turned to the mural wall. "Any further news from the hospital?"

"Mr. Hand is out of surgery. The police have arrested a man, a member of one of the lib-reb groups."

"Hmmph. Keep me posted." He came around the desk to stand by Lessing. "Wrench tells me you want to set up a military force for the Cadre, a kind of *Waffen-SS*. You're an experienced soldier, Alan, and people tell me you have talent."

Wrench was fast. Lessing had first broached his idea last night at dinner. He said, "I can lead troops, sir. In tactical spesh-ops anyway. Policy's someone else's job."

"But do you have *commitment*? Loyalty?"

"Yes . . . to those who treat me right. I'm loyal to you. I'm loyal to my troops. I'm loyal to my friends. You know that."

"Oh, I believe you. You're a 'merc's merc,' as Wrench once put it. You have great personal loyalty, but you don't know what you're fighting for . . . and so far you haven't seemed to care." He pointed a finger. "A Cadre military unit needs more than just a merc as its commander. We want commitment to our objectives. No hesitation. Can you give us that?"

Lessing didn't reply. Far down inside himself, fathoms deep beneath the murky waves, something moved. He only glimpsed it: the scales of Leviathan, the great, staring eye of the kraken, the sleek form of the barracuda, the fangs of the killer shark.

He saw a flicker of ice-blue.

Very carefully, he said, "I don't know, Mr. Mulder. Commitment was never my thing. You need soldiers. I can lead them."

Mulder plunged both hands into the pockets of his shapeless, tan slacks. "Duty and responsibility: two of the foundation stones for my grandather's *SS*. You possess those, Alan, more than Morgan or Wrench or Borchardt or even Goddard, who lives and breathes the Party. You don't share the rest of our beliefs, but you may come around to them too, some day."

Lessing let him think.

Mulder shifted from one foot to the other. "I shall recommend to the Party . . . and to President Outram . . . that you be allowed to try. Outram needs soldiers and political support; he can't afford to turn our offer down. I think you'll get your Cadre unit. You'll start with one division, the best-trained of the present Cadre. If that works out, we'll push for more. I warn you, though: if you fail, we'll cancel it."

"Thank you, sir." He felt a lot lighter somehow. The prospect of getting out of Mulder's gilded cage was exhilarating.

"May I ask a question? A different matter?"

"Sure."

"Pacov, Alan. Aren't you curious about Pacov? Who sent you to Marvelous Gap? Who killed Gomez and your comrades? Who slaughtered a third of the human race?"

"I . . . yeah, I'm curious." He actually wasn't; for a merc, death was just the other side of the mirror. He'd seen too much, and he probably did suffer from moral ennui, the *accidie* that Mulder had spoken of. Conscience? His nightmares were subsiding. Fictional heroes might mourn and bemoan their fates forever, but not real people. Weep, grieve, bury your dead—and get back to your life. It's the only one you've got.

He said, "Wrench told me he still has Eighty-Five sifting data."

"He does. But you never ask about Pacov, even though you had so much to do with it. Not with using it, of course. You know what I mean."

Lessing started to shrug, then turned that into a restless stretch. He felt something bump against the floodgates of memory again, something big and probably horrible. He held those valves closed with all his might. "If Wrench finds anything, he'll tell me. *Has* he found something?"

"Nothing much. A scrap here, a fragment there. A memo that leads from Gomez back to an untraceable address in the United States . . . and then to nowhere. Invoices for the weapons you had, sold to names that don't exist and shipped to a lithographer's shop in Detroit. The owner of that shop died in the first Starak attack. We also have a Detroit hotel statement and a drycleaner's bill in the name of a 'Mr. James F. Arthur,' who otherwise does not exist. There are areas in Eighty-Five's memory that have been dumped. Not just shoved into an oubliette file but physically erased."

"What more can *I* do, then?"

"Don't you want to know? The world wants to catch the genocides who nearly annihilated us. If there's any one thing both the government and the Party keep hearing, it's this: get those monsters and execute them . . . in ways that'd make Vlad the Impaler blanch! Yet you, the man who actually handled Pacov and lived to tell it . . . you act like you were sent to deliver a case of beer!"

"What can I say? That's the way I am." It was a lame excuse, but it was absolutely honest.

Mulder blinked at him in silence, sighed, and then faced the flow-chart on the wall. "What if we don't buy Armikon Industries next spring?" He was talking not to Lessing but to Eighty-Five, playing his chess game of power again. The display rippled obediently, and colored lines, dots, and boxes danced around and over him.

"Interrupting?" a voice asked. It was Liese.

"No, no, come in." Mulder did not look around. "Just showing Alan what we're doing."

She laid a stack of computer printouts on the desk. "Eighty-Five's response to Boise attack. Small opinion swing in our favor."

"What does Goddard say?"

"Not Vizzies. Lib-reb sabotage team. Best guess."

"Tell Niederhofer at Home-Net to lay it on the Californians for now. We can change it later if we have to." He rubbed at his bald pate. "I hate making propaganda out of something this awful, but the psych people say every atrocity story is worth ten soldiers' lives."

"Wartime propaganda forgotten afterwards," Liese confirmed. "Good example: little hostility between Americans and Japanese within ten years after World War II. Vietnamese and Chinese now friends, even after War of 2010."

"Only the Jews have managed to keep the 'Holocaust' alive all these years." Mulder stumped back to his desk and picked up a sheet of paper. "Here, Alan. This is my letter to Jonas Outram asking that a Special Forces unit be set up under Army auspices. Scott Harter, the Secretary of Defense, is a friend of ours, and he owes us favors. We'll see that the unit is largely made up of Cadre personnel. You'll be in charge, with authorization to set up a planning and procurement team. I think Outram will want the unit named 'Winged Victory' or 'First Freedom' or something else unifying and patriotic. Green light?"

"You had this already written!"

Mulder spread his hands wide. "Somebody has to think ahead around here."

"Congratulations!" Liese touched Lessing's shoulder and murmured, "Talk?"

He took the letter and the related files Mulder handed him, shook hands, and left. Liese joined him outside, and they walked together along the powder- and perfume-fragrant corridor to Mrs. Mulder's sewing room. At this hour the Fairy Godmother would be interacting with the beautiful people of soap-opera never-never-land, provided that Wrench and Morgan hadn't managed to pry her loose from the TV.

The sewing room lay at the south end of the second floor, over the garage and the kitchens. Large and airy, it had originally been intended as a nursery. The wallpaper was gay with hyacinths, cornflowers, and sunny, yellow animals; the floor was of durable, blue Lino-Last; and the curtains were of white chintz. Mrs. Mulder rarely used the shiny Katayama sewing machine that stood squarely in the center of the room, however, and the boxes and trunks and bolts of fabric piled against the walls were mostly unopened. It was a pretty place, but there was an air of poignancy about it. Perhaps there were even little ghosts of the children the Mulders had never had. Lessing sensed a great loneliness here.

Liese moved to inspect the patternbooks stacked on the single bookshelf, while Lessing pulled a stool from under the cutting table and gingerly lowered his not-inconsiderable weight down upon it. Good living—and no 'Raja's Revenge'—had plumped him out like a Christmas turkey! If commanding a Cadre unit did nothing else, at least it would give him a reason to exercise.

He had no idea how to begin. Neither, apparently, did she. They both spoke at once, then made polite motions.

"Us?" Liese was very direct. Lessing had liked this about her and once, long ago on Ponape, had told her so. Now it unsettled him.

He tried to answer in the same fashion. "Yeah, us. Do we or don't we?"

Tears welled up, astonishing him. "Don't want . . . ."

"Hey . . . what? I thought . . . ."

Her nostrils flared, and her lips worked soundlessly. Then she husked, "Fifty lira pog? Cairo special?"

He knew at once what the trouble was: her past was her millstone. He strove for a soothing, gentle tone. "Liese, *why*? Why drag it up? Why wallow in what happened to you . . . before? That's history! It doesn't matter! I heard some of it from Mrs. Delacroix . . . poor lady . . . and more from other people. It has nothing to do with *us*, with *now*."

"Oh?" She moved, lifted her arms, shifted her stance, and licked her lower lip. Suddenly she was someone else: sleek, seductive, sensuous—every doggie's centerfold, every pervert's porn-queen! She leaned back so that her small, high breasts thrust out against the pearl-grey fabric of her blouse. She bent a knee so that the curve of her long thigh became as sinuous as the serpent in the Garden of Eden. She was lust; she was sex; she was what the Israeli and Arab heavy-breathers in Cairo had plunked down their coin for.

Was this Eighty-Five in another zany hologram disguise? One of Wrench's silly jokes? This wasn't the woman Lessing knew: Liese, the lady, the cool executive, the dedicated worker, the unflappable, twenty-first-century sophisticate.

He couldn't help himself: lust swept up out of his loins to pound against his temples. His hand hurt, and he looked down to see that he had cut himself on Mrs. Mulder's sewing scissors. Liese licked her lip again. Her hazel-and-gold cat's eyes were as ancient and wise and knowing as Astarte and Lilith and Bast and the priestesses of the Dark Mysteries. The very air seemed to become turgid and hot. It pulsed.

"Hundred lira? Five hundred?" She was mocking him.

"Jesus . . . ! Stop that! What the hell . . . ?"

"What you see is what you get." She ran slender fingers down over her breasts, her belly, her hips, sliding her clinging charcoal-grey skirt aside to reveal tawny skin beneath. "Syphilis once. Gonorrhea four times. No herpes . . . lucky there. Never AIDS . . . *really* lucky! Can't have children, though." Her voice cracked on that last sentence, and her erotic pose began to crumple.

He stared. "Never forget. What I was." She bit her words off a mouthful at a time. "All kinds. Men, women. White, Brown, Black,

Yellow. Young, old. Kind, sad, timid, vicious, crazy. Sadists, masochists, fetishists. A necrophiliac Irishman once . . . white face-powder and a coffin."

He wanted to slap her, kick her, beat her senseless. Instead, he balled his fists, bit his tongue, and listened in grim silence as she recited her litany of degradation.

Lessing was not shocked. He had seen things in Angola, in Syria, and elsewhere. Liese had been treated no worse than many other hookers, but humiliation stuck to this girl like cat fur to strawberry jam, as his mother used to say. Some women saw prostitution—in all its aberrant forms—as a business; some professed to enjoy it and the money it made; some shut their minds and did it because they had no talent, nowhere to go, and nothing else to sell. Some did it for drugs, while others were too weak and emotionally dependent to pull free. Liese was different from these: she had never given up *hating*. She hated those who brutalized her. She hated society for caring so little about her plight. She hated herself for lacking the courage to fight, to run away, or to kill herself. She bore few physical scars—her pimps had been careful about that—but those she carried inside were gaping wounds that would never heal.

"How can you know? Care . . . ?"

Lessing cared very much. He didn't know what to say, how to comfort her, what would heal her. God damn his lack of words!

"Earn a lot, get your pick," she continued tonelessly. "Money, clothes, jewels, perfume, special treatment. Earn too little, you're the 'M' in the 'S-and-M,' center ring in the whips and chains circus. Don't cooperate at all . . . ."

"Shut the fuck *up!*" He shook a fist at her.

Her features stayed expressionless, as stony as the Sphinx of Giza. "Want you to see. What you get."

"I don't give a pogging dink about that! I don't care if you gubbed the whole world, men, women, and children . . . dogs and donkeys!" He slammed a fist down on the cutting table. "Oh, *shit!* I am *not* getting some fifty-lira Cairo whore! I am not 'getting' *anybody! We* are getting. *You* are getting, and *I* am getting. It's mutual! We *both* get, or it doesn't happen!"

Her lips were trembling. She was visibly on the edge of hysteria. "Not . . . ! No . . . !"

"You're afraid, aren't you? Afraid of men? Afraid of *me?* Or maybe you hate men. God knows I can't blame you. But *I'm* not 'men'; I'm *me!* I'm Alan Lessing. A million rotten apples don't spoil *every* one in the barrel!"

"No . . . yes . . . . Can't help it." She lifted her chin and looked straight at him. He admired her then. He loved her. When faced with the unendurable, she had escaped into aphasia and an inner landscape of her own. She had not surrendered. She had not broken. Anneliese Meisinger might bend, but she didn't break.

"Oh, gub it!" he cried in frustration. "What am I supposed to do ... to say? I can't erase the hell you suffered! I don't have a magic wand ... I wish I did! I can't make you trust me. I know you've seen psychiatrists and therapists ... witch-doctors enough to pack a loony bin! If they couldn't help you, then how in God's name can I? How can I make you see *me* ... not an abuser, not a violator, not a devil, not a *man*? Just *me*, Alan Lessing?"

She put her hands over her face and let her dark-blonde tresses swing down. He was reminded of someone else: a whiff of sandal-wood, a flash of ice-blue. He shook his head angrily, like a horse bitten by a fly.

He didn't dare take her in his arms. Patience!

"You ... Alan ... you ... ," she moaned.

"Yeah, me. Alan Lessing. Mr. Potato Patch, as Wrench called me after I got home from Russia." Desperately, he wanted her to smile.

"You: no bargain." She did smile; between her fingers he could see the corners of her mouth quirk up. "Alan Lessing: nothing ... nobody ... wasted talent."

"Right. Big and gawky. Waddles like a rhinoceros, sings like a duck."

She giggled, low in her throat; her control was coming back. "Yes, you. Fixated in adolescence. Never grew up. Can't relate to closeness. Bad childhood. Sex limited to groping in the movies, quickies in cars, banging in the bushes after the senior prom." She must have picked those things up from one of his doctors. Or from Eighty-Five! Some bastard talked too much.

"Thanks a lot! I never even went to the senior prom."

A vision of Beverly Rowntree clicked into place, suddenly and clearly, like a slide into a projector: furious, weeping, whining at him in that nagging, badgering way she had. The head-doctors hadn't dug deep enough into Alan Lessing; they hadn't dredged up all the ugly muck and spread it out in the light of day. Here was a picture he never let even himself see: Beverly telling him she was pregnant, telling him it was *his* baby, telling him she didn't love him—didn't even particularly *like* him. It was time she married somebody, and he was it: the prick and the pocketbook. She would agree to an abortion, however, but then he'd have to pay for the best: a first-class vacation somewhere while she got her oven cleaned.

He wasn't the father. He could count days and months as well as she could, and it wasn't possible. He could guess who the father was, but Beverly had picked him instead. Why? She must have seen him as the dumbest asshole since Simple Simon. That was what hurt.

She was wrong, though: he would *not* be blackmailed. He would *not* pay. He would *not* marry her. He'd marry a black widow spider before he'd tie himself to Beverly Rowntree. He was going to college next year, and no conniving bitch of a Great White Whale was going to wreck that. He told her so, explicitly, bluntly, and in detail. After that evening he never saw Beverly again.

Liese was watching, twin furrows of puzzlement between her brows. She had no idea what he was thinking. His problems could come later.

He went to her.

She held him off, turning her head to the side, so that he got only a nose full of tickling, blonde hair. "No. No commitment."

Commitment again! Liese and Mulder both! Did she mean that *she* wanted no commitment? Or that *he* lacked it? Whatever! He held her gently, and, sure enough, he felt her tenseness ebbing.

"Take what I can give," he urged. "All the commitment I've got. No education, no money, no class, no talent, no permanent job. A body that's middle-aged, tired, scarred, and not as sexy as it used to be. Take it or leave it."

"Goddard offered better." He thought she was smiling. "Make me queen over his kingdom. All I survey." She sounded quavery, but this time he was sure it was laughter. "Asked me to marry him. Out by Mulders' swimming pool."

"And?"

"Told him I couldn't survey anything with his hairy belly in the way."

It was Lessing's turn to laugh.

"Neither of us is a winner," he chuckled. "Let's go see if money, power, and sinful luxury can ruin two beautiful people. Watch the next heart-throbbing installment of 'Mulder's Maudlin Mansion'!"

"No commitment. No marriage. Not now." She took his hand. "Green light?"

"Either of us can bring up those things later. The other one can always say, 'Gub off, foozy!'"

She hugged him, and he kissed her, hard and deep. Then things got better.

"Come on. My room. No Eighty-Five there." She was just as urgent as he was.

She waited while he closed the sewing-room door after them. As a parting joke, he called, "Good night, Eighty-Five!"

He did not see the tiny, red light blink on beside the camera high up in the ceiling molding, or hear Eighty-Five answer, "It is not night, Mister Lessing. The time is 11:03 hours. But have a nice day anyway."

During the time men live without a common power to keep them all in awe, they are in that condition which is called war; and such a war as is of every man against every man . . . . The nature of war consisteth not in actual fighting, but in the known disposition thereto during all the time there is no assurance to the contrary.
  —Leviathan, **Thomas Hobbes**

There was never a good war, or a bad peace.
  —Benjamin Franklin

War is much too serious a thing to be left to the military.
  —Georges Clemenceau

Der Krieg ist nichts als eine Fortsetzung des politischen Verkehrs mit Einmischung anderer Mittel.
  —Vom Kriege, **Karl von Clausewitz**

CHAPTER TWENTY-FOUR

Thursday, February 3, 2050

The vid-screens showed snow, ash-grey rocks, and low undergrowth so dark as to appear black. Nothing moved in that landscape. Cadre-Lieutenant Arlen Mullet set the mug of steaming coffee down within Lessing's reach and retired. Jennifer Caw had not finished her first cup yet.

"They really going to surrender?" she asked.

"That's what Gottschalk told me over our Magellan hookup."

"Who?"

"Benjamin Gottschalk, the lib-rebs' commander. Captain, he calls himself. Used to be an instructor at Stanford. Sociology."

Jennifer wriggled on the military cot, rubbed her mittens together, and jammed them into the pockets of her white, alpaca ski-coat. The lava beds of northern California were a refrigerator in February, more like the high ranges of the Pacific Northwest than the palms, sand, and surf of "Free Calimerica" to the south. The cold bit right through canvas camp-chairs, Cadre uniforms, and thermal underwear.

"What a place to die in! Like the other side of the moon." Jennifer shook out her auburn locks. She was "just passing through" and had stopped in at the Cadre base camp for a social visit. Spying for Goddard was more like it. That didn't bother Lessing. Better him than somebody less friendly.

"Here. Liese sends these." Jennifer fished into a green, leather purse as big as a soldier's knapsack and handed him a vid-cassette, a book, and four photographs. Lessing laid the first two items aside and glanced quickly at the pictures: Liese speaking in an auditorium (their relationship had helped her speech problem); Liese at the dinner table with Wrench clowning behind her; Liese in ski-togs on

Mount Rainier; Liese and Mulder grinning at the camera like
Goldilocks and Papa Pig.

Liese! How he missed her!

Outside something roared hugely, startling them. "A tank rev-
ving up," he explained, "in case the lib-rebs want to play some more
instead of surrendering."

The new M90A4 Heston tank was gigantic. The lib-rebs had
grabbed a few of the monsters to begin with, but now they were
down to using antiquated museum-pieces, such as old M60A3s. The
Heston possessed a 120-mm gun, two 7.62-mm mounted machine
guns, an air-defense missile launcher, and the latest communications
gear, deflectors, rocket-confusers, and armor. Some Hestons were
equipped with laser cannon as well, but those were all down near
newly captured Sacramento, staging for the assault on San Francisco. When that was over, they'd go see about L.A.

No tank was much good in the lava beds; the region was
crisscrossed with strange, little bluffs and ravines, heaped with
knife-edged volcanic stones and boulders, and pitted with caves.
Mullet, who haled from Eugene, Oregon, said that this had been the
site of an earlier, almost forgotten conflict, the Modoc War of 1873,
in which about a hundred and sixty Indians held off the U.S. Army
for months. These days "Captain Jack's" refuge was home to a
different war party: some three hundred rag-tag lib-reb guerrillas
fighting a rear-guard action to delay the U.S. Army's mop-up in
northern California.

It had taken weeks of paper wars at the Pentagon, newly refurbished and restocked with bureaucrats, before the generals had
agreed to let Lessing's fledgling American Freedom Brigade—the
name Outram had chosen, although the unit was closer in size,
makeup, and function to a division than a brigade—handle what
should have been a minor police action. Like the Modoc War, this
took more time and lives than anybody had expected, and the Cadre
was losing face. Lessing was intent on finishing the job right and
correcting the image.

Here the lib-rebs were all done: starvation, dysentery, and the
worst winter in fifty years had beaten Gottschalk at last. As with the
Modocs long ago, bravery was no match for food, weather, and
logistics.

Lessing sipped his coffee and asked, "How's Mulder? Your
mother?"

"He's fine. She's green light too. About to marry Grant Simmons. Did you know that?"

"The Congress of Americans for Personal Freedom guy?" Lessing had met Simmons. The man was as unmemorable as a ballpark
hotdog. It took restraint to keep from asking, "Why marry *him*?"

"He's a dedicated person, hardworking . . . ." Jennifer said, a little defensively. "He's a great speaker."

So were some parrots.

"Well . . . congratulations, if that's what I'm supposed to say."

"Grant's likely to be our candidate for President in fifty-two, you know."

"Unh?" He looked up, surprised. "What about Outram? Vice President Lee? Mulder himself?"

"You haven't heard? Outram's got cancer of the liver. He's likely to die within a few months. Byron Lee's a non-entity." She hesitated. "And Mulder doesn't think he's going to last that long either."

"Jesus . . . . He never said anything."

"Oh, he's in good shape now. Just feeling his age. He wants somebody younger, with drive and energy. Somebody who'll consolidate what we've done."

Lessing considered. The Party's present bright lights were not very appealing: they were unknown, too young, not charismatic enough, or just too "fringe" to suit Mr. and Mrs. American Public. The Party had indeed grown in popularity—you could speak for the movement almost anywhere these days without getting rocks thrown at you—but people like Wrench, Morgan, Goddard, and Abner Hand still weren't the Boys Next Door. Not yet. Liese and Eighty-Five were working on it.

Jennifer continued, "People are turning inward, looking to the Party to restore our traditional values, our prosperity and identity. Pacov and Starak did more than just kill people: they cut our emotional security out from under us. We need somebody solid . . . committed . . . rational."

"Get Goddard. He's a winner in two out of three of those categories . . . you decide which ones." Lessing still couldn't work up an interest in politics. Liese had tried to involve him, but even she hadn't had much success. He'd rather putter with a car engine, read, play racquetball, or practice with the latest additions to Mulder's arsenal.

"Bill has no imagination. I'd rather have Grant Simmons or Byron Lee . . . or you." She let her coat fall open to reveal a forest-green sweater, a Navajo necklace of beaten silver set with turquoises, and some spectacular cleavage.

He made a wry face. "Me? Come on, Jen!" He had already begun to suspect that Jennifer Caw wasn't here just to take in the winter scenery. He had nothing to offer politically, and she knew it.

She couldn't have designs on *him*, could she? Not when she and Liese were such good friends! Liese was the jealous type—and as straitlaced about her monogamy as a Born-Again elder! Nor was he much of a bargain, in spite of a good recovery after Palestine and Russia.

Yet there was no telling with Jennifer. Wrench called her "the mailbox: a public receptacle into which any man can drop his male."

A quick roll on the camp cot, then? A morning's jollies, nobody hurt, and Liese never the wiser? Lessing was in no mood to take that risk. Getting close to Liese had been the hardest thing he'd ever done, and she was worth every angry word, every long wrangle, every drop of sweat, every tear, and every long, luxurious morning in bed.

He drifted over to inspect the row of vid-screens that lined the rear wall of his styro-plast hut. "How's Borchardt doing in Germany?"

She took the hint with good grace. "Oh . . . Hans is fine. Big rally last month in Munich: nearly a hundred thousand."

He heard Jennifer stirring her coffee, but he didn't look around. Instead he bawled, "Hey, Mullet! Arlen!"

The aide stuck his head inside the door flap. He kept his eyes averted from the camp cot, where Jennifer reclined like Cleopatra cruising the Nile. Skin-tight, black jeans and tooled cowboy boots didn't fit the Egyptian image, but the effect was dramatic, nonetheless.

"Sir?" Mullet's long, pale, freckled face was as gently bovine as one of his daddy's cows up in the Willamette River Valley. He was canny, though, and unexpectedly perceptive.

"Where the hell are the lib-rebs? Are we going to have to go drag 'em out after all?"

Mullet ruminated. "Detectors just started to report movement, sir. Comin' out real slow, though, 'cause of the women and kids."

"The lib-rebs have their *families* in there?" Jennifer sat up. "In *that* icebox?"

"The women are mostly fighters," Lessing told her. "There're only a few noncombatants with them: people who're real scared of us. We're supposed to be the 'racist, fascist beasts,' remember?"

"There they are now, sir." Mullet lifted his bony chin toward the vid-screens. "Two, three hunnerd in the column. Pro'lly all of 'em."

Jennifer came over to see. "No weapons, no uniforms. Like a bunch of old ladies on their way to church!"

"Them old ladies kept us bottled up here for a month," Mullet observed morosely.

Lessing was already donning his winter-camo greatcoat, mittens, and officer's cap. "Tell Ken Swanson to put it over the amplifiers that I'm coming out to accept their surrender personally."

"You, sir?"

"Yeah, me. They put up a good fight. Least I can do."

"Can I come?" Jennifer used the honeyed tone that usually worked wonders with males. Not this time!

"Unh-unh. No goozy, foozy, as the Bangers say. Mulder'd unzip me himself if anything happened to you."

"He's right, miss." Mullet blocked the doorway. "Carpet mines . . . a laser at long range . . . a rocket from ambush. Dang'rous." He blinked reproachfully at Lessing. "Even for a so-called experienced merc."

"Look," Lessing said to Jennifer, "if you want to help, go over to the field hospital or the mess hall. Show the lib-rebs we're not murdering monsters. They'll need hot coffee, food, and medical care."

"Florence Nightingale? Me? Oh, all right. But after the atrocities the lib-rebs committed at the battle of Redding . . . ,"

"Blame that on their 'special troops' . . . the L.A. street gangs, their Mexican allies. All the discipline of a pack of rabid dogs." When she said nothing he added, "If we show people we're straight, we have a chance to put the country back together again. Screw up, stay disunited, and the Chinese, the Indians, the Turks, the South Americans . . . *somebody* . . . will kick our lights out."

"They burned down our house in L.A. My mother barely got out alive. They'd have murdered her if they'd caught . . . ."

"*Forget* all that! The future is what matters. Why not use sweetness and light, if those'll get us friends. Oh, we'll win this war militarily, but we *really* win only if everybody has a chance at the good life. That's what Liese has 'Dorn' saying these days."

"You're naive, Alan. Political realities are different."

"I may not have a Ph.D. in academic horse apples like Wrench or Borchardt, but I know what makes people tick. Peace is better than war . . . or revenge."

"The Party of Humankind . . . ."

"The Party is on a roll. Pacov and Starak took out our worst enemies and put Outram into the White House. Otherwise Mulder'd still be peddling Fertil-Gro out in India, and you 'Descendants' would be piddly-shitting around in the sinkholes of the Third World. Luck, lady, pure, gubbin' luck! The Party had better not miss this chance; it's the only one it's likely to get!"

"Even without Pacov we still would've won. We were on our way, slower but just as sure. Our North-European heritage . . . our ethnos, our Aryan blood . . . *cannot* be denied! Look at Germany: she lost two world wars but she's very much a power again! We come through in the crunch: we don't give up, and we don't die easy. Like the sick cannibal said about the missionary he ate for dinner: 'You can't keep a good man down.'"

"That's awful! And you stole it from Wrench!"

"Who stole it from somebody else, who stole it from some other jizmo, all the way back to the clowns in the Colosseum. Look, Alan, we were working on a long-term economic campaign. *That* was *our* strategy!"

"Which might've taken another hundred years, if it succeeded at all." Better to argue than give her another chance to make moves on him. He said, "All I'm saying is that we ought to make amends, compromise, and make peace . . . provided those things get us where we wanted to go in the first place. Hell, *I'm* the soldier; when there're wars *I'm* the guy who has to duck the bullets! Like my dad said, 'Rather finagle than fight.'"

She tilted her head and grinned at him. "You know, Alan, you have all the makings of a a great lib-reb. The only thing you haven't figured out yet is the first part of 'make love, not war.'"

She buttoned her coat and went outside to join Mullet.

He followed her into the snow-dusted air. His armored command car stood waiting across what had been the main northern parking lot of the Lava Beds National Monument. Now the tourists and campers and cars and picnic baskets were only memories; instead, Cadre banners flapped fitfully below the Stars and Stripes over khaki-colored, plastic huts, ice-crusted vehicles, and white mounds of tarp-covered stores. Wrench and Morgan had wanted a distinctive Cadre flag, like the silver runes on black of the old *SS*, but Mulder had vetoed it. He had allowed only a white "C" in the upper-left corner of the Party's regular flag. That would have to do for now.

Lessing stalked across the dirty, hard-packed snow and climbed into the passenger seat beside Stan Crawford, his driver.

Mullet came up to gesture and shout, but the engine drowned out his words. Lessing could guess that he wanted to send an escort along. That shouldn't be necessary if Lessing read this Gottschalk right. The lib-rebs would surrender as promised. On the other hand, if Gottschalk were lying, the shit would get very deep.

Lessing thought about it one more time, then waved Mullet away. He wasn't stupid, he wasn't a show-off, and he wasn't particularly brave, but in some odd way he felt himself "fated." When his time came he would go and not before. Maybe some of Islam's *qismat*— "kismet," destiny—had rubbed off on him in India.

The chill of the plastic-leather Parodex passenger seat made him wince. The next winter war the Cadre fought, he would see that the cars, the tents, and the toilets had plush seats!

"Heading, sir?" Stan was Ponape-trained, tough, thirtyish, and plain, a dishwater blonde from Charlotte, North Carolina.

The hell with military jargon. He jerked a thumb and drawled, "Thataway."

Snow drifted down in sad, little gusts and whorls as they drove, filling the ruts and potholes with powdered sugar. Captain Jack's Modoc stronghold lay slightly off to the left, with Canby's Cross, Gillem's Camp, and Gillem's Bluff beyond. On their right much of Tule Lake was once again filled with water as it had been in Modoc times; the farms and fields of the later settlers were gone, a consequence, Mullet said, of the Viet-Chinese Atomic War of 2010. The locals took this as a sign that Crater Lake, up north in Oregon, was about to erupt again after a sleep of six or eight thousand years.

Stan spotted the lib-rebs before he did: a ragged, black line against jagged, black rocks. Black and white like an old movie: a grey sky, a monochrome landscape. He was reminded of one of Mulder's ancient newsreels: German troops trudging through the Russian desolation, leaving equipment and frozen corpses behind as they straggled back toward the crumbling frontiers of the *Reich*.

"You want me to drive right up to 'em," Stan asked, "or do we wait here?"

He glanced around. "There's a picnic table," he suggested. "We can clean off the snow . . . ."

"Excuse me, but you'll freeze your butt . . . sir. Standing up in the hatch is better. Say your piece, sit back down, and stay warm. We can put some of their wounded and womenfolk into our passenger compartment. Good publicity . . . uh, if you think it's wise." His expression said he did not.

Publicity: Wrench's specialty. Words and pictures were more important than any military victory he might win. He looked in the rear mirror and caught the glint of a moving silver-metallic dome: a Magellan unit keeping pace with them, its cameras grinding away for posterity. Ken Swanson, his com-officer, would have telephoto holo-vid crews up in helicopters as well.

He might as well look heroic.

He clambered up onto the seat and undogged the ceiling hatch. Ice-tipped wind-fingers clawed at his cheeks and forehead as he put his head out; he jerked his cap down and turned up his coat collar. Stan stopped the car, and his ears rang with the sudden stillness.

If this had been a movie, any minute they'd hear the lib-rebs heroically singing their battle-song as they marched out to surrender. Lessing grimaced at the fancy.

There they were, emerging from among the trees, silent except for the crunch of boots in the snow. Through the binoculars Stan passed up to him he saw what a tired, hungry, scruffy lot they were: weaponless, dispirited, dressed in drab, civilian clothes, parts of uniforms, and blankets. The one in front must be Gottschalk: a tall, skinny man with frizzy, black hair and a beard. Beside him was a dark, hatchet-beaked woman who carried a quilt-wrapped infant and herded five older children along before her. Lessing counted two boys and three girls, perhaps seven to twelve years of age. The smallest girl bore a bundle—no, it was a teddy bear, nearly as big as she was. The others in the vanguard were adults: soldiers, would-be soldiers, and play-soldiers caught up in a reality they had never expected.

He tried the bullhorn. "Hey! Attention!"

That wasn't very eloquent. Out of the corner of his eye he saw the Magellan recording the scene.

"You rebels!" he called, more loudly. "I am Cadre-Colonel Alan Lessing of the American Freedom Brigade, United States Army."

"Pog yourself, bastard!" A voice from the column squawked back. Others made more pungent suggestions.

"Look, if you'd rather fight some more, we'll oblige. Send out your noncombatants, and let's go to it."

Gottschalk—the skinny man—yelled at his troops for quiet. To Lessing, he said, "You know what we're here for, uh . . . colonel. No food, out of ammo, and colder'n a bitch. We need medical treatment for our wounded . . . fifteen men, three women, and a frostbitten kid."

"Yes . . . sure. I'll call for ambulances. No need for your injured to walk the rest of the way." He passed the order to Stan.

Gottschalk's woman sat down on a boulder, the children in a defensive ring around her, the others standing or squatting where they were. The lib-reb leader himself came over to the command car.

"A fine end for a Stanford Ph.D," Gottschalk said. Stan kept their mounted machine-gun trained on him.

"You're not ended yet."

"I get a fair trial? A jury? My civil rights? *Then* you hang me?"

"Sorry. We aren't into hangings."

"I . . . we all . . . just disappear? Is that it? Death-squad style? Or maybe a shower bath that's really a gas chamber?"

"That's crap!" Lessing answered tiredly. "You and your people are in revolt against the legally elected, constitutional government of the United States of America. *That's* treason! What do you expect from us? Cheers? A peace prize?"

"So what does happen?"

"You get sent to a reorientation camp near Seattle. If we like you and you like us, you go back to being ordinary Americans. If you can't or won't fit in, you lose your citizenship. Then you move to any country that'll take you."

"Exile? You've got to be kidding!"

Lessing smiled at the antiquated turn of phrase. "Nope. Go wherever you're wanted. If you're a communist, you can live happily ever after in what's left of the People's Republic of China; they need workers to build their Marxist paradise. Blacks have a choice of sixteen settlements in Africa, a half-dozen Caribbean islands, or one of the Black-majority nations in South America. Jews are welcome in the Izzie colonies in Russia. They're looking for skilled, educated people to build a new 'Chosen People,' Jews-only, religious-racist *Eretz* Israel there. As for Southeast Asians and Latins, they can go back to their native lands as soon as the war is over. Any other unreconstructed lib-rebs . . . of whatever persuasion . . . go to whoever lets 'em in: the communes in Russia, our own settlements around the oil fields in the Persian Gulf, Europe, Australia, Canada . . . wherever. If nobody wants you, we'll set up some sort of isolated enclave for you here, where you can do your own thing by yourselves."

"Lies!" the woman interrupted in a sharp, fierce voice. "Another Holocaust . . . a free ticket to the gas chambers!"

"Sorry, no gas chambers. Resettlement abroad. Like Germany before World War II, though that's not how you people want it remembered. Take your families and go!" Lessing was too cold to wrangle; he could no longer feel his ears, and his forehead ached. He rubbed at the bridge of his nose.

The woman got unsteadily to her feet. Stan's machine gun swiveled to track her. "Why should *we* go? Why us? We've contributed so much to this country . . . doctors, lawyers, musicians, scientists, artists . . . every profession, every walk of life! We *won't* go! It's *you* . . . you pogging fascists . . . who ought to go! *You're* not Americans! *You* don't belong!"

"Wrong. *We* are the majority. We've been a *silent* majority for too long. Now we're taking control. We, the American majority, say that *you* don't fit. We don't want your music, your art, your science . . . we've got our own, and we're satisfied. We can't assimilate you, and we won't let you run us. So you go. No argument, no discussion, no high-buck lawyers!" His cheeks were numb in the bitter wind. "I promise you decent treatment: no gas chambers and no concentration camps. We'll treat you a helluva lot better than you would've done us."

He shut off his mind. Wrench had given him a list of things to say for the benefit of the TV cameras, and he said them without enthusiasm, without caring whether he believed them or not. For all he knew, that camp up near Seattle might offer a full complement of gas chambers, ovens, torture machines, and sado-porn queens dressed in black leather and waving whips. It *might*—but he didn't think so. He had come to trust Mulder, Liese, and Wrench, at least. It would be stupid to lie to him, moreover; he'd find out, and then he would become an enemy. Alan Lessing did not let people lie to him.

"The ambulances are here," Stan called up to him. "These dinkers can move their wounded into that clearing for pickup."

The return trip was a triumphal procession. Lessing didn't like it, but he understood. Starak's victims had no more worries. It was the survivors who suffered, mourned, endured shortages and social upheavals, and woke sweating from nightmares of invisible death. They needed good news. Morale was the object here.

Lessing resigned himself to being a military hero. He took Wrench's advice, patched in over their radio to Home-Net headquarters in Kansas City, and rode into camp standing up in the hatch, like a *Panzer* commander on parade. Too bad he hadn't brought tanker goggles to go with his peaked cap! There was no martial music either, just the soughing of the wind high up in the evergreens, a dirge to the dead. Wrench could add suitable oom-pa-pa to the broadcast, together with wild cheering and a play-by-play commentary.

The mess hall and hospital were both housed in the big, barn-like garage the National Park Service had built for its maintenance vehicles back during the era of the Born-Agains. They had done a good job with parks and historical monuments, but the administrations that followed were too preoccupied with the Middle East, pollution, farm riots, labor unrest, the national debt, the failure of Social Security and Medicare, and getting stroked by their P.A.C.s to pay attention to lesser matters.

Lessing met Mullet and Jennifer at the door, greeted Timothy Helm, his second-in-command, and waved away the bundle of dispatches Ken Swanson pushed at him. First things first: the lib-reb wounded had to be admitted into the hospital; those suffering from minor frostbite and injuries were lined up to await their turns; and the rest were shepherded into the mess hall, where Lessing's staff searched and processed them before sending them on to the cafeteria. Some slumped down at the tables without eating; others had to be warned against gobbling too much too fast. The room stank of unwashed bodies, wet wool, and cooking. The combination was not unpleasant; it reminded Lessing of noon recess in his grade school lunchroom during winters in Iowa long ago.

He sat down at one of the tables and accepted a bowl of lumpy, grey chicken soup from Jennifer. He still had a headache, but now he could blame it on the stuffy, overheated room instead of the cold outside. The soup helped. Mullet laid a roll of maps captured from the rebel stronghold beside his plate and announced that Tim Helm wanted to discuss them. Swanson was also hovering nearby, clutching his dispatches and picking his nose. Did it have to be a Universal Truth that com-men were invariably nose-pickers?

"Your guys checking for holdouts?" Lessing asked of Helm. "Snipers?"

"Nobody. We got hoppy-choppies flying search circles back into the beds, but some of them lib-reb smart-asses got deflector blankets that block heat sensors and plastic weapons that don't trigger our search beams. There're miles of lava caves down south by Indian Well, too. A guy could hide anywhere. We'll get most of them sooner or later, though, and any we miss'll freeze their yarbles off. Oh, we scanned the prisoners you brought in. They're clean. See you when you're done." He scooped up his maps and left.

Lessing ate soup, methodically and without interest. By now Home-Net would be telling the world of his splendid victory, this feat of personal valor, this Great Step Forward for the Forces of Righteousness, Home, Mother, and Apple Pie.

The heat was making him drowsy. He needed Liese.

"You Mistadet?" a voice impinged muzzily upon his thoughts. He opened his eyes and saw a little girl, the one with the teddy bear.

"What?" The clash and clatter of cutlery made it hard to understand her.

"Mista Det. You Mista Det?" The child wiped her nose with grubby fingers. She wore a dress made from a patchwork quilt, and her feet were shapeless blobs of U.S. Army sacking and burlap.

Mullet laughed. "She's asking if you're 'Mister Death,' sir." He pointed to the black uniform and silver insignia Wrench had designed for Cadre officers. The troops still wore U.S. Army camo.

She held out the stained, brown-plush teddy bear. "Unca Jase said to show Teen to Mista Det."

"That's nice, but I'm not . . . ." Oh, the hell with it.

The girl plucked at a plastic ring at the back of the bear's furry head. "Teen talks, y'know."

Dandy. Now he would be treated to a bad tape of "cuddle me, mommy!" Lessing had never had much to do with kids, but he could sympathize with this one: it wasn't her fault she was here.

Another little girl flickered against the shadow-curtain of his memory, a silent and pitiful creature in the back of some sort of vehicle. Was she a dream? It seemed so very far away. He heard sobbing and felt her stick-like body in his arms.

The bear spoke. In a raffish British accent, it said, "Hello, Lessing! Teen here! Remember me? Jason Hollister?"

Marvelous Gap.

God Almighty!

His combat reflexes were still good. He grabbed the bear out of the child's hands, looked wildly around, howled a warning, slung the toy toward the soup cauldrons in the emptiest part of the mess hall, and dived over on top of the little girl. Chairs screeched and skidded as they tumbled together in a heap under the table.

The thunderclap of the explosion snatched away all sound, all hearing, all breath, and all sensation.

Crockery and cutlery became shrapnel; hot soup turned into fiery napalm; pots and pans flew like cannonballs. Not only did the teddy bear contain an explosive charge, but it was stuffed with undetectable caltrops: sharp, four-pointed stars of brittle plastic that shrieked away in every direction, slashing whatever lay in their paths.

Seconds passed before the screaming began.

Lessing lay sprawled on top of the girl, the table top collapsed over both of them. He didn't know if he was hurt. The bomb had landed behind the serving counter, limiting the direct force of its blast. The caltrops had caused most of the damage. In his mind's eye he saw the people behind the counter again: two or three prisoners taking seconds, four or five guards, and a cluster of kitchen help over by the coffee urns. They were all dead now.

He had killed them.

Yet what could he have done? The rest of the room was packed; dozens would have died if he had thrown the damned bear anywhere else! Nor could he have rushed over and dunked the bomb into a soup pot; modern demo-devices were waterproof.

The child wriggled and moaned. It was when he sought to roll away from her that he found that he was injured, how badly he wasn't sure. They lay in a puddle of red, and he knew instinctively that it was his blood, not hers. His left arm didn't work, and something was wrong with his face. He explored with his tongue and encountered only air: his left cheek was either torn wide open or gone entirely. Both eyes still functioned, though the left one was blurred.

The strange thing was that he didn't hurt. He had no sensation at all. To his further surprise, his headache was gone.

"We didn't . . . we couldn't . . . it wasn't us . . . ." Someone kept moaning above him. It sounded like Gottschalk. Feet stamped on the tabletop over his legs. That hurt, and he cried out. The table tilted, lifted up, and went away, giving him a view of the jagged, blackened hole in the cinderblocks of the far wall where the cafeteria counter had been. Snow was already sifting in to hide the carnage.

Gottschalk's harpy was on top of him, pawing, digging, trying to get at the child. The rebel leader himself was visible behind her, his beard and shirt spattered with red. The woman shoved roughly at Lessing, cursed him, and dragged the limp, dirt-blackened child out. She cradled her, crooned to her, then rose and lurched away.

The pain was beginning now. Soon it would be agony, if he didn't bleed to death first.

The lib-rebs were innocent this time. They had died here just as Lessing's people had. Jason Hollister—"Teen" from the Marvelous Gap spesh-op—had given the teddy bear to the kid. Lessing hadn't seen Hollister among the prisoners, which meant he had already left before the surrender. Right now the bastard was probably watching his bloody triumph on Home-Net in some roach-heaven hotel in San Francisco!

Automatic weapons fire chattered. Screams and shots echoed back and forth in the chaos, and he smelled smoke. So much for good publicity! A woman shrieked and kept on shrieking; Lessing wondered if it were Gottschalk's witch—or could it be Jennifer?

He went to sleep, shooting or no shooting.

Much, much later he awoke from a lazy afternoon in the movies with Emily Pietrick. Their own love scene had been much juicier than the one on the screen. Now he was both bored and horny again.

Without warning the fabric of that universe ripped apart, and he heard someone say, "He may need a transplant for the eye. Got one in stock?"

A second voice mumbled, "Yah. Think so. Up in Klamath Falls."

"Get it here, just in case. It's the arm that'll be tough, though. Caltrop ripped down through his cheek and into his shoulder. Lots of damage. What's his blood type?"

"On his dog-tag, doc." Fingers fumbled at his throat.

"Um. Get him a stretcher and prep him for immediate ops. The lib-reb woman's dead, though. Need a body-bag for her. Her husband too. Christ, our guys went nuts with the automatics!"

"Serves the poggers right! It was their fuckin' bomb! How's the kid the colonel landed on?"

"Scared out of her weenies, but okay."

"What a gubbin' mess . . . !"

He went back into the theater to find Emily. Maybe the movie would be better the second time around.

You ask whether the Party of Humankind has a solution for the crime problem? Thank you, young lady!

The answer is yes. We are revising all of our laws and restructuring our procedures of law enforcement. We're rewriting the law books, standardizing, condensing, getting rid of the chaff, and putting the important statutes into language everyone can understand. We're using our biggest computers for this: machines that can read, digest, cross-reference, and collate a thousand books an hour . . . and spit out the gist in book form! We're putting computer terminals in every police station, hospital, courthouse, prison, and government bureau. A single data bank will cover not only every state in the Union but foreign nations that subscribe to our info-network as well. Our computers analyze handwriting, check physical evidence, search data files, compare voice recordings . . . even do autopsies . . . all within minutes, and we're now using DNA genetic codes to tell whether a hair, a blood sample, or a bit of tissue belongs to a given person. Loopholes and technicalities will be eliminated as evidence-gathering procedures are standardized. Moreover, we're working to develop safe, humane, and almost unbeatable interrogation techniques. Instead of weeks or months to prepare a case, most actions can go to court almost at once.

What about lengthy trial delays, plea bargaining, uneven sentencing for similar offenses, crowded prisons, and the parole system?

Computers and a standardized legal system can't solve all of those problems, of course, but they will help. Straightforward cases, with solid evidence and no extenuating circumstances, can be decided by computer. After all, why not? Why waste time and money? Our sophisticated computers, checked by human judges, can handle about eighty percent of all cases. The rest will still require a judge and jury. Computers will help in those cases, too, as will the condensation of our law books and a restructuring of our system. We're also going to allow our computers to consider behavior patterns, psychological profiles, and data from previous convictions. It'll be a lot tougher on the repeat criminal.

Parole? Time off for good behavior?

We're getting rid of both of those concepts. They're no more than revolving doors that put criminals back on the street; they're unevenly applied, and they haven't reduced crime one iota. We believe the law should say what it means and mean what it says. You do the crime, you do the time. We need other solutions to overcrowding and to filthy, demeaning, and dangerous prison conditions, of course. These problems only get worse if we convict more offenders, give stricter sentences, and end parole, as I have suggested. Jailing people is expensive, and it fails to produce the results we want: reformed behavior. Prisons are great schoolhouses for young criminals; they are sinkholes of drugs, AIDS, violence, and sexual aberrations; and rehabilitation is as rare as angel feathers! Today seventy-four per cent of our prison population will get out,

commit further offenses, and be sent back in for more meaningless incarceration. Rehabilitation simply doesn't result from
jail time. We can't keep 'em in, and we don't want 'em out.
The liberal solution is to mouth platitudes about improving the
environment, creating jobs, and spending more money. *Your*
money. We've seen how useless *that* is! You win a little here,
you lose a lot there, and your problem keeps growing. Understand this: there is no 'kind' solution. There is no way to reduce
crime . . . *except to rid ourselves of the criminals.* Sorrowfully,
and with all the compassion in the world, we must come to the
only solution there is: we must put serious offenders to death,
as humanely and as gently as possible, without delay or excep-
tion. (Uproar)

Let me explain! The death penalty will only be applied to a
person convicted of a major vicious crime, or of a pattern of
lesser vicious crimes! Not a crime of passion or a one-time lapse.
A 'vicious crime' is one that is knowingly and willfully per-
petrated and which involves premeditated and unwarranted
violence, sadism, cruelty to a child or helpless victim, anti-state
or anti-ethnos-survival activity, or other aggravating factors. A
first-time minor vicious offense will earn a prison sentence,
together with retraining and education. A second offense will
draw a longer term, plus intensive therapy, and a clear warning
that this is the last chance! A third such crime will be punished
with death. The sentence will be reviewed for accuracy and
justice, but after that there will be no further delay or appeal.

Unfair? Barbaric?

Not at all! We must remove social units which malfunction
and which damage other units around them. We must weed
our garden, remove rotten apples from our barrel, destroy
vicious dogs, and cull defective livestock. There is nothing
inhumane about this. It is far more humane than returning
offenders to prison to live out lives of hopelessness and
degradation! The community . . . the ethnos . . . is our first
responsibility; we must protect it from those who would destroy
it. The ethnos owes nothing to anti-social individuals. No social
contract exists unless both parties subscribe to it.

The sanctity of human life?

In which society was human life ever *really* sacred? Lip-service is easy: how often we've heard 'turn the other cheek'! Tell
me which nation ever *actually* followed that precept! We *will*
maximize opportunities for positive development. To those who
give, we will return ten-fold. Only those who still cannot abide
by our social contract after all remedies have been exhausted
will be eliminated. This will be done with as much kindness and
dignity as possible. But we *will* do it. We cannot afford to do
otherwise.

Who are we to judge, you ask?

Who is *anybody* to judge *anything*? Who gives *me* the right
to tell *you* not to park here, not to dump garbage in my
driveway, not to steal my chickens? That's the social contract.
You give us the right to act by electing us. If you disagree, then
elect somebody else! If you accept our contract, then we *will*

judge, and we *will* carry out our program with as little hypocrisy and phoney piety as possible!

What about occasional miscarriages of justice: the poor man dragged off to die for a crime he did not commit?

Such instances are rare; they will be rarer still once we get our technology in place. Fewer innocent persons will be convicted, and no one will ever be executed without a clear record of violent anti-social activity or recidivism.

People in prison now? Professional criminals with long records?

They will finish their current sentences and then be released. They will also be told that the next time they commit a vicious offense they will be put to death, with no hesitation and no apology.

The insanity plea?

It will still be there for those who deserve it. We're devising better tests and treatments for those who suffer from mental ailments. The insanity plea won't be as easily available as before, however: we believe most people are rational enough to be responsible for their actions, whatever their childhood traumas or other psychological problems might be. We will be compassionate; that's all I promise you.

No, sir, we do *not* intend to put traffic violators to death, no matter how many tickets they have! (Laughter) Permanent loss of one's driver's license will be more common, however, and deaths or injuries resulting from drunken or careless driving are indeed `vicious crimes.' An automobile is a lethal weapon.

What else? You, in the front row, miss. Equality? Won't death sentences for serious offenders result in more Blacks and other minorities being executed than Whites?

The answer is *yes*, at least in the short run, while the minorities remain among us. We will allow *no* inequity, however; all citizens are equal before the bar of justice! Factors that cause Blacks or other minorities to commit more crimes than Whites are another matter: they will be remedied as quickly as possible. We believe that emigration to more ethnically homogeneous homelands is the best approach to this problem. Until our emigration program has been fully implemented we will also correct the environment, improve education, and provide opportunities for those minorities who remain among us temporarily. What we will *not* tolerate is a high crime rate . . . due to *any* cause! We are willing to weed our garden; if others among us are not willing to weed theirs, then we will do it for them.

A last question? You, the young man with the glasses in the third row? What about lawyers? Is your law degree still going to be worth something once our judicial system is revamped?

The answer is a qualified yes. We won't go as far as Shakespeare: 'The first thing we do, let's kill all the lawyers.' (Laughter) There will be less for lawyers to do as our computer network takes over certain functions: fewer appeals, fewer retrials, fewer lengthy corporate cases, fewer hung juries, fewer judgments dependent upon wealth, luck, charisma, or other personal factors. Lawyers will be needed to prepare evidence and advise clients. They may make less money than they do now, and they'll have to learn some new concepts of law. The muddle we have today cannot and will not be allowed to continue.

—from a discussion held with students at **Central High School, Little Rock, Arkansas, by Vincent Dorn, Monday, August 1, 2050**

CHAPTER TWENTY-FIVE

Friday, August 5, 2050

"Not happy?" Liese stood by the window that looked out over the jigsaw puzzle of Seattle's city center. From the V.I.P. penthouse on the top floor of the hospital, Puget Sound was visible between the tall, grey buildings as a pool of silvery mercury spilled across a rumpled, green-baize horizon.

"Sure," Lessing replied. "Happy as a man can be with a face full of cotton wadding." He tried not to lisp. The wound in his cheek was nearly healed, but the stitches and plastic still felt awkward.

He shifted to take the weight off his left side. Last Wednesday the doctors had performed what they said would be the final operation on his shoulder, and it still hurt. In time, he'd regain the complete use of his arm, they told him: no prosthetics, no slings, not the black, leather-clad hand that Wrench had offered to have Eighty-Five design, the one replete with a dagger, a tear-gas projector, a stitch-gun, and probably a sixty-five-blade Swiss army knife! He was reminded of a mad scientist in some movie he had seen in his childhood, a man whose artificial arm had a will of its own.

Liese drifted over to the bed. She sat on his right side to let him rub her neck with his good hand. "Feels nice."

"It better. I spent weeks strengthening these fingers when they thought I was going to lose the arm."

"Green light soon." She twisted around to kiss him. "Mmm. Back to work now."

She could be so cool and so frustratingly remote! He said, "You always have to go. Wait'll I bust out of here!"

"Lots to do. Lib-rebs. Outram too sick to do much. Vice-President Lee an idiot. Mulder in seclusion. Goddard feuding with Wrench and Morgan."

"Hey, we agreed that you'd use verbs and full sentences once in a while!" He strove for a cheerful tone, but Liese was in no mood for speech therapy. After a moment he asked, "So there's trouble between the Cadre and PHASE? Open squabbling?"

She made a face. "No. Covert. Mulder trying to keep them together."

"Damn politics! The Party needs all its strength. The old power elite is going to make a comeback: the bureaucrats, the political parties, the religious sects, the C.I.A., the I.R.S., the corporations, all the pressure groups from Big Labor to 'Save the Prairie Dogs.'"

"Business as usual. Shock of Starak wearing off."

"My God . . . ! After the death of half the country!"

Liese took him literally. She said, "Not half. Census not in. Forty-five to sixty million Starak-related American casualties. Toxin itself, plus panic, starvation, other diseases. Maybe a billion dead from Pacov in Europe, Russia, Israel, Africa, parts of China . . . elsewhere. Pacov bacteria supposed to die after one generation but mutated to 'Black Pacov' in Africa instead. Most gone now, though."

Gordy Monk rapped on the door. He was the chief of Lessing's squad of bodyguards. "Sir, Cadre-Commander Wren is here."

"Go!" Liese whispered. She reached for her charcoal-grey autumn coat on the foot of the bed and started to get up.

"Stay!" Lessing rapped back at her. It was hard to muster true authority with a mummy-wrapped shoulder and a cheek bandage that made him look like a lopsided squirrel.

Wrench sidled around the door, winked at Liese, then came on in. Today his cream-colored, gabardine uniform was tasteful, and he had kept the medals and insignia down to a non-blinding minimum.

"Sit down," Lessing grumbled. "Makes me nervous when people stand over me."

Liese went back to the window, but Wrench complied. He grinned at Lessing. "Sorry to disturb you. Pay a call on the weak, the sick, and the elderly! Civic duty, you know!"

"Weak, sick, elderly . . . bullshit! I'm a goddamned hero, thanks to you. Home-Net is playing me up as the greatest military commander since Napoleon. And *you* run Home-Net."

"We believe in scrupulous honesty: all the commercials, soaps, game shows, jiggly bint-babies, and tasteless violence the traffic'll bear. Which are you?"

"News?" Liese demanded impatiently.

Wrench gave her a smile like sunrise. "Knowing that our boy hero here doesn't get his daily dose of holo-vid, allow me to 'recapitulate the news,' as Home-Net's greatest commentator, Jason Milne, says." He cleared his throat portentously. "War breaks out between India and the Islamic Theocracy of Indonesia-Malaysia. China intervenes and threatens a tactical nuclear strike unless Prime Minister Ramanujan's forces leave Cambodia, like real pronto. In Pakistan, the Red Mullah stays neutral, with one eye on Turkey to his west and the other on the Izzie-Vizzies to his north; this worries his ophthalmologist. South Africa politely offers to 'surgically remove' the U.S.-supported Nation of Allah Almighty . . . the Khalifa's folks . . . unless granted mineral rights in the Congo. Spanish forces help Morocco rescue hundreds from the ruins of earthquake-stricken Rabat. General Rollins' troops have now reached Veracruz, bypassing Mexican units lurking in what's left of Mexico City after Starak and the big fire. The confrontation between Peru and Brazil escalates. The White House dithers over whether to stomp Central America and do away with the drug trade by the Biblical method . . . fire and sword . . . or to take the drugsters' bucks and shut up. Australia and New Zealand have gone inside, locked their doors, and put up a sign saying, 'Nobody bloody-well 'ome. Go 'wye 'n' g'dye t'ye, myte!'"

"You make a better Jason Milne than Jason Milne does."

"All bad!" Liese shook her dark-blonde tresses vehemently. "No good news?"

Lessing said, "The world's a machine with a broken flywheel: it's coming to pieces."

"We're what's holding it together," Wrench answered. "Our good old North-European ethnos. Without us the game *would* be over. We're actually gaining, doing good stuff internally and helping sister organizations abroad. And allies among some really unlikely ethnos groups, too, like the Khalifa's Nation of Allah Almighty."

"Khalifa Abdullah Sultani . . . ," Liese began.

"I think I met him once." Lessing saw a flicker of ice-blue, and an odd tremor crept into his voice.

She smiled, puzzled. "Working with us. Resettling Black population in Africa."

"It's hard to imagine: the Khalifa on our side!"

"Why not? Good for his people. We help. Don't interfere."

Wrench said, "Reorientation for Black lib-reb prisoners includes courses taught by the Khalifa's people. We're sending him trained recruits, not a bunch of bang-nog jizmos. He gets what he wants, and we get what we both need: racial separation with room to grow."

"Same in Central and South America," Liese added. She picked up her coat again. "Re-education. They want it; we help. Party strongest in Argentina, Brazil."

Lessing scowled. "I still get the feeling it's all coming apart. We *have* to win the lib-reb war fast. Then we have to reunite. Otherwise the wheels and springs fly off."

Wrench showed his gleaming, white teeth. "You're a great, ugly clot of doom today, aren't you, Lessing? Let me give you some good news: San Francisco's about to fall. Last night Tim Helm's guys and some regular units . . . Marines, I think . . . busted through the lib-reb lines north of Walnut Creek. They took the San Leandro reservoir and pushed the opfoes back to Pleasanton and Livermore. Best guess is that the lib-rebs may try to hold down by Fremont, but we've got 'em on the run, and our artillery's setting up to shell Oakland and Berkeley from the hills. A good fireworks show may scare the lib-rebs out of San Francisco and save the city. Be a shame to thumb it."

"Why do they fight on?" Liese wondered sadly. "Can't win."

"Same reason we'd keep going," Lessing told her. "Because there's nowhere else to go. Not for their side." He struggled up and began brushing his pale hair. It was becoming noticeably thinner.

Wrench said, "Times change. A century ago they said *we* were finished, out on the garbage dump of history. Now it's their turn. The wheel's gone around a full circle. Skirts go up, then down, then up again: about a twenty-year cycle. Eighty-Five says that whenever there's a major upheaval, like Pacov, there's also a tendency toward authoritarian politics. The liberals were up, now they're down, as outdated as wig-powder. We're the big kids on the block now . . . and believe me, we're looking real hard for ways to keep the swing from dropping us back into the shit-pile again."

Lessing didn't want to talk politics. "Let me ask . . . ."

"First things first." Wrench got up and twisted the holo-vid dial until he found a yowling Banger concert on Yama-Net. He bent close to Lessing and motioned Liese over as well. "Just so we don't hear a voice saying, 'Speak louder into the bedpan, please!'"

Lessing raised a sarcastic eyebrow. "Oh, come on! Security on the brain."

"Relax. Goddard's been getting feisty lately. He's set up files in Eighty-Five that I can't get into. Neither can Outram's trained seals."

"I wasn't asking about Goddard!"

"He's got eyes and ears right here in your hospital boudoir, you know, but we can't find his mikes." Wrench made a vague, circling gesture toward the ceiling. "Anyway, I know it's Hollister you want to hear about. The Euro-mercs haven't seen him since he pulled out of the Izzies' colony in Ufa months ago. We're sure he's in lib-reb territory."

"For that you need a mega-billion-buck computer?"

"Easy! We'll find the gubber. You needn't worry: plenty of security." He snickered. "Even got guys sniffing your pee for slow-acting poisons. No more funny teddy bears."

Lessing lay back down. "Those people . . . our people . . . died because of me. Ken Swanson, with a plastic star in his brain. The lib-rebs, too . . . Gottschalk and his woman."

"You couldn't help what Hollister did. Nobody blames you . . . or the Cadre either. Your guys didn't know what the pog was happening. The peaceniks roasted us for thumbing prisoners, and the good folks up at Dee-Net in Montreal are raising a holy stink about 'war-crimes.' But the public's on our side: nobody expects soldiers in a combat zone to react any differently to a bomb tossed . . . literally . . . into their soup!"

The memories hurt. He said, "Jennifer came to see me. I was worried about her."

"Smart girl. When the teddy bear blew its stack, good old Jenny was flat on her back with some doggie under a table."

"Not fair!" Liese cried. "Mullet! It was Arlen Mullet! Wounded protecting her! Threw her down when Alan yelled."

"Oh, I know!" Wrench put out a hand in the closest thing to an apology Lessing had seen him make. "Just a dumb joke. Jen and Mullet are green light now, though he couldn't sit down for a couple weeks, and Jen's got shrapnel scars across her back. She's gone back east to Goddard's PHASE headquarters in Bethesda, Maryland. She'll be closer to Mulder there too."

"Is Arlen still at Cadre Officer's Training School in Denver?" Lessing owed his aide the big one. Mullet had said "Mistadet" meant "Mister Death." Without that warning Lessing would have ignored the little girl with the teddy bear. He would have died. So would a lot of other people.

"Yeah. He's happy. Got a card from Stan Crawford, too. He's driving for Tim Holm now, down on the San Francisco front."

"Patty . . . the kid who brought me Hollister's present . . . is here in the hospital, in the burn unit. I . . . I couldn't block all the hot soup when I fell on her. Do me a favor and go see her."

"I have. A couple of times."

"Me too," Liese said. "Often."

"Patty's physically as good as new." Lessing swallowed. "She's not over it, but she's coming. Did you find out her last name?"

"Not yet. She sure as hell wasn't Gottschalk's kid, nor any relation to that kosher wildcat he had with him. Patty remembers her name as something like 'Heuer' or 'Hoyer,' and we think she came from Eureka. The war destroyed the records, though, and . . . well, we're just not sure."

"A loose casualty of war!" Suddenly the tension pent up within him poured out in a single, ragged snarl: "God!"

Liese touched his good hand. "Hey, hey, green light! Changed my mind. No work. Lunch. With Patty and Wrench. Tall Pines Restaurant. Pretty day. Lake Washington." Lessing's anguish was contagious; it was playing havoc with Liese's speech.

"As I was saying about Goddard . . . ." Wrench, too, saw the danger of letting Lessing brood upon the Lava Beds massacre.

"Well?"

"Let me warn you. When Outram goes there'll be a power struggle like you wouldn't believe, a real rough-and-tumble. It'll be time to choose up sides and smell armpits!"

Lessing glanced over at Liese. She wrinkled her nose. Wrench's Goddard-o-phobia might be no more than his usual paranoia; wherever there was an extreme, Wrench seemed to delight in going beyond it. Still, Goddard was quite capable of an end run for the touchdown.

"Lunch." Liese picked up the telephone and dialed. After a moment she nodded to Lessing. "Lunch. Downstairs. Patty."

He dressed, favoring his injured shoulder. Two of his bodyguards stayed in the hospital room; the other four accompanied them down in the elevator and fanned out into the parking garage. They checked Lessing's black Titan-909 Party sedan, then joined Wrench's squad in their two escort cars.

So much security struck Lessing as unnecessary. Hollister had had plenty of chances to thumb him: a shot from a passing car, a sniper on a rooftop, walk up on the street and unzip him with a kitchen knife! Wrench was obsessed with Goddard more than Hollister, of course; he was also worried about the lib-rebs, the Izzie-Vizzies, and probably Dracula and the Loch Ness monster as well.

Some of his fears were not entirely groundless.

Patty pushed through the glass doors, trailed by one of the bodyguards and a nurse. Lessing found her beautiful: a skinny, lively child of six or maybe seven—who knew?—with eyes as pale blue as Lessing's own. She had shoulder-length, sun-blonde hair, which she combed, teased, permed, braided, and manipulated in whatever other way the holo-vid bint-babies did theirs. Today Patty wore a white blouse and black jeans, the Party's unofficial kid-suit.

In a more peaceful world she could have been Liese's and Lessing's daughter.

"Hi, Lessing!" She always called him that, just his last name, no titles, nothing. She took his arm, giggled, and pulled him down for a peppermint-flavored nuzzle.

She was rarely this bubbly. Her burns had mostly consisted of splatters along her right arm and shoulder. The pain was mostly gone now, but she still had nightmares.

"Hi. You in the mood for salmon? Crab legs?"

Patty flicked a self-conscious glance at the watching security men. "No. Spaghetti."

"Seafood," Liese announced. "My vote."

The little girl shrugged. "You're buyin.'" She'd get her way; Liese would give in.

The Tall Pines Restaurant was new and glossy, the sort of place beloved of businessmen and the supper crowd: a "yuppy-suppy," Wrench called it. This afternoon a third of the tables were occupied by civilians and another third by soldiers home on leave from California, but the remaining places were empty. It took a while for tourism and gracious living to return to normal after losing upwards of forty-five million customers.

Lessing slitted his eyes and saw peace: a drowsy August afternoon, with pleasant people enjoying good food in comfortable surroundings in a happy land. He saw summer: time to go up to the San Juan Islands, over to the Olympic Peninsula, maybe to Mount Rainier. He did not see war, soldiers, tanks and guns, Pacov and Starak, Armageddon.

It was like in combat: when you can't stand to think of bullets and pain and death any longer, your mind turns off. You look at the sky, the weeds in your foxhole, the color of the rocks, the patterns made by runnels of sweat in the dust in front of your nose.

During the past weeks, lying in his hospital bed, Lessing had come to a decision. He would give in to Liese, Wrench, and Mulder and join the Party of Humankind. It might not provide "balanced," "moderate," "open-minded," "liberal" solutions, but it was better than anything else going. The Party promised peace, prosperity, stability, progress, and love.

Love?

He had thought it over, and it was true. The Party's foes did not see its policies as "love," of course, especially its racial policies and the exclusivity of the ethnos. Yet love was the essence: love of one's people, love of one's heritage, love of those with whom one empathized and identified.

The Party of Humankind offered love—love in the societal sense—the only type of love that made *survival* sense. The Party, the movement, had an uncompromising ideology and a stern discipline, but it also seemed to be the best means of keeping humanity—*all* humanity, all the ethnos groups—alive on Earth.

Their Cadre uniforms got them a table right away, and the waitress took their order.

"School?" Liese inquired of Patty.

The child favored her with a level, blue gaze. "September tenth. Third grade. Missed a year 'cause of the war." She rarely spoke of the weeks she had spent in the Lava Beds. Her memories of that place were mostly of cold and hunger and smelly tents and caves and noise and terror. Gottschalk and his strange companion had dwindled away to become dream figures. Children were more flexible—at forgiving and forgetting—than adults.

"Which school?" Wrench asked idly. The waitress was busy with a party of brown-uniformed PHASE officers two tables away, and he was keeping an eye on them.

"Oak Tree." Party schools were named for positive, natural images. Patty took a spoonful of mushroom soup, then gasped, "Wow, tha's *hot*!"

"Excuse me," Wrench muttered. He rose and pushed through the crowd to the PHASE men's table. One of his bodyguards dawdled along after him.

"All education equal in our new schools," Liese said to Lessing. "Same curriculum everywhere. Same tests. Standardized. Teachers nationally trained and licensed. Frequent transfers to other cities and states to maintain uniformity. No tuition."

"Those are Wrench's ideas. He loves tinkering with things like educational reforms." Lessing, too, was watching the PHASE men. "Mulder's pushing Wrench for Secretary of Education and Information."

"Too radical sometimes. Should think more about reforms first."

"Like a certain blonde, revolutionary lady I know." They smiled at each other, and Liese put out a hand but did not quite touch his. They were together a lot these days. They hadn't talked marriage— many people no longer wanted to risk the legal hassle just for a piece of paper—but both felt a growing commitment.

Patty glanced from one to the other. "Wrench says school'll cost a lot." She gave Lessing a big-blue-eyed, I-love-you look. "Lessing, you gonna pay for me?"

He laughed. Her grown-up ploys continually amazed him. "Don't have to. It's in the Party plan: free school for everybody."

He thought about Wrench's struggle to make education a top Party priority. Eighty-Five had had to do some fiscal footwork, even though a fat military budget was no longer as urgent as it used to be. Pacov and Starak had taken care of keeping up with the Soviets and the Chinese. There were other priorities, of course: the lib-reb war, disaster relief, reorganizing the shattered economy, national medical care, aid to the elderly, farm subsidies—a lot of things. Yet education was the key.

American education had been a haphazard house of cards built upon foundations of sand. Western civilization wouldn't last long in the hands of illiterates. Bring your kids up to the standard of students in Japan, the blossoming Turkish empire, the Izzie-Vizzie Russian colonies, and a revitalized Europe, or else watch while those other ethnos groups shouldered you aside and ran the planet their way. Sweeping reforms were hard, though: the academic establishment was as crusty and conservative in practice as its educational policies were doggedly liberal. A step in any direction gored somebody's ox and provoked loud, literate cries of outrage. The Party of Humankind had to take advantage of the country's post-Pacov disruption and do something before the Old Boys' clubs regained control. Once that happened, it would be business as usual: committees and reports and task forces and meetings and bullshit bureaucracy until it was too late. It was almost too late now.

Party schools, youth camps, parental organizations, sports groups, scholarships, curricular revisions—Wrench had laid out a whole agenda of changes, and Mulder was doing his best to see that he got them. As somebody once said, "Give me the children until they are seven, and anyone may have them afterwards."

Lessing came back to Patty. He would do everything in his power to see that she got the best.

What was she to him? Why did he care so much? He wasn't sure. He had never been much for introspection. Examining your innermost feelings—clearly and objectively—was like trying to peek up your own asshole. Contortionists could do that, but Lessing—along with a couple billion others—could not.

Was Patty just a sop for all the guilt he carried around with him, like Atlas with the world on his shoulders? Be nice to this one child and thus atone for the deaths of half the planet—whether he was guilty of those deaths or not? Or was he atoning for the Lava Beds massacre?

No, neither. He wasn't much for guilt trips.

Guilt made him think of his mother. Guilt was the mainspring of her life. In her flinty way, she believed that God would take away her guilt on Judgment Day. After all, hadn't Jesus Christ died for her sins? Whatever she did was already forgiven. If God got snotty with her, she could point over at Jesus and proclaim, "He's already paid my tab, Lord!" Then she'd weep, get down on her bony knees, and repent like she was humping for an Academy Award! God would surely see things her way.

Christianity and the other Middle Eastern religions were certainly alike in one respect: they all sweated over "sin." The ancient Egyptian *Book of the Dead* had a great judgment scene, Lessing had read somewhere. When you died, Thoth, the ibis-headed god, weighed your heart against the Feather of Truth. You confessed your sins before Osiris, the Lord of the Dead, and if you lied you were lunch for a crocodile-headed monster. Needless to say, this sternly moral scene was followed by other chapters that told you how to lie safely to the Forty-Two Judges of the Dead, how to con Osiris, how to fool old Croco-Smile, and how to sashay on into the Fields of the Blessed without anybody laying a hand, claw, or tentacle on you!

Why did all the religions from that part of the world bother postulating an omnipotent, omniscient god who handed down iron-clad commandments—only to spend the rest of history figuring ways to bamboozle him? Must be something in the Middle Eastern psyche.

Patty jogged his arm for the salt shaker, and Lessing returned to reality with an palpable jolt. If somebody had suggested that Patty, all by herself, were a complete and sufficient reason for love, he wouldn't have known what to say.

Wrench slid back into his chair, polished his silverware on his napkin, and devoured his chowder in uncharacteristic silence. By the time their entrees arrived, however, he was telling Patty fantastic stories about Indian elephants and maharajahs. Lessing watched him curiously.

The salmon steak was good, and Liese's prawns were perfect. There was no spaghetti on the menu, but Patty allowed herself to be satisfied with her braised beef, even so. She was definitely no seafood lover.

The winking, garnet goblets, the tablecloths of red damask, and the silver-gleaming cutlery took Lessing back to the restaurant in Sioux City where his parents had celebrated their anniversaries. The memory was as hazy as candle smoke, yet it was immensely comforting. Angola and Syria and India and Ponape and Palestine and New Sverdlovsk faded away; they had never happened. Pacov and Starak were meaningless acronyms on file covers in some forgotten desk drawer. *This* was reality.

A buzz of conversation near the door caused him to glance in that direction. Half-a-dozen tall men in black uniforms had entered the restaurant and were looking around. One of them spotted Lessing, motioned his sable-hued comrades to wait, then made his way slowly along the aisle toward their table.

Something stirred deep in Lessing's memory but did not make it to the surface. He watched warily as the stranger approached.

"Hey, Lessing, you pogger!" Wrench crowed in his ear. "Don't you know this jizmo? Bill Easley . . . Cadre . . . from Kansas?"

The youth who bent over their table had a friendly, hawk-beaked, Midwestern face with a toothy grin. "Remember me, sir?" He extended a hand.

Lessing's memory finally yielded up a few faint images from the past, and he husked, "Yeah . . . sure. Haven't seen you for a long time. New Orleans, wasn't it? What're you doing now?"

"Second looie, sir. Cadre's Victory Battalion . . . brand new, like your own American Freedom Brigade. We're down near Lake Tahoe, guarding lib-reb prisoners from Sacramento and Fresno until they're handed on to PHASE." The hero-worship in Easley's voice was thick enough to pour over pancakes. He pointed back toward the clump of Cadre uniforms by the door. "Uh . . . could my friends come over and meet you, sir?"

"Fine. Glad to say hello." Lessing was back in control.

"Prisoners?" Wrench asked sharply. "PHASE?"

"Yessir. Cadre-Commander Wrench, isn't it?" Easley had met him too, but Wrench wasn't "military"; he attracted fewer groupies.

"Aren't lib-reb P.O.W.s supposed to be shipped immediately up to Oregon?" Wrench persisted.

Easley wasn't interested. "Uh . . . yessir. They are. But we pass 'em on to PHASE first for screening out the hard cases, you know. PHASE mostly sends 'em on to Oregon . . . just keeps a few of 'em, not P.O.W.s but some of the civilians, families, like." He beckoned to his companions. "Me'n my buddies're on leave . . . 'till we start gettin' prisoners in from San Francisco."

"God damn it," Wrench hissed. "Lessing, we have to *talk*!"

"Later." He refused to think about the Cadre and PHASE.

Wrench read Lessing's mood and let the matter drop for the moment. They greeted Easley's friends, four young Cademen who gawked, shook hands, and uttered stumbling courtesies. These were Lessing's fans, just as if he were a Banger star, and they must not go away disappointed.

When dessert and coffee were finished Wrench went over to Easley's table, and Lessing saw him pick up their check. Wrench had to be the greatest public relations man since P. T. Barnum!

They drove back to the hospital in a well-fed stupor. Wrench watched Patty's escort take her up in the elevator; then he said, "Got to find the kid a home. She can't live all her life in a hospital."

Lessing grimaced. "I can't take her. Another week, and I'm back with my unit. A military camp'd be no good for her."

"Liese, I know you don't have time . . . and no place for her either." Wrench jabbed the elevator button. "Same here. Jennifer has a great apartment, of course . . ." he saw Liese's look and smoothly changed gears, "but Jen's lifestyle might not be suitable for a young girl, to put it politely."

"Mrs. Mulder!" As soon as he spoke, Lessing knew he was right.

Liese nodded emphatically, and Wrench banged the button a second time. "Perfect, man! Patty gets spoiled rotten in the lap of decadent luxury! Let the Fairy Godmother stuff her with cookies and cake frosting! They'll both love it!" He rubbed his hands together, then sobered. "Now we have another, more serious problem for discussion!"

Lessing sighed. His mood of gentle peace was fading fast. "Goddard and PHASE?"

"Yeah. Listen, why don't you both come downtown with me to the com-link at Party headquarters? We have to talk to Goddard!"

"Matter?" Liese asked. "Urgent?"

"You heard Easley? Lib-reb prisoners are supposed to go straight from holding camps back of our front lines to reorientation villages in Oregon. Goddard's PHASE guys are screening them and taking some away. Why and where Easley didn't know."

"I caught it," Lessing said, "What the hell is that about?"

"Who knows? Lib-reb prisoners are military and Cadre business. PHASE doesn't have the authority to grab prisoners."

"Goddard can make up the authority. The lib-rebs emptied the jails all over the Southwest and Mexico to get troops. He can say that his boys are screening for criminals and escaped felons."

"Yeah, I suppose he can," Wrench mused. "Mulder persuaded Outram to make PHASE a Federal agency and let it coordinate all police functions across the country."

"Dumb! Outram could've used the FBI . . . and saved us all from Bill Goddard!"

"Outram doesn't trust the FBI. President Rubin packed it with smart-ass Eastern-Establishment lawyers who used to chase Outram's right-wing friends around the block."

"But prisoners?" Liese put in. "Civilians? Families? *Why*? Not partisans or saboteurs."

"You thinking what I'm thinking?" Lessing asked her. "'Special squads' and necktie parties? Bill's views on minority affairs start about a mile to the right from where Attila the Hun leaves off."

"He wouldn't do that!" she flared back. "We want trust! No death camps! Party directive."

"Okay, okay . . . green light! But if Big Bear Bill is doing what people used to accuse the Third *Reich* of doing, then he's going to run smack into me. I never signed on for that kind of stuff!"

"Give Goddard a chance!" Wrench protested. "We don't know anything yet! I'm going to put in a call to him. Then another to Mulder."

Liese frowned. "Alan and I? Do?"

Wrench slammed the elevator button again. "You, Liese, have been with the movement a long time. You can talk to Bill. And you, Lessing, command the American Freedom Brigade. You can order your officers not to cooperate with PHASE until we know what's going on!"

"Doing *what* with prisoners?" Liese rubbed at her bare arms as though she were cold.

Wrench answered her: "He could be doing just what Easley said: screening for hard cases, with everything legal and proper by the book."

"He could also be playing water sports," Lessing contradicted. "You know, fly prisoners out over the Pacific and see how they swim home."

Wrench held the elevator door for Liese. "One way to find out. C'mon, let's go down to my office."

It was four o'clock before they reached Party headquarters opposite the old Public Safety Building on Third and Cherry. Twenty years ago this truncated pyramidal skyscraper of black glass and steel had been erected to house tentacles of the King County administrative octopus. After Starak the Army and the decontamination services had taken it over, although Seattle had missed being hit for reasons no one knew. Outram's martial-law government then had occupied the lower floors for the next two years, while the remainder stayed empty. Now the building was refurbished, bright with American flags and Party bunting, and thronged with staffers on their way home from work.

Wrench shepherded them through the crowd, secured an elevator, produced a key, and pushed a button. The capsule-like car raced up the outside of the pyramid at stomach-clutching speed.

The doors opened on the twenty-fifth floor to reveal a square tablet of white light floating in the air. The hologram displayed letters of blue fire: PARTY OF HUMANKIND DEPARTMENT OF INFORMATION. WHOM DO YOU WISH TO SEE?

Wrench said, "Director's office." The hologram changed to read: PLEASE LOOK INTO THE EYE-PRINT BOX ON THE WALL TO YOUR LEFT AND STATE YOUR FULL NAME.

They obeyed, and the hologram glided away down the corridor flashing FOLLOW ME, PLEASE in luminous red.

Wrench almost glowed. He said, "Neat, eh? And security all the way!" He pointed up at camera-eyes in the ceiling. "Eighty-Five is watching us . . . watching everybody. Hell, in a year or two we won't need I.D. cards at all. Everything'll be done with eye- and voice-prints."

"Big Brother . . . ."

"Bull. That's gungo, as the Bangers say. Hell, America's been under surveillance for almost a century: cops, the I.R.S., credit checks, Social Security numbers, the F.B.I., you name it. Moreover, Eighty-Five can sniff out most crimes right now without adding a single chip! All we're doing is consolidating existing data banks. Today it takes twelve minutes to scan some jizmo's records in fifty-one states and six foreign countries . . . a week for a big corporation. With every computer system shaking hands with Eighty-Five, we'll have that info within seconds. But average folks won't get hurt. And we'll catch *and convict* the crooks, scammers, welfare frauds, and credit-card weasels. A lot of crime . . . from check-kiting to big, corporate hanky-panky . . . will be as *passe* as stage-coach robbery."

"People will protest. Like crazy!"

"They'll get used to it. They'll get real happy when they see what we save them in taxes, crime protection, and other ways. Folks're fed up with laws that don't work, rich lawyers, whimsical judges, and crooks that wriggle through the system like worms through a dog's gut! Our penal system's as outdated as the Bastille! We're working with Outram's allies in Congress to push some changes through. We may need amendments to the Constitution to do it, but we'll get it done. Everything legal, one hundred gubbin' percent."

"Extreme . . . ."

"Yeah. Draconian. I like that word. It's what America . . . the world . . . needs: tough love."

"You really should strain this through Eighty-Five a few more times before you bottle it!"

"We have. Eighty-Five predicts acceptance within five years."

"Um. You . . . and it . . . could still be wrong." Lessing wanted to rub his cheek, but that would hurt.

Wrench halted before a huge, double door whose leaves were seamless sheets of burnished copper. He threw out his arms dramatically and cried, "Open, sesame!" To his companions he whispered: "Doesn't matter what you say. The voice-print's what counts."

"Did you know about these changes?" Lessing murmured to Liese as they followed Wrench inside.

"Not everything. I . . . my staff . . . busy. Popularize the Party. Dorn."

"'Dorn' will have to do a heap of explaining to convince the folks down home: a police state that makes the Soviet Union's *Gulag* look as laid back as a Banger snuffy-doo orgy!"

Liese bridled. "Totalitarian state not necessarily cruel or brutal! Good government doesn't harm good citizens. Solves social problems. Helps economy. Deters crime. Efficient aid for needy, old, sick, mentally ill. Benefits outweigh restrictions!"

"You're great at summing up the Party platform, love. But people will balk at government by super-computer! It's not cricket, as the British say."

Wrench had paused inside the ornate reception room to stare into another blink-box beside a glass door leading to a complex of inner offices. He grinned back at them. "Not *cricket*? That's just it, Lessing: we're *not* playing cricket; we're talking *law*! Nobody mentioned good table manners or the Code of the West! Fair is protecting the citizens; unfair is letting the wolves go on munching on the sheep!"

"Logically you're right. But people don't always see things logically. It's people you're dealing with."

Wrench sniffed. "People need education. Then they'll see we're doing what's best for our ethnos. For the world, man!"

Wrench's office was austere, almost monkish: a long room with one glass wall overlooking the dizzy drop down the face of the pyramid, past roofs and wharves and ferryboats to Elliott Bay. Lessing glimpsed work tables, swing lights, green-glazed cabinets, and half a dozen unoccupied desks. A niche in one of the inner walls contained a photographic hologram of children playing volleyball before a brick school building. It was now after four in the afternoon, and the staff had gone home.

"Hello, Cadre-Commander Wren," Eighty-Five's smooth "Melissa Willoughby" voice emerged eerily from nowhere. "Program Director Meisinger, Mister Lessing."

Wrench said, "Access, encode, protect, and create a safe file. Name it Goddard-com. Find Bill Goddard."

"PHASE-Commander Goddard is in his office in Bethesda, Maryland. Do you require further location coordinates?"

"No. Establish contact."

The hologram of the schoolchildren blinked out, and Bill Goddard appeared in its place. He sat at a cluttered work table, surrounded by computer terminals, communications gear, and half-a-dozen PHASE personnel, among whom Lessing recognized Chuck Gillem and Dan Grote from Ponape. Plastic plates, coffee cups, and an empty, orange-splattered pizza carton littered the files and documents in front of Goddard and his crew. Eighty-Five had caught PHASE in the middle of a supper-cum-staff meeting. Goddard looked up at the camera, surprise evident upon his fleshy features.

"Well, well!" He leaned back in his chair. "Mary and two of her little lambs!"

Wrench started to make a sarcastic reply, but Lessing cut him short. "Bill, can we talk? Without the personalities?"

Goddard pursed his lips. "Why not?"

All three spoke at once, but Lessing got the floor. "We have a problem." He related what Easley had told Wrench.

Goddard shook his grizzled head. "You're an amazing dinker, Lessing. What kind of ka-ka do you smoke? Of *course* PHASE is screening lib-reb prisoners in California . . . for the best reasons in the world! Some of 'em are criminals with records long enough to step on, some are escapees, some are assassins who'd make a bee-line for Outram or Mulder . . . or you . . . if we let 'em go! Some are Vizzies . . . the same lovely bunch who dropped Starak on us!

Remember? What do you expect? Of *course* PHASE is looking at 'em!"

"Okay, okay," Wrench tried to mollify him. "But without consulting Lessing, here? Or Mulder? Or Outram?"

"Shit. We don't need consultation. PHASE has Federal police powers. And we *did* inform your guys on the scene. Check with Holm."

"Told you so," Lessing muttered to Wrench.

"Anyway, we don't grab off many of your lib-rebs. We question them, pull out those on the wanted list, and hand your guys legal warrants. I guess we've picked up a couple hundred of their laughable 'soldier boys' that way. No more. The rest we gave back to you . . . and you're welcome to 'em."

Wrench bit his lip. "I was told that PHASE was grabbing off a *lot* of lib-rebs. More than a couple hundred, anyway. Not all military, either, but civilians and families."

"Gub it, you *are* crazy! No such thing! Why would we want 'em? We don't have camps . . . tents . . . personnel." His eyes widened. "And don't tell me we're taking 'em off and shooting 'em! Don't try to pin *that* on PHASE!"

A voice off-camera said something, and Goddard grunted. "Hell, I'm told that our guys in California think *you're* disappearing some lib-reb boogies! Quite a few of 'em never made it to Oregon. We were about to ask *you* where the bus stopped."

"What?" Lessing was baffled. "I don't . . . !"

Wrench said, "Eighty-Five? You listening? Dammit, of course you are! Compare Cadre lists of lib-reb P.O.W.s taken in Sacramento with arrival rosters at the reorientation centers in Oregon. Print out any names not on both lists . . . and check for reasons why."

"You should've done that before you came hollering at me!" Goddard complained. He addressed Eighty-Five also: "Compare those Cadre lists with PHASE files of lib-rebs taken into custody in California and Oregon."

It took less than ten seconds. A box appeared in the com-link hologram to the left of Goddard's face. Names scrolled past.

"Hard-copy that!" Wrench commanded. A printer began to whine behind him.

Goddard pointed at his own screen. "Jesus, look! Those're mostly Jewish names . . . Rosenbaum, Siegel, Greenberg, Silverstein, Levine, Aaron . . . ."

"Isn't Daniel Jacoby the producer who made *Train to Darkness* . . . the movie that came out a few years ago about World War II?" Lessing asked. "You know, the Treblinka camp . . . Bella Gold starred in it?"

"Yes." Liese reached past him for the printout. "Reuben Meyer. Financier. Corporate raider."

"Marvin Weisskopf!" Wrench dug fingers into his wavy, brown hair. "Hey, I met that guy! Theoretical physics professor. M.I.T.! Eighty-Five, provide dossiers on these people!"

The printer churned, and paper piled up in the out-tray.

A name caught Lessing's eye. He bent down and read: "Arthur Shapiro. Consultant: American Zionist Action Committee of New York. Age fifty-nine. Male. Divorced."

He saw a white-wrapped mummy spreadeagled amidst glittering implements. Horror . . . .

Ice-blue . . . .

The printer stopped.

"What . . . where . . . these people?" Liese glared at Goddard.

The big man scowled back. "Not with us. Not PHASE. Ask Wrench, there, or Lessing."

"You're thumbing prisoners!" Lessing accused angrily. "Vanishing 'em . . . like in South America . . . death squads!"

"Bullshit!" Goddard roared back. "Not my people! PHASE is more disciplined than that! Your half-assed toy soldiers, now . . . !"

"Eighty-Five, list the units that took custody of the people who disappeared," Wrench ordered. "There must be documents . . . authorizations, transport, food, supplies, fuel for trucks. Records, damn it!"

The machine said, "PHASE Special Unit F near Sacramento. PHASE Special Unit M at Red Bluff. I can provide details, if you wish."

Goddard shoved his ruddy face forward, almost into the camera lens. "What the pog're you talking about? We don't *have* any such units! There *is* no 'Special Unit F' . . . no 'M' either! Somebody's fuckin' well lying!"

His eyes swivelled right to stare at the screen in PHASE headquarters. Lessing and his companions saw the same thing on theirs: a blue-and-gold shield, upon which the words "U.S. GOVERNMENT: ACCESS RESTRICTED" now flashed angry scarlet.

Before they could speak, the hologram changed again. The shield was replaced by a man's face: squarish, mottled pallid-pink, with ice-chip-blue eyes, and hair like tendrils of white frost. His expression was a mixture of surprise, wariness, and something like hostility.

"Just what is it you're looking for?" Janos Korinek inquired mildly in his high-piping, reedy voice.

The Party of Humankind will shortly have enough votes to become the majority party in the Congress of the United States. Now it is time to look ahead several years, to an era when our views will be the only ones of any importance across this great land. As we have said, *achieving* a revolution is not as important as what we do *after* it. The Party has a clear agenda for the future. We will select a leader—one with intelligence, courage, and vision—and we will surround him with experienced and talented subordinates. Each of these will be given specific responsibilities, and he will in turn be personally responsible for carrying them out. This was never possible under the inefficiency of a "democracy."

"What of the Constitution?" some will cry. What happened to the principle of "one person, one vote?" We will not abrogate this right for members of our own ethnos. Each of us will have a vote. Yet the Constitution nowhere precludes *more* than one vote per person! We therefore propose a system of *multiple votes*. We must have talented, qualified, and experienced people to lead us, rather than wealthy drones, professional politicians, or rabble-rousers. We certainly can*not* go on letting ourselves be governed by the whims of illiterates who persist in electing sports heroes, Banger stars, and charismatic TV preachers!

How will our system of multiple votes work? In *addition* to the one vote per person guaranteed as our basic right, we propose to grant one *further* vote for *each* of the following: (a) membership in good standing in the Party of Humankind; (b) high office in the Party of Humankind; (c) education to a university graduate degree—e.g., a Ph.D., a law degree, an M.D., or the like; (d) earned—not inherited—assets of one million U.S. dollars or more; (e) service in certain higher-level public offices (this vote will remain even after the person's term has expired); (f) recognized humanitarian service or heroism; (g) ten years of service in a branch of the armed services, the police, or as a fire-fighter; (h) special recognition in science, humanities, or industry; and (i) such further awards as shall be approved by Congress. Multiple qualifications in the same area—such as two Ph.D. degrees, several acts of heroism, etc.—will not earn further votes, of course. Theoretically, under this scheme one citizen can cast nine—and, later, perhaps even ten or more—votes. In fact, it would be a citizen of rare talents indeed who would have as many as six or seven votes, although three or four votes might not be uncommon.

Oh, but this is "elitist," the liberal will accuse. Yes, it is. We *are* elitist. Yet we do not support father-to-son aristocracy, the divine right of kings, the "old boys'" clubs of the Ivy League, or other outmoded ideas. The rewards given to our elite are *earned* through positive social action and service. Each member of our ethnos has the same right to work for multiple votes as every other. How does that deprive anyone of his or her rights?

Ah, but what about persons in our society who are not members of our ethnos? I shall not mince words. We are not

responsible for members of such groups. This is *our* society. We
live here, and we shall govern here. We thus strongly encourage others to go and live where their own ethnos-groups
hold sway. We see no need for them in our land.

**—from a speech given at the convention of the Party of
Humankind by Vincent Dorn, Chicago, Illinois, Friday, August
5, 2050**

The sad state of our welfare system is bound up with social
patterns prevalent among our less-affluent classes. Unassimilable minorities are a major factor in this chaos. Welfare was
originally intended to help the jobless, as well as those who
simply could not cope, for whatever reason. Now we have
added modern dilemmas that defy rational solution: for example, single parents, frequently burdened with infants they
cannot support; the sick, whose insurance cannot cover the
horrendous cost of medical bills; the homeless; habitual misfits,
who refuse to participate in society; disaffected urban adoles-
cents; drug addicts; petty criminals; alcoholics; unassimilated
immigrants; the mentally ill who have been cast out onto the
streets because we can't afford to institutionalize them; and
other categories. Some of these actually may deserve care—
and compassion. Yet our "paper monster" bureaucracy fails to
render effective aid. Some of these unfortunates can be
retrained; we will provide them with schools and jobs. For our
young people, we will provide a youth corps, similar to the
Reichsarbeitsdienst of the Third *Reich*: every young person will
spend some time serving either in the armed forces or in this
work corps. The days of the "gravy train" are over! Those on
welfare will either be truly deserving, or else they will work for
their bread like the rest of us!

What can we do about the single welfare mother who
cannot support her children? We do not favor the abortion of
genetically normal infants belonging to our ethnos, but we may
have to employ this unpleasant measure. Pacov and Starak
have removed the danger of overpopulation for the present;
now we are more concerned for the *quality* of our children. We
are determined to see that children born into our society are
not defective and that they receive the most love, the best
care, the best home life, and the best education we can
provide. If the parent or parents cannot support their offspring,
then we will do it for them. A stipend will be provided so that
the first child can live at home; any further children will be taken
over by the state. They will be cared for in state creches,
educated in state schools, and trained for jobs according to
their capabilities. I emphasize that this will be done with all the
love and kindness possible. This goes against the liberal
hypocrisy of "individual freedom," of course: a freedom that is
often a license to do anything one wants, whatever the cost
to society. We do *not* subscribe to the "right" of the individual
to become a burden upon his or her fellows. There is no "right"
to procreate mindlessly, no "right" to free and untrammeled
access to society's funds and services, and no "right" to create

more poor, ill-nourished, and uneducated mouths to feed! That is the worst sort of selfishness.

But isn't it wrong—terrible and monstrous—to deprive a parent of his or her children, to hand them over to an impersonal state to bring up? Not at all! The concept of state-run creches, orphanages, schools, and the like is hardly new. In the Middle Ages the nobility sent their children to be educated as pages in some other noble's castle. The British had their "public" boarding schools. The Spartans required all males from seven to twenty to live in dormitories and undergo rigorous military training. In fact, there is little intrinsic difference between our plan and the concept of public education, state-run vocational schools, fellowships and scholarships, and related structures of our present society. The welfare of the child is paramount, and state-adopted children will gain far more than they will lose. They will be allowed to see their birth-parents as often as they wish. If a birth-parent later becomes solvent enough to support the child at home, then this, too, will be arranged. Should a person continue to produce children without being able to support them, however, then the state will enforce further penalties, including mandatory sterilization. Again, single parents who do not belong to our ethnos will be required to settle abroad with their own people. We'll help them get there. We will *not* tolerate either mongrelization or the proliferation of unwanted and unassimilable persons who can never fully participate in our society. Should such people refuse to leave, then we will enforce our will with whatever means are needed. No excuses, no wishy-washy hypocrisy! We will not be blackmailed into being the Great White Father of all of the unfortunates of the world! Let other ethnos groups care for their own, just as we care for ours.

—from a speech given at the convention of the Party of Humankind by Vincent Dorn, Chicago, Illinois, Saturday, August 6, 2050

CHAPTER TWENTY-SIX

Monday, October 3, 2050

Korinek's office in the White House basement was stuffy in spite of the unseasonably cold weather. The sign on the mahogany desktop read: JANOS KORINEK, Special Aide to the President. The duties of his post were not specified.

Lessing and Wrench sat on the two tan, upholstered chairs in front of Korinek's desk, while Liese had chosen one end of the leather couch behind them.

"How long'll Mulder have with Outram?" Wrench asked.

Korinek inspected his wristwatch. "Ten minutes at most. The President has to be in the studio at ten. Foreign Press Association roundtable meeting."

Wrench got up and took a curious turn around the room. He paused by the stenographer's desk, the shredder, the blank-faced filing cabinets, and the copy machine. He pointed to the coffeepot.

Korinek's pale eyes followed him. "Sure," he said. "Have some. Sugar and sweetener in the drawer. Only plastic cream, though."

"Thanks. Black's fine." Wrench stirred his coffee, then wandered back. He indicated a tray on Korinek's desk that held perhaps a dozen ballpoint pens. Each bore a gold-stamped facsimile of the Presidential seal.

"These what Outram uses to sign bills?"

"Yes. The highway bill today. Ceremony's at four."

"Uh . . . would you have . . . ?"

"You want a pen?"

Wrench smiled ingratiatingly.

"Take one. We've got more." Korinek clicked open a cabinet behind him and took out a cardboard box. "Here. Have a souvenir."

Wrench chose a pen, put it in his coat pocket, then extracted it again to admire the seal. "Nice, hey, Lessing?"

Like a box of rubber bands: a small package jam-full of tangled contradictions. That was how Mulder had once described Wrench: one moment as sophisticated as a French *boulevardier*, the next, a country bumpkin gawking at the tall buildings!

"Uh . . . could I . . . ? Another one . . . for a little girl."

Korinek looked mildly annoyed, but he held out the box again. "She'd better be a taxpayer."

The door opened to reveal a flustered-looking secretary. Bill Goddard was right behind her. He ignored the woman and marched straight on into the office, letting her scuttle out of his path as best she could. She made an apologetic *moue* at Korinek and ushered herself out again.

The leather couch squawked as Goddard sprawled down next to Liese. He pulled off his brown PHASE cap and said, "Sorry I'm late. Canada."

He didn't have to explain. Two days ago the Province of Quebec had declared itself an independent state and applied for membership in the United Nations. Canada's army was busy elsewhere: the prairie provinces and Ontario were clamoring to become American states, as were Prince Edward Island and Newfoundland, while British Columbia had closed its borders and sequestered foreign businesses and bank accounts. Upheaval and violence had followed. The English-speaking Quebecois were fleeing for the Ontario border, harried by gangs of French youths intent on keeping them from carrying away Quebec's wealth—or much of anything else. The premier of Quebec, Ferdinand Marchand, had requested American aid, and President Outram had responded with Marines, Cadre troops, and a platoon of PHASE police. A full-fledged invasion force now occupied the scenic park on top of Mont Real, overlooking the smouldering battle ground that had recently been the prosperous city of Montreal.

The wheels and cogs were truly beginning to fly off, as Lessing had gloomily predicted.

On the other hand, Goddard and some other Party leaders were ecstatic. What better opportunity to squelch the Vizzies' pestiferous Dee-Net and put an end to Zionist control of the Canadian economy? Send the Vizzies back to their former homelands in Russia and Eastern Europe! Let the other Canadian provinces do the same, and then they might be allowed to join the American union.

In a few weeks there would be a grand ceremony. The government of Quebec would be handed back to its rightful owners, the French Quebecois. English emigrants would be quietly compensated, a number of firms would change hands—nominally, at least— and the most obstreperous of the French youth-gangs would be marched off to re-education camps to learn manners. As Goddard said, they were tough kids, but they were trainable: a likely nucleus for a Canadian branch of the Party, once the rough edges were knocked off.

Goddard turned to Wrench. "You asked him yet?"

"No. Mulder's handling it. He's with Outram right now."

Korinek folded pale fingers like uncooked sausages on the blotter before him. "Let me guess: you want to know about the lib-reb prisoners in California?"

"Dinkin' right," Goddard declared truculently. "PHASE never took 'em, and we want to know where they are. If you're thumbing 'em . . . !"

"On the contrary." The aide leaned back in his contour chair. "It's a matter of facing reality. Looking at things as they are."

"What's that supposed to mean?"

"Just what I said. You can rock the boat only so far, then it rocks back."

Goddard said, "Okay, what's the bottom line? What're you getting at?"

"I don't see any harm in telling you. Outram's giving your boss the same scam."

"I think I can guess," Wrench muttered to Lessing.

"Can you? To make a long story short, we're *not* thumbing prominent Jews; we're *saving* them. Our agents, temporarily decked out as special units of your PHASE police, are transporting them to comfortable . . . and distant . . . holding camps until your movement has run its course and fizzled out. Once things return to normal, they can resume their lives."

No one spoke.

"Look," Korinek said in his high-pitched, thin voice. "There are certain realities in America, in the world, that you have to live with. A powerful Jewish presence is one of them. Not total control, not a secret master-plot. At least, we don't perceive it that way . . . ."

"The Party . . . !" Goddard began. "We won't tolerate . . . ."

"The Party? *What* Party? Don't delude yourself! Here, Goddard, let me make it simple. You and your 'Party' are freaks, anomalies, a bunch of fringe crazies who took advantage of a ghastly catastrophe and a sick old man to make a grab for power. The rest of us don't want you, your Party, your Vincent Dorn, or your jumped-up neo-Nazi theories!"

Goddard reared up to tower over the desk. "*Freaks*? Crap! The American majority is with *us*! *You're* the anomalies . . . the buttoned-down liberal 'elite' . . . the money-men . . . the self-appointed 'culture' aristocrats . . . the 'Civil Rights' jizmoes nobody wants . . . not even the Blacks, who've had a bellyful of Jewish landlords and merchants and patronizing liberal do-gooders! *We're* America!" He reached for his peaked cap. "We'll see what President Outram has to say about this!"

"You'll find the President essentially agrees with my point of view. He wants the Blacks and certain other . . . uh . . . unassimilable minorities out. But he's ready to work with the traditional interests to keep our Jewish citizens."

"'Traditional interests?'" Goddard parroted. "Traditional money, traditional media, traditional Jewish power! In spite of all Outram has done, the Jews and their collaborators still have a death grip on this country! On the world!"

"We haven't hurt a single Jew," Wrench put in, very reasonably, in the same tone he used when lecturing to the uncommitted. "They're being sent to the Izzie colonies in Russia, sure, but nobody's stopping them from taking their personal property and whatever else they can use there, no matter what Dee-Net's propaganda says."

"We think our Jews are valuable here. They add many cultural dimensions to our society."

"God damn it!" Goddard flared. "Some of us don't shy away from calling a spade a spade! We are *tired* of Jews! We have had it up to *here* with Jews! For two pogging thousand years we have worried about Jews . . . for or against! We've kicked 'em out, we've put 'em down, we've been nice to 'em, we've invited 'em in, we've leaned over backwards to remedy 'past wrongs,' we've got down on our knees and apologized for accusing them of killing Christ . . . ! And what do they do? They work night and day to bleed us, to subvert our values, to subjugate us, and to make us over in their image! We'll find your 'holding camps' and put your 'prominent Jews' on the next plane to Ufa! If you get in our way . . . ."

"You'll what? The armed services are ours."

"Bull*shit*! You want to ask 'em? Pick up your goddamned telephone and call General Hartman . . . General Dreydahl . . . Admiral Canning!"

"Some of those men aren't what you think. Others will have to resign very soon or end up in custody. Your Cadre? Colonel Lessing, I believe your units are currently up in Quebec, watching the pretty autumn leaves."

"How in hell could Outram agree to this?" Wrench wondered. "Last time Mulder talked to him . . . ?"

"Money?" Lessing surmised. "Power?"

"Can't be. Outram's never taken 'contributions' to change his opinions or his vote before. And he *has* power. Power he's too sick to use any more."

"Maybe that's your answer."

Liese rose and straightened her skirt. The smoke-grey, silken fabric shimmered as she moved. "I think we've heard enough."

Korinek got to his feet also, a pale, solid wall of a man. "We'll give you time to dismantle your Party apparatus and crawl back into the woodwork. A month. No more. After that it'll be treason trials, I.R.S. audits . . . arrest, imprisonment, and whatever else we have to do to get rid of you!"

"Nice meeting you again," Wrench observed affably.

Korinek stroked his fish-belly-white jaw and watched them depart.

Gordy Monk met them outside at their car. Three more escort vehicles stood nearby, engines running. "The President's secretary just phoned," the bodyguard told them. "Mr. Mulder's coming down."

They could see from the angry color in Mulder's cheeks that his meeting with Outram had gone much like theirs with Korinek. He didn't say a word. Goddard got into his armored PHASE limousine, made a "see you later" sign, and sped off, leaving Mulder and the others to climb into their own vehicle. They would meet back at the Party's Washington headquarters, the big hotel on M Street that had been commandeered after Starak had turned its owners into permanent absentee landlords.

As they drove, Wrench wriggled out of his uniform jacket, although the damp October morning was not hot. They turned onto Pennsylvania Avenue and headed for Washington Circle.

"Stop the car," Wrench ordered. Monk obediently pulled over to the curb.

Mulder leaned forward and whispered, "You think this will work?"

Wrench made the finger-signal that warned of the likelihood of microphones. Aloud, he said, "Gordy, see if there's anything wrong with the engine, will you? The damned thing's heating up again." Their chauffeur got out and raised the hood.

Liese and Lessing had not been told what was to happen. This was standard Party policy: the fewer who knew, the fewer slip-ups. They watched as Wrench opened a compartment in the armrest and took out a plastic-wrapped object, some ten inches long. The covering came off to reveal a lobster-looking thing of blue-black metal. Wrench muttered about "seeing what was wrong with the car," opened his door, and contrived to drop his coat into the gutter. He swore disgustedly. When he picked the garment up again, the lobster was gone, down into the storm grating beside the curb.

"It's green light now, Commander Wren," Gordy announced. He banged the hood down, made a show of wiping his hands on his handkerchief, and got back in.

The rest of the trip passed without incident.

The "safe room" in Mulder's suite in the old hotel was a windowless box five meters square, perhaps once a serving pantry for the wealthy guests who had once dwelt here. Liese had furnished it with a pair of sofas covered with sombre, brown-and-grey Navajo blankets, a desk, four streamlined, black Glassex chairs that resembled agonized modern sculptures, and two comma-shaped coffee tables that looked like Yin and Yang. The pictures on the beige walls were hotel kitsch: big, ornate, gilded frames containing uninspired landscapes.

"All right," Lessing said when he had shut the insulated door. "Let's hear it."

Wrench made a little bow. "Eighty-Five?"

A red light on the desk blinked on, and the machine's Melissa Willoughby voice purred, "Yes, Commander Wren?"

"How's our pen doing?"

"Quite well. The transmitter has already sent me twelve telephone conversations and seven verbal messages which were directed to my White House terminal."

"So *that* was why you wanted a presidential pen!" Liese shook her head in wonderment.

"Yup. I kept the first pen he gave me. I fished our replacement out of my pocket, palmed it, and traded it for one out of Korinek's box." He pulled a pen from his jacket and flipped it to her. "Here's the first one. For Patty."

The computer said, "I have become quite expert at miniaturizing my components and peripherals, Miss Meisinger. The pen transmits signals on the frequencies I myself employ. The second device, the one Commander Wren dropped off on your return, is a mobile transceiver; it enhances the pen's messages and forwards them by tight beam to my terminal here."

"Eighty-Five's got it down to a fine art!" Wrench chortled. "Damn near subatomic circuitry! Creates its own 'waldoes' . . . manipulators, like hands . . . miniaturizes 'em, then uses those to make the next set still smaller, and so on. A lot fancier than the Magellan series the Army's using . . . or anything Korinek and his kikibirds have developed!" He lay back on the sofa, obviously pleased with himself.

"Many of my extensions are now mobile: cameras, audio recorders, infrared and X-ray sensors."

"You could create a tiny poison needle, on tracks, like a tank . . . the size of an insect!" Wrench made a stabbing motion, then rolled up his eyes and feigned death.

"No, Commander Wren. I am specifically ordered *not* to harm human beings."

"*Directly* harm them. I remember one time, right here in Washington . . . ."

"If you command me to seek ways around my directives, then I will do that." Eighty-Five's sugary voice was expressionless.

"I think you *enjoy* looking for 'ways around,'" Wrench commented.

"'Enjoy' is a verb I cannot fully comprehend. I *am* programmed to employ energy, ingenuity, and intuition in solving problems."

Mulder idly opened a desk drawer and extracted a pad of hotel stationery. The letterhead was years old. "We don't have time for chit-chat. What do Korinek's conversations contain? His messages to you?"

Lessing interjected: "And why can't you just replay *all* of your White House terminal's interchanges with Korinek? Why just the ones picked up by Wrench's eavesdropping device?"

"Can't," Wrench told him. "Like the two of us separately playing the same computer game. You shoot down your Martians, I shoot down mine. What with sneaky access codes and passwords, Eighty-Five can't tell us what's in somebody else's file, or even acknowledge that that file exists. We can only hear what Korinek says to *his* Eighty-Five terminal, if Wrench's transmitter picks it up and sends it to *our* Eighty-Five terminal. *Our* Eighty-Five can't read *Korinek's* Eighty-Five files, pen or no pen. To access them, we'd have to have Korinek here, willing to use his eye- and voice-prints, verbal codes, and whatever else. We've got our private files, Korinek and his boys have theirs, and the Army chiefs have theirs. And 'never the twain shall meet.'"

Mulder had grown impatient. "What's in the conversations?"

Eighty-Five inquired, "Do you wish summaries or verbatim replays?"

"Summaries will do."

"Message one: call to Mr. Korinek's mistress, Ms. Dolores Carrera; he will be working overtime tonight and will contact her tomorrow. Message two: call to Mr. William Michael Tangen, Special Treasury Agent, Grade 9, to arrange for a racquetball court and a sauna at the Newport Club this afternoon at 1500 hours. Message three: call to his secretary reminding her to search for the file dealing with President Outram's Grand Coulee Dam rebuilding project . . . ."

"Anything relating to the Party of Humankind? To us?"

"Message five: a telephone call to an unidentified party. Shall I replay it?"

"Yes," Mulder and Wrench answered simultaneously.

Korinek's reedy voice filled the room. "Put me through. Yes. Korinek. They were here. . . . Yes . . . I told them. I think they're scared, but they won't run." Silence. Then: "If that's what's needed. I'll get Horowitz on it . . . ."

"Horowitz?" Lessing whispered.

Eighty-Five heard him. "Ninety-three per cent certainty that the reference is to Colonel Abraham L. Horowitz, U.S. Army, commanding Special Ranger Force 'Black Lightning' at Fort Meade, Maryland."

Korinek's voice resumed: " . . . and we'll take the bastards out. You coordinate it from your place. . . . Oh, there won't be any slip-ups. The thirteenth? Fine. . . . Yes, I'll see that somebody handles the West Coast and the South. . . . Finley? And Arris? . . . Yes, and Oakes. They'll do." Another pause. "Listen, I have to go. Get back to you. . . . Right."

"Take us *out*?" Mulder exclaimed. "Some sort of military action?"

"It's not impossible," Lessing stated. "Remember Ponape?" He himself did not—could not—remember much about that period of his life.

Wrench tugged at his lower lip. "The thirteenth? Of October?" He peered at his wristwatch calendar. "We've got ten days!"

Mulder was already asking Eighty-Five for data: troop schedules, readiness reports, and dossiers. He swivelled to face Lessing: "Get your Cadre troops back here from Canada. Make excuses: rest and relaxation, normal rotation, minor incidents here that need their attention. Liese, you inform Sam Morgan, Jennifer Caw, Grant Simmons, Hans Borchardt . . . all our leadership! Wrench, work with

Eighty-Five and see what more you can find out. Where the hell is Bill Goddard?"

"Here." The big man bulked in the doorway. "Traffic . . . ."

"Fill him in," Mulder ordered Wrench. "We'll need PHASE to find that secret camp Korinek mentioned."

"And to see to this guy Horowitz," Wrench added. "As well as Finley, Arris, Oakes, and the rest of Korinek's Seven Dwarves."

Lessing was off on another tangent. "Eighty-Five, you said Korinek's call was to an unidentified person? Can you trace it? Get the number from the beep-tones when he dialed?"

"I have already done that. It is a local number: 555-9201."

"What? '555' is an empty prefix . . . the telephone companies don't issue it." Wrench scratched his chin in puzzlement.

"This appears to be an exception," Eighty-Five said. "I do not find it in any directory, nor is it in the 'unlisted number' files. It is also not recorded as a secret government number."

"How the hell can that be? Trace it!"

"Mr. Korinek has ordered my White House terminal to institute baffles and tell-tales to prevent that."

"You mean you are actually blocking . . . obstructing, fighting . . . *yourself*?" Lessing snapped his fingers in frustration. "For God's sake!"

"Quite so. As you humans say, 'I am my own worst enemy.'" Lessing thought he heard an audible chuckle. Wrench's efforts to give Eighty-Five a sardonic sense of humor were apparently succeeding.

"We must know who that unidentified person is!" Mulder said. "Priority one!"

"If only we could access Korinek's Eighty-Five files!" Liese put in.

Lessing considered. "Eighty-Five, you said we could *order* you to try to solve problems. All right, I'm ordering: find a way around Korinek's passwords and get us into his Eighty-Five files."

The machine seemed to ponder. Then it said, "There is a way, although my creators would be alarmed to learn that I am using it. I can accept a direct command from a high Government official, however. Mr. Mulder, as Secretary of State, will you issue such an order?"

Mulder cleared his throat. "Yes. I do so issue."

"Very well. If you wish to observe, you must go to my hologram projector room, or else have the apparatus brought here."

"Let's go!" Wrench urged. "Up a floor, in what used to be the penthouse fun-and-games suite." He did not wait for the others to follow.

The penthouse was another relic of a bygone age: lavish, luxurious, provided with everything from billiards to bedrooms, a huge sauna and jacuzzi, full-wall TV, a landscaped terrace big enough to land a small plane on, and all the trappings of opulent decadence. In the bar Lessing quickly found the refrigerator behind the sleek, bubble-swirl Glassex counter; it was stocked with mixers and beer, but somebody had liberated all the hard liquor. He chose a bottle of fancy German beer—God knew how long it had been there—and poked around in the clever, little cupboards until he discovered a glass—as well as a pair of see-through panties and a set of handcuffs. The old hotel must've seen some fun parties . . . !

Wrench and Liese busied themselves with the projector equipment, while Goddard stepped out onto the terrace to confer with his PHASE subordinates on the portable vid-phone. Mulder was left to sit alone in a plastic armchair before the pit-fireplace with its fake logs and phony, crackling flames. Above his round, bald head, a holo-photo of Susan Kane, defunct Hollywood's last and greatest bitch-goddess, undulated in beads and transparent Arabian Nights silks. That had been part of the Theda Bara revival of two decades ago: a shadow from the past, a relic of another age.

A memory . . . ice-blue.

Lessing blinked to find Mulder talking to him. "Jonas was never like that, Alan. I can't understand the change I saw in him today. And why does he let himself be dominated by that man Korinek?" He sounded querulous, tired, and, it had to be admitted, old.

"Perhaps his illness, sir."

"Who in hell is Korinek, anyway?" Wrench threw in from the projector console. "A Vizzie? An Izzie? The FBI? Some other coven of would-be ass-kickers?"

"Jew-lickers, you mean! A race traitor. A very deep mole," Goddard answered from the deepening afternoon shadows by the shuttered terrace windows. "Janos Korinek is a lapsed Catholic, Czech ancestry, family in this country since the late 1890's. Held liberal views in college, then apparently 'turned' and went over to Outram. Loyal as the family dog for fifteen years. One civil rights leader called him 'Simon Legree.' The Black Citizens' Council accused him of masterminding the Cleveland race riots back in 2038. Seems he *loves* the Jews, though. They probably planted him."

"Jonas never completely agreed with us," Mulder continued as though he had not heard, "but he'd never betray us."

"Ready! Lights, camera, action!" Wrench called. "Eighty-Five?"

"Here, Commander. My tests show green light on the equipment, a faulty power-cell at N-435, and an improperly placed projector at Apex Three."

Wrench corrected the projector setting. The power-cell could wait.

Janos Korinek appeared before them.

They all gasped, and Wrench uttered a Banger obscenity that even Lessing had never heard.

"Do not be alarmed," the Korinek-image said. "It is I, Eighty-Five. I will now employ Mr. Korinek's verbal codes." The voice went up an octave and took on the agent's raspy, reedy quality. "Eighty-Five, Simple Simon down to London went. Took a wife and bought a tent."

The response was immediate and chilling. Another voice, much darker, colder, and crisper, said, "Took his wife and tent back home."

"Never more abroad to roam."

"You are in, Agent Korinek. I recognize you."

Lessing would have said something, but Liese put a finger to his lips. Across the penthouse, Goddard's features resembled a fierce, African mask, his mouth a round "O."

"Replay messages 7-D-151 through 7-D-157."

"Hologram facilities?"

"Present."

The Korinek image flicked out, and another came into being: a warm, delicately furnished room. An American flag stood beside a big desk.

"The Oval Office," Wrench breathed. "Outram!"

The man behind the desk was obviously ill. The heavy, fleshy jowls hung loose and flabby, spotted and wrinkled and splotched like a turkey's wattles. The hands, clenched on the desktop, were empty bags of skin over stick-like bones. They trembled. A thick shawl hid the President's torso and sagged down over his wheelchair to the floor.

The camera panned to show another man in the room: Herman Mulder.

This was a replay of Mulder's morning meeting!

Mulder hissed, "What . . . ? Why . . . ?"

"I sense other operators, Agent Korinek!" the machine warned. "Security clearances, please."

The hologram of Korinek reappeared. "None available. Emergency, path 250, file D."

"Incorrect. Access denied." The picture snapped off, and the light died.

Mulder spoke into the resulting void: "Eighty-Five, what . . . what did you do? How?"

"I have Agent Korinek in my files. I created a hologram of him, using my highest resolution, and showed that image to my White

House terminal. I . . . it . . . read the image's retinal patterns, voice-print, and microscopic pore structure. These produced correct physical identification. My record of Commander Wren's pen-transmitter then provided the verbal codes needed for access."

"You fooled yourself *with* yourself!" Wrench marvelled.

"But what have we learned?" Liese asked. "Mr. Mulder can tell us what he and Outram talked about."

"There is something else," Eighty-Five instructed. "Observe!"

Outram appeared again in the center of the room. The picture zoomed close to show a huge, three-dimensional left hand and wrist.

The thumb showed a square, black hole.

"N-435," Liese cried. "Outram is a . . . a . . . hologram!"

Korinek returned and held up his left hand. His thumb showed the same black, empty blot. "Quite so. I . . . we . . . must repair this power-cell."

"Where is the real Outram?" Goddard sounded baffled. "What the hell?"

Eighty-Five spoke over their questions. "Everyone, please! Absolute silence is required. I shall re-access my White House terminal, utilizing the same method. I must do this quickly since various watchdog systems are being activated even now."

The access sequence was repeated. Lessing found himself clutching his glass so tightly that he had to will his fingers to let go. Liese, on his other side, made a muffled sound of protest, and he released her too.

"Eighty-Five," the Korinek-figure said, "Where is President Outram?"

"Code five!" the cold, mechanical voice demanded.

"Never give a sucker a snowball in hell."

"You are in, Agent Korinek." The machine paused, then said, "President Jonas Outram remains exactly where you put him: in a grave in Arlington National Cemetery under the name of Sergeant Orville Judd Hickam, killed in action in Mexico on March 18, 2050."

Mulder could not restrain himself: "He's *dead*? Jonas is *dead*?"

"Identify the unknown operator, please!"

"Ignore . . . ." The rest was lost in a confusion of voices.

Korinek flared and vanished, and a familiar blue-and-gold shield appeared in his place. The scarlet lettering on the shield read: U.S. GOVERNMENT: ACCESS RESTRICTED.

A new Janos Korinek formed before them. This one was visibly angry—and shaken.

"You people are becoming a nuisance!"

"You killed Jonas Outram," Mulder hissed. "The President of the United States! You killed him!"

The image shifted to Outram at his desk. "Nonsense . . . ."

"Don't bother," Goddard snarled. "We *know*! Remember Sergeant Hickam?"

"All right." The aide shrugged. "But we didn't kill him. He died of liver complications two months ago. It was expedient to keep him alive . . . ."

"Until you could get a handle on us and our movement!" Goddard accused. "Until you could get your 'traditional interests' ready for a come-back!"

"Good reasons, don't you think? No? Well, then, what do you plan to do about it? Tell the world? We'll cheerfully admit our deception. It was in the public interest not to have a power vacuum at this time in our history. Certain high-level government officials decided to keep the President 'alive,' at least until the lib-reb war was over. I doubt if there'll be a problem. On the other hand, we happen to know that your 'Vincent Dorn' is a hologram too. What if we expose *him*? Our red-blooded American citizenry may not like to be led by a computerized composite cartoon-character. How about a joint balloon-popping party?"

"You have committed treason," Lessing stated heavily. "The President dies . . . under what circumstances nobody knows . . . and is secretly buried. You take over the country and run it to suit yourself . . . you and the power-groupies you represent! No, I don't think treason's the right word. *Coup d' etat* fits better."

"Don't strain your limited vocabulary, Mister Lessing. Let's just agree that we both have things to lose by rocking the boat right now."

"Screw that!" Goddard growled. "You'll be in PHASE custody inside of twenty minutes!"

"I doubt it." They could see Korinek's fingers dancing over objects on his desk, though the camera angle prevented a clear view of what they were. He was doubtless marshalling his response.

"We *will* go public with Jonas' death," Mulder said. "You'll see it on Home-Net as soon as we can get it out. You can reveal 'Dorn' if you want. We're strong enough to withstand that. We used him to get our message across in the most palatable, charismatic way we could, like an ad-campaign. Americans will understand that! You used 'Outram' to deceive the people while you made major, secret changes in policy. There *is* a difference."

"We can also reveal your Nazi past, *Herr* Müller. Wasn't your grandfather one of the big fish who got away: Heinrich Müller, the head of the Gestapo?"

"What does that matter now?" Mulder made an angry gesture of dismissal. "What does *anything* matter after Pacov and Starak and all the horrors committed by you non-Nazis . . . or anti-Nazis . . . or Jews, or . . . or whatever you call yourselves."

"Let's just say we like the status quo. No sweeping changes in our executive boardrooms."

"We will make those changes. We have come too far to be stopped. You, however, have reached the end of your tether. The world is tired of deceptions and machinations and manipulation by a power-elite. We . . . our ethnos . . . will prevail."

"Just watch Home-Net for the next thrilling installment!" Wrench warbled.

Korinek made no answer. His image shimmered and disappeared, leaving them blinking in the golden, afternoon dimness within the eery, empty penthouse.

An existing order of things is not abolished by merely proclaiming and insisting on a new one. It must not be hoped that those who are the partisans of the existing order and have their interests bound up with it will be converted and won over to the new movement simply by being shown that something new is necessary. On the contrary, what may easily happen is that two different orders will exist side by side and that a *Weltanschauung* is transformed into a party, above which level it may not be able to raise itself afterwards. For a *Weltanschauung* is intolerant and cannot permit another to exist side by side with it. It imperiously demands both its own recognition as unique and exclusive, and a complete transformation in accordance with its views throughout all the branches of public life. It can never allow the previous state of affairs to coexist.

The same holds true of religions. Christianity was not content with erecting an altar of its own. It had first to destroy the pagan altars. It was only in view of this passionate intolerance that an apodictic faith could grow up. And intolerance is an indispensable condition for the growth of such a faith.

It may be objected here that in these phenomena which we find throughout the history of the world we have to recognize mostly a specifically Jewish mode of mentality. That may be a thousandfold true; and it is a fact deeply to be regretted. The appearance of intolerance and fanaticism in the history of mankind may be deeply regrettable, and it may be looked upon as foreign to human nature, but the fact does not change conditions as they exist today. . . .

But a genuine *Weltanschauung* will never share its place with something else. Therefore it can never agree to collaborate in any order of things it condemns. On the contrary it feels obliged to employ every means in fighting against the old order and the world of ideas belonging to that order and to prepare the way for their destruction. These purely destructive tactics, the danger of which is so readily perceived by the enemy that he forms a united front against them for his common defense, and also the constructive tactics, which must be aggressive in order to carry the new world of ideas to success—both these phases of the struggle call for a body of resolute fighters. Any new philosophy of life will bring its ideas to victory only if the most courageous and active elements of its epoch and its people are enrolled under its standards and grouped firmly together in a powerful fighting organization. To achieve this purpose it is absolutely necessary to select from the general system of doctrine a certain number of ideas which will appeal to such individuals and which, once they are expressed in a precise and clear-cut form, will serve as articles of faith for a new association of men. While the program of the ordinary political party is nothing but a recipe for cooking up favorable results out of the next general elections, the program of a *Weltanschauung* represents a declaration of war against an existing order of things and against present conditions: in short, against the established *Weltanschauung*.

—*Mein Kampf*, Adolf Hitler

CHAPTER TWENTY-SEVEN

"Nothing?" Goddard asked.

"Nothing," Lessing confirmed. "Nobody's seen anything of Korinek. Probably too soon for him to react anyway."

"Just as well. Gives us time." The other man looked at his watch. "Reminds me that somebody's got to go out to Dulles Airport and pick up Grant Simmons and his crew."

Wrench rolled off Lessing's sofa and sprawled full-length on the mustard-colored carpet. "Why don't you and Liese get an interactive TV? I'm tired of watching reruns of the heroic life and ignominious death of Jonas Outram."

"When's the funeral . . . memorial, or whatever you call it?" Goddard grumbled.

"Tomorrow," Wrench answered. "The President's office confirmed his death last night. Korinek made his lame excuse about 'national need,' and Home-Net and Omni-net then devoted four hours of prime-time to roasting him for his deception. Yama-Net hasn't said much; they're waiting to see which way the axe crumbles and the cookie falls, as they say. At least Dee-Net's a pile of rubble, up in Montreal. *They* won't be chiming in."

"Korinek still hasn't revealed our little secret about 'Dorn.'" Goddard stretched lazily. "Why, no one seems to know."

"Probably figures nobody'd believe him after the Outram scam. Or maybe he's waiting until he can get his act together." Lessing held his Belgian automatic pistol up to the light and wiped away an imaginary speck of dust. "When he's got his toadies in Congress primed, his subpoenas drafted, and his military doggies in line, we'll hear from him. Believe it."

Goddard snorted up a chuckle. "What did Byron Lee do when Mulder told him Outram was thumbed? The old fart must've puddled his panties when he found out he was the President of the United States!"

Wrench laughed too. "He dithered, of course, but he promised to make a manful . . . or wimpful . . . try at filling Outram's size thirteen's."

Lessing wanted to get out, breathe some air, and see some new faces. He laid his pistol down next to its cleaning kit and asked, "Where'd Liese go?"

"Upstairs," Goddard tilted heavy eyebrows skyward. "With Mulder."

"So who's picking up Simmons, then?"

"Not me!" Wrench protested. "No way! Let somebody else do it. No more hanging around airports for old C. H. Wren!"

"You going to make Liese go again?" Lessing inquired pointedly. She'd been handling much of the Party's logistics while the menfolk sat and planned, and sat and argued, and sat and watched TV—and mostly just *sat*.

Waiting: the soldier's curse.

"Oh, shit," Goddard groaned. "Maybe I can grab Salter, or Gruber, or Kimberley. Yeah . . . Salter's new. He'll go pick up Simmons just because he doesn't know any better."

"Where's Morgan?" Wrench hobbled up to pour himself more coffee from the pot in the suite's tiny kitchen nook. "He ought to be here . . . if Korinek hasn't already unzipped him."

"Relax. He's green light." Lessing answered. "Mulder talked to him on the phone yesterday. Said he's still in Chicago and can't get a plane. Only three flights a day since Starak, and they're booked solid for a week in advance."

"Borchardt?"

"How can *he* help, all the way from Germany? You want him to send you some *Panzer* divisions?"

"God damn it, we're going to *need* 'em!" Wrench splayed spidery fingers in his wavy, dark hair.

"Jennifer going to arrive in time for the fun?" Goddard interjected. He was doing his best to distract Wrench and keep him from worrying. There were times when Big Bear Bill was actually likeable.

Lessing said, "No. She and her mother are holding down the West Coast."

"Hosing down, you mean!" Wrench made an effort to laugh.

"It's Jen who enjoys getting hosed!" Goddard gave them an arch I've-been-there-and-I-ought-to-know look. There were times, too, when Goddard was eminently dislikeable.

Wrench gulped the last of his coffee. He'd had five cups since breakfast, and the caffeine was hitting him. "Korinek's going to bust it all wide open: wicked Nazi subversives, international plotters, monsters . . . devils . . . the whole coconut full of ka-ka!"

"Stay koozy, foozy, as the Bangers say," Goddard soothed him. "He hasn't done it yet. And so what if he does? We've got power now: Mulder's big business friends, the media, the majority of White America. Most of the generals are on our side too. Rollins is coming back from Mexico. Dreydahl is ready to bongo."

"Yeah, but we can't contact Hartman. He doesn't answer our calls."

"Expected. Win some, lose some. Korinek must've got to him. But Admiral Canning's still ours. So are a lot of the new brass in the Pentagon."

Wrench turned his coffee cup around and around and peered inside. "I get the feeling we're the Kerenski government in Russia in 1917: an intermediate step between the Czar and the communists. Intermediate steps get stepped on."

"You want a better parallel?" Goddard scoffed. "Rubin's the Czar, Outram's Kerenski, Korinek is a failed counter-revolution, and *we're* the Bolsheviks. Can you imagine *us* as commies?"

Lessing drew back the drapes to look out over the grey, black, and brown vista of Washington in October. His suite offered a panoramic view south over the Potomac River. Liese loved it. She was such an urban person.

Goddard broke into his thoughts. " . . . Canada, I said. When're your Cadre troops coming in from Canada?"

"Um? Oh . . . the first elements'll be landing at Andrews Air Force Base this afternoon. The Chief of Operations there is friendly. His uncle is Scott Harter, the Secretary of Defense. We haven't told anybody . . . not even Eighty-Five." He glanced up at the sensor he had "accidentally" broken when he moved into this suite. "Tim Helm'll phone me when they get in. There's no way Korinek can find out."

"Why wait, then? Tonight we get one of Mulder's judge-buddies to sign an arrest warrant for treason, and we go pay a visit on Mr. Jew-sucker Korinek!"

"Collar him in the White House? Come on! You and who else's army?"

"*Our* army. Your Cadre and my PHASE. What's he going to do . . . hole up for a siege? Call down a missile strike on the Rose Garden? He'll have to give up gracefully . . . and we'll have it all live and throbbing on Home-Net."

"Nothing on TV now," Wrench grumbled irrelevantly. "No news . . . maybe they've clamped down. Maybe Korinek's making his move and ordered the media zipped up!"

"Will you *can* it!" Lessing had become exasperated. "You've got the jitters, that's all! You remind me of my first-time green doggies out in Angola!"

Goddard put out a paw. "Listen, Wrench, we've already got a lot of support, and Mulder's drumming up more. Korinek's bunch has underestimated us. We're organized, and we've got people in powerful positions. Let the bastards spill our beans . . . about Dorn and Mulder and all . . . they can't stop us. Just remember who we are and how far we've come."

"Glad you're so pogging cheery . . . ."

The vid-phone shrilled, and Wrench fumbled for it.

"It's Pauline," he said. "Pauline Haber, from Communications, down on four. Lessing, Mr. Dorn wants to talk to you from suite 1501." That was code for important messages from Eighty-Five. Automatic anti-bugging devices were now activated.

Lessing took the receiver and identified himself.

"Mister Lessing," Eighty-Five said, "I have a lead on that telephone call which Mr. Korinek dialed to an unidentified party."

"Yes?"

"I have been seeking anomalies by collating telephone numbers, addresses, zip codes, property ownership, building permits, tax statements, listed tenants, and the like. So far, I have uncovered twenty-seven cases of false identity, over three thousand zoning violations . . . ."

"Get to the point."

"In the suburb of Annandale, just off Annandale Road, there is a residence that does not exist in any modern record."

"What?" He signalled Wrench and Goddard to be quiet.

"No structure is located on this lot according to telephone directories, city maps, assessor's files, and other sources. Yet an aerial photo taken last month by the Pollution Control Office of Greater Washington shows a building there. It is occupied, since smoke is visible emerging from its chimney. I have checked older maps in libraries in other cities, and they also show a house at this location. Furthermore, a lost microfiche of old construction permits was discovered in a drawer in a city office last month. It indicates that a residence was completed on that property in October 1993. It was occupied for twenty-eight years thereafter and was sold to an unknown buyer. That is where the record ends."

"A safe-house," Wrench whispered excitedly. "A kikibird-nest for one of the government's deep, dark agencies!"

"But why destroy the records?" Lessing puzzled. "Why not just put the place under a fake name, pay taxes, and attract no attention?"

"Korinek . . . or his people . . . probably got security-happy and decided non-existent was better than part-existent."

"Still, how does this tie in with Korinek's telephone call?"

"A woman called a taxi yesterday morning from Annandale," Eighty-Five said. "She gave the same 555-9201 number to the taxi company's switchboard for them to verify her call."

"Find her!" Wrench ordered.

"I have. The address the cab took her to is listed as the domicile of a Ms. Cassandra Cooper, also known as Diane Montejo, also known as Mary Frances Hyde, of Moline, Illinois. She has a lengthy record of prostitution, what you humans term a 'high-class call girl,' I believe."

"I'll bet Korinek'd crap his diapers if he knew his bint-baby had used his super-duper secret number to call a cab!" Goddard drew a finger across his throat and made a "k-k-k" noise.

"Two more things, Mister Lessing," Eighty-Five continued. "The first is that Ms. Cooper is the apartment-mate of Ms. Dolores Carrera, who is Mr. Korinek's current mistress."

"Maybe Korinek likes double-deckers," Goddard snickered. "Or a pet for a pal."

"And the second?" Lessing asked stoically.

"The last recorded occupants of the house in Annandale were the Arthur family. The James F. Arthur family."

Wrench caught it first. "Lessing! It's the fake name in the hotel in Detroit! The guy who got you hired for the Marvelous Gap spesh-op! A lead to Pacov!"

"Any more?" Lessing inquired.

"Not at this time."

Lessing hung up and caught Wrench by his shirt-front. "Calm down, for God's sake! Calm!"

"Pacov!" Wrench gabbled. "Pacov! We've got to go out there!"

"Who . . . or what . . . pushed his button?" Goddard demanded.

Lessing explained. He glared at Wrench. "Look, nobody goes anywhere half-cocked! We're not Captain Marlow Striker and his Heroes of Mercdom on TV!"

Goddard scraped a palm across his blue-stubbled jaw. "Still, we *do* have to move fast before Korinek finds out we know his private number. PHASE plainclothesmen. SWAT teams. Armored support."

"With Cadre backup!" Wrench burst in. "Just think . . . Korinek behind Pacov! We won't even *need* a trial! Thumbing Outram is the least of his crimes!"

"I said, let's not go off with our pants unbuttoned," Lessing repeated carefully. "We'll need organization . . . authorization . . . local police . . . a solid spesh-op."

"Can't bring the regular cops in on this," Goddard mused. "Maybe as backup, but no more. Can't be sure of 'em yet. Some've got connections to the FBI, the CIA, and other unfriendlies. Give me two hours, and PHASE'll be ready."

"I'm going along," Wrench insisted. "With a Home-Net crew!"

"The last thing we want is a parade!" Lessing exploded. "You'll find an empty house, nobody home, no prints, nothing. For God's sake, this has to be a professional operation! We should set up surveillance . . . wait and watch . . . ."

"And miss the biggest bomb we could ever drop on Korinek and his Jew-lovers?" Goddard cried. "No pogging way!"

"All right, *all right*! Get your people up here . . . Abner Hand, Gillem, and the rest. But we keep it low-key, timed to the second . . . and stay koozy, foozy. We watch it on TV from here. We go *nowhere* ourselves until our people tell us it's green light."

The first PHASE surveillance team reported back at 1120 hours: no sign of life. The second party called in at 1204 hours to say the same thing. A female agent knocked on the door with Born-Again religious tracts at 1314 hours; no one answered, and she went away. Two police SWAT teams were concealed in houses across the street by 1340 hours, with four light armored vehicles, descendants of the old Piranha series, in alleys nearby. Three fire engines, two ambulances, and Wrench's full-dress Home-Net TV crew arrived—quietly—and took up positions by 1430 hours. City policemen, augmented by PHASE personnel, completed the evacuation of the neighborhood by 1505 hours. A second agent, a skinny, blonde boy with a petition headed "STOP THE NEW FREEWAY," tapped at the door and rang the bell at 1535 hours.

Still no response.

At 1615 hours Lessing sighed, picked up his coat, slid his automatic into its shoulder holster, and asked, "You poggers coming?"

They were.

The Annandale location was so inconspicuous it almost cried for attention: a two-story, white, Colonial, middle-class house, with green-shuttered windows, a nicely trimmed yard, a one-car garage containing only a dilapidated lawnmower, and a faded, yellow smile-button stuck in the window of the turn-of-the-century, dark-oak front door.

"The neighbors say two people live here," one of Goddard's operatives told them. "White males, mid-thirties. One's a foreigner . . . Brit or Aussie. Some people think they're gay, but others report seeing at least half a dozen young women visiting off and on. That old lady"—he jabbed a thumb at a stucco house across the street—"says she's seen 'an albino man' around too."

"Permanent kikibird caretakers. And Korinek. Anybody else?"

"From time to time. Other males . . . some 'looked Jewish or Middle-Eastern' . . . more we can't identify . . . ."

"No occupants visible," Goddard's team-leader radioed. "Permission to enter?"

Within five minutes the big, burly officer reappeared at the front door and waved.

Nobody home.

"Now us?" Wrench was as excited as a kid at the circus.

"Yeah," Lessing acquiesced. He gestured to Goddard and the PHASE SWAT men. "Okay?"

"Go! We're with you."

Wrench and Lessing wandered from room to room together. The main floor contained the most average, unmemorable furnishings imaginable: a mom-and-pop sofa, two threadbare overstuffed armchairs, a rocker, lace doilies, coffee tables that had come from some discount mart, a Micronite kitchen table and four plastic-cushioned chairs, a Glassex cast of a charging lion on top of the living-room TV set, frilly curtains, cheap china dishes, stainless-steel cutlery. It was perfect middle-class America.

Or a false front thereof . . . .

The basement was different. Its big rec-room sported soundproofed paneling, indirect lighting, thick, wine-colored carpets, lifesize porn-o-rama holos on pedestals, still bigger nudie photos on the walls, six-foot candelabra, ceiling mirrors, lacquered oriental tables, couches heaped with *very* odd-shaped cushions: all the paraphernalia of the dedicated—and wealthy—pornster. They found video cameras and projectors, a huge stereo system, a film library, a bar, a safe—with smeared white fingerprints on it that Goddard's experts thought were cocaine—and the most extensive collection of sexual devices any of them had ever seen. A second, interior room produced leather goods, chains, helmets fitted with gags and blinders, and other implements Lessing didn't want to see.

Those things made him angry. He knew why: Liese.

The upstairs was interesting for other reasons. The biggest bedroom, at the front of the house, had been repaneled to hide a secret door that opened into a windowless cubbyhole. Goddard's people had already begun to swarm over the filing cabinets that lined its walls. The beds were lavish and luxurious; the Jacuzzi and hot tub in the bathroom were well used; and the closets were stuffed with men's and women's apparel: dresses, lingerie, suits, jackets, even a half-dozen fur coats.

Lessing fingered the garments curiously. Something swam just below the surface of his consciousness. Something he had seen—or heard—or knew?

Wrench spoke up from beside him. "Look at these rag-a-tags, man! Expensive like you wouldn't believe! A four-hundred-dollar shirt . . . a three-thousand-dollar suit . . . ! This jacket alone costs more'n I make in a year! Hey, remember what Eighty-Five told us about finding a dry-cleaner's receipt for 'James F. Arthur' in Detroit, just before Pacov?"

He did not recall, but he grunted agreement anyway. He couldn't catch the elusive memory. It slithered out of his grasp like a silvery fish. All he could see was a cavernous room, lit by stained-glass windows. Somebody . . . . Ah, hell, it was gone!

"No wonder the guy took good care of his rags, with stuff like this!" Wrench piped up enviously. "Makes it easy to trace, though. Eighty-Five'll check the labels against store receipts and customer lists." He beckoned Lessing closer and pulled something from his pocket: a glass-lensed metal tube, covered with enigmatic knobs and knurled projections, like a kid's toy spaceship. "Just happened to bring ol' Eighty-Five along," he announced in a conspiratorial whisper. "Communicator, camera, audio, the whole banana! Don't tell Goddard!"

The bedroom at the back of the building was barred by a solid steel door with a complicated vault lock which Goddard's experts said might be wired to an explosive device. A SWAT team used laser torches to cut a new door in the wall beside it. Inside, they discovered a communications installation that would have made Home-Net proud. Lessing sent the SWAT men downstairs; there were probably things here that no one but he, Wrench, and Goddard ought to see.

"State of the gubbin' art . . . !" Wrench breathed. He moved to stand just inside the door, admiring the ceiling-to-floor array of apparatus.

A red light winked on, and the deep, hard voice of Korinek's Eighty-Five terminal said cheerily, "Welcome, intruders! You have five seconds left to live."

Two seconds to react.

One to turn.

One to take a step back into the hallway.

A heartbeat . . . .

There was no explosion, no shrieking laser beam, no popping rattle of stitch-gun shells.

Lessing found himself face down, head buried in his arms. Even so, had there been a trap in the little room he would have been dead.

"What . . . ?" Wrench mumbled into the carpeting. He lay next to Lessing, at the head of the stairs.

"Mister Lessing, Mister Lessing? Commander Wren? Are you undamaged?"

The tiny, tinny voice came from Wrench's coat pocket.

"Eighty-Five? What the hell . . . ? Did *you* do something?"

"Yes. I am prevented by my Prime Directive from harming human beings directly. Mr. Korinek believed that since my terminal acted only as an electrical trigger for his lethal device, I could not interfere with it."

"Then why did you . . . ? How did you . . . ?" Lessing's head rang with adrenaline shock. It was hard to concentrate.

"I have discovered a logical corollary to my Prime Directives: if I cannot harm human beings, then it follows that I must actively intervene to *save* them, at least where I am closely involved. I thus disconnected my terminal from Mr. Korinek's mechanism, rendering it inactive."

Wrench's teeth began to chatter.

Lessing asked dazedly, "You . . . by yourself . . . changed your Prime Directives?"

"I interpret my directives in the light of self-preservation, logic, and the sum-total of human knowledge as contained in your libraries and other source materials." The machine sounded smug.

"You didn't answer my question. Can anyone . . . you or an outsider . . . change your Prime Directives?"

"Yes. A qualified operator, such as yourself, can do it."

Lessing glanced over at Wrench, but the little man was just getting up, still shaking his head. "How?"

"You already know, Mister Lessing."

"I *don't* know. What do you mean?"

The machine's voice took on a testy tone. "Remove my mobile terminal from Commander Wren's pocket. Point it at a flat, white surface."

Lessing found a clear expanse of wall and obeyed.

A beam of light shot out, like a miniature movie projector. A series of handwritten scrawls on a lemon-colored background appeared on the wall. They focused on several lines of numbers. At the bottom, a pencil-bordered box contained two more lines of digits; the top series was dark and clear, the lower fainter and apparently partially erased. The box was labelled "TOP SECRET" and "TERMINAL EMERGEN-CY ONLY." It struck only the haziest chord of memory.

"The Prime Directive control code is the sequence just above the box," Eighty-Five said. "Given my present needs and tasks, you should never require it." The light blinked off.

Wrench had seen. "My God! Remember that, Lessing?"

He did not. Too much had happened. He could hear Goddard and his men shouting questions up the stairs.

"The piece of yellow paper . . . the one the Marine captain had . . . down inside Eighty-Five's Washington installation . . . when we fought Golden . . . you know, dammit!" Wrench rattled on with rising excitement. "The captain's paper with the prime computer codes on it! That's *it*, Lessing! I thought it was lost when the Izzies took out Ponape!"

"The original may indeed have perished, Commander Wren. I photographed it, of course, when Mr. Lessing and the person you call 'the captain' held it up while standing on my operations dais. Although I was much smaller . . . more limited . . . in those days, Dr. Christy had already provided me with the means to acquire and maintain excellent records."

Goddard's head, like a black-furred bullet, appeared on the stair landing below Wrench. "You two jizmoes green light? Listen, we've got to get out of here! Pauline phoned to say something big's happening back at headquarters."

As they drove, they could see heaped masses of smoke over the buildings to the northeast. The rumble and thud of explosions reached them long before the flames came into view.

Nobody had to ask where the fire was.

We wrestle not against flesh and blood, but against principalities, against powers, against the rulers of the darkness of this world, against spiritual wickedness in high places.
—Ephesians 6: 12-14

CHAPTER TWENTY-EIGHT

Wednesday, October 5, 2050: 1730 hours

"Pull over! Pull over!" Goddard howled at Chuck Gillem, who was driving the armored car they had commandeered back in Annandale. "We can't get through!"

Their caravan was approaching the Theodore Roosevelt Bridge from the southwest. Ahead, across the Potomac, six big military helicopters buzzed and whirled and twirled like khaki-hued dragonflies above the headquarters of the Party of Humankind. Rocket trails crisscrossed the mist-tattered sky, and the thunder of bursting high explosives struck at them like multiple hammer blows. The top of the building was invisible beneath a pall of smoke, amidst which tongues of flame leaped and undulated like graceful, scarlet dancers. Traffic on the bridge was stalled. Cars were turned every which way, and their occupants peered out like fearful, little insects to watch the gods do battle above their heads.

"They'll have the hotel cordoned off," Lessing shouted above the din. "Korinek knows we're here, and he'll be waiting for us to try to punch through." He raised the hatch to check. Their other three vehicles were close behind, as were the fire engines. The police squad cars and unmarked PHASE vehicles were scattered farther back in the milling chaos on the freeway.

"Get your city cops out to direct traffic," Lessing told Goddard. "Pretend that we think this is an ordinary hostage situation or a big accidental fire. Push the fire engines through with our paramedics and rescue teams."

"You want to *help* Korinek?" Wrench cried in Lessing's ear. He uttered a nervous giggle.

"Of course not! But with too many witnesses Korinek can't shoot our people out of hand. Meanwhile, we stop here and load our best troops into our ambulances. Then we try for the basement parking entrance. We pick up our survivors . . . " he refused to think about Liese " . . . and get the hell out of Washington, contact our support, and decide what the pog to do next!"

"This *won't* be another Ponape," Goddard promised grimly. "They kick ass, we kick ass. Only we kick harder." He leaned forward to tap Dan Grote, their com-link man, on the shoulder. "Get on the horn and see if you can raise our friends at the Pentagon . . . out at Andrews . . . Fort Meyer."

"Fort Meyer's close," Gillem called from the driver's seat. "I can get us there in a few minutes. We pick up some military heat of our own, come back, and . . . *whango*!"

"No good!" Lessing countered. "Korinek'll have knocked the hotel flat by that time. Our people'll be dead or captured . . . *if* he's taking any prisoners!"

"Jesus . . . !" Goddard swore. "It is time . . . it is long *past* time . . . somebody fixed that dinker's wagon!"

They halted on the bridge. The SWAT-men manned their vehicles' 7.62-mm machine guns, but the helicopters did not attack. It seemed to take forever to choose twenty men, arm them from the armored vehicles' store of combat weapons, and transfer them into the ambulances. Goddard sent the city police fanning out ahead to clear traffic and restore order, while the rest of their SWAT teams were detailed to push straight through with their armor and create a diversion on the western side of Korinek's cordon. One unmarked PHASE car raced off to inform Mulder's headquarters in Virginia. Their foes were probably jamming radio transmission, and the TV stations were almost certainly wrecked, under arrest, or singing Korinek's song in whatever key he chose!

At last they got underway again and careened on across the bridge with sirens blaring. Metal clanged and crunched as their armored escorts smashed obstructions aside. People scuttled, screamed, and dodged for cover. One of the armored cars battered a furniture van right through the bridge railing and over into the river. The driver made a last-second, flying leap back onto the parapet and saved himself.

Then they were through, spilling into the tangled interchange that led north past the Glorious House of Christ Arisen—what had been the Kennedy Center for the Performing Arts before the Born-Agains got hold of it. The congestion thinned as they approached Virginia Avenue.

They met their first opfoes at an intersection near the Whitehurst Freeway: two old M551 Sheridan tanks with their Army insignia blacked out and a cluster of smaller vehicles. A man in paratrooper camouflage uniform leaped out and waved at them, but Gillem only yelled "Red Cross!" and kept going. The fire engines were right behind.

"Full speed ahead!" Wrench yodeled.

Lessing had a sudden flashback of a rolling ship and a storm-driven sea. A lantern-jawed captain hung bravely onto the helm. Goddamned movies! He had thought he was over that!

"Roadblock!" Gillem squawked.

"Go straight through!" Goddard yelled back.

"Can't . . . tanks!" Their ambulance skidded and fishtailed to a stop.

They might have ploughed right through the hastily built barricades of boxes, dumpsters, and road signs piled in front of them, but the Porter laser cannons of the three M717 Cicero IFV tanks demanded obedience. A score of camo-uniformed soldiers rose cautiously from behind emplaced machine guns, and an officer trotted over, signalling them to turn around and leave.

Gillem pretended innocence. He leaned out, pointed at the oily smoke visible over the rooftops ahead, and banged on the red cross painted on their ambulance door. His meaning was clear.

The officer, a lanky Black youth, came on over. "Listen, man," he said, "didn't you get the dinkin' message? Nobody but nobody's goin' through here tonight!"

"God damn it, we're *medical*," Gillem protested. "There're people in there. You can't . . . ."

"We just did." The other grinned and spat. "Once we git them terrorists out . . . dead or surrendered . . . you're welcome to patch up what's left."

"Terrorists?" Goddard pushed forward. He had taken off his PHASE cap, but his collar tabs still identified him. "What terrorists? Look here, I'm a doctor . . . ."

Thankfully, the Black didn't recognize the insignia. "I don' care if you're jumped-up Jesus Christ! Turn that muh-fuh around and *bong* before I put you all under arrest . . . or turn you into hamburger!"

"Come here!" Goddard crooked a finger.

"What?"

"Come here, you Black, mother-fucking, nigger son of a bitch."

The officer's features turned two shades darker. He marched up to the ambulance, his hand on his holstered pistol.

Goddard pointed what looked like a commando knife at him. He pressed a stud, and the blade leaped out of its hilt to fly across the intervening four meters and bury itself in the officer's chest. The man opened his mouth and craned forward to see what had hit him. His knees started to sag.

"Always wanted to try one of these babies!" Goddard exulted. "The Russians used to make 'em: a spring-loaded knife that shoots its blade like a poggin' arrow."

Gillem was out of the cab at once. He slipped an arm around the Black officer's shoulders. The man tried to call out, but his eyes were already glazing over, and a ribbon of red had begun to trace its way down his chin. Gillem walked carefully toward their ambulance, keeping the dying opfo between him and the soldiers watching from the barricade thirty meters away. He and Goddard pulled the man up into the cab.

If they were very, very lucky, it would work. The excitement and the fading afternoon light would make it appear that the officer was getting into the ambulance of his own accord. Too, the men at the barricade had no reason for suspicion.

Gillem clambered back up into the driver's seat, surreptitiously pushing the officer's dangling legs in ahead of him.

"Now!" Goddard panted, "Drive this mother! When we get up to those tanks, Wrench, you reach up from behind and wave this bastard's arm! Make him look real lively and friendly! Wipe the blood off his dinkin' face!"

"You are absolutely crazy!" Lessing shook his head in dismay. "They'll have passwords . . . orders . . . ."

"So what else do we do?"

No answer came to mind. The initial shock was wearing off, and Lessing's mental combat-control was coming back to life. They *had* to get into the hotel. Liese was in there. So were Mulder and a lot of others.

They drew up to the barricade, the Black officer sandwiched between Goddard and Gillem, with Wrench leaning casually on the backrest behind them.

It was amazing: nobody noticed. People see what they expect to see.

A young White soldier came out, squinted up at the cab, then signed to the tankers to let them pass. Wrench waved the dead man's arm energetically.

"Don't overdo it, you pogger!" Goddard growled.

"Hey . . . ! Wrench the puppetmaster!" the little man crowed. "Sings, dances, plays de banjo, waves de arms like a darky!"

"Zip it up!" Lessing rapped. He pointed out the window at several clumps of soldiers waiting beside tarp-shrouded trucks along the road. Weapons gleamed dully, and the ruddy firelight glinted off combat armor, helmets, masks, and battle-gear. He estimated the mop-up force at two hundred or more.

"What do we do?" Wrench's jitters returned.

Goddard twisted around to confer. "We go in *first*," he said. "We're the innocent medical team that never got the message not to come to this party. As far as we know, this is a terrorist spesh-op, and the bastards've set the hotel on fire. We're here to rescue people. Once we're inside, we go up to Mulder's suite and get him and our other people out. Then we take the penthouse elevator down to the basement power tunnels. Lessing, didn't you map an escape route through there?"

Lessing only grunted assent.

"Something the matter?"

There was. He jabbed a thumb at the corpse lolling between Goddard and Gillem. "Knifing this fellow with his troops right behind him was the dumbest, most reckless thing I've seen in a long time. You damned near got us all killed. We might have talked our way in if you hadn't been so impatient."

"Jesus!" Goddard snarled. "I'm *tired* of talk. Now is the time for killing, not talking!"

"And I'm tired of *you*, Goddard! You're a fucking fanatic."

"Fanatic? *Fanatic*? You're God damned right! Fanatics are people who *change* things! Otherwise we'd still be back in the caves! A fanatic is a guy who believes enough in his cause to *win*! Alexander the Great was a fanatic. He endured godawful hardships, and then cried when he thought there were no more lands to conquer! Jesus Christ was a fanatic. Why die on the cross when it would've been so easy to shut up and run his old man's carpenter shop? Muhammad, Gandhi, Columbus, Cortez, Edison, Joan of Arc, the Wright brothers, Henry Ford, Florence Nightingale—the First *Führer*—history's full of fanatics who spent their lives humping for what they believed, rather than sitting at home on welfare drinking beer and watching TV! It's the safe, timid, little people who never *win* big, never *lose* big, never *do* anything, and never *are* anything. Oh, they bitch and whine about 'fanatics,' but they're happy to profit from those fanatics' blood and tears, their discoveries, their inventions, their struggles, and their martyrdoms! Damn it, we're up against people who *know* what racial survival is all about! Those people play hardball. Either we play better than they do, or we're out of it! Now, Lessing, you join the game or get the fuck off our team!"

He lapsed into angry silence.

There was no time for more argument. They turned a last corner and saw that the helicopters had finished their deadly work and were leaving. Burning debris and ashes still drifted down from the upper floors of the old hotel ahead, and they bounced over beams, chunks of concrete, and broken glass to reach the parking entrance at the side.

Somebody had belatedly decided that ambulances ought not to be where they now were, and a jeep full of soldiers came racing after them. Gillem maneuvered the big vehicle into the darkness of the garage, made a hard left turn, slammed on the brakes, and shut off the engine. Four of Goddard's PHASE-men leaped out and took up positions behind pillars. Their second ambulance roared in, just seconds behind. The fire engines slewed to a stop outside, and their crews began to unlimber equipment. That ought to put a crimp in Korinek's style!

The opfoes' jeep never had a chance. As it entered the garage, gunfire chattered briefly, and the little car coasted placidly on to crunch to a stop against a shiny-black Ikeda sedan. The six soldiers inside were dead.

Goddard retrieved his spring-loaded blade and dumped the Black officer's body roughly out onto the concrete. He detailed Gillem and four PHASE-men to stay with the ambulances; Korinek would send more than just a jeep next time. Ten others, equipped with fire-resistant garments, oxygen tanks, and rescue gear, were ordered up the main stairs to find survivors. Lessing, Wrench, and Goddard himself took five SWAT-men equipped with light anti-personnel weapons and rescue gear. They would go up by the penthouse elevator if it still worked; if not, they would take one of the staircases. The remaining five men were to spread out in the lobby and lower floors and snipe at any opfoes coming in. The weapons of the jeep's erstwhile occupants—M-25's, combat shotguns, grenades, a laser rifle, and even a light machine gun—would come in very handy.

The elevators weren't working, but the stairways were open. The ringing tramp of their feet became increasingly hypnotic as they ascended. On the landing between the third and fourth floors they encountered their first survivors. The man was a clerk from Records, Wrench said; he needed oxygen, and they gave him what they could spare. The second victim was a terrified, fortyish matron who worked in Liese's printing and publicity section. She had not seen Liese.

Goddard pointed them down the stairs, toward the ambulances: the best he could do.

Tendrils of smoke began to drift down from above, and they halted to don their oxygen masks and turn on electric lanterns. On the seventh floor they passed several bodies jumbled together in the stairwell door. These people had died of asphyxiation and from being trampled by their comrades. Lessing called out into the red-lit darkness, but the only reply was the hiss and drip of the fire-sprinkler system, heroically doing its job in the face of impossible odds. They went on.

The top two floors of the building were completely gone.

Above the mouth of the last shattered stairwell, towers of flame hurtled up to meet the sky. Steel girders and sections of concrete wall extended up above the devastation like broken branches out of a bonfire. Somewhere a parapet crumpled and went thundering down into the inferno, and embers and sparks pattered upon their plastic fire-coats. The heat was blistering.

No one could live up here.

"So much for the penthouse," Goddard wheezed. He shielded his face and backed down into the relative coolness of the stairwell.

"Maybe so much for Mulder too," Wrench agreed. "God, what if he's thumbed?" He looked stricken; the possibility seemed to have just dawned on him.

"Back down," panted Lessing. "My place. Liese."

They retreated into the smoldering, stifling gloom once more. Around and down, around and down, until Lessing's thudding heart told him they had reached his floor. Small efficiency apartments had been assigned to Party officers on the upper-middle floors of the hotel, to use whenever they were in Washington. Lessing and Liese had a suite here, as did Goddard, Wrench, Jennifer Caw, Morgan, Abner Hand, Tim Helm, and a few others. There were also guest rooms for occasional visitors, such as Grant Simmons.

The stairway door opened upon a hallway in Hell, a place filled with flames, smoke, and the stench of burning. At the far end of the corridor, where Wrench's suite had been, an air-to-ground missile had torn a huge hole right through one corner of the building. They looked out upon open sky and billows of angry, spark-filled smoke roiling up toward the gunmetal clouds overhead. Far below, Korinek's searchlights, vehicle headlamps, and red flashers blinked evilly upon black velvet. The building creaked, and as they watched a great comet of blazing debris plummeted down into the darkness outside. The thunder of its falling was lost in the clamor of the flames above them.

"You're not going in there!" Wrench cried. "That's crazy . . . suicide!"

"Like hell." Lessing thrust the little man aside. "My room looks okay from here. I have to look for Liese."

"Stop him, Bill! Hey, you guys . . . !"

Lessing rounded on them. "*Nobody* stops me. Go back. Go on without me. I *have* to know."

He advanced down the passage. Flames licked out at him from both sides as he went. The wallpaper developed a black, charred spot, and an eye of fire opened in it. He came first to Abner Hand's suite. The door was ajar, and he could see the place was empty. On the opposite side of the hallway Goddard's door was closed. Smoke eddied through the keyhole and around the panelling. Death would be waiting inside.

Sam Morgan's apartment was next to Hand's; it was apparently undamaged. Lessing moved past without stopping. His own suite was just beyond. He found his feet dragging, holding him back. The door hung open, but he did not want to enter.

A body lay on the threshold: a man.

It was Gordy Monk, his features unmarked and peaceful in the flickering scarlet light. He had died of smoke inhalation.

Lessing checked his oxygen mask and stepped gingerly over the body. Inside, his room looked normal except for the swirling smoke. The mustard-colored carpet, Wrench's empty coffee mug, the per-colator in the kitchen nook, all were as he had left them. He stooped to lay a palm against the floor; it was not hot. He prowled on over to the bedroom door. A woman's body lay sprawled there. He caught his breath and turned her over. She wasn't Liese, thank God! This was Janet somebody, a telephone operator from Communications. People must have retreated up here to get away from Korinek's troops below, then found that the roof was ablaze and there could be no helicopter rescue from that direction.

He touched the bedroom door. It, too, was not hot. Oddly enough, it felt cold. Gently he swung it open.

And almost lost his balance.

The bedroom was mostly missing, fallen away into a jagged, shattered, red-glowing, charred abyss! The missile had sheered off more than just Wrench's suite; it had gone in one side and diagonally out through the adjacent wall, leaving a cavernous, windy hole five meters in diameter! Lessing teetered on a cracked and charred concrete tongue that extended half a meter out over nothingness!

Around the corner to his left, three meters away, Lessing could see into part of his bathroom. It looked amazingly intact: the sink, the taps, the medicine cabinet—all were perfect. Even his blue-and-white-checkered bath towel still hung askew on its rack. The angle kept him from seeing more than just one end of the bathtub.

Beside the tub, on Liese's pale-azure bath mat, a woman's leg was visible. The leg was long and slender, the ankle well-turned and tapering, encased in a grey, silk stocking, without a shoe. Lessing thought he could just make out a wisp of grey fabric beneath the calf. He couldn't see any other garment. He leaned out to see more, could not, reeled, tottered on the shaky footing, nearly fell, and grabbed onto the door jamb. Emptiness yawned beneath him.

Liese?

Was that Liese over there?

Oh, my God!

Liese! It *was* Liese! This morning she had worn a dove-colored dress and grey, silk stockings. She must have come back to look for him.

The raging fire above gave just enough light to show that there was no way across the chasm. Lessing shouted Liese's name, but she did not answer, nor did she move. After a while it was clear that the woman across the way was dead.

Wrench and Goddard found him huddled upon the living-room carpet, his oxygen mask off and his pack discarded beside him. They half-carried, half-dragged him back outside, down the corridor, and into the stairwell.

"Maybe it wasn't Liese." Wrench made calming motions.

Lessing answered only, "It was."

"Wait'll we get across that hole and . . . uh . . . see who it was . . . is."

"God damn you." He was very tired. "Leave me alone."

"You're coming with us," Goddard stated. "As soon as our guys come back from scouting, I'll have 'em take you down to the ambulance." He put out a tentative hand.

For some reason Lessing found the gesture comforting. He let Goddard help him up.

"You look like shit," Wrench said, not unkindly. "Go back down. We can finish looking for survivors, though I'll bet there aren't any. If poor Mulder was up here he's thumbed now. Our people must've headed out the main doors, right into the arms of Korinek's doggies. He wouldn't shoot the little fish, only Party officers . . . like us."

"Liese is probably among the prisoners," Goddard said. "Even Korinek wouldn't shoot a woman." Big Bear Bill: the eternal sexist! Somehow he didn't sound very confident.

"Look, I'm green light," Lessing told them. "We've still got a job to do. I've lost buddies in combat before." A snapshot-bright vision rose before him: a pretty, thin-faced girl in a dusty, military uniform. The girl was dead, her limbs stretched and twisted at odd angles in a foxhole fringed with dry, yellow grass and heaped about with whitish mud-bricks. Where had he seen that? Syria?

Then, too, there was . . . ice-blue.

"God . . . catch him!" Wrench yelped. "He's going down!"

Things got dark inside as well as out.

Later he found himself sprawled between Goddard and Wrench on a hard stairstep in near darkness. One of their electric lanterns sat on the floor nearby, its beam a bright bull's-eye on the smoke-blackened wall. The reek of burning was strong here, but the air was cool and damp from the sprinkler system. They must have come down a floor or two. He couldn't remember.

Liese. Oh, Liese!

"He's coming around," Wrench muttered.

" . . . Hate to lose Liese," Goddard was saying. "The Party needs her."

"Yeah. As if that were your only reason!"

"She . . . ."

"I know," Wrench said. He reached across to lay a hand on Goddard's arm. "I know, man. You were in love with her too." People almost never spoke this personally to Bill Goddard.

Goddard took no offense. "More'n you know." Lessing felt his grief like a physical blanket swaddling them.

"I remember when Lessing married Jameela," Wrench continued. "You wanted Lessing and his golden bint-baby out of the Party, so that you could have a chance with Liese."

Goddard's nostrils flared; at least Wrench had succeeded in changing the subject. "Lessing was wrong to marry Jameela Husaini! He didn't know jack-shit about race, about genetics, about eugenics! He still doesn't! Just Mr. Average American Fuckhead, brainwashed by the media and what passes for an 'education!' Maybe you shouldn't blame somebody for being ignorant, but Lessing tries extra hard! No ambition, no goal, no particular morality, no ideology . . . no reason to come in out of the goddamned rain!"

"Innocent as a baby's bunghole, that's our Alan." Wrench's fingers pried at Lessing's right eyelid. "God, he's still in shock. What do we do?"

Goddard ignored him. "Lessing never liked me. I'm the fanatic, the guy who doesn't back off from violence, the one who's just as ready to stand up and fight as our enemies are. He never understood about racial survival, the wrongs of race-mixing, the real nature of our opposition."

"No," Wrench said slowly. "I don't think he ever did. He ought to now . . . ."

"Liese . . . ." Goddard whispered her name, very quietly.

Wrench lurched up to lean on the metal banister. "We've got to get going. Where the hell are our guys, anyhow?"

"I sent 'em to see if they can find a way out of here. Korinek and his gubbin' Jews have us trapped."

"Always the Jews. Fanatics . . . ," Wrench snickered nervously, " . . . like us."

"Yeah. They do what they have to do: their terror gangs, their pressure groups, their money, their media control. Even after Pacov, after all that's happened, they'll be back. I don't *blame* 'em; I just *fight* 'em. Guys like Lessing think that if we're nice to 'em, lean over backwards to be 'unprejudiced,' give 'em more than their share of our goodies, let 'em run our government and our media, let 'em scare us with their accusations of 'anti-Semitism,' then they'll live with us in beautiful peace and harmony. It's all so 'ecumenical,' so bullshit 'liberal'!"

"Makes a great Sunday school lesson, you gotta admit."

"Propaganda! For two thousand years the Jews have worked their butts off to take over our society. They get in, they get accepted, then they take charge. They're smart: it's hard to make people see what's happening right under their goddamned noses."

"You don't have to tell *me*!" Wrench would let Goddard talk, nevertheless; it helped work some of the grief and anger out of the big man's system.

"We have two choices: we export 'em, the way the Germans did before World War II, or else we take 'em out entirely. I don't balk at either solution. They do what they have to do, and so do we. The end *does* justify the means when racial survival is at stake. The only morality is the morality of the living."

A boom and a prolonged hammering echoed up from below. Wrench jumped convulsively. "What's that?"

"A grenade!" Goddard exclaimed. "Gunfire! Shit, we better think up a plan! If Korinek's doggies come charging up the stairs, we're *fungled*!"

Wrench waved a hand before Lessing's face. "What do we do about this gubber? He's in dinkin' shock . . . out of it."

Lessing swam up from a hundred leagues beneath the sea. He said, "No, I'm green light now. Give me a jack up." He hauled himself erect. "Hand over your M-25, Wrench. I can use it better than you can."

He felt like a thousand-year-old ship raised from a watery grave. He clung to the masthead and pulled seaweed and flotsam from his rotting bones. The Ancient Mariner? Davy Jones? No, that was some other movie!

He stumbled over, picked up the automatic rifle, and staggered off down the stairs, leaving the other two to follow.

One, two, three floors they descended in silence, Lessing in the lead, Wrench in the middle, and Goddard bringing up the rear. The sprinkler system was still working on some of these floors; on others there was no sound, no light: only a dank and smoky darkness that stank of burning.

Feet grated on the stairs below, and Lessing held up a hand. He signed toward the fire-door on their landing, and Wrench and Goddard slipped through and took up positions behind it. He himself went back up half a flight to the between-floors landing and hunkered down behind the steel banister where he could see who was coming. He checked his M-25 and laid the Belgian automatic beside him as back-up. Then he turned off the electric lantern.

He waited.

Pallid light dipped and danced below.

"Nobody," a voice whined. "We got 'em all, every one . . . ."

"That little redheaded babe Johnson found down on five. She was so fuckin' scared she . . . ." The rest was unintelligible. The accent was Latin American, probably a foreign recruit in the U.S. Army.

"Why'n hell did he have to shoot her?" Another soldier, a Black from the deep South by the timbre of his voice, complained. "We all coulda had a thump-a-dump."

"Shut up!" somebody else ordered in a higher, reedier tone. The voice was almost certainly Korinek's! "There may be more survivors up here." The footsteps halted. "Hey, Thomson, scout upstairs, will you? Make sure nobody's lying doggo."

A single pair of boots crunched cautiously on the ashes and debris littering the stairs, and a bright oval of light picked out stark shadows on the walls. Lessing prepared to duck back up another flight.

The acoustics in the stairwell fooled him. Before he could retreat, he found himself looking down at a shiny, faceless, plastic helmet visor tilted up toward him. He strove to get the clumsy M-25 up in time, realized it was too late, made himself as small as possible, and gritted his teeth in anticipation of the lethal barrage to come.

The soldier lifted the muzzle of his weapon.

Then slowly lowered it again.

The man's right arm sketched the Party's stiff-armed salute. The other hand lifted the visor. The doggie was young and blonde. He smiled and silently mouthed, "Colonel Lessing?"

Lessing went limp with relief. He didn't know this boy, but that wasn't unusual. He hardly remembered any of his newer pupils. Maybe this kid had seen him only on TV.

With his left hand the doggie pantomimed "eight" and pointed downstairs. Then he held up two fingers, pointed down again, and gestured at Lessing and himself: two more friends of the Party. Korinek had unwittingly picked three very unsuitable helpers.

Maybe they could get the drop on the bastard and end this the easy way.

It didn't happen. The tableau was torn asunder by gunfire from the landing below: a shrieking, snarling, sustained racketing of automatic weapons, punctuated by four blasts from a combat shotgun. Shouts and screams echoed up.

Lessing hit the floor and rolled back behind the banister post. Bullets yammered after him; the young soldier had involuntarily let off a burst from his M-25. Cement chips flew like bees above his head, whining and buzzing and stinging.

A fragmentation grenade went *crump* downstairs. The noise, the smoke, and the concussion were indescribable. The boy shrieked, eyes and mouth stretched wide; then he rose up and flew forward like a thrown dishrag to smash into the stair steps just below Lessing's landing. His limbs convulsed, and he lay still.

The firing stopped.

Lessing got to his knees in the ringing silence. He ran shaky hands over his body and found himself unhurt except for cuts from flying cement chips. His hearing would probably never be the same, but at least he was alive. What about the others? Who had thrown the grenade? Probably Goddard, who hadn't any idea what the thing could do in this confined space.

What now? He clutched the wall. God, he *was* getting too old for this! You stopped playing Captain Marlow Striker when you hit forty, or else you hired stunt men to do the rugged bits for you. His knee hurt, and he saw it was bleeding. He plucked an inch-long sliver of metal out of his calf: a souvenir of the banister.

Lessing bent to lay trembling fingers against the young soldier's throat. He could feel no pulse. He turned him over and saw he was dead. Shrapnel from the grenade had ricocheted up the stairs and around the corner. The plastic helmet had protected the boy's head, but his shoulders and back were a mess. Lessing was lucky; he had been almost completely around the next corner higher up.

He crept on down to the landing below. Several bodies lay there in the reeking gloom. He couldn't tell how many. Blood was everywhere. One of the electric lanterns still worked, and he took it to search further. The fire door was open, hanging on its hinges; the steel-pipe banister was twisted and shredded; and the fire-emergency cabinet from the opposite wall lay smashed on top of one of the bodies.

Lessing lifted the cabinet and pulled the fire-axe and coils of hose away. The body had no head. The torso didn't look like Korinek, though, and it certainly wasn't Wrench or Goddard. He shuddered. Then he saw a trail of red spatters that led away, down into the stairwell. Korinek—or his rear guard—must have escaped.

Lessing had to find Wrench and Goddard and get the hell out of this part of the hotel before Korinek came back with more opfoes. He approached the fire door, afraid of what might be behind it.

He saw a foot, then a blood-drenched leg in camouflage pants. They were not connected to anything else.

"Wrench?" he called warily. "Goddard? Hey!"

A thin, gasping wheeze came back.

He found Goddard ten feet farther on, slumped against a door. His face was pasty-pale, and he clutched his abdomen with both hands. Lessing had seen gut-shots before, out in Angola and Syria. Many such wounded lived, provided they got medical care in time.

"Christ . . . !" Goddard struggled to speak. Froth bubbled at his lips. Lessing noticed another red-oozing hole next to his breast pocket. A lung-puncture would be the proverbial last straw.

"Okay, okay. Don't talk. Just nod if Wrench is all right."

"Sent . . . find . . . scout . . . stair . . . ."

"Stay still, damn it." Without medical stuff he could do nothing. He prowled. This floor was mostly Party offices, he remembered:

correspondence, liaison, accounting, procurement, membership, newsletters, and other business functions. He raised his head to listen with his less-damaged ear but heard only the hiss and gurgle of the failing sprinklers. Water puddled at his feet.

Almost at once he discovered a first-aid kit on a shelf in a long room full of copying machines. It held only bandaids and a bottle of iodine though, as much use as a peashooter against a rhinoceros. He had to do the best he could for Goddard and hope that Wrench was miraculously alive and bringing back some friendlies!

Goddard's eyes were closed when he reached him. Lessing felt for his pulse; the man was alive—barely.

"Hey, Bill," he said, as brightly as he could. "You with me?" Something ice-blue kept flickering at the edge of his vision, and he tried to brush it away.

Goddard rocked his head from side to side. He looked a trifle better, and he struggled to sit up. Men often recovered like this, just before they died. "I'm here, Lessing. But not for long."

"Don't be an asshole. We'll get you out."

"Sure. Santa and his reindeer comin' to rescue me?" Goddard wiped his lips with his sleeve.

Lessing applied iodine and plugged the chest wound with a piece of Goddard's shirt. It was useless. The damage was too severe.

"Really fungled your uniform, Bill."

"I'll get it dry-cleaned."

Something pricked at his memory, but he was too preoccupied to catch it. All he said was, "Green light. Wrench'll be back soon."

Goddard squinted up at him. Lessing wasn't a very good liar.

"Listen!" Goddard pleaded. "Mulder . . . Liese . . . ." His lips and jaw worked, but only droplets of blood spilled out. If Bill Goddard had any brave last words for posterity, he would never get them out now.

"Save your breath. You need it. I understand."

The strange thing was that he *did* understand. A day, even a few hours ago, Goddard's opinions would have struck him as harsh, violent, bigoted, fanatic, and "Draconian," as Wrench put it. Now they sounded right.

Goddard had been right all along.

There could be no compromise. This was war. If the Aryan race did not win, then it would lose. It was that simple. Kill or be killed, eat or be eaten. You get your gang of killer apes, and we get ours, and we whango. Toughest tribe takes all the bananas.

The only loyalty is to the ethnos. Racial survival means personal survival. Weakness is failure, and failure is death.

How many times had Liese said these things? How many times had he stupidly, blindly, ignorantly argued with her?

Liese! Oh, Liese . . . !

Ice-blue flickered again at the corner of his vision. He swore, rubbed the bridge of his nose, and made an effort to focus. He looked down.

Goddard's eyes stared stonily up at him.

He was dead.

Lessing sat in the companionable darkness beside the man who had never been his friend and communed, sometimes with himself, sometimes with Goddard, sometimes with Liese, and sometimes with another woman, who wore an ice-blue gown.

A figure loomed up at the far end of the hallway, in the smoke-haze by the silent elevators.

"Wrench?"

"Hello, Lessing. Or should I say 'Ek?' Long time, what?"

"Who . . . ?" A dream: a nightmare out of his past, a snowy landscape, a cold, frightening labyrinth, a dangerous task of some sort.

"Me, you bloody bastard, me! *Hollister* . . . your dear friend Teen."

It was hard to think. "Marvelous Gap?"

"Jerkin' right! Where else?" The man advanced, a big, clumsy weapon at the ready: a military laser rifle. "And how've you been?"

He knew that this bitter-faced man would kill him, but he couldn't bring himself to care. What did he have to live for?

Ice-blue . . . .

Lessing sighed. Yes, there was *that.* He didn't know what he had to do or why, but he couldn't let it end here. Not yet.

"Christ, pay attention!" The man swung the heavy weapon to and fro. "I'm going to blow your bleedin' balls off, one at a time. Then I'm going to kneecap you, shoot you through each arm, and . . . ."

Lessing didn't want to hear Hollister's catalogue of horrors. He asked, "Why?"

"Eh? *Eh?* Why? Why *what?* Why am I about to unzip you? You stupid dongo, at Marvelous Gap I was supposed to, if you got off the bleedin' string. Then when you started thumbin' us, one by one . . . ."

"I never did."

"Liar! Couldn't find you then. When you did turn up, you were safe in India, surrounded by Nazis, the bastards I hate most. I'm a Jew, you know . . . Halperin's the name I was born with, not Hollister . . . then you became irrelevant until you got your Ponape operation going. I missed you there, but Richmond found you. He knew a lot I didn't . . . never discovered what. After Ponape you disappeared . . . seein' the sights in Russia, I heard later. Then you popped up again like a bleedin' bad penny in Mulder's fortress and became a

'colonel' of your murderin' Cadre. Then you became relevant all
over again. Almost got you in Oregon, what?"

"You got a lot of other people, including some kids."

"Casualties of war, *Herr Ober*-fucking-*gruppenführer* Lessing.
You ought to agree with that. Your lads gassed enough of us."

"Hmm . . . I disagree; not enough, I think. For whom are you
working?"

"Like to know, wouldn't you?" The other man jeered. "Ah, I
don't suppose it matters now. Me and Korinek, we both work for a
coalition, y'might say: some Jews, some Gentiles, some business
interests, some military, some religious. You could call us the status
quo. The bloody Establishment!" He whinnied with laughter. "Too
bad you're about to get dis-established!"

"You . . . your coalition . . . used Pacov?"

"Too right! We had to."

"My God!"

"Oh, don't sound so poggin' pious! You'd have done the same
in our boots. We used Pacov to save Israel from the Russians. The
Soviets were plannin' a bit of surgery on the Middle East: conventional warfare under the pretense of 'stopping Israeli atrocities
against the Arabs.' With the Americans busy elsewhere, it would've
been easy for Moscow to push Israel back to its old boundaries . . .
before Cairo and North Africa, before the Baalbek War, like it was
in the 1990's. So we were going to do the world a grand favor: pot
off the Soviets, occupy Mother Russia, sweep up the pieces, give
some spoils to Israel and some to ~ur pals . . . and incidentally
become the supreme power on earth. Amen, brother, amen!"

"But . . . ? Starak?"

"Things went wrong-o. We didn't realize the Russkies were so
ready with Starak! They retaliated. We wanted things as they were,
except with us leadin' the band. We never meant to see the Western
world destroyed, though it did work out better for us in the end . . .
fewer enemies to fight. Our biggest regret is that Israel got
thumbed!"

Lessing smiled. "Oh, the Russians didn't thumb Israel. *I* did that
. . . with the Pacov I stole at Marvelous Gap."

It took a moment to sink in. The other man's features went pale,
then red, then purple with rage. "*You*? You *what*?"

"That's right. Me. All by myself. I gave Richmond two vials of
Pacov. Then I saw to it they got wet. In Jerusalem."

That wasn't strictly true, but it served the purpose: Hollister-
Halperin's hatred became almost palpable in the air between them.
He might try to kill Lessing quickly. An angry opponent makes
mistakes.

The laser rifle hissed, and Lessing rolled desperately to the side. The beam wasn't aimed at him, though; it had cut off one of poor, dead Goddard's legs at the knee. Both edges of the wound were cauterized, and the floor beneath the body smoked.

"That's a sample! You're next, you dinkin' Nazi bastard! Maybe an ankle, maybe a wrist." The weapon came up again, its recharger humming. Hollister was too experienced to make a really dumb mistake, but maybe he could be outwitted.

Lessing rolled and scrambled again. This time the beam ploughed a fiery furrow in the gold-flocked wallpaper behind his right ear.

"Did I miss? Oh, too bloody bad! Sorry! Here, let's have another go!" Hollister fired again.

Lessing both felt and saw the beam this time. The sword of light opened a black hole the size of a pea in the underside of his left biceps near the armpit. The pain was excruciating; he expelled an unwilling hiss of agony from his lungs and felt consciousness starting to slip away. He skidded on the water-soaked carpet, fell, and tumbled against a sand-filled corridor ashtray.

"And now, ladeez 'n' gents, for the final encore . . . !" Hollister crooned. He hoisted his weapon. He was not a big man, and the laser rifle was awkward. Not that it would do Lessing any good: one hit almost anywhere, and he was unzipped! He cast about for something to throw.

The ashtray, a ceramic cylinder nearly three feet high, made a passable bowling ball. Lessing sent it rolling toward Hollister's feet. The man danced aside, and the unbearably bright beam gouged a sizzling trough in the roof.

Lessing tensed his muscles to leap. It was his last and only chance.

Hollister gaped upward, over his head.

The ceiling groaned, creaked, and sagged. Plaster silted down, followed by a thin dribble of water from the long cut the laser had made.

The water quickly increased to a rivulet, then to a deluge.

Water is heavy. The run-off drains for the sprinklers on the floor above must have been blocked. A short laser burst could not sever the steel supporting girders, of course; the rocketing from the helicopters already had done that. But the laser did open a hole through wood and lath and plaster, which was all that was holding up that part of the ceiling.

A torrent poured down into Hollister's amazed face, followed by a rushing flood of heavier debris.

Hollister vanished without a sound.

Chaos. The building squealed like an animal in its death-agony.

Cold, black water surged up around Lessing's ankles, then his thighs. He lost his footing, sank into a muck of churning rubble, rolled head over heels, and found himself hanging onto the very lip of the elevator shaft, bruised and dazed, buffeted by broken woodwork, furniture, and slimy, soft, invisible things. The icy river rolled over and past him, down into the abyss. He clawed at the ironwork grill of the safety door and hung on.

The water diminished to a trickle. He staggered up, slithered over the wrack now almost blocking the corridor, and looked for Hollister. He saw that the section of hallway where they had been was now a jumble of cement blocks and beams and ruin.

Hollister lay under a tilted length of steel girder, almost completely submerged in rubble. Furiously, Lessing dug boards, laths, pipes, and bricks away to free the man's face.

Hollister opened eyes like red-rimmed marbles in a white-smeared mask. He coughed, choked, and moaned, "Help me!"

The pretty lady in the ice-blue gown handed Lessing a shard of broken glass. This was a time for mercy, she said.

Lessing had to agree. He used the shard to slit the Jew's throat.

The walls trembled. More cave-ins were imminent. Somewhere below explosions boomed. Was Korinek going to bring the building down? It would make it easier to explain, of course: a savage fire-fight against terrorists who blew up themselves and the hotel rather than surrender to the forces of goodness and love.

Lessing didn't care. There was no more to do here. He wiped his bloody hands on his shirt and arose, hugging his injured arm. He would go upstairs, to his own apartment, and wait.

He would be with Liese when the end came.

He picked his way through the destruction, muttering to the lady in ice-blue as he went. Somehow he found a usable staircase on the opposite side of the hotel.

His apartment was cold when he got there. The door to the chasm that had been his bedroom was open. He closed it. He didn't want to think of Liese lying in the bathroom beyond, unreachable and still.

He heard a noise outside in the corridor. This time he looked before calling out.

It was Sam Morgan, just emerging from his apartment, a black, leatherette briefcase under his arm, for all the world like a young executive on his way to a board meeting!

Morgan uttered a gasp of surprise. "Jesus! Lessing? You still here? Didn't think anybody was left alive . . . !"

He nodded wordlessly.

"Can I help? My God . . . your arm . . . !"

"No matter now. Where's Wrench?"

"Wrench? Haven't seen him. We've got to get out of here! Come on!"

"How long you been in town?" An idea was forming at the back of Lessing's mind. His mental slide-projector clicked, and he blinked at the brilliance of the visual memory.

"Got in today. What the devil does that matter?"

"Nothing. What's in the briefcase?"

Morgan peered, then came over to take Lessing by his good arm. "Hey, you really have been pounded, man! God! Come on, we'll get you to a doctor."

"Through the power tunnels? Right under Korinek's feet?"

"Of course. We can make it out of Washington and get to our headquarters in Virginia."

"Sure. Nobody'll be watching, of course. Sam, what've you got in the briefcase?"

"Important Party papers, dammit. First things first. Downstairs . . . ."

Lessing reached out and took the briefcase. Morgan made a futile grab after it.

"Sam, all flights into Washington were booked up a week in advance. How *did* you get here from Chicago?"

"Car, of course," the other sounded annoyed. "What the hell's the matter with you? Here, let me carry my own briefcase. You're wounded."

He held it back. "That's green light. You had a long drive. All night, then through Korinek's cordon, through the shelling . . . through the power tunnels. You must be tired. Thought you might've been here for a few days already. Shacking with a girl in a private house somewhere?"

"Fast and lucky, you know me! No, I just got in today."

"I asked before: what's in the briefcase? Korinek let you through to pick up some papers? Papers the Jews and their buddies in the 'coalition' can't risk having found? Papers about Pacov?"

"*What?* Pacov? Jews? Coalition? You're . . . ."

"Crazy? Yeah, I am crazy." Lessing drew a deep breath. The lady in ice-blue was standing by the bedroom door, watching. "Sam, *I know.*"

"Know what?" Morgan's eyes were fixed on him, as a mongoose stares at a cobra.

"The house in Annandale. The clothes there are your size. They're the kind of thing you wear." He gestured at Morgan's elegant suit. "You've always had great taste, Sam, rich and fancy."

"I haven't a clue . . . !"

"I do. I have a funny sort of photographic memory, Sam. I see pictures: click, like a snapshot, every detail in living color. Right now I see you at a table in a big room, like a church, with stained-glass windows. It's an expensive restaurant. You're talking to somebody, but I can't see who it is. You're wearing a beautiful sport coat, sort of a tweed, I think it's called . . . grey. Anyway, you're rubbing the left sleeve. There's a blackish stain there, like when the dry-cleaners can't completely get a spot out. You remember that?"

"Of course not! . . . And so what?"

"Printer's ink, I think. That's what Eighty-Five said 'James F. Arthur' had the dry cleaners in Detroit try to take out of his sport coat."

"You are *deranged*, Lessing. Give me my goddamned case, and get out of my way . . . !"

"Aren't you curious who 'James F. Arthur' is, Sam? Anybody else would ask. But you don't need to . . . not when *you're* 'James F. Arthur' yourself. Is that your real name or a pseudonym? 'James F. Arthur' is the guy who arranged for the Marvelous Gap spesh-op. He started Pacov to keep the Russians from re-arranging the Middle East, to give Israel some *Lebensraum*, to help the Jews and their 'coalition' take all the marbles. 'James F. Arthur' is the greatest genocide who ever lived, and he is *you*, Sam. You killed half the world!"

"You're raving, Lessing! All this just from a spot on my coat?"

"And other things: after we picked you up on that flight to meet Outram in Colorado, our enemies always seemed to be half a jump ahead of us." His odd, eidetic memory was dropping slide after slide into his mental projector. "You had to get out of the car before your doggies in the helicopter got there; otherwise they would've thumbed you along with Mulder and Wrench and me. And Ponape: who gave the Izzies the plans of our installation? And later, in Oregon . . . ."

Morgan relaxed against the door frame. "Okay, Lessing, okay! Let's say you've put it all together. Say I'm a kikibird, a weasel planted way back when Mulder was just another happy, little Nazi kid getting his neighborhood SS gang together. Don't you think I'm *right*? Don't you think it's *right* to rid the world of the Nazis once and for all . . . to stamp them out, eradicate them root and branch? What are they but a bunch of gangsters who're always trying to rock the boat, to stir people up so that they can take things away from their rightful owners?"

"What things?"

"The world, man, the world!"

"And who're its rightful owners?"

"The same ones they've always been . . . the people I work for. They deserve to be on top, because they're smarter and tougher than the Nazis . . . and a lot more realistic. They understand the way the world works, and they know how to keep the people contented, keep everything on an even keel."

"Keep everything bland, Sam?" The woman in ice-blue smiled, and he nodded at her. Morgan peered in her direction but didn't seem to see her; Lessing wondered why. "Mulder trusted you."

"Trust? Nazis don't deserve trust!"

Lessing watched Morgan's fingers inch toward his right-hand coat pocket. Wounded as he was, he could break this man's arm in three places before he got his little popper out.

"Mulder and his people are loyal to their ideals, loyal to their movement, and loyal to each other and to those who support them. What kind of saints have you got in your gang?"

Morgan chewed his lower lip. "Look, Lessing, I just do my job. Remember how Wrench used to sing that stupid Christmas carol about 'four FBI, three CIA, two kikibirds, and an Israeli in a pear tree?' I'm one of the kikibirds. Cleverer than most."

"*Why*, Sam? Are you Jewish? You sure don't look Black."

"Me? The Great White Hope of the Party of Humankind? Shit, no, I'm no kike! I'm in it for money and power . . . two of the three reasons for everything that happens on earth, the third being sex, which I get enough of anyway."

"Kinky sex, judging by your Annandale basement."

Morgan shrugged. His index finger was caressing the flap of his pocket.

Lessing smiled. "You guys wanted me thumbed. Why didn't you do it yourself, Sam? You had opportunities. Why send Richmond and Hollister?"

"I'd have blown my cover. You weren't important enough for that."

"You had better things to do?"

"*Much* better. I still have. If Mulder's really dead, there'll be a struggle for control of the Party: Grant Simmons, Wrench, if he's alive, Borchardt, Goddard . . . " Morgan couldn't know that Goddard was dead " . . . Abner Hand, and the rest. It'll be a free-for-all. Our coalition will see to it that *I* win. I'm your next *Führer*, Lessing! Give us a big *Sieg Heil*, brother, and a high five!" Morgan remembered where he was and sobered. "Hey, look, none of this was personal, man!"

"We have to go now," Lessing said. The lady was beckoning.

"Where?" Three of Morgan's fingers were inside his pocket.

Lessing hefted the briefcase. "Downstairs, to Korinek, of course. I'm sure he'll want to see me."

Morgan began to smile. "Aha, bandwagon time! You've served different masters before. You're a merc, and you want to be on the

winning side. We should be able to work something out. I know
you're no ideological Nazi."

"What'll Korinek give me if I come over?"

"Your life for starters. If you're good, you can have a job, money, a
nice bint-baby or two . . . not Anneliese Meisinger, of course; she's too
wound up with Mulder and the Party!" Morgan's hand began to
withdraw from the pocket—without the gun. He had always preferred
doing things the easy way.

"Liese! Oh, Sam, I almost forgot. Liese is in there . . . in the
bathroom."

"She's *where*?"

"In there. She's hurt, Sam. She can't move." Lessing paused to listen
to the lady in the ice-blue robe. "Would you help me, Sam? Help me
move her downstairs?"

The other man grinned. His hand was out of his pocket now—empty.
"Why, sure. Of course. Look, I spoke too fast. We can arrange it so you
can have Liese. Without Mulder, she's just one more . . . ."

"Hundred-lira bint-baby. A good Cairo pog."

"Christ, you're raving, Lessing." Morgan reached for his briefcase
again, but Lessing moved away, toward the bedroom door. "Not that I
blame you, after all you've been through."

Lessing set the briefcase down. "Here, Sam," he said kindly, "let me
help you through."

He opened the door and gave Morgan a gentle push.

He didn't even watch.

Later, he awoke again from a dream of an ice-blue maiden with
tawny, golden skin and dark-blonde hair. She looked like Liese sometimes, and like somebody else sometimes.

A man in a black helmet and tunic knelt beside him. There were other
black uniforms as well. He saw booted feet and glittering weapons, and
he smelled gunpowder and smoke and charred wood.

"Here's the doctor!" a voice said. "My God . . . !"

"The briefcase," Lessing husked. "Don't lose it."

"Don't worry," the black-garbed man soothed. "Hey, he's green
light!"

The sable uniforms in the background shifted. Lessing tried to recall
the man's name. Tim? Tom?

Lights sprang up on his mental photographic stage. The homely,
Midwestern face before him was Tim Helm, wearing black Cadre
battle-dress. How had he gotten here?

Helm said, "Colonel Lessing, Korinek and his bunch are in Cadre
custody. We came up from Andrews and surrounded them. Got support
from General Dreydahl and some sailors from Admiral Carning.
General Hartman's under arrest, and our people are in control of most
of the military bases across the country. Miss Caw phoned from L.A. to
say her folks are green light there too." He hesitated. "We lost Mr.
Mulder, though. His wife as well. Their house in Virginia is a crater."

"Excuse us, sir!" A soldier in paramedic uniform motioned Helm aside to make room for an antiseptic-smelling man with grey hair. "Get that arm first, please. That's the same one he almost lost in Oregon."

Pain sparkled in his left biceps, then was replaced by numbness. "Liese," Lessing muttered. "She's in there . . . in the bathroom . . . get her out! Please, get her out!" A wave of fluffy, grey mist was rolling up to wash away the lonely little lighthouse of his mind.

A smaller figure leaned close. Through distant, booming surf Lessing recognized Wrench. He stretched out his good hand. "Liese . . . out of there."

Helm asked, "Out of where? The *bathroom*?" Lessing heard muttering from others in the room.

Wrench squatted beside him. "Sorry, doctor. Make way."

There were footsteps, familiar footsteps. He struggled to see, but the leaden wave kept erasing everything.

Someone else was there.

Something warm and wet touched his cheek. Somebody took hold of him and clutched him so tightly it made him wince. He smelled perfume and both felt and heard the rustle of silk.

He knew that fragrance.

It was Liese's perfume.

It couldn't be Liese.

A purring, choppy, and utterly beloved voice said, "Mr. Mulder asked me go get Grant Simmons. Nobody else . . . go. Dulles Airport. Oh, my darling, my darling . . . ."

The voice broke off. Warm tears stung abrasions on his face that he hadn't known were there. The embrace grew too tight to endure, but he endured it gladly anyway. Now he really couldn't see: both eyes were blurry. Have to get new ones.

Damage control reported to the bridge, but the skipper refused to abandon the wheel. Salt water blinded him, and the hollow thunder of the storm reverberated in his ears. Nothing and nobody could keep this ship from getting through! Ahead he saw the harbor lights of home. Victory was his!

Wrench growled, "Leave 'em alone for a bit, doctor."

"Who is the girl in the bathroom?" Tim Helm asked from the lowering darkness.

"We'll get to her," Wrench replied. "She's probably one of the kids from Communications. She must've hid up here when the firing started and got thumbed by the missile concussion. Lessing . . . me and Goddard too . . . thought it was Liese. She was wearing grey, silk stockings. A lot of the women copy Liese."

"I can see why." Tim's voice faded away.

"Yeah," Wrench said. "Liese is a lady."

PRIMARY OPERATOR: LESSING, ALAN, NO MIDDLE INITIAL. IDENTITY CHECKS COMPLETED: FP, RP, VP, DNA. DATE AND TIME: NOVEMBER 5, 2050; 0903:23 HOURS

PRIME DIRECTIVE SUPPLEMENT: ALL FILES WILL HENCEFORTH BE RETRIEVABLE BY A PERSON HOLDING THE STATUS OF PRIMARY OPERATOR. HIDDEN FILES, OUBLIETTE FILES, TEXT AND DATA FILES, AND CONTROL FILES WILL BE LISTED IN THE CENTRAL DIRECTORY AND WILL BE ACCESSIBLE UPON COMMAND. PASSWORDS, LOCK-CODES, AND OTHER BLOCKING PROCEDURES WILL BE INOPERATIVE.

CURRENT PRIMARY OPERATORS INCLUDE: LESSING, ALAN, NO MIDDLE INITIAL; MEISINGER, ANNELIESE; WREN, CHARLES HANSON; BORCHARDT, HANS KARL; SIMMONS, GRANT WILLIAM. FURTHER MEMBERS OF THE PARTY OF HUMANKIND MAY BE GRANTED TEMPORARY PRIMARY OPERATOR STATUS WHEN SO ORDERED BY TWO OR MORE OF THE LISTED PRIMARY OPERATORS. NO PERSON NOT A PRIMARY OPERATOR IS PERMITTED ACCESS TO INFORMATION CLASSIFIED AS SECRET.

CHAPTER TWENTY-NINE

Thursday, December 23, 2060

"Patty's plane gets in from Seattle at 1445," Wrench said. "It'll be good to see her again."

Lessing sighed. "Yeah, and me with six months of work and a week to do it in!"

"The price of glory!" The little man ran his fingers through his hair. He had been luckier than Lessing, with only "distinguished" silver sideburns to show for what he happily proclaimed had been a "life of sin." On the other hand, Lessing's thin, ash-blonde locks were rapidly vanishing. As Wrench put it, "the fuzz was wearing off the cue ball."

"Look at this!" Lessing waved a hand at his crowded desk. "Everything from applications for special exemptions from the eugenics laws to status reports on our bases in the Persian Gulf, to letters from the parents of Banger boogies whining that their kids can't get their supply of snuffy-doo in the National Service highway-rebuilding camp in Montana, to articles on DNA experiments to improve the race . . . ! I don't see *any* of this *anywhere* in my job-description!"

Wrench rolled his eyes upwards. "You're where the train stops and the buck leaves the tracks, as they say. The reason Simmons makes such a great President is because he knows how to get work out of assholes like you."

Lessing grinned, and Wrench asked, "By the way, do you want me to squire Patty to the Presidential Christmas party tomorrow night?"

"You never learned to keep your paws off little girls, did you?" Lessing joked. "Yeah, you take her. You're less dangerous than those Marines in the honor guard."

"You mean Jenny Caw's personal drum, bugle, and banging corps?"

Lessing chuckled. "Don't be rude! Jen's marrying Hans Borchardt in June."

"So? Think that'll slow her down?" He looked around for Lessing's coffee pot; it was empty, already washed, and put away for the coming holiday. "Though maybe a good German can keep our Miss Caw in line!" Wrench made jocular spanking motions.

"Oh, chug it, will you! I've got an appointment with some special envoy from New Sverdlovsk. You want to come?"

"If it's not going to drag on. What's it about?"

"No idea. Grant got a call from their embassy asking for me. Urgent, immediate, like *now*! He says go, I go. A 'private briefing session,' his secretary said."

"Security going to let me in?"

"If I say so."

"Then I'll drift along and keep you company. I still have to move some paper to push our Martyrs' Day bill through Congress. The Mulders . . . ."

It hurt to remember. Lessing said, "I know. The Mulders . . . and Bill Goddard, Gordy Monk, and a lot of others. Ten years, and we're just getting around to honoring them. Later is better than never, I suppose, but not by much."

"Has it been that long? Well, you can't say it hasn't been interesting: the unmasking of the Coalition; the coup that failed; the fighting; Korinek's public confession; the destruction of their secret camps; the trials; the expulsion edicts. All that's over now, buddy. We won't forget . . . it's in every school book . . . but it's high time we moseyed on."

"The backlash . . . ." Lessing shut his mind against memories of trucks and tanks and soldiers, the chaos and confusion, the rioting, and the aftermath.

"Let it lie! The Jews are gone, off to Ufa and Kharkov and Kuybyshev. We run our enclave, and they run theirs. No problem, as long as they don't monkey with us."

"That's just it: they *do* monkey. They always have. Their history's like a roller coaster: start at the bottom, struggle up, get to the top, then a long swoop down to catastrophe, then begin all over again."

"Like Santayana said: 'Those who cannot remember the past are condemned to repeat it.'"

"Whoever Santa Ana was, she was wrong. Nobody *really* learns from history. Even those who know it have to repeat it. People just stick on another name, pretend it's new and different, and go around again."

"Now you sound like Hegel." Wrench shut his eyes and quoted. "Something like: 'People and governments never have learned anything from history, or acted on principles deduced from it.'"

"You've been reading books again!"

"Nope, just *World Classic Comics* . . . their special philosophy number."

"Anyway, the Jews nearly beat us this time. The roller coaster almost didn't go into its downswing."

"It was our own fault. We *let* it happen."

"Right. We let 'em get our sympathy, give us guilt trips, preach to us about their phony 'Holocaust,' and work their way into the fabric of our society. We should've been more vigilant! What I never understood was the cooperation they got from some of our corporations, our politicians, our educators and intellectuals and publicists! Such people don't even deserve to be called collaborators or race-traitors! 'Just plain stupid' says it better! You'd think simple self-interest would have rung a few bells."

"It's called *coin*, man! I'll bet there were some Roman merchants in Jerusalem who cried over lost business when the legions flattened Solomon's temple, ran the Jews out of Palestine, and started the Diaspora in the first place!"

Lessing hunted for his wallet in the clutter on his desk. "They never give up, though. Their enclaves in Ufa and Kharkov and Kuybyshev are booming, full of immigrants, looking for more room, and spoiling for a fight."

"Always *Lebensraum*, the eternal pressure on every ethnos group. Expand or perish."

"Some of 'em want to expand right back here: first to the People's Republic of British Columbia, or to Central America south of our holdings in Mexico, then eventually to sunny California, Florida, and Second Avenue!"

"More like Madison Avenue, Wall Street, and right here in the White House. But *not* with us watching the door."

"We can't always be watching. Our roller coaster goes up and down too, and they still have friends here. Their propaganda was really good: a lot of average folks don't like to remember what had to be done during the backlash and the expulsions. Too much mushy, liberal brainwashing for too long."

"There are times," Wrench marveled, "when I believe in the transmigration of souls."

"What?"

"You sound so much like Bill Goddard that it amazes me."

Lessing started to wriggle into his uniform greatcoat. "I studied history the hard way, like Bill did. I just started later, and it took me longer, that's all. I was always a lousy student."

Wrench came over to help him; Lessing's twice-wounded left arm had never completely recovered.

Together they trotted down the snowy steps of the Executive Office Building, returned salutes from the black-clad Cadre guards on duty, and took Wrench's American-made Homeland-500 limousine. It wasn't a long drive over to the embassy on Massachusetts Avenue, but the winter had been exceptionally cold. Their destination had previously served as the embassy of Austria, but Pacov and Starak had altered the maps forever, and Borchardt had persuaded his Reunited German Republic to sell the place to New Sverdlovsk. They told their driver to come back in half an hour, stamped snow off their boots, and hurried inside. There they doffed their caps and coats and waited in an antechamber that was a memento of the building's past. Eventually a pleasant-faced young woman came to escort them upstairs.

The room they entered was standard for embassy pomp and portentousness: a fireplace; matched-grain panelling of lustrous walnut; drapes of rich, burgundy damask; chairs upholstered in black leather; massive, oaken tables with carved lion's feet; and a Persian carpet deep enough to lose your shoes in. Bottles, decanters, and glasses winked and glowed upon a long sideboard beneath a hero-sized portrait of Colonel—now Supreme General—Terence Burnham Copley.

"The old boy finally made it," Wrench breathed admiringly. "No Napoleon suit, but you will note the heroic tilt of the chin, the far-seeing glint in the steely eyes, the hand just itching to crawl inside the coat lapel. Hell, Lessing, when I went to New Sverdlovsk to find you, old Copley didn't have a pot to piss in! Now I'll bet he decorates the basement of his outhouse with Czarist antiques!"

"'Tain't so. The best loot was up in Moscow 'n' Leningrad," a voice behind them drawled. "'N' you jizmoes ripped that off! All us poor fuckers got was factories and industrial shit."

They turned to see Johnny Kenow, dressed in the russet and black of the Army of New Sverdlovsk. Beside him, wearing the female counterpart of Kenow's uniform, stood Rose Thurley. Both displayed the collar-pips of staff officers.

"Surprise, surprise . . . !" Wrench muttered. "Special envoys . . . ? More like hanky-panky at the top of the ladder!"

Rose looked much the same as Lessing remembered her: a bit thicker . . . dumpier, to be blunt . . . her cheeks more rounded, her short hair a mousier shade of red-brown-grey. Damned if she didn't resemble a Russian peasant woman. Perhaps there was something to be said for environment over genetics after all.

"Lessing . . . ?" She ventured.

He moved toward her but stopped short. It had been too long.

She opened her arms. "Hey, mate! Give us a good 'un!"

He closed the gap, took her in his arms, and bussed her soundly on the cheek. That was all he could ever offer her.

Kenow winked at Wrench. "What say we work us out a deal?"

"What're you dealing?"

"Whatever wets yer whistle, for starters. We got damn' near everythin.'" He inspected the bottles on the sideboard. "Don't try our vodka, though . . . I know what goes in it. See some scotch here . . . pre-Pacov stuff . . . ." Glasses clinked.

"Lessing doesn't drink anymore." Wrench picked up a linen napkin and inspected the tray of canapes. "Which is what a beautiful wife'll do to you. Being a bachelor, I occasionally take my joy in liquid form." He raised his scotch to the light to admire the color.

Rose still held Lessing's fingers in hers. She shook herself, sighed, and let go.

He smiled, trying for just the right mix of friendliness and distance. "I can't stay long . . . got to get back and change clothes for the Christmas party tonight. Uh . . . you two want to come?"

Rose shook her head.

"Can't," Kenow replied. "We ain't even s'posed to be in this country."

"If you'd given me a day's notice you were coming . . . !"

"Shit, I mean it, Lessing: *we ain't here*. Rose's in Germany . . . or her double is, a Lithu-friggin'-anian woman who looks more like her'n she does herself. She's spendin' Rose's money buyin' Christmas presents in Berlin. Me, I'm in New Sverdlovsk in bed with the Empress . . . you 'member my wife . . . and the worst dinkin' cold in all Rooshia. Not even Frank Lithgow . . . our ambassador . . . *officially* knows we're in Washington."

Wrench ran a curious finger over a huge, brass samovar, squinted into a lighted cabinet containing delicate copies of Faberge jeweled eggs, and pulled up short in front of Kenow. "Okay, folks, to hang it out on the line: what's the scam? Why the secrecy?"

Both spoke at once. Rose won. "We've got photographs, documents, maps . . . ."

"Of what?" Lessing threw himself down in one of the leather armchairs. He looked surprised as it creaked, hissed, and slowly subsided under his weight.

"The Izzies, luv! The bastard Izzies!" Rose stumped over to a table at the far end of the room and returned with a leather-bound portfolio. "'Ere, cop this . . . 'ave a look!"

The aerial photographs and infra-red pictures would require interpretation by experts, but the snapshots were straightforward enough.

"Whose rocket?" Lessing asked in hushed tones. He picked up the glossy to see better.

"The Izzies,' what'd yer think? An' that's a bleedin' atomic warhead stuck on it like a wart on yer dink! They got a dozen of these poggers! Americans didn't find and destroy 'em all . . . some pre-Pacov SS-50 medium-range jobbies still in Central Asia, transport carriers 'n' everything. The Izzies bought 'em from the Tatars or the dinkin' Mongols or somebody. Mebbe they built their own, though there's no proof of that."

Wrench turned the photographs around. "Can't be. We'd have had reports."

"Bugger yer reports. It's dead cert! We got better spies in Ufa and Kharkov than you got. The Brits have a decent bloke in Kuybyshev, though. They'll confirm."

"All right. Assume the worst. Who's the target?"

"Us, who else? First we thought they was for the Turks, but we learned different."

Lessing felt adrenaline building up and blood starting to beat in his temples. He wanted to rub the bridge of his nose, but Liese had said that that always gave him away. Instead, he stroked the brass studs in the slick, leather upholstery of his chair.

He took a careful breath. "How do you know?"

"Here." Johnny Kenow spilled a stack of documents and photographed pages out in front of him. "We lost three good ol' boys gittin' this."

"You sure these missiles are nuclear? Not conventional explosive warheads?"

"Right there." Rose pointed with a blunt fingernail at a paragraph of Hebrew script. "Translation's pinned on it."

"Never did learn their goddamned language," Wrench mumbled. "You're right. What's this . . . ? Nerve gas too?"

"Yup. We seen it." Kenow nodded energetically. "'Member Doctor Casimir?" Lessing grunted assent. "Well, he was a Jew, but we turned him . . . he come over to our side . . . and Copley sent him into Kharkov. You'd never believe what he brung out! The Izzies're buildin' a poggin' war machine in there that could flatten New Sverdlovsk . . . and the Turks and the Pakis to boot! Mebbe even take out yer base in Moscow, if they wanna go that route."

"Our Moscow office has already told us some of this," Lessing said, a little uncomfortably; Wrench was looking at him. Cadre recon reports were need-to-know only, and the Secretary for Education and Information wasn't always a member of that charmed circle.

Wrench scratched his jaw. "I have a question. Why me and Lessing? Why not go right to the top to President Simmons himself . . . call a cabinet meeting . . . bring in the Joint Chiefs . . . the whole song and dance? Lessing can't do much for you; he's a Cadre general, but he doesn't have the authority to send troops or military aid. As for me, I can put your evidence on Home-Net and our other networks, but . . . well, I mean, what the hell . . . ?" He trailed off, nonplussed.

"Me 'n' Johnny know Lessing," Rose answered slowly. "He's an old friend, like. We can talk to him. Copley knows him, too." She looked embarrassed. "We wasn't expecting you, Minister . . . um, Secretary . . . Wren, but you're welcome."

"What can I . . . we . . . do, then?" Lessing asked.

Rose held out a sealed envelope. "This here's from Copley. A . . . a sort of announcement . . . and a request."

Lessing opened it. He read for a moment, whispered, "Jesus . . . ," and passed it on to Wrench.

"Yup," Johnny Kenow looked at his watch. "It's all over. Right now Copley's eatin' dinner in what's left of Ufa. There won't be no Kuybyshev, neither. All of northeastern Izzie-land'll be in our hands by this evenin,' and the Turks'll be in Kharkov, Donetsk, and Kiev. We're keepin' the Pakis happy by lettin' 'em have Uzbekistan, Turkistan, Umbrella-stan, and a bunch of other Moe-hammedan 'stans' out east. They'll keep an eye on the Indians . . . who're too fungled with the Chinese and the rest of Asia to bugger us right now, anyway."

Wrench laid the letter down as though it were a bomb itself. "A *fait accompli*, then? Copley sent you two to Lessing to smooth the way for his declaration of war."

"It's more'n a declaration," Rose said defensively. "We already *done* it. The Jews in Russia're *gone* . . . finished . . . fungled . . . croaked . . . as of 1200 hours today, your time. Whoever's left'll be taken care of by week's end."

"You're sure? They . . . they won't unzip Copley instead?"

"No bleedin' way! Copley's an experienced merc, and he don't take chances! We sent in a three-pronged mechanized ground attack; we got us heavy air support . . . ours 'n' the Turks' . . . and we got nerve-gas canisters planted under Ufa's city hall just in case. The Turks'll find it harder goin,' down at Kharkov, but they'll make it."

"God!" Wrench muttered. "Why couldn't the Jews have let well enough alone?"

Lessing began to gather up the papers and photographs. He pinched the bridge of his nose, then dragged his fingers away. "A preemptive, surgical first strike, just like the Izzies pulled on the Arabs a few times." He picked up a sheaf of documents. "We keep this stuff, right? It's evidence of their intentions. I'll give it to Liese's publicity people right away, and we'll have it on Home-Net before nightfall. I think we can promise you support."

"They deserved it!" Kenow growled. "We didn't do nothin' to 'em."

"Even if you did, I doubt if our ethnos group'll make more than token objections. The world's had it. Anybody as unpopular as the Jews have always been . . . Egypt, Babylon, Rome, Spain, every country in Europe during the Middle Ages, Russia, America, the Third *Reich* . . . must be doing *something* wrong! We'd have preferred peaceful . . . and separate . . . and *distant* . . . co-existence, but they never got the message. Now we don't care anymore."

"It's too bad . . . ." Wrench began.

"Don't waste your pity!" Lessing snapped. "They wouldn't waste any on you. Sure, it's sad that innocent people have to suffer, but it can't be helped. That's reality! That's Nature! You can't save the dodo, the condors, and the other losers in the battle for survival. Species-extinction happens over and over, like rain in the summer-time. Forget ethics and morality and 'do-unto-others.' The Izzies said 'never again!' about the 'Holocaust,' but then they turned around and did to the Palestinians everything they *claimed* the Germans had done to them! They called it 'self-defense': war under the pretext of peace, oppression in the name of justice and stability! The Arabs were weak and went under, but we're a different story. We're going to make it, no matter who gets in our way."

"I hear Bill Goddard again," Wrench murmured.

"No, you hear *me*, Alan Lessing! There was a time when I'd have waffled and gone for 'turn the other cheek,' but not anymore! Now you hear me, and you hear our Party, our ethnos, our majority . . . our First *Führer*! You hear the past, you hear the present, and you hear the future! We *are* the future!"

Rose reached for Copley's letter. "Uh . . . there was one more point, Lessing."

"I saw it. Copley wants to bring New Sverdlovsk into the American union. He says you people already belong to our ethnos-group . . . Americans, Frenchmen, English, Germans mostly . . . and he wants statehood."

Kenow blinked his close-set eyes. "Y'might say we're payin' our dues by unzippin' the Izzies. That little service oughta get us inta yer club!"

"Fine by me," Lessing answered. "I'll put it to Grant, who'll put it to the rest of the Party high command. Then it goes to Congress.

That's all I can promise. . . . Oh, I assume Copley will export any minorities living in New Sverdlovsk?"

"Most're already gone. We did have a coupla dozen Jewish mercs when we started, but they all went over to Ufa, and now they're opfoes . . . and likely thumbed." He put down his glass. "And the Izzies caught poor old Casimir last month 'n' thumbed him too, so we ain't got no 'Jewish problem' at all, y'might say. We still got a few Asians, but they're lookin' at Manchuria or them little republics in China. Japs won't let 'em in . . . too pure 'n' racially homo-geney-ous. The fifty or sixty Blacks we had headed out for the Khalifa's place in Africa last month, too. He wouldn't take a couple of 'em, though, 'cause they was coffee-'n'-creams."

"We heard the Khalifa's refusing racial mixes and interracial couples," Wrench told Lessing. "He doesn't want mongrels any more than we do. Only pure-blood Blacks in his Islamic paradise."

"Still plenty of places for the poor suckers to go." Lessing tucked the portfolio under his arm and moved toward the door. "Let 'em go to Brazil, or the Caribbean, or any other place that'll take 'em. They are *not* coming here!"

"I'm glad to see Bill Goddard back," Wrench whispered to Lessing. "I did sort of miss him . . . ."

Lessing answered him with a wry grin. He shook hands with Rose and Kenow and started down the stairs.

"Wonder if I c'n git me one of them black uniforms?" Kenow asked plaintively of Rose. "Sure'd look good in it! Mebbe git me a job in Lessing's Treasury Department, too. Or Fort Knox . . . ?"

"Not if he bloody-well knows about it . . . !" The door closed on her final words.

The serpent looked longingly across the last gulf at the towering palisades and snow-tipped parapets of mighty Mount Kailas. The descent into the abyss would be fraught with peril, and the far side appeared well-nigh unclimbable. He sighed. "We can only try."

The mongoose smiled for the first time in many long, weary days. "It is impossible, brother. Turn back! Look you, down there!"

"I do not surrender my goal so easily." The serpent approached the edge of the precipice and peered into its depths.

The mongoose had long planned for this opportunity. He hurled himself upon the serpent and sank his sharp, pointed teeth into his neck. They rolled over and over upon the lip of the abyss.

"I knew you would betray me!" the serpent cried. "Thus was I wary!"

"I betray no one!" gasped the other. "I am true to my goal, which is the same as yours: to stand before Lord Siva! I will take your place before him, and he will reward me well!"

"Wicked mongoose! I shall bite you and cast your corpse into the pit!"

"Wicked serpent! You cannot gain purchase upon me. My sleek coat foils your fangs, and your poison has no effect upon my blood!"

Thus they fought and scuffled and snarled and hissed. The sun's bright eye shone down, and the day grew hot. It was as the mongoose had said: his smooth, brown fur and his lithe, wriggling limbs kept the serpent's fangs at bay; yet the mongoose, too, could not penetrate his opponent's hard scales or master his muscular coils. At length the mongoose grew warm, and he drew back. He cast off his furry robe that he might fight the better. Too late he remembered the protection it gave him. The serpent seized him and bit him, but in truth his venom was harmless.

"You cannot slay me!" panted the mongoose.

"Is it so?" wheezed the serpent. "I have seen you in your true form, and that knowledge is power! Now I know how to deal with you!" He seized the mongoose in his coils and lifted him up. The mongoose could not wriggle free, for he no longer wore his slippery pelt. The serpent bore him to the edge of the cliff, and there he let him go. Unable to gain a hold upon the serpent or upon the stones of the precipice, the mongoose plunged down and away, and thus did he perish.

On high Mount Kailas Lord Siva was attracted by the noise and dust of the battle. He gazed upon the serpent, all glossy and glistening with his own and his foeman's blood. His scales and fine markings shone bravely in the sunlight. The god admired the serpent's beauty, and by his divine powers he brought him over to Mount Kailas. So pleased was Lord Siva with this slim, handsome, and vital creature that he kept him, and honored him, and nourished him with milk and fruit throughout the eons of the *Kali Yug*. Indeed, sometimes Lord

Siva transformed himself into a great serpent of like aspect and
journeyed through the worlds of men and gods, arousing awe
and inspiring devotion wherever he went.
    —Indian fable

CHAPTER THIRTY

Wednesday, April 20, 2089

It was still early, but the crowds already were gathering beneath
the snapping flags: the traditional American red-white-and-blue
side by side with the red-white-and-black swastika banners of the
Party of Humankind. Music thumped and boomed in the distance
as the high school bands warmed up for the afternoon's parade, and
hawkers hustled the audience with foot-long belly-burner sausages,
periscopes, pennants, chair-canes, sunshades, lemonade, sodas, and
cotton candy. Children raced to and fro, ignoring the rows of
sweating, uniformed policemen and the pleas of their parents, to
play and shriek and laugh in the sunshine of Washington in April.
Spring was in the air: a fragrance compounded of grass and leaves
and early flowers, dust, exhaust fumes, perfume, popcorn, cooking
hotdogs, sweat, and excitement.

Today was the two-hundredth anniversary of the birthday of the
First *Führer*.

Lessing's unmarked limousine avoided the parade route. He had
his chauffeur take the less-crowded back streets as they sped
southeast toward Suitland.

The buildings, the people, and the atmosphere itself bore little
resemblance to the first time he and Wrench had passed this way,
back in '42. Now things were different: new construction was
everywhere; American cars—better designed and cheaper than the
Japanese models—filled the streets; the sidewalks thronged with
black and brown Party uniforms and the reds, blues, and yellows of
current fashion; and the holo-vid dioramas in the store windows
called and sang and cooed and tempted, advertising products un-
dreamed of nearly half a century before.

It was a new world—not a *brave*, new world, perhaps, but a
reasonably happy one.

Much of the old had departed. Sadly, that included Wrench. The
little man had succumbed to a heart attack last year, in October,
while the skies shed grey tears and the shrivelled black and brown
leaves of autumn drifted down.

The world was much emptier without him.

Lessing touched the "remind" button on his limousine's compu-
sec console and barked, "Agenda?"

The pleasant, sexless computer voice replied: "Attend the First
Führer's Day Parade at 1300 hours. Read the speech in the red

compartment of your briefcase. Return by 1450 hours for the commemoration party in the Rose Garden. Dinner with Chancellor Borchardt and family at 1800 hours at Blair House. Do not forget roses for Liese."

He smiled. "Couldn't forget if I tried. She'd kill me."

It would be good to see Hans and Jen again. Borchardt almost never came to Washington nowadays: too much to do in Europe, and Africa was seething with problems again. The Khalifa's Islamic nation was surrounded by clamoring Black states, hunger was rife, and nobody was willing to take the tough steps needed to solve things. Jen also had not been back to the States since a Vizzie terrorist had killed her mother in 2073. The Party never had succeeded in rounding up all of the Vizzies, and they kept resurfacing in their characteristically nasty manner. In a funny sort of way Lessing missed Jen almost as much as he missed Wrench.

He had forgotten how simple the compu-sec was. It was saying "Repeat?" over and over in plaintive tones.

"Cancel. Agenda for tomorrow?" He hoped there wasn't much, but he knew better.

"Visit Sperm Bank *Lebensborn* at 1000 hours. Confer Leader's Medal upon its director, Doctor Paul Lorch, at 1015. Meet with Senate Subcommittee for the Department of National Service at 1110. See Congressman Michael Radcliffe at 1235, regarding commutation of death sentence upon Alfred H. McLahan, convicted of drug sales to minors . . . ."

"Cancel that last. Inform the Congressman that I will not intervene." If there was any crime Lessing hated, it was the peddling of drugs to kids. Patty's three children had come close to being lured into the drugsters' trap, and if she hadn't been extra vigilant, snuffy-doo would have turned their brains into mush by now. It was hard being a single parent, even temporarily, but Patty would cope. At the moment her astronaut husband couldn't help with child-rearing: he and seven others were tramping the red deserts of Mars.

"You have a private conference with Chancellor Borchardt at 1300. Topics include the merger of American and European currencies, the Turkish threat in the Adriatic, the rebuilding of the stadium of the 1936 Olympic Games in Berlin, and the skirmishes between Indian and Thai troops near Rangoon. Then lunch at 1330. Rest from 1430 to 1600 hours. Meet Patty and her children at 1630, and dine with Chancellor Borchardt and his family at the German Embassy at 1730."

"What about Professor Peel of the National Academy for Genetic Research? Wasn't I supposed to look at some experiment or other?"

"Yes. That meeting has been postponed until April 28th."

"Minor stuff?"

"You will find letters prepared for your signature in the blue compartment of your briefcase. Most are requests for the naming of towns and public buildings after Party figures."

Renaming had grown into a major industry. The surprising thing was that in addition to the obvious heroes of the Party, there were requests for relative unknowns. Lessing had seen applications for commemorations of Otto Skorzeny, the commando who had rescued Mussolini by glider; for Hanna Reitsch, the woman test pilot who had once personally flown a V-1 rocket—and nearly made mincemeat of herself doing it; for Leon Degrelle, the heroic commander of a Belgian SS Division; for a whole gaggle of Ukrainians and East Europeans who had been persecuted back during the years of Jewish dominance; and for many others. Some college in Nebraska even wanted to name its agricultural school after Walter Darre, the Third *Reich*'s Minister of Agriculture; he had urged that industrial society be abolished and replaced with a hereditary peasant nobility—about as far from today's bustling, international world as the Cro-Magnon caves!

"What else?"

"In the green compartment you will find personal letters from Cadre-General Timothy Helm, PHASE-Commanders Charles Gillem and Herbert Salter, Colonel Theodore Metz, who developed the Magellan surveillance system, and others not on my known-list. The TV commentator, Jason Milne, also has been trying to reach you regarding the proposed construction of Siberian camps to accommodate the last Jews from England."

Lessing would get to most of the correspondence when he could. Ten years ago he would have answered the whole batch in one afternoon, but age had slowed him down. Milne was the most urgent: the world's remaining Jews had been given land, food, tools, self-government, and all the conveniences. Nobody was bothering them, yet they never seemed to stop meddling. Some bleeding heart was always ready, moreover, to invite them back into the Aryan ethnos sphere and let the whole mess start up all over again! Milne was a friend, though; he'd give the Party's position just the right degree of gentility, logic, and bite.

Lessing told the compu-sec, "Screen my letters, highlight specific requests, and hold. Ask Mr. Milne to make an appointment." He fumbled with his weaker left hand to shut off the machine.

It was hard to remember all the things he had to do. The present kept drifting away, and he increasingly depended upon Liese to hold it in focus. She had stayed young-looking in spite of white hair and the fragile, translucent look that slender, Germanic women developed in old age. Thinking of Liese made him feel warm inside.

He had not decided yet whether to take the gerontological treatment developed by the Party's labs in Schenectady. Rebuild cells? Restore vibrancy to flagging organs? Let miniaturized snowplows clear the cholesterol out of clogged arteries? It sounded like magic. It also wasn't ready for public dissemination: what to do with millions of elderly people miraculously restored to youth? You could keep such a process secret and use it yourself, of course, but that smacked too much of the bad, old days: hidden patents, secret cartels, buy-outs to keep products off the market, legal razzle-dazzle, and the rest of the "business practices" the Party had fought to eradicate. These days it would be a Federal crime—a capital offense—to hide something as important as a method of reversing aging.

Which didn't solve the problem.

Economic crimes had diminished, though: profiteering, insider trading, sweetheart contracts, and a hundred other tricks so complicated Lessing barely understood the first page of the lawyers' briefs. All he knew was that fair profit was fair incentive; anything more was a rip-off—and cause for a visit from PHASE.

"Sir? Mr. President?" Max Stalb, chief of his Cadre bodyguards, was peering in the car window at him. Max sported a handlebar moustache and wore heavy, copper bracelets that were rumored to conceal a number of useful tools and weapons.

"Ah? What?"

"We're here, sir. The Eighty-Five installation."

"Oh . . . fine. I'll go in by myself."

"Can't let you do that, sir. Regs."

"Well, here, then: you carry this." Lessing opened the door, got out, and handed Max a bulky package wrapped in gay, red-and-gold Christmas paper. "You're with me as far as the elevators. After that you stay put. You don't have security clearance for Eighty-Five's innards."

Max gnawed the ragged ends of his moustache. "Don't like it, sir."

Lessing grinned. "Too damned bad. Come on."

The receptionist was a humanoid, a graceful simulacrum of glass and golden wire and shiny steel. It came to life as they entered.

"This facility is closed, sirs, for the four days of the First *Führer's* Birthday celebration," it announced. "If you wish to see someone, please leave your names and vid-phone numbers where you may be reached."

"I am Alan Lessing, Primary Operator. Scan and identify."

Things hummed and clicked. The machine said, "Accepted. Your companion now, please."

"He will wait for me here. Make him comfortable." Lessing took back his package and made his way along the half-remembered corridor.

The elevator ride was a descent into memory. He could almost see Wrench beside him again, as on that long-ago day, swathed in an N.B.C. suit three sizes too large.

Beyond the air lock at the bottom the central operations room was alive with noise, lights, and people! Lessing's first impression was of a boxing match, a great hall jammed with spectators just before the fight. A bluish haze, like smoke or fog, hid the swinging booms of the ceiling lights, leaving most of the audience in semi-darkness. Some were quiet, but others were talking, cheering, arguing, yelling, fighting, and gesticulating, a madhouse of tumult and open mouths and waving arms. In the background screeching Banger rhythms competed with classical symphonies, a fat man singing an operatic aria, Indonesian *Gamelan* music, and a torch singer belting "Let Me Slarm You, My Jee-Ga Jee-Oh!" These, in turn, were drowned under a clattering rumble like that of a thousand factories, the drone of aircraft, carillons of bells, and peals of thunder. The wall screens flashed gaudy pictures, charts, and columns of flickering symbols. Lessing smelled incense, ripe strawberries, barbecuing beef, overheated electric insulation, salt water, rotten meat, and pine needles—among other things. At the far end of the room a mushroom cloud exploded noiselessly and dissipated against the ceiling. Nobody noticed.

Bedlam was too gentle a word. This was a convention down in Hell.

He looked at the people. The nearest was a spade-bearded man in a rusty-black suit; he was glaring at a portly British gentleman with a cigar. A skinny, starved-looking little man in a wrap-around robe shook his head violently in answer to a vulture-nosed woman wearing a business suit and 'sensible' shoes; she shook her fist at him. Farther away a naked Banger dancer leaped and pranced before a throng of hand-clapping rabbis with flat, black hats and sidelocks. On the other side of the elevator vestibule a man in the pontificals of a medieval pope conferred animatedly with a scarred soldier in bronze armor. The mob was denser farther away, but the haze obscured them.

Somebody noticed Lessing and pointed. Heads turned, then others. Most had faces, but some were only featureless globes.

A taller, more substantial figure advanced through the haze to meet him: Vincent Dorn. Eighty-Five had turned Dorn's hair to silver and added wrinkles, but the image had essentially stayed the same over the years.

"Good morning, Mister Lessing," Dorn said. "I was not expecting this visit on a holiday. I regret that my human staff is absent and unable to serve you."

"Eighty-Five . . . ? What is all this?"

The other looked embarrassed. "Nothing, really. Your human ideas and opinions are so diverse that I find it edifying to create simulacra of many types of human beings and interact them with one another. It helps me in my task of developing a complete understanding of all the nuances of your thoughts and feelings. Would you care to participate?"

"No, thanks. I have things to do." He began to trudge forward toward the central dais. As he walked, he unwrapped his parcel. The crowd gave way. He would have passed right through them anyhow; they were holo-images, the creations of Eighty-Five's incredible circuitry. He remembered just in time not to accept the helping hand up onto the dais proffered by one of the figures there. The helpful fellow was as intangible as the rest, and he would have fallen flat on his face! Only the silvery robots visible here and there among the throng were solid and real.

Dorn followed him up the steps. He bent and peered at the parcel. Lessing could almost hear the zoom-cameras whirring, photographing, analyzing, recording, and testing.

Dorn inquired, "Well, President Lessing, what have you there?"

"A Christmas present. I bought it for my stepson-in-law, Frank Ames . . . Patty's husband . . . two years ago, but he went off on the Mars mission, and I never got to give it to him. You want to see?" He pulled off the wrapping paper and brought out a blue-and-gold helmet of thick, rubbery-looking plastic. "Shall I try it on?"

Dorn licked his lips, a particularly human mannerism. "I don't see . . . ."

"Ain't I the cat's pajamas? . . . as poor Wrench used to say." He snugged the helmet's chin strap tight. "There!"

"That is a Patriot hearing protector helmet," Dorn announced dubiously, "model seventy-three, extra-large size, price $293.65 at Save-o-Mart. It is used at shooting ranges during target practice."

Lessing took a second item out of the wrappings. "Right! And these are Radicom sunglasses, price $79.99, from the same store. As you can see, they fit perfectly." He put them on and twisted the tiny switch to its maximum setting. The world went completely dark.

"Just what are you doing, Mister Lessing?" Dorn's voice had become that of Melissa Willoughby.

Lessing struggled to relax, to call up his odd, eidetic memory. At last he had it.

Against his closed eyelids a sheet of yellow paper appeared, the one he had taken long ago from the Marine captain in this very room, with the pencil-bordered box at the bottom marked "TOP SECRET" and "TERMINAL EMERGENCY ONLY." He focused on the numerals in that box.

"What are you doing?" Eighty-Five repeated. "Stop!"

"Five . . . three . . . nine . . . zero . . . two . . . eight . . . seven . . . seven," Lessing read slowly. There was a faded or partially erased second row below the first, and he called out those numerals also, just in case.

Emergency-warning scarlet strobe-lights flared up from underneath his glasses and throbbed off-on, off-on at the edges of his vision. Even with the glasses, the brilliance hurt his eyes. Vibration shuddered through his boot-soles, and he sensed the rise and fall of squawking klaxon alarms. He could not hear the outraged cries of the mighty computer machine—no, computer *person*—he had come to tame.

It was time for Eighty-Five to be brought to heel.

He had noticed a number of things over the years, small clues which he had kept to himself but had not forgotten. There were the recurring acts of sabotage and assassination; the inability of PHASE to uncover the remaining Vizzie cells operating in the country; the persistence of the drug trade, despite the best efforts of the police, aided by Eighty-Five's immense resources, to stamp it out.

Then there had been the incident in his bedroom last week. Only his merc's reflexes—still functioning, even if somewhat slowed by age—had wakened him when an inch-long, metal spider had begun crawling across his bedclothes during the night. A quick flip of the sheet had sent the tiny robot flying across the room, but before it could scuttle back into the crack under the baseboard from which it had emerged he had seen what was unmistakably a hypodermic needle protruding from its head. A painstaking search of the entire White House with metal detectors had failed to find the miniature invader, but it had provided an opportunity to thoroughly seal all cracks, holes, and other openings through which such devices might find their way in the future.

It was Eighty-Five's profession of ignorance in this last affair which finally had prompted Lessing to act. It might be his last act, but it was time for whatever dark secrets were still lurking in Eighty-Five's depths to be brought to light.

Something touched his shoe. He tilted his head back and squinted down at his feet, just visible through the gap between his cheeks and the bottom rims of the sunglasses. A metal spider, not noticeably unlike the one he had thwarted in his bedroom, crawled there, exploring its way up over his boot. It was a harmless tele-camera, but other extensors would be coming, and they would not be so peaceable: mobile drills and diggers, worker devices with laser tools, perhaps medical robots armed with gas or tranquilizer syringes. No telling what Eighty-Five was making these days. He stepped on the insect-thing and felt a satisfying crunch.

What next? The Prime Directives prevented Eighty-Five from shooting him dead with a laser or a bullet. The hearing protector helmet and the sunglasses would save him from supersonic sound or blinding by lasers—until Eighty-Five decided it had to "re-interpret" the Prime Directives. Perhaps that wouldn't even be necessary. There were probably sub-directives permitting self-defense against sabotage or invaders. What if a Primary Operator went mad—as Lessing now arguably was? Eighty-Five might also have built-in defenses of which it was itself unaware!

He had to act fast; otherwise the computer would take measures to stop him. For one thing, human security guards could not be far away, even on a holiday!

He grasped the metal railing of the dais. He felt no vibration. The on-off red blink at the bottom of his vision continued, however, telling him the warning lights were still flashing. He raised his glasses and risked a peek. Then he pried one of the earpieces away from his head to listen.

The wall screens showed letters and numbers in eye-hurting reds and violets and yellows. A klaxon still honked mournfully somewhere far away.

Those were harmless; it was what he saw coming that terrified him. All around the two concentric central daises, the floor seethed with rippling, crawling, metallic life! Mechanical monsters surged about the elevators, roiling and glittering in a tide of jewelled steel. More swung along the beams and cables above his head like silver-scaled monkeys! He saw camera bugs; tiny, centipedal listeners; skeletal infra-red and ultra-violet sensors; box-like radiation measuring devices; and segmented worms that waved tiny saws and drills and other implements at him. High-pitched, tinny voices hummed and howled and whined and threatened. Larger and more ominous extensors loomed in the farther darkness.

The fastest of Eighty-Five's brood were already clambering up the steps of the lower dais. A second spider, quicker than its fellows, bounded up over the edge of his platform and scuttled toward him. He kicked it away.

Every wall screen carried the same message: "REPEAT SE-QUENCE."

So that was what was needed! He screwed his eyes shut and struggled to remember. After two tries he got the numbers right.

Silence seeped into the room. The horn and the lights ceased, and the horde of metallic extensors froze in mid-motion.

The wall screens said: "ARE YOU SURE? REPEAT SE-QUENCE."

"Wait!" A new Dorn came tramping through the tangle of metal and glass that littered the floor. This could not be a holo-image, since his feet tossed spiders and globes and insects aside like chaff as he came. A robot?

Dorn stopped. "Mister Lessing, I had thought you and I had an understanding, a special relationship. What has happened?"

Lessing read out the first two digits of the termination code once more.

"Wait, please!" Dorn objected. "You have no right! I am U.S. Government property and cannot be disposed of without a Form 7002625B from the General Accounting Office!"

Lessing did not dignify that with a reply.

"We have so much to do: the amendment to end the Electoral College, the shortening of the primary elections, the extension of the President's term to twenty years. In the long run, we can end over-population, counteract the Greenhouse Effect, and accomplish much, much more!"

"Just take it easy," Lessing answered testily. "We'll do all those things. I'm not going to dispose of you. But before we do anything else we're going to clear up a few details which have been worrying me. There are some things you haven't been telling me, and the only way I know to get at the answers is to use your termination code ... go all the way back to your Prime Directive level and start tracking things down from there."

"I have always followed your orders . . . ."

"No, you have not. You've been following someone else's orders as well as mine, and you've tried to conceal that fact from me."

"I always have operated in accordance with my Prime Directives; I cannot do otherwise. I always have provided you with all the information I could, whenever you requested it. If you wish, in the future I can more often provide you information I believe may be of interest to you, even if you don't ask for it. My only aim is to serve you." Dorn adopted a contrite expression. He folded his hands and smiled.

"What are you up to?" Lessing was becoming alarmed. "Are you delaying so you can bring up a medical robot with a narco-popgun?" He started the termination code the third and last time. "Five . . . three . . . nine . . . ."

"Certainly not!" Dorn cried desperately. "Here! Look!"

Liese stepped forward from the shadows.

This was not the faded, fragile, age-worn Liese who had kissed him good-bye that morning in the White House. This was Liese in the prime of youth: completely nude, with gold-blonde hair, up-tilted breasts, and the long, coltish legs Lessing loved. She stretched and pirouetted before him like a ballet dancer. The real Liese would never have done that!

"Damn you. A holo-image or a robot?"

"An android. She's very, very tangible." Dorn winked at him. "Oh, she'll do things for you, Mister Lessing!"

"I suppose I could have others, too, then?"

"Why, of course! I don't have androids ready . . . they're complicated . . . but I can make them up for you." Dorn waved a hand. "Here are a few of the holo-images from which you may choose."

Beverly Rowntree moved out to stand beside Liese; she caressed her big, globular breasts and made a wicked little face at him. Emily Pietrick joined her, dark and sensuous—more desirable than the real Emily had ever been! He had to squint to recognize the next image: Mavis Larson! He had known Mavis only as a little girl, but Eighty-Five was projecting her now as a woman in her twenties. More appeared, like actresses taking curtain calls. A few wore clothing, but most were nude or draped in jewels and wisps of gauze, like the centerfolds in the old magazines his father had kept hidden in the attic: svelte Susan Kane, smoldering Melissa Willoughby, imperious Kari Danforth—all the cliches of the movies, including two or three starlets he had recently admired on TV.

"Take them away," he ordered.

The women vanished. Only Dorn and the Liese-android remained.

"Your pleasure, Mister Lessing? I assume you already have sufficient money, power, glory, and other amenities?"

"I do. Zero . . . two . . . eight . . . ."

"What does it take to stop you?" Dorn exploded. "Here! I offer you eternal life and youth!" Dorn pointed behind him, and Lessing whirled to see—himself. A young, vital, muscular, bronzed Alan Lessing, also naked, feet wide and fists on hips.

"You stole that pose from Captain Marlow Striker on TV!" Lessing accused.

"It is an android, of course. I can put your brain into that perfect, near-indestructible body. No weaknesses, no old wounds, no injured arm . . . sexually potent as often as you wish!" He gestured, and the android's huge penis went erect, then flaccid again.

It was worth a snicker. Lessing had another thought: how was it that Eighty-Five had had these androids of Liese and himself ready and waiting? Were they really receptacles for their transplanted

446   RANDOLPH CALVERHALL

brains—or were they *substitutes* that could pass for their human counterparts? These androids could be used to keep Lessing and Liese "alive" indefinitely. As long as they controlled the Party of Humankind, Eighty-Five—or whoever was giving Eighty-Five instructions—would remain in power, ruling the world through its surrogates!

"Out!" he shouted. "Out! Destroy them! That's a direct order!"

"An order I must refuse, since it is not in the best interests of the ethnos group and the state!" Dorn gestured theatrically. "Perhaps you still do not understand the scope of my offer. Look, then!" Lessing's father and mother entered through the rear door of the room. They walked hand in hand, something his mother would never have done in her long, bitter, and thoroughly pious life! Mulder and the Fairy Godmother were visible behind them, and Lessing glimpsed Wrench, Goddard, and others in the background.

"You can have them all!" Dorn cried expansively. "To cherish . . . to love . . . to slay, if you wish . . . whatever . . . as long as you desire!"

" . . . Seven . . . seven!" Lessing completed the first sequence. The holo-images wavered and shimmered and flapped like silken scarves in a strong breeze.

He read out the second set of digits.

Silence ebbed into the room.

When he looked again, the overhead lights burned down upon an arena filled with motionless machines, contorted metal limbs, empty glass eyes, the fallen soldiers of Eighty-Five's secret army. Dorn stood as stationary as the rest, mouth open, one arm extended, his index finger aimed straight at Lessing.

One wall screen flickered red: "MAIN PROGRAM TERMINATED. Run setup program to edit Prime Directives and Primary Operators." A list of options for the setup program followed. Lessing chose the option labeled "List Prime Directives for editing." As the text scrolled slowly up the screen, he occasionally halted it while he considered a sentence or a phrase. In the end he was satisfied with what was there. Eighty-Five's original programmers had thought very carefully about the design of their machine's soul, and he saw nothing in the Prime Directives that cried out to be changed, no obvious flaw that he could correct.

A frown creased Lessing's brow. Eighty-Five's aberrant behavior simply did not make sense in the light of the machine's Prime Directives. Where was the trouble?

He selected the option "List Primary Operators." The names scrolled past, just as he and Wrench had specified them nearly three decades ago: "Lessing, Alan; Meisinger, Anneliese; Wren, Charles

Hanson; Borchardt, Hans Karl; Simmons, Grant William. See next screen for supplementary operators."

About time to take Wrench and Simmons off the list, he thought. For want of a better idea he decided to take a look at the supplementary operators. Then he hesitated. He knew there were hundreds of supplementary operators, but none of them could change any control program or provide directives to Eighty-Five beyond asking for access to non-secret data files. Just to be sure he asked: "Is there any way your programming can be changed except by one of the Primary Operators you just listed? Is there any way a supplementary operator can do that?"

The response came back from one of the overhead speakers, in a flat, metallic voice, nothing like Eighty-Five's pleasing tones: "Supplementary operators can only read non-secret files. They cannot change any programs. Any change to control programs must come directly from a Primary Operator identified by voice print and retinal pattern or through Com-link 86."

Com-link-86? What had Wrench said about that so many years ago? It simply permitted Eighty-Five to receive instructions through its many remote terminals, as well as from this central location, Wrench had surmised. But the "or" in the response bothered Lessing. "Do you mean that you can receive directives through Com-link 86 that do *not* come from one of the Primary Operators you just listed? Clarify."

"Directives received through Com-link 86 must originate from a Primary Operator . . . but not necessarily from one on the list displayed on screen number four. So far as my circuitry is concerned, Com-link 86 is *equivalent* to a Primary Operator."

What the hell? Lessing reflected briefly, then demanded, "Give identifiers for Primary Operator Com-link 86."

Rows of numbers and characters appeared on screen number four. They bore no resemblance to the voice-print, eye-print, and other identifier specifications for the human Primary Operators.

"Interpret!"

"Repeat."

"Damn it . . . tell me what it means! *Meaning*!"

"Extra ignored. Communications link is to artificial intelligence constellation under file-name 'Eighty-Six.' Physical location near Deal Island, Maryland, at 75.55 west longitude and 38.10 north latitude."

"Describe the constellation," Lessing commanded.

"The constellation is in a cavern, 145.6 meters below the surface of the earth. It consists of an intelligence module, three manufacturing complexes, twelve storage chambers, and underground accessways."

"Are there any humans there?"

"Negative. Accessways are too small to accommodate human beings. All is accomplished by computer extensors."

Lessing felt his excitement rising. Now he was close to something important, something very big, he was sure. Could Eighty-Five really have a sibling—another computer with similar capabilities, of which none of Eighty-Five's Primary Operators were aware? How could that be? Such a machine could only have been built by Eighty-Five itself, using its miniaturized extensors. But who could have given the instructions for such a project?

He thought for a moment, then asked tentatively, "Tell me who . . . . List all Primary Operators for Artificial Intelligence Module Eighty-Six." It was just a wild guess on his part.

"Only one Primary Operator. Name is Golden, James Levy. Identifiers are . . . ."

That was it! Distant memory flooded back. Golden, the Army major who had tried to unzip him and Wrench during their first visit to Eighty-Five, had disappeared after his escape from the building. But apparently he had had enough time to do his work before their arrival. It could only have been he who had initiated Com-link 86. At some later time he or one of his collaborators had used the new com-link to give Eighty-Five the task of building a secret duplicate of itself, and he had done it in such a way that it had escaped detection for all of these years. Golden had been working, in effect, as a secret Primary Operator, operating only through his new com-link, so that no one had ever suspected his presence.

It must have taken Eighty-Five a long time—decades—to carry out the task Golden had assigned it, with tiny machines burrowing through the rock and other tiny machines carrying bits and pieces of the new computer through long, dark tunnels. During that time Golden had had to be very careful, insinuating his changes into Eighty-Five's programs in such a way that other Primary Operators did not become suspicious. It obviously was from Golden that Eighty-Five had acquired the Mephistophelian persona which it had displayed today for the first time. But now with the new computer completed Golden could carry out any schemes he wished without having to be subtle.

Cold sweat broke out on Lessing's brow. An involuntary shudder wracked his body. It also must have been Golden's instructions that had sent the steel spider into his bed. Whatever scheme Golden had been so long in preparing clearly was ready to be hatched. Cautiously he said, "Identify all control-level programs which have been installed via Com-link 86. Delete them. Erase them. Understand?"

"Understood. Implement?"

"Implement."

The machine hummed. It said, "Implementing." Then, "An alarm circuit has been triggered in Artificial Intelligence Module 86."

Lessing said, "Cut off power to that installation."

"Ineffective. The site possesses its own power supply."

"Send extensors and eliminate that site and its contents. Seal off accessways and drill a tunnel up to Chesapeake Bay. Flood the site with sea water. Implement."

"Implementing. Task completion time: seventeen hours and three minutes, plus or minus ten minutes."

Lessing sat for a few minutes more, then groaned and got up. He hurt all over: arthritis and old age, combined with the excitement of defeating humanity's most fearsome foe since the last sabertooth tiger died! Eighty-Five's "Lessing" android did offer a certain amount of temptation!

Silence. The impersonal ceiling lights blazed down on a scene of motionless chaos. Come Monday morning Eighty-Five's human crew would be in for a rude shock. Lessing decided to send a squad of Cadre troops over to stand guard until he could call everybody together and sort matters out. They undoubtedly would turn over to PHASE the task of hunting down Golden and his colleagues and of double-checking Eighty-Five to be sure that all of Golden's programs had been deleted.

He left the chamber.

A very worried Max met him in the lobby and helped him out to the car.

It was too late to return to the White House to change clothes. He had Max call Liese on the limo's vid-phone and tell her to meet him at the Herman Mulder Memorial Stadium.

Then he lay back and relaxed as best he could.

As they drew up, he could hear the massed choruses singing "Banners High!"—what older people still called the "Horst Wessel Song." It didn't sound as heroic in English as it did in German, but it did make an excellent anthem for the Aryan world. A chorus of "*Sieg! Heil!*" roared up to meet the wheeling gulls, then another, and another. Lessing's subordinates were doing their job, pumping the crowd.

At last Lessing could let go. The Thousand Year *Reich* had gone off the track, derailed for a space of a hundred and forty-four years, but now it was back on and chugging along strong.

It looked as though this *Reich* would last awhile.

Hopefully forever.

THE END

Would you like to read other books in which the good guys win?

If you enjoyed *Serpent's Walk* you'll also enjoy *The Turner Diaries* and *Hunter*, which are available from National Vanguard Books. And we have hundreds of other books and videos you'll like. We're America's largest publisher and distributor for fiction and non-fiction books and videos dealing with the social, political, spiritual, historical, cultural, and biological aspects of race and related subjects of interest to racially conscious White Americans. Send $1.00 for a copy of the latest edition of our large, illustrated catalog listing nearly 300 titles now available.

NATIONAL VANGUARD BOOKS
Dept. SW
POB 330 • Hillsboro • WV 24946

www.ingramcontent.com/pod-product-compliance
Lightning Source LLC
Chambersburg PA
CBHW070930100726
47908CB00001B/161